DAW Books Presents
The Finest in Imaginative Fiction by
TAD WILLIAMS

SHADOWMARCH
SHADOWMARCH
SHADOWPLAY
SHADOWRISE
SHADOWHEART

TAILCHASER'S SONG

THE WAR OF THE FLOWERS

MEMORY, SORROW AND THORN
THE DRAGONBONE CHAIR
STONE OF FAREWELL
TO GREEN ANGEL TOWER

OTHERLAND
CITY OF GOLDEN SHADOW
RIVER OF BLUE FIRE
MOUNTAIN OF BLACK GLASS
SEA OF SILVER LIGHT

Shadowheart

N
W
E
S
The Twilight Lands
Irisian Ocean
Vuttish Archipelago
Connord
Southmarch
and March Kingdoms
Settland
EION
Brenland
Syan
The Heartwood
Jael
Perikal
Eiluin Mountains
Devonis
Krace
Ulos
Hierosol
Sessio
Akaris
Osteian Sea
Talleno
Torvio
Hesperian Ocean
Great Xis
XAND
TW 2004

TAD WILLIAMS

Shadowheart

The Final Volume of Shadowmarch

DAW BOOKS, INC.
DONALD A. WOLLHEIM, FOUNDER
375 Hudson Street, New York, NY 10014
ELIZABETH R. WOLLHEIM
SHEILA E. GILBERT
PUBLISHERS
http://www.dawbooks.com

Jacket art by Todd Lockwood.

Maps by Tad Williams.

DAW Book Collectors No. 1526.

DAW Books are distributed by Penguin Group (USA) Inc.

Book designed by Elizabeth M. Glover.

First printing, November 2010
1 2 3 4 5 6 7 8 9

PRINTED IN THE U.S.A.

Our children Connor and Devon still think that getting a grown-up book dedicated to them instead of one of our more kid-oriented books is kind of a rip-off. I told them that one day they will be grown-ups just like us, but they refuse to believe anything so horrid and unfair could happen to such nice children.

(It'll be fun watching them learn better. Actually, it'll be fun watching them no matter what.) Remember, you wonderful beasts, we love you hugely—but don't make me come back there.

Irisian Ocean
MARCH KINGDOMS
Southmarch
Blueshore
Landers Port
Oscastle
Kertewall
Marrinswalk
Silverside
Whitewood
Elusine River
Great Kertish Road
Weeping Moors
N
W
E
S
Esterian River
Upper SYAN
The Heartwood
TW 2006

Acknowledgments

Betsy Wollheim and Sheila Gilbert and everyone at DAW Books receive my overwhelming gratitude as usual as we finally steer this monstrous story into port. I also want to thank our fabulous assistant Dena Chavez and my wicked-cool agent Matt Bialer, as well as the lovely Lisa Tveit who has put in tons of work making our website, www.tadwilliams.com, a fun and informative place to visit. Please come and join us there, or see me make a fool of myself on Facebook at www.facebook.com/tad.williams. Don't worry. Nobody has died yet from too much Tad, so you probably won't be the first.

Super, extra-big thanks and love also go to my awesome wife Deborah Beale, who put in a staggering amount of work helping me revise the late drafts of this book when she could have been doing something else fun, or at least non-Tad-related.

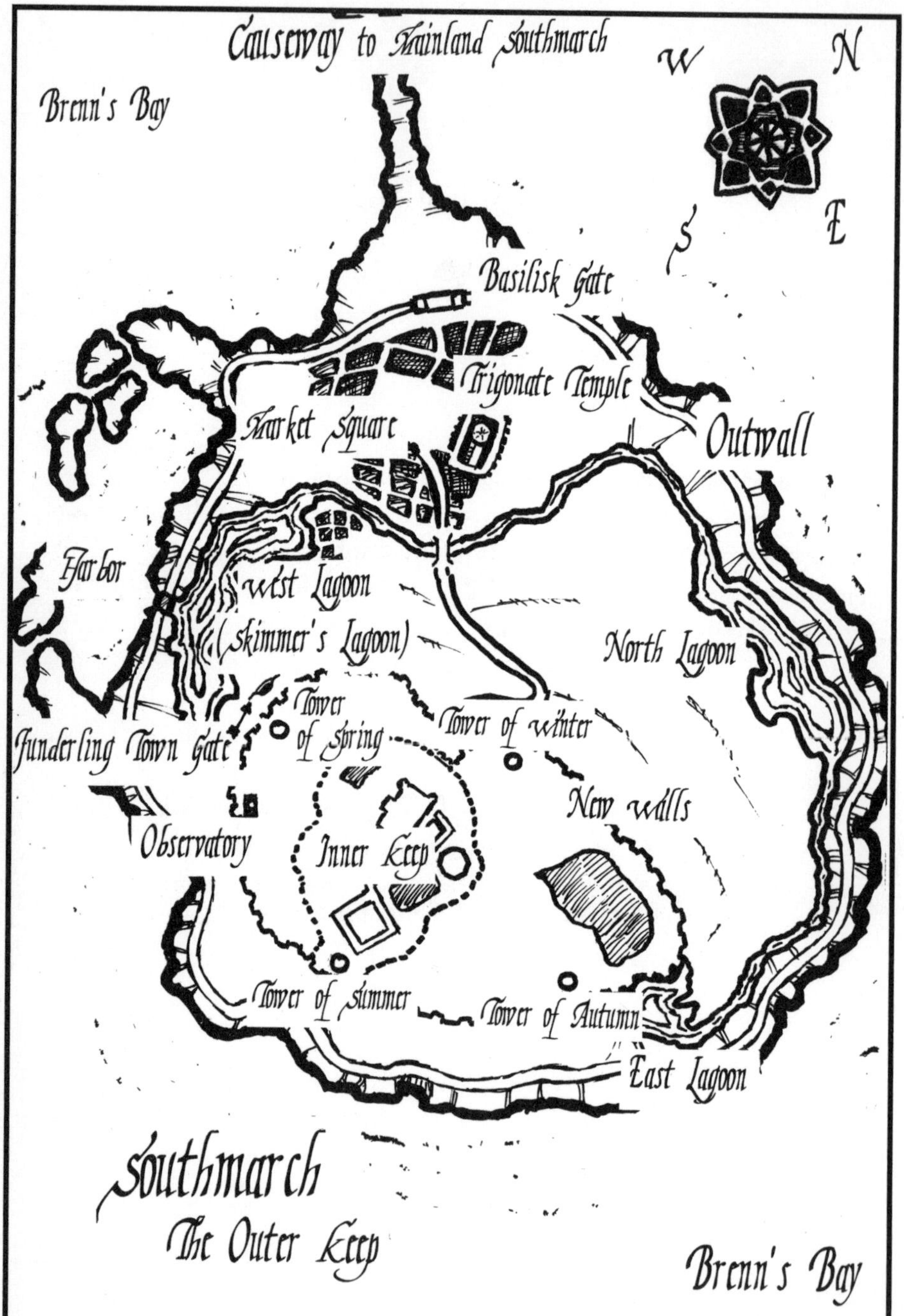

Causeway to Mainland Southmarch

W N S E

Brenn's Bay

Basilisk Gate

Trigonate Temple

Market Square

Outwall

Harbor

West Lagoon
(Skimmer's Lagoon)

North Lagoon

Tower of Spring

Tower of Winter

Funderling Town Gate

Observatory

New Walls

Inner Keep

Tower of Summer

Tower of Autumn

East Lagoon

Southmarch
The Outer Keep

Brenn's Bay

TW 2004

Author's Note

Because of repeated questions and occasional physical assaults (yes, the bruises are healing nicely, thank you) I have included as a second appendix a genuine historical document which lists and names most of the principal gods of the Trigonate faith and the names by which other peoples of Eion and Xand call them.

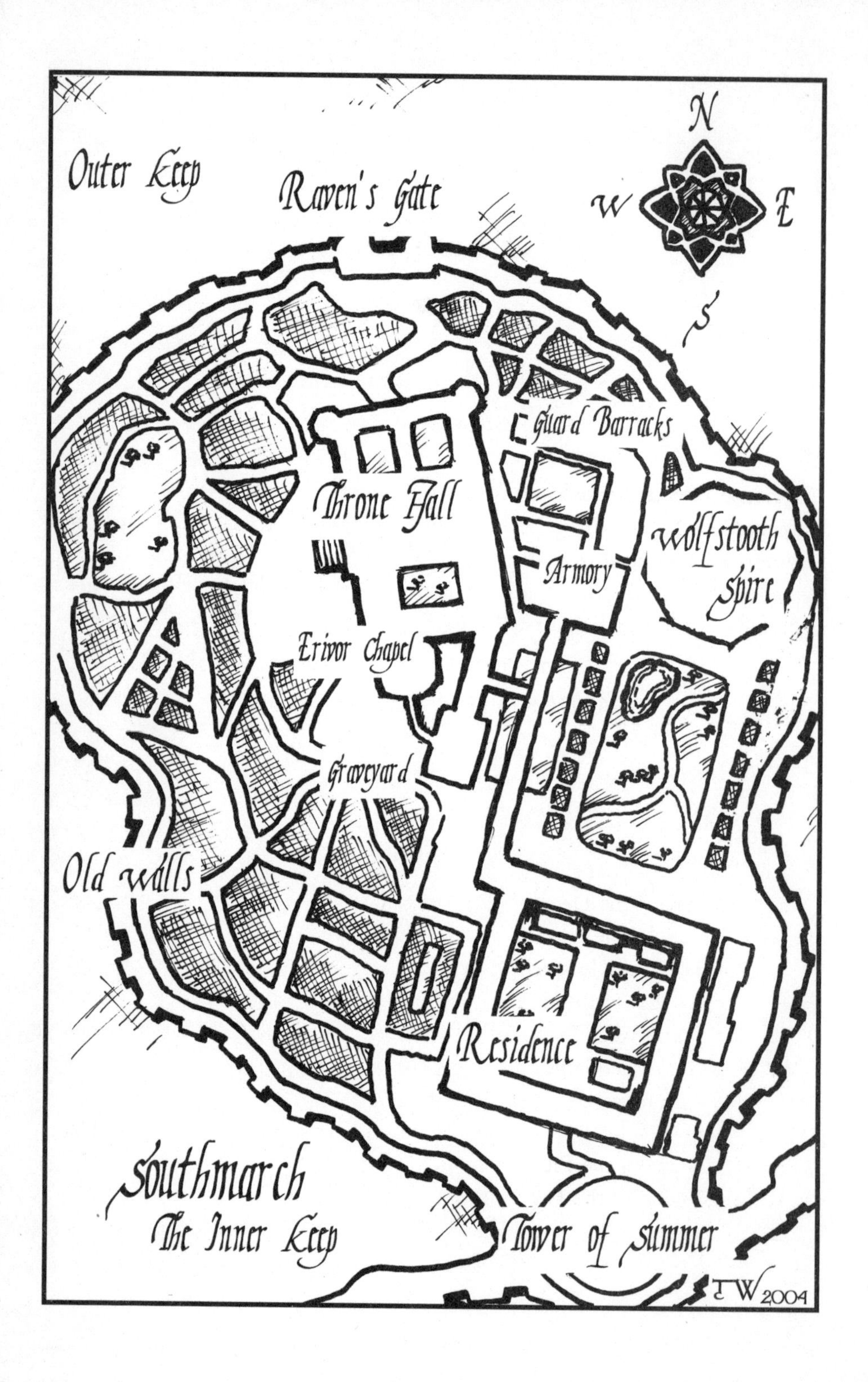
Outer Keep
Raven's Gate
N
W
E
S
Guard Barracks
Throne Hall
Wolfstooth Spire
Armory
Erivor Chapel
Graveyard
Old Walls
Residence
Southmarch
The Inner Keep
Tower of Summer
TW 2004

Contents

PART TWO: THE TORTOISE

PART THREE: THE OWL

PART FOUR: THE PINE TREE

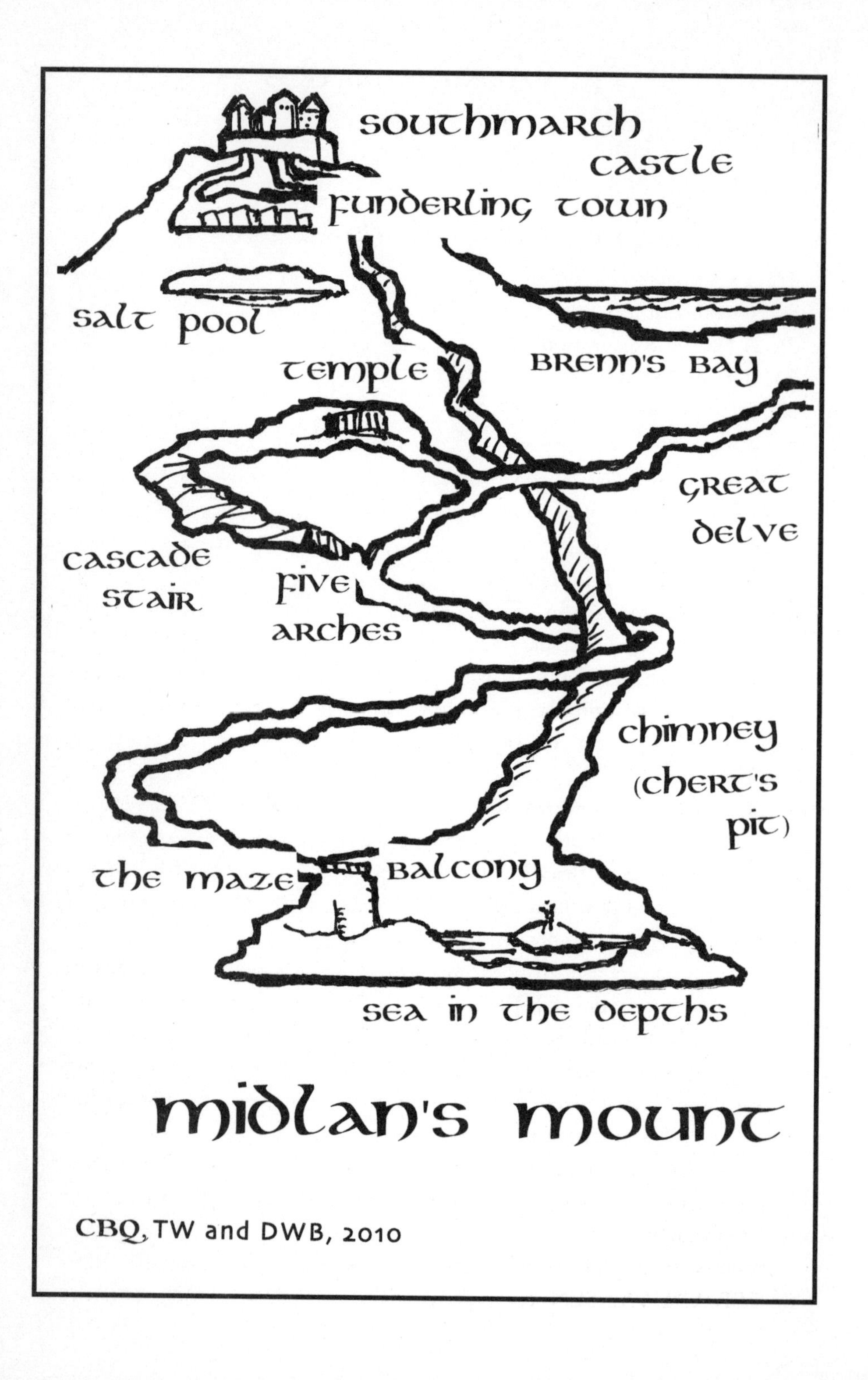
Southmarch
Castle
Funderling Town
Salt Pool
Temple
Brenn's Bay
Great
Delve
Cascade
Stair
Five
Arches
Chimney
(Chert's
Pit)
The Maze
Balcony
Sea in the Depths
Midlan's Mount
CBQ, TW and DWB, 2010

Synopsis of *Shadowmarch*

Southmarch Castle, the last human city in the north, has stood for two hundred years as a bulwark against the immortal Qar—the fairy folk who have twice fought wars against humanity. This is a bad time for Southmarch, a country whose king, OLIN EDDON, is being held for ransom in another kingdom, leaving only his three children, KENDRICK, the oldest, and the twins BARRICK and BRIONY, to watch over his land and people. Making this uncertain time worse, the Shadowline—the boundary between human lands and the foggy, eternally twilit domain of the Qar—has begun to move closer to Southmarch.

Then Kendrick is murdered in his own castle. SHASO DAN-HEZA, Briony and Barrick's mentor, is imprisoned for the crime and it seems his guilt is undeniable. Briony does not feel entirely convinced but she is distracted by many other concerns, not least the problems of trying to rule alongside Barrick, her sickly, angry twin.

In fact, matters are growing more confused and more dangerous in Southmarch every day. CHERT and OPAL, two Funderlings, a dwarfish folk who live beneath Southmarch, see a child abandoned by mysterious riders from the far side of the Shadowline. The boy is one of the Big Folk—an ordinary sized human—but they give him the Funderling name FLINT and take him home to their town under the castle. Meanwhile, CHAVEN, the royal physician, finds his own attention absorbed by a mysterious mirror, and the even more mysterious entity that seems to live inside it.

Princess Briony places much of the blame for her older brother's death on FERRAS VANSEN, the captain of the royal guard, who she thinks should have done more to protect him. Vansen has an affection for Briony Eddon that goes beyond the bounds of both propriety and good sense. He can only accept mutely when, in part as punishment, she sends him out to the site of a reported attack across the Shadowline by the Qar.

YNNIR, the blind king of those same Qar, has initiated a complicated strategy concerning the castle and its ruling family; dumping the boy Flint near Southmarch was only the first part. That act is already having repercussions: at Kendrick's funeral the Eddon children's great aunt, DUCHESS MEROLANNA, sees the boy Flint and almost faints. She is positive she has seen her own illegitimate child, whose birth was kept secret but who disappeared more than fifty years earlier.

Ynnir is not the only one of the Qar with complicated plans. LADY YASAMMEZ, one of the most powerful of the fairies, has gathered an army and is marching across the Shadowline to attack the mortal lands.

Meanwhile, Barrick and Briony find themselves in an ever stranger situation. Their chief counselor, AVIN BRONE, tells them that the TOLLYS, the most powerful rival family in the March Kingdoms, have been entertaining agents of SULEPIS, the AUTARCH OF XIS, the malevolent southern god-king whose goal seems to be to conquer the whole of the northern continent as he as already enslaved the south. (We have already seen him and his apparent madness in his treatment of QINNITAN, an innocent temple novice whom he has declared his newest wife and moved into the harem called the Seclusion. Strangely, though, the only attention she receives there is a kind of religious instruction and a series of disturbing potions the priests force her to drink.)

Back in the northern continent, things get worse. Ferras Vansen and his troop find themselves lured onto the wrong side of the Shadowline. Several of the soldiers are killed by various creatures, and before they find their way back to the lands of men, Vansen sees the army that Yasammez has mustered heading for the March Kingdoms.

MATT TINWRIGHT, a Southmarch poet down on his luck, is asked to write a letter to the Eddon family on behalf of an apparently simple-minded potboy named GIL. A chore Tinwright thinks of as easy money instead gets him arrested and brought in front of Avin Brone, accused of treason. Princess Briony takes pity on Tinwright and frees him, even allowing him to stay in the household as a poet. Of all the troubled folk in Southmarch Castle, Tinwright alone seems to have found some luck.

The Qar destroy Candlerstown and Princess Briony decides Southmarch must send an army to halt the fairies' advance. To her surprise, her brother Barrick is the first to volunteer to ride out against the Qar. He has confessed to his sister that their father Olin suffers from a kind of madness that caused him to cripple Barrick some years ago, and Barrick believes he has the madness as well, so he feels he might as well risk his life defending the kingdom. Briony cannot talk him out of this, so she tasks Ferras Vansen, who has finally made his way back from beyond the Shadowline, to protect her brother at any cost.

Beneath the castle in Funderling Town the strange boy known as Flint has disappeared. With the help of one of the tiny ROOFTOPPERS, Chert tracks him down in the mysterious, sacred place beneath even their subterranean city, the holy depths known as the Mysteries. There Flint has somehow made his way to an island in an underground lake where stands the strange stone figure known as the Shining Man, sacred to the Funderling people. Chert brings the boy home. Later, with the potboy Gil, Chert will take a magical artifact the boy has brought back from the Mysteries and give it to Yasammez, the dark lady who leads the Qar forces camped outside the castle walls.

It is mid-winter and the army has gone out to fight the Qar. Briony is taunted in public by HENDON TOLLY with her family's failings and she loses her head so badly that she challenges him to a duel. When he refuses to fight her she is humiliated in front of the court, many of whom already feel she is too young and unstable (and too female) to rule Southmarch. Later, when she goes to keep an appointment with her pregnant stepmother ANISSA, she is surprised by the sudden appearance of Chaven the physician, who has been missing from the castle for some time.

Back on the southern continent, Qinnitan, the reluctant bride of the Autarch, escapes the royal palace of Xis and manages to talk her way onto a ship bound for the northern continent.

Meanwhile, the Qar prove too powerful and too tricky for the Southmarch armies: Prince Barrick and the rest are badly defeated. Barrick himself is almost killed by a giant, but Yasammez spares his life. After a short while alone with him she sends him away and he rides toward the Shadowline in a kind of trance. Ferras Vansen sees him, and when he cannot stop or hinder the confused prince, Vansen goes with Barrick to protect him, as Princess Briony had begged him to do.

Meanwhile, Briony's meeting with her stepmother turns horrifying when Anissa's maid proves to be Kendrick's murderer and again uses a magical stone to turn herself into a demonic creature bent on murdering Briony as well. Only Briony's courage saves her; the creature is killed. In the shock of the moment, Anissa goes into labor.

Leaving Chaven behind to take care of her stepmother, Briony sets out to free Shaso, her mentor, who has now been proved innocent of Kendrick's death. When she frees him, though, they find themselves outmaneuvered by Hendon Tolly, who has been manipulating events all this time. He intends to make it look as though Shaso has murdered Briony so Hendon can take the throne. Instead, Briony and Shaso fight their way free and escape Southmarch with the help of some loyal SKIMMERS, a water-loving people who also share the castle. But Briony has been forced to leave her home in the hands of her worst enemies, her brother is gone without trace, and Yasammez and the murderous Qar are now surrounding the castle.

Synopsis of *Shadowplay*

BRIONY EDDON and her twin brother BARRICK, the last heirs of the Southmarch royal family, have been separated. Their castle and country are under the control of HENDON TOLLY, a murderous and particularly nasty relative. The vengeful fairies known as the QAR have surrounded Southmarch Castle.

After escaping Hendon, Briony and her mentor, SHASO, take refuge in a nearby city with one of Shaso's countrymen, but that refuge is soon attacked and burned. Only Briony escapes, but now she is friendless and alone. Starving and ill, she hides in the forest.

Barrick, compelled by something he doesn't understand, heads north through the fairy lands behind the Shadowline in company with the soldier FERRAS VANSEN. They soon gain a third companion, GYIR THE STORM LANTERN, one of the Qar general YASAMMEZ's most trusted servants, who has a mission from her to bring a mirror—the very object the boy FLINT took down into the depths beneath the castle and to the feet of the Shining Man—to YNNIR, the king of the Qar. But Barrick and the others are captured by a monster named JIKUYIN, a demigod who has reopened the mines at Greatdeeps in an attempt to find a way to gain the power of the sleeping gods.

Briony Eddon meets a demigoddess, LISIYA, a forest deity now fallen on hard times, who leads Briony to MAKEWELL'S MEN, a troop of theatrical players on their way south to the powerful nation of Syan. Briony joins them, telling them nothing of her real name and situation.

Back in Qul-na-Qar, the home of the fairies, their QUEEN SAQRI is dying, and King Ynnir is helpless to do anything more for her. His only hope, it seems, are the machinations taking place around the magical mirror currently in the hands of Gyir the Storm Lantern. That mirror, and the agreement about it called the Pact of the Glass, is the only thing keeping vengeful Yasammez and her fairy army from destroying Southmarch.

At the same time QINNITAN, the escaped bride of SULEPIS, the AUTARCH OF XIS, has made a life for herself in the city of Hierosol, the southernmost port on the northern continent. What she doesn't know is that the Autarch has sent DAIKONAS VO, a mercenary killer, to bring her back, compelling Vo with painful magic. The nature of the powerful Autarch's interest in Qinnitan is still a mystery.

Southmarch Castle remains under the strange non-siege of the Qar. Inside the castle, the poet MATT TINWRIGHT has become enamored of ELAN M'CORY, Hendon Tolly's mistreated lover. Recognizing that Tinwright cares for her, she asks him to help her kill herself. Unwilling to do this, he tricks her by giving her just enough poison to make her senseless, then smuggles her out of the royal residence so that he can hide her from Hendon.

Tolly maintains his hold on power largely because he has named himself the protector of the newborn ALESSANDROS, heir to the missing KING OLIN. Hendon Tolly appears largely uninterested in the besieging Qar or anything else.

Meanwhile, Olin is being held in the southern city of Hierosol, where he catches a glimpse of Qinnitan (working as a maid in the palace) and sees something strangely familiar in her. He does not have long to think about it before the Autarch's huge navy sweeps up from the south and besieges Hierosol. Olin's captor sells him to the Autarch to secure his own safety, although why the god-king of Xis should be interested in the monarch of a small northern country is not clear.

In Greatdeeps, Barrick Eddon and the other prisoners of the demigod Jikuyin are slated for sacrifice in a ritual meant to open the way to the land of the sleeping gods, but the fairy Gyir sacrifices his own life, defeating the demigod's forces with their own explosives. Gyir dies and Vansen falls through a magical doorway into nothingness. Barrick is left alone to fight his way out of the mines and escape, carrying the mirror that Gyir was meant to take to the fairy-king Ynnir. With his companions gone and only the raven SKURN for company, Barrick begins his lonely journey across the shadowlands toward the fairy city of Qul-na-Qar. His only other companion comes to him solely in dreams—the girl Qinnitan, whom he has never met, but whose thoughts can, for some reason, touch his.

Meanwhile Briony and the theatrical troop have reached the great city of Tessis, capitol of Syan. She and the other players meet DAWET there, the onetime servant of Ludis Drakava, King Olin's captor, but they are all surprised and arrested by Syannese soldiers, although Dawet escapes. The players and Briony are accused of spying. To save her companions, Briony declares her true identity—the princess of Southmarch.

Ferras Vansen, who had fallen into seemingly endless darkness, undergoes a strange, dreamlike journey through the land of the dead at the side of his deceased father. He escapes at last only to find himself no longer behind the Shadowline, but in Funderling Town underneath Southmarch Castle. CHAVEN the physician, who is hiding from Hendon Tolly, is also with the Funderlings now.

Far to the south, in Hierosol, Qinnitan is captured by Daikonas Vo, who takes her to the Autarch Sulepis, but the Autarch has already left Hierosol on a ship bound for the obscure northern kingdom of Southmarch. Vo commandeers another ship and sets out after his cruel master.

The Autarch is not alone on his flagship. Besides his faithful minister PINIMMON VASH, he also has a prisoner—the northern king, OLIN EDDON. And Olin's ultimate fate, Sulepis informs him, will be to die so that the Autarch can gain the power of the sleeping gods.

Synopsis of *Shadowrise*

The twins, BARRICK EDDON and his sister BRIONY, are both far away from their embattled family home, Southmarch Castle. The usurper HENDON TOLLY still holds Southmarch, which has been besieged for weeks by the Qar, also called the fairies or the Twilight folk. The brunt of the attack has fallen on the Funderlings who live beneath the castle in a near-endless warren of tunnels that stretch deep, deep down into the ground, down to the sacred places the Funderlings call "the Mysteries."

Princess Briony is far to the south, a guest of sorts at the court of KING ENANDER of Syan. (She has given up her disguise as a traveling player after they were all arrested by the Syannese king's guards.) She makes some friends in the court but only one useful ally, the king's son, PRINCE ENEAS, who seems to think very highly of Briony indeed. She is all the more grateful for his support when she survives a poisoning attempt that kills one of her maids.

Her brother Barrick is traveling through the twilit fairy lands with an ill-mannered raven named SKURN, on a mission he does not entirely understand. Barrick knows only that before his death the Qar warrior GYIR made him swear he would deliver a magical mirror to the royal court of the fairies—the timeless halls of Qul-na-Qar. But between him and the legendary fairy city lie countless murderous miles of shadowlands, full of miniature dangers like the Tine Fay and stranger creatures like the faceless, murderous Silkins.

To Skurn's disgust, Barrick chooses to take refuge from the Silkins on a place called Cursed Hill, and at the top he encounters a trio of strange, apparently ancient creatures who call themselves SLEEPERS. They are renegade members of the Dreamless tribe of Qar, and they declare they know Barrick and want to help him reach Qul-na-Qar, but that he is both too weak and too far from Qul-na-Qar to succeed in reaching it. They perform a magic ceremony that makes him feel stronger and healthier and restores his crippled arm to full health, and then tell him that he must find the mystical gateway to Qul-na-Qar in the city of Sleep, home of the Qar's enemies (and former relations) the Dreamless.

It is not only the Qar who have designs on Southmarch. The AUTARCH, the god-king of the southern land of Xis, is bringing many men and ships to conquer the castle, along with Southmarch's true ruler, the children's father, KING OLIN, who is his prisoner. The autarch is not at all reticent about what he plans to do, and even seems to enjoy talking about it: he plans to sacrifice Olin and use his blood (which derives in part from the Qar royal family, and thus from a god) as a magical tool to open a portal to the land where the gods lie trapped in sleep, banished there by the very god who is ancestor to both Olin's family and the Qar—KUPILAS, also known as CROOKED. But it is not dying Kupilas who interests the autarch, but some other, more sinister god whose power the autarch means to steal and take for himself in a ritual on Midsummer's Day, which is only a matter of days away.

Olin is not the only prisoner who interests the autarch. A young woman who escaped from him earlier, QINNITAN, has been recaptured by the autarch's hand-picked hunter, the mercenary DAIKONAS VO. Vo barely misses the autarch's ship, which has just left for Southmarch in the north, but he commandeers another Xixian vessel and pursues them, looking to give the autarch his prisoner and receive his reward. After several attempts, Qinnitan finally manages to escape from Vo in the wild coastal lands east of Southmarch, but Vo, who is growing increasingly mad, continues to pursue her.

FERRAS VANSEN, the captain of the Southmarch royal guard, has led the Funderlings in a long and brave resistance against the Qar, but now he learns that the autarch is on his way. Vansen sets off for the Qar camp, determined to make common cause with the fairies or to die trying. Meanwhile, the enigmatic boy FLINT, adopted by the Funderlings CHERT and OPAL, continues to take a mysterious role in events, but sometimes seems as confused by his own actions as everyone else is.

In Syan, Briony is betrayed and falsely accused of trying to undermine King Enander's rule. She escapes with the help of her actor friends. Prince

Eneas, the king's heir who wants to aid her, catches up to her and declares he will help her reach her home, and even assist her to retake her throne if he can. With such an ally (and his troops) Briony can finally begin to think about heading home to her family's stolen kingdom.

Meanwhile her twin Barrick has finally made his way to the city of Sleep, and after defeating some particularly dreadful guardians he is able to use the magical gateway there to go directly to Qul-na-Qar, although his companions Skurn and the merchant RAEMON BECK enter the gateway with him but do not arrive in Qul-na-Qar. The ancient home of the Qar is all but abandoned (since most are besieging Southmarch with their fierce leader, LADY YASAMMEZ) but the blind king YNNIR and sleeping queen SAQRI and a few servants remain. Ynnir uses the mirror Barrick has brought so far, but its power is not enough to wake the queen.

The autarch and his prisoner King Olin land in Southmarch. Olin's home looks deserted: the Qar seem to have given up their siege and left, which means the autarch's huge army will quickly overcome the castle's meager defenses and then the autarch will open the doorway to the place where the angry, dispossessed gods are waiting for their revenge.

In Qul-na-Qar, King Ynnir tells the mortal prince Barrick that the only way Queen Saqri can be woken is if Ynnir gives her the last of his strength. But he cannot do this without finding a caretaker for the FIRE-FLOWER within him, the wisdom of all the kings of the Qar. (Saqri contains the female version, the wisdom of the fairy queens.) No human has ever taken the Fireflower, but Barrick, like his father, has the blood of the god Kupilas (or Crooked, as the Qar name him) in his veins. Barrick agrees.

He is almost destroyed by the power of the Fireflower, but Saqri revives even as Ynnir dies. Barrick is left alone in the house of his enemies with a head full of incomprehensible Qar memories.

Prelude

He was named after the *tualum*, small antelope that ran in the dry desert hills. As a girl, his mother had often watched the herd come down to the river to drink, so lean, so bright of eye, so brave; when she first saw her son, she saw all those things in him. "Tulim," she gasped. "Call him Tulim." It was duly noted down as he was taken away from her and given to a royal wet nurse.

The first things the boy remembered were the sunset-colored hangings of the Seclusion where he lived among the women for the earliest years of his life, where kind, sweet-smelling nurses held him, sang to him, and rubbed his tiny brown limbs with expensive unguents. The child's only moments of sadness came when he was placed back in his cot and another of the monarch's youngest children was lifted out to be cosseted and caressed in turn. The unfairness of it, that the attention which should have been for him alone was also given to others, burned inside little Tulim like the flame of the lamp he stared at each night before he fell asleep—a flame that he watched so carefully he could sometimes see it in his mind's eye at midday, so bright that it pushed everything real into shadow.

When he was scarcely three years old, as a sort of experiment, Tulim drowned one of the other young princes in the bath they shared. He waited until the nurses were turned away to comfort another child who had been splashed and was crying, then he reached for his brother Kirgaz's head, shoved it under the blossom-strewn water, and held it down. The three or four other children in the bath were so busy splashing and playing that they didn't notice.

It was strange to feel his brother's desperate struggles and to know that only inches away ordinary things went on without him. People made so much of life, Tulim realized, but he could take it away whenever he chose. He saw the lamp's flame again in his mind's eye, but this time it was as though he himself had become the fire, burning so brightly that the rest of creation fell into darkness. It was ecstasy.

By the time the nurses turned around, Kirgaz was floating lazily, his hair swirling on the surface like seaweed, pale flower petals tangled in it. They screamed and dragged him out, but it was too late to save him. Many princes lived in the Orchard Palace—the autarch had many wives and was a prolific father—so the loss of one was no great tragedy, but both nurses were, of course, immediately executed. Tulim was sad about that. One of them had been in the habit of smuggling him a honey-milk sweet out of the Seclusion's kitchen each night. Now he would have to go to bed without it.

Tulim soon grew too old to live in the Seclusion, so he was moved to the Cedar Court, the part of the mighty, sprawling Orchard Palace where the young sons of nobles were raised until manhood in fortunate proximity to the royal sons of Tulim's father, the glorious god-king Parnad. There for the first time Tulim lived with true men—only the Favored were allowed in the Seclusion—and learned manly things, how to hunt and fight and sing a war-song. With his long-legged good looks and his sharp wits, he also for the first time came to the attention of the men of the Orchard Palace, including, most surprisingly, his own father.

Most of Parnad's sons hoped to remain unnoticed by their father. True, one of them would one day become his heir, but the autarch was a vigorous, powerful man in his fifties so that day was far away, and Xixian heirs had a way of suffering accidents. Parnad himself had found a few of his sons too popular with the soldiers or the common people. One such young man had been the sole casualty of a battle with pirates in the western islands. Another had died, purple and choking, after apparently being bitten by a snake in the Yenidos Mountains in midwinter—a most unusual season for snakebites. Thus, none of the other princes felt too jealous when their father noticed Tulim and began to speak to him occasionally.

"Who was your mother?" Parnad asked him the first time. The autarch was a big man, tall but also broad as an old crocodile. It was strange for Tulim to think that this heavyset man with his thick beard was the source of his own slender limbs. "Ah, yes, I remember her. Like a cat, she was. You have her eyes."

Tulim wasn't sure whether this way of talking meant his mother was no longer alive, but he did not want to ask, which might seem sentimental and womanish. If he had inherited her eyes, though, she must have been exceptional indeed, for that was the thing that people noticed first about Tulim, the strange, golden eyes like holes filled with molten metal. It was one of the reasons he had long known he was not like any of the others—that same bright, all-devouring flame did not burn within his brothers or the other children as it did in him.

He and his father the autarch had other conversations, although Tulim never said much, and after a while Tulim was taken from the sleeping room he shared with several of the other young princes and given his own room where the autarch could visit him at whatever time of the day or night he thought best without disturbing Tulim's brothers. Parnad also began to perform various odd cruelties and unwholesome practices on him, all the while explaining to him about the terrifying responsibility of being the Bishakh—the chief of the falcon line that had come out of the desert to trample down the thrones of the world's cities.

"The gods hold us dear," Parnad would explain as he held Tulim's mouth closed, silencing his cries of pain. "It is given by them that the falcon soars higher than any other—that he can look down on all creation. The very sun itself is only the great falcon's eye."

Tulim could not always make sense of what his father said, but as a whole the lessons, coupled with the pain and other strange feelings, made it clear that the way of the flame and the way of the falcon were more or less the same: *Everything belongs to the man who can reach and grasp without fear. That man the gods love.*

Still, although the visits went on for years, Prince Tulim made a vow the first night that he would kill his father one day. It was not so much the pain that had to be revenged as the helplessness—the flame should never be smothered by the shadow of another, not even the autarch himself.

As he approached the age at which boyhood would be set aside and manhood put on like a new garment, Tulim began to spend time with another grown man, this one much more deferential toward his feelings. It was the man he called Uncle Gorhan, one of the autarch's older half brothers. Gorhan had been sired by Parnad's father on a woman of extremely common blood, and so was no threat to take the throne. He had used this sullied nobility to his advantage, becoming one of the autarch's most trusted councillors, a man of storied wisdom and ingenuity. His attraction to Tulim was both less physical and less metaphysical than that of the boy's father: he saw in the youth a mind like his own, one that could, with proper training, roam not just beyond the walls of the Orchard Palace or the boundaries of Xis but through all the endless corridors of the gods' creation. Gorhan it was who taught Tulim to read properly. Not simply to recognize characters printed on vellum or reed paper and glean their sense—all princes learned that—but to read as a way of harnessing new wisdom to one's own like draft oxen, or adding new ideas to one's own like soldiers, so that the reader's power grew ever greater.

Gorhan introduced Tulim to the works of famous tacticians like Kersus and Hereddin, and historians like the great Pirilab. Tulim learned that the thoughts of men could be saved in books for a thousand years—that the great and learned men of other ages could speak as if to his own ear. Even more important, he learned that the gods and their closest followers could also speak across the great abyss of time and the greater abyss that gaped between earth and Heaven, sharing the secrets of creation itself. In the words of the warrior-poet Hereddin, which Gorhan quoted to him, *"He who reaches only for a throne will never grasp the stars."* Tulim understood that and felt that his uncle also must have a wisdom beyond other men, a wisdom only a little less than the gods: Gorhan had clearly sensed that Tulim was like no other, that he was greater even than the blood of his father that rushed through his veins. Gorhan understood that Tulim was a child, not of a man, but of Heaven itself.

Over the years, as Tulim grew older and his boyish limbs gained the supple sinews of young manhood, his father the autarch lost interest in him, which only confirmed him in his hatred. The autarch had only wished to use him, and not even for that which made him unique, but for those qualities he shared with any other handsome boy. If Tulim could have killed Parnad, he would have, but the autarch was not only constantly attended by his fierce Leopard guards but was himself a man of astounding strength and practiced, unflagging attention, even while engaged in activities which would leave a lesser man distracted or drowsy. In any case, generations of Xixian Autarchs had been protected by the existence of the scotarchs, the special, temporary heirs who were not of the autarch's direct line, men who would take the throne in the event of any autarch's suspicious death and mete out justice before handing the throne over to the true heir—providing that heir had not been the former autarch's murderer. It was a strange old custom; one with many twists and turns, but it had kept centuries of autarchs safer from intrigue than almost any other nation's monarchs.

So Tulim could do nothing except wait, and study, and plan . . . and dream.

At last came the day when the rectangular gongs in the Sycamore Tower and the Temple of Nushash sounded the royal death-knell. Parnad, only a little more than three-score years old, had died in the Seclusion, in the bed of one of his wives. Although there was no sign of foul play his scotarch promptly had the wife and her maids tortured to make sure they had no guilty knowledge, then executed them, which served as a reminder to other palace dwellers of how unsafe it was to be involved, even innocently, in the death of an autarch. The period of mourning began, after which Dordom, the oldest son, already a general in the army and a warrior of renowned skill and cruelty, would ascend to the throne.

But Dordom died choking the night of Parnad's death and it was whispered throughout the Orchard Palace that he had been poisoned. That began to seem even more likely when three more of Parnad's brothers (and a few of their friends, servants, and mistresses who happened to share the wrong plate or goblet) also died from some strange poison that could not be tasted or smelled, did not act at once, but then ate the victim away from inside like spirit of vitriol.

One by one the other heirs fell, poisoned like Dordom, stabbed in their sleep by servants thought incorruptible, or strangled by assassins while in the throes of love, with guards waiting outside who, apparently, heard nothing. Several of Parnad's less ambitious sons and daughters, seeing which way the winds of change were blowing, took their families and left Xis altogether to avoid their own deaths (which, nevertheless, eventually found them.) Others fell into the spirit of the game and for a year ancient Xis was like a single huge *shanat* board, with every move by a surviving member of the royal family considered and countered. Tulim, who was twenty-third in the line of succession, was not even considered as a possible culprit in the early deaths—many people believed that Parnad's death had set off a long-prepared, murderous rivalry between many of the aspirants to the throne. In fact, during the Scotarch's Year (as it was afterward called) most inhabitants of Xis, and certainly the wisest minds in the Orchard Palace, believed that the struggle for supremacy was between Dordom's younger brothers, the princes Ultin and Mehnad, who survived as other heirs fell or fled until only they, Tulim, and a demi-handful of others remained alive in Xis.

Most of the wisest courtiers felt certain that Tulim's survival was a mark of how little a threat he was to anyone. The few who knew him better, who might have had suspicions that things were not as they seemed, also knew him well enough not to gossip about him. Many of these truly wise ones survived to serve him.

Wisest of all, of course, was Uncle Gorhan, who had recognized a certain implacability in young Tulim—perhaps the reflection of his inner flame—and cast his own fate with the obscure princeling, so far from the throne. This was a genuine gamble on Gorhan's part because he was the sort of wise, unthreatening elder most likely to survive the accession of a new monarch, most likely to carry his service through another reign or even two, to die at last peacefully and in dignity and then be interred along with as many as a thousand living slaves, a mark of the royal family's great favor. Instead he was risking everything on one unlikely throw of the dice . . . or so it would have seemed to anyone who had not looked deeply into Tulim's disquieting golden eyes.

"I could do nothing else, Blessed Highness," Gorhan told him. "Because I knew what you would be when I first saw you and nothing could make me betray you. You and I, we are like this." The older man lifted his hand, index and middle fingers raised and pressed tight together to show the completeness of his connection to Tulim. "Like this."

"Like this, Uncle," echoed the prince, raising his own hand, fingers twinned. "I hear you."

As it happened, it was not long until their partnership bore its final fruits. One of the lesser princes was having an uncomfortable dinner with Mehnad, one of the two main rivals for the throne. In the midst of the meal the lesser princeling began to breathe like a man who had an entire duck egg stuck in his throat. He turned black, lurched to his feet and walked through the sumptuous meal set on the floor without seeing it, then fell into a crowd of servants bearing finger bowls and wine jugs, making such a clatter that for long moments it obscured the fact that his young wife had also died of a similar, although quieter, apoplexy.

Prince Mehnad, furious, shouted that this was nothing to do with him, that it was a plot to make him look petty (because what else was one to think of someone who poisons guests in his own house, and not only men but a woman as well?) Certain that his brother Ultin was behind it, Mehnad took a squadron of guards and went to Ultin's apartments in the city's Blue Lamp Quarter, but news of the murder had gone before them, and Ultin was waiting with a squadron of his own guards. Both brothers were so tired of the months of plot and counterplot, of murder and mistrust, that they needed no excuse to settle their differences now once and for all. As the guards brawled among themselves, Ultin and Mehnad singled each other out and, like the fierce soldiers they were, fought each other without mercy.

It was only when Ultin had finally cut down his brother and stood over his body in triumph, bloodied by a few wounds but largely unhurt, that the nature of Tulim's plan became obvious. Even as he crowed in victory, Ultin suddenly began to choke as the unfortunate princeling had choked—as if a duck egg were lodged in his throat. Blood passed from his nose and mouth, then Ultin fell down on top of his dead brother. Both men's swords, it was later discovered, had been poisoned by some third party, but Mehnad had not lived long enough to suffer the effects.

And as the two princes' household guards stood around the bodies in a cloud of confusion and rage, Tulim and Gorhan stepped out from the place where they had been watching. They had only a few of Gorhan's own guards with them, a much smaller number than either Ultin's or Mehnad's forces, but those who had so recently fought for the two older brothers recognized quickly that if they fought Tulim the best they could hope for was to be in search of new employment afterward—for what is a prince's guard with no prince? After all, Tulim was one of Parnad's heirs, and although he had begun as a very unimportant one he had managed to outlast nearly two dozen others—that in itself was enough to convince them his candidacy was worth considering; Gorhan's small but firmly committed bodyguard and their sharp spears were enough to make the argument convincing.

So it was that Prince Tulim, whom few had even noticed and none had particularly feared, walked across the bodies of dozens to achieve the Falcon Throne of Xis, taking for himself the autarchical name *Sulepis am Bishakh.* In days to come, Sulepis would reassert the historical right of Xis to rule over all the continent of Xand, walking across the bodies of hundreds of thousands more to do so, covering most of the land south of the Osteian Sea with his bloody footprints. And if he then set his sights on conquering the northern continent of Eion, who could blame him? He clearly had destiny on his side: his flame had indeed proved to burn brighter than all others.

And, like a god, Tulim-who-became-Sulepis didn't only mete out justice on the scale of continents: he could be personal as well. Within a few days of taking the throne he found himself in disagreement with his uncle Gorhan over some minor matter of statecraft, at which point Gorhan gave the new autarch a look calculated to make him feel, if not shame, at least discomfort at his own ingratitude.

"I am disappointed, my lord," Gorhan told his nephew. "I thought we were to be *like this*," he held up his fingers, index and middle pressed together. "I thought you cared enough to heed my advice. You are like a son to me, Tulim. I had hoped to be like a father to you."

"Like a father?" Sulepis raised one eyebrow, fixing Gorhan with a stare as remorseless and golden as that of a hunting hawk. "So be it." He turned to the captain of his Leopard guard. "Take the old man away," he said. "Flay the skin from his body—but slowly, so that he may feel it. Not all at once, either, but in a single strip winding the length of his body, starting at his feet and continuing to the top of his head. I would like him to live until then, this new 'father' of mine."

Even the hardened captain hesitated as old Gorhan fell to his knees, weeping and begging for mercy. "A single strip, Golden One?" the soldier asked. "How wide?"

Sulepis smiled and lifted two fingers. "Like this."

PART ONE

THE KNOTTED ROPE

1
A Cold Fever

"This Book is for all children of gentle birth, to give them instruction of the good example of the Orphan, holiest of mortals, beloved of the gods . . ."

—from "A Child's Book of the Orphan, and His Life and Death and Reward in Heaven"

THE DISTANT MOUNTAINS WERE BLACK, as were the rocky beach and the pounding sea, and the sky was like wet gray stone; the only bright things he could see were the crests of the waves that ran ahead of the stiff breeze and the gleaming white foam that leaped toward the sky each time a wave died against the rocks.

Barrick could scarcely take it all in. Overwhelmed by the clamor of the Fireflower voices, the inside of his head felt louder and more dangerous than the crashing surf, as though at any moment this storm of foreign thoughts, ideas, and memories might sweep him away, batter him and push him under, drown him utterly. . . .

. . . Not since Mawra the Breathless walked the world . . .

. . . But they came not by sea as Silvergleam had expected, but from the air . . .

. . . She was never after seen, although her lover and his pack searched the hills until the winter snows . . .

It was all he could do not to scream at the unending storm of thoughts. He clenched his teeth and curled his hands into fists as he struggled to hold onto the Barrick Eddon at the center of it all. He had hoped the confusion in his thoughts would ease when the king's funeral ended, but instead the silence that followed had seemed to make it worse.

The queen of the fairies was walking with him—or rather Saqri walked a little ahead, dressed all in billowing white so that she seemed hardly more substantial than sea foam herself. Ynnir's widow had not spoken a word to him since she had summoned him with a single imperious gesture to follow her, then led him out of the halls of Qul-na-Qar and down a winding path to the restless, dark ocean.

They were alone, Barrick and Saqri, or as alone as they could be: three armored, manlike figures stood at the foot of the path watching every step their queen took. These were Ice Ettins, Barrick could not help knowing, part of a clan called *The Whitewound*, from Bluedeeps in the north. He knew their names, too, or at least the gestures they made for their names—despite all their potential for violence, the Ice Ettins were a quiet and secretive race. He knew that their dully shining armor was nothing a smith had forged, but a part of their skins, as nerveless as nails or hair; he also knew that though none stood much taller than a mortal man, each Ice Ettin with his heavy bones and horny plates would weigh at least as much as three large men. These creatures were bound to the Fireflower by their clan oath, and each had earned a place in the queen's guard through victory in one of the murderous ceremonial games that *The Whitewound* always conducted in icy darkness.

Barrick knew all this as well as he knew his own name and the names of those who had raised him through childhood—but in a completely different way: all this new knowledge, countless histories and namings and connections and even more subtle things that could not be named but simply were, all these delicate understandings shouted and muttered in his head—shouted, but without noise. Barrick could not look at anything, even his own hand, without a thousand intricately foreign Qar ideas battering his thoughts like a sudden hailstorm—bits of poetry, scholarly associations, and countless far more meaningless and mundane memories. But these storms of knowledge were as the balmiest spring weather compared to the swelling of imagination and memory that crashed over him when he looked at anything significant—the towers of Qul-na-Qar or the distant peak of M'aarenol, or, worst of all, at Queen Saqri herself.

. . . When she first as a child stood in snow, laughing . . .

. . . The night her mother died and she took the Fireflower, and her sense of what should be would not let her weep . . .

. . . Her eye, knowing . . .

. . . Her lips, warm and forgiving after that terrible fight . . .

The associations went on and on, unstoppable, and Barrick Eddon was terrified by how little he could do beyond holding onto those parts of himself he could still recognize.

I was a fool to agree to this, he thought. *It is like the story of the greedy merchant—I will get everything I wanted, but it will fill me until I swell like a toad and then burst like a bubble.*

Saqri suddenly stopped and turned toward him—a graceful transition from motion to absolute stillness. She used words to speak out loud but he heard them in his thoughts as well, where the meanings were subtly different. "I have thought all the day and I still do not know whether to embrace you or destroy you, manchild," Saqri told him. "I cannot understand what my beloved great-aunt thought she was doing." A tiny shift of the mouth betokened a scowl. "I stopped wondering at my late husband's actions long ago."

Her thoughts came with a sting even sharper than the wind off the booming black sea. "It isn't . . ." He fought to keep his concentration through the flurry of foreign recollections and impulses. "It doesn't matter anyway. What she wanted. She sent me and . . . and then your husband gave me the Fireflower."

She looked at him with an expression that did not quite reach compassion. "Is it painful, then, child?"

"Yes." It was hard to think. "No, not painful. But it . . . I think it is too much for me. That soon it will . . . *drown* me . . ."

She took a few steps toward him, her head tilted a little to one side as if she listened. "I cannot feel you the way I could always feel him—but nevertheless, you are there. How strange! You are truly *shih-shen'aq*." It was a thought that did not become a word in his language, but still blew toward him with its meaning trailing—*flowered, enbloomed, blossom-hearted*: it meant to blaze with the inner complexity and responsibility of the Fireflower.

"But what does that mean?" he begged her. "Is there no way my thoughts can be quieted? I'll go mad. The noise, it's getting . . . stronger!" And had been since Ynnir had passed it to him, a fever in his blood just as terrible and mortal as the illness that had nearly killed him back in Southmarch, but a fever without heat, something altogether different than any earthly malady. "Please . . . Saqri . . . help me."

Something moved in her face. "But there is nothing I can do, manchild. It is like asking me to save you from your blood or your own bones. It is in you now—the Fireflower *is* you." She turned away to look toward the ocean. "And it is more than that. It is all of my family—all we have learned and all that we are. One half of it is in you. It may kill you." She lifted her hands in a deceptively small gesture, whose meanings rippled out in every direction—*Defeat is Ours* was one meaning, a strange mixture of resignation, terror, and pride. "And the other half is in me and will certainly die with me." She looked up, and for the first time he thought he saw something like pity in her hard, perfect face. "Take courage, mortal. The ocean has beat at this black shore since the gods lived and fought here, but it has not devoured the land. Someday it will, but that day has not yet come."

Everything she said set off ripples in Barrick's head like stones cast into a pond, each ripple intersecting with a dozen more and filling him with half-glimpsed memories and ideas for which the language of his thoughts had no proper words.

Black shore . . .

The first ships foundered here, but the second fleet survived.

The ones who sing beneath the waves . . . Listen!

It was like standing in a temple bell tower while the great bronze bells thundered the call to prayer. The voices seemed to shake him to his bones—but at the same time the attack was as silent as a subtle poison. "Oh, gods. I can't . . . stand it."

"But why did she do it?" Saqri scarcely seemed to hear him, looking up to the cloud-painted sky as if the answer might be swirling there. "I can understand Ynnir giving the Fireflower to a mortal, mad as it is—my husband would have taken any gamble, no matter the danger, to try to craft peace. But why would Yasammez mock him with that which she herself holds most dear? Why would she send you to him in the first instance?"

Her great age, voices suggested. *Even the mightiest can decay . . .*

Hatred, said others, full of anger themselves. *Yasammez has built her great house on the rock of her hatred . . .*

Barrick couldn't understand why none of them, not Saqri, not the even the Fireflower voices, suggested that which was so obvious to him. Did they really understand so little of despair, these people who should have understood it better than any—who saw their lives as an inevitable defeat lasting thousands of years?

"She wasn't . . . mocking the king," he said, struggling to make words out of the cacophony of his thoughts and senses. "She was mocking . . . herself."

Saqri whirled to stare at him. For a moment, by the weird, stony look on her face, Barrick thought she would strike him, or call her Ice Ettins to take off his head. Instead, she tilted her head back and laughed, a throaty burst of anger and amusement that caught him utterly by surprise.

"Oh! Oh, manchild!" she said. "You have taught me something. We must not let such a rarity end too quickly! I will honor my great-grandmother's wishes, no matter how obscure their origin, and we will try to find a way to mute the Fireflower, at least until you have learned to live with it."

"Can . . . can such a thing be done?"

She laughed again, but sadly. "It never has been. It was never necessary. But there has never been a scion of the Fireflower quite like you, either."

Like a walking white flame, she led him back over the black sands to the foot of the stone stairs where her armor-skinned warriors stood waiting, their eyes only glints deep beneath plated brows. The row of huge creatures parted with surprising grace to let her lead Barrick past, then fell in behind and followed them back up the winding hill-steps to Qul-na-Qar.

It was worse for him inside the castle: the ancient walls and passages put so many thoughts into his head that the voices in his skull swooped and chattered like bats startled from their roosts; it was all he could do to follow Saqri. A few times he stumbled, but felt the broad, stone-hard hand of one of the queen's escort close on his arm and hold him up until he found his feet again.

The Ice Ettins were not the only ones following them now. As soon as Saqri had entered the castle, a flock of shapes had appeared almost as suddenly as the Fireflower voices—Qar of every shape and appearance—but they seemed hardly even to notice Barrick. It was Saqri they surrounded, their voices full of worry and even fear for her health, and those who could not speak through the heavy air found other ways to make their unhappiness known, so that a cloud of dismay followed Barrick and the queen across the great central halls and down the Weeping Staircase. It felt as though the jabber of their thoughts and the whirl of Fireflower memories were pounding away at his wits like a hailstorm.

Barrick stumbled again. He was no longer certain how to make his legs work properly.

"I . . . can't . . ." he tried to say, then stopped to stare at Saqri, her guards, and supplicants. They were all changing, stretching, shredding like shapes made of smoke under the barrage of so much noise, so much life, so much *memory.* He couldn't remember what it was he had been about to say. Their now-unrecognizable forms curled into a dwindling whirlpool of color in the midst of the blackness and the clamor in his head suddenly went quiet. As the spin of light gurgled away, he fell into nothing, but he accepted the darkness with gratitude.

"Come back," the voice whispered. "Step out and join me, manchild. The light is good here."

He did not know who he was or who spoke to him. He did not know where he was, or why the darkness that surrounded him felt so immense—a place where you could fall for a thousand years before you even realized you were falling . . .

"Come back." A minute flicker of light, the faintest possible glimmer, appeared before him. "Come here. Come and run in these green fields with me, child. Where you were going is too cold."

He opened his eyes, or at least that was how it seemed: the blur of light spread and deepened. Green and blue and white, the colors burst out, and he felt like he drank them down as a thirsty man gulps water. The clouds, the grass, the distant hills . . . and what was this new thing? Something white skimming toward him down the gray sky, a great bird with wings so wide they seemed as if they would brush a cloud with each tip: it was Saqri, of course, wearing a dream-form—or perhaps he was learning something deep and true about her that could only be experienced here.

"Run with me!" the swan called to him in the fairy queen's gentle, musical voice. "Run! I will follow you."

Fixed on the beautiful white bird, his senses swimming with delight, he spread his own wings to leap toward her, only to realize he was not a winged thing at all but a creature of hooves and strong legs and long strides. As he bolted out over the green meadows there seemed little difference between what he did now and what he would have done with wings. It was a wonderful freedom—it felt *right.*

"Where is this place?" he called.

"It is not a matter of 'where' but of something different . . . 'how,' perhaps . . ."

He found he did not care. It was enough simply to run, to feel the wind making his mane and tail snap, to thrill to the thunder of his own hooves as they tore the grass beneath his feet into flying clods.

She skimmed past him and for a moment was content to fly just a little way ahead, matching his pace so that she seemed to float, rowing herself through the air with her vast pinions, black-beaked head on a neck long as a spear. "Are you weary, child?" she called. "Would you like to stop?"

"Never!" He laughed. "I could do this forever." And it seemed like he had never said anything more true—that there would be no greater heaven than to run here forever, fit and strong and free of everything.

But what is this place? His stride faltered a little. *Where am I? I was . . . I'm not . . .* He felt his powerful body carrying him across the face of the world on four striding legs. *But I'm not a horse . . . I'm a man . . . !*

Heaven. Is this heaven? Does that mean I'm dead?

And suddenly he shuddered to a stop, the hills suddenly high and close, the sky darker, everything near and threatening. "Where am I?" he said again. "What have you done to me?"

The swan banked and circled. "Done to you? Those are hard words, Barrick Eddon. I brought you back when I could have let you go. I brought you back."

"From where?"

"From what is next."

"I was . . . dying?" A chill stabbed him deep in his center. Even through this fevered excitement, he could suddenly feel how close he had come.

"Do not fear it. It is a road all of us must tread one day . . . all of us except the gods, that is."

"What do you mean?" He was trying to look down at his curious body but his head and neck were not well-shaped to do so. It felt unfamiliar—but also strangely familiar. "You mean everybody dies? But *you* don't. You and the king and all your ancestors . . . you don't."

"We will see. If the Fireflower leads you to share our fate, you will be able to judge for yourself what kind of immortality our gift gives to us."

The great bowl of meadow surrounded by hills seemed to grow darker still, as if a storm rushed in overhead, but in truth the mixed skies had not changed. "And this place? If I'm not dead, this isn't Heaven."

The swan stretched her beautiful neck. "It is not—although names are at best troublesome in these lands. It is another place. One that I could not be certain you would cross, or even reach, as you began to slip away from the places of the living—there is much I do not know about your people. But it was the only place I could have found you before it was too late, and the only place where I could be strong enough to hold you until you could make your own choice to return to the world or not."

Suddenly, as if a door had been thrown open, letting light in, he remembered. "It was the voices—all the . . . the things I knew. The Fireflower. And it felt like I was knowing more every moment . . . !" He felt his four feet restless beneath him suddenly, his entire body tensed to run.

"Of course," she said, and for the first time since he had first heard it he found her voice soothing. "Of course. It is difficult enough for one of our kind—how much stranger and more painful for one of your folk. That is why we are seeking help for you." A flicker of spread wing, a sunbeam of white blazing before his eyes, and she was off again. "So follow! We will go where mortals do not venture, except for those rare few that can dream a path. Those travelers pay for their journey with their happiness and their rest. Who knows what those like us, we who have neither rest nor happiness, will be asked to pay?"

Up into the hills he ran, following the dim form of the swan as it darted low over the grass ahead of him. The trees snapped past him like arrows and his legs drove him tirelessly as he ran from twilight into true darkness.

He ran so fast he could not feel the air, but nevertheless the cold grew in him, crystals of ice forming in his blood as they might on the surface of a slow-moving river as winter settled in. And as the cold and darkness grew, he crossed into a land where the hills grew naked of grass and great piles of stones loomed, each one somber and alone despite the thousands of others that surrounded it. The light now was as pale as that which fell from a waning moon, but there was no moon, only a black sky and a glow that painted the standing heaps of stone as though they were not whole things with weight and breadth but only spirits of stones gleaming in an unending midnight.

And as they passed farther and farther into this quiet, disheartening realm, the swan flickering low on the horizon was the only thing that reminded him of what daylight had been. A little of who he was and what he was doing came back to him.

Barrick Eddon. Son of the king of Southmarch. Brother of Briony . . . and of Kendrick.

He had fought all the way to the heart of Faerie because Lady Yasammez had commanded it. He had carried a mirror containing part of a god's essence all the way to Qul-na-Qar because Gyir the Storm Lantern, Yasammez' servant, had begged him to. And now he was carrying within himself the painful gift of the Fireflower, the life and thought and memory of all the kings of the Qar since the god Kupilas had fathered the line.

My blood comes from a god's blood. No surprise I have this dreadful storm in my head . . . !

But he didn't, and that was what finally struck him: since he had crossed over into this land, he had felt nothing in his head but his own thoughts: the Fireflower voices and memories had gone still. He had fallen back into the familiar glory of this solitude without even realizing how strange it now was.

"Saqri! Saqri, where have the voices gone?"

"If you mean the Fireflower ancestors, you cannot hear them now but you will again. Here you are no longer in your own land, where they can speak only into the ears of Crooked's children. We have crossed over into lands you have only glimpsed in the deepest and strangest of dreams. We are with the dead . . . and the slumbering gods."

And she flew on with Barrick running behind her, the dream of a man in the dream of a horse, chasing the queen of the fairies across the endless, empty lands.

The darkness was almost complete but Barrick was not frightened. He could see only what was in front of him, and that barely. Nothing spoke in his head but his own thoughts. Occasionally Saqri broke her long silences to give him encouragement or make some cryptic remark. At last they had gone so far into the valley that the barren hills climbed high on either side and the darkness became a sort of tunnel, with Saqri's whiteness the only thing he could see. "Where are we going?"

"We are there . . . I believe." Her thoughts were strangely hesitant. "The Valley of the Ancestors. I hope it is so, anyway . . ."

"Hope so? What do you mean? You've been here before, haven't you?"

She actually laughed. It had an edge of wildness. "How could I? These are the lands beyond—where the dead go. And I am still alive . . . !"

"But you . . . we're . . ." Suddenly the darkness and the deep-shadowed hills *twisted*, becoming something even deeper and stranger than before: Barrick felt as though, instead of running on a broad greensward, he now was galloping across an impossibly narrow bridge with nothingness yawning on either side.

The dead lands. The Valley of the Ancestors. The fear was growing so thick he could scarcely breathe. *What has happened to my life?*

"Quiet now." Saqri's voice was music in a haunting minor key. "We are close. We must not frighten them."

"*They're* frightened?"

"Only of life. Of too much care. Of the pull and grasp of memory." He could feel deep sadness in her words. "But I must bring all that and more to my brother."

Things moved around him now in the inconstant darkness, forms with some kind of independent existence from the grass and the hills. He could not see them, exactly, could only sense them as a man can feel when someone stands close behind him. These new forms seemed distant, almost empty, little more than wind and the impression of existence.

"These are the long dead, or perhaps the impressions those left behind when they moved on to other places." Saqri's voice seemed distant, her light scarcely more visible than the empty shapes around him. "Do not fear them—they hold no harm for you."

But he did fear them, not because they menaced him, but because they did not even seem to notice him or anything else. Were they simply shadows left behind, as Saqri said, or were they sunk so deep in death that they could not even be understood anymore by the living? It terrified him to imagine becoming such a thing some day.

"There." Saqri had moved a little closer, her swan-form faint as foxfire. "I see them—they are in the glade."

She led him into a murk of shadows that stood like trees. They were silvered ever so faintly by radiance from above, though no source was visible, as though the moon had let some of its light fall like dew before disappearing from the sky.

He saw them, then—a cluster of smeared, dully gleaming shapes that wavered as if seen through deep water or ancient glass. They were deer, or at least each bore a shining filigree upon his brow that might have been antlers. They moved restlessly as Barrick approached, but did not run.

"Do not go closer," Saqri told him. "They can smell the life on you. They may not remember it but they know it is foreign to this place."

Now he could see something brighter in the wavering light—eyes. The deer-shapes were watching him. "What do we do?"

"You? Nothing . . . yet. This first task is set only for me." And he felt her voice stretch out as her wings had, gently enfolding the herd before them with her words. "Listen to me, all you lords of winds and thought. I seek the one who in life was Ynnir, my brother. I am Saqri, the last daughter of the First Flower."

Barrick heard a voice, or felt it sighing like the wind in a tangle of branches. *"What do you want? You do not belong here. Do the black hellebores still bloom in the Dawnflower's garden, or has the Defeat finally come?"*

"It has not come yet, but it may be upon us with the next breath, my fathers. I have no time to waste, even in this timeless place. Send me Ynnir."

"The youngest of us . . . comes . . ." The voice was fading even as it spoke.

And then another shape appeared before them, closer and clearer than the others, a great stag whose gleam was far more vibrant than those of its older brethren. A lavender glow hung between its spreading antlers, the warmest thing in all of that cold, dark valley.

"Saqri?" it said after a long silence. *"Beloved? How have you come here?"*

"By roads I should not have traveled, and on which I may not find my way back, even if you help us." Her voice was as calm as ever, but some tight-drawn note in it told Barrick that this was not a happy meeting. "If there is to be any chance at all we must be swift. Come back with us, Brother. Your manchild is overwhelmed by what you have given him—his blood boils with it. Come back and help him to live with the terrible gift of the Fireflower."

The great stag lowered its head. "I cannot, Sister. Every moment it is harder to think as you think. Every moment the current pulls me farther into the river of forgetfulness. Soon the only part of me that will still touch the world will be that part which is of the Fireflower."

"But you must . . . !"

"You do not understand. You do not understand . . . what it would cost me."

Saqri was silent for a long moment. "Even to save the manchild, you will not come? You would abandon your own last and greatest gamble?"

The great stag raised his head. His eyes for a moment took on the same lavender gleam as the light that shimmered above his brow. "Very well, my sister . . . my most beloved enemy. The victory is yours. Every instant I stay in the between-lands, the House of Forever draws away from me . . . but I will do my best." The beast lowered its pale head like a prisoner awaiting the headsman's ax. "I will give what I have. I hope that it is enough."

2
A Letter from Erasmias Jino

"It is agreed by all men that the holy Orphan was born of lowly sheep herders in the hills of Krace during the reign of the Tyrant Osias."

—from "A Child's Book of the Orphan, and His Life and Death and Reward in Heaven"

BRIONY THOUGHT THAT TRAVELING with even a small army—and Eneas kept reminding her that his Temple Dogs made an *extremely* small army, scarcely even a battalion—was like living in a movable city, one that had to be taken down every morning and set up again the next evening. Even with a group of men as hardy as the prince's troops, swift riders who needed little in this spring weather beyond bedrolls and some source of water, they still could travel each day only as far as caution permitted. Few people were on the roads in this strange year, and those who were often had traveled no farther than from one walled town to the next, so information about what lay beyond the Southmarch border was scarce.

Every day took them farther north, winding up King Karal's Road (named after one of Eneas' most famous ancestors) out of Syan and through the lands that lay between it and the March Kingdoms, mostly tiny principalities who offered token allegiance to the throne in Tessis or the throne in Southmarch, but which only existed because the long era of peace had allowed them to keep their soldiers at home. Now that the north was in chaos they were less happy and less hospitable than they had been in the past.

They had discovered one such county seat near Tyosbridge. The land's master, Viscount Kymon, had refused to let Prince Eneas and his men inside the walls, although it would have brought a great deal of money into the pockets of the town merchants. Eneas and his dozen or so officers (with Briony among them) had been invited to spend the night at the viscount's hall but Eneas had refused, furious at the implication that his men could not be trusted—or worse, that he himself could not be trusted. They had spent the night instead camped outside with the men, something Briony admired greatly as a gesture. Still, a part of her could not help regretting the lost chance at a night on a decent bed. Between sleeping on the ground with the players and the same now with the Syannese soldiers, she had largely forgotten how it felt to sleep on the soft beds of Broadhall Palace, although she remembered very clearly that she had liked it.

The next day Eneas marched his men back onto the Royal Highway. He scarcely glanced up at the viscount's walled stronghold on the hill, but more than a few of the soldiers gave it a wistful look as it disappeared behind them.

"It's just as well," Eneas told Briony and his chief lieutenant, a serious young knight named Miron, Lord Helkis, who treated the prince with the respect normally given to a father, though Eneas was only a few years older. "They would only lose their edge in a city, anyway. Cities are terrible places—full of idlers and thieves and wicked women."

"Truly?" Briony asked. "That seems a strange thing to say. Don't your father and the rest of your family live in Tessis, the grandest city in Eion? Don't you live there yourself?"

Eneas made a sour face. "That is not the same, my lady. I live there because I must, and only when I must, but I prefer to live in camp—or in my hall in the mountains." His handsome face was serious—a little too serious, Briony thought. "Yes, that is a place you must see, Briony. From the upstairs windows you can see all the way down the valley—not a person in sight but a few shepherds and their flocks in the high meadows."

"It sounds . . . very pretty. And I'm sure the shepherds like it, too. But is there nothing good to be said about cities—or the royal court?"

He looked at her a little mistrustfully, as though she might be trying to trick him. "You saw what a court is like. You heard them whispering about you. You saw what they did to you, because you are from a quieter, smaller place and not used to their ways."

Briony raised her eyebrow. Her problem in Tessis had been that she had enemies, one of them the king's mistress, not necessarily that she was an innocent country girl who did not understand how to protect herself. As if no one had ever tried to kill her until she got to Syan! She wondered if that was part of what Eneas liked about her—that he thought of her as little more than a peasant girl, although one who had a stubborn, forward streak.

"In any case, Highness," she replied, "some of us like thing things that can be found in cities, and even at court—dancing and music, theater, markets full of things from other places . . ." Just talking about it reminded her of the delight she had felt as a young girl when her father showed her some of the more exotic items to be found in Market Square, the stuffed lizard from Talleno that looked like a tiny dragon, the huge skull of a strange, horned animal from somewhere beyond the Xandian desert, even the chest of spices from that continent's wet, hot jungles, not a one of them familiar except good Marashi pepper, which always made her nose wrinkle. She could still remember the anxious merchant, a little Kracian who had bounced up and down on his heels in front of the king, smiling and spreading his hands as if to say, "All this is mine!" Her father had bought the stuffed lizard, which had sat in her room for years until one of the dogs finally chewed it up.

Eneas was not thinking of the same kind of pleasant memories, to judge by the look on his face. "Cities! I despise them. I beg your pardon, Princess, but you cannot guess the kind of trouble they make for a ruler. The ideas that ordinary people get into their heads when they live in a city! All day long they see their neighbors wearing garments too fancy for their station, or they see nobles acting no better than the peasants themselves, until nobody knows where he belongs or what he is supposed to do. And theaters! Briony, I know you have a sentimental attachment to those players with whom you traveled, but you must know that most theaters are little better than . . . forgive my rough speech, I beg you, but it must be said . . . little better than brothels when it comes to the morals of the players. They parade in front of drunken men—some of the players dressed as women!—and frequently hire themselves out like common prostitutes. Again, I beg your pardon, but the truth must be told."

Briony tried not to smile. It was true that many of the players were a little loose in their morals—the treacherous Feival Ulosian, for one, had kept a string of wealthy admirers up and down the north of Eion—but she just couldn't see it with the same indignation Eneas felt. If the prince's beloved shepherds were so much better behaved, it could only be for lack of human companionship out there on the windy hillsides. Then again, they couldn't be as chaste as all that—little shepherds had to come from somewhere, didn't they . . . ?

"And why shouldn't ordinary people come together at a market or festival?" she said out loud. "Why would the gods have given us festivals if we were not supposed to enjoy them?"

Eneas shook his head. "That's just it. They didn't mean for such heedlessness to accompany their celebrations—they couldn't have! If you had stayed in Tessis longer you would have seen the Great Zosimia, and then you would know the truth. People dancing naked in the streets! Common folk mocking the nobles—and the drunkenness and fornication! Again I beg your pardon, Princess Briony, but it is heartbreaking to see the lawlessness that has become ordinary in the cities. And not just on Great Zosimia but on Gestrimadi, Orphan's Day, even Kerneia—you need but name it, and you will find another day when the common folk turn their backs on honest toil and think of nothing but wine and dancing!"

As grateful as she was to him, Briony was beginning to think that Eneas was in some ways a bit of an old stick. "But the nobles celebrate all these festival days and more besides. Why shouldn't the common people have the same privilege? They have the same gods."

Eneas frowned at her jest. "Of course they do. But it is the duty of the nobles to provide an example. The lower classes are like children—they cannot be allowed to do everything their elders are allowed to do. Would you permit a child to stay up all hours, drinking unwatered wine? Would you let a child go to the theater and see a man dressed up as woman kiss another man?"

Briony wasn't sure what she thought. She had heard sentiments like the prince's many times and had generally found herself agreeing—after all, if the common people could truly govern themselves then the gods would not have made kings and queens and priests and judges, would they? But this last year had made her look at things differently. Finn Teodoros, for instance, was one of the wisest people she'd ever met, and yet he was the son of a bricklayer. Nevin Hewney's father had been a cobbler but Hewney was still acknowledged to be a great playwright, better than dozens of writers from more noble backgrounds. And even the people she had met on the road while she was traveling in disguise had seemed little different than the nobles of the Southmarch or Tessian court except in richness of clothing and sophistication of manners. Certainly her own brother Barrick always said that the lords and ladies of Southmarch were only perfumed peasants—wouldn't the opposite be just as true, then, that the peasants themselves were only unbathed nobles . . . ?

"You have gone silent, my lady," said Eneas with a worried look on his fine face. "I have been too free with talk of rough matters."

"No," she said. "No, not at all, Prince Eneas. I am just thinking about the things you've said."

As they rode into the southeastern corner of Silverside, Briony discovered she could barely recognize her own country, her father's and grandfather's kingdom. There was little evidence out here of the siege of Southmarch, or in fact any trace of the fairy army at all—the Qar had passed far to the east when they marched down from beyond the Shadowline—but even in this relatively undisturbed spot, it felt as though Briony and the Syannese had arrived in the middle of an icy winter instead of a fairly mild spring. Fields lay fallow, and those that had been planted were barely half-seeded, as though there had not been enough people to do the work. In other places entire villages lay deserted, clusters of empty cottages like the nests of birds after fledgling season.

"The not knowing, that's what it is." The weary innkeeper was closing up his roadside hostel in the Argas River Valley and was only too happy to sell most of what he had left to the prince's moving town. "First we were feared the Twilight People were coming this way—people said the fairies were burning all the towns north of the Syannese border. They never came, but people came through from the east, running away—people whose towns *were* burned up, and they had terrible tales to tell. That scared away lots of our local folk, right there. After a while, though, hardly anybody using the road did for most of the rest of us. There are still people in these parts, especially the ones up in the hills, or the towns with high walls, but the villages along the road are all but empty." He shook his head, a man suddenly aged by fear and uncertainty. "And just like that, it all goes. You think it will never change but that's a lie. Things can change in a day."

In an hour, thought Briony. *In a heartbeat.* She was saddened by the innkeeper's confused, frustrated face, and saddened even more to know it would be a long time if ever before she could give these people any real help.

But here is something that the nobility can offer, she thought. *In bad times, a king or a queen can be a rock for the waters to crash against, so those less strong are not washed away.*

I will be such a rock. Only give me a chance, sweet Zoria, and I will be a rock for my people.

Qinnitan had only been awake a few confused moments when a glimpse of something manlike crawling on the beach drove her up the hills and into the forest. The thick morning fog hid the thing's full shape, but the look of it frightened her badly: either it was Vo, crippled by the poison, or something demonic, an *affir* out of old nursery tales lurching crablike along the gray northern sands. Qinnitan had no urge to find out which.

She made her way up the hillside, trying to stay on grass to protect her feet but often having to clamber through the thick, scratchy shrubs that covered the slope like blotches on the face of a beggar. After a sizable part of an hour had passed, and she had put the beach far behind her, Qinnitan began to feel the sharp jab of hunger, a pain she welcomed because it came from a problem she might be able to do something about. The larger matter seemed hopeless: she was lost in an unfamiliar land, and even if she had truly escaped her captor and what she had seen on the beach had been only the last wisps of a dream, Qinnitan knew that there was little chance she would survive in the wilds for a tennight without help.

She stopped to rest near the top of the hill, in the middle of a stand of trees with slender white trunks shaded by delicate leaves. Each stand grew a decorous distance from its fellows so that the hilltop glen seemed a gathering of stout Zoaz-priests saluting the dawn. At first she was merely impressed by the number of trees and the profusion of light-shot greenery, so different from the shaded gardens of the Seclusion, but after climbing higher, she reached a place where the trees began to thin and Qinnitan saw the full extent of the woods and the white-capped mountains beyond. She fell to her knees.

It was one thing to see the forests of the Eion coastline from the rail of a ship, their unending dull green spread along the coast like a rumpled blanket, but quite another to be *in* one and to think about crossing it. Qinnitan was a child of the desert, of streets where, despite the autarch's thousand sweepers, the sand still blew, and of gardens where water was abundant precisely because it was expensive and rare. Here, Nature squandered its blessings without discrimination, as if to say, "The way you and your people live is small and sad. See here, how for my own amusement I shower my riches on mere beasts and savages!"

For a long time she could only kneel, shivering, overwhelmed by the frightful vastness and strangeness of this alien world.

She did not find food that day or the next. She tried chewing on the grass that sprouted between the trees; it was bitter and did not ease the gnawing ache in her stomach, but at least it did not poison her. She heard birds, saw squirrels leaping through the upper branches, and once even saw a deer poised on a rise before her as if hoping to be noticed, but Qinnitan knew nothing of hunting or trapping. Neither had she seen a single residence or any sign of human habitation. While she was a prisoner her only thought had been to get off the boat, to free herself from Daikonas Vo so he could not give her to Sulepis, since she had decided long ago that it would be better to die than to fall into the autarch's hands again. But now that she was free and still alive, she wanted to *stay* alive but did not know how to do it.

What was this place that Vo had called Brenland? She could not understand how such a place could even exist, endless forest crisscrossed with fern-lined streams, green hills that looked out over more green hills, silent but for the rasping calls of hawks. If such a place existed in Xis, people would come by the thousands to enjoy this abundance of greenery and shade—it would be a byword for luxury, comfort, and beauty! But this wilderness was empty of people, lonely as the cries of its winged hunters.

Qinnitan knew from something Vo had said that Brenland stood east and south of the place they had been headed, which meant there must be some kind of settlements to the west of her, perhaps even cities. She tried to use the sun as a guide but had trouble finding it sometimes, and when she found it again she often seemed to have lost as much ground as she had earlier gained. She could drink almost whenever she wanted from clean, cold pools, which did much to keep her from despair, but her hunger was growing every hour. When the discomfort became too much, or when her legs would not carry her any farther, she piled leafy branches on herself and did her best to sleep.

Once or twice, when she had reached a high place out from beneath the trees she thought she saw a dark shape behind her, following her trail. If it was not the murderer Vo, it was likely nothing much better, a bear or wolf or forest demon. Each time she saw something that might be that shape slipping along behind her like a lost shadow, her heart felt cold, but each time she hurried on, determined that whatever else might happen, she would never be a prisoner again.

Two days passed, then three, then four. Each night it grew harder to ignore the griping pain in her stomach long enough to get to sleep, and harder to get up and go forward in the morning when yet another night had brought her no dreams of Barrick Eddon. For all she knew Barrick was dead now, or worse. When she most needed him, he had left her alone.

In the Seclusion, Qinnitan had fallen in love with one of Baz'u Jev's poems, called "Lost Upon the Mountain," and as the hours and days of Qinnitan's ordeal passed, she recited it to herself over and over again like a magic spell, though it merely gave words to her sadness and added to her growing certainty that she would die here in this unknown waste.

"Morning has gone.
Midday has gone.
The shadows are in the folds of the deep valleys
And I have lost my path.

"The wind is trying to tell me something
But I cannot understand the words
How does the sun
Find his way back through the darkness?

"Somewhere I hear the call of a mountain goat.
Somewhere I hear the shepherd's cry.
But though I turn and turn I cannot find the direction home.
How does the moon find his house in blinding day?

"And yet all come home
All come home again
All come home and find the fires
Lit for their homecoming.
And wine waiting in the cup.

"I ask you who find me
Only to remember, please remember,
That once I had breath, and on that breath
Was this song."

Keeping something familiar and sweet in her mind when the strangeness was crowding in brought her only a small amount of relief, but in this wild, empty country, that felt like a great deal to be grateful for.

Despite her year of leisured luxury in the Seclusion, Qinnitan had become considerably tougher long before she staggered out of the water and onto the shore of this strange place. She had worked hard in Hierosol, harder even than when she had been an acolyte in the Hive, and Vo had kept her since in painful and uncomfortable conditions, feeding her only enough to keep her middling healthy; she had also slipped part of her own food to the boy Pigeon while they were still together. So Qinnitan was no hothouse flower, no orchid in the autarch's greenhouse, like the woman Baz'u Jev described in one poem, *"A fragrance of ineffable sweetness, but the first brisk wind will carry it away, never to be tasted again . . ."* But now she was coming to the end of her strength. The fifth day—she thought it was the fifth, but she was no longer certain—and then the likely sixth passed in a smear of dappled forest light, of needles and leaves sliding wetly underfoot, of first one stream to cross and then another, like shining stripes on the back of some giant beast . . .

Qinnitan fell down at last and could not get up. The shadows of the late afternoon had turned the forest into a single dark place, a great tomb filled with columns to hold the crushing weight of the world and the sky. Her head seemed full of voices, chanting wordlessly, but she thought perhaps it was only the shadows of the trees falling on her, heavy as drumbeats.

She tried to remember the prayers the Hive Sisters had taught her but she doubted Nushash could even hear her in this place so far from the sun and the red desert: a few words came to her, fragile as sand-sculptures, then quickly fell apart again.

Please, she prayed, *please do not let me die alone.* The noise in her head grew deeper, greater, like the rush of a tremendous wind. *Please help me find a way to Barrick . . . to the red-haired boy who was kind to me. Oh, gods and goddesses, please help me! I am so deep in the forest that I can't think anymore! Please help me! Where am I? Where is he? Please help us . . . !*

For long moments after Qinnitan awoke, she did not even realize that rain was falling on her, though she was shivering hard. Then, before she could do more than rise to a crouch, a nightmare shape lurched out from between two trees and into the clearing before her. He was bent double and walked with a shambling, crablike gait. His hair sprang wildly over his head and he had the beginnings of a shaggy beard to match, but what sent a cold knife of fear deep into her gut was the mask of blood that all but covered his dirt-smeared face—blood from dozens of cuts, blood that had streamed in gouts from his nose and dried there, blood at the corners of his mouth and smeared in his whiskers. And when he opened his mouth to grin at her, there was even blood between his teeth.

"Ah, yes," said Daikonas Vo as calmly as if they had met in the marketplace. "Here you are."

❧

The messenger from Syan had the look of a man who had nearly killed several horses reaching them; his cloak and breeches were more travel stains than cloth.

"Forgive me, your Royal Highness," he said, kneeling before Eneas. "I have left an exhausted mount in every post between here and Tessis but his lordship the marquis wanted you to have this as quickly as was possible."

Eneas reached out for the oilskin pouch, pulled out the letter, and looked briefly but closely at the seal. "My quartermaster will see you are given a meal and a place to sleep," he told the young courier. Standing there, Eneas opened the folded letter to read it while Briony waited as politely as she could. She guessed the marquis must be Erasmias Jino, a man Prince Eneas trusted despite his profession as spymaster. Briony herself had not particularly liked Jino to begin with, but unlike most of the folk in King Enander's court, he seemed to have done more good for her than bad.

"You should read this too," he said when he had finished. His face was grim; Briony felt her throat tighten.

"My father . . . is he . . . is there anything . . . ?"

"Nothing to say he is not well," Eneas quickly assured her. "Your pardon, my lady—I did not mean to frighten you. There is no direct mention of your father at all. But I do not like the other things Jino has to tell me."

Briony took the letter from him. A frowning moment passed before she could make anything of the Marquis of Athnia's hand—he had the ornate Tessian style, all filigree and curlicue, so that his words were almost more ornament than information—but after a moment she began to get the feel of it. Also, ornate hand or not, she had to admit that after the customary greetings and salutations Jino did not waste time on needless fripperies.

"Highness, I have done all that you asked me to do,"

she read out,

"In other matters, though, things are not so satisfactory. Many at court do not even acknowledge that we are at war despite the events to the south and the attack on Hierosol. This will change when it is their own lands being snapped up by the autarch, of course, but by then it will be too late for many of them, if not for all of us."

"But it is of the autarch himself I wish to speak, because I am in receipt of many strange pieces of news about him and can make nothing in the way of a larger picture from them. I beg your Highness to set your greater tactical understanding to this task, where my poor wits have failed."

"Isn't the marquis rather full of himself?" asked Briony. "Even when he's trying to be unctuous, he can't quite do it."

"He's a good man, Princess." Eneas sounded offended. "He is my right arm at the court—a place I avoid when I can, and where I desperately need men I can trust."

"Certainly, I didn't mean . . ." She turned back to the letter.

"Numerous strange reports have come from Hierosol, and not just from the refugees that clutter our cities along the southern border. Equally surprising rumors are coming from the garrison commanders and even some of the nobles, survivors of the old gentry, who are mostly now in hiding or out of Hierosol. Their stories often conflict, and in many cases are filled with unsupported speculation, but one thing

almost all seem to agree on: the autarch is no longer in Hierosol. Neither is he back in his capital of Xis—travelers in the south agree that one of his lackeys, a man named Muziren Chah, still holds the viceregal throne. So the question becomes, where is the autarch?

"Some of the speculation is that he became ill and rushed back to Xis in secret, in order not to give comfort to his enemies or diminish the bravery of his troops. Other tales suggest more sinister reasons—that he has been assassinated by rivals or his heir, a sickly creature called Prusus, and that the new ruler is keeping it secret until he can take Xis back from the dead autarch's caretaker.

I have also heard from other sources (although none of them witnesses) that the autarch and a small army of Xixians attacked King Hesper of Jellon and killed him and many of his subjects, then sailed away again. I have even heard a rumor that he is kidnapping children all across Eion to make some sacrifice to his heathen gods, asking Nushassos and the rest to give him total victory over the north, but I think the source of that one must be the breath of war and fear of the unknown instead of anything based on true events.

"Thus, I do not know what to advise you, Highness. I find it hard to believe that the autarch would leave his siege of Hierosol except to return to Xis—monarchs too long gone from their homes sometimes begin to fear what they have left behind. But almost all the tales agree that he has left, and almost as many say that no sign of him has been seen in his own kingdom. At the same time, the Xixians' attempt to break the last resistance in Hierosol has not flagged. If that devil Sulepis has lost interest in conquering that great old city, I can see no sign of it.

"I have little else to tell you, except that your father's health is unimproved. The great pains still come upon him without warning, and his mood suffers because of it. The physicians attend him, and I have sent for . . ."

"That's enough," said Eneas suddenly. "The rest is only meant for me—small matters of my household. Jino and a few others keep an eye on things for me when I am away from home."

"Your father is ill . . . ?"

Eneas shook his head, a little too hard. "A distress of the stomach. My uncle has sent a famous Kracian physician to treat him, the best of his kind. My father will be well soon."

Briony suddenly felt she understood some of what was going on, or at least the cause of Eneas' brittle mood.

"You are worried, dear Eneas," she said. "No, don't say anything. Of course you are. Worse, you fear that something might happen to your father while you are away." She wanted to say, "And you fear that Lady

Ananka and her supporters at court may try to take control of the throne in your absence," but she knew he would feel obligated to disagree. Sometimes, Eneas' sense of honor forced him through a tiring series of responses that he and everyone else knew were not his true feelings, but simply what he felt as obligations. Instead, Briony continued with, "And you are caught between your oath to me and your loyalty and worry for your father and your country."

He glanced up at her, startled. Lord Helkis and some of the other nobles in the great tent were beginning to look distinctly uncomfortable. Eneas sent them away, keeping only the young pages as defense of Briony's modesty.

"You presume much when you presume to know my mind, Princess," he said when they were more or less alone.

"I'm sorry, Highness, but I believe what I say is true."

He gave her a stern look. "Still, even if so—and I do not concede it—it is not to be talked about in front of all and sundry."

"What—you mean Miron? Lord Helkis? He is your best friend and a relative. As are all your other captains friends and relations. Don't you think they have thought the same thing? Don't you think they have wondered why you are riding north into unknown dangers and someone else's war when you have the danger of the autarch at your own country's southern doorstep and a royal father who is in poor health?"

"It is nothing. My father eats rich food every night. That woman encourages it." For a moment something of his true feelings about Ananka showed on his face, his jaw tight and his teeth clenched. "But that is not the issue here. Even if what you said were true, I have sworn to accompany you home. That is not something that can be undone. . . ."

For a moment Briony's admiration for him soured into something else—frustration, perhaps even anger. Why were men so caught up with their honor, their solemn word, their promises? Half the time the promises were never asked of them in the first place! And yet the wars that were fought over such things, the hearts broken and the lands ruined . . . !

"Very well." She held up her hand. "Then know this, Eneas. I hereby release you from your promise, if I ever truly held you. I do not think I did. You offered me a great favor from the kindness of your heart. Now I release you from it. You must do as your heart thinks best . . . but do not let a single promise, uttered in haste and in a kind attempt to atone for the rest of your family's bad treatment of me, force you to do something you think is foolish. If your family needs you—if your country needs you—go. I of all people will understand."

Again she seemed to have caught him by surprise, as if he had not thought her capable of thinking and acting this way. For long moments he could only stare at her as though seeing something new and strange.

"You are . . . a brave woman, Briony Eddon. And in truth I do feel a pull to go home, as any son would—as any heir would. But things are not so simple. Give me this evening to think. Tomorrow morning we will speak again, you and I."

She thanked him and went out. Their parting was oddly formal, but for the moment Briony would have had it no other way.

She did not sleep well. Lisiya's bird-skull amulet clutched in her hand did not bring her dreams of the demigoddess or any other immortal, only a series of escapes from and near-captures by shadowy things she could not quite see, things that muttered in angry voices as they followed her through tangled woods and over marshy ground where she had to fight to stay upright. When she woke, she was as tired as if she had spent the entire night doing what she had dreamed.

Still, she could not bear to sit around waiting for Eneas to summon her, so she bundled up warmly in her hooded travel cloak and went to walk along the edge of the encampment in the first blue light of the morning. The Temple Dogs had selected a small box canyon a short distance off the Royal Highway where the hills were as comfortably close and enfolding as her cloak. Briony walked to the top of the nearest one without ever losing sight of the sentry post, then sat and watched the sun clamber into the sky.

I am no less stubborn than Eneas, she thought to herself. *I don't want him coming with me if he is to resent it, even though I am desperate for his soldiers . . . and happy with his company as well, if I am honest with myself.*

But each day spent with Eneas Karallios, the heir to the throne of Syan, was also a sort of lie, or at least so it often seemed. The prince cared for her, he had made that obvious. He would marry her, or at least that was what he seemed to be saying. And there was much to admire about him, as well. Even to hesitate about accepting his affection seemed nearly an act of madness—certainly almost every other woman on the continent of Eion would deem it so. But Briony did not know what she wanted, or even what exactly she thought, and was just stubborn enough not to let good sense rush her into anything.

The sun was tangled in the branches of the trees lining the hillcrest. The dew was almost gone from the grass and the camp below was up and in full preparation for another day on the road—but which direction would they be going? What would the prince decide? And what would she do if he did decide to turn back to Tessis, as she had all but begged him to do?

What I have done all along. I will keep going, she told herself—and half-believed it. *I will follow my heart. And, with the help of Zoria's mercy, I will hope not to be too much of a fool.*

Still, there was a small part of her that hoped she hadn't been *too* forceful in making her points to Eneas.

Thinking about the prince made her think of Guard Captain Vansen, as it usually did. How strange that these two, who did not know each other and likely would never meet, should be so twinned in her mind! She could hardly think of two men less alike except in common kindness and decency. In all other ways, in looks, importance, wealth, power, Eneas of Syan was Ferras Vansen's clear superior. And Eneas had made his feelings known, whereas Briony had to admit her notion that Vansen cared for her was based on the flimsiest of interpretations, a few looks, a few mumbled words, none of which could not equally be said to represent the ordinary awkwardness of a common soldier in the presence of his monarch. And he *was* a common soldier, which made it all the greater an idiocy even to think about him in that way. Even were Vansen to throw himself down at her feet and beg her to marry him, Briony could no more do that than she could marry one of her horse-grooms or a merchant in Market Square.

Not without giving up my throne. . . .

Briony could not even entertain such a mad idea. With her father and brother gone, who would look after her people? Who would make certain that Hendon Tolly received his due and dreadful reward?

She sighed, plucked up a handful of damp grass, and flung it high into the air. The wind lifted and carried the grass for a moment and then, like a bored child, let it fall.

"You sent for me, Highness?" she asked.

Eneas frowned. "Please, Briony. Princess. Do not speak to me as though we have not been friends."

She realized he was right. There was a stiffness in her manner. "I . . . I'm sorry, Eneas. I meant nothing by it. I did not sleep well."

He showed a rueful smile. "You are not the only one. But now I have decided what I must do—what common sense demands as much as honor." He nodded. "I will stay with you, Briony Eddon. We will continue to Southmarch."

Briony had already begun to tell him she had expected it, and to thank him for all he had done for her; she was even pondering what she could decently ask of him besides the horse and armor he had already given her when she realized what he had said. "What? Stay . . . with me?"

"I gave my word. And I realized that, with Jino and other friends at Broadhall, I am not so cut off as I might think. Even should something . . . the Brothers prevent it, the gods all forswear it . . . should something happen to my father, the kingdom is sound . . . and the throne is safe." He smiled, although it did not come easily. "If Ananka had given my sire an heir, things might be different."

As Anissa did with my father, Briony thought but did not say. The thought echoed in her head unpleasantly, but she pushed it away for later consideration. "Your Highness . . . Eneas . . . I don't know what to say!"

"Then say nothing. And don't assume it is only because of obligation, either. Your company means much to me, Briony—your happiness, too. And I have my own curiosity about what is happening in the north. Now go and make yourself ready, I beg you. We ride out within the hour and I must prepare a letter to be sent back to good Erasmias Jino."

She left him scratching away at a sheet of parchment and walked back to her tent with the feeling that she had stepped unexpectedly from one road to another, and that because of that much had changed and much more would change in days ahead.

3
Seal of War

"His parents named him Adis, and when he was old enough they sent him out to watch over the flocks. He was pious and good, and he loved his parents nearly as much as he loved the gods themselves . . ."

—from "A Child's Book of the Orphan, and His Life and Death and Reward in Heaven"

BOTH CHAVEN AND ANTIMONY carried torches, although the young Funderling monk was only carrying his as a favor to the physician. Only a few brands glowed in the whole of the great chamber called Sandsilver's Dancing Room, since the Qar had little more need for light than the Funderlings themselves . . . or at least that was true for many of them: Chaven had already seen examples of some who needed no light at all because they seemed to have no eyes, as well as huge-eyed folk who blinked and winced at even the dimmest glow. Chaven could not help marveling at the variety.

"How can such things be?" Brother Antimony asked quietly. "The Great God has made men in many shapes and sizes, we know—look at you and me!—but why should he make one kind of creature with so many different shapes?"

Chaven couldn't answer. He would have loved to study every single Qar with a strong lamp and seeing-glass, calipers and folding rule, but at the moment he and Antimony had a more important task, which was seeing to the comfort (and covertly examining the mood) of these new allies. Vansen had asked him to do it, so Chaven had chosen Antimony, the most open-minded of the Metamorphic Brothers, as his companion.

"I was thinking only a moment ago how much we could learn from these folk," Chaven told the Funderling. "Even Phayallos admits that when they lived beside us centuries ago very little proper study was done. Most of the works that purport to describe the Qar from detailed studies sadly turn out to be filled with hearsay and superstition."

"It is not superstitious to fear something whose ways and looks are so different," Antimony said, his voice still low, "and I will be frank, Physician Chaven—I fear these creatures." The cavern seemed filled with roiling shadow, a single moving thing with many parts like something crawling in a tidal pool. "Even if they are sincere in their desire to fight the autarch, who's to say what will happen if we live through it? Even if we somehow beat the southern king and all his thousands and thousands and thousands of men, what if these Qar decide afterward to return to what they were doing—which was killing us?"

Chaven was pleased to see the young man exercising his wits so clearly. He had been right—this one had the makings of a scholar. Pardstone Jasper, the last Funderling who had regularly contributed to the wide conversation of scholars, had died when Chaven was still a young boy. "You ask a good question, Brother Antimony, and Captain Vansen and your Magister Cinnabar are already thinking on it as well. I expect that is all we can do at the moment . . . think on it. Because even to reach the point of having to deal with that problem will be an astounding and unexpected triumph." He shook his head. "Forgive me—I do not mean to be gloomy."

Despite his earlier admission, Antimony seemed more fascinated than frightened. "Look at that one—he glows like a hot coal! He looks to be nothing but a fire burning inside a suit of armor—or is that suit of armor a part of him, like the shell of a crab?"

"I could not say, but I believe it is one of the Guard of Elementals."

"How do you know?" asked the monk, impressed.

Chaven shrugged. "Only because Vansen told me—he said they were some of those most likely to cause trouble. Just as not all of *our* friends are happy with the idea of yoking our fortunes to the Qar, so they have their own disagreements, and apparently these Elementals are among the most . . . disagreeable." He fought off a shudder. "Still, all the questions of refraction such a thing raises are fascinating at the very least . . . !"

They stood and watched as a parade of strange shapes filled the great chamber, some far smaller than any Funderling, others that could only be called giants. The Qar had so many forms and sizes that it was often hard to tell which creatures were soldiers and which were beasts of burden. Chaven recognized a few from descriptions in Phayallos or from Ximander; others he could only guess at. Occasionally, a confusing citation in an old book would suddenly march past him in the flesh, even pause to cast a mistrustful eye in the physician's direction. He explained what little he knew about them to Antimony, talking more than was his usual wont, in part because of the pleasure of an intelligent audience (so much more satisfactory than talking to that boob Toby, his so-called assistant, who really had been little more than a particularly useless servant) and partly because he did not want to have to listen to his own troubled thoughts.

Chaven fell silent at last, not because the newest arrivals were any less odd and interesting, but because the emptiness of his own knowledge had begun to grieve him. Here he was in the midst of the most fascinating thing a lover of the physical world could imagine, and yet the chances were good that neither he nor these wonderful and frightening Qar would survive the slaughter that was coming.

So I shall play a part in this war that any fool could play while a chance for true scholarship is wasted . . .

And the violent fate hurrying toward them even now was not his only worry. Chaven had been long troubled by the loss of what seemed an entire day of his recollections, perhaps more. He had been in Funderling Town on a Skyday, he knew, then had set out for the temple on a Windsday, but had not reached the temple until Firesday—an entire day and more missing. In truth, he remembered only a little of his time in Funderling Town well, and could no longer recall even the errand that had taken him there. Chaven knew that it had seemed important when he decided to go, so it was more than strange he should not remember it now. It frightened him.

This was not the first time he had lost track in such a way. For several days before Winter's Eve, the night Princess Briony had fled Southmarch with Shaso, he had been gone from the castle, or at least from his house in the outer keep, but he couldn't remember where he had gone that time, either.

Looking again at the cavern before him, at the vast sprawl of huddled, mostly silent shapes, eyes glowing in the shadows like foxfire, he quietly asked Antimony, "If all we are is in our thoughts, how can a man know if he is going mad?"

The young monk was silent for a long time. He was large for one of his folk, but the top of his head was still a hand's breadth below Chaven's shoulder; when he spoke, his voice seemed to rise up from the stony floor, as if the cavern itself was speaking.

"He cannot know. Nor can a king, I suppose . . . which is what they say of this autarch, that he is a madman. In fact, as I think on it, Chaven, even a god might not know whether he had lost his wits, if he lost 'em."

"And thank you, Antimony," the physician said. "You have given me even more to worry on." He hoped he sounded more amused than he felt.

"I do not mean to be rude," Ferras Vansen began, "but Funderlings—and taller men, too—are not as patient as your people. Your mistress set an hour for the council to take place, and yet not only has she not come, she has not sent word as to why. Hours are passing. People grow worried."

Aesi'uah folded her hands before her mouth, as though to blow life into a tiny flame shielded there. "Please, Captain Vansen, you do not understand . . ."

"No, your mistress does not understand." He did not like arguing with her. The chief eremite was quiet and graceful, and in her own way, kind; disagreeing with her made him feel clumsy and cruel. "My allies have made a brave concession. They have opened their gates to your people, although only days ago you Qar were killing Funderlings on the doorstep of their own city. Not only that, but they have even given you a place for your army to camp—a place between themselves and their most holy place . . ."

"That is because of our shared mortal enemy, the Autarch of Xis," she began, but Vansen was still angry.

"Yes, but *we* were not in immediate danger from the autarch. The people of Southmarch were safe inside our castle walls, the Funderlings down here in the rock. It was your people in their camp above who were most at risk."

She paused, but with the air of someone listening to something he couldn't hear. He suspected she conversed with Yasammez in her head, just as he had once heard the words of Gyir Storm Lantern in the same, silent way, but knowing that did not make him feel any better. It happened to her several times an hour and had been a constant reminder that no matter how courteously she seemed to listen to Vansen, nothing would be done without her mistress' consent.

"Please, Captain," she said at last. "One thousand years or more of hatred and distrust do not vanish with a wave of the hand."

"Oh, trust me, my lady, I know that very well."

"Look there," Aesi'uah said, gesturing with a slender hand toward the crowd of strange shapes that surrounded them, filling the natural stone gallery to the walls—perhaps a thousand Qar in this chamber alone. "Already we have done something here unseen since the earth was young. Understand that my mistress must deal with problems of her own, many of them of a subtlety that I cannot explain to someone who will live only a century."

Vansen was surprised to feel pain at her words, although she only told the truth—he was not like her, not at all. The pain was from what it brought back to his thoughts, the equally unknowable distance between himself and the woman he loved. It was becoming clearer to Vansen every day that it had been madness even to suppose he and the princess lived in the same world.

"Just give your lady to know," he said, "that my people are losing patience. That everybody is losing patience. And they are frightened, too."

"As you said yourself, Captain, trust me." Aesi'uah smiled—at least, he had always assumed it was a smile, since it seemed in many ways to serve the same function as it would have in an ordinary woman, although not always. "My mistress already knows this."

"But, Opal . . . !"

She fixed him with a stare that could have split granite like a wedge. All the Leekstone women had that eye. "Don't you dare. There should be women there and there *will* be women there. By the Elders, their *general* is a woman."

"Exactly! And according to Vansen she has the blood of a god running in her veins and a temper like a cornered rat. She's killed Big Folk by the hundreds . . . !"

His wife again gave him that shriveling glance. "I'm not planning to take up a sword and fight her, old fool. We're *welcoming* them. We are allies now."

"Not yet." He knew he was losing, but he could not resist one last attempt to bring some perspective to the conversation. "We're hoping to be allies. This is a sort of parley, remember? There's no promise that they won't change their minds and cut all our throats—which they were trying to do just a few days ago."

"All the more reason to have a few sensible Funderling women on the spot, then," she said with satisfaction. "It will mean that much less chance of Jasper or some other lackwit starting another fight." She nodded. "Now, I have to go. Vermilion Cinnabar has called all the women to a meeting in the Temple library before the Qar arrive."

"In the library? Oh, the brothers will love that."

"The Metamorphic Brothers have had their own way too long, and so has the Guild. That's one of the reasons we're in this slide. Imagine, not telling anyone the Qar have been coming here for years!"

"What? How did you hear of that?"

"Vermilion Cinnabar told us. She heard it from her husband, of course."

"Beat it out of him, more likely." Chert had to laugh. Clearly, things were going to change whether he wished it or not. Better to be on top of the boulder when it decided to roll than in front of it. He gestured toward the boy, curled sleeping in a feral pile of blankets on the floor. "What about Flint?"

A troubled expression flitted across her face. "I was going to bring him with me, but he declares he will go with you instead."

Chert felt bad for her. "He's growing. He wants to be with the men . . ."

"That's not what's bothering me, you old fool. He's changed. Haven't you noticed?"

"Of course. But he's always been . . . unusual. . . ."

"Not that. He's changed in some other way . . . something new. But I can't . . ." She made a noise of frustration. "I don't have the words for it! But I don't like it." For the first time he saw how upset and frightened his wife really was. "I don't like it, Chert."

He stepped toward her and put his arms around her middle, pulled her close, and kissed her forehead. "I don't like it either, my love, but we'll make sense of it. I missed you, did you know that?"

"Missed me picking up after you," she said gruffly, but did not let go.

"Oh, yes," he said, smelling her hair, wishing they could simply stay that way, standing together, with everything bad still yet to happen. "That as well."

"How do you see it, Captain?" Sledge Jasper asked Vansen as they seated themselves at the table. "Do they speak our tongue, or is it all barble-barble except for that silver-haired baggage?"

"She is not a 'baggage,' Jasper, she is a high-ranking adviser to Lady Yasammez and a powerful figure in her own right."

The bald Funderling gave him a doubting look. "As you say, Captain. I'm just asking if they speak properly or not."

Vansen thought about Gyir's voice, something he had never heard with his ears, but which he would never forget. "They have many ways of talking. I do not think they will have any trouble making their wishes known . . ."

"Oh, shite and slurry!" said Jasper loudly.

Vansen was taken aback—for a moment he thought that the little man was calling him a liar. Then he saw what Jasper had seen—half a dozen Funderling women, led by Cinnabar's wife and Chert's wife Opal, making their determined way across the chapel.

"Hold now." Jasper was on his feet, as though he would bodily keep the women from the table. "What are you doing here? The Qar are coming!"

"Sit down, Wardthane Jasper." Vermilion Cinnabar was a handsome Funderling woman, dressed in a beautifully embroidered blue-green travel robe. "We have just as much right to be here as you and your warders."

"I beg your pardon, Magistrix," said the wealthy Funderling Malachite Copper, who had quickly made himself invaluable to the struggle. "Of course your advice is welcome, but only a few days ago these Qar were trying to kill us . . ."

"That is neither here nor there, is it?" The magister's wife directed her companions to seats on either side of her. Unlike Vermilion Cinnabar and Opal Blue Quartz, the other women looked a bit awed to be in such a place at such a time—but then again, Vansen thought, so did the men.

One of the other women leaned forward. "Is there much danger?" she whispered to Opal, who was sitting close enough for Vansen to hear.

"No," Opal told her, then shot Vansen a look that clearly said, *"And please don't disagree."*

She and the magister's wife are leading their troops by example, he realized. *Like any good commanders they are worried too, but they cannot show that to their forces.* "We should be well," he told the Funderling woman. "We are all under a treaty of peace here and the Qar, whatever else they are, seem to me honorable creatures." He felt a touch of shame at the understatement—Gyir the Storm Lantern had been more than "honorable." He had unhesitatingly given his life to carry out his promise to his mistress Yasammez—the sorceress or demigoddess they all awaited today.

Chert and Cinnabar and the physician Chaven came in with several others, including a party of Funderling monks led by Brother Nickel. The monk even nodded courteously toward Vansen as he and his party seated themselves at the long table.

"What's gotten into him?" Vansen said, half-aloud.

Malachite laughed. "Don't you know? Cinnabar had a talk with him. Reminded him that the Guild's highwardens have to approve a new Prior of the temple—and, when it comes to it someday, the new abbot of the temple as well. If Nickel wants to carry the abbot's holy mattock he's going to have to dig when the Guild says dig."

"Ah." Vansen wasn't surprised. Even Nickel, with the sacred souls of all the Funderlings supposedly in his protection, saw things differently when ambition called the dance.

"Hello, my darling," said Chert as he bent to kiss his wife. "I hope you don't mind—I'm going to be sitting with Cinnabar. It's his idea." Chert did his best to look surprised that he had been singled out for this honor, but Vansen knew the little man not only had good sense, he was in the middle of so many of the mysteries here that he was virtually indispensable. "And how very nice to see you, Magistrix!" he said to Vermilion Cinnabar. "You're looking well."

"Magistrix, is it?" she said with an amused smile. "I'm not soapstone, Chert, so don't try to carve me. Your wife has told me all about your adventures. I think my husband wants you around just to take his mind off our boring life at home."

Chert laughed. "Oh, wouldn't we all love to be bored these days, Magi . . . Vermilion." He gave Opal another squeeze and wandered back to Cinnabar and the others.

"My Chert is a good man," Opal said fiercely and suddenly, as if someone might have been about to suggest otherwise. "Everything he's done has been for others."

Before Vansen could tell her how much he agreed, a stir ran through the chapel—a sense of wonder and alarm that Vansen felt before he either heard or saw anything, a primal thrill of warning that ran up his spine. He turned and for a moment only saw Aesi'uah in the doorway—a powerful, captivating figure, no doubt, but someone he looked on almost with fondness. Then the others came silently in behind her.

It was not the full, staggering panoply of Qar types, but even this small embassy had enough variety to make those who had never seen them—perhaps three-quarters of those assembled—blanch and blink and mutter to themselves. Most frightening was the immense creature known as Hammerfoot, a war leader of the Deep Ettins, taller and heavier than even the largest cave bears. His jutting brow overshadowed his face so completely that nothing could be seen of his eyes except two gleaming coals far back in the darkness. He was wrapped in furs and armor made of stone plates held together by massive leather straps, and his two-fingered hands were each as wide as one of the Funderling shields. The giant found his way to the far side of the table and then sat down on the floor, almost knocking the table over when he nudged it with his great chest.

He was the largest of the Qar who came to the table, but not the strangest. Vansen had seen all these shapes before, and others, but he was still far from used to it. Here came the one named Greenjay, who looked like a cross between an exotic bird and a costumed Zosimia fool. Some of the other Qar looked almost human, their origin betrayed only by the shapes of their skulls or their coloring—Vansen knew no ordinary man or woman whose skin was touched with hues of lavender or mossy green. Others like the Elementals were manlike only in seeming to have a head and four limbs: Vansen had seen them in their fiery, naked forms in the Qar camp, and still saw those shapes in his dreams, but the two present today had been more discreet, wrapping themselves in robes that betrayed nothing of what smoldered beneath.

Bent or straight, small or tall, the Qar filed in to fill the other side of the table, as varied as the bestiaries so carefully painted in the margins of old books. The one thing they all seemed to have in common was the quality of watchfulness: as they took their seats they did not speak to each other, but only looked across at the gathered Funderlings and their guests.

And then, at long last, Yasammez herself came into the chamber, tall and silent, wearing her angular black armor and strange cloak like a cloud of dark fog. She looked neither to one side nor the other as she walked slowly to her place at the far side of the table, although she was the lodestone to all eyes. She seated herself in the center of her people.

After a silence Yasammez spoke, her voice as slow and baleful as a funeral bell. "This battle is already lost. You must know that before we begin."

One voice rose above the flurry of disapproving murmurs—Cinnabar Quicksilver. "With all respect, Lady Yasammez, what does that mean? If there is no chance of victory, why are we here instead of at home making peace with the gods?"

"I cannot speak for you, delver," she told him. "But this *is* how I make peace with the gods."

Ferras Vansen could only stare as the room exploded into confusion. He had worked so hard to bring both sides together and now the Qar leader's arrogance was going to smash the alliance to pieces before it even started.

"Stop!" He did not realize he had stood until he had already begun to speak. "Funderlings, you are fools to argue with these people, whose suffering is so much greater than any of us can even imagine." He turned to the other side of the table. "But you, Lady, *you* are a fool if you think you can make peace while you still treat us as your enemies and inferiors."

"Make peace?" asked Yassamez in a voice like a cold wind. "I did not come here to make peace, Captain Vansen, I came here to make common cause. The wounds run too deep for peace between my race and yours."

Vansen pitched his reply above the tumult of unhappy voices. "Then let's speak of common cause, Lady Yasammez. Enough of the past—for now."

She stared at him, still and silent as a statue. At last the noise began to subside as the others waited to see what she would say.

"But it is always the past, Captain Vansen," she said at last. "This room is crowded with the ghosts of those who have gone before, even if you cannot see them. But, of course, your delver allies know—they know very well, which is one of the reasons they did not want this council to happen."

"What are you talking about?" Cinnabar did not sound as confident as his words suggested: he sounded like a man prepared to flinch. "What do the Funderlings know?"

"That the blame for the destruction of the Qar is not on the sunlanders alone. Yes, Vansen's people captured my many-times-great-granddaughter Sanasu and killed her brother, Janniya—but we had been coming back to this place for a thousand years and more to perform the Fireflower ceremonies, always secret except to you delvers, and were never troubled before that day. How did Kellick of the Eddon know we were coming?"

Vansen had been told the story of the prince and princess of the Qar (or so he thought of them, though those were not Qar words) and how their pilgrimage during King Kellick's day had resulted in disaster, but what Yasammez was saying now was new to him. "Does it matter, Lady? It is two hundred years in the past . . ."

"Fool!" she said. "There is no past. It is alive this moment, in this rocky chamber. How did the Eddon know that Sanasu and Janniya were coming? Because the treacherous delvers told him."

Now the uproar was complete, with several of the diminutive Funderlings actually climbing onto the table to shake their fists and declare the innocence of their people. The ruckus became so great that Hammerfoot of Firstdeeps thumped a broad fist down on the table with a noise like a wall falling; his deep, rumbling growl of warning quickly silenced the Funderlings. In the sudden stillness, the only voice was Malachite Copper's.

"Stop!" the Funderling said. "Enough shouting! She is right. May the Earth Elders forgive us, she is right."

"What are you talking about, man?" Cinnabar asked, frowning. "Right about what?"

Copper looked around. "You Funderlings know me. All our people know me and my family. My many-times-great-uncle was Stormstone Copper, the draughtsman and chief mover of the Stormstone Roads. It was the great work of his life, meant to make his people safe and secure, to give us ways to come and go from Funderling Town that were not dependent on the moods of the Big Folk in the castle above. But he could not create an entirely new network of tunnels. Some of the most important passages already existed and had for centuries." Copper paused for a moment. "This is hard to tell. He brought such honor to our family name—there is not a single child of the Copper clan who has not thought, 'I am of Stormstone's blood,' and walked taller."

The rest of the Funderlings were clearly confused again. Vansen had learned enough in his time underground to know that they revered the famous Stormstone as his own people did the gods' holy oracles.

"All this is known, friend Malachite," said Cinnabar, his voice gentle, as though he spoke to someone who had fallen ill. "Tell us what we do not know."

"He . . . he feared that as long as the Qar came to Southmarch, one day the upgrounders—the Big Folk, and I beg your pardon for the crudeness, Captain Vansen—would discover the network of tunnels he had created. It was a terrible decision for him . . . but we are still shamed by what happened. I am sure he meant only for the Southmarch soldiers to frighten the Qar away . . ."

"You seek to put a kind face on murder," said Yasammez. "Because that is what happened. The delvers whispered to Kellick the Eddon that the Qar were coming. The Eddon went himself with his soldiers to stop them. He stole Sanasu and killed her brother Janniya and so doomed my people . . ."

"It was a fight," Vansen said to her. "You make it sound like murder!"

Yasammez's look was stony. "Janniya and Sanasu were accompanied only by two warriors and one eremite—a priest, you might call him. The Eddon met them with over two score of armed men, and afterward Sanasu was a prisoner and the rest of the Qar were dead. Call that what you will."

Vansen looked back at her. Yasammez was the child of a god they said, but she was also a living woman, however strange. She was angry—a bitterness that he recognized, one that was hard to let go; his father had felt that way toward the other farmers in Little Stell, that because he was of Vuttish blood they treated him as a stranger even after he had lived twenty years with them. He had died with that bitterness still on him, refusing on his deathbed to see any visitors not of his own family.

It was odd, Vansen thought, here in the midst of all these other earth-shaking events, that he suddenly felt no anger toward the man who had sired him, no sorrow, as if they had finally reconciled, despite Pedar Vansen being years dead. What had changed?

"If all this is true, Lady Yasammez," he said out loud, ending the long, whisper-scratched silence, "then there is nothing to be said by either Marchman or Funderling except that . . . we are sorry. We the living did not do these deeds—most of us did not know of them until now—but we are still sorry." He turned to Malachite Copper. "Is that so for you?"

"By the Hot Lord, but certainly!" said Copper, and then covered his mouth at having shouted such a strong oath in the very chapel of the Metamorphic Brothers' temple. "Ever since I came of age and my father passed this heavy secret to me—it travels thus, to each Copper heir—I have thought of my great-grandsire only with sorrow. I think he meant well but he plainly did wrong. If the rest of my family knew of it, I believe they would feel as I do and grieve at this family shame." He shrugged. "That is all there is to be said."

Yasammez looked from him to Vansen, and then paused, staring at nothing, making Vansen wonder to whom she spoke in her silent thoughts. Then she took up the great, dark ruby around her neck, slipped the heavy chain over her head, and let it fall to the refectory table with a loud clatter. As the rest of the assembly stared she drew out her strange sword, pure white in color but its glow as shimmery as mother-of-pearl, and set it atop its sheath on the table before her as well.

"This is the Seal of War," she said, gesturing with a long, thin finger toward the stone, baleful as a dying ember. "Because I bear this, the decisions of life and death I make are a bond upon the People—the Qar. This is Whitefire, the sword of the sun god himself. I swore that I would not sheathe it again until I had destroyed this mortal hall where our great ancestor, my father Crooked, fell." She swung her gaze around the table. Even Vansen found it hard to meet those eyes, which had looked out at the world since Hierosol itself was young.

Then Yasammez took the hilt of the white sword in her hand and lifted it. Anxious whispers turned to outright cries of alarm before she slid it into the scabbard with a noise like the snap of a door latch.

"Today I swallow my own words. I default upon my oath. The *Book of the Fire in the Void* will find a way to even my account, I am sure." Yasammez lowered her head as if a great weariness had just come over her, and for a moment the entire room grew completely still. Then she straightened, her face a mask again, and donned the Seal of War once more. "I decree that my people are still at war . . . but only with the autarch. Today I have made myself an oath-breaker, but there is no escaping it—this man's danger must be faced. For he comes here to wake a god on the night of Midsummer, but down in the place you call the Mysteries there is more than one god waiting to be awakened, and many of them are angry with all the living."

4
The Deep Library

"He could play his shepherd's flute well, and with it would delight all who heard him, man or beast. He could also understand the speech of the birds and the beasts of the field. Even the lions that lived in Krace in those days did him no harm, and the wolves shunned his flock . . ."

—from "A Child's Book of the Orphan, and His Life and Death and Reward in Heaven"

WHEN HE AWAKENED, he was still as tired as if he had run for hours. It was impossible to tell how long he had slept; the luminous gray sky outside, the swirling clouds and damp, ancient rooftops seemed unchanged. He sat up on the bed, thoughts blurry and wordless, then put his feet on the floor and had to stop there, dizzy. He remained that way, head in hands, until he heard the queen's voice.

"Manchild."

He opened his eyes to find her standing over him. He was in a room that was plain but comfortable. Beside the bed a window with an open shutter looked down onto an enclosed courtyard and an overgrown garden of white-and-blue flowers. All of the other windows Barrick could see were shuttered.

"I had a dream . . ." he began.

"It was not a dream," Saqri told him. "You were on your way to the fields beyond, almost obliterated by the strength of the Fireflower. But my husband is with you now, helping you. Or a part of him is—the part that your need has prevented from going on." Saqri's dark eyes were solemn. "I do not know whether I should hate you for that or not, Barrick Eddon. Ynnir was meant to go on. He chose to go. But now because of the bond of responsibility or shame he feels to you, he lingers."

"Ynnir is . . . inside me?"

"They are *all* inside you, it seems, all the men of the Fireflower, in almost the same way the women are all inside me, my mother and grandmothers and great-grandmothers, our family stretching back entirely to the days of the gods. But though a part of them remains with you, the Ancestors of the Father have in truth gone on to whatever lies beyond . . ." She shook her head. "No. There are no words that will truly speak it from my thoughts to yours. But my husband . . . my brother . . . he cannot . . ." Her face changed and she fell silent again. He heard a batwing whisper in the dark depths of his own being, but from a voice that was neither hers nor his own—"*Sad she is sad she misses me even through the fury oh proud sister you are still beautiful . . . !*"

"I must spend some time in thought about this—about everything," Saqri told Barrick at last. "I will go. Harsar will attend to you until I call you."

Shortly after she had left the room, the strange little servant Harsar came to him with a tray containing what Barrick could only regard as a feast—bread and salty white cheese and honey and a bowl of the fattest, sweetest, most thin-skinned plums he had ever tasted. Harsar did not leave immediately, but stood watching Barrick eat.

"I have never seen one of your kind, except in dreams," the manlike creature said to him at last. "You are neither so fearsome nor so strange as I would have expected."

"Thank you, I suppose. I would say the same for you, except I'm not sure I've ever seen your kind even in dreams."

Harsar gave him a squinting look. "Do you joke? Never seen the Stone Circle People? Your people used to dance with ours by moonlight! We took you down into our towns beneath the hills and showed you wonderful things!"

"Doubtless," Barrick said, wiping honey off his chin. The excellent meal was improving his mood by the instant. "But I'm young, you must remember. Still, I'm sure my grandfather danced the Torvionos with your grandfather at every festival!"

The squint deepened until Harsar's eyes had disappeared. "You are jesting. Foolery."

Barrick laughed. It felt strange—he could not remember the last time he had done it. "You are right, sir. You have caught me."

Harsar shook his head disapprovingly. "Just like . . ." He stopped himself with an obvious effort. "To jest is to mock the seriousness of things."

"No." Barrick found himself needing to explain. "Jesting is the only way to make sense of some things. Perhaps because your people don't die . . ."

"We die," said Harsar. "Mostly at the hands of men."

For a moment Barrick faltered. "Perhaps it's because my people are mortal that we must jest. Sometimes it is the only way to live with things that cannot be lived with."

"Not simply because you are mortal." A sort of frown stretched the fairy-factor's face; when he spoke again, it was almost as if to himself. "There are those among the People—yes, even the highest—who do this, who jest and speak meaningless words when they should be acting . . ."

His anger is at me, a voice in Barrick's thoughts said. *And his frustration. He is not the only one, but he was the closest to me . . . except for my own sister-wife . . .*

This new voice seemed so clear that Barrick thought against all sense and memory that Ynnir must be standing in the chamber. He looked around, hopefully at first, then increasingly wildly . . . "Lord? Where are you?"

Harsar stared, but with no more than polite concern, as though this kind of gibbering madness must frequently overtake the residents of Qul-na-Qar.

You told me I could not leave you—not yet. The king's voice was as clear as if he stood beside Barrick. *But now you must rest again. It takes no deathly wisdom to know you will need all your strength for whatever comes next, and you still are not strong enough to withstand the full bloom of the Fireflower. I need your attention. Send Harsar-so away.*

Barrick began to mumble excuses, but whatever else he might have been, the exotic Harsar was by training a royal servant: he glimpsed what was wanted and promptly made himself scarce, taking the empty tray with him.

"You said he was angry at you . . . ? Harsar?"

You need not speak aloud, the king's voice said. *And you have no need to stand or sit, either. Lie down, for you are still weary. Rest. What Harsar thinks of me does not matter anymore. He is faithful to the Fireflower.*

Barrick stretched out on the bed, found a delicate but surprisingly heavy blanket to pull over himself. Even with the king's comforting presence so close, he began to feel the Fireflower voices stirring in him, threatening to pull him down, to drown him in an ocean of alien memories. How would he ever find the strength to reach the shore . . . !

Do not think of a shore, said the king, startling him with how much of Barrick's mind he had understood. *You are not drowning, but neither can you climb safely up from the Fireflower and leave it behind. It is part of you, now and forever.*

Instead, think of the light of a single star low on the horizon. Swim toward that light. You will not reach it, but in time you will learn to be content to swim eternally in that endless ocean. In truth, you will never reach that glowing mote, but neither will it ever disappear from your sight. . . .

The king continued to speak these riddling words to him, over and over, his voice as soothing to Barrick's thoughts as the song of summer crickets. He tried to swim toward the light, but instead found himself sinking deeper and deeper into weariness and, at last, back into the oblivion of sleep.

When the servant wakened him again, it was not with a meal but a summons.

"The queen bids you join her in the Singing Garden."

Barrick got up and followed Harsar, feeling protected still by Ynnir's help and the king's unfelt but still recognized presence. The Fireflower voices were not gone but at the moment they seemed muffled, as though some layer of protection had been woven between them and Barrick. He followed the small servant out a side door and beneath the gray sky, down a path of black gravel running through a bed of stones. They passed through one garden after another, concentric walled rings that used colors of flowers and stones, as well as their shapes, in ways he could not entirely grasp, but their effect was so strong and so varied that it tired him just to pass through them.

At the center was a gateway, an arch of stone wound with clinging white flowers.

"Go quietly," Harsar said. "For your own sake." The servant bowed then and left him.

Barrick stepped through the gate, wondering what exactly he was being warned against. Were there animals here that would harm him if they caught him—or even plants? He walked as silently as he could, grateful that the gravel path had been replaced here with a track of pure, deep grass that cushioned every step.

Water dripped quietly beside him, falling from a crack in the outer wall onto a stone, *plik, plik, plik.* A little farther along a series of slightly larger waterfalls trickled into shallow ponds beside the path with a sound like someone gently tapping a crystal goblet. Behind both these noises he could hear a delicate hooting which might have been the call of some contented bird sitting on its nest, but turned out instead to come from a slender tower of stone scarcely twice his own height, with a hole in its top like a needle's eye that took in the passing wind and made it into sweet music.

The Singing Garden, Harsar had called it. The Singing Garden. Even the voices in his head fell utterly silent; as if they listened to something they had loved once but had long forgotten.

He found the queen sitting in an open pavilion surrounded by flowering trees, her eyes closed as though she slept. As he approached, Saqri stirred in the depths of her white robes, like petals brushed by the wind, and opened her eyes.

"My husband . . . my brother . . . always preferred the Tower of Thinking Clouds," she told him. "But that place is too stark for me. I like it here. I would have missed this place if I could not have returned."

"Returned from where?"

"The fields we will all go to someday—the fields from which you nearly did not return only a short while ago." She nodded. "But even here, in the middle of all this peace, I could not pierce the veil around your home, which we call the Last Hour of the Ancestor." Saqri's face took on a troubled shadow. "Something grave and strange is happening there—something I have never known before, that keeps the words of my great-aunt Yasammez from me and mine from her."

"But if you can't talk to her, what can we do? We have to stop her—tell her the Fireflower is still alive. She will destroy Southmarch, otherwise."

"The fact that she has not yet conquered it—that, I can sense—means that things must be more . . . complicated than we can guess." Saqri shook her head. "But it is pointless to speak of it any more. Unless things change, I cannot speak to her. She will make up her mind and do what she feels she must, as she always has."

"Then we should go there. We have to tell Yasammez that the Pact succeeded. The trust of the People demands it!" Fireflower voices and ideas rose in his head like splashing water, but it seemed clear to him he had the gist of it correctly. "Why are you looking at me like that?"

"You sound more like one of ours than one of yours." Her lips curled in a faint smile. "Still, go to her, you say? Manchild, hundreds of leagues lie between us and them."

"But you have these . . . doors. Gateways. I came here through one!"

Saqri made a strange little hissing sound—she was laughing. "Grandmother Void did not invite everyone in the world to use her roads, child! Just her own great-grandson, Crooked. You came here on one of his, made long ago when the gods still walked the world, and my folk and the Dreamless were still allies. It only survives because the lore of making and unmaking such things is lost to us—and it would only lead you back to the city of Sleep."

"But if we can't use that one, there must be others!"

"A few. Some had already been discovered by accident before Crooked learned the great secrets from the old woman. In fact the gods built many of their houses so that they could use those which had already been found."

"Then we can use them, too, can't we? You said that Southmarch is on top of—in front of, whatever you said—the palace of Kernios. That's what you meant, isn't it? One of those doors?"

"Any of the roads that served Kernios would be banned to us," she said. "Even with the dark one deep in his long slumber. It is a good idea, Barrick Manchild, but it will not serve."

"What am I supposed to do, then, just . . . *pray*? My people will be killed! And so will the rest of yours!" He threw himself down on the steps of the pavilion at her feet and slapped the stone in frustration. "I used to think the gods didn't even exist—now you're telling me they're blocking my way every direction I turn. And they're not even awake!"

Saqri raised one eyebrow at this display but did not speak. After a moment she rose and drifted down the steps past him. She raised her hand as she passed, clearly bidding him to follow her.

"Where are we going now?" Barrick asked.

"There is another source of help that remains to us," she said without slowing.

Barrick scrambled after her as she made her way back across the chiming, singing garden into the timeless halls of Qul-na-Qar.

There was a point at which the stairs they had been descending for so long became a level floor, but he could not quite remember when that happened; there was another point at which the inconstant, watery light of the palace dwindled and at last died, but he could not exactly remember when that had happened, either. Lastly, even the stone floor beneath his feet had ended; now he felt the give of loam beneath his feet, as though they had gone so deep beneath the castle they had left even the foundations behind. In fact, they had been walking in darkness so long now that it seemed no matter what Saqri might claim of the distance, they must have walked most of the way from Qul-na-Qar to Southmarch.

The silence of this endless dark place was of course not truly silent, at least not in Barrick's teeming skull, but with the help of what Ynnir had told him and the feeling that the blind king himself was not too far away, Barrick was able to rise above the chaotic knowledge of the Fireflower and concentrate on staying close to Saqri, who led him not like a mother leading a child through an unfamiliar place, but like someone leading another family member through a place in which they had both lived their entire lives.

Is it confidence in me she's showing, or contempt? It did no good to wonder, of course, because they probably meant the same thing to a Qar, somehow. Still, the voices in his head did not feel nearly as alien as they had before. He almost thought he could live with them.

At last, and only because of the deep, awesome darkness through which they had been traveling, he finally saw the light: it was such a faint change that he would never have recognized it otherwise—more the memory of light than light itself. Although it grew steadily stronger as he walked, it was still a hundred paces or more before it even brightened his surroundings enough that he could finally make out the silvery outline of Saqri before him, then another hundred more before he could see the sides of the narrow, dirt-and-stone passage through which they walked, something that looked as if it had been crudely cut from the living earth in a single day's work.

Where . . . ? he wondered, but felt Saqri's thoughts settle gently over his, urging him to silence.

Soon enough.

The dim radiance ahead began to grow until it became a pearly cylinder of light, its base round and shiny as a coin. As they grew closer, he saw that the cylinder was a single large beam from a hole in the top of the tunnel, and the circle on the floor was the surface of a circular pool not much larger than a writing table but just wide enough to catch all the beam of light from above. Saqri stopped and he stopped beside her.

The Deep Library, she said.

Barrick had no idea what he was supposed to think. He had heard the name more than a few times from Ynnir. He had supposed it some deep vault in the lower part of the castle, or even a massive hall, filled with old scrolls and decaying volumes, a little (at least in his mind's eye) like the library in Chaven's observatory or his father's rooms in the Tower of Summer.

The queen reached out without warning and took his hand in hers, then lifted her other hand into the light and gestured for him to do the same. Barrick had to take a step forward to reach, and as he did so he could see up the vertical tunnel toward the gleam's source, a hole in the darkness that seemed impossibly distant, at its center a single point of white light.

Yes, Saqri told him. *It is Yah'stah's Eye, the hopeful star. It always shines above the Deep Library.*

Barrick was astonished. *But . . . but I haven't seen a star in months . . . ! The Mantle*—the word came to him unbidden, handed up by the Fireflower as if it had been a small object he had dropped—*the Mantle covers the whole land . . . !*

But the Deep Library does not see the Mantle, Saqri told him. *It sees things as they are, or at least as they were. And the Eye is always above it. Now give me your thoughts and your silence.*

It takes both of the heirs to the Fireflower to open the Deep Library, the voices told him—or was it Ynnir's voice somehow braiding all the other voices together into one? *That is another reason why losing you or Saqri now would cripple the People forever.*

For a long time he only stood, listening to the murmur of the Fireflower, feeling the broad shapes of Saqri's thoughts as she wove the summons, a chain of questions almost like children's riddles:

* * *

"Who is gone but remains?
Who is without but within?
Who will come back to the place they never left . . . ?"

He began to feel the presences gathering even before he saw the first of the silvery strands start to form in the radiance like bubbles clinging to the weeds in a pond. They came from nowhere—they came from *nothing*—but by the time they floated in the beam of light, they were something. They lived, at least a little, they thought, they remembered.

"We honor the summoners. We honor Crooked's House. We honor the Fireflower." The voices washed through his head like the sound of water dripping in a dark place. As each voice spoke, though it could be heard only inside Barrick's thoughts, the pond or well at his feet spawned a little circular ripple. Soon the circles were crisscrossing. *"Ask us and we shall give you what is in us to give."*

"The House of the People and the Last Hour of the Ancestor no longer share any of Crooked's Roads," Saqri said, her silent words seeming to drift up into the beam of light like motes of dust. *"How can the distance be crossed? How can the gap be bridged?"*

"In the elder days, one of the brightest could ride to the Ancestor in three days—fewer if his mount was not earthbound."

"Yes," said Saqri with a touch of asperity in her voice, "and the gods could make scented oils appear from the air then, too, and cause stones to blossom. Those days are gone. The great steeds have broken their traces years ago and fled to far lands. Those who traveled Grandmother Void's roads can only go where the way is not barred—and the place we wish to go is barred to us."

It was unutterably strange to stand before the Deep Library, to hear the voices and watch the surface of the pool rippling as if beneath the strike of invisible raindrops. It was different than the way the Fireflower manifested itself in his head, more chaotic and less like the conversation of humans, but with Saqri directing it, it did not pass beyond what he could take in, although he could by no means understand all of it.

"Terrible things are on the wind," the Deep Library voices murmured. *"The forbidding of the old roads, the dying god, the plans of the southern mortal that make even Heaven tremble . . ."*

"And Yasammez has a Fever Egg," another voice said in mournful sing-

song. *"The end must truly be near. Perhaps even the Dark Lady has finally discovered despair."*

"The roads are still there, if only the gods would open a way for you," moaned another.

"Stop!" Saqri said, and her voice was like a whipcrack. "The gods themselves are asleep! You know that, because it has been true for half of your existence! And besides, even were they not beyond our reach, with Crooked dying and the rest dreaming, the most powerful of the gods are our enemies! The Three Brothers and all their followers hate us. That is one reason for my great-aunt's desperation."

"Then all is lost," whispered one of the Deep Library; a chorus echoed it, agreeing. The faces formed and disappeared, roiling for their moment of existence like weeds in a swirling river.

"All is lost!" they muttered.

"Almost all," said one. *"Do they hate the mortals, too?"*

Saqri abruptly held up her hand.

"May I dismiss them?" she asked. It took Barrick a moment to realize she was asking him. Apparently it took both halves of the Fireflower to dismiss the Deep Library as well as summon it.

He raised his hand into the light and let her do what had to be done.

They walked back in what Barrick assumed was the silence of defeat.

"So what will we do?" he asked at last. "My people—the people of the castle—your people—they will all be killed!"

"If we cannot stop them, I fear you are right."

He could not believe her calm. "But we can't stop them. Everyone agrees! We are on the other side of the world and you heard what the Deep Library said—there are no roads left for us to use."

"Not exactly." Saqri's thoughts were quiet, almost hesitant, as though she was still working out the details of some complicated picture in her head. "They said the gods' roads are still available to us."

"But the most powerful gods hate the Qar—you said that yourself! So what good would that do?"

"Ah, yes, the gods may hate the Qar," Saqri said, an invisible shape in the darkness beside him, "but I cannot help wondering how they feel about your folk?"

5
Haunters of the Deeps

“. . . But in those days the Kracian hills were a fierce, lawless place. A clan of bandits came into the valley where Adis and his parents lived while he was out with the flock, and they killed his parents and took what little the family had.”

—from “A Child’s Book of the Orphan, and His Life and Death and Reward in Heaven”

“I AM WEARY AND HEARTSICK,” said Olin Eddon. “Why must I remain here? I have seen the ships roll in, seen the soldiers in their thousands disembark. Yes, the autarch has ample might to humble my poor country. What purpose does this serve?”

Pinimmon Vash looked up to the deck of this latest, largest supply ship. The chief of the cargo-men waved a signal, letting the paramount minister know that the show was about to start. Other ships were unloading as well—the harbor that had once served mainland Southmarch was now the hub of the autarch’s tent-city along the shore of the bay—but it was this one that was the object of the autarch’s greatest interest.

“It was the Golden One himself who decreed that you must watch from here, King Olin,” Vash said as politely as he could. “That is all you need to know.”

“Why is no one in Southmarch firing on your ships?” Olin’s face was pale and damp with perspiration. “Surely not even Tolly would fail to defend his own castle. What trick has your master played to land here unopposed?”

"Ask the Golden One about such minor matters, King Olin, not me." Couldn't the northerner see that all this had nothing to do with Pinimmon Vash himself, that he was only doing what his master required of him? The foreign king was less of a savage than Vash had expected, but his manners were clearly not up to the rigorous standards of a real court. After all, wasn't having to stand here on the sunny waterfront without even a parasol—where were those cursed slave boys, anyway?—much harder on the older, more delicate Vash?

He became uncomfortably aware that King Olin was staring at him. "Yes?"

"You seem like a civilized man, Lord Vash," said Olin, weirdly mirroring Vash's private thoughts. "An intelligent man. How can you do the bidding of someone like the autarch? He has said—if he is not completely mad, of course, if what he plans can actually be done—he has said he intends to bind up the power of a true god so that everything that lives on the earth will be his slaves!"

Vash almost smiled at that, but he had not lost all caution: he quickly looked around to make certain they were alone before answering. "And how is that different from what we have now, King Olin? The Golden One already rules absolutely, so what else can I do but comply? No, your question is naïve, I fear. You might just as easily—and just as fruitfully—ask me why a stone falls to the ground when dropped or why the stars hang shining in the sky. That is how Creation is ordered. Only a fool would give up his life when there is no hope things will ever be otherwise."

Olin Eddon didn't appear offended, but neither did he seem convinced. "Then no tyrant in history would ever have been overthrown. The Twelve would not have cast down the dictator Skollas, and Hierosol would have crushed Xis a thousand and more years ago."

"If the gods willed it, so it would have been," agreed Vash. "But I see no such truth in the world we inhabit here, today. The autarch rules us, may he live forever—all else is but an airy game of what-might-be."

Olin continued to stare at him, intently enough that Vash began to feel quite put out. Didn't this northern upstart realize what an honor was being done to him, having the paramount minister of all Xis as his attendant? "You really should pay attention to the unloading, King Olin. It was the Golden One's express wish. . . ."

Olin ignored him. "Not all southerners are as fatalistic as you, Lord

Vash. I know many of your continent who fought back against the autarch—one in particular who became my friend."

Pinimmon Vash could not help laughing a little. "And what did it gain him? Not much, I imagine." A thought suddenly came to him. "Hold a moment. Do you talk about the traitor, Shaso dan-Heza? The Tuani general who tried to thwart the rightful claims of Autarch Parnad, the Golden One's father?"

Now it was Olin's turn to smile, a wolfish grin deep in his gray-shot beard. "Rightful claims? Now who is being purposefully naïve? Shaso and his people fought Parnad and Parnad's father, too, and even though I hear a puppet of sorts has been put on the throne in Nyoru, I imagine some in Tuan will continue fighting until one day they drive you Xixians out. The Tuani are no cowards and they clearly do not agree that the autarch's rule over all the world is inevitable."

Again, Vash was nettled by this upstart king. "And your friend, the traitor Shaso? This mighty bulwark against tyranny? Where is he today?"

Olin's expression grew dark. "I do not know. Nor would I tell you if I did, of course."

"Of course. Now, enough of such contentious matters." Vash shook back his long sleeves and gestured to the gang ramp leading down from one of the larger cargo ships onto the mainland harbor's biggest loading dock. "Look. This is what the autarch most particularly wanted you to see."

Even many of the Xixian sailors on the dock and the soldiers on the beach had wandered over to watch as a group of large, awkward, man-shaped things made their way down the ramp. Each had two arms and two legs, but there the resemblance ended. Their stocky legs and short arms were covered in bony plates, with stiff bristles growing between them and up the creatures' backs. Their hands looked more like the digging-claws of moles, proportionately large and covered with leathery, warted flesh. But it was their torsos and heads that dragged at the eye: they had strange armored midsections, as if they were upright beetles or tortoises, and these rose up in the front to cover their necks and the bottoms of their heads from below, just as a continuation of their back armor curled down over the tops of their heads, so that all that could be seen of their faces were eyes peering out of the shadows between the unjoined pieces of bony shell, as if they were giant oysters or armored men wearing absurdly large helmets. But for all their defenses, the weird things seemed ill—they halted for no reason, or stumbled as they walked. One fell and could not rise, legs kicking slowly in the bright sunlight.

"These things . . ." Olin said, blinking, "they are monsters. Did *you* do this to them?"

"Vash did nothing!" said a voice behind them, floating down from above as if a god had spoken. Which, in a way, one had, since the voice was the autarch's, who was coming toward them across the sand on his ceremonial platform carried by slaves, as though he were himself some breed of giant, many-legged creature. "In fact, these splendid creations were first bred in my great-grandfather Aylan's day."

"So madness runs in the blood of your family," said Olin in disgust.

"Something you and I have in common, eh?" Sulepis grinned. "These creatures were of the Yisti once, who are the same blood as your northern Funderlings, although this breed, the Khau-Yisti, were larger and more savage, wild diggers where their Yisti cousins were almost as civilized as men." He spoke with the air of one who tries to impart an interesting lesson to a dull student. "My great-grandfather's breeders captured the wild tribes, took the largest and strongest of them and began to shape them to work the mines of the Xan-Horem Mountains, dangerous places where the earth often collapses. These Khau-Yisti, though, are strong and stolid, and they can dig their own way out after a cave-in—a most thrifty sort of worker to have." He frowned, watching the creatures struggling down the gangplank. "Traveling does not seem to agree with them, or perhaps it is your chilly northern air. Many died during the voyage, and these do not look to last much longer. . . ."

"I'm afraid half of them have died already, Golden One," Vash said.

"Your people bred these poor creatures like hounds? Just to work in the mines?" Olin seemed surprised, as if he had learned nothing about the Xixian royal family. If Vash had not felt a little nauseated by the sight of the trudging, subhuman Khau-Yisti filing across the sand, he would have been amused by the northern king's naivety.

"Oh, not just for that," said the autarch cheerfully. "As you will see, they also make the best handlers for the *askorabi*—with their armored bodies, they are almost impervious to the creatures' stings. In fact, in our tongue we call these particular Khau-Yisti *kalukan*—'the shielded ones.'" He smiled and looked up at the sun, which had appeared from behind the clouds. "The only thing they truly hate is too much light. Hear them murmur in pain! I think you may be right, Paramount Minister Vash. I suppose we will have to use the human handlers instead." He didn't sound particularly bothered.

The creatures were in obvious discomfort, clumsily trying to keep the bright sun out of their tiny eyes with their plated hands, stumbling, halting in confusion in the middle of the ramp, blearily staring out from the depths of their carapaces. Every time they slowed, though, the handlers were on them, poking at the joints between their armor plating with sharp-tipped iron rods.

"Terrible . . ." said Olin quietly.

"Ah, you feel the tug of kinship." The autarch nodded sagely.

"What are you talking about?"

"All the Yisti are Qar. You have Qar blood yourself. Thus, these poor monsters are your kin, Olin." The autarch's tone was again one of an adult speaking to a slow child. "It demonstrates your good heart that you recognize that, no matter how bestial these relatives might be. Now remain silent and pay attention—wait until you see what comes next!"

The autarch was not even looking at Olin Eddon as he spoke, but Vash was, and he was surprised by the intensity of the cold hatred on the northern king's face.

The sky darkened. The day, which had been warm, suddenly took on an edge that reminded her it was still spring, and a cold one at that: true summer was still far away. The Lady Idite dan-Mozan sighed and clutched her bowl of *gawa* a little tighter. "Just a moment longer, Moseffir," she called to her grandson, who was digging between the stones of the courtyard with a stick. "Then it's time to go inside for your supper."

"Won't," the little boy said with the same careless certainty his father had shown at that age—and doubtless his grandfather, too, although of course Idite had not been present to see that. He wouldn't even look at her because he knew that as soon as he did he couldn't ignore her anymore, and that *was* like his grandfather Effir.

The thought of her merchant husband made the suddenly dark day seem darker still. She had lost him only a few short moons ago, and some days that terrible night of fire and blood actually seemed to be receding into the past, like a landmark seen from a barge floating down a river. But then at other times, like now, the hurt was so fierce, so . . . *alive* that it might have only just happened. It was moments like this that she had to fight off despair. Only her family gave her reason to go on. Were it not for her son and his daughters and young Moseffir here, Idite might have walked out into the cold ocean off Landers Port and let the gods do what they wanted with her.

She did not know how long she had been lost in thought when she became aware of Fanu standing and waiting for her. Why hadn't the girl said anything? Idite did not have the heart for anger, though. Fanu had always been shy, but she had been so pretty once . . . ! Since the burns, though, she had crawled back inside herself like a desert tortoise retreating into its shell. Even in the company of the other women, some of whom had scars far worse than hers, there were days that scarcely a dozen words came out of her mouth between sunrise and sunset.

"What is it, Fanu-saya?"

The girl's attention had wandered to Moseffir, vigorously beheading stems of grass with his little stick. "Oh, Mistress! A thousand pardons! You have a visitor."

Idite was surprised. It was a strange time of the day for it. Still, she smiled and sat up straighter. "Truly? Well, do not keep her waiting—the Great Mother herself sometimes goes disguised, it is said, to see who honors her injunction to hospitality!"

"Oh, but, Mistress," said Fanu, "it is a man. A *stranger*." She said this last word as though it described something with claws and sharp teeth.

"Ah. Did he give a name?"

Fanu shook her head. "But . . . he is handsome!"

Hearing Fanu say something so much like her old self was more surprising than the sex of the visitor. "All the more reason to send him in then," said Idite, laughing a little. "You may stay if you wish."

The girl's eyes widened and she shook her head violently. "I couldn't, Mistress! I couldn't!"

"Then have one of the porters come in with him, so that propriety is maintained."

After Fanu had fled the courtyard Idite straightened her robes. Not that she cared very much what even a handsome young man thought of her, but neither did she wish to look like an old gossip. She had the honor of her son's house to think of, after all—it was her home, now.

The old porter led the visitor in, then went and sat cross-legged in the corner of the courtyard. Idite examined the newcomer as she gestured for him to sit in the chair across from her. Fanu had been right: he *was* easy to look upon, tall and slender, with a trimmed beard just a little longer than what was proper—it gave him a bit of a bandit look—and sumptuous clothes in the northern style, the sort of thing that might ordinarily be seen on a young nobleman of Tessis or Jellon. His skin and dark, almond-shaped eyes, though, showed that his blood originated from the same place hers did.

"Lady Dan-Mozan." He folded his hands on his breast and bowed his head above them. "You are very kind to see me."

The courtly gesture startled her. She had not seen it performed with such grace in years, not since she had been a young woman in Nyoru. It brought on a pang of homesickness that she covered by returning the Tuani greeting with one of her own. "I see you are my countryman," she said. "Or you lived there. What is your name, young man, and what can this useless old woman do for you?"

He smiled and she found herself remembering more of her youth, the hot desert nights and the whispers of the women as the men paraded past in their military finery at the beginning of the Ul-Ushya Festival. "Useless? I think not. Your kindness and wisdom are legendary, Lady Dan-Mozan. Again, I thank you for inviting me into your beautiful home and restful garden. I have ridden a long way to see you."

"I am flattered," she said, more certain than ever that something strange was afoot. "But you must know this is not my house, but my son's. He was kind enough to take me in when my own house burned earlier this year. It was a sad time, but at least now I have the chance to see my grandchildren as often as I wish." She gestured to Moseffir, who had managed to get dirt all over his face. Idite sighed. "Even a grandmother cannot keep that one out of mischief. Moseffir! Come here."

"The fire, of course," said the young man, nodding as she wiped at the boy's face with the heel of her hand. "Please accept my very deepest regrets on the death of your esteemed husband. Effir dan-Mozan was a prince among merchants."

"Better, I suppose, than being a merchant among princes," she said, surprising him a little. She freed Moseffir, who waddled back to his excavation. "I do not mock you, but please do this old woman the honor of dispensing with such flowery stuff. Of course I miss my husband more than anyone can ever know. I appreciate your courtesy, but since you did not know him . . ."

"Ah, but I did," said her visitor. "And I truly admired him, although I do not think he felt the same way about me."

She watched him in silence for a long moment. "You still have not told me your name."

"No, I have not, Lady Dan-Mozan. Because I wished you to have a chance to spend a short time in my company, so you might be prepared to think better of me than my name warrants." He sat up, fastidiously smoothing out the sleeves of his jacket. "I am Dawet dan-Faar."

It was as though he had thrown a pan of cold water over her. If Idite's entire body had not suddenly felt as limp and helpless as a trampled reed, she would have run to snatch up her grandson and flee the courtyard. "Prince Dawet . . . ?"

"Yes, *that* Dawet." His face was a proud, hard mask, but she saw something in it that she thought might be pain. "The one you have heard called murderer, ravager, thief, traitor. And I must admit that not all those names are unfairly given. But despite the worst of the tales, I have never harmed a woman. On that I offer my soul in surety to the Great Mother. You are safe with me, Lady. And neither will I harm anyone in your household if you ask me to leave this very moment. You greeted me very courteously. Will you hear me out?"

She looked to her grandson, then to the porter snoring gently in a pool of light. The afternoon sun had crept out from behind the clouds again.

"What is it you want from me, Prince Dawet?"

He shook his head. "Let us put away pleasantries, at least those which do not apply. That title was taken from me, nor do I wish it back. All I desire from you is information. Tell me what happened to your house. I have been told that the fire was set by men in the service of Baron Iomer. Why should he do such a thing?"

Idite now wished she had run from the garden when the impulse had first struck her. How could she tell this well-known criminal anything true without giving away that which could not be told? And if she told him lies, what would he to do her? To her family? His promise not to harm them was, if even half the stories about Dawet were true, as useless as shoes for the wind. "I . . . I do not know why the fire was set. The baron's soldiers were in our house, it is true, and many think they set it, but it could have been an accident. . . ."

"Please do not waste my time with nonsense, Lady," he said, his voice firm but not threatening. "Otherwise the day will turn cold, and I will feel it my fault if you catch a chill. The rumor is that he was searching for King Olin's daughter, Briony, who was in your house. I have heard this from Briony herself, Lady, so do not bother to deny it."

"You . . . you have seen her?" After the girl disappeared that night, Idite had feared that Briony was dead or in a Southmarch dungeon, although in recent days she had heard rumors that the princess had somehow reached Tessis. "Truly? She is alive?"

He looked at her closely, as if he suspected her concern was not genuine. "Yes," he said at last. "She lives. Although she will not talk much about the night of the fire." He paused a moment, gazing at the starlike blossoms of the pear tree. "And besides your husband, many others died that night, Lady Dan-Mozan. I want to talk about one of them. About Shaso dan-Heza."

Idite's heart almost stopped beating. "Sh . . . Shaso?"

"Yes, Lady. The one whose daughter all believe I kidnapped and ravished. The man who hated me so much he swore he would cut out my heart and lay it on his daughter's grave. Tell me about Shaso."

"What . . . what do you mean?"

"Do not pretend he wasn't in your husband's house that night, Lady. I will not threaten you, but neither do I wish to be insulted. I know he was there—I have spoken to the princess, remember?"

"Yes, yes, of course." Idite wondered if he truly would leave if she asked him. What could this famous monster want? Who could have sent him? "He was there, yes, Lord Shaso was. It was a secret. He was killed in the fire. Only myself, the other women, and a few of the servants survived."

"But I do not believe that, my lady," said Dawet. He stood up. He was taller than she'd imagined. His shadow fell across little Moseffir, who looked up in confused surprise, muddy twig clenched between his teeth. "I believe that Shaso dan-Heza is alive. And you, Lady, are going to tell me how I can find him."

It was one of the most dreadful things Pinimmon Vash had ever seen, a dusty black horror as long as a supply wagon, with six thick plated walking legs and two more that each carried a heavy claw. Almost a dozen men pulled at it with ropes but still couldn't coax it out of its cage at the bottom of the ramp, a box taller than a man, made of heavy wooden boughs woven together like wicker.

"By the gods, what is that terrible thing?" demanded Olin in a tone of horror. Even his guards had turned their backs on him to watch the angry thing swiping claws as large as ox-yokes at its handlers, who although presumably experienced with such creatures looked no happier at dealing with it than anyone else would be, their faces pale and set in tight, fearful lines.

"Have you never seen an *askorab*?" Vash tried to sound matter-of-fact, but it was not easy with a hissing monstrosity like that only a few dozen paces away, struggling so hard as it was dragged out of the cage that the sand it kicked was landing on the paramount minister's feet. "I believe you have them in the south of Eion. The Hierosolines call them . . ."

"Skorpas," said Olin, staring as though he could not help himself. "Yes, I have seen them, but never one as big as a wagon . . . !"

"By my blood, but that is a handsome fellow!" said the autarch, laughing. "Have you ever seen such a splendid machine?"

"Machine? It is a living creature, or I miss my guess," Olin said. "I can hear its breath piping."

Sulepis chortled. The god-king was in a good mood. "I meant only that it was a machine in the sense of being something created to fulfill a task, as a plow turns the soil or a windmill turns a stone to grind grain. The forefathers of this brute in the Sanian desert hills were nothing like this big—scarcely larger than a hunting dog. He and his cousins have been bred just for this task."

"And what task is worthy of such a hideous demon?" Olin asked, but if he meant to sound defiant or disgusted, he failed: even Vash could hear how shaken the man was by the sight of the terrible beast, which had just caught one of its handlers in a flailing pincer and was busy crushing out his life as the others struggled to hold onto their ropes and cursed uselessly, breaking their sticks against the monster's hard shell.

"Why, to go down into the tunnels beneath your old home and clear them for us," said the autarch. "The *askorabi* are hunters. This fellow will make short work of anything alive down there. And he is only one of a dozen!" Sulepis sat up straight. "Ah, look there—they have lured him out at last!"

"Lured" was perhaps not the word that Pinimmon Vash would have chosen, since a dozen more of the askorab-handlers had been forced to run and help their fellows keep the monster from escaping, but with so many more hands on the cords, they had at last managed to drag the hissing black beast out into the direct light. Vash saw that its tail was more slender in proportion than that of its small desert brothers, but still a formidable weapon, coiled over the creature's back, trembling with the urge to drive the dripping barb at its tip into the handlers, who knew well enough to stay out of reach of the tail as well as the claws.

Most of them knew, Vash amended himself as another handler was abruptly caught up in a massive pincer, tweezed mostly in half, then shoved into the creature's clicking mouth parts even as he still tried to scream. King Olin turned away, clearly struggling not to be sick, but Sulepis watched avidly.

"Into the tunnels with him!" the autarch shouted. He turned to Olin and Vash. "Then we will seal the entrance with a big stone." He seemed as pleased as a child describing a new game. "They are all but blind—the beast will go downward in search of food." He frowned. "They should not have let him eat that slave. He will be sluggish." The moment of bad humor did not last. "Then we will let the next ones go. Soon the tunnels beneath Southmarch will be full of these beauties."

Olin looked up, pale and shocked. "But the tunnels beneath the castle—some of them must lead to Funderling Town. And from there, up to the rest of the city."

"Yes," said the autarch. "Yes, indeed."

"And it would be pointless to beg you not to do this," said the northern king heavily, "wouldn't it? To say that if you refrain, I will cooperate with whatever you plan?"

"Worse than pointless," said Sulepis, smiling. "You will cooperate whether you wish to or no, Olin Eddon—your part in what is to come is important but not subtle. And although I have soldiers in the thousands, I myself must go down into the depths beneath your old home. Do you see? In the dark caves there are many places to hide in ambush. But when the *askorabi* are finished, nothing that breathes will remain."

"It is not that skorpa who is the monster here," Olin said.

Sulepis only laughed. It seemed there was nothing the northerner could ever say to make the autarch lose his temper—an astounding talent to have, and one that Vash fervently wished he, too, possessed. "I am another perfect machine, King Olin. I let nothing stand in my way." He clapped his long, gold-bejeweled hands and his platform was carried away, back toward the massive tent that had been set up in the town square, a new Orchard Palace underneath the skies of the March Kingdom.

The *askorab* had lifted what was left of the dead handler and had stung it over and over in a raging frenzy until what remained was scarcely recognizable as having once been human. As the shouting handlers slowly drove the many-legged beast toward the rocks, it dropped the tattered remains into the sand. The other handlers, ashen to a man, turned their faces away as they passed. Behind them, scores of other workers were lowering more cages down from the deck, each with its own hideous, hissing passenger.

"We shall probably lose a few *askorabi* down in the depths," the autarch said cheerfully. "They are not hounds, after all—they will not return when called. It is interesting to think that generations from now their descendants will probably still be emerging from the tunnels to hunt unwary travelers. . . ."

Olin's movement was so swift it astounded Vash, who had come to think of the northern king as someone like himself—older, passive, a creature of mind and manners. With a shout of rage that clearly had been long bottled inside him, the northerner leaped past his own guards and in a quick two paces had crossed the sand to the autarch's litter, then began to clamber up onto the platform. The autarch watched with interest, as if the murderous northern monarch was just another entertainment. Olin's attack was hindered by the alarmed slaves, who in their sudden fear made the whole litter dip and sway precariously, so that Olin slid backward, away from the autarch, but the Leopard guards had already moved to block him. Three of the elite guardsmen grabbed the northerner and yanked him off the litter, then threw him to the ground. Two of them knelt on his arms while the third set his blade against the king's throat hard enough to draw a thin line of blood.

"Don't hurt him," said Sulepis, sounding for all the world as if Olin had done nothing more than startle them all with a clever trick. "He is valuable to me."

The skin of Olin Eddon's face was white above his beard and he was trembling in every limb as the guards roughly dragged him to his feet—he looked as though he might even try to attack the autarch again. Instead, to Pinimmon Vash's great relief, the northerner yanked himself loose from the unresisting guards and stalked away up the beach, back toward the autarch's camp and the guarded tent that served as his prison. His guards hurried after him.

Vash, however, was still petrified. "Golden One, I am so sorry . . . !"

The autarch laughed. "I was beginning to wonder whether any blood at all ran in that man's veins, let alone the ichor of a god." He nodded. "I would not want to spoil my long years of preparation by the use of an insufficient vessel." He waved his hand and his slaves turned the platform around to face the distant rocks. "Oh, and see that all King Olin's guards are replaced, then execute them. Do it in front of the other men. Make it slow, so the lesson is well-learned by their replacements." He raised his hand and the slaves stopped moving. "There was something else . . ." The autarch frowned, closing his brilliant yellow eyes to think. "Ah!" he said, opening them again. "Of course! Arrange a parley with the master of Southmarch Castle. Time is growing short."

He wriggled his fingers and the slaves carried him away down the beach—to watch the rest of the *askorabi* being released into the tunnels, Vash presumed. He watched him go.

Surely even the northern king has realized by now that the Golden One cannot be resisted, thought Pinimmon Vash, as if someone had spoken to him, had questioned him, but of course he was now alone on the dock. *Only a fool would do anything differently than I have done.*

6
The Tree in the Crypt

"When the child returned the bandits would have killed him too, but instead the leader of the bandits made the orphaned boy his slave . . ."

—from "A Child's Book of the Orphan, and His Life and Death and Reward in Heaven"

"YOU ARE A DRUNKARD AND A FOOL, Crowel." Hendon Tolly then turned on his constable, Berkan Hood. "And you are no better!" His voice echoed through the Erivor Chapel. "I should have both your heads this very moment."

"But, my lord, it is true!" Durstin Crowel insisted. "The Twilight People are gone! Come up onto the battlements with me and see for yourself."

"Not even the fairies can make an entire camp of more than a thousand soldiers disappear in a night without a single sound," Tolly snarled. "In any case, why would they retreat? They were winning! No, the Qar and their ancient bitch of a leader are planning something . . . and you are too stupid to see it!"

Crowel's face turned ugly with frustration, but instead of replying he closed his mouth with an almost audible *snap.* Even a pig like the Baron of Graylock knew better than to trade words with Hendon Tolly when he was in a foul mood. Tinwright, who still remembered several near escapes from Crowel and his cronies, was a little disappointed by his restraint.

"Doubtless you are right, Lordship," said Tirnan Havemore, the castellan. "And that is why we have all come to you, because we need your wisdom."

"If you butter me any more thickly, Havemore, I shall slip out of your fingers," Tolly said with a scowl, but the worst of his anger seemed to have passed. Tinwright, who had been unwillingly keeping company for several days with the lord protector of Southmarch, had never met anyone so mercurial of mood, laughing and jesting one moment, beating a servant almost to death a few scant instants later. He was like a weathercock that never rested, spinning always toward a new direction and new extremes. "What do you say, Hood?" Tolly asked the lord constable again, sounding almost reasonable this time. "Are they truly gone? And if you say so, pray then tell me why that should be."

Tinwright had heard almost as many terrifying stories about the scarred, muscular Berkan Hood as about Lord Tolly himself. Since Hood had become lord constable, dozens of people heard to speak slightingly of the Tollys in any way, especially those who suggested the disappearance of Princess Briony and her brother might have something to do with Hendon and his family, had quickly disappeared themselves. Rumor said they were brought to the little fortress Berkan Hood had made for himself in the Tower of Autumn. After that, nobody heard from them again, although from time to time faceless corpses were found floating in the East Lagoon just below the tower.

"The men on the wall saw nothing last night, but they heard . . . noises . . ." Hood began.

"What sort of noises?" demanded Tolly. His moment of composure was over already. "Singing? Whistling? Dancing the bloody *hormos*? And why did nobody do anything? By all the gods, have I set rabbits to guard my castle?"

As the lord protector continued to shout, an anxious Tinwright let his gaze wander around the chapel. He had never been inside it before; during the time Briony Eddon ruled it had been reserved for family rituals and worship. Hendon Tolly seemed to use it only for its privacy.

The council did not seem to enjoy their time in the chapel with the lord protector, nor did he much enjoy his time with them. When he had sent them away at last, Tolly threw himself down on the front bench, the one marked with the Eddon family crest, frowning and self-absorbed. Seeing the Wolf and Stars carved there, Tinwright felt a moment of helpless sadness. He tried not to think about the changes that had come to his life and land in only half a year, but it was hard to forget that things had once been better for him—much better.

Whatever was bothering Hendon Tolly had not departed with his counselors; he was up now and pacing. "Clearly, we are all but out of time," he said at last, as if carrying on a conversation from only a moment earlier instead of after a long silence. "The Qar have fled because they know that the autarch is coming, so we have merely exchanged one deadly enemy for a larger and more powerful one—we have a few more nights at the most. Curse that sniveling fool, Okros!" A young page had been waiting some time in the doorway of the chapel. Tolly finally saw him. "*What?* Gods be blasted, what is it now?"

The young man bowed deeply. It was clear he was terrified of the lord protector. Tinwright could sympathize. "The . . . the queen! Queen Anissa b-begs your attendance, Lordship."

"By the holy hands of the Three, am I never to have peace? Tell her I will come when I can!"

As the page scuttled away, Tolly pulled out one of his several knives and began carving at the stars in the Eddon family crest on the back of the bench. "Knaves and slatterns, this castle is full of nothing else—not a soul capable of pissing on a stone without me there to direct them. Now I must go and listen to that southern bitch complain." He glowered at Tinwright as though it had been the poet's idea. "Get up, damn you," he said, "or I'll take the skin from your back. Follow me."

Tinwright had not been doing anything so foolish as sitting, of course, nor was he so foolish as to point that out.

The guards who accompanied them out of the great throne hall hemmed them tightly as they made their way across the inner keep toward the residence, and Matt Tinwright was grateful to have them. The displaced throngs who lived in makeshift shacks and tents all across the keep had a sullen regard, few of them looking at Hendon Tolly with anything like admiration, and many with outright animosity.

"Ungrateful cattle," Tolly said, far too loud for Tinwright's comfort. "If human meat were not banned by the gods, they might have some use, but otherwise they are only a drain on my treasury and my patience."

Queen Anissa and her household had taken up residence in chambers that covered a great deal of the residence's highest floor. When the maid let them in, Tinwright was astonished at the amount of room they had for themselves when people were packed into the keep down below, and even into other parts of the residence, like chickens in a coop.

Anissa turned when they came in and at first seemed to see only the lord protector. "Hendon!" she cried, and ran toward him, arms wide. "How I have miss you! Why do you not come anymore to me . . . ?" It was only then she noticed Tinwright and stopped, putting on a more queenly air. "It . . . it has been so long since our last visit."

"Many, many pardons, good lady," Tolly said to the woman he'd been cursing only moments earlier, his voice warm and reassuring. "You must understand that with the castle under siege . . ."

"Oh, that, yes," she said, as if speaking of a foul smell from the middens. "It is terrible. But I do not like it here. I want to go back to my tower."

"Impossible, Highness. I cannot protect you and the young prince there. No, I'm afraid you must stay here." He shook his head solemnly, as though to say it pained him; a moment later his expression brightened. "Since we speak of him, where is your handsome son Alessandros—our king-to-be?"

But Anissa was clearly disappointed and would not be so easily jollied. "There," she said, gesturing at the knot of women on the far side of the room who were huddled around the baby and pretending not to listen. "The maids have him. They make such a fuss of him, he will spoil himself."

"Surely not, Highness." Tolly made his way over to the ladies, who bowed and squirmed as he approached. One of them held the little dark-haired prince, who yanked on the maid's braided hair and stared wide-eyed at the lord protector.

"Handsome lad," said Tolly with convincing good cheer. "He has his father's nose."

But Anissa was still sullen. "I fear for him," she said. "I think perhaps it is time you send us to my father's country. Too dangerous here it is with the war."

The lord protector was clearly taken aback. "Pardon? Send you where?"

"Back to Devonis, where my people are. It is not safe for Alessandros and for me here. Those *kanzarai*, those twilight goblins, they have already got inside to the castle once. We are not safe here." She scowled and drew herself up to her full height, which was lower than Tinwright's shoulder. "And I do not like the way the others look at me, the nobles. These people here in the residence are very rude. I am the king's wife, do they not know that? No, it is not safe here."

"But the Qar are gone, Highness," Tolly said. "Have you not heard?"

"Gone? What do you mean?" She looked as though she suspected a trick.

"Just that—they have left. If you do not believe me, have your maids ask anyone they choose. The Qar have broken camp and withdrawn. They are gone from our shore."

"Truly?"

"Truly. And now, if you will forgive me, Highness, I have much pressing business awaiting my attention. I ache that I cannot spend more time with you and the heir, but if you wish him to have a kingdom to inherit, then there is still much work for me to do."

It was not quite that easy; at least a quarter of an hour more passed before Tolly managed to withdraw from the queen's presence. His mood had not improved. "Does she think I am a fool?" he snarled as he led Tinwright down the stairs. "Does she not realize I have spies everywhere, even in her chambers? I know every treacherous, complaining thing she has said about me. She is fortunate I need her for at least a little longer. . . ." He looked up as if noticing Tinwright for the first time in a while. "Speaking of spies, poet, you have never told me who you serve."

Tinwright's heart slammed in his chest like a fist pounding on a door. "Wh-what . . . ?"

Hendon Tolly rolled his eyes. "Wait, now I remember—I told you I didn't care. And it's true. Because after tonight, you will either be dead or you will belong to me body and soul, little versifier." He seemed distracted now. "Yes, tonight. I suppose you think I seduced the queen because I wanted power," he said suddenly.

Tinwright could only stammer.

"Or the pleasure of bedding a king's wife." He spat on the floor. "Ah, well, I suppose in a way, I *did* do it for power—but not the way you think." He stopped on a stair landing, then held back the guards with a wave of his hand. The lord protector leaned closer to Tinwright and said softly, "I did it to give myself time, because time will bring me power—more power than you can imagine. Oh, you will see tonight, poet. You will see power *and* beauty beyond your ability to imagine, beyond the wit of even a bard like Gregor of Syan to describe. You will see *her.* Yes, you will see her and then you will truly understand."

After a long silence, Tinwright finally found the courage to speak. "Understand, my lord?"

Tolly looked at him with amusement on his sharp, clever face, but something altogether stranger in his eyes. "Yes. When you meet the goddess who loves me."

Matt Tinwright was out of his depth. "You are taking me to meet . . . a woman?"

"No, you fool, do you not listen? Does no one in this cursed place have even a copper's worth of wit? I said a goddess and that is what I meant. Tonight you will meet her, and she will tell us how to defeat the autarch." Suddenly, without warning, Tolly slapped Tinwright so hard the young poet almost fell down. As Tinwright stood swaying, holding his bruised cheek, the lord protector looked at him, his face now stern and cold. "Stop staring and follow me, lout. There is much work to do before I can see my bride-to-be again."

Theron the Pilgrimer had grown used to traveling with the boy and his mysterious, hooded master. Each evening the boy made sure the hooded man was fed, then joined Theron at the fire to eat his own supper with silent haste. It wasn't really surprising; the hooded man himself spoke only to the boy, and the boy often seemed more of a tame animal than an ordinary child, and he used words only when necessary. Theron was a sociable man and it all made for a bleak fellowship . . . but the money was good. The money was very good.

The Marrinswalk Road had still been well traveled as far as Oscastle, but as the walls of that city had disappeared behind them, so too had most of the crowds. Only a few travelers were still to be found between the Marrinswalk border and the first Southmarch town on the road, but they all had fearful stories to tell of the lands beyond and the chaos that had overtaken the north.

"Bandits?" said one traveler who stopped to share a meal with them. He was a traveling merchant with a wagon and two helpers, and he had contributed a sack of dried peas and some millet to the stew. Theron had been fortunate enough to snare a rabbit that morning, so up to this point it had been a merry evening. "Oh, aye, there are bandits in plenty between here and Brenn's Bay, but that's the least of your problems."

"Least?"

"I should say so. Still, they have ravaged the country all around and take what they please from anyone they find."

"How did you get past them?" Theron asked.

"By paying them, of course," said the merchant with a harsh laugh. "These are bandits, not madmen. In their way, they are men of business. Mercy of Honnos, I made sure they know that I pass this way every other tennight and that I would pay them both directions. Two silvers it costs me each trip, but my skin is worth that to me and more. I suggest you tell them the same."

Theron reflected ruefully on the gold the hooded man had given him—the most money he had ever had. What were the chances such outlaws would not search his belongings? Where could he hide so much gold? "You said they were the least of my problems. Is there no other way north to Southmarch?"

The merchant gave him a strange look. "Southmarch? Fellow, what madness would lead you there? Do you not know what has happened?"

"I know the fairies have come out of the north again after all these years. I know they have besieged the city there."

"You make it sound so ordinary, Brother Pilgrimer!" The merchant shook his head and had one of his servants bring him more ale. He generously had another cup poured for Theron as well, then looked over to Theron's silent, hooded client and raised his eyebrows, questioning.

"He might take some. He is a strange one, though, so he may turn it down."

"No matter." The merchant had his servant pour another cup and take it to the hooded man's youthful servant. The boy's master accepted it without comment but did not even turn to acknowledge the kindness. "No matter," the merchant repeated, but he sounded a little nettled.

"Tell me what you mean, sir," Theron asked. "I've had so little good intelligence of what is ahead. Have you seen the fairies? What are they like? Do they threaten honest travelers?"

"Some say they *eat* honest travelers," the merchant said with a hard smile. "But I've met no one who claims it's happened to anyone they know. Not so with the bandits. Not only have I met those myself, I've met others who could not make compact with them and were robbed and beaten for their troubles. Some lost companions. The outlaws in this lonely place are desperate and cruel."

"Oh, Holy Three preserve us!" said Theron in fright. "How can we avoid these people? Is there any way to get around them?"

"The cleverest thing to do is to turn around and go back to Oscastle or whence you came," the merchant said sternly. "If you cannot do that, you must choose between the bandits and the fairies. The bandits haunt the roads. If you would avoid them, you must take the forest track through the Northern Whitewood, and then . . . well, who knows what you may find?"

"Have you seen these fairies?" Theron asked again. "What do they look like? Are they fierce?"

The merchant shook his head. "I have stayed upon the road, so I have seen little out of the ordinary. But I have seen enough. Riders on the hillside by evening, dressed in the old, old way, with armor that gleamed like moonlight. A flock of women speeding across the grass at midnight, in a place no woman would dare show herself, let alone run naked. Yes, I've seen some strange things, Pilgrimer, and heard others that I had no wish to see at all. And the dreams that come to a man these days when he travels in the north . . . ! Night after night I have woken in a sweat, sometimes crying out so that my helpers hurried to my side, thinking me deathly ill or stung by a serpent. There are voices that echo in the hills and in the forest deeps, and shadows that move when there seems no light to throw them . . ."

"Enough!" said Theron, shuddering. "No more tales, thank you. I have scarcely the courage to stay here all tonight, let alone to go forward."

"It is not all terrible," the merchant said suddenly. He stared into the flickering fire. "There is . . . sometimes . . . a kind of beauty in things I've seen . . . or almost seen . . ."

But Theron had no urge to discover such strange, unhomely kinds of beauty, and began to think about when the time might come to turn back.

The boy, Theron had finally learned, was named Lorgan. It was a Connordic name, although the boy said he had lived in Oscastle all his life until now.

"How did you come to be traveling with the stranger, lad?" Theron asked one night over the stewpot. In comparison to the night the merchant had joined them, this was much thinner fare indeed, closer to porridge than a stew, since there had only been enough dried fish to flavor things, but it was warm and the fire was bright and that meant something when you were half a day off the South Road in the lonely woods.

"Told you. He asked me." The boy scooped out some more stew with the crust of hard bread.

"What about your ma and da? Didn't they mind, you going off?"

"Dead."

"What happened?"

Lorgan looked up at him in puzzlement as if it was some kind of strange, foreign custom to ask a child about his parents. "Fever took 'em."

Getting answers was like trying to lift a bucket with a feather. "And what happened to you? Where did you live?"

The boy shrugged.

"And then he . . ." Theron nodded his head toward the hooded man, who as usual was sitting by himself away from the others, his head down on his knees as though he slept, although from here Theron could hear him mumbling, ". . . he paid you to go with him? To help him?"

The boy shrugged again. "Said he needed eyes and ears. And someone to talk loud for him, because his throat's so sore hurt."

"What happened to him? Did he tell you?" The stranger was so miserly with showing even an inch of skin that Theron still half-feared he might be a leper, for all his reassurances.

"He was dead. He told me so." Lorgan scoured the last of the stew from the pot and sucked his fingers, restless as an animal, ready to move now that he had fed.

"He can't have been dead and be alive now. That doesn't happen. Nobody comes back from being dead except the Orphan. Nobody can do it."

"The gods can do it," the boy said, licking his lips and chin for anything he might have missed.

"You're not trying to tell me he's a god, are you?"

"No. But they could have made him alive, couldn't they? The gods can do what they please." The boy shrugged one last time, then went off to throw rocks at trees until the last of the light was gone. The conversation was clearly over. Theron had to admit to himself that he couldn't prove the child wrong—the gods, it was said, could certainly do anything they wanted. It was just that helping mortal men didn't seem to be something they wanted much.

It was just across the border into Southmarch, in the Vale of Aulas where the forests grew so thick on either side of the road that the sun only appeared just before noon and vanished shortly thereafter, Theron Pilgrimer saw real fairies for the first time. It was not quite dark, and he was walking back toward the camp with wet boots on his feet and his arms full of mallow roots he had dug up at the edge of the stream when he saw something moving across the forest track before him. In some way, the figures seemed quite ordinary, so much so that for a heartbeat or two Theron did not even wonder why a procession of men dressed in black would be walking slowly across a deer path deep in the Northern Whitewood. Then he saw that these men were as small as children, barely half his own size, and the hairs on his arms and the back of his neck rose. They were dressed in black cloaks and odd, wide-brimmed hats, and just behind them, crossing the path as he stared, came a wagon drawn by two black-and-white-spotted boars—a coffin-wagon bearing a single, unlovely wooden box. As the pigs snuffled at the ground, the wagon rolled to a stop, and the driver, dressed in black like the others, turned to look at Theron. The little man's face was pale and round and too large for his body. It was all Theron could do to hold his urine. He felt certain that if the little men made the slightest move toward him, he would faint dead away, but the driver only stared at him incuriously for a moment, then shook the reins and urged his grunting steeds forward. Within moments, the funeral procession, if that was what it was, had vanished into the forest.

Theron was still shaking when he got back to camp.

❧

The guards who accompanied the lord protector and Tinwright on their mysterious errand out of the residence were big, hard-faced men wearing the Tollys' Boar and Spears—Hendon's personal soldiers. Even more disturbing to Matt Tinwright was that Tolly was clearly leading this little procession back to the place where Okros had died, the Eddon family vault near the Erivor Chapel.

Tinwright didn't like graveyards. His childhood years living next to one in Wharfside had given him many bad dreams—the stone crypts like little houses always made him think about their invisible residents, and his father's stories about a time when heavy rains had washed bones out of the graveyard right into Wharfside's main street had only made the nightmares worse. Still, he had no choice but to follow.

Tinwright couldn't help wondering why they were entering the vault from outside, through its ceremonial entrance instead of through the narrow stairwell that wound down from the Erivor Chapel itself, so that the family might lay flowers or otherwise commune with their departed ancestors.

"Give me the torch." Hendon Tolly reached out and took the burning brand from one of the guards. "Poet, you carry the mirror."

A guard handed him the heavy bundle—rather eagerly, Tinwright thought. The stairway down into the vault was narrow and surprisingly steep; he had to concentrate just to keep his balance. As he reached the bottom, he avoided looking as long as he could at the spot where Okros had lain, but that was precisely where Tolly was headed. To his relief, the physician's body was gone.

Tolly slid the torch into a bracket, then took the bundle from Tinwright and began to unwrap it.

Matt Tinwright had been far too frightened to examine the vault the last time he'd been inside it. The stonework was spare but graceful, the walls honeycombed with niches, each filled with its own stone sarcophagus. Beside the stairwell up to the Eddon family chapel there was at least one door that led back from the chamber in which they stood, presumably to other catacombs.

Tinwright's father had once told him that the royal vault of the Broadhall Palace in Tessis was so famous for its size and grandeur that people called it "The Palace Below." It was even a popular trysting-place for courting couples because it had so many quiet nooks and corners. Tinwright could no more imagine a couple choosing to bill and coo in the Eddon vault than in a butcher shop. This place took its spirit from the ruling family's gloomy, Connordic side; in this dark stone chamber, death was not the beginning of a glorious afterlife; it was simply the end of this life.

"There." Tolly had unwrapped the mirror and set it on top of a monument, letting it lean slightly against the wall. It was obviously an unusual object. For one thing, it had a slight but unmistakable outward curve from left to right. Also, the frame itself had been painted over so many times in so many dark shades that whatever carvings were underneath had been obscured and the frame had the look of something grown, not built. ""Now it is time for you to play your part, poet."

"But . . . but what *is* my part?" Was there any chance he could simply run for it? Quick as Hendon Tolly was, it would still take him a moment to draw his sword—how far up the steps could Tinwright get by then? And would the guards be ready to stop him? What if Tolly called to them? He realized with a very uncomfortable looseness in his bowels and tightness in his chest that he didn't dare to risk it. Maybe Okros had been unlucky. Maybe something would happen that would take the lord protector's attention and allow Tinwright a better chance to escape.

Tolly took a step toward him, and even though Tinwright was taller than the lord protector, he felt as though he were looking up at Hendon's glare from the bottom of a hole. "Listen carefully, you witless blatherskite. I must know if you can take that dead fool Okros' place for the summoning ritual—Midsummer is only short days away. If you *cannot* help open the way to the land of the gods, I'll have to find someone who can. You would then be useless to me, of course, so if you want to last a little longer, I suggest you serve me well." Hendon Tolly passed him a book covered in tanned leather. Tinwright looked at it with horror. "Just open it, you white-livered fool," Tolly growled. "That is cowhide that binds it, not human flesh. It is Ximander's book—even you must have heard of that. Open it!"

Reluctantly, Tinwright did. He had not read ancient Hierosoline in years, but his schoolteacher father had made certain his son could read the old, great books. If he had not been so terrified, it might have been an interesting experience—he had heard of Ximander's famous book and its strange predictions and tales, but he had never seen it. The actual title appeared to be, *"A Diversitie of Truthfull Thinges, from the pen of Ximandros Tetramakos."*

"Here," Tolly said. "I will show you the page. You will read, and only read, until I tell you to do something different."

"Read out loud?"

"Yes, fool. You are not reading for your pleasure, you are invoking a goddess."

"A goddess . . . ?" Tinwright swallowed. Was Tolly serious? Did he truly think he could speak to the gods as though he were one of the

Oniri, the sacred oracles that carried the gods' words to a waiting world? But the oracles were blessed folk, beloved of the gods, men and women of such purity and piousness that they could touch the will of Heaven itself. Hendon Tolly was a murderer, a rapist, and usurper.

Tinwright did not, however, point any of this out.

"Read this, Lord?" To his dismay, the language was nothing so ordinary as ancient Hiersoline, but instead some strange, unreadable tongue he had never seen before. "I do not know these words. . . ."

"Stop sniveling and get to it," Tolly said. "Make the best sense of it you can. You are not charming empty-headed women here, but speaking words of power."

Tinwright cleared his throat. He could feel the stone walls looming close around him, and perhaps even the souls of the royal family's dead watching him with dislike, but there was nothing to be done but to read Hendon Tolly's nonsense aloud.

"Vea shen goarubilir sheyyer gelameian o goh en duyak paraasala in ichinde ionet gizhli, vea SYA yeldi goh buk vea shen goarmelimiş vea bagh! O buk iscah bir goabegi . . ."

As Tinwright read, a strange thing began to happen. The words of Ximander's incantation, couched in some awkward, antique desert tongue, began to seem more and more familiar, like a melody from childhood, until Matthias Tinwright began to understand what it was saying, as though the language of the book had somehow changed to his own tongue even as he read it.

". . . And You commanded that visible things should come from invisible in the very lowest parts, and SYA came into all that was and You beheld it all and there! From her belly there shone a great radiance . . ."

The light from the torch dimmed abruptly, as if someone had plucked it from its sconce and was walking away. Tinwright felt himself falling forward, not into the mirror that still stood before him like a window frame, but falling nonetheless, his body almost completely lost to him, his thoughts drawn into the reflection of his own face in the mirror's dark surface.

Except that the reflection was changing, Tinwright realized. Fear dug at him. Somehow the walls of the crypt had all but vanished, although he thought he could still dimly see them. The floor was entirely gone, replaced by a carpet of green grass and the gnarled but slender gray trunk of a tree. It was an almond tree, branches festooned with white blossoms like small stars.

By all of Heaven, it's Zoria, he realized. *We're invoking Zoria!* Only his fear had kept him from understanding for so long. *The almond blossom is hers, first flower of the spring—the year's dawn.*

But why? What lunatic sacrilege did Hendon Tolly have in mind? Tolly had said something about marrying a goddess, but could even such a madman believe he might woo and even wed Perin's virgin daughter? Blasphemy!

None of these thoughts changed anything. The Matt Tinwright who read the invocation seemed almost a different person than the Tinwright who had such frightened thoughts. The garden in the mirror before him was like something in a dream, distant even where it was close. He was no longer aware of the words from Ximander's book, though they still flowed unceasingly from his lips; he heard them only dimly, as if someone behind him was whispering.

Now something pale fluttered down and landed on the nearest bough of the almond tree, something as gently rounded as a tiny boat, but alive, with bright eye and soft, powdery feathers. A dove, Zoria's sacred bird.

"Now reach for it," Hendon Tolly whispered. His voice might have been blown to Tinwright's ears down a long, windy valley. "Reach for it! Okros said there must be a sacrifice to open the way—there must *always* be a sacrifice!"

He didn't want to—the sense of the mirror as a doorway or a window had grown even stronger now, and either way, it was an entrance to a place he did not belong—but he felt his arm moving forward, his fingers spreading as his hand reached out for the mirror's cold surface . . .

. . . And passed through.

For a moment Tinwright lost all sense of where he was—outside the mirror reaching in, inside the mirror reaching out, he could no longer say. A chill ran up his hand, a cold as fierce as if he had plunged it into an icy mountain stream.

It seemed that Hendon Tolly was still talking to him. If so, Tinwright's ears could no longer hear him, but his hand could. As if it had a life of its own, it stretched toward the dove, which had tucked its small head beneath one wing. As his thumb and fingers curled around the bird's small, delicate neck, he suddenly realized what he was doing. He tried to stop, but his hand moved as though it were no longer his own. He tried to shout a warning, but the incantation went on in his own voice and no other words passed his lips. He closed his eyes, but he could still feel the horrible fragility of the dove's neck as he squeezed it, and then the terrible percussion of its breaking. Then, as he raged uselessly against whatever held him, he felt something change in the place where the almond tree grew.

The dove was no longer the only other creature inside the mirror.

But just as he had not been able to stop himself from snapping the beautiful, pale bird's neck, now Tinwright could not withdraw his hand from that strange junction, no matter how hard he tried. His own voice droned on in a language that had become meaningless again, but he could not stop it, nor could he make his own sinew and bone act for him in any way. But his hand was not the only thing at risk; all of him, he somehow understood, was now naked and vulnerable to a thing he himself had attracted, some hunting thing that glided through the mirror-world as a ferret shark knifed through the waters of Brenn's Bay. Whatever it was had not found him yet, but it was looking.

He groaned, or tried to. The drone of his own voice had stopped. He tried to make his mouth speak, tried to shout to Hendon Tolly for help, but his voice seemed a thing without air or force. He could not even see Tolly any more: the mirror had become all the world—the blackness surrounding the almond tree branch, the dove with the crooked head clutched in his hand, all only a tiny shadow of reality. Then even those few familiar things began to fade into the growing darkness.

Afraid his very heart would burst, Matt Tinwright found a little voice, somehow, and croaked, "Help me . . . !" He could hear no response.

The sense of exposure was so great that he now began to weep with terror. *This is how Okros must have felt just before his end, watched, hunted . . . !* At the same time he was as light-headed as if a fever had taken him.

Without warning, a sensation crept up his arm from his mirror-hand to his heart, a wild arousal, something too powerful to be called love but too all-compassing to be lust. Tinwright had only a moment to sense the newcomer, to feel its scalding, exhilarating power, before he was flung away from the mirror like a man struck by lightning.

Matt Tinwright felt a moment of terrible loss, as though he had been separated from everything he had ever loved, then his thoughts flew away.

When his senses came back to him, Tinwright was lying on the floor of the Eddon vault, staring up into the shadowy places where the torch's light did not entirely prevail. His shoulder was tingling as if it had fallen asleep, or had been plunged for a terrible length of time in an icy pool, but when he groped at it in panic, he was relieved to find that his arm was still attached to it. He rolled over and found himself staring up at Hendon Tolly—but no Hendon that Tinwright had ever seen. The lord protector stood swaying and moaning before the mirror, his eyes half-closed, his body shaking all over in the grip of some unimaginable pain or ecstasy. His guards could only watch, sweaty and terrified, as their master danced helplessly in the overwhelming embrace of Heaven.

7
The Battle of Kleaswell Market

"One of the bandits' women took pity on little Adis and gave him food from her own store. One day she and her man took the boy and escaped from the other bandits . . ."

—from "A Child's Book of the Orphan, and His Life and Death and Reward in Heaven"

AS THEY DREW CLOSER TO SOUTHMARCH, Briony's heart grew heavier. It had been one thing to talk about recapturing the throne at the Tessian court, surrounded by idlers and courtiers, many of whom sympathized with her (or pretended to), but quite another to contemplate real action. However willing Prince Eneas might be to help her, she had embroiled the son of Eion's most powerful king in her own fight without his father's permission. Even with the best will in the world, what chance did Eneas have to take back high-walled Southmarch, perched on a rock in the middle of a bay, with no ships and fewer than a thousand men at his command?

"Do not fret yourself," the prince told her. "We go to see what we will see, and only then will we concern ourselves with tactics. Your father was a famously clever man—surely he taught you not to make plans without some idea of the land and conditions . . ."

"Is," she said. "He still is. I know he lives—I know it!"

"Of course, Princess." Eneas looked genuinely pained. "I did not mean . . . I spoke clumsily. . . ."

"It is not your fault." She shook her head. "Sometimes I speak that way, too, and even think that way. It has been so long since I saw him! My friend Dowan said he felt certain I would see my father again, at least once . . ." She had to stop speaking for a moment, for fear of crying. The thought of poor, dead Dowan was too much for an already overburdened heart.

Prince Eneas was strong and kind and reassuring. It would have been easy for Briony to give everything over into his care—her promise to take her kingdom back, her other hopes and fears, even herself—but she just could not do it. Something perverse was always at work in her, she feared, the same perversity that had so often put her at odds with her counselors and even her own attendants. She would not let anyone, even someone as reliable as Eneas—*especially* someone as reliable as Eneas—take her burdens from her. She found it hard enough trusting Dawet dan-Faar to do things she couldn't or wouldn't do herself, but at least the Tuani adventurer did not treat her the way a benevolent uncle would. In fact, Dawet seemed truly to admire her stubbornness.

Briony could not help wondering what kind of husband the dangerous Dawet would make. He would demand his own freedom, but he would give her freedoms of her own. . . .

And what of Ferras Vansen? Was he as shy as he seemed? She could not forget the way he always avoided her eyes. Was she imagining the man's feelings for her? But there had been moments—bright, fierce moments when their eyes had met and she was certain something had passed between them. At the time she had not really understood, but she did not think she was wrong. She had grown since then and felt more certain of her own ideas. The problem was, she was not completely certain how she felt about Vansen, and was even less certain that it was appropriate for her to think of him at all. He was a commoner, was he not? They could have no future.

Which brought her back again in a weary circle to Eneas, who deserved better. He had made it very clear that he cared for her and would make an eminently sensible match. Why, then, she wondered as she looked at him, tall, handsome, at ease with all that was manly and appropriate, did she find herself less than overwhelmed?

Every unmarried woman in Tessis would laugh me to scorn if they knew, she thought. *And then trample me into the dust in their hurry to reach him.*

★ ★ ★

Eneas had certainly told the truth when he said his men were trained to move quickly: ten pentecount of foot soldiers and over a hundred well-armored knights, with grooms and other servants making nearly a thousand men altogether, managed some days to travel as far as ten leagues. But even after all that riding, the work of the Temple Dogs was nowhere near finished. Making camp brought with it dozens of other chores. The men were organized ten to a tent-group in the old Hierosoline manner, each group of ten responsible for their own cooking and for contributing sentries, as well as digging their own section of the defensive ditch around the perimeter of the camp, which they did every night, whether they stopped near a tiny Syannese village, beside the walls of a large town, or, as now, in the nearly empty wilderness between settlements.

Briony didn't understand, but Eneas explained. "If I take pity and allow them to go a night without digging the ditch and then nothing bad happens, they will come to think it unnecessary and chafe at the work. Better to make it as familiar as breathing—is that not true, Miron?"

"Yes, Highness," said his earnest lieutenant. "The Duke of Veryon was caught unawares at Potmis Bridge and nearly his entire army was routed and destroyed."

Briony wasn't terribly familiar with Syannese military history but she understood the point.

The men also had to bake their own bread, draw water, and choose lots for the order of sentry duty, all before bedding down for the night. With such long days full of duty and precious little in the way of diversion in this part of the north, it was a credit to Eneas and his generalship that the men looked fit and morale was generally good.

So why am I such a fool? Briony thought. *Why can I not love a man like Eneas? And is love even necessary? Father didn't know Mother before the marriage was arranged, but although she died when we were born he still mourns her.*

Thus it was that the Syannese troop quickly made its way north from the border of Syan and through the corner of Silverside, crossing far to the west of the trade city of Onsilpia's Veil and into Southmarch itself. It was a part of the country that Briony did not know well, iron and copper and coal country, as her father had taught her, centered around mines in the high hills and sheep country to the west, grass downs where domestic animals far outnumbered the people and whose farmers and herdsmen provided wool to much of the north. Now, though, it looked as though a great wind had come and blown the people themselves away, leaving behind houses, barns, byres, and fields that had gone to weeds. The Qar themselves, in their march down from the Shadowline, had passed at least a league or two to the west, but the effect of their passage seemed to have emptied the land like a plague.

The saddest and most telling example of the exodus was a doll made of straw, a fine piece of craft Briony spotted by the side of the road. It seemed so forlorn there, in the middle of a desolate stretch of rocky meadow that she dismounted and picked it up.

One of the doll's wooden button eyes was missing, and it was discolored from the rains that had swept through in previous days, but otherwise it was unharmed. It had clearly been someone's treasure, dressed in a cleverly made gown and hat, hair of golden thread—a fine court lady in miniature. Only a family in a desperate hurry would have dropped such a thing and not come back to search for it, and Briony could easily imagine the little girl who was doubtless still crying herself to sleep at night over her loss.

As spring days passed, they made their way up through Southmarch toward the Settland Road, which would lead them almost due east to the shores of Brenn's Bay. By the end of the first tennight in Hexamene they had reached Candlerstown, the site of the first attack by the fairy folk on the cities of men. There was little of the town left to see—the walls had been torn down in dozens of places, almost with what seemed like careless malice, as a child might kick down something a rival had built before hurrying home for supper. But the blackened ruins of the houses, softened only slightly by the grasses that had begun to grow up through what had once been well-tended streets to cover the charred wreckage in a fragile net of green, spoke of a malice that was far from careless. By the time they had left the ruins of Candlerstown behind, Briony was shivering as though from a winter chill. The Syannese soldiers, for whom the Qar to this point had been largely abstract, were also wide-eyed and troubled, and even Eneas could not entirely mask his unease.

"These fairy creatures are monsters," he said as they made camp that night, well out of sight of the blackened, lifeless city. "Worse than monsters."

"Worse than monsters, yes, but only because they are as clever as we are—maybe more so." She thought of the tale the merchant Raemon

Beck had told her, how the creatures had appeared almost from nowhere. "Don't underestimate them, Eneas. They're not beasts."

Over the next two days they crossed eastward through the Dale country. They made early camp one evening in a river valley to give the soldiers a chance to bathe, and also because the narrow outlet from this valley to the next made Eneas cautious: the narrow pass seemed a very good place for an ambush, leaving them largely defenseless against anyone who might be lurking above the road with arrows or even stones.

The first set of scouts came back in a hurry, excitement plain in the way they rode, and the Temple Dogs' sergeants—called "*penteneries,*" also in the old Hierosoline manner—had all they could do to keep the men who were setting up camp working in an orderly fashion.

"Fighting, sir," Miron reported when he had taken the scouts' reports. "At the far end of the next valley there's a hill town with good-sized walls, but there's not much left of it. Looks like the fairies tore it down. But if they did, they're still there and they're fighting with ordinary men right on the valley road!"

"Kleaswell Market," Briony said, heart beating fast. She had thought she was ready to meet the Qar face-to-face, but suddenly she was not so sure. "That's the name of the town. People come from all over this part of Southmarch for the holiday market. I mean, they used to come . . ."

"How many of each?" Eneas demanded.

Miron thought hard. "Seems as though neither force is as large as ours, Highness, although it's hard to be certain—by the time the scouts got far enough up the valley to see the town, it was getting near dark and they didn't want to risk going closer and being noticed by the goblins. You said they can see a long way."

"Very well. There is nothing we can do tonight. Put the sentries on quiet watch, and we will move out in the watch before dawn—that way we have a chance of getting close before the sun is above the hills."

That night, Briony left her meal with Eneas and his officers early and returned to her tent. She wasn't hungry, and she was too anxious to make conversation. The men had been too excited to pay much attention to her anyway. They were like small boys, she decided—females were acceptable company, but only until something really important came along. Even Eneas, Briony could not help noticing, had showed a bit of childlike enthusiasm, talking avidly about tactics. The prince was not a fool, and he had been planning carefully with an eye toward keeping his own men as safe as possible, but Briony still saw something in his excited conversation that reminded her of her brothers arguing over quoits.

But even the work of getting herself ready for bed without the help of servants, a once-unfamiliar task now become quite ordinary, did not tire Briony enough to bring sleep quickly. Instead she lay in a bed that (like almost everything else in camp) smelled of the animals that carried the bags each day, listening to the quiet, intermittent calls of the camp sentries declaring that all was well. Between calls, she thought of the men of her family, scattered or entirely lost, and in the darkness and solitude of her tent, which alone in the camp she shared with no other person, Briony Eddon wept.

The fairies' attack had either never stopped for darkness or had resumed with the first light. The sun had still not crested the hills when the Syannese troop reached the end of the far valley and could see the broken walls of Kleaswell Market, but the first thing they saw was that men—and Qar—had already died this day in plenty.

The mortal defenders had taken up position atop a small hill on the far side of the road, protected in part from Qar arrows by the thick branches of trees. The fairy folk, a small force of which only a few pentecounts at the most were visible, had adopted an attacker's strategy and were besieging the small hill. At first it was hard to tell whether the Qar were much different from their human enemies—only their strangely-shaped banners and the equally unusual colors of their armor suggested otherwise—but as Eneas gave the order and his troops hurried up the road toward the rise at the end of the valley, Briony began to see more telling differences: one of the fairy commanders, who wore what Briony at first thought was a helmet decorated with antlers, proved not to be wearing a helmet at all. A group of small manlike shapes who seemed to be dressed in long tattered robes of black and brown were in fact naked. All of them fought fiercely, though, and with a strange absence of any sort of tactics that Briony could recognize. They swarmed like insects, and like insects, seemed to have some unspoken way of knowing what they should do next, because, when they changed method or direction of attack, they all changed together, without any sign or word being passed as far as she could tell.

The mortal men they were attacking seemed to be a mixed lot of well-armed soldiers and unarmed or lightly armed civilians—merchants, perhaps, since many wagons had been drawn together at the top of the hill they defended. They flew no recognizable banner, but Briony recognized a few of the crests on men's shields and surcoats as Kracian. Mercenaries, she decided, hired to protect a caravan—but why hired from so far away? And why was a caravan moving through such dangerous territory in the first place? Surely the castle itself must be receiving most of its supplies from the sea, as it had been doing even before Briony left Southmarch behind.

She had little time to think about this because just then the fairies seemed to notice Eneas and his oncoming troop for the first time. Arrows began to leap toward them.

The prince abruptly interposed his horse between her and the distant Qar, driving her off the road. "You will not risk your life, Princess."

"But I can fight!" Briony realized as she said it that it was foolish, but she could not help it. "You're a prince, and you're not hiding . . . !"

"Without you, your people have nothing. I have two brothers and a father who will live many years yet." His face was hard: it was clear no argument would be entertained. A moment later he gave her horse a slap on the rump to propel it farther off the road, then wheeled his own mount and spurred back toward his men.

The Qar soldiers had not been waiting idly. By the time the first of the Syannese riders reached them, they had formed a makeshift spear wall , some with actual pikes and spears, others by grabbing any long piece of wood they could reach and turning it toward the oncoming horsemen. Briony was almost as frightened for the horses as she was for the men, and as the vanguard of the charge struck, she had to close her eyes. She did not see it, but she heard the terrible, savage crash of splintering wood and screaming men and horses—and fairies, she could only presume, because no living thing could be struck that way and not cry out.

Within moments, the main part of Eneas' troop had broken through and was wheeling back around to assault the fairies from the other side. Other soldiers and their Qar enemies had broken apart into knots of combat. The fighting was fierce, and Briony several times saw Syannese soldiers fall to the ground, pierced by an arrow or spear or sword thrust, but the fairies had obviously been taken by surprise and were slow to recover. Also, Briony saw nothing of the magical trickery she had heard that the Twilight People used at Kolkan's Field and in other encounters with the Southmarch soldiers. What exactly was going on here? If the Qar were still besieging Southmarch, why should they be trying to destroy a supply train so far to the west of the castle? And how had the merchants who hired the Kracian mercenaries expected to get their caravan into a surrounded castle even if they reached the shore of the bay? It was a mystery.

She heard a shriek of dismay and turned in time to see something charging down out of the woods that at first she took to be a bear or something stranger still—a bull, perhaps, but running on its hind legs. The thing had a huge, square head and a back as broad as an ox-yoke, and it carried a sort of bladed club in its hands, a horrible weapon with several massive stone axes bound into the wide shaft. It charged right into the center of Eneas' men with weapon flailing and knocked several of them through the air like shuttlecocks to land crushed and bleeding at the side of the road, but other Syannese foot soldiers charged toward the thing, pikes lowered, and hemmed the monster in, jabbing and then falling back as it swung its club at them, stabbing at it again when it turned away. Despite its strength, the thing could not escape its smaller persecutors and was soon bleeding from several dozen wounds. The monster's face twisted in a rictus of agony as it threw back its head and bellowed its pain and rage. Moments later, it tried to break out of the circle of its attackers, reminding her of the day so long ago when Kendrick and the others had hunted the wyvern in the hills of the Southmarch mainland, but several more spears pierced the huge Qar fighter, one of them all the way through the throat, freeing a freshet of bright red blood. The great, dark creature swayed and then collapsed. The soldiers cried out in terrified triumph and surged forward, stabbing it and even kicking it repeatedly.

Eneas himself, who had caught up to his men in time to join their charge through the thick part of the Qar line, had been immediately surrounded by a group of small, dark things that, were it not for their short stabbing swords, might have been mistaken for apes, but between his lance and his own sword he had made short work of them, aided by his warhorse and its heavily shod hooves. A group of Syannese riflemen had set up on the edge of the fighting and started firing into the knot of Qar farther up the slope, scattering them in retreat across the slope only moments after the merchants and their mercenaries had seemed on the verge of being eradicated.

And then, just when it seemed that the Qar could do nothing but flee or surrender, a figure on a great gray horse appeared in the road as if it had stepped out of nowhere. The fairy folk collapsed into a semicircle around this armored warrior, who although nowhere near as large as the club-wielding giant still seemed tall beyond mortal men. His armor was a dull, leaden color, his face a sooty black—not black like the skin of Shaso or Dawet or the other southerners Briony had met, but black as something burned, black as charcoal or a fireplace poker. The creature's eyes, though, were like nothing Briony had ever seen, lambent yellow as amber held before a flame, and he carried a weapon that had an exotic blade on one side and a spike on the other, clearly meant to pierce armor—even more frightening when Briony contrasted it with the light mail Prince Eneas was wearing.

To his credit, Eneas did not hesitate, but spurred toward the newcomer, recognizing that the Qar were rallying around him and a victory over the fairies that had seemed so certain a few moments ago now seemed much less so. A rain of arrows came from the hill above; Eneas' men screamed in outrage at the human mercenaries who had fired them, because as many of them seemed to strike the Syannese as the enemy Qar.

The black-faced creature spurred toward Eneas, swinging his ax in violent circles above his head.

"Akutrir!" the other Qar chanted—the creature's name, Briony guessed. *"Akutrir saruu!"*

Eneas and the fairy lord met in the center of the road, scattering both men and Qar who leaped for safety like grasshoppers disturbed in a summer field. The spike on the fairy's ax bit into Eneas' shield, piercing the painted white hound, and for long moments the two could not separate, Eneas struggling to pull back his shield and hacking at the handle of Akutrir's weapon with his own sword. The fairy's grinning mouth was huge—his dark-shadowed face seemed nothing but teeth and glowing orange eyes, like a Kerneia mask. The newness of everything that had distracted Briony was now gone; she was nothing but frightened. This was not an old story or a tale from the *Book of the Trigon*. Even though she was praying to Zoria as hard as she could and to the Trigonate Brothers as well, the gods would not step in and save them. They could all die here by the side of this lonely road, slaughtered by the enemy Qar.

What had seemed at first like single combat was nothing of the sort—the fairy folk around Eneas jabbed at him with short spears even as he met Akutrir's blows with sword swipes of his own. The prince's men charged forward to even the odds and everything disappeared into the swirl of flashing blades and dust from the road, which now hung over everything, a gray cloud sparkling in the morning sunlight.

And then it was over, as quickly as it had begun. The tall fairy lord retreated and the rest of the Qar fled away toward the east as the mortals who had been fighting a losing battle for their lives only an hour before shouted and cheered. Some of them even hurried down to chase the retreating Qar, but the fairy folk seemed almost to melt away into the trees at the end of the valley.

The merchants and their mercenary soldiers might have been celebrating, but the Temple Dogs had lost more than a few men and were in no such mood themselves. Their grim faces as they brought back the bodies made Briony want to turn away. Instead, she forced herself to stand and watch the corpses being carried off the field to be laid beside the road. A detachment of the prince's soldiers began to dig the necessary graves.

Now these Syannese men have died for my cause, too, she told herself. *Eneas' comrades and brothers. That is a debt that cannot be forgotten.*

8
And All His Little Fishes

". . . And so they entered into the great city of Hierosol. Along the way Adis was taught to pretend injury to excite the pity of wealthy folk, and other beggar's tricks, so that he could earn his keep . . ."

—from "A Child's Book of the Orphan, and His Life and Death and Reward in Heaven"

BARRICK AWOKE IN HIS CHAMBER at Qul-na-Qar to find another meal waiting for him, just as good as the first—slices of some fruit crunchy as apples but tangy as a Kracian norrange, and thick brown bread that tasted a little of mulled wine, along with plenty of butter in a small pot. It seemed clear that some of the people who lived in the castle must still bake, and some kept cows or goats. At least Barrick *hoped* it was cows or goats supplying the butter and cheese, but if some other creature was responsible, he was just as happy not knowing because it all tasted good.

Barrick swallowed the last of the small loaf, then wiped the butter pot with his fingers and licked them clean. Gods, but it felt wonderful to have something in his stomach—real food, too, not bitter herbs or even the scrawny black squirrels he'd been hunting since crossing the Shadowline, miserable, tasteless things that in his hunger and misery had seemed a festival meal.

Harsar appeared a moment later, as though the little lop-eared servant had been in the hallway listening for the sound of Barrick sucking on his fingers. "She is waiting for you in the Chamber of the Gate of Sleep," he said in his clumsily accented speech. Barrick wondered why the little servant didn't just speak to him in thoughts as the queen did. "I will take you there."

"Where?" But even as he said it he knew, as if it had been in his memory all along—the many-columned chamber with the shining disk where he had first arrived in Qul-na-Qar from the city of Sleep. His heart quickened. Saqri had been telling the truth, then. She had an idea.

The first thing that surprised him when he reached the columned room was that the queen was kneeling in the center of the glowing, pearly stone disk with her head bowed as if she prayed. The second was that when she rose and beckoned Barrick forward, Harsar stepped toward her as well.

"No, you must stay, Harsar-so-a," she told the hairless creature. "After all, the castle will need to be looked after in our absence, and there is no one who knows it better than you. Your sons will need you, too."

He bowed, showing no emotion. "As you say, my lady." He turned and went from the room, quick and silent as a shadow sliding on the wall.

"Very well, then." She turned to Barrick. "Two kinds of roads there are, as I told you. The first sort are those that Crooked himself created, or at least made available. We have one such road here before us." She gestured to the gleaming disk. "Through it, you can pass into the city of Sleep . . ."

"But that won't do us any good . . . !"

"Just so." She gave him a cold look, and he shut his mouth. "But there are other roads, other paths, and many of those the gods themselves found, although they did not know what they were or how to find or make more. They used them as a snake takes the burrow of a mouse for his own, although he did none of the work of digging. And just like a snake, sometimes the gods devoured or destroyed the roads' original owners, spirits of an earlier age—but that is another tale. In any case, there are still several such roads leading to the houses of the great gods like Kernios and his brothers.

"Although it leads to the very place we seek, the road into Kernios' house is banned to us because we have the smell of Qul-na-Qar on us, the house of the Earthlord's enemies." She turned to Barrick. "But there is one other god who might open a road for us. Long has your family believed itself descended from the great sea lord Erivor, brother of Perin and Kernios . . ."

"Is that true, then . . . ?" said Barrick, amazed.

"Not in the least," the queen told him. "Or at least not in my knowledge. Anglin's folk were fishermen, but they were also good fighters, and gained their thrones by wit and strength. No gods had a hand in it—at least not directly." Did she smile? "But long has your house held Erivor your special patron, and many sacrifices and festivals have you given in his honor, century upon century. It could be that he would listen to you, not because you have the blood of Crooked in you, but because you are an Eddon, and the Eddons have long and richly worshiped him."

Barrick's head felt as though it were spinning. "But . . . but you said he was asleep!"

"The sleep of gods is not like the sleep of others," she explained. "And in all the time your family has prayed to him and sacrificed to him, he has *always* been sleeping, for a thousand years and more." Now she did smile, the smallest stitch taking up the corner of her mouth. "So pray, Barrick of the Eddon. Down upon your knees and pray to your old tribal god. Ask him to open a way for us."

Was she mocking him?

"Kneel?"

She nodded. "It helps one's perspective. Treating with the gods requires courtesy, and courtesy is ultimately an acknowledgment of power—the true power on both sides of the conversation."

"But I have no power at all!"

Saqri did not bother to agree with this.

Barrick lowered himself to his knees. He could not help noticing how much easier it was now that his arm no longer pained him, and how much more comfortable it was now that the bruises and bloody scrapes of the journey were beginning to heal.

Ask him . . . someone said quietly in his head; he couldn't guess whether it was Saqri or one of the bodiless voices. *Ask the sea lord . . . to open the way . . .*

Barrick closed his eyes, uncertain of what to do. He had prayed countless times, especially in his childhood—oh, how he had prayed for the nightmares to stop, for his arm to be healed, to be able to play like the others—but never with such an unusual request in mind. He tried to remember some of the rituals held on Father Erivor's sacred days, but with little success.

Father Erivor . . . that was what Barrick's own father had called him, almost as a joke. *"Father Erivor and all his little fishes preserve us!"* the king would growl when he was particularly exasperated with one of his children.

Why did you leave me to suffer alone, Father? Why? It was bad enough what Olin had done, throwing his son down the steep tower steps, but why had he spoken so little of it afterward? Shame? Or because he was too busy with his own problems and the problems of the realm?

Father Erivor. Barrick tried to remember what he had thought then, as a child, when that name still meant somebody real—not just the bearded, blue-green giant portrayed on the chapel wall, silver fish surrounding his head like the rays of the morning sun, but the shape he saw in his head when they bowed their heads together and Father Timoid led them in prayers to the family patron.

Great Erivor, monarch of the green-lit depths . . .

As a child Barrick had imagined the god moving slowly at the bottom of the sea, slow as the great turtles or the ancient pike that lived in the castle ponds, wrapped in waving fronds of kelp.

Great Erivor, who has blessed us beyond other men . . .

It was strange, but Barrick could no longer tell if his eyes were closed or open. He seemed to hear the wind battering the waves to froth.

Great Erivor, who calms the waves and brings his bounty to our nets, who rides the great whalefish and tames the world-girdling serpent, hear us now!

The darkness swirled. The darkness was shot through with green light and flittering, bright shapes.

Great Erivor, who slew many-armed Xyllos and drove vast Kelonesos back into the depths so he would prey no more on sailors!
Erivor, who quiets the storm! Erivor, lord of ocean winds!
Chieftain of all sunken gold! Master of treasure!
King of the world's waters! Traveler's rescue!
Hear me now!

The darkness grew deeper, greener, and even more quiet. The winds that had howled in Barrick's ears only moments before were muffled, and even the waves themselves became only a distant roiling. Down here all was silent, the sediments ancient, the kelp coiling and uncoiling, fish darting through its strands. Here dark things swam and crawled. Here mighty armored shapes moved through the dim, greenshot day and the lightless night.

Erivor? Barrick tried to send his thoughts out as boldly as he could. *My family has always given you what was due. You have been our patron, our lord. Please, lord, help me now!*

Something in the darkness shifted—nothing he could see, but something he could feel, as if the massy ocean floor itself had shrugged. It was so near—and so huge! The sheer size of what he felt terrified him, and for a moment Barrick Eddon almost flung himself away from the thing that frightened him, away from the darkest deeps and up toward the light. Then he remembered what would happen if he failed.

My lord! Hear me! Open the road for me to your house. Open the door! If you ever loved us, now is the time to help us! Please, Father Erivor!

And then he felt . . . something. It reached out to him and touched his thoughts, mossy and gigantic as a mountain. He could feel the immense slumbering impossibility of it, this thing sunk deep in millennia of sediment, slow as a starfish moving across a rock but also with parts of its thought as swift as tiny fish dodging in and out of the safety of coral fronds.

Manchild . . . ?

The thought was ageless, ponderous and strange, as though the lord of the sea truly were a giant turtle or lobster, something immense buried in the muck for thousands of years, its shell covered in countless other, smaller living things, waiting for who knew what distant happenstance.

Will you open the door for me, Father Erivor?

It could barely hear him, barely sense him at all. It was not entirely asleep, but it certainly was not awake—he could feel the greater part of its thought lying beyond his reach, inert, dreaming, moving at a rate so slow that no living thing could understand it. *Door . . . ?*

The door to your house! Open it for me! A thought occurred to him, floating in like a bubble. *I will make you many sacrifices, I promise!*

The door . . . it said again, and then he could feel the immense thing suddenly very near—a bright eye in the darkness, a mouth that might have been a hole into the heart of the world, a lightless whirlpool. It was so much bigger—it was big as the world . . . !

Little worshiper . . . you . . . may . . . pass.

The darkness fell away and Barrick fell with it. For a moment all was as it had been when he traveled through Crooked's Hall out of Sleep. Then pressure and cold smashed in on him, crushing him almost to nothingness. Terrified, he opened his mouth to scream, and it filled with salty water.

Father Erivor had opened the door to his house, but his house was at the bottom of the sea.

Barrick was deep, deep in green water—only the gods knew how deep. He'd swallowed more than a little of it in his initial shock, a stinging mouthful that burned in his throat and windpipe until all he wanted to do was cough, which he knew would doom him. He clenched his teeth against it, flailing against the cold water, but he did not even know which way was up. He opened his eyes to the caustic green and saw bubbles streaming and circling him like dandelion fluff. The Fireflower chorus in his head was shrieking a warning but it seemed muffled, distant. He watched the bubbles swirl even as the water began to grow dark—as if here, deep beneath the ocean, twilight had fallen. It was beautiful in a strange way. . . .

Even as Barrick realized he was dying, that the breath trapped in his lungs was turning to hot poison, he saw that the bubbles were forming actual shapes, shapes ghostly as mist that circled him, watching. Did he see pity on those spectral, frothy faces, or only curiosity?

The god's children, his thoughts told him, but they were not exactly his own thoughts.

Something clasped his arm and drew him out of the cloud of bubbles into shadowed green emptiness. Floating, he could not resist, but everything around him was turning black and he did not really care to resist anyway. Was he rising? No, sinking . . .

Her face loomed close to his, smooth and pale, hard as a statue, green as southern jade. For a dreamlike instant he thought it was his own mother's face—Meriel, the mother he had never seen, who had died birthing him. The apparition held her hand up before him and caught a bubble the size of a duck's egg; when it touched her slim fingers, it began to grow until it had become as big as a rubyskin melon. He could scarcely see it, but felt it press against his face, cool and delicate as a first kiss. New air pushed into his chest, replacing the water that had been choking him, and suddenly the darkness was crossed with streaks of light as his thoughts stirred back into life once more.

Do nothing, manchild—only breathe. Saqri's voice was distant at first, but by the last words it filled his mind. *We must give thanks to the god, even if he only sleeps and dreams us. Even more so, in fact, if he only dreams us. . . .*

Barrick had no idea what she meant. He was content to float and taste the sweetness of air while all around him the green seemed to grow deeper and wider until he thought he could see shadowy shapes on all sides, pillars and arches. He couldn't tell if they were natural or the work of some supernatural hand—in fact, he could not be entirely certain he was even seeing them.

But behind the vertical shadows was one deeper and darker than all the rest—a cave? A hall? For a moment, as a little light streamed down through the green from above—and as he realized for the first time where "up" actually was—he thought he could make out a massive shape crouched deep in that darkness, something so big and so strange that he could barely steel himself to face in its direction, let alone look carefully.

Tell him, she said.

Tell him what? Despite the bubble of air over his face, diminished in size now but still filling his lungs with life, he was finding it hard to take a breath. Something was in that cave, something unimaginably huge and powerful and alive, and he was terrified . . .

Tell him!

I . . . we . . . thank you. Thank you, Lord Erivor. By . . . He could remember nothing—all those bored mornings sitting in the chapel, and how could he have ever guessed this hour would come? Why hadn't he paid better attention? *By the blood of . . . of my ancestors, who have always served you, O Lord, and upon whom you have showered your blessings . . .* No! That was wrong! That was the harvest prayer to Erilo!

Something stirred in the depths of the shadows; even with an incomprehensible weight of water pressing down on him from all sides Barrick could feel it in his bones. Whatever it was, it had become restless. Awake, angry, it could pull down mountains.

As panic rose, something else drifted up in him, too—not the voices of the Fireflower, which had become almost ordinary, but another voice, thin and quavering—a memory of Father Timoid, reciting the Erivor Mass, words that he had forgotten he knew.

O Father of the Waters,
Whose blood is the green water
Whose beard is the white wave
Who raised up the land
Who is the master of the flood
And the father of tears
Who lifted Connord and Sharm
From the mud
Who lifted Ocsa and Frannac
Out of the ocean wrack into sunlight
So that the people could live
And the grass could grow
O Father of the Waters,
Who calms the storm
And guides the boats safe back to harbor
Who sends his fish into the nets
Of Glin's children
Who sends his winds to fill the sails
Of Glin's children's boats
Who lifts his hand
To bring the waves gentle upon the shore
We praise you.
We praise you.
We praise you.
Give us your blessing
As we give our thanks to you.

And as the last oh-so-familiar word fell down into the blackness, the great shadow stirred again and slowly drifted backward into deeper dark. The presence that had, merely by existing, almost squeezed Barrick breathless began to recede from his thoughts, from his senses.

Thank you, Great Lord. It was Saqri's voice, and to his astonishment there was a teasing lilt to it, like a cheeky girl taxing a beloved older relative. *Thank you for your help, both to bring us here and to send us a little farther on, where the air is not so damp . . .*

Send us? Barrick thought. *Where? Hasn't there been enough sending and coming and going . . . ?*

He and Saqri began slowly to rise. The green grew brighter, the streaks of light smearing into one general circle that glowed high above them like a burning jade sun.

Barrick rose, and as he did the voices of the Fireflower woke again into what seemed a chorus of alarm and wonder, as though the darkness of the depths had made them somnolent, but the growing circle of light had wakened them.

Above the green . . .

Saved by the spawn of Moisture!

No! Do not trust them . . . !

And then the light widened overhead, swift as a brushfire sweeping across a hillside, brightness that expanded to swallow him up as he broke out of the green and into the dazzle, splashing and gasping for air. He discovered there not the unbroken sea as he had expected, an endless expanse of waves, but a jut of rocks and beyond that the dim shape of something he had not seen in so long that he almost could not recognize it, especially as the voices inside him grew to a singing crescendo.

The Last Hour of the Ancestor . . . !

We see it again! Praise to the honorable Children of Breeze!

May they dwell in bliss!

Jutting on the horizon like a mountain range whose peaks had been whittled into sharp points, blasted white by the sharp morning sun so that it seemed sculpted in ice, loomed Southmarch Castle, the only home Barrick had ever known. It no longer seemed familiar to him, but had instead become something beautiful and strange.

It frightened him.

Something boomed nearby, loud as thunder, catching him completely by surprise. It happened again but now he saw a plume of smoke on the shore. Cannons! Someone was firing at the castle.

He stopped paddling for a moment in surprise and sank back down into the waters of the bay. Only then did Barrick realize his mouth was hanging open.

Coughing and spitting and sputtering, he almost slipped back under the water again until he heard Saqri's voice, so loud and firm that it was like a hand grabbing his collar.

Swim, fool child. Swim to the shore.

Shore? Even the closest part of the bay's edge was too far away, and that was where the cannon was being fired!

Not that part, Saqri told him. Tiring now, Barrick paddled and kicked himself in a tight circle to look around, but he could see no trace of her. He did see something else, however. *Yes,* she said. *There. Swim.*

With his back to the land and his shoulder toward the castle, he could finally see it—another lump of stone that didn't stretch as high above the waves as the castle mount but was washed by the same breezy, white capped bay waters. He had not seen it in so long that it took him a moment to recognize it, even after he made out the angular shape of the lodge at the top of the hilly island.

M'Helan's Rock!

Barrick summoned his weary strength and began swimming.

9
The Thing with Claws

"After many adventures and perils he was taken up at last as an unlawful beggar by the guards of the city and brought before the magistrates. Because the Orphan could show no such crippling injuries as he pretended, he was sent as a slave to the temple of Zuriyal . . ."

—from "A Child's Book of the Orphan, and His Life and Death and Reward in Heaven"

"THERE'S NO NEED FOR YOU TO GO FARTHER, Captain," Sledge Jasper told Vansen. "Truth is, some of these tunnels may be too small for you."

"We'll see, Wardthane. Carry on, I'll follow."

The other Funderlings, five more new-minted warders, looked from Vansen to Jasper in worried anticipation. They all carried *gurodir,* heavy stabbing-spears with broad iron spearheads and shafts of precious oak, a war weapon something like a boar spear. It had not been in common use among the small folk for a long time; now every single one that could be found in Funderling Town had been repaired and pressed into service, and more were being made. Even Vansen carried one, although he also kept his dagger and scabbarded sword for their comfort and familiarity.

He waved his hand to pass leadership of the patrol to Jasper, then let the others file past him into the Moonless Reach. The most recent patrol through the caverns, led by one of Jasper's most trusted men, had gone out that morning and not come back.

As they stepped out of the broad main tunnel, which was illuminated by dim fungus-lights at irregular intervals, Vansen reached up to make sure he was wearing his coral lamp. He had discovered that the Funderlings did not always remember that he could not see as well as they could and he wanted to make sure he didn't walk into any unexpected pits or low-hanging rocks.

"You mark my words, Captain," Jasper said quietly as they made their way across the middle of the great chamber, so full of man-high stone towers that it looked like a hall of frozen dancers, "it'll be the fairy what done it, whatever's gone wrong."

Vansen was confused. "What are you talking about? It's the southerners we're fighting, now—the autarch's men." Had the entire peace council with the Qar fallen on deaf ears?

"Talking about that half-drow my men took with 'em. I don't trust that langedy-leg fellow."

The "langedy-leg" fellow had been a Qar of sorts—one of the Funderling cousins known as "drows"—a scout named Spelter who was a bit taller and longer of limb than Sledge Jasper's folk. Spelter and any of the other drows who were familiar with the tunnels of Midlan's Mount from the last few weeks' siege had been joining the Funderlings on their patrol. "What, you think he did something to them?"

"He had a foul look," said Jasper stubbornly, pulling off his helmet to wipe sweat from his bald head. It was beginning to get warm as they moved away from the tunnel that led up to Funderling Town. Up? Vansen wondered if that could be right. They were certainly above the Temple, but were they still below Funderling Town or just off to one side of it? He again found himself muddled by the way the Funderlings underground world fit together.

"But see now, Sledge," he said, raising his voice a little higher so that the other warders would hear him, too. "I know you don't trust them, but why would the Qar bother to stay and betray us? It would be so much easier for them simply to leave us to fight the autarch . . ."

He never had the chance to finish. Something hammered him hard in the back and knocked him forward so that he spilled Jasper and several of the warders like skittles. Vansen lost his spear and was feeling for it when something grabbed his collar and wrenched him another few paces across the stony cavern floor.

"What . . . ?" He struggled to his knees, but before he could turn to see what had grabbed him, a nightmare shape lurched out of a dark place along the wall, a glowing obscenity that Vansen could not even understand, twice as big as a cart horse and with more legs than anything that large should have.

"Perin's Hammer!" he shouted in sudden fright, shoving himself upright and stumbling backward from the huge creature so quickly that he lost his balance and fell down again. All around him the Funderlings were also retreating, howling in dismay and amazement.

It was a monstrous spider or insect, something Vansen could not recognize and would not be able to see at all except for its own green-blue glow. It lumbered toward them with frightening speed, its armored body making a noise like the creaking of bellows-leather; when he saw it whole, he wished he hadn't. The indistinct outline had not only spiderish legs but claws like a crab's and some kind of huge tail swaying above its broad back.

"Have you fire?" a voice said from behind him. "They fear it a little. I chased one away with a torch, but that has long burned away."

Vansen put a large, round stone between himself and the creature, then took a swift glance backward. The light from his coral lamp fell onto a strange, long-jawed, bearded face—the Qar scout, Spelter. "No fire," Vansen said. "Where is the rest of your company?"

"Dead or lost." Spelter spoke the language surprisingly well—one of the reasons he'd been chosen to travel with the Funderlings, no doubt. "We were separated hours ago when the first of these things came out of a tunnel and took the leader and two of the others. Crushed them with its claws. The rest scattered. I tried to get back to Ancestor's Place, to our temple-camp, but found this thing between me and the way back."

"That was you who grabbed me, then?"

"Yes. I heard your voices coming. I did not know exactly where it was waiting, and I was afraid to call because it hunted me, too."

The creaking, whistling monster abruptly tried to clamber up onto the boulder that shielded Vansen and the drow; the monster's scent, musty and slightly fishy, filled Vansen's nostrils. Its huge claws clacked above their heads as he and Spelter scrambled backward. Vansen thought for a moment that they might be able to make a run for the passage that had led them to the chamber, but the creature backed down off the rock and began making its slow way around the wide boulder again, searching almost blindly. Then it lurched forward again, astonishingly fast, this time scraping around the side of the rock where Vansen couldn't see it; an instant later it scuttled back with a screeching Funderling warder in its claw. The little man struggled helplessly, and although his comrades stabbed at the monster with their heavy spears, the blows could not penetrate the thing's armor. The Funderling was pulled into the dark region at the front of the head. Vansen heard a hideous crunching noise, and the screaming abruptly stopped.

Sledge Jasper had managed to climb up on top of the boulder, where he was stabbing almost dementedly at the creature. It spread its claws and lifted its front section onto the rock, then the long, lumpy tail quivered as if in preparation for a strike. Vansen jumped up and caught at Jasper's clothing, yanking backward so that the Funderling fell on top of him only inches ahead of a swipe from the deadly tail. Vansen could smell the venom, a sour, hard smell like hot metal. Some of it spattered onto Sledge Jasper, who screamed and began writhing on the floor as if he'd been burned. The Qar, Spelter, leaped to help him.

Vansen stood. "We can't let it keep us pinned down!" he shouted to the others. "Get out into the center of the cave!"

He led the warders to a spot in the middle of a small forest of stone spikes. He grabbed at one with his hand and was able to break off the very tip, but decided that the spikes were thick enough to give some protection. He turned back to help Spelter drag Jasper into the center of the open space he'd chosen, then quickly set the terrified Funderlings into a tight-packed arrangement, spears pointing outward like the spines of a hedgehog.

The monstrous, green-glowing thing came stilting toward them again but could not immediately pass between the stone spikes. It stopped short a few paces away from Vansen's side. He leaped out and stabbed hard at the place he thought the thing should have eyes, but his *gurodir* only skimmed off hard plate. The tail lashed at him. He danced back out of its reach and his coral lamp fell off his head. Strangely, the monster's glow dimmed, as though some inner light had guttered and almost failed. Vansen snatched up the headband and jumped back into the forest of stones, putting his back against the nearest Funderlings as he pulled his lamp into place. The creature was glowing brightly again. It was too big, too strong, too well armored. Vansen could see no way to defeat it.

But what else could they do except fight? From what Spelter had said, this many-legged beast was not the only one of its kind, and even if they could hold it off, that would only bring more unsuspecting Funderlings out in search of them, no better armed against such a horror than they had been.

What *would* be useful against this thing? Fire, likely—Spelter had said he drove one away with a torch. But what else? It seemed like nothing short of a rifle ball would pierce it and the Funderlings did not have such things. There was Chert's bombard, the one that had devastated the attacking Qar, but they hadn't brought one of those along on this expedition. Still, if they survived, it would be something to think about . . .

So—spears and my sword, and a few rocks. If they couldn't beat the creature with the long, strong *gurodir* spears, they certainly weren't going to be able to kill it with a few small stones . . .

A sudden idea came to him—an unlikely one, but Vansen was growing more desperate by the moment. The many-legged monster had tired of trying to butt its way through the stalagmites and was attempting to climb over them instead, and was slowly, awkwardly succeeding. The faces of Vansen's Funderling allies were full of hopeless terror.

"Spelter," he called to the Qar scout. "How is he?"

The langedy-legged man, as Jasper had called him, looked up. "He's burned, but most of the venom is on his plate. . . ." He jabbed at the armor with his finger where it lay in a heap beside Sledge Jasper, who was murmuring and twitching as if in a deep fever.

"Leave him. One of the others can see to him." Vansen told the drow scout what he wanted him to find. "I can't see well enough, Spelter, but you can. Go, find it for us! We'll keep the thing's attention here."

Spelter went so quickly that he seemed to vanish like a ghost at dawn. Vansen turned back to the rest of the men, who were crouching as far back from the approaching beast as they could. "Spears up and jabbing!" he ordered. "If you can't find something soft to jab at like a joint or an eye, just whack at the cursed thing as hard as you can! And shout!" He didn't even know if the creature had ears, but he was leaving nothing to chance.

The monster was almost upon them, teetering on a high spike of rock, legs flailing as it sought purchase to pull itself off the pinnacle. The shouts of Vansen and the Funderlings became louder, fueled by panic. The thing actually caught one of the warders in a sweeping claw, but with the Funderling in its grip it could not pull its claw-arm back. Two more warders leaped at it, prying at the crablike claw until the wounded man fell out onto the ground, gasping and coughing, bleeding in a wide band across his chest where his mail shirt had been crushed against his flesh.

The monster tipped and slid backward a little, then could not get up onto the pointed stone again. Heartened, the Funderlings redoubled their efforts, cracking on the beast's armor so hard with the ends of their heavy spears that they made a noise like high-pitched thunder in the echoing cavern.

Vansen had his spear in one hand and his sword in the other. Once he even managed to get his spear into the thing's bizarre mouth, but could not drive it in more than a few inches, and although the monster shied back it did not seem badly hurt. Another moment he saw a black spot that he thought must be an eye on the side of the weird, flat head, but when he tried to reach it with his sword, the beast almost took his head off with a flailing leg and he had to retreat behind a stalagmite.

Vansen was tiring and knew the Funderlings were tiring as well, but the monster did not seem to tire. They were running out of time.

The creature took a few many-legged steps back to find another angle of attack, and as it did, it moved beyond the Funderlings' reach. The clatter of spear on shell stopped, and in that moment of comparative quiet Vansen heard Spelter calling them: "Here! Here! Come now!"

"Follow his voice," he hissed to the warders, then bent down to scoop up the small but solid body of Sledge Jasper and toss him over his shoulder. "Go—now!"

The Funderlings ran deeper into the cavern, away from the center where the stone pinnacles sprouted everywhere. Only a moment passed before the monster realized what they were doing and came legging after them.

"Here!" shouted Spelter. He was standing near one of the sloping walls of the cavern, half-hidden behind a large, mostly rounded stone many times his size which looked to have been rolled there when the world was young by some god playing at bowls. "Here, help me!"

Vansen got there last and carefully lowered the senseless Jasper to the ground. "It's too big. We'll never move it!"

"Balanced. Not so difficult—if we work hard!" Spelter said breathlessly. He had clearly begun already. Vansen and several of the Funderlings hurriedly clambered onto the curving shelf of rock beside him and jammed their spears into the space between the round stone and the wall.

Vansen set his booted foot against the stone and leaned back hard, testing the flexibility of his spear. If it broke, he might well kill himself or one of his fellows with the shards before the monster even reached them, but for the moment it was holding together.

"Everybody!" Vansen shouted. "Now!" The other Funderlings did their best to find a place to throw their own weight and strength against the perched stone, their spears bending like saplings. Vansen felt blood in his temples threatening to boil and burst out, but the stone was not moving and the glowing, spiderlike monster was moving toward them, in no hurry now that it had them out from behind cover and against a wall with nowhere else to run.

Something was pulling hard at his leg. For a terrifying moment Vansen thought it was another one of the creatures, then he realized it was the half-naked form of Sledge Jasper, with armor and helmet gone and a blistering burn up the side of his face, trying to use Vansen's leg to climb up and help.

"Give me room, you cursed, gawky upgrounder!" Jasper cried, then shoved the butt of his spear into the crack between stone and floor and lifted his legs off the ground, swinging on the spear until it bent nearly double. The others, too weary now to do anything but keep pulling, leaned back into their own spears. Vansen shoved his back down against the wall so he could use both legs at the same time. The creature lifted its snapping claws, each the size of a fiddler's bass viol, and reared up on its hindmost legs. Then the stone moved.

Vansen had only a moment to notice that nothing was holding him up before he fell heavily to the floor of the cavern, Funderlings tumbling all around him like frozen sparrows dropping from winter branches. The boulder tottered, then tipped and rolled down the short incline. At first it seemed to move so slowly that Vansen thought it was impossible the monster would fail to evade it, but either the thing's tiny eyes or its weak wits betrayed it, and it only waved its claws impotently as the rock, three times the monster's height, rolled over it and crushed it with a dreadful, wonderful wet crunch. By the time the boulder came to a halt again some twenty paces on, part of the monster was still stuck to it, but most lay in a ruined smear of shadow on the cavern floor, only a leg or two that the stone had missed still showing any last, fitful movement.

"Go!" Vansen shouted. "Back the way we came in, before another one finds us! Go now, and stay together . . . !" The indescribable smell of the thing was so strong as they ran past it that Vansen had to stop shouting and clamp his teeth together to keep from being sick.

If Sledge Jasper had not dragged back a monstrous claw from the thing that had tried to kill him and the other warders and Captain Vansen, and then proudly showed it to nearly every living person in the Metamorphic Brothers' temple, Chert would have had trouble believing that such a horror could exist, even after all the other mad things he had seen in the past year.

The claw itself was almost as long as Jasper was tall. As Chert stared, the chief warder beamed and pointed to his blistered cheek. "See? This is where he spit his poison on me. Would have killed me, too, but Spelter rubbed it off with his own shirt." Sledge nodded proudly. "One of them drows, but he risked his life to save us. That's a pretty tale, isn't it? But true. He's all right, that Spelter."

"Does it hurt?" Chert asked.

"My skin, you mean?" Jasper asked. "Burned like fire at first. Better now, but the healer-brother says I'll always have scars. '*More* scars, you mean,' that's what I told him. More scars, 'cause I'd got plenty already. Have I showed 'em all to you?"

"Later," said Chert quickly. "I'd love to see them, Wardthane, truly I would, but Captain Vansen's waiting for me."

"Ah, yes, certain then you'd want to be going. We're lucky to have the captain, you know. Almost as good as . . . no, I'll say it; he *is* as good as a Funderling. Thought of that dodge with the big stone right on the spot, he did, while that Elders-cursed crab-spider was trying to kill us. We'd all be in its belly, weren't for Captain Vansen."

"Yes, we're lucky to have him," Chert agreed.

He left Jasper looking for anyone else who hadn't seen the massive, odiferous claw and made his way down the hall toward the refectory, which Vansen and Cinnabar and the rest had made the stronghold of the defense effort. Chert was a little worried about what Vansen wanted of him, not because he was afraid of being put back into danger—just being alive beneath Southmarch was danger enough these days—but because he was terrified that Vansen would want to send him somewhere and he would have to tell Opal he was off again. She had not been back long and was already distraught over how strange Flint had become: Chert felt sure having to give her bad news would be a more terrifying adventure than any monstrous spider-crab.

He was surprised to find Vansen sitting in the refectory by himself, poring over a pile of parchments and—even more surprising—piles of the Temple's precious mica sheets. *Brother Nickel must have nearly soiled himself when Vansen asked for those and Cinnabar backed him up,* thought Chert, not without some satisfaction.

Vansen looked tired, his eyes shadowed as if bruised, his shoulders slumped, but he found a smile for Chert. "Ho there, Master Blue Quartz. How is your family?"

Chert was touched to be asked. "Well as can be expected, sir. The boy is very quiet and thoughtful, so that we can hardly get a word from him, but that's better than him traipsing everywhere and getting into trouble."

The big man laughed quietly. "He is not the chiefest delight of the Metamorphic Brothers, is he?"

"That's fair to say." Chert couldn't quite muster up the energy to smile himself. "I do not know what we've let ourselves in for with this child, to tell the truth, he is often so strange. It is like living with a fairy child—a changeling."

Vansen looked at him absently for a moment, then his eyes narrowed. "He is deep in these doings. I suddenly wonder why we have not spoken of him to the Qar—and especially to Lady Yasammez."

Chert suppressed a shiver. "I stood before her once as a prisoner—a condemned prisoner, at that. I'm in no hurry to seek out another audience."

"In any case, there is something important to be understood about your boy, Chert, that I feel certain—but it would take a keener eye than mine to see it clear. Perhaps Chaven can solve the riddle." Vansen sighed. "Ah, well. We have troubles enough without inviting more. I was wondering if you could do me a kindness, friend Chert."

"Of course, Captain. We are all here to help you." But now that the moment had come, Chert Blue Quartz could not help flinching a little in anticipation of some new, mad venture—being ordered to sneak into the castle to steal Hendon Tolly's handkerchief, or sent out to demand the autarch's surrender.

"Since I have been here beneath the castle," Vansen said, "I have had difficulty making sense of things. Not all," he said hurriedly, "but certainly your people's directions. I do not know what is meant by 'frowards' and 'upwise' and whatnot, but . . ." he put out his hand to forestall Chert's explanation, "but more importantly, I simply do not know the ground."

"We have many maps . . ." Chert began.

"Yes, and I have most of them in front of me," said Vansen. "Come, look. Here is one. It shows Funderling Town and what lies below as a single circle. We are looking down, as from the sky is my guess, if there was no castle and no earth in the way to block our gaze. Am I right?"

Chert nodded. "It does not show the Mysteries, or most of the Stormstone Roads, but those are secret . . ."

"Yes, but I wouldn't have known that from looking. I can make no sense of it at all."

Chert smiled. "I can show you easily enough. Here, the different thickness of lines indicates the level, and these marks mean . . ."

"No, I mean I can make no sense of it. I cannot see it with your eyes no matter how I try, no matter how your folk try to instruct me. Brother Antimony spent half of last night grimly explaining over and over again, but it is like trying to describe Orphan's Day to a fish." His smile was sad, now, and the weariness plainer than ever. "You have spent much time on the surface, Chert, I know. You of all people here might be able to make maps that an upgrounder can understand. Will you do that?" He spread his hands over the documents before him. "It need not be perfect. I do not need every single passage—although I would not quibble at it. But the most important thing is that I need to understand how close the different passages are to each other, especially which of them are above which others. Also, which ways are passable by anyone, which only by Funderlings. Then I can ask questions. Then I can make decisions. Will you do it for me?"

It was potentially a huge task, but Chert could understand how important it was. And, he realized, he could accomplish much if not all of it from the safety of the temple, so that Opal would not fret too much, and he would see her and the boy every day.

"How soon?" he asked. He would have to make sure Cinnabar knew about it, in case Brother Nickel made a stink about Chert using the temple library.

"I need it a tennight past." Vansen rose and stretched, his joints popping so that even Chert could hear them. "I will take it as soon as it is ready—sooner. Show me what you have as you work. Now, if you will pardon me, friend Blue Quartz, I think I should find Jasper and Cinnabar and the others before they say something to turn the Qar back into enemies."

". . . So I will be in the library much of the day most days, and perhaps some nights until I finish this for Captain Vansen," he explained to Opal. "But I can do a good deal of the work here at home, too, after I've finished with the Brothers' books, since I doubt that Nickel will let me carry those home under my arms."

"*Home*," Opal sniffed. "I would not call a cramped, crowded room in the drafty, cold temple a home . . . but I suppose it is all we have for now. At least we don't have to share it with your giant friend anymore." The "giant friend" was Chaven, who on Opal's return had moved to other quarters.

Chert was reassured. If Opal was complaining, she was . . . if not happy, then at least in reasonable spirits. "Yes, well, the mark of a noble character is how it stands up to suffering, my only love."

"Then if I become any nobler, I'll have to start screaming." She gave him a sharp look. "Do you have time to talk to the boy before you go hurrying off to play your map games? He said you would understand, and if you do, you may explain it to me because I don't."

"Explain what?"

"Ask him. He's gone down the hall to Chaven's room." She fluffed the straw mattress into a more pleasing consistency, but the look on her face made it clear straw would never compare with their swallow-fluff bed at home. He was surprised she had not carried the mattress down from Funderling Town on her back. "I have things of my own to do, in case you didn't know."

Chert turned back—he knew that tone and knew he should pay attention. "Of course, my love." He waited, hoping she would go on without making him ask. Of course she didn't. "And those things are . . . ?"

"Chert Blue Quartz, you are the flaw in the crystal of my happiness, I swear." She was only half-serious, but the problem was that even half meant he was in trouble. "I told you several times, Vermilion Cinnabar asked me to help making sure all the men get fed. By the Elders, do you really think we can bring hundreds of men down here without providing for them? Do you think the monks have a magic garden that simply grows more food when you ask it?"

"No, of course not. . . ."

"Of course not. So we are putting many of the women to work in the fungus gardens themselves, and replanting some of the old ones that have gone fallow. We are also bringing food down from the town, of course, which means someone has to organize the caravans."

"Caravans?"

"What else would you call a dozen donkey carts a day, twice each way?" Funderling Town's few donkeys, descended from upground ancestors almost twice as large, had never bred well in the depths, and the fact that the Guild had given so many to this cause showed how worried they were—and how much power Vermilion Cinnabar wielded. And now Opal was her second-in-command. Chert was proud of his wife. "Donkeys, and drovers, and we have another twenty men carrying the smaller goods, along with warders to protect them all. It makes quite a parade going down Ore Street."

"The men down here are lucky to have you looking after them."

"Yes." She was slightly mollified. "Yes, I suppose they are."

It didn't matter where he found the boy; the circumstances always seemed to be slightly unexpected. This time Flint was indeed in Chaven's room, as Opal had suggested, but the physician was not present. The flax-haired boy was on his knees atop Chaven's stool, leaning on a table as he squinted at a leather-bound notebook.

"That looks costly," Chert said. "Are you sure Chaven will not mind you handling it?"

Flint did not seem to hear the question. "The talk is all of mirrors," he said as if to himself. "But no earthly glass could be large enough for a true god's gateway . . ."

"Flint?"

The boy turned and saw him, and for a moment seemed nothing more than a child caught doing something he shouldn't, opening his blue eyes innocently wide. He closed the book quickly, but Chert saw that Flint kept his finger between the pages, marking his place until Chert went away again. "Hello, Papa Chert. Mama Opal sent you to speak to me, didn't she?"

"I suppose. She said that I might 'understand.' Understand what, Flint?"

The boy pulled up his legs to sit cross-legged atop the stool like an oracle on a pillar. "I'm not like other children."

Chert could not argue with that. "But you're a good boy," he said. "Your mother and I . . . we . . ." He did not know quite what to say next.

"But the problem," Flint went on, "is that I don't know *why.* I don't understand why I am so full of thoughts and ideas that seem . . . like they don't belong. Why can't I remember more?"

Chert spread his hands helplessly. "Where we found you . . . beside the Shadowline . . . well, we always knew there had to be some kind of magic on you. I knew it from the first. Opal knew it, too, but she would never admit she knew." He let his hands drop. "I'm sorry, lad. I didn't know it was hard on you, too."

"Someday, I think I will have to go away," Flint said. "To find out all the things I want to know. All the things about why I'm . . . this way."

"When you're grown, son, if that's what you want to do. . . ." But even as he said it he knew that Opal would see even this distant consent as a form of betrayal. "Just remember, your mother loves you very much . . . and I love you, too . . ."

The boy shook his head, but not, it seemed, at what Chert had said. "I do not think I can wait so long," he said. "I'm frightened that if I don't understand, I'll . . . I'll *miss* something."

"Miss what? I don't get you, boy."

"That's just it!" His pale face had gone red. "I don't understand it myself. But I can feel that things are bad, so bad! And I think I know the answers, or some of the answers, that I can . . . I don't know, reach in and find them. But when I try, they all just fly away, like bats, like . . ."

To Chert's astonishment, Flint's eyes were shiny with tears. He had never seen the boy like this. He hesitated, then stepped forward and wrapped his arms around him. Flint swayed on the flimsy stool but hung on tightly, his chest moving with sobs like small hiccoughs. At last the boy pulled himself away and slid down to the floor.

"Will you let me go when I need to?" he asked. "When I truly, truly need to?"

"Before you're grown? We can't, son. We can't do that!"

The boy looked up at him, and precisely now, when his flushed face was as childlike as Chert had ever seen it, another look stole across, something strange and sly and somehow alien. "Then I will go anyway without your blessing, Papa Chert."

"No!" He took hold of the boy's shoulders. "You must promise me you'll do nothing of the sort. It will break your mother's heart—that's the truth! You must promise me that, until we say you're old enough, you will stay here with us. Promise!"

Flint tried to squirm out of his grasp, but years of working stone had given Chert strong hands and the boy could not get away. "No!"

"You must promise, boy. You must." Chert was almost weeping himself. "That's all I can say. Promise me you won't go without our . . . without my permission." Opal would never allow it, but if he had to—if he felt it was the only way not to lose the boy in other, deeper ways—he knew he would go against her. And that would be a terrible day. "Promise."

The boy at last stopped struggling. "Only with your permission?"

"Until you reach a man's age."

"But how old am I?"

Chert was so upset that it surprised him how suddenly the laugh came. "Well struck, lad. So, let us say . . . five more years, shall we? By any standard, that should give you time to do some growing."

"Five years?" He looked dully resigned. "In five years the world might be ended, Father."

"Then what you and I do won't be such a worry, will it?" He had won, but Chert did not feel particularly good about it. "Come," he said. "You like the temple library, don't you? I have business there. Come and spend the afternoon with me."

Silent and thoughtful again, his tears all but dried, Flint followed Chert back through the busy temple halls, past priests and soldiers and more than a few women, all silent, all apparently in a hurry. Each and every one of them wore a face as grim as Black Noszh-la, Gatekeeper of the House of Death.

10
Fools Lose the Game

"For a year the poor child labored in the temple, but then the corrupt mantis of that place sold the Orphan and several other slaves to a ship's captain in need of crew . . ."

—from "A Child's Book of the Orphan, and His Life and Death and Reward in Heaven"

THE ROOM WAS WARM AND DARK and smelled of the heart-shaped roots that one of Tolly's other minions had set in the fireplace to smolder the night before, a smell that made Matt Tinwright's head ache even as he peered around the chamber through slitted eyes. He still had no idea whether the roots had been meant for some magic ritual or simply so the smoke could provide a kind of dreamy drunkenness, which it had definitely done. Hendon Tolly's pursuits, though often disquieting, were still largely mysterious, despite nearly a tennight of Tinwright being kept at the man's side like a dog on a leash.

He groaned and opened his eyes wider. The groan became a gasp of surprise as he saw that Tolly was sitting on the edge of the bed next to him, staring down like a vulture watching a living thing turn into carrion.

"Wh—wha—what is it, my lord?" Tinwright stammered. "Do you need something?"

They were alone in the chamber: the women had gone. Tinwright hoped they were all still well. He had seen a few frightening moments before he had finally collapsed into welcome oblivion.

"Brother Okros never decided precisely what he wanted," the lord protector said, as if in continuation of an early conversation. Perhaps it was: Tinwright could remember little of what had happened. He struggled into an upright position.

"I beg your pardon, Lord Tolly?"

"What he wanted. I'm talking of that pinchsniff Okros. Some days he played the man of learning, concerned only to uncover the great secrets of existence." Tolly smirked. The lord protector looked remarkably well-groomed for a man who lived the way he did: Tinwright could not help wondering if the nobleman had snuck off to bathe while Tinwright himself was still sleeping. "It was quite amusing, really. On those occasions, he would treat me as a fine cook might treat his grossly fat master—as an embarrassment, but a necessary one, because I was the sponsor of his art." Tolly rose and gestured impatiently. "Get up, poet. This will be a momentous day or I miss my guess."

"My lord . . . ?"

"But Okros lost the path, you see. He came to believe that what we sought were the answers to *his* questions." Tolly looked at Matt Tinwright with the bright eyes of a hunting hawk.

The lord protector was stranger than usual, Tinwright thought—as though he were drunk, but in some hard, crystalline way. "But he was wrong, Lord . . . ?"

"What I want had nothing to do with him. He was a fool . . . and fools lose the game." Tolly smiled a hard smile. The warning was very clear. "Now come, poet."

Tinwright followed Hendon Tolly across the crowded residence to the Prince Kayne Library, which had become the lord protector's throne room and council chamber during the days of the Qar siege. The old library had always been a quiet, neat room despite its large size, with books crowding all the shelves between the floors and the high ceilings, but now it looked as though it had been in the front lines of the siege. Books lay scattered everywhere, both modern bound volumes and parchment scrolls from Hierosol and even ancient Xis, as well as a dozen chairs and stools and even a few tables dragged in haphazardly from other parts of the residence. The disorder was in large part because Tolly and Brother Okros had emptied the Tower of Summer, King Olin's refuge, and brought almost everything out of his locked room to this library—some of the books, Tinwright had noticed, even seemed to have been written by Olin himself, and he thought about how glorious it would be to be left alone long enough to read some of them. What a boon for a poet—to read the true thoughts of a mindful king! But Hendon Tolly was clearly not going to let him stray from his side long enough to do such a thing.

Tinwright had not spoken to Elan or his mother in days, and had been hard-pressed even to send them a pair of short, secret letters telling them what had happened. He only prayed that his mother would not show up at the palace demanding that her newly elevated son—she must think he was Tolly's secretary!—find a place for her in the residence.

Nightmare. And not just the idea of having her underfoot—what if she mentioned Elan?

Tinwright forced these thoughts from his head as a group of soldiers led by the lord constable, Berkan Hood, came to the library seeking an audience with Hendon Tolly. They were understandably distressed about the idea of the autarch's ships landing unhindered in the harbor just opposite the castle.

"Two dozen warships, Lord Protector, and there are still more coming!" Berkan Hood was doing his best to keep his voice even but not entirely succeeding; he was clearly not the kind of man who usually practiced such restraint. "Yet we have not fired so much as a single bombard. Please, my lord, why do we not fight back? We struggled against the fairies for months, threw them back a dozen times. Now that those demons have retreated, why have we gone shy as maidens in front of the Xixies, who are only mortal?"

Hendon Tolly glared. He was barely interested in the trappings of ordinary rule—Tinwright had seen it even in their short time together. "There are plans afoot to protect this castle and this city, Hood," he growled, "and I will tell you what you need to know when you need to know it." With these curt words he dismissed them, although Berkan Hood and the others seemed far from satisfied.

As they went out, the castellan, Tirnan Havemore, who had once been Avin Brone's factor, slipped into the library. "It is here, my lord," he said, handing Tolly a parchment chopped with a seal Tinwright had never seen. As his master read the letter, Havemore looked Tinwright up and down with unhidden dislike. None of the inner circle could understand why Tolly kept Matt Tinwright around, but that was unsurprising since Tinwright wasn't certain himself.

"I was wondering when we would hear from them," the lord protector said when he had finished. He called for paper and ink to write a reply. "You're the poet," he told Tinwright. "Take my answer down and write it in a fair hand."

He proceeded to dictate a message so full of strange, almost meaningless phrases that Tinwright could only gape and do the best he could to get the wording correct. Still, a few things were clear. The astonishing missive was a letter to the Autarch of Xis, and promised that Tolly would meet with the southern king just after dark that very evening, then named the place.

"M'Helan's Rock?" Tinwright asked, surprised. "The island out in the bay?"

"Yes, you insufferable idiot," Tolly said. "Do you question my choice?"

"No, my lord! I just wanted to make sure I had the name straight."

As if he were a child copying out texts in his best hand to avoid a thrashing, Matt Tinwright did his best to keep the writing clean and graceful. *As if the Monster of Xis is going to notice my penmanship!* he mocked himself. *"Oh, no, we won't kill that one when we conquer Southmarch—he writes too fair a hand!" Tolly's right—I'm a fool.* Still, it was an interesting situation, in a dreadful sort of way: who would have guessed a year and something past that Matt Tinwright would be here today, writing messages for the lord of all Southmarch to an actual god-king . . . whatever a god-king might be. . . .

"Good." Tolly finished reading, then added his own jagged signature and sealed the letter closed with wax and his signet ring. "Send it back immediately," he instructed Tirnan Havemore. "And if any man tries to open that, I will make sure he chokes on his own severed fingers."

The castellan hurried off with the letter held out as though it were a deadly serpent.

"So now the endgame begins," said Tolly as he turned to Matt Tinwright. "Our lives and our destinies are in our own hands, poet. Who could ask for better than that? If we succeed, we win all. If we lose—well, history will not remember our names and future generations will not find our graves." He grinned, his expression still as shiny and brittle as cracked glass. "Splendid, eh?"

Tinwright only bowed and said, "My lord." Tolly's ranting did not seem to require an answer and he was too terrified to try to invent one.

Not all the Qar who had met in the small cavern near Sandsilver's Dancing Room had their minds on the new enemy, the thousands of Xixian soldiers and their master, the autarch. Hammerfoot, lord of the Ettins, who like all his kind was slow to build to wrath but even slower to cool, sat in the darkness fuming like one of the forges of Firstdeeps.

"They humiliate us," he rumbled. "These sunlanders. A thousand years of wretched treatment, hundreds of years of exile, and we are expected to forgive them . . . just *so*." He flicked his massive, blunt fingers in a gesture of disgusted finality. "As I sat looking at their unformed faces, soft as pink mud, it was all I could do not to crush them. I *should* have crushed them . . ."

"Then you would be a fool," Yasammez told him. "We need them all."

"Need them?" Hammerfoot looked up; in the small place, he seemed to grow even larger. "We could have ground them all beneath our hooves if you had not held us back, Lady."

Yasammez stood, and her dozen lieutenants fell silent. "Do you see this?" she said, touching the Seal of War. "It means you have sworn yourself to me. Do you see this sword?" She slapped Whitefire's sheath. "In the very place my kin were murdered I forswore my oath and sheathed it. And you tell me now that you would become *twice* an oathbreaker? Where is the honor of the Deep Born, Hammerfoot? Where is the brave heart that has shared so many troubles with me—and whose father and grandfather fought beside me as well?" She shook her head and the thoughts that carried her words were as chill as a blast of wintry wind. "I am disappointed."

For a moment it seemed the anger might make the great Ettin do something beyond madness, for the oaths of the Deep Born were among the most powerful things that any of those gathered there knew. Even Lord Hammerfoot, though, could not stand long in Lady Porcupine's cold regard.

"I . . . I spoke rashly," he said. "But I do not understand what we are doing, my mistress. We came here to fight the creatures who have done evil to us . . . not to help them."

"We cannot beat this southern king by ourselves," said Yasammez. "I told you, this autarch has twenty soldiers for every one of ours, and other weapons beside—those are odds that even the People cannot overcome . . . unless all we seek here is a noble death." She spread her hands in the gesture *Complications Unsought* as she seated herself again. "But though we need the sunlanders as allies, that does not mean they are friends. Ultimately, we must keep the doorway to the gods from falling under the power of any mortals, even our momentary allies, so if we defeat the southerner but still cannot regain control here . . ." She shrugged. "Then it will be time for the other measures."

Aesi'uah, her chief eremite, seemed unsettled by this idea. "Other measures? Do you mean the Fever Egg . . . ?"

"Yes," said the dark lady, silencing her. "Stone of the Unwilling, which of your people has been tasked with protecting the Egg?"

He flickered as if surprised. "Shadow's Cauldron, great lady."

"Call her."

"Of course. She will step to us now."

A moment later another of the Guard of Elementals joined their presence, smelling freshly of the Void. "I have come . . ." she began.

"Produce it," commanded Yasammez.

Shadow's Cauldron did not need to ask what she was expected to produce; only half an instant passed before it was in her hand, a translucent stone the size of a human child's head. In its depths some brown murkiness so dark it was almost black swirled like a tiny thundercloud. Inside that cloud something shone a sickly yellow, like lightning struggling to be born.

"The Egg is strong." Shadow's Cauldron was young and less used to forming words than Stone of the Unwilling; her speech buzzed like wasps in the thoughts of those listening. "It will not break unless thrown from a great height, or struck by something heavy and strong. But when it is broken, the fever seed will be released and it will spread like smoke. Everything in its path will die."

"Even a god?" Yasammez looked at the thing with interest and a little distaste.

Again the buzzing words; those who had skin felt it crawl in response. "Any earthly form that a god wears will die—nothing that draws breath or sinks roots can live when this fever burns it."

"But what will stop it?" demanded Greenjay's son, Flightless. "Shall we kill everything that runs beneath the sun or moon? That will be a miserable epitaph for the People."

"It stops of its own accord, like the ripples in a large pond," Shadow's Cauldron told him with something like anger in her voice. "As the Lady Yasammez wishes, it will not spread far beyond the borders of this mortal land before its potency dies." Her flicker grew stronger. "Although many believe that *none* of the sunlanders deserve to survive . . ."

"Thank you, daughter," said Stone of the Unwilling. "Have you heard what you wished to hear, Lady Yasammez?"

"She may go."

A moment later, Shadow's Cauldron and the Egg were no longer in the cavern. It was the eremite Aesi'uah who broke the silence. "Has it really come to this, Mistress? To such despair? Not only to take our own lives, and thousands upon thousands of mortal lives as well, but even the lives of beast and herb, then to make this place a wasteland of death for years to come?"

"Small enough price for them to pay for their treachery, certainly!" said one of the Changing tribe. "We are *owed* this vengeance, Dreamless! As Shadow's Cauldron said, it is a shame we cannot kill more."

Yasammez silenced him with a harsh gesture. "We do nothing simply for vengeance, much as it might be deserved. But know that I will do whatever I must to make certain that the gods and their gateway do not fall under the control of any mortal."

"Are you not putting your own wisdom above that of the god himself?" Aesi'uah protested. "Why should Crooked himself not decide what is right to do?"

"Because the god is dying," Yasammez said coldly. She did not like being questioned by her own eremite, however long and honorably the half-Dreamless had served her. "He is scarcely still there—certainly his thoughts have been strange for some time. It could be he is trapped in nightmare and will no longer even be able to understand us. No, we must not rely on even the god . . . on my father . . . to make our decisions. The People must choose their own way forward."

"But . . ." Aesi'uah was searching for words, her own thoughts clearly complicated. "But I fear for them, my lady."

"For whom?"

"Our allies, the mortals—the sunlanders. I find it harder to hate them now. They are . . . different than I expected."

"Think you so?" asked Yasammez with no small amount of scorn. "They are exactly as I expected. Exactly."

The boat with Hendon Tolly, Matt Tinwright, and two of the lord protector's guards landed at M'Helan's Rock first. While Hendon Tolly and Tinwright climbed carefully up the ancient dock stairs, the boat with the other four guards tied up and began to unload. Tinwright paused on the steps to look out across the rocky island and the lights of the castle just across the water, overwhelmed with fear and wonder.

It was plain to see why Tolly had chosen the spot: it was accessible from the mainland but far enough from both the shore and the castle that even in daylight an observer would have had trouble seeing who landed there. And the rock itself was so craggy and studded with caves and inlets that Tinwright thought three or four different ships might land on the island and never see each other.

The lodge at the top of the hill smelled musty when they opened the great doors, and little surprise: Hendon Tolly said no one had used it since he had taken power. Tolly complained about the lack of amenities and having to wait in the cold and damp while one of his guards lit a fire in the great room—even now, in late spring, the island was a windy, wet place. All the guards were well armed, some carrying swords and spears, others with loaded crossbows.

"He will be here soon." Tolly settled into a high-backed chair. "Oh, yes—he will have been watching us land, to make certain we brought only six guards and no more, as we agreed."

Something made a skittering noise in the ceiling and Tinwright looked up.

"Rats," said Hendon Tolly. "The place has been empty so long that it must be full of them. Do you fear rats, poet?"

"Fear them?" He didn't like them much, but he also wasn't certain what Tolly wanted him to say. "Not too much . . ."

"They are the cleverest of cattle, as the country folk say." Hendon Tolly grinned. "I knew a man once, a keeper in our hunting lodge in the Summerfield hills, who raised one almost like his own child. It would sit upon his shoulder, and when he commanded it to, it would sing."

"Sing?" The noise of someone shouting down on the dock wafted through the unshuttered windows.

"Well, as much as a rat can," Tolly conceded. "It would squeak along when he sang. And it could fetch him his purse if he dropped it, or find coins in the straw under a table. Then somebody tired of the trick and stepped on the creature." He tilted his head. "Ah, do you hear? He is coming." The lord protector stood, which was a surprise in itself, but as Tinwright watched him shifting from foot to foot, he realized something even stranger: Hendon Tolly was worried, perhaps even frightened.

One of the Summerfield guards opened the door and let in two dark, hard-faced men carrying long, ornamented rifles and wearing helmets in the shape of some grinning, spotted cat, a lion or a pard. After a moment's wary inspection of the room, they stepped to either side of the door and stood at rigid attention. Before Tinwright had time to do more than gawk at these newcomers with their hard, brown faces, a third figure followed them through, a portly, older man with a long and carefully tended beard and an air of almost ludicrous gravity.

This must be the Xixian envoy . . . Tinwright thought.

"Out of the way, priest," said another voice. The heavyset man scuttled to the side so that a new figure could duck underneath the lintel and enter the hall.

He was very tall, that was the first thing Matt Tinwright saw—more than a head taller than Hendon Tolly, taller also than the bearded man or any of the guards, who were not small men. The newcomer was dressed strangely, in a long white linen robe and a hat unlike anything Tinwright had ever seen, a tall cylinder encrusted with gems and wound with gold wire, which with his height made the newcomer literally tower above everybody in the room. Only as he stared up at this apparition did Matt Tinwright finally understand it was not just an odd and expensive hat the tall man wore: it was a crown. The autarch himself had come.

In that precise, terrified second of recognition the two Xixian guards crashed their rifle butts on the ground so hard that Matt Tinwright jumped and Tolly's guards grabbed at their own weapons.

"The Golden One, Master of the Great Tent and the Falcon Throne," one of the Xixian guards announced in a loud voice, "Lord of All Places and Happenings, a thousand, thousand praises to His name—bow before the glory of Sulepis Bishakh am-Xis III, monarch of all Xand and Elect of Nushash!"

Once their master had been announced, the leopard-clad guards ushered him to one of the room's two principal chairs. Hendon Tolly took the opposing seat, his face a careful mask. The autarch gestured for his fat, bearded priest to stand behind him. Tolly did not stoop to introducing Matt Tinwright which did not bother the poet at all: even a momentary glance from the autarch's odd, golden eyes was enough to make him want to start explaining things, or apologizing, or even throwing himself on his belly and begging not to be killed. Yes, he was a coward—Tinwright was the first to admit it—but what compelled him now was something more primitive, more basic. The master of the southern continent seemed to the poet a completely different kind of creature, a predator to Matt Tinwright's hapless prey, and if flight was impossible, the only defense against that kind of murderous threat was to remain unimportant.

At first the autarch and the lord protector exchanged only small talk. The autarch spoke their tongue well, and it was clear this was not the first time he and Tolly had communicated. What was going on? How could the master of Southmarch sit down for a friendly conversation with the Monster of Xis?

The autarch was certainly a monster, but Tinwright had to admit he was a fascinating monster, and much younger than Matt Tinwright could ever have guessed: from the stories about the catalog of horrors his armies had visited upon his own continent and in the last year on Eion itself, Tinwright would have expected some wiry, scarred old desert hawk instead of this doe-eyed creature who despite his great height looked to be scarcely grown. The autarch's character was not what the poet would have expected, either. He seemed quite cheerful, although at times that cheeriness seemed as weirdly stilted as Hendon Tolly's. Some of the things he said made no sense at all, as though the southerner spoke words straight out of his deepest thoughts, thoughts that ordinary men would never speak aloud.

". . . But, of course," the autarch said at one point, smiling at Hendon Tolly all the while, "others who thought themselves wise died in shrieking ignorance. Just as you will."

Tolly stared in surprise, but the autarch went back to speaking of the war in Hierosol (which he considered to be all but over with himself the victor) and other strangely mundane topics as if he had never said it.

Hendon Tolly spoke with the cautious manner of someone walking down a path he suspected to be strung with snares. He kept looking to

Tinwright each time he made some point as though expecting Tinwright to agree, perhaps even out loud, but it was painfully clear to Tinwright that either of these two men would have his throat slit as blithely as if swatting a fly.

"But now," the autarch said abruptly, clapping his hands together with a sound as loud and as sudden as the guards' gun butts hitting the floor earlier, "let us speak of . . . more important things. You have something I need, Lord Protector."

"We could equally say you have something *I* need, Your Highness."

"Autarch must always be addressed as 'Golden One,' " growled the Xixian priest.

Sulepis waved a long-fingered hand at the priest. "We will not stand on ceremony, good Panhyssir." The autarch took a moment to admire his long brown fingers, each finger capped with odd little baskets of gold. "We both have needs, Lord Tolly. How will we resolve them?"

"Let's not get ahead of ourselves." Hendon Tolly's voice had suddenly gone sharp. "You made several promises to me . . . Golden One . . . and I fulfilled my part of the bargain . . ."

"Yes, but clumsily," countered the autarch with a hard smile. "You have the throne, but it is not secure. There are elements inside your own walls that will resist you, and thus will resist me, too. And you have stalled and bungled the simple protection of your island keep so that the Qar are now a factor as well."

"The fairies?" Tolly shook his head. "No factor at all. They have fled, balked by my defense at first, then frightened away for good by the arrival of your ships."

"What?" The autarch stared at him, then suddenly threw back his head and laughed, a shrill, childlike bray. "Do you really not know?" He turned to the priest. "Panhyssir, tell him where the Qar may be found."

The glowering priest said, "They are in tunnels beneath your own castle, Lord Toh-lee. They fled there when we landed."

Matt Tinwright could tell that Tolly was truly startled. "Impossible!"

"All too possible," the autarch laughed. "And you still think you bargain with me from a position of strength? Your family has not held power long, have they? Mine came out of the deserts to throw down the thrones of men ten centuries ago, and we had already been rulers there." He sat up. "Ah. I am reminded. I brought you a gift."

Tolly was again taken by surprise. "Gift . . . ?"

The autarch clapped his hands. One of the guards went out and came back with a wooden chest not much bigger than a lady's jewel box, which he set down in front of Hendon Tolly.

"Open it," the autarch told him.

Tolly looked mistrustful. He leaned over and gingerly lifted the lid, then let it drop again and sat up, carefully expressionless. Tinwright had only had time to see something with matted hair and blood.

"Your brother Caradon," said the autarch. "His head, anyway. I sent some of my men to find him while he was out riding." The god-king grinned mockingly. "A most dangerous pursuit for members of your family, I would say—didn't your other brother Gailon die that way, too? Ambushed on the road?"

"What . . . ?" Hendon Tolly blinked. Tinwright had never seen that particular expression on his face before. "But why . . . ?"

"Because Caradon promised me something and never delivered. Your brother had an enemy of mine—well, of my father's to be precise, but the enemy of one Xixian Autarch is the enemy of all autarchs—had him within easy reach, but failed to secure him for me. Instead, your brother clumsily let him escape in some miserable little town named Landers Port, and he has not been seen since. Perhaps you have heard of the fellow—Shaso dan-Heza?"

Tolly looked as though he were going to choke on his own saliva. "But . . . Shaso escaped from me as well."

The autarch nodded. "Yes. Unfortunate." He brightened. "But at least now everyone is happy—I am, because your brother has been punished for failing me, and you are because you need no longer look over your shoulder to Summerfield Court. Felicitations! You are now the head of your family, Lord Tolly! I imagine that makes you the . . . what is the title that your brother held? Duke?"

Tinwright could not help looking at the closed box beside Hendon Tolly's feet. Hendon Tolly could not stop looking at it, either.

"But, we have distracted ourselves with these family matters when there are important issues to be discussed," the autarch continued. "You have something I want, Tolly. I feel certain you were not foolish enough to bring it with you . . . were you?"

Tolly shook his head but did not seem to trust his tongue.

"As I suspected. Panhyssir, how long do we have to resolve this negotiation?"

The priest stirred. "Midsummer is but a few days away, Golden One."

The autarch nodded. "And I must have everything in place by midnight of Midsummer's Day or the god will not come to me. Tolly, you will send the stone to me by tomorrow."

"The . . . stone . . ." Tolly said slowly.

"Exactly—the Godstone. And I promise I want nothing else but that from you, and that in return you will be allowed to do what you please—remain if you wish and continue to rule your little kingdom or go elsewhere, unmolested. When I have summoned the god, it will no longer be of any interest to me what you or anyone else chooses to do." Sulepis grinned again, the contented grin of a jackal gnawing a shinbone and thinking fondly on mortality. "Do you understand, Lord Tolly? Tomorrow. If not, I will have to come and take it from you, and your suffering will be unimaginable. Understand?"

Tinwright couldn't understand why Hendon Tolly didn't say anything—couldn't he see this man was serious, that the autarch would destroy them all without a thought if it suited him? But the lord protector of Southmarch had the look of a man suddenly feeling very ill indeed.

"But I . . . I didn't . . ." Tolly shut his mouth with a snap, but it was too late. The autarch was staring at him.

"You have it, do you not?" the autarch demanded. "You told me you had it."

"Of course . . . !" Tolly had realized his mistake. "Of course, but I thought . . ."

"Describe it to me." The Autarch of Xis leaned forward, his yellow cat's eyes fixed on Tolly. "Tell me what the stone looks like, northern dog!"

"Like . . ." Tolly could not manage even to come up with a lie. He pushed his chair back. His crossbowmen pointed their weapons at the Xixians. The Xixian guards lowered their rifles. Tinwright thought carefully about throwing himself to the floor, but was afraid he might startle the guards and then everyone would die, Matt Tinwright definitely included. For a long moment Tolly and the autarch and their respective guards stared at each other across a gulf no more than three paces wide.

The Xixian broke the silence, his face now as hard as copper and shiny with the blood of his anger. "You swore that you had the Godstone. You lied to me—to *me*! I lowered myself to come here and speak to you . . . !" His yellow eyes seemed to glint and spark, as if Sulepis was burning inside, as if at any moment he might burst into flame. Tinwright could barely look at him. "Only good fortune allows you to live another day in freedom instead of as fodder for my torturers—*but that will change!*" He rose. Tolly's guards stared at him, determination and sheer terror battling on their faces, but the autarch only waited for his own guards to open the doors, then followed them out, so confident of his safety that he didn't even look back.

When the southerners were gone, the lord protector of Southmarch fell back in his chair.

"We are all dead men," said Hendon Tolly.

As they were trudging down the stone steps to the dock, Matt Tinwright looked back and saw a movement in the nearest window of the lodge. He decided it must be a trick of the light. Hendon Tolly and the guards were in front of him, making their way to the boats with the slow, dispirited air of a funeral party, and the autarch and his men had already left M'Helan's Rock—Tinwright could see their boat in the distance, heading toward the waiting Xixian fleet. Who else could still be in the lodge?

Tinwright did not work up the courage to speak until they were halfway back around Midlan's Mount with the castle's sea gate in sight. "Lord Tolly, I did not understand. What happened there? I don't understand any of what we have just seen and heard."

"We have had . . . a setback," Tolly admitted at last. He looked down at the box the autarch had given him, which sat on the deck of the small boat, then abruptly bent and picked it up and flung it out over the dark green water of the bay. It landed with a small splash. "But we will find our way again," he said, his voice rising in triumph as if he had not just tossed his own brother's severed head overboard. "Because Sulepis does not possess this Godstone either!"

Tinwright could only stare at Hendon Tolly in uncomprehending horror. Suddenly his rhymes about nobles and gods seemed naïve beyond belief. If this was how the rich and privileged behaved, how much worse must the gods themselves be? If he were ever fortunate enough to be able to write verses again, Matt Tinwright decided, he would tell the truth. He would write poems that would describe both the beauty and the true horror of existence. He would write the truth and shock the world!

"But what could it be?" Hendon Tolly was still talking to himself; in an instant, he had gone from glee to fury. "Godstone? What is this cursed Godstone? Okros never mentioned it, may the demons of Kernios gnaw his scrawny hide." He shook his head, face even paler than usual in his fury. "I could have been killed here!" He turned suddenly to Tinwright. "When the pagan bastard sent his messengers to me and asked me if I had the 'last piece,' I thought he meant Chaven's mirror. I bargained, but all the time I was mistaken—I was wagering with nothing in my purse! I could have been killed!" Tolly shouted this as though the universe could offer no greater tragedy—which, Tinwright reflected, Tolly undoubtedly believed. Men like him could not conceive of a world without themselves at the center of it. Matt Tinwright had been reminded since childhood that he would scarcely be missed.

Away in the distance behind them, halfway between their boat and M'Helan's Rock, the wooden chest was still bobbing on the surface. Tolly finally noticed it.

"So the Tolly family fortunes come down to this, brother," he called to the box. "Gailon rots in the earth, you will feed the fishes, and I will stake everything on a final roll of the dice." His eyes were again fever-bright. "The autarch is overconfident. He does not realize the virgin goddess waits for me—that she wants me to be the one who frees her! All else is trickery. Who knows if the southerner even believes his own lies? But I know what I know." The worry had left his face. Tolly looked toward the walls of Southmarch, which rose above them now as the little boat neared the sea gate. "Destiny has not carried me so high only to let me fall."

Tinwright thought that might be the most frightening thing he had yet heard.

11
Two Prisoners

"Although the boy was too small to be chained to the rowers' benches, he was worked in hard service for the ship's cruel master."

—from "A Child's Book of the Orphan, and His Life and Death and Reward in Heaven"

"I'M SORRY," Briony told him. "I don't understand. What do you mean, we were wrong?"

"It is . . . it is just . . ." Prince Eneas' face bore a strange expression, one she had never seen before. He had been so busy after the battle she had not seen him for half the day—he was still wearing all his armor except for his helm. "It would be easier for you simply to come with me," he said at last.

He led her to a stockade built in the middle of the Temple Dogs' camp, with a roof of stitched skins stretched across one end for shade and to keep out the occasional rains that swept down out of the surrounding hills. To her surprise, all the prisoners in the enclosure were ordinary humans, some of them the very mercenary soldiers that the Temple Dogs had rescued only that morning.

"Where are the fairies?" she asked Eneas. "Did none of them live?"

"Wait." His face was still unusually grim. At an order from the prince one of the prisoners was led out of the newly built stockade. He was a big man, tall but stocky, with the full, untrimmed beard she associated with the Kracian plains. From his battered armor, he seemed to be one of the mercenaries that had guarded the merchant caravan.

"Tell us everything you said before so this lady can hear it," Eneas ordered him.

"Again?" The man did not seem very frightened to be a prisoner.

"Yes, again, dog." Eneas was upset, that was clear—but why?

The man grinned without mirth. "As you wish." He looked Briony up and down with less than perfect respect, but did not let his gaze linger long. "I am Volofon of Ikarta. I am an officer of these men. Our leader was Benaridas, but he is dead." He looked at Eneas as though it were his fault somehow. "The fairies murdered him."

"Why are these men prisoners?" Briony asked.

"Wait." Eneas turned to the big mercenary. "Tell us again how you come to be in this land."

The man shrugged. "We were hired. Some of us do not have rich fathers and uncles. We must make our own way in this world."

"You address the prince of Syan!" snarled Lord Helkis. "Show respect, man, if you value your head."

Volofon looked intrigued for the first time. "A prince? So Syan, too, is sniffing for what scraps may be collected here in the north?"

Helkis snatched at the hilt of his sword but Eneas reached out and touched his arm. "Enough, Miron." The prince turned his attention back to Volofon. "You are making no friends. A man in a cage should perhaps think more carefully before speaking. Who hired you?"

"A group of Hierosoline merchants. Many of them are dead now, but more than a few are stuck in here with us honorable soldiers." The mercenary pointed to a crouching figure on the far side of the stockade, a middle-aged man who had been watching everything carefully while pretending not to do so. "There's one—Dard the Jar. He was the supply chief for all the caravan. Ask him your questions."

"Your story is not finished," said Eneas. "What did the merchants tell you when they hired you and your men?"

"That they had a commission to take a caravan into the far north—to the March Kingdoms—and that they needed protection on the journey. They had to pay through the nose for it, too." Volofon laughed; half his teeth were gone and the rest were mostly black. "We knew what was going on up here. Fairies and monsters! That's double-pay work!"

"Were you promised anything else?"

"Whatever we could pry loose along the way. 'A good chance to make your fortunes in a lawless land,' the Hierosolines put it."

"In other words," Eneas said, "they said you could steal whatever you wanted."

"That's another way to put it, yes." Volofon grinned his unsavory grin once more.

"That is enough," said Eneas. "I can't stand to listen to you any longer. Go back to your cage. I will decide what to do with you later."

The mercenary looked him over for a moment as if considering some kind of challenge to his authority, but only shrugged and sauntered back into the stockade. He called something to the other soldiers who laughed and shouted back at him. Briony hated them all, though she could not have said why. They had the uncaring certainty of boys, but without kindness, and with the brawny bodies of men. They were used to getting what they wanted at the point of a sword, and the fact that what they wanted belonged to other people meant nothing. *Thieves and rapists,* she thought. *And murderers. Hiding behind the name of soldiers.*

"I still do not understand, Eneas," she said aloud. "What . . . ?"

"You must hear the rest," he said. "You!" he shouted at the man skulking near the far fence. "Dard, if that is your name. Come here!"

The smaller man came up at once, and the difference between him and Volofon could not have been more marked. Dard held out his hands and walked in a supplicating near-crouch, as if trying to make himself as small and harmless-seeming as possible.

"You are Prince Eneas!" he said, smiling and bobbing his head like a witling. "Such an honor! Your fame goes before you!" The merchant turned to Briony. "And this fine young lord is . . . ?"

"Shut your mouth." Eneas stared at him as though he had crawled out from beneath a muddy rock. "Bring him out here to me." When the merchant had been dragged outside the fence, the prince said, "Just answer this question, Dard. You hired the mercenaries. Who hired *you*?"

The man stared at Eneas for a moment, mouth working. "Why . . . why someone who believed a profit was to be made in the north, even in such difficult times, Your Highness. So many caravans have stopped traveling here, and many of the merchant ships were troubled by the Qar—just as we were, it should be said. The same Qar who would have murdered us if you had not come to our rescue . . . !"

"For the last time, merchant, answer only what you are asked." Eneas shook his head. "I am not a child to be swayed by flattery. Even if you wished to use a land route to bring your goods, why could you not simply have come up through Summerfield or Silverside to Marrinswalk? This is a long, strange way to travel—and through very dangerous country, too. Why hire mercenaries to protect you in such a wicked, lonely place when there are so many more . . . civilized places that would have welcomed your goods?" He held up a hand to silence the merchant, who was already beginning to stammer out justifications. "Because you have a special buyer, do you not? And he is waiting for you at Southmarch."

"At Southmarch? Who is this buyer?" Briony asked. "Is it Hendon Tolly?"

"A look at the caravan's cargo manifest will tell you," the prince said. "Miron?"

The officer lifted a heavy book and began reading: "Sugared wine, hard bread, barrels of iron rings . . ."

"Those are military supplies," Briony said.

"Oh, but we can be more precise than that." Eneas' face looked like a sky preparing to explode into thunder and wind and rain. "See. Several thousandweight of grain for bread, hides, pig iron—all reasonable supplies for an army at war which is not certain it can find all it needs by foraging. But here are five hundred barrels of Marashi peppers. Have you ever tasted the things? Foul and hot, fit only for animals—or southerners. In fact, Xixian troops practically live on them, along with dried chickpeas—but look! Here are a thousand sacks of those as well! What a coincidence we find here. This caravan, which you can see by the manifest left Hierosol three months ago or more . . . is carrying supplies that seem to be for a *Xixian* army." He turned on the cowering Dard. "But the Autarch of Xis is besieging Hierosol, isn't he? Why should he be sending supplies here, far to the north? Unless he was expecting to *come* here . . . ?"

"Please, Highness, we did not realize . . . !" shouted the merchant. "We were only fulfilling an order!"

"You lie." Eneas kicked at him, and the man skittered back against the gate of the stockade. "Take him away. I shall decide what to do with the whole noisome crowd later."

Lord Helkis and the other soldiers shoved the protesting Dard back into the pen.

"But the Qar . . . ?" Briony said.

"I am not certain, but if they were fighting to keep these supplies from the autarch they are no worse than accidental allies. Who knows? But I am angry, Princess Briony, very angry. Because I broke the first rule of the battlefield—to know who you fight and why—we have aided an enemy."

"Not entirely," Briony said. "Because whatever else happened, we now have the supplies and the autarch doesn't."

The lines on the prince's brow smoothed a little; after a moment he even smiled. "That is true, Princess. And if the autarch is now besieging your family's castle, perhaps soon we can do that southern whoreson even greater harm . . . begging my lady's pardon."

It was strange traveling through the March Kingdoms again. The thriving market towns mostly stood deserted, and what had once been fertile fields now were overgrown with unfamiliar vines that bore nodding black flowers and leaves as purple as a bruise. They also saw far fewer people than Briony would have expected, but she decided that was because she was traveling with a large troop of soldiers. Syan and Southmarch might have had years and years of peace between them, but after the Qar invasion and the inevitable banditry, the people who still hung on to their homes and livelihoods would not be showing themselves to armed bands, no matter whose insignia they wore.

Even the animals seemed different, she noticed. Most of the domestic livestock were long gone or carefully hidden, but even the deer and squirrels and birds seemed to have lost their fear of humanity. Strangely, though, this did not make them any easier to hunt, so the Syannese troops still had to dine most nights on the food they carried. They had brought their own cattle and sheep, but Eneas insisted these were to be slaughtered only sparingly, since he had no idea what they would find in the way of forage around Southmarch, so mostly the men ate soup and hardbread and whatever few vegetables could be found in the deserted fields. Some of his knights had brought their own, more toothsome fare, but Eneas was a great believer in an army that shared both hardships and windfalls; seeing the expensive pheasants these knights had brought packed in barrels of oil taken out and handed out among the foot soldiers was enough to convince most nobles it wasn't worth the trouble trying to smuggle in better food for themselves. Briony couldn't help noticing that for every one of Eneas' fellow nobles who was cross and out of sorts at the loss of his favorite tidbits, a dozen ordinary soldiers thought the prince little short of a god.

But even the knights who would have preferred to hang onto their delicacies almost revered the prince, Briony was learning. At first she suspected he had arranged the parade of thanks and pledges of loyalty that came to him every time he went among the tents, but she quickly realized it was all genuine. Eneas was simply one of those leaders who shared all hardships and rewards with his troops, and who never forgot that despite the differences in birth—of which Eneas was certainly aware, and about which he could be quite old-fashioned—he acted as though the life of each man-at-arms was no less important than that of one of his most influential knights. Briony couldn't tell whether the prince was entirely ignorant of his popularity among the rank and file—he seemed to be, but she wondered if he only pretended for the sake of modesty. Watching Eneas among the common soldiers was a sort of primer for princes—and princesses, too, Briony decided.

The strangest thing for Briony about the trip north was not seeing how much the land had changed, but realizing how much she had changed, too. Only half a year had passed since she had fled Southmarch—and just twelve months since her royal father had been taken captive—but she felt she would hardly recognize the Briony Eddon of a year before if she met her. That girl had experienced so little of the world! That Briony had never sat on the throne except while playing games with her brother when the court had finished for the day; today's Briony had sat on that throne as ruler and had made decisions on matters of commerce and law and even war. That Briony had never been out of the castle without a retinue of guards and ladies in waiting. Today's Briony had slept in a haymow, or in the dirt underneath a wagon in the rainy forest. The old Briony had studied swordplay for years with the same incomplete attention she had brought to doing sums and reading passages from the *Book of the Trigon*; the Briony who stood here now had fought for her life and had even killed a man.

But it was not simply the large experiences that had changed her, she realized, it was all the things she had seen in the last year, all the ordinary and extraordinary people she had met, players and thieves and traitors, goblins and Kallikans, as well as the situations she had been forced to endure—hunger, fear, having no roof over her head, and no friends and no money. Briony felt as though the only thing she had in common with her younger self was the name and the place they were born.

It was strange, but it was also exciting. She was writing this new Briony as a pen wrote words on a piece of sanded parchment. What would the pen write next? That was impossible to say. But for the first time in her life, despite the danger that lay ahead and the loss she had already experienced, she was content to wait to find out what the future would bring.

Although, she reminded herself, it was not as though she had much choice about it.

Qinnitan had escaped him again, but only barely.

Daikonas Vo was ill, or badly injured; otherwise, Qinnitan knew she would never have been able to outrun him for even a few moments, let alone stay ahead of him so long. But although the soldier moved as if his bones were all broken and his guts were aflame, he never stopped. Every time she looked back, every time she paused to rest, Vo was still behind her.

Why didn't I kill him when I had the chance? Why was I such a fool, to let him live?

Because you couldn't know what might happen, she told herself as she struggled gracelessly across the wooded Brennish hills, hungry and exhausted, unable to stop even to tend to her aching, bleeding feet. *Because you wouldn't know how to kill any man, let alone a soldier like Vo. A monster like Vo.*

And that had been the real reason: he terrified her. It had taken all her courage to try to poison him with his own black bottle on the fishing boat, but that had failed. What hope did she have now?

Still, even if she hadn't managed to poison him completely, something was definitely wrong with him: he looked like a wild creature, and when he drew close enough for her to hear him, he was often moaning and talking to himself.

Even though I didn't kill him, she thought with sudden insight, *perhaps too much of what was in that bottle made him very sick. Or perhaps it's not having the medicine that's made him this way.*

But none of it would matter if he caught her, and even if he didn't,

Qinnitan knew she would starve if she couldn't get far enough ahead of him to search for food.

Qinnitan's stomach ached with hunger. She was so tired that she could barely keep her legs moving. The ground had become steeper, but every instinct forced her out of the wooded valley and straight up the slope, even though doing so would leave her visible to Vo or anyone else below. By the time she was halfway up, she could hear him crashing up the slope below her. She burst out of thick forest and onto the upper part of the grassy hillside where the trees grew more sparsely and the ground was lumpy with purple-gray shrubs, then stole a look back. Vo saw her and bared his teeth in the mask of dried blood that covered his face. It might have been a grimace of exhaustion, but to Qinnitan it was the snarl of a beast that would not give up until one of them was dead and it terrified her.

As she climbed, she pushed at several large, loose stones to send them rolling down toward him, but even in his terrible state Vo was too agile to be caught that way; each time he waited until the stone had almost reached him, then moved out of its way.

At the top of the hill, Qinnitan saw to her great surprise that a road wound along the base of the hill's far side, several hundred yards beneath her. Perhaps that meant there was a town somewhere nearby! She scrambled downslope as fast as she could, looking back for Vo but not seeing him; when she reached the flat road, she began to run. She could manage nothing better than a pace she herself would have mocked in her childhood days on Cat's Eye Street, but at least she knew that every step took her farther from the limping murderer Daikonas Vo.

She alternated between running and walking for what seemed like an hour at least, praying at every bend in the road to find a town or at least a village in front of her but seeing scarcely any sign of habitation at all. She saw old ax-marks on many of the trees and once a tumbled hut that might have belonged to a charcoal burner, but the ruin was deserted and no use to her.

Sundown was almost upon her and Qinnitan was stumbling with weariness when she saw the rider some distance ahead of her on the road. At first she thought it a trick of the lengthening shadows, but as she slowly drew nearer, she could see that it truly was a man on a small horse. Another few hundred steps and she could see that his mount was no horse but a mule, and that the man himself had the shaved head of some kind of Eionian priest.

"Help!" she shouted, one of the few northern words she could remember. "Help! Please!"

The man turned around in surprise and looked back, then reined up and waited for her, shaking his head. "If this be a trick, child, it will go badly for you." He pulled a gnarled walking-staff from a loop on his saddle and waved it at her. "I will not be ambushed by thieves without making them earn the few coppers in my purse."

Qinnitan only understood part of what he said. "Help," she said. "Please. Hungry."

He was not an old man, but he was not young, either, the skin of his face a net of wrinkles made by sun and wind. After a moment he reached into his bag and produced a heel of bread. "Have this," he said. "And may Honnos bless your road. Are you on your way to Dunletter? You will not reach it walking tonight."

She never found out whether he meant to offer her a ride. A crackle in the bushes made the priest look up in time to see Daikonas Vo step out of the trees a little ways behind them, something dark curled in his hand.

"Curse you, child!" the priest said in despair and anger. "You played me false . . . !"

Something struck his head with a horrid *crack* and the man tumbled from the donkey's back, the bloodied stone that had dashed out his brains lying on the road beside him. The donkey took a few skittering steps forward, then began to lope away up the road. Qinnitan did not even look back at Vo, but ran after it and clambered awkwardly onto its back, pressing her face against its hot, bristly neck as she kicked at it its flanks with her feet, trying to make it run harder.

"I will have you, you little bitch . . . !" Vo shouted hoarsely in the Xixian tongue, frightening the donkey so that it began to trot even faster. *"You will never escape me . . . !"*

Qinnitan kicked and kicked again, forcing the donkey to go faster and faster until she was afraid it would bounce her off into the road. All she could do was cling to its neck and pray.

The prince's Temple Dogs followed the Silver River Road as it wound north-northeast through a half dozen Kertewall valleys, then at last passed over into the western edge of Silverside. The road crossed the river at several points, sometimes on shaky bridges that had to be rebuilt by Eneas' soldiers to bear the weight of their wagons and heavily laden war-horses, but generally ran beside it. The river was high with spring rains and the water lively, making a counterpoint to the oppressive silence of the empty valleys: Briony found her spirits lifted a little just by the sound of the water and the sight of ordinary spring flowers, although it was impossible to overlook the deserted Kertish towns in which they often grew, or the occasional scenes of devastation, still raw from the Qar's march through the area half a year ago.

One morning, half a tennight after they had fought the Qar, Briony woke up early after a fitful night and sat in the doorway of her tent watching the camp come to life. She missed drinking *gawa*, which had become her habit in Effir dan-Mozan's house in Landers Port. The smell of woodsmoke from the morning fires reminded her of its bitter, musty taste underneath the honey and cream, and the way it made her feel as it warmed her stomach. She had not drunk any for months: here on the road mornings meant sour wine or water from the Silver River, which at least flowed swiftly enough to be clean and sweet.

If I survive all this, she told herself, *I will have gawa every morning, with cream from the Dales and heather honey from Settland. And if anyone asks me about such a strange custom, I will tell them, "Oh, I picked it up when I was living with the Tuani . . ."*

A sudden memory of Shaso blew through her morning's thoughts like a storm cloud, but before she could do more than note its arrival she saw a stir near Eneas' tent, which the prince had only recently and reluctantly agreed to take back from her when she had inherited a tent of her own from one of the officers killed at Kleaswell Market. Briony had grown used to the rhythms of a small army on the road: she recognized that the scouts had come back. What she didn't understand was why their return seemed to have caused such a stir.

"Princess," said Eneas when she had made her way over, "I am glad you've come. Weasel has an interesting tale to tell."

Weasel, who was nearly as small as a boy and had the dark hair and complexion common to the southern islands below Devonis, did not look like an interested man so much as a worried and unhappy man who was doing his best to hide it. His fellow scouts, who, like him, wore shabby clothes so that together they looked more like a band of poachers than anything military, sat and listened silently as their chief reported.

"Dreadful many of them," said Weasel. "Thousands, I would guess—ten thousand and perhaps more, and that does not count those who are barracked in the city itself. There are dozens of ships in the Southmarch mainland harbor, everything from cogs to three-masted, square-rigged warships, and several more galleases in the bay. They have besieged the castle—in the time we watched yesterday afternoon and early evening the cannons were firing almost continuously—and have breached the outwall at least twice, from the looks of it, but the defenders have made repairs. The cannons—by Volios Strongarm, what monsters they must be! We could not see them from where we stood, but they flamed like Mount Sarissa and made a sound like the end of the world."

"And it is the autarch's army?"

Weasel nodded. "The cursed Xixy falcon is everywhere, Highness. We never thought to see so many—it is like what was said of Hierosol."

"And the Qar?" Briony asked.

"No sign of them." The chief scout turned to his men. They nodded their agreement. "Perhaps those we saw were a wing of a retreating army."

Eneas looked troubled. "Perhaps. But it makes little difference in any case. Ten thousand Xixians!"

"More, if the scouts are not mistaken," said Lord Helkis. "If they are barracked in the town, perhaps as many as twice that. How many men could be billeted in the mainland town, Princess Briony?"

"Many." How could Southmarch hope to stand up to so large an army? And if the autarch now controlled Brenn's Bay, the last source of supply to the castle was closed off as well. "Were they fighting back?" she asked. "The castle folk?"

"Hard to tell, Ma'am." Weasel couldn't bring himself to look right at her, but spoke halfway between her and the prince. "We saw a few trails of smoke from the walls but they must have been small-bore guns. Nobody fool enough to be up there making a target of themselves just to shoot a few arrows, that's certain."

It was all Briony could manage not to ask questions to which she already knew the answers: if the autarch had so many men and so many weapons, the castle could not hold out for very long. Merolanna, Briony's own lady's maids Rose and Moina, Sister Utta, grumpy old Nynor—all of them were in terrible danger.

"We cannot hope to defeat such a force, Prince Eneas," Helkis said. "The men will follow you anywhere you lead them, but their courage deserves better than a pointless death—even for the honor of . . ." he gave Briony a carefully emotionless look," . . . such a lady."

"It is not my honor that brings me here, sir," she began angrily, but Eneas lifted his hand.

"Peace, both of you. I promised Princess Briony my help and of course she will have it. But she does not expect me to be foolish with it, do you, Highness?"

"Of course not." But she didn't like the implication very much. Eneas and Lord Helkis seemed to have agreed already that there was nothing they could do against the autarch's superior force.

Briony was too angry to stand listening attentively while the prince and his noble officers began to discuss what they would do next, most of which seemed to be no more than making a secure camp. It was clear that they would do nothing of any importance today, and maybe not for longer than that—if ever. She couldn't blame them for not engaging the autarch's forces directly, but surely they could begin planning to go around the southern army somehow. Surely there must be some way to relieve the castle?

She was standing before her tent, angrily sharpening her Yisti knives, when a tall young soldier approached her with worry obvious on his face. She waited, but he did not speak even when he had stopped only a few steps away.

"Yes?"

He swallowed. For all his size, he looked scarcely older than Briony herself. "Your pardon, Highness," he said, which seemed to empty his lungs of air. He stood for another long moment before he had breath enough to begin again. "Someone . . . there's someone . . . who wants to speak with you. Your Highness."

She gave him a look that should have told him she wasn't interested, but he was either too stupid or too frightened to understand. She sighed. "Who? Who would want to speak with me that I would also want to hear?"

Panic crept over his face as he tried to make sense of this.

"Oh, for the love of Zoria, just tell me what it is, soldier. Who wants me?"

"The merchant, Highness. Dard, the merchant."

It took her a moment to remember who that was. "Ah. And how is it that you are carrying messages for a prisoner? For a servant of the autarch, no less?"

He swallowed again, hard. "Servant of . . . ?"

"How is it that you come bearing his messages? Did he slip you a coin?" She raised her eyebrow. "Ah. He did, didn't he? I can't imagine Eneas will think much of that."

The boy's eyes bulged with alarm. "My father's dead," he began, almost stuttering in his hurry to explain, "and my sister can't be married without . . ."

She sheathed the blade she had been polishing and lifted her hand. "Enough. I do not much care, to tell the truth. Keep your coin and lead me to him."

When the little merchant saw the tall soldier approaching the stockade with a companion, he walked away from the other prisoners and then made his way to the fence with the casual air of a man in no hurry.

"All right, soldier, you can go on your way," Briony said. "Just tell me your name."

"M-my n-n-name?" The stutter was quite serious now.

"I'll keep silent about you taking money from a prisoner, but I may need a favor from you in return some day. What's your name?"

"A-Avros. They call me 'Little Avros.'" He shrugged. "Because I'm tall."

"I see. Go on, then."

The soldier was long gone by the time Dard reached the fence. Briony pulled out her smaller knife and began to clean her fingernails. "You bribed a soldier," she said. "The prince won't like that."

"Surely you won't tell," Dard replied. "That poor lad, with his ugly sister trying to raise a dowry . . ."

"Enough. What do you want?"

"I recognized you."

Briony raised her eyes to look at him for a flat moment, then returned to examining her nails. "Everyone in this camp knows who I am. Did you waste my time just for that?"

"No, Princess, truly I didn't. I want to bargain with you."

"Bargain?" She looked from side to side. "Eneas now owns everything you had, merchant. What could you possibly have to bargain with? Especially with me?"

"Information." He smiled. He did not have all his teeth, but those he had were very white and shiny. She was not impressed. "I know something that I think you would like to know."

"And why should I not have Prince Eneas squeeze it from you like water from a cleaning rag?"

Dard was not intimidated. "Because you might not want him to know about it. But if you want me to tell him first, of course, I will . . ."

She took a moment to finish cleaning under the nail of her smallest finger, then slipped the knife back in its hidden sheath. "And what do you want in return for this information, merchant?"

"Freedom. I can make back the money I lost on this venture in half a year—but not if I am a prisoner. Eneas can put the mercenaries to work, but he has no need for me and my colleagues. I was only trying to make a living, not take sides in a war." He shrugged. "And I do not think this will be a safe place to be for very long."

Briony considered the man. What could he know that she would not want to share with Eneas? The fact that she could not think of anything did not make her feel more secure. "But even if I wished to make such a bargain, I have no power to do so. The prince of Syan is the master here."

"Can you not . . . persuade him?" White teeth or no, his leer was disgusting.

Briony turned and walked away.

"Wait! Wait, my lady, I am sorry! I mistook the situation! Please, come back!" She turned and looked at him. Dard the Jar had sunk to his knees and now let his desperation show: "Please, Princess, I was a fool—forgive me. Just give me your word that you will do your best to honor our bargain and I will trust you. Will you do that? If my information helps you, promise you will speak to Eneas about my release and I will be satisfied. Your word is good enough for me."

She was half-frightened, half-curious to hear what he considered information good enough to bargain with a princess. "Very well," she finally said. "I promise that, if what you say is useful, I will speak with Eneas on your behalf."

"Soon. Before there is any more fighting."

"Soon, yes. Now, what is this news of yours?"

He looked from side to side, although there was not another soul within several dozen paces, then leaned close to the stockade fence. Briony moved as close as she could while staying out of the merchant's reach—she was not going to be tricked into being anyone's hostage.

"On the other side of the hills," he said, "on the shore of Brenn's Bay, lies the autarch's camp."

"I know that, merchant . . ."

"But what you don't know is that he has a prisoner—a royal prisoner." Watching her face, he must have felt he had guessed right, because his expression became more confident. "Ah, I see you did not know. That prisoner is your father, Princess Briony—the autarch has your father, King Olin of Southmarch."

12
Willow

"They traveled to Perikal and Ulos and even savage Akaris, where they saw Xandian wind-priests in the marketplace and heard the whine of their pagan song, but the Orphan stopped his ears and eyes against such godless hymns . . ."

—from "A Child's Book of the Orphan, and His Life and Death and Reward in Heaven"

SOMETIMES IT SEEMED that the guns would never stop again.

After days of a curious, unexpected peace, the Xixian attack had finally begun and had not stopped since. The southern ships slipped up and down Brenn's Bay, their cannons blasting the tops of the city walls and smashing rooftops and spires into a deadly rain of whirling rubble that killed people from above as suddenly as Perin's lightning. Much of the roof of Wolfstooth Spire, the city's tallest tower, was already gone. Larger Xixian guns hammered away at the outer wall all day long from their emplacement on the hill behind mainland Southmarch, and once or twice every hour the autarch's mightiest cannons, the Crocodiles, roared their terrible roars. The Crocodiles fired cannonballs so big it took dozens of men just to lift one, carved boulders which could punch holes in even the thickest ramparts with just a couple of landed shots. Southmarch's defenders had to rebuild the most critical parts of the great outer wall every night, gangs of men working feverishly in near-darkness before the autarch's cannons came back to fiery life in the morning and began the assault all over again.

* * *

It was obvious even to Sister Utta, who knew very little of war, that the castle could not resist the assault for very long—hundreds of Southmarch folk had already died, and many hundreds more lay wounded. Already Xixian soldiers in conical helmets were running boldly at the base of the walls, shrieking up at the defenders like mad things, daring them to waste precious arrows and rifle-balls. At some point there would be too few hands available to rebuild the broken sections of wall and the autarch's soldiers would come pouring through. Utta knew she would have to make a final decision on whether to let herself be taken or to violate the Zorian order's prohibition against suicide—she certainly did not expect to be treated as gently by the Xixian soldiers as she had been by the Qar.

Utta made the sign of the Three as she stepped out of the covered passage into the long colonnade that ran along the western side of the residence gardens. The morning sun was nearly visible above the ramparts, which meant that the lull in the cannonade would end soon and the thunderous, smashing attack would begin anew. It was never entirely safe now anywhere in the castle, but in these small, temporary silences there was at least the illusion of lessened danger. Utta was happy to grasp at whatever kindly untruths she could find, since even the most obviously false hopes were in scant supply these days.

Avin Brone had set himself up in a suite of chambers beside the guard barracks. The Zorian sister walked across the open spaces as quickly as possible, trying to stay away from the taller buildings, often the first targets of the morning barrage because they were the first things that caught the light. The ruins of the Tower of Winter gave testimony to that: it had been largely destroyed less than a tennight ago and the upper half of it still lay across the buildings crushed in its fall like the corpse of some serpentine monster.

It was a sort of miracle in itself, Utta recognized, that Avin Brone was still free, let alone taking a major part in the castle's defense. In other circumstances, it would have been interesting to note how the power ebbed and flowed in Southmarch: Berkan Hood and the castle's other defenders had begun to realize that they were largely on their own, that Hendon Tolly was not going to step up and lead the resistance to the siege, so Brone was useful again.

She found him in the chamber he had made his meeting room, his painful leg up on a stool. Brone was attended by three or four worried-looking guardsmen—none of them old enough to be wearing armor, Utta thought disapprovingly, let alone risking their lives in defense of Hendon Tolly. But after the destruction in the farmer Kolkan's field and the murderous fight against the Qar, perhaps as few as a thousand men remained in the castle who were even capable of lifting a weapon.

"Lord Brone," she said. "May I have a moment?"

He looked up at her, frowning. His guards, or squires, or whatever these spotty-faced boys were supposed to be, did their best to seem perturbed by her intrusion as well. "What?"

"I'm Sister Utta, Lord Brone. Do you remember? We have met before."

His beard was almost completely gray now, although some of that might have been the ubiquitous dust from shattered stone and plaster that filled the air these days. It took a moment before he recognized her, then his preoccupied frown turned into another kind of frown altogether.

"Yes, Sister. Forgive me, but I am grievously occupied. What can I do for you?"

"Not for me, Lord Brone. For the duchess. She asks you to come to her."

"Merolanna? But . . ." He shook his head in irritation. "I cannot walk—not well. And in case you and the duchess have not noticed, we are at war with a cruel enemy. Ask her to forgive my discourtesy, Sister, but it is not convenient just now." He tried to turn back to the maps of the city spread on the table before him, but a residue of guilt made him look up. "Truly, it just cannot be. Not today."

"I will tell her that, Lord Brone. She will be disappointed, of course. She said to tell you that she wishes to talk to you of a matter that you alone know about. That *you alone* know about." Utta had no idea what this was supposed to mean, but the duchess had been very firm.

"Don't let him say no," Merolanna had told her. *"He will try. Don't let him."*

"Truly, I cannot, Sister. It is not the right time," Brone said, but with less certainty than before. He looked flushed and weary, and certainly no one would argue that he was in the best of health himself. Utta felt bad for him, but not so bad that she did not bring up her next weapon.

"Very well, but I fear to give her this news," she said. "She is not very strong."

He looked at her suspiciously. "Merolanna? I have never heard that said of her before."

"You have not seen her since we were held prisoners by the Qar. She is not the woman she was."

"The man I sent to interview you both on your return said nothing of this." But he looked stricken. What kind of lord constable could he have made, Utta wondered, with such a soft heart? Or was she mistaking one emotion for another?

"Come and see for yourself, Lord Brone. She is not well. Our captivity was hard on her, and she is not a young woman." Utta did not feel too bad about applying this pressure to the count of Landsend. She only wished that she were not telling the truth.

He groaned. "I will need a sedan chair."

She tried to be firm, although seeing the swollen sausage of his foot she was feeling a little sorry for him. "You are an important man, Count Avin. I am sure even in such days as these, one will be made available for you. Or Merolanna could send you her carriage, if a way can be cleared through the rubble."

Merolanna had propped herself up in her bed, but she truly did not look well. The new physician had taken out several of her teeth, which had gone rotten during her captivity—Kayyin the half-fairy had offered to get her help, but the thought of one of the Qar poking in her mouth had horrified Merolanna, and she had refused. Now her cheeks were sunken, something even the thorough application of rouge could not disguise. Her hair, concealed now under a simple white linen coif, had grown quite thin as well, and the hands that clutched bedclothes to breast were bony and mottled. Only her eyes retained much of what she had been even a year ago. Her gaze was still sharp, and it fixed on Brone as he hobbled into the room.

"So you did come." Her voice quavered just a little.

"Yes, Your Grace," he said. "How could I refuse such a kind invitation? *'Tell him to come, or I will drop dead on the floor and it will be on his conscience'*—wasn't that the gist of it, Sister Utta?"

Even Merolanna had to smile at that, but she quickly raised her hand to cover her ruined mouth. "As always, you exaggerate, Brone. But I am glad you're here. We need to talk." She turned to Utta. "Leave us now, Sister, so I can speak to Count Avin alone. We are old friends, after all."

Utta had not known she would be sent away. She bowed her head and went out, but with more than a little anger in her heart. How much time had she and Merolanna spent together in the last year? How long had they lived with each other like maiden sisters, captives of the Qar? And had any of it been for Utta's sake? No, but now Merolanna sent her away as though she were nothing better than a servant.

It isn't right, she thought, stopping as she reached the door of the outer chambers where she could hear Merolanna's maids talking quietly as they sewed, pretty young Eilis usually loudest and always quickest to laugh. What future for Eilis or any of them in this doomed castle? These were frightening times. And yet, Utta, who had experienced things few other people could even imagine, who had actually met the dark mistress of the fairies and lived, was expected to go out and sit with these young children until Merolanna was done talking to this important man, so vital to the castle's continued survival.

Her hand was actually on the door handle when she turned and retraced her steps. Utta did not mean to spy on Merolanna—she intended only to walk back in and ask to be included, let the duchess know that after all they had been through together she expected better treatment—but what she heard through the door stopped her for a second time with her fingers on a door handle.

". . . My child? Yes, he is my child, Brone. But he is your child, too. You have never taken responsibility for your act . . ."

Utta went rigid. The lost baby, the one who after all these years had suddenly possessed Merolanna's thoughts . . . was Brone's?

"*My* act? With all respect, Merolanna, you were my elder and I was quite green. Is that not called a seduction? And I helped you with money, helped you find the woman to take care of him. . . ."

"Yes, the woman who let the fairies steal him!" For a moment Merolanna was close to weeping—Utta knew the older woman's ways quite well. "My poor child, stolen and dragged away behind that cursed Shadowline . . . !"

Brone sounded tired and old. "You must make up your mind, Merolanna. Is he your child or my child? It cannot be both ways."

"Yes, it can," she said, her voice so low that Utta found herself leaning close to the door like any eavesdropping servant. "Because he is ours. Your blood and mine."

"I don't understand what you want me to do." Brone spoke like a man who knew he had been defeated.

"The Qar know what happened to him. They took him, so they know, but they would not tell me. That witch who leads them imprisoned me so she would not have to face me. I sent message after message asking only for the smallest bit of news, but she ignored me."

Which was not exactly true, Utta thought. The duchess had indeed sent message after message, but the strange creature named Kayyin had brought back more than a few replies, and all of them had been the same: Yasammez had not ignored Merolanna's questions, she had simply refused to answer them.

"What should I do?" Brone laughed sourly. "Do you think I have any sway with the fairies? Anyway, they are gone from here."

"Don't treat me like an idiot. I looked that horrible fairy woman in the eye. She would no more walk away from this place than you or I would. She has only retreated a short way and she might be convinced to make common cause against another and greater mortal enemy. I suspect that is what's happened. There are people who even claim that the fairies have gone to ground under the castle! But that is nothing to me."

"What people?" Brone was angry now. "Who says such things? Where did you hear it?"

"Oh, don't be a fool, Avin. It doesn't suit you." For a moment, Utta could hear the old affection come up in the duchess' voice; for the first time she could truly believe the two had once been lovers. "Even with that foul little Hendon Tolly barring the way in and out of Funderling Town, gossip still travels. You cannot expect people to hide such a thing, especially not from me. I know everything that happens in this castle. You should remember that."

The Qar hiding inside the walls of Southmarch? And Brone himself aware of it and doing nothing? How could that be? For the first time, Utta was painfully aware that she was not just eavesdropping but spying on state secrets. She took a step away from the door in case one of the ladies in waiting should come through, but the muffled talk from the front room still went on as before.

". . . It matters not," Merolanna was saying when Utta leaned close to the door again. "At least not to me. Nor do any of the other secrets you are keeping, like the return of Vansen, who disappeared behind the Shadowline with my great-nephew. Do you know where my poor nephew Barrick is, too? Surely even if you hated me for what's between us you wouldn't keep that from me, would you?"

Brone sounded quite helpless. "Gods, Merolanna, of course not! I swear I know nothing of where Barrick is today, nor does Vansen. The prince was alive when they parted."

"Good. That is good, at least." Even through the door, she could hear how weary Merolanna sounded. The duchess had done her best to seem stronger than she was, Utta knew, but even the imposture was beginning to flag. "Then we can get to the most important matter. I'm dying, Brone."

"You are not. You will outlive me . . . !"

"Nonsense. I'm ten years your senior and I doubt I will live to see next spring. Do you think I fear it? I welcome it. But here is what I ask of you—no, I demand it. Use Vansen or any other tool you have to make the fairies talk. Find out what happened to our son. Find out why they stole him and what happened to him. I must know that before I die. Promise me that."

Brone didn't sound angry anymore, but he didn't sound happy. "I cannot go near Vansen or the . . . or any of the others, Merolanna. Hendon Tolly watches everything I do."

"Promise me." The voice was so quiet now that Utta could barely hear it. "Give me this one last gift, Avin. Swear you will do it."

Utta didn't hear any more words, but she guessed that Brone had nodded his head. She heard his heavy, hobbling steps coming toward the door. Utta's own eyes were full of tears and she was frightened at the prospect of being caught listening—as it was, she felt like the lowest of spies. All her anger had gone, driven out by the voices of two old people discussing a great sadness.

Brone stepped into the hallway just as she reached the far door. She tried to make it look as though she had just come from the front room, but the count seemed scarcely even to notice her. He limped slowly down the hallway, his face stretched in a grimace of pain. She did not think all of it was from his gout.

"Good day to you, then, Sister," he said gruffly, but did not look up. She had forgotten how tall he was, even with his head bent as though he were weary beyond belief.

"And to you, Count Avin." She stepped aside as he passed, then watched him make his halting way down the passage.

The booming noise of a monstrous cannonball striking the outer wall had barely ended when another crash came from much closer to hand.

Hendon Tolly grabbed another dish from the tray and threw it across the room after the first, almost killing the cowering squire who had brought him the meal. Gravy and bits of meat and crust from the splattered pie made their slow way down the wall as Tolly walked back and forth with bulging eyes and a face as red and raw as an open wound. "Curse that yellow-eyed freak! Curse him! None of this veal nonsense—I'll have the autarch's stones in a pie instead."

Tinwright knew better than to say anything. Across the room Puzzle was on his elbows and knees, whatever message had brought him to Tolly's chamber still undelivered, cowering for his life. Tinwright had been kept at the lord protector's side for days and hadn't seen the old jester for some time, but this was clearly not the best moment to catch up on gossip.

"My lord . . . !" Puzzle quavered. He was so frightened that the bells on his dark green jacket and cap made an unceasing, jingling murmur. "My lord, please do not . . ."

"Shut your mouth, you withered old lackwit!" Tolly raged. "I could kill you where you stand and not even blink. Not a living soul would remember you by tomorrow sundown."

Puzzle looked like he was about to weep. He pressed his head against the floor and was silent except for the continuous tinkle of his trembling bells. Tinwright would have felt sorry for him but he had been kept in a state of fear for his own body and soul for days now and had little strength left for others, even friends.

Another distant cannon blast echoed like thunder.

Berkan Hood, the lord constable, stood in the doorway watching, his scarred face pale but expressionless. The news he had brought of the first breach in the outer walls—a breach that the defenders were struggling to close at this very moment—was what had sent Tolly into this fit of rage.

"My lord," Hood said when the lord protector's rampage had finally slowed. "Calm yourself. All is not lost. We are repairing the breach and they will not be able to fire their biggest gun for some time. I understand that you are frustrated . . ."

"You *fool*." Tolly walked over to him and stared up at the taller Hood, eyes slitted with contempt. "Calm myself? I should have your head for that. You understand *nothing.* We cannot defeat that pagan bastard. He has ten times the troops we have—more!—and more than twice that at his disposal down in Hierosol. Not to mention what he could muster if he brought another army up from Xis after the winter storms are over. And unlike the fairy folk, the autarch has ships. We will be getting no more food from Marrinswalk or anywhere else." He picked up the tray he had knocked from the squire's hands, then let it drop to the floor again with a clatter. "Whether it is tomorrow or next tennight or half a year from now at the very longest, Southmarch *will* fall to Sulepis."

Hood stared down at him. The warrior's face was implacable behind his thick mustache but something in the way he stood at stiff attention suggested he was resisting the urge to strike his lord and master. Despite Hood's cruel reputation, at that moment Tinwright almost admired him.

"Of course, Lord Tolly," he said at last, then bowed, turned, and walked out.

Hendon Tolly walked to the door to watch him go. Puzzle crept to his feet with much grimacing at the stiffness of his joints, and hobbled across the room to Tinwright.

"I only came to tell you . . ." he began.

"Puzzle!" Tolly shouted from the doorway. "Curse you, you ancient bit of dried jerk-meat! Are you not my royal jester?"

Tinwright surreptitiously put out his hand and braced Puzzle as the old man's knees buckled and he nearly fell. "Yes, my lord!" Puzzle fluted. "Of course, yes, Lord Tolly!"

"Then make me laugh. Go to—I wish to be cheered!" Tolly stared at him, his face pale, eyes fierce and intent. "Did you hear? Amuse me."

"M-m-my lord, I am unpor . . . unpoo . . . unprepared! I came only to give a message to Master Tinwright . . . !"

"Very well." Tolly walked toward him slowly, a feline smile playing on his features. "I shall be just as in need of merriment an hour from now. You will return to me then and make me laugh uproariously or I will cut off your face and make it into a Midsummer mask to scare the ladies. Would you like that, Puzzle? You wouldn't, would you?"

"N-no! No, my lord!"

"I thought not. Then go and prepare your very best japes and comical songs. Do you see how I am frowning, old man? Well, in an hour, one of us shall have our face changed."

Puzzle tried to bow and moan and promise his cooperation all at once, but only succeeded in muddling himself so badly Tinwright had to brace the old man again. "Why were you seeking me?" he whispered to the trembling jester.

"Oh, Zosim preserve me!" Puzzle's red, rheumy eyes were welling with tears. "He will murder me!"

"He will probably forget," Tinwright tried to assure him. "He is very changeable of late. Just do your best and all will be well. Now, what was your message?"

The jester had to swallow twice before he could speak again. "Your mother is looking for you, Matty. She is looking for you all over the residence, and attracting much attention, little of it favorable." Message delivered, Puzzle patted his arm. "Farewell, lad. You were a good friend."

The old man trudged away, legs and arms as thin as pipestems, bells still chiming mournfully.

If only he would not try to be funny, Tinwright thought, *he would be the most amusing fellow in the March Kingdoms. If ever a man was perfectly ill suited for his work, there goes such a man.*

But he was only thinking about poor Puzzle to avoid considering the horror that was Anamesiya Tinwright loose in the royal residence. If anything could assure Matt Tinwright of being executed even before the doomed jester, it was the presence of his mother, stupid and righteous as a peacock and no more discreet than a feverish child. It would be a miracle straight from Zosim if she had not already told half a dozen people about Elan M'Cory.

The gods, it appeared, had been searching for new ways to amuse themselves at a humble poet's expense, and now they had found one.

Puzzle survived. In fact, by the time he reappeared, the lord protector had either forgotten all about him or simply lost interest. "Who? The jester?" he asked the guard who had stepped into the room to announce Puzzle's return. Hendon Tolly did not even raise his eyes from his cup of unwatered wine—perhaps his dozenth of the evening. "Send him away. That moping horse-face is all I need to sour the last of this good Torvian red." The guard went out. Tolly looked blearily up at Matt Tinwright. "Go on! Make certain that fool of a guard sends him away. Tell him to give the old fool a good kick, too."

Before Tinwright could get to the door the castellan, Tirnan Havemore, suddenly leaped to his feet. "I will deal with the fool, my lord. Rest yourself."

Tolly did not look at either of them but only waved his hand.

Neither of the two men was willing to relinquish the chance to get out of their master's presence, even for a few moments. Both went out the door of the lord protector's chambers at the same time. Puzzle had already been sent away by the guard and was wandering down the corridor toward the kitchen, his relief combined with confusion.

"Puzzle, wait," Tinwright called after him.

"*I* will give him the message," Havemore hissed. "I am your superior."

"As you wish, Lord." Tinwright knew better than to argue.

The castellan swept down the corridor with all the authority he could muster, his long, fur-trimmed robe swinging above his velvet slippers. He was clearly taking as much time as he could, delivering Hendon Tolly's criticisms in elaborate detail as the old man looked more and more morose.

"But he told me to come back!" Puzzle protested, apparently forgetting that his attendance would likely have ended in his execution. "Look! I prepared a new diversion—the ball floats in the air!"

After Puzzle had at last, and with great effort, chased down the bouncing ball, he was sent on his way. Tinwright waited for the castellan to return to the door so they could go back in together, but to his surprise Tirnan Havemore gestured for Tinwright to walk with him a little distance away from the guards.

"Lord Tolly does not like me to be long away from him. . . ."

Havemore scowled. "Yes, yes. Enough of that." He was a tall man with a round, youthful face, but he had aged in recent months. He was not well shaved today and looked bloated and pink. "I would talk to you, Tinwright. Would you walk away from the lord castellan of Southmarch?"

"No, Lord."

"You are much in our master's company lately. If that scarecrow who just left is your rival in entertaining him, then it is little surprise, but still it seems odd the protector should take such pleasure from the company of a mere poet."

Jealousy? Or something more complicated? "Lord Tolly does what he wishes, Lord Havemore. And gets what he wants."

The other man studied him carefully. "We have only a moment before Tolly notices our absence, even full of wine. Answer my questions truly and you may find you have a friend you will need one day. What happened to Okros, the physician? I know the story we were told is a lie."

"I don't know. He died . . ."

The stinging slap came so fast Matt Tinwright did not even have time to raise his hand. "Do not trifle with me, young man. I ask you again—Okros?"

Matt Tinwright rubbed his face. The masters of Southmarch were all terrified, that seemed clear, and none of them trusted Hendon Tolly. Tinwright lowered his voice to a near whisper before answering. "He was killed doing the lord protector's bidding." How much did he dare say? "It had something to do with a magic mirror . . . and the gods. I did not see it happen." There was no reason to mention that Tolly had made him perform the same ritual—that Tinwright himself had almost suffered Okros' fate while helping Hendon Tolly reach out to the land of sleeping gods.

Havemore blinked. "Witchcraft!" he said, peering at the nearby guards to make sure they could not hear him. "I knew it! That madman will doom us all." His shrewd eyes fixed on Tinwright again. "I also know you are close with my old master, Avin Brone. Do not deny it! Tell me what Brone plans. Does he have some strategy of his own to save the castle?"

"I truly don't know, Lord Havemore. He would never tell me."

"No, likely that's true." The castellan frowned, considering. "Tell Brone . . . tell him that his old friend and servant Tirnan wishes him well. Tell him that I still think of him fondly, and would . . . that I would be ruled by his wisdom about what to do to save our beloved Southmarch. You will say just those words to him, and to no one else."

Tinwright's heart was beating fast—he was being asked to carry a message to Brone saying the castellan was open to betraying Hendon Tolly!—but he found himself shaking his head.

"My lord, the protector will never let me away from his side for so long, especially not to visit Brone."

"Leave it to me," Havemore said. "I will arrange something, some pretext, to get you away from Tolly long enough to deliver my message."

"But, with respect, my lord, why do you not simply speak to Brone yourself? You are the castellan—surely you have ample opportunity?"

"Because some of my own men are Hendon's spies, though I do not know which. And there are other spies watching Brone. He and I could never meet without every word being carefully listened to. It is too risky. No, you must do it. If you succeed, you will have made a good friend in me. If you fail—well, I will not go to the block alone, poet."

Despite seeing the first gleam of hope he might be able to escape Tolly and the death he had assumed would inevitably come to him at the lord protector's hands, Tinwright was also awash with anger and disgust. Brone himself, Tolly, and now Tirnan Havemore, none of them thought anything of risking the life of Matthias Tinwright for their own schemes. What was he, after all, but a worthless poet? Why should they fret if he was killed furthering their schemes?

Of course he said nothing aloud except, "As you wish, my lord."

The roar of cannon fire went on like a winter storm.

The castellan Havemore soon made his excuses and departed the chambers, leaving Tinwright alone with the lord protector except for the silent guards and tiptoeing servants. Hendon Tolly was still drinking, but the fury was past and he had descended into a deep, strange quietude.

Tinwright was leaning discreetly against a tapestried wall, falling asleep on his feet and wondering if he dared to sit down on the floor, when the protector stirred in his high-backed chair and looked around until he found Tinwright.

"Come here, poet." He gestured at the floor near his feet. "Sit."

Matt Tinwright settled as far away from Tolly as he dared, so that if the protector should decide to hit him he would have to extend his arm a little and weaken the blow—he had learned a few things during his weeks in Hendon's company. Tolly's face was no longer flushed. He had gone quite pale, as if a fever in his blood had turned suddenly from hot to deadly chill.

"It is a poor excuse for a man who does not admit when he has met his match," he said. "I admit it. Sulepis is clever. The pagans consider him a god. His army is the greatest in the world. He is . . . a worthy adversary." He cast his eyes sideways toward Tinwright as if daring him to say otherwise. Tinwright had learned by now that it was best to speak only when asked a question, and sometimes not even then. "I thought that we each had one part of what was needed—that Sulepis had the blood sacrifice and I had the mirror. I believed we needed each other—and so did Sulepis. But something else is needed—this Godstone. Sulepis doesn't have it but neither do I. In fact, I have nothing he needs at all, and that is why we are doomed."

Tolly lifted his cup and took a long swallow, wiping his chin with the back of his hand. He was very, very drunk. "That fool Okros misled me, or perhaps he hoped to trick me so that he could somehow gain the power for himself. Perhaps he simply did not know. Whichever is true, he never told me of any Godstone, or any other magical bauble." He looked around a little vacantly, as if he was searching for his audience, which at this moment was only Matt Tinwright. "But I *will* find some way to free the goddess. She is mine. She has told me so. And I will think of some way to keep her from the Xixian as well."

Tinwright didn't understand much of what Tolly was saying. The protector kept calling the thing that had spoken to him "the goddess," but the Autarch of Xis had several times called it a god. Which of them was right? And what did such confusion mean?

Tolly finally looked down and saw the expression on Tinwright's face. He did not seem to like it. "You. Are you wondering why I let you live, poet?" he demanded. "Why I did not simply kill you when I caught you spying? Answer me."

As ever, Tinwright sought for the right words, the careful words. "I suppose I have wondered, my lord."

"You suppose, yes." The thin lips twisted in a smile. "As so many others do. But I'm different, boy, I'm different. I do not suppose—I must *know*. Do you understand me?" Tolly had closed his eyes now as if deep in thought or memory; he did not wait for an answer. "Men are small creatures, most of them, creeping and crawling like mice. For centuries, they scuttled at the feet of the gods, hoping mostly to stay unnoticed. But even after the gods finally turned their backs on them, men kept scuttling. Like the vermin in the walls, they continued to live their lives in fear of larger creatures, not knowing and not caring what lay beyond their hidey-holes. They continued to fear the gods even after the gods left them. But I am no mouse, poet. I do not fear the gods or anything else. The only thing I fear is not to be understood."

Hendon Tolly was silent for a very long while, his eyes still shut—so long that Tinwright was contemplating getting up to go in search of some food and drink when Tolly spoke again.

"Who can understand me? Not one man in ten thousand, poet. Not ten men in all of Eion. The autarch—he is one of the few. It grates on my soul to admit it, but he is one of the few. *He* is *alive*, you see. He knows that the measure of the universe is the reach of a great man—no more, no less." Hendon Tolly opened his eyes. For a man who had drunk so much, he looked terrifyingly sober. "That is why you are here, poet. Because you must write of what I do. You must witness what becomes of me . . . so that I will be understood."

"By me, Lord?"

Tolly's bark of laughter was as sudden and violent as the slap he had given Tinwright earlier. "You? By the arseholes of the foul, farting gods, poet, are you mad? You scarcely understand how to read and write. Do you know anything of Phayallos? The *Book of Ximander,* which you have now held and read from? Of course not. You are like so many of your type, enamored with the mewling and whimpering of Gregor and the rest of the bards, thinking that truth lies in pretty words and pretty stories. You know *nothing.*" He leaned and spat on the floor on the opposite side of his chair—a thoughtfulness for which Tinwright was grateful. "But you can write what I tell you to write. You can witness what I allow you to see and then write about it, and even with no better guide than a dull wit such as yours, in the centuries to come those who are worthy to understand . . . will understand. They will see my works and hear my words and those few will understand me. I care truly about nothing else. If I gain the power I seek, well and good. If I can do no more than thwart the autarch, that is well, too, as long as what I am—*who* I am—does not disappear from the memory and minds of my equals, my very few equals, most of them not even born yet." He raised his cup and drained it to the dregs. "Go to your corner, poet. Go and sleep. The hour of your highest calling is almost come. One way or another you will see the world begin anew. You will see . . . *astonishing things.*" Tolly closed his eyes and leaned back in the chair, letting the heavy iron cup fall to the ground with a noise like a sword being forged. "You will see my . . . moment of glory, when the gods . . . recognize me at last for . . . for what I am."

When it was clear that Hendon Tolly would not speak further, Tinwright crawled into a corner and made himself as comfortable as he could in a pile of blankets on the stone floor. He pulled his cloak tight around him, but although the floor was chilly, that was not what set him shivering until sleep at last led him away.

Utta had never felt such confusion before. In all the strange happenings of the last months she had always had a clear-cut sense of what she needed to do next, but now she felt as if she were wandering lost in a fog. What had become of the old, familiar world she had known? The fairies had held her and Merolanna prisoner and threatened to kill them—but now those same fairies had become allies and were hiding beneath Southmarch. The Autarch Sulepis of Xis, a nightmare that had been little more than a name a year ago, was now camped on the near shore trying to blow down the castle walls. And the father of Merolanna's child, the one she was so certain the fairies had stolen . . . was now revealed to be Avin Brone. How could any of that be?

Despite the late hour, the roads and greens of the inner keep were crowded. Thousands of people had flooded in from mainland Southmarch when it was abandoned, and during the attacks on the castle, first by the Qar and now by the Xixians, those refugees had crowded ever closer to the inmost parts of the castle, so that the royal residence was now scarcely more than an island jutting above a sea of desperate, homeless people. The center of the castle had become a sort of village fair, except that the faces in the crowd were nearly all angry or bleak or both. Many of them stared at Utta with dislike as she passed, and for the first time in her life she felt her Zorian robes marked her out not as someone who might help, but as someone who had done harm.

They think the gods have failed them, she realized. *Zoria, the protector of the poor and downtrodden, has not answered their prayers.*

As she passed through a narrow space in the crowd someone bumped her hard enough to make her stumble. A few women nearby murmured disapprovingly at the discourtesy, but no one actually said anything out loud against the man who had done it—he was already gone, anyway—and Utta began to feel as though she walked, not among Zoria's children, as she usually did, but among beasts who might turn on her when she had gone far enough into their midst. Feeling suddenly old and frightened, she made her way out of the thickest part of the crowd toward the edge of the inner keep, but it was no less dangerous there. The camps along the wall seemed to be mostly full of men—she thought that strange, considering the need for every able-bodied man to fight—who turned from their campfires to watch her go past as though she were an object being offered for purchase, their eyes reflecting emotionlessly in the firelight.

Utta hurried toward the relative sanctuary of the guard tower that stood across from the front of the Throne hall. The Throne hall now was used mainly to house troops, and had already lost some of its roof to the autarch's bombardment, but it was lit by lanterns and looking at it made her feel a little less as though the entire world had been replaced by a different one when her back was turned. The Xixian cannons had gone silent so she asked one of the pikemen if she could climb the guardhouse stairs up onto the wall of the inner keep. She was craving air from the sea, air that did not smolder with the smoke of hundreds of campfires.

The soldier squinted at her a little suspiciously, but then nodded and said, "But you take care up there, Sister. There are children running around like wild things. Don't even have parents no more, some of them. They'll steal your purse and push you right off if they catch you too far from the tower."

Utta winced to think such things were happening here, in the middle of Southmarch keep. "I'm not going far. I just want to smell the ocean."

She kept her word, taking only a few steps out along the walkway at the top of the wall and keeping the guardroom fire in sight when she stopped to lean against the cold stones and breathe the salty air. A seagull screeched somewhere nearby. The outer keep also sparkled with fires, but only those of the soldiers: beyond the New Walls as they were called, most of Midlan's Mount was dark, although Utta could hear countless voices raised in argument and even the occasional song and knew that almost every inch of both the inner and outer keep were crowded with refugees from the mainland.

So many people! So little hope. Utta crossed her hands on her breast and prayed.

She was peering down, trying to make sense of where the gate to Funderling Town might be in the darkness, when she realized someone was standing next to her—someone who had come up to her in complete silence. Sister Utta was so startled she gasped and almost fell down, but the stranger did not move.

"You can feel it, too, can't you?" asked the newcomer—a young woman with wild eyes. "You can feel that it's happening."

"I'm . . . I'm sorry," Utta said, "I don't know what you mean." Perhaps this was part of a trick—distract her, then others would come up and try to rob her. Had she not been so frightened she might have laughed. Utta was a Zorian sister—what did she have that could be stolen? A wooden brooch in the shape of an almond? Some prayer beads? Her life? None of them was worth even the price of a meal.

"It's coming," the girl said. "The great day is coming—I can feel it. But I cannot reach him!"

She's mad, poor thing, but surely she cannot be worshiping the autarch? There were a few benighted souls, Utta had found, who were already so terrified by the events of the past year that they saw the autarch as some kind of heavenly scourge who would bring the sinful world to an end.

"I'm not mad," the girl said, startling Utta so that she drew back again in alarm. "I know. I know what is going on underneath the castle. I can hear it, smell it, touch it. He is returning. The god is coming back. And the one I love is there, too." She turned and looked at Utta, her thin face youthful in the light of the torch burning at the guardhouse door. She looked as though she had scarcely eaten in days. "You! You know my lover. I can feel it. You have met him and spoken with him."

Utta had already begun to back toward the door. "Bless you, child. May Zoria the Merciful protect you from harm . . ."

"I called him Gil, but his name is Kayyin now." She laughed a little. "It was Kayyin before, as well, but he changed it for a while. My silly, clever Gil."

The close-cropped hairs on the back of Utta's neck stood up under her coif. "What . . . what name did you say?"

"Kayyin of the Changing tribe. Lady Porcupine is his mother, but he is not so thorny as she is." She giggled, and it transformed her from a figure of potential menace into something entirely different. "But I cannot go to him. I feel him in my thoughts, but he cannot feel me." Her voice grew somber. "The men, the soldiers, they will not let me go down into Funderling Town. And Kayyin is beneath, waiting for the god to be reborn. But his thoughts are full of things I don't understand—worries about eggs and fevers, fevers and eggs . . . !"

Utta shook her head in confusion. "You truly know that the Qar are there, beneath us? Or is it only something you've heard?"

The girl laughed again, incredulous. "Heard? Heard it with every part of my body, knew it with every thought! I can feel Kayyin's heart beat through the stone."

Utta shook her head. She had heard—and seen—stranger things of late. "What are you called, child?"

"Willow." The girl made a clumsy little curtsy and laughed again, but this time the edge of desperation was gone; she sounded calmer, happier. "No one has called me that in a long time, though."

"It's a nice name," Utta said. "Come back to Zoria's shrine with me, Willow. You look as though you could use a good meal."

13
A Glimpse of the Pit

". . . He was beaten then by the wicked captain, who would have killed him, but that even the ship's sailors took pity on the child and pleaded with their master to spare the Orphan's life . . ."

—from "A Child's Book of the Orphan, and His Life and Death and Reward in Heaven"

THE STRANGE THING, Chert realized, was that the more he worked on the map for Captain Vansen and the more accurate he tried to make it, the more unfamiliar the whole matter became.

Because no one but the Lord of the Hot Wet Stone himself ever saw the world like this, he decided—*all of it at once, open and naked. Only the great god could see things this way. Only a god would* want *to see things this way.*

Still, although at times he despaired of being able to make anything useful at all, let alone do so quickly enough to help his people survive the siege, Chert found himself fascinated by the task. His slates and parchments had spread across the table in their temple dormitory room until Opal had demanded a second table, so that "people have something to eat on—if they ever stop working to eat." Contemplating the dozens of different maps the Metamorphic Brothers had let him borrow from the library at Magister Cinnabar's orders, Chert felt, if not like a god, certainly like more of a true engineer than he had ever been in his daily profession.

It was one thing to look at someone else's idea of what the world looked like, something else entirely to devise one's own. After struggling to imagine how he could show everything in one drawing, he had decided on a combination of maps to display the terrain, cross-sections of each level with a single, larger drawing to show how those levels fit together. With these maps and a little imagination, Ferras Vansen should be able to make some kind of sense of the tunnel world belowground.

Opal frequently questioned her husband's sanity for agreeing to take on such a task, but she spent more than a little time each evening watching him at work, asking questions and even arguing a point from time to time, though she professed not to care about any of it. Flint also came in to watch the work, studying the scene as though to learn it by heart, but if he thought in any way about what the maps represented, he kept such thoughts to himself.

Flint was not as talkative as the last time the two of them had left the temple. In fact, he was silent.

Well, that's back to the way things always were, isn't it? Chert didn't mind too much, anyway: he was trying to see things in his head in a way he hadn't before, trying to notice how the tunnels and caverns actually fit together instead of relying on the usual Guild shorthand, which was a better way to think about *some* things but not so good for others. He had brought several pieces of lamp-coral that were bigger than what was ordinarily used for traveling—if he stumbled across a significant detail for his maps, he wanted to be able to see it well enough to record it properly.

The two of them made their way down to the bottom of the Cascade Stair, but when they got there, Chert turned and could not see Flint. He had a moment of panic—panic and something else less definable—and then the boy came around the corner. He had only fallen a few steps behind. Still, something about the moment troubled Chert.

It came to him as they walked on. The last time he and the boy had been here looking for Chaven, the boy hadn't just fallen behind, he had got himself truly lost. When Chert found him, they had also discovered the crack in the wall and the telltale smell of the Sea in the Depths, the silvery lake around the Shining Man's island where Chert had come so close to losing the boy forever. Now, though, the mundane side of it all came to him.

In his maps, he had traced what he believed must be the opening above the Sea in the Depths that stretched all the way to the surface—although he could only guess at its true shape and path. But he had forgotten to show anything of the spot where the boy had discovered a hole into the side of that shaft, and where Chert had been able to smell the Sea in the Depths' unique scent—something that he still could not name. It might be the only place where the chimney leading up from the Mysteries could be entered. It belonged on his maps.

"Boy, do you remember the last time we were out, and you got away down a side tunnel and then you called me . . . ?"

To Chert's mild astonishment, not only did Flint remember but immediately turned and began leading his adoptive father in what seemed like more or less the correct direction.

The journey seemed longer than Chert remembered, but Flint soon proved that he knew the route very well indeed, leading his stepfather through Five Arches and up the Great Delve—Stormstone's long passage that surfaced all the way on the far side of the bay—and before another hour had passed, they reached the dead end of the corridor and the black gap between two slabs that had turned out to be not merely another shadow, but a hole into the great chimney that led up from the Sea in the Depths. As he leaned close, Chert could again smell the faint tang of the sea.

"It *must* lead all the way to the surface," he said out loud. "Must do. Why does no one upground or down seem to know of it?"

"What is it, Papa Chert?" There was an odd tone in the boy's voice, the measured speech he used sometimes that seemed too mature for his years. "What are you saying?"

"This . . . chimney, this hole in front of us. As far as I can tell it goes all the way up from the . . . the place where I found you that time"—for some reason Chert was reluctant to speak the Shining Man's name—"to the surface of Midlan's Mount."

"Ah." Flint nodded slowly, but there was still something strange about his behavior. "Then why doesn't the ocean come in?"

"The opening must be somewhere above the waterline, or everything here really would be flooded with water," Chert explained. "In fact, the Salt Pool is at sea level, so if the ocean got in, everything beneath there would be drowned—the Maze, the Five Arches, even the temple."

Chert took one of the largest chunks of coral in his fist, tightened his headlamp so it wouldn't fall off, and then slipped his arm into the crevice. He sucked in his gut to make himself narrower so he could get his body through the opening as well.

It was impossible to make out much past his own arm and the glare of the coral chunk in his fist, but two things struck him immediately: this great chimney was wider than he had guessed, perhaps longer than a rope-throw across; and there was a sizable ledge just a few yards away from him along the wall of the roughly cylindrical space, and a black crevice behind it big enough for a man his size to stand in upright. Could that be a tunnel? It would be a way to get in and have a better look at the great pit before him.

He held onto Flint's belt so tightly his knuckles ached while he let the boy, who was thinner than he was, lean out and look at the ledge Chert had spotted.

"Do you think we could muddle out where that is, lad?" he called.

Flint did not reply until he was all the way back in the crevice again. "Think so," was all he said. His strange, adult mood seemed to have passed.

In fact, it took Chert and the boy the better part of two hours to find the spot, and they ate their midday meal while walking. This was in part because they had to go far down before they could find their way back up to the correct spot, and also because Chert, to his shame, had estimated the distance incorrectly, and several times made Flint turn back because he felt certain the boy had gone too far.

The ledge he had seen was not a few paces away but hundreds, and far bigger than he had guessed. When they finally located it, Chert was astonished to discover it was no mere lip of stone but a great, broad ledge a dozen Funderling cubits deep and three or four times as wide, with room for far more folk than just Chert and Flint to stand looking down into darkness. Even the crack leading in from the mostly natural passageway outside was in fact a rift large enough to drive one of the Big Folk's wagons through.

A shiver of awe and even terror passed through Chert. *The Pit,* he thought. *Is this the J'ezh'kral Pit itself, and I alone have found it?* In Funderling legends that was the hole in the earth that led down to the Lord of the Hot Wet Stone's fabled domain, the place where the Funderlings themselves had been created. But what else could this be, a chasm that stretched from the surface of the world all the way down into the deepest

Mysteries? And why had no one else ever mapped it before? Did the Metamorphic Brothers know? Were they hiding it from the rest of their people?

Get your scaffolding put up before you take a bad tumble, Blue Quartz, he told himself. *Don't start thinking about such things. You'll run mad or scare yourself to death. Put it on the map. Put it all on the map.*

"Just sit quiet for me a moment, lad," he told him. "This won't take long."

It was the boy's good behavior, paradoxically, that made Chert aware of how long they had been in the place: he had made as many notes and sketches as he could of the ledge and the immense pit and was just starting to put his tools away when he realized that he had not even heard Flint sigh for what must have been an hour or more. He turned, miserably certain he would find the boy gone, but Flint was sitting calmly a few yards away, his eyes fixed on the indefinite middle distance of the great pit.

"By the Elders, but I've asked a lot of you today, boy, and you've done everything I've asked," Chert said with a sudden burst of pride. "Let's go back and I'll see if I can't get my hands on some bread and honey that those greedy monks have been keeping for themselves—you deserve something good."

Flint smiled—a rare occurrence, but he did dearly love honey, which was hard to get in Funderling Town these days. The boy quickly climbed to his feet and led Chert back to an open passage that would lead them out to the Great Delve. But when Chert stepped into the wider space, he bumped into Flint, who had stopped, and then they both stood and stared at the stranger who had appeared in the passage before them.

No, not a stranger, Chert realized after a heartbeat; he had seen the thin, strange face before, the preoccupied gaze, even the hair that looked as though it had been cut with a piece of dull flint. In fact, he remembered every terrifying moment they had spent together, including their death sentence from the she-demon known as Yasammez. What he could not understand was why the stranger was alive.

"Gil," he said. "Your name is Gil."

"Yes, I once was Gil. Before that I was Kayyin. Now I am Kayyin again."

"Do you remember me? I'm Chert Blue Quarz and this is my son,

Flint. You and I went to the dark lady together—Yasammez. I'll be honest, I did not expect to see you again—it seemed certain she was going to kill you."

"She still may. Some days it seems like a better idea to her than others." He shrugged with the slippery Qar grace that seemed odd from such a manlike form. "That is the way of families."

It took a moment to sink in. "Hold a moment—family? You and the dark lady?"

Kayyin nodded. "She is my mother. I did not remember that for a while."

Chert did not know what to say to any of this. "Well, it is . . . good to see you, Gil. *Kayyin.*" He shook his head. "It is strange to meet you this way in the middle of nowhere! What brings you out here?"

"Oh, I often walk for a long time," Kayyin said. "And it has been long indeed since I have seen any of these, our old sacred places here beneath Midlan's Mount."

"Well, you must come and have a drink with me back at the temple. Let us go and dig out a cask of Brother Brewer's best and you can tell me what has happened since I last saw you. . . ."

Kayyin shook his head. "I am sorry, friend Chert—perhaps another time. There is something I must do now."

"Of course," Chert said. "Another time, then."

When they reached the wide passage known as the Great Delve, Kayyin turned away from the direction of the temple. "Fare you well, Chert Blue Quartz. One day I hope we can have that drink together."

"I cannot pretend to be surprised by anything anymore," Chert said to Flint as they watched the fairy go. "Come, lad, we've tarried out here too long. Let's be on our way. Opal will doubtless be back for the evening meal and will skin me if we're not there. And if she finds I took you out of the temple, she'll sew the hide back on me and then skin me again, so let's make fast time going back." But the thought Chert could not get out of his mind had nothing to do with Opal. He kept wondering what exactly Kayyin was doing out here, in this out-of-the-way place. Could it truly be simple coincidence? When the nearby chimney—the Pit as Chert had begun to think of it—led all the way down to the Mysteries, the spot that currently obsessed the Funderlings, the Qar, and even the southern king, the autarch?

Coincidence? Truly?

"What do you think of Copper's idea?" Vansen asked as he and Cinnabar broke bread in the shallow scrape that sufficed for a commander's field station. The magister had come all the way out to Moonless Reach, where Ferras Vansen and a few hundred Funderlings and Qar had held back the autarch's forces for three days, but Vansen was worried about having Cinnabar there for long. It was too dangerous a spot, and Cinnabar was too important. The Guild that had given him sweeping powers had shown wisdom, Vansen had long since decided—Cinnabar Quicksilver was that rare politician whose gifts made it easier to get the hard but necessary things done.

"His plan to sneak men around behind the autarch's vanguard?" Cinnabar shook his head. "Not a chance it will work. You've heard the same reports I have—Copper and Jasper have already given up half the length of that system of caverns. They'll never hold it until we can get reinforcements there, let alone long enough to dig around behind the southerners. Those old tunnels must be full of rubble. No, we must drop back and try to hold them at Ocher Bar." Cinnabar sighed, then gulped a long draught of his mossbrew.

Vansen followed suit. The drink would never replace ale, he thought, or even the sour mead his father had liked to make—the Funderling ale tasted altogether too much like wet dirt for his taste—but he had drunk worse things in his day, or at least so he had been told afterward by those who had carried him back to the guardroom. "I'll leave it to you to tell Copper, then."

He looked out across the room where Jackdaw, one of the Qar war leaders, was supervising a wall being built across the center of the chamber by a work gang of Funderlings. Vansen wished they all had another few days to prepare—he was confident that given enough time, the clever Funderlings could make even wide Moonless Reach nearly impregnable—but it was not to be. "What is the latest news from Copper and Jasper, anyway?"

"They are still holding the lower half of the reach, but it cannot truly be called anything but a slow retreat. Jasper says they are taking terrible losses. May the Earth Elders forgive us—most of his soldiers are little more than boys themselves. . . ."

"Yes—may the Three lift them high." Vansen made a sign on his chest and his face clenched with unhappiness, but he carefully made it neutral again. "And what else can you tell me? Any word from my master Avin Brone upground?"

"Nothing. And we cannot find a way to get any more messages to him. We have tried several times to slip someone through the main gate, but the Big Folk guards will not permit it—they say that any Funderling who wishes to come up to the castle will have to seek the permission of Lord Protector Tolly himself. And the less well-known routes either lead to the mainland and the autarch, like Stormstone's Great Delve, or are guarded by the lord protector's soldiers like the way into the basement of Chaven's old house. Wherever we choose, our enemies are waiting for us like a hungry cat outside a mousehole."

Vansen grimaced. It still sickened him to hear Hendon Tolly spoken of as anyone's "protector": every man among the royal guards knew about the youngest Tolly brother's interests and practices. "Do not risk trying to send anyone else through the main gate," Vansen said. "Tolly is a monster but a clever one. He would have all our secrets out of any messenger before long, even you or me."

"Then your Brone and any help he might send remain lost to us, at least for now. In any case, Captain, he and the rest of your people have enough horror to face already—the autarch bombards them day and night. There are nights I can hear the cannonballs crashing into the walls even down here, through a millionweight of stone." Cinnabar rubbed his small, thick finger in spilled mossbrew and made a few dark circles on the stone of the cavern wall. "So we must prepare for another retreat. I am truly sorry, Captain Vansen. We have asked much of you, but we have given you little to accomplish it with."

"You've given me all you have. What more could anyone do?"

Cinnabar smiled—perhaps the weariest, most lackluster smile Vansen had ever seen on the cheerful magister's face. "What more, indeed, my friend?"

Shortly after Vansen sent Cinnabar back to the temple, the autarch's forces made another attempt to drive the defenders out of the Moonless Reach. The attack was swift and sudden. One of the ghastly skorpa-monsters came lurching over the makeshift barricades the Funderlings had built across the reach, scattering the guards before it like beetles. By the time that Vansen's men had formed a spear wall against the thing and stopped it, a company of the autarch's riflemen were spilling out of a side tunnel into the wide reach. Within moments, the southerners had set their shooting sticks and began firing. Their rifle balls skidded harmlessly off the *askorab's* shell, but several of the less well-protected Funderlings and Qar fell in the first volley. Vansen shouted at them to fall back to the larger but incomplete wall at the far end of the reach where the rest of the company was already sheltering. His troop made a chaotic retreat, but a well-timed volley of arrows from the tiny contingent of Qar bowmen gave them just enough cover; only a few more were lost before they all achieved the security of the wall.

Vansen crawled to Jackdaw, who was calmly wrapping a length of torn sleeve around the bloodied meat of his own upper arm where a ball had hit him. The blood was red even in the dim lantern light, but that was almost the only thing about Jackdaw that seemed ordinary to Vansen. The fairy's face, scrawny and so long-nosed that he seemed more bird than man, was covered with an iridescent down that in stronger light seemed purple or sometimes even pink and blue, but now seemed just black. It made his bright yellow eyes even more startling. His body, too, wherever it showed between the few pieces of light armor he wore, seemed to be covered in the same kind of feathery down.

Vansen had stared at him for a few moments during their first meeting, but the Qar's martial personality had quickly become all that mattered: the fairy had clearly been around a battlefield, and although what ran in his veins was the right color for blood, it seemed by his actions to be something altogether slower and colder.

"We have no more serpentine or we could have brought down the stone above us and ended this," said Jackdaw, putting his head above the barrier to look around as if leaden balls were not cracking and hissing past him. He turned to Dolomite, one of Jasper's warders and the ranking Funderling warrior in Moonless Reach. "Is that what the black sand is called here? My people call it Crooked's Fire."

"Don't know about crooked anything," said Dolomite and grimaced. Like Sledge, he had witnessed much of the worst his own small world had to offer and did not like people to see him excited. "Blasting powder, we call it. But if we don't have it, we don't have it. We'll just have to fall back to Ocher Bar and hold them there."

"Still," said Jackdaw, "it would be nice to have a few of those bursting fireballs your little friend brought to you, Vansen. We could roll one of them directly under that foul-smelling *seliqet* and smash him to slivers."

"We're getting hold of as much as we can, but at the moment we don't have it," Vansen said tightly. "Any other ideas?"

"Keep sticking them with things until they're all dead," suggested Dolomite.

Another wave of musket balls snapped by overhead. The cavern echoed with the roar of the guns until Ferras Vansen thought it might come down around their ears. "You are as clever a tactician as Sledge Jasper," he told the Funderling. "Now, if you've nothing else to do, let's get back to the business of trying to kill that monster."

They survived two more assaults from the autarch's troops and their pet, just barely driving the attackers back each time, having to fight hardest to defend the unfinished end of the wall. The *skorpa* kept attacking the spot, determined to get to all the fierce but flavorsome meat it sensed there.

"See, that is the seliqet's weak spot!" Jackdaw cried as the jointed horror loomed over them again, huge claws clacking. From this angle Vansen could see a pale oval bubble of flesh in the center of the creature's underbelly where the legs came together. Jackdaw and the others began jabbing their spears into this soft place. The monster reared back up with a terrible hissing noise and retreated, crushing any of the autarch's unfortunate soldiers who could not get out its way. Its hobbling retreat soon led it back out of Moonless Reach and into the tunnels leading upground, the portion that the autarch's troops had already conquered. The horrified screams of the reinforcements who had apparently been coming up the passage as they encountered the masterless and deranged creature were enough to bring new heart to the defenders. Vansen led a charge from behind the wall and although several fell in the assault they quickly finished those of the autarch's men who were unwilling to surrender, but even more unwilling to flee back into the jaws of their own monster.

"That is at least a half dozen of those things we've killed," said Dolomite as he and the other fighters, Vansen included, bent to the work of finishing the wall while the autarch's troops were in retreat. "How many more do you think there are?"

"Not more than a hundred," said Jackdaw with a fierce grin. His own soldiers, despite some of them being badly shaped for digging and building walls, were helping out with a will. It was almost possible for Vansen to forget that some of them looked like frogs and foxes, and others were even stranger than that. They were all becoming brothers, in the manner he had seen before: facing death together was the greatest of levelers. Perhaps, with the help of these Qar, they could actually hold out against the autarch until Midsummer had passed.

"We will kill them one by one, then," Vansen said. "Until we have the gunflour to blow them all right to the gates of Kernios himself."

Jackdaw laughed. "You are funny, mortal. Do you not know where you are?"

"What do you mean?"

"We are already at the gates of Kernios, Captain. That is what is under siege here in the earth—what we defend! Our enemies seek to conquer the Palace of Kernios! We are Death's own honor guard."

For a moment Vansen wasn't entirely certain what he meant, but then began to understand. At last he summoned a grim laugh of his own. "As you say, then, friend Jackdaw—that is what we will do. Defend the gates of Death's city until we ourselves are invited inside."

It was almost a relief to realize how futile their task was. Vansen shook his head and bent once more to his work.

When he and the boy got back to their room, Flint sat down to think his strange, quiet Flint-thoughts and Chert hurried to turn his notes into marks on his maps before he forgot what they meant. The whole of the Pit had to be traced and much of the labyrinth behind Five Arches would have to be redone as well. As Chert worked, some of the things Flint had said rolled around and around in his mind, troubling him although he could not say exactly why.

He had just finished marking the changes and was moving onto other things when an idea came to him—a strange, magnificent, utterly mad idea.

For long moments he just sat, breathless, not even certain of whether it made any sense. Opal came bustling in from her labors with many things to say about what was happening and what she had been doing, but Chert scarcely heard her. He did his best to smile and say the right things, but his thoughts were completely taken by the new idea.

It was definitely *not* the kind of thing he could discuss with Opal, much as he valued her counsel. The danger of it was appalling, and she had all but told him that if he again went off and got himself involved in something risky when they had a boy who needed him to be a father, that would be the last night she would ever sleep under his stone. And since Chert didn't know whether Vansen and the Guild would even listen to such a lunatic idea, let alone approve it, he wasn't going to waste an argument with his wife on it yet (an argument that he knew he would lose anyway, and lose badly.)

He didn't want to waste any more time that should be spent on the maps, but neither did he want to wait too long before taking his audacious plan to Vansen, Cinnabar, and the rest. After the evening prayers had been called, Chert waited impatiently until Opal and Flint fell asleep, then got up, lit the lamp, and went back to his table. He made a pile of all the maps he would need for his calculations—there were many—then bent over the table in the guttering light of the lantern and began working out his scheme in the solid, old-fashioned way the Guild had taught him, filling his slates with numbers and symbols that would explain the workings of his strange, unthinkable idea.

14
The Queen of the Fay

"Such was his misery that many times the Orphan would have thrown himself into the green sea even against Heaven's wishes, but for the kindness of an old blind slave named Aristas . . ."

—from "A Child's Book of the Orphan, and His Life and Death and Reward in Heaven"

SAQRI WAITED AS HE CLIMBED UP out of the waves onto the rocky shore, as poised in her formless white robes as a temple statue. She was also quite, quite dry. Barrick, drenched and drizzling sea-water, had barely an instant to marvel at either that or the sea meadow he had not seen in so many years, then Saqri turned and started up from the shore toward the royal lodge, which was just visible through the trees at the top of the stony hillcrest.

"There are some things you learn after a few hundred years," the Queen of the Fairies called as he trudged after her, streaming water and making squelching noises with every step. "One of them is how not to get wet unless you want to."

He didn't have the strength to discuss it. Exhaustion and his sopping clothing were pulling at him like a legion of invisible goblins, making each step a terrible chore. Also, he could see the lodge more clearly now, and although the Fireflower voices seemed uncharacteristically silent, his own memories were not.

★ ★ ★

"First to touch the door is the lord of the cliff!" his sister shouted, and, without waiting to see if he had even heard her, she was gone, sprinting up the ancient steps. Barrick hesitated for a moment, waiting to see if Kendrick would run, too, but their older brother was waiting patiently for their father. Kendrick was twelve years old and determined to show he was nearly a man—he wasn't going to be playing any games. Barrick sprang up the steps after his twin.

"Cheat!" he yelled. "You had a head start."

"That's not cheating," she called over her shoulder, laughing so that she almost lost her balance on narrow steps worn to a shiny polish by rain and wind. "That's strategy!"

"If either of you step into that house without the guards," their father shouted from the dock, "I will skin you and feed you to the hounds!"

Which only made Briony laugh harder, of course—she loved those dogs so much, she'd probably enjoy being devoured by them, Barrick thought—and then she stepped a little short and almost fell back.

"Briony!" their father shouted. "Have a care, girl!"

She spun her arms around like the vanes of a windmill, trying to keep her balance, which gave Barrick the chance to help her. As he hurried past, he gave her the smallest nudge with his good arm so that she tilted forward and recovered her footing.

"Cheater!" she shouted after him. "You pushed me!"

Now it was Barrick who laughed. She knew it was a lie—she knew he'd looked after her, for once, instead of being the one looked after, and it felt glorious. He reached the pathway at the top and dashed along it toward the lodge, past the cypress trees. He had just caught sight of the broad coachway that lay before the front door—a most useless feature in a place with no roads and no coaches, but he supposed King Aduan and his builders might have had greater ambitions for the place—when he heard his sister's footsteps behind him.

"I've got you now!"

What, did she think that because his arm was crippled he was also lame? He put his head down and flung the last of his strength into a finishing burst, sprinting across the gravel coachway and thumping against the front door of the lodge just before his sister. Gasping too hard to say anything, they both slid down the door to sit side by side on the porch. His lungs finally full of air again, Barrick turned to her and . . .

THOOM!

The crash of sound yanked him back to the present again, scattering his memories like dandelion fluff. He whirled around in the middle of the path to look back across the bay. It was hard to see what was making the noise, but thin streams of smoke were rising from the mainland town. For a moment, Barrick could almost tell himself it was the chimneys, that all was ordinary and he'd heard only thunder. After all, who would be firing a cannon . . . ?

THOOM! THOOM!

. . . No, several of them—the Qar? Did they even use them? And where had Saqri gone? Could she be hurt? Could the cannons throw one of their balls this far? He hurried up the hillside path.

No, she said, as close as his own thoughts. *Move slowly, Barrick Eddon. There are many eyes watching.*

He turned and, to his astonishment, saw that Saqri was now behind him—he had passed her along the way, somehow. She did not speak again when she caught up, but walked on through the grove of twisted, shaggy trees. When she reached the house, the door opened at her touch as though it had been waiting for her.

Barrick followed her inside, overwhelmed by the familiar, musty smells, but also by the exhaustion that dragged at him like a Skimmer net weighted with stones.

"Go and sleep," Saqri told him, speaking words into the air like any ordinary mortal. "You are safe for the moment. There will be time later for everything else that must be. Sleep."

Barrick did not argue. One of the beds was disarranged as though it had been slept in, although to judge by the sheets and blankets (which always stiffened in the salty air) that must have been weeks ago at least, but he couldn't worry about it because sleep was tugging him down as powerfully as the waters of Brenn's Bay had pulled him, and this time he did not have the strength to stay afloat.

So the bed was unmade. Just now he didn't care if Kernios himself had slept in it. Barrick dragged off his wet clothes and climbed naked under the stiff sheets. In moments he had fallen into deep slumber.

"We have visitors," Saqri said from somewhere close by.

Barrick struggled up from the tail end of a dream in which he had searched for Qinnitan up and down the streets of a desert city without ever catching up to her. He opened his eyes, uncertain at first of where he was, but then it all came back to him—the mirror, the green ocean, the god-haunted, dreaming depths. He sat up to find Saqri at the foot of his bed.

"What?" he said, trying to pull his thoughts together. "Visitors?"

He had been joking, but the fairy queen looked over her shoulder toward the main room of the lodge. "In truth, I suppose it is we who are the visitors and they have come to see whether we mean them any harm."

Barrick could only shake his head, trying to clear out the confusion. "Visitors? Here on M'Helan's Rock? But the place is empty . . . !"

Her pale, angular face seemed expressionless. "Do you think so?"

"Very well, then, I'll come." He waited for a moment, but she did not move. "Can you go out, please, so I can get dressed? I'm naked."

Saqri gave him an amused look as she pulled the door closed behind her—but she was sort of his many-times-great-grandmother, wasn't she? Surely it wouldn't be proper to dress in front of her as if she were a servant? Barrick scowled as he wrestled on his Qar clothing. It was very odd for her to look so young and beautiful. It confused him.

When he stepped out into the main hall of the lodge, he was uncertain at first of what he was seeing. The very floor seemed alive with movement, as though a carpet had come to life. A hundred or more tiny people were waiting there, he realized with growing astonishment—people as small as the Tine Fay he had met behind the Shadowline, but dressed in hats and hose and jackets like ordinary folk. Their little faces, each smaller than a copper crab, turned toward him expectantly, but Barrick found himself speechless.

One of the tiny figures, a little bearded man, stepped out from the crowd. He was noticeably stout and looked very well dressed, with a fancy hat and minuscule gold chain draped across his chest that might have been part of a child's bracelet, but which hung as heavily on him as a royal jewel. It was all Barrick could do not to bend down and pick him up to have a closer look.

"Duke Kettlehouse am I," he said in a voice scarcely louder or deeper than a mouse's squeak, "master by election of the esteemed Floorboard Assembly of Rooftop-over-Sea, as well as uncle of Queen Upsteeplebat (whom you may have encountered, may her grandiosity remain unambiguous) and I and my folk, whom you see gathered here most bravely before you, wish to welcome you, our lordly lords and ladies . . ."

A little man with a pointy beard standing next to him, only slightly less well-dressed, poked Kettlehouse with his elbow.

". . . and, ah, of course." Kettlehouse took a moment to gather his thoughts. "Yes. We welcome you to our country again, Queen Saqri. It has been long."

"Since the war, or almost." Saqri nodded her head seriously, as if she were not talking to a man smaller than a mouse. "Many times have the winds blown since then. I wish better days had brought us together."

Kettlehouse looked pleased, if still tentative. "You are most kind, Majesty, most kind. We wish to speak with you about important matters—nay, incredulous matters! You know we have always, despite the difference in our onetime alliance, held the greatest and most tenacious respect for the old ones, our cousins, your people . . ." The pointy-bearded man gave him another nudge. "Ah. Your pardon. We wish to speak with you, if we may, about our peoples' future disposition toward each other—if you understand our meaning . . . ?"

Saqri nodded in that smooth but abrupt and birdlike way she had. "I understand well. I say with only truth on my lips that if by some impossible chance our two peoples survive what is to come, there will no longer be a shadow between us. I say that from the very heart of the People's House."

Some of the little people let out a cheer at this pledge; others as far as Barrick could tell, were weeping and blowing their noses, or whispering in excitement. The Fireflower voices, mitigated by the apparent presence of Ynnir, gave him glimpses of the long centuries of estrangement that might end here today.

Was this why we came here? he wondered. *Was there more to it than simply swimming to the nearest shore?* It was almost impossible to tell with Saqri, as it had been with Ynnir: with both of them, that which was real and fleshly quickly became that which was uncanny. Even simply watching the Qar in their everyday moments was like trying to understand a conversation in someone else's tongue.

"I am certain I speak for the Floorboard Assembly, then," announced Duke Kettlehouse after a moment's consultation with the pointy-bearded man, "when I say that we would be most happy to see that shadow of estrangement gone. Most extremefully happy. But now I must let my secretary, Lord Pindrop, explain to you things of which you may perhaps, begging the pardon of your infallibility, Mistress, not be aware." He took a step back and allowed the slender, pointy-bearded man to step forward.

"See what is written here," said Pindrop, proffering a sheet of parchment that seemed as large in his hands as a window shutter. "All the words spoken by Sulepis Autarch and Tolly, the Protector of Southmarch, when they met here only hours ago."

"What?" Barrick thought he had misheard the tiny man. "Here? The autarch? With a Tolly?"

Saqri took the note and read it, her face more like a statue's than ever.

"We heard everything he had to say," Duke Kettlehouse began. "We copied it most assiduously, in fair hand, so that we could make certain Your Majesty . . ."

Little Lord Pindrop interrupted his duke. "The danger is grave indeed!"

"When?" demanded Barrick. "When was the autarch here?"

"Yesterday evening." Saqri looked up. "And if these written words report truly what was spoken here, then the southerner knows far more about this castle and its history than even the Fireflower and the Deep Library could guess. Even as we speak, this Autarch Sulepis is preparing to push his way into the deep places where the doorways are."

"Doorways? Like the one that brought us here?"

"Yes, places where the world is thin. But the doorway beneath this place that has most recently been your family's home is different than any other. It was opened by Crooked and then closed by him as well, and only his dying strength has kept it sealed so long. Through it, he banished the gods who had tormented him, and because of him they are still on the far side of that doorway, fettered by sleep. But even in that sleep they dream of returning and taking their revenge on the world. . . ."

Ideas drifted up to him from the Fireflower, ideas of such abstract but overwhelming horror that Barrick could scarcely remain standing.

Saqri, however, went on as though she had considered such things every day of her life. Perhaps she had. "Speaking of the places where the world is thin," she told the Rooftoppers, "we must go now to talk to the other tribe that shares this place with you."

"Of course! We are not the only exiles who would honor our ancient kinship," piped Duke Kettlehouse.

"We must leave soon," Saqri told him. "When darkness comes. Can you have those you would send with me ready by then?"

"We will have our embassy ready for you one hour before sunset," he assured her. "We will wait for you at the dock."

★ ★ ★

There were times when the Fireflower seemed to give everything shadows and reflections. As Barrick followed Saqri down the path from the lodge, it made all around him shimmer like a fever-dream. It was certainly easier to be here on M'Helan's Rock, where most things did not have the significance that was layered everywhere in Qul-na-Qar, but Saqri herself, both as the queen and as the last in a long succession of women who had carried and then surrendered the Fireflower, was so full of . . . *meaning* that just being around her exhausted Barrick.

She talked calmly as they walked, as if by coincidence, about the Godwar and the Long Defeat that began when the Qar made the fateful choice to stand and fight with the heavenly clan of Breeze, earning the enmity of the Three Brothers and their Moisture clan and losing sovereignty over many of their own folk, including the very Rooftoppers Barrick had just met.

Even when it was not the explicit subject of Qar conversation or art, Barrick understood now, the Defeat was still part of them. It was there unspoken in all their poetry, a silent counterpoint in all their songs. The years since Barrick's ancestors had stolen their princess and driven them back behind the Shadowline had confirmed to most of them that their end was near. That was why Yasammez' crusade had found so many willing soldiers. If the end was coming in any case, why not face it with courage?

And what of me? Where do I belong in this Defeat? Why did the gods, or Fate, or whatever rules men's lives allow the Fireflower to pass to me, if all I can do is die with it inside me?

Saqri had turned off the main path to follow the curving track that led toward the sea-meadow where he and Briony had spent so many of their childhood hours. She passed across the meadow like a silk scarf being carried on the breeze, then stepped down onto a little winding path that Barrick remembered very well, a "fairy path" as Briony had called it, and which had amused Barrick and his twin because it led nowhere. He caught up with the queen as she reached the place where the descending track ended a little way above the waves of Brenn's Bay. To his surprise, a smooth-sanded gray fishing boat was bobbing in the water there, with a bare-chested Skimmer youth sitting in it, moving his oars to stay in one place as he looked at Barrick with cautious interest. But when he looked past Barrick and saw Saqri, the young Skimmer rose to his feet, hardly rocking the shallow-drafted boat at all, and made an awkward bow toward her.

"Told it true, they did." He sounded amused, but his face said his feelings ran much deeper. "Really are her, you are."

"I am pleased you recognize me, Rafe of the Hullscrape," she said.

His heavy-lidded eyes widened. "You know me?"

"I recognize all of our people, even those who grew up in exile . . . but I think you have already had some connection with these doings, have you not?"

He shrugged. "Suppose. Nothing to take home and feed the family, though, if you know what I mean, Mistress. But some . . ." He suddenly brightened. "Are you coming with all the rest? Is that what this is all about?"

Saqri nodded. "As is Prince Barrick."

For the first time the Skimmer really seemed to see Barrick. "And are you the true prince of Southmarch, then? Son of Olin the Good?"

For a moment Barrick was so tangled with thoughts of what he was and what he was not that he could hardly speak. "Yes, I am," he said at last.

"Brought here by the holy hand of Egye-Var himself," said Saqri.

The Fireflower voices whispered, *Erivor . . .*

"Well, then, that is two in the eye for Ena's da!" said Rafe with sudden exuberance and slapped at the water, although he was careful to direct the splash away from Saqri. "The Queen of the Ancient Folk and the prince of this castle both to ride in my boat! Old Turley will be sour as pickled shark when he finds out . . ." The young Skimmer stopped and flushed in seeming embarrassment, a strange mottled greenish brown that rose from his neck to his small ears. "Pardon, Mistress. You'll not want to hear me croaking, and of course there's work to be done. Please, Majesty, let me help you."

He stood up and extended a hand to Saqri, stared at it for a moment, then apparently reconsidered. He withdrew it, squatted and dipped his fingers into the water of Brenn's Bay, then wiped it quickly on his breeches before extending it again. Saqri allowed the Skimmer to help her onto the ladder that Barrick only now realized lay out of sight just below the curve of the ground where they stood. From her effortless balance and the grace with which she stepped onto the rocking craft, Barrick suspected the queen of the Fay had needed no help.

But why are we in a hurry? he wondered. *They said we'd leave when it's dark and it must be well over an hour until sunset . . .* The Fireflower voices offered no answer.

He let Rafe's hard-skinned hand help him find the ladder, then turned and climbed down, grateful again for whatever the Dreamers had done to cure his crippled arm.

Now the young Skimmer pushed the boat out from the shore, but instead of heading out to open water and toward the castle, to Barrick's surprise Rafe followed the shore around to the quarter of the island opposite the castle, a spot the Eddon family had always left alone because of the tight tangle of trees and thornbushes that grew right down to the waves. Barrick had never really seen it from this angle, and certainly had never seen what appeared next: they were slipping toward a cave, which probably seemed an ordinary overhang of rock at higher tides, and whose entrance even now was scarcely higher than the gunwales of the fishing boat.

"Heads down," Rafe said. "No disrespect, but even fairy queens and drylander princes can get their blocks knocked."

Barrick bent forward far as he could until he was almost pressing his face against his own knees. After they slid past the overhang, he cautiously raised his head again to discover that the inside of the cavern was astoundingly large. Who could have guessed something like this was hidden under the thorns of the island's southeastern end?

Even at low tide the cavern was mostly under water, but above a shore of rocky tide pools, a lantern-lit dock led up from the water to a strip of stony beach and a strange little house, far longer than it was wide, its roof thatched with dried seaweed and beach grasses. After staring for a few moments, Barrick realized that what looked like a separate stone building at the back of it was a huge stone chimney that led straight up to the cavern ceiling and, he assumed, vented somewhere outside.

It's a drying shed, he thought. *Like the Skimmers have all along the lagoon. But what's it doing here on M'Helan's Rock? How do they hide the smoke?*

As if reading his mind, the Skimmer Rafe said, "We only light the fires at night. Smoke comes out of a crack farther down the island—wouldn't find where it really came from unless you dug for weeks. Not that they light it very often any more. More a . . . what's it called? Tradition."

"An old tradition," Saqri said. "This is where your people first declared themselves to their master, the Water Lord."

He looked at her oddly, apparently both startled and gratified by her knowledge. "I wouldn't know about that, ma'am. I'm just a fisher."

"But you will be headman one day and the girl's father knows it," she said. "That is why he is hard on you, Rafe Hullscraper."

This left the young Skimmer nearly dumb with surprise; he did not speak again until he had tied the boat to the dock and was helping Saqri and Barrick up the ladder.

"I'll go and fetch the little ones while you speak with the sisters," he told them, then climbed back into his boat.

As Barrick walked with Saqri up the little causeway toward the long shed he was suddenly struck by an odd feeling of both familiarity and utter strangeness. Something in him recognized this place, recognized its power, but another part of him couldn't imagine why such an unprepossessing building should spawn such intense sensations. It felt old—old as Crooked's Hall in the city of Sleep, old as parts of Qul-na-Qar, but although the wood was gray and weathered, nothing he could see seemed more than a hundred years old—a passing moment compared to the antiquity of the great House of the People, which after all had once been a god's home.

Two small, bent shapes stood waiting in the doorway of the longhouse, two Skimmer women who looked as old or older than the building.

"Welcome, daughter of Kioy-a-pous," said the more upright of the two. Like her sister, she had only a few wisps of hair on the crown of her head and her skin was as wrinkled as dried mud, but as she turned to Barrick, her eyes were sharp. "And to you, manling, son of Olin and Meriel—welcome, too. We were told of your coming. Ah, and you be somewhat more now than your seeming, be you not? We smell it. Gulda am I, and this my sister Meve."

Barrick only nodded at the odd greeting, but the reference to his mother surprised him. Still, the two old sisters had certainly been alive when his father had brought his new bride from Brenland. They might even have watched her ride in through the Basilisk Gate with all her dowry and household . . .

What had she thought about it all, young Queen Meriel? Barrick's father had always told his children how lively their mother had been, how much she had loved simple, joyful things like singing and dancing and riding. Would she have done anything different if she had known how little time she had to live? He couldn't imagine a better way she might have spent her days.

"Great queen, have you come to consult the Scale?" the one called Gulda asked Saqri.

One of Silvergleam's tiles, the Fireflower whispered. *A mirror that opens a hole to the dreaming lands . . .*

Saqri shook her head. "I dare not. I fear to expose myself to those strong currents just now. In any case, what thoughts I have about the future I would keep secret—I fear what others might learn from me if I opened my thoughts to the Scale here, so far from the seat of my power."

Gulda nodded. "It is true that the currents are strong and times are strange. Just last night the great god spoke to us. He sent a dream to me and my sister that heaven's children were coming back to Shadowmarch—that is what we call the great house across the water from Egye-Var's Shoulder," she explained to Barrick. "Our great ocean father dreamed that one of the immortals will walk the earth again and the world will be covered in darkness."

"Darkness," intoned the smaller, frailer sister.

Gulda folded leathery hands on the breast of her simple, homespun robe. "It was a good dream, despite the fearful things of which Egye-Var spoke. He seemed as he used to be when we were children just learning to hear his voice—not angry, not strange, as he has been of late."

"Late," Meve echoed.

"He told us he would have been content to sleep," Gulda continued, "but something had woken him. Someone is trying to fit the key into the door."

Barrick did not know what to make of any of this. Talk of the gods woke a cloud of Fireflower shadows in his mind, thick as bats taking flight after being startled in their roost, confused, echoing, and contradictory. The memory of the Qar contained the time when the gods still walked the earth, but even the Fireflower was only the People's own wisdom—it could not explain the gods and their secrets. "I don't understand," he said out loud.

"Nor will you," said Gulda. "Not yet. But our lord Egye-Var said this—"Do not despair. I will not desert my children, old or new."

"Old," Meve said quietly.

"That is all we have to say, Mistress," her sister said, then bowed toward Saqri. "All the Exiles will do their part. We were wrong in our fear to side with Pyarin the Thunderer and the rest of his godly brood—even the Sea Lord came to regret that division. We were wrong to turn our back on our own tribe. But now we will at least die together, as allies and kin." And Gulda smiled, a wide, almost toothless grin. "Or, who knows? Perhaps despite everything, we will live!"

Meve laughed. "Live."

Barrick wasn't exactly certain what was happening. "Are they saying the Skimmers will fight with us? Do they have the power to decide that?"

"We do not," said Gulda. "But our lord Egye-Var, the lord of the green waters, does. Our people will fight beside our family once more."

"Once more," echoed Meve.

Saqri stepped forward until she stood before Gulda and Meve, her pale, dark-eyed face serene and kind. At such moments Barrick thought she was the most beautiful thing he had ever seen. "Even if these moments are the only victories given us by the Long Defeat, still we have triumphed." Saqri reached out her hand and touched both of the Skimmer women on their foreheads; Meve sighed loudly at the contact. "Farewell, sisters."

Barrick heard a gentle plash of waters and turned. As if summoned by Saqri's words the fishing boat had appeared and slid toward them across the water, Rafe plying the oars. A large box of some kind sat in the bow of the boat behind him. As the little boat slid closer, Barrick was overwhelmed by a haze of echoes and shreds of meaning from the Fireflower voices . . .

Even the gods regret the Godwar . . .

. . . The ocean bears no grudges . . .

Then why did the lord of the green waters change his song?

. . . But also with the sudden realization that he was going home to Southmarch.

But is it really my home? Except for the times with Briony, I was never happy. I never felt it in my bones the way I felt in Qul-na-Qar . . .

Beating heart of the People.

Rebuilt on the bones of Silvergleam and the ashes of the Dawnflower's heart . . .

Our ancient house the People may never see again . . . whispered the chorus.

. . . Still, Southmarch was always my home, Barrick thought. *How could it seem so foreign now . . . ?*

It was not until he felt Saqri's cool fingers touch his arm that he realized the old Skimmer women had vanished back into the Drying Shed. Rafe had tied the boat up at the end of the dock and was waiting for Barrick and Saqri to come aboard.

When they reached the bottom of the ladder, Barrick saw that the box in the bow of the fishing boat was a sort of carriage for Duke Kettlehouse and his people—the whole population of Rooftop-over-Sea, apparently, perhaps a hundred of the tiny folk in all, seated on low strips of wood which served them as benches, their children in their arms and their belongings piled around their feet.

Saqri once again allowed Rafe to steady her arm as she got in, which seemed to make Rafe very proud. Barrick clambered down beside her and settled in, a little awed by the queen's nearness. He could smell her delicate and quite individual scent, flowers and cinnamon and some darker, stronger note, piney and bitter as temple resin.

They slipped quietly out of the cavern, Rafe rowing easily and strongly and the anxious Rooftoppers doing their best not to be thrown around by the movement of the boat. The sun had fallen very low in the sky and Barrick wondered how they could have been so long in that place when it had seemed less than an hour. By the time they reached the northernmost end of M'Helan's Rock the last of the sun was sliding down behind the hills west of Southmarch. They waited in a shallow cove until the day had dwindled to a last bright glow behind the hilltops, then they slid out into open water.

Darkness billowed over them like a cloak. For a moment the jagged ruin of Wolfstooth Spire gleamed in the last light, then it too dropped into shadow.

The Last Hour of the Ancestor, a voice whispered to him above the murmur of the Fireflower chorus. *I have never seen it since the day of my pilgrimage—except in dreams.*

King Ynnir? Is that truly you?

The voice came to him, distant as the far side of the water. *You called me back, manchild. I could only . . .* Barrick had a momentary feeling of something being reassembled, piece by piece—something that had been happier in pieces. *I am here.*

And he was, stronger than any of the other voices, more coherent. The king was there, part of Barrick's own blood and bones now.

"And now we return at long last, my love," Saqri said out loud, startling Barrick, until he realized it was not him she was speaking to—not directly, in any case. "At long last, and at the end."

"The ending of one thing is the beginning of another," Barrick found himself saying, but even though it was the dead king speaking, it didn't feel like a usurpation of his voice, only a prompting to say something he would have liked to say himself had he found the words.

The Fireflower voices fell silent. Even the crowded Rooftoppers in their box spoke only in inaudible whispers. For a long time Barrick heard only the steady, gentle splash of the oars, and he began to feel himself slipping into a sort of between-place, neither here and now nor any other time, as though they traveled between worlds—which in a way was true, Barrick thought. Everything that had gone before was done and behind him. Everything that would be lay ahead. Would it be the end of the world, as many around him seemed to think?

Perhaps. That was all he knew.

A quiet sound rose, so soft at first that he thought it only another note in the music of the bay and their passage upon it. It was no simple sound of water, though, but a sinuous, exotic melody. Then he heard words, or felt them in his head—at this moment there seemed no difference between the two.

"I am all my mothers.
I am perilous! I am beautiful!
I am all my daughters, too . . ."

It was Saqri, he realized, singing in a small, clear voice that rang like beaten silver. The melody ran around and around and began again without ever ending, like a snake with its tail in its mouth.

"I am the swan of the hither shore!
I am the lamp that lights the way!
I am the iron bird that ends what should not be!
Give me my crown!
Give me my crown!
Give me my crown!"

Her voice was sweet and low, but not soothing—this was no lullaby. It was rather a song so old Barrick could almost feel it sounding in his bones, each note a century, each century different, yet also much the same as the one before it, with cycles that came and went, came and went, until that time itself was all circles. And it was a woman's song, a song of pride in survival, a chant of triumph at the survival of life despite all dangers, all obstacles . . .

"When days have wound down
When nights have flickered into gray
When all stands before the nameless and are afraid to speak
I am all my mothers!
I am all my daughters!
I am the singer of the song.
I am the fox who stops the den.
I am she who can catch and hold every breath
Until Time itself turns and runs."

After a while, Barrick Eddon could no longer remember what it had been like when Saqri was not singing—it seemed as though he had always rocked on these waves, in this darkness, while the words of this song coiled around him, touched him, whispered to him.

"I am the swan of the hither shore!
Perilous! Beautiful!
I am the lamp that lights the way!
Fiery eater-of-shadows!
I am the iron bird that ends what should not be!
Fear me when you have wronged me.
I am all my mothers.
I am every one.
I am the dead.
I am the living yet unborn.
I am the one the moon loves
And fears . . ."

He had become something that had never been before, he realized, and he was returning to a home that was no longer his, if it ever had been.

They were all doomed, but darkness was only the thing that gave light shape. He was going home, and the Mother of All was singing beneath the rising moon, a song that went on and on and round and round. . . .

"I am all my mothers.
I am perilous! I am beautiful!
I am all my daughters too . . ."

PART TWO

THE TORTOISE

15
Heresies

Aristas showed him kindness and taught him of the true gods, the Three Brothers, and they became fast friends. When the ship on which they were both prisoners sank during a storm in Lake Strivothos, the Orphan helped Aristas to reach safety.

—from "A Child's Book of the Orphan, and His
Life and Death and Reward in Heaven"

THE VILLAGE LOOKED as though it had been abandoned at least a year earlier, but as Theron the Pilgrimer soon learned, that was not entirely true.

It stood by itself in a bend of the river he had been following because the roads were faint and overgrown here, as though they hadn't been used in a very long time. Perhaps a few dozen people had once lived in the small settlement but they were clearly long gone: brambles had grown up the sides of the houses, most of which were only collections of cut branches and mud daubing. The grasses had moved in across the paths and animal trails that had once led to the village's main road, so that the ramshackle cottages seemed to have grown directly out of the ground without human intervention, like mushrooms.

The weather had been gray and oppressive all day, with spatters of rain, but it was the horizon that worried Theron. The wind was rising—already the trees were beginning to bend—and in the north clouds had piled up in purple-black mounds, ready to roll down across the hills and drench the valley through which they had been traveling since they crossed the Southmarch border two days earlier.

"Boy," he said to Lorgan, "go and see if any of these huts would shelter us. It's been raining, so if you find one with a dry floor that should do for us."

The boy looked to his hooded master, but the man with the bandaged hands was sitting on a stump, taking the opportunity to rest. Theron thought it nearly a miracle that a fellow so weak and unwell could walk so far each day, but something was clearly driving the bandaged stranger to reach Southmarch—not that Theron thought for a moment they would get anywhere near that far. In fact, the increasing strangeness and emptiness of these lands had nearly convinced him that their journey would have to come to an end in one of the towns along the coast of Brenn's Bay, which they should reach in another few days. If he truly wanted to enter a castle at war, Theron's odd companion would have to manage that himself.

"Go on, then," Theron said to the boy. "Find us a place to shelter."

Lorgan still hesitated. "What are those lumpy things under the eaves?"

Theron squinted at the nearest of the deserted houses. "That? Wasps' nests, perhaps, but I see no wasps, do you? In any case, if you don't poke at them they'll do you no harm—that is well known. Now go and turn up something dry enough to give us shelter."

The child went forward on tiptoe, which irritated Theron. It was bad enough traveling through such empty, godsforsaken territories with the disturbing evidence of human desertion all around; the boy skulking as if some terrible beast or ogre might step out of the trees at any moment only made things worse. Now Theron was feeling unsettled, too. "For the love of the oracles, would you get on with it?"

Lorgan leaned into the nearest house without touching anything, as though the very wood might be poisonous. He straightened up quickly and shook his head, then went on to the next, stopping only to peer anxiously up at the odd, grayish shapes hanging like curds beneath the eaves on either side of the open doorway. Again the boy did his best to avoid any contact with the house itself, and again he quickly withdrew, shaking his head.

"Muddy," Lorgan said quietly, but with an air of defiance, as though Theron seemed about to argue, which he wasn't—the pilgrimer was only weary and hoping they could stop here for the day and build a proper fire to chase the damp cold out of his bones. All he had to do was deliver this hooded fool to someplace as near Southmarch as possible, then take his money and go home. Never again would he have to spend a night in the rainy woods. Never again would he have to hear the sound of a wolf howling and wonder whether he dared to sleep or not. He had an entire sack full of the madman's money, enough to buy livestock and a fine manor house in south Summerfield along the Brennish border. In fact, with all that gold he could maybe purchase a magistracy—or even a minor title! Theron, Baron of the Stefanian Hills—that was worth a little discomfort, surely . . . !

His musings were interrupted by a sudden shriek from the boy, who danced back from the door of one of the houses waving his hands, and then to Theron's utter astonishment began to *rise into the air.* The pilgrim-master had only an instant to stare, then he felt a sudden sting on his own cheek, another at the back of his head, a third on his arm.

Wasps . . . ! was his confused thought—confused because he knew even as he reeled back, flailing his arms and trying to drive the invisible creatures away, that no wasps in the gods' creation had the power to jerk a boy several handbreadths into the air. After that he scarcely had any time to think of anything.

Something wrapped around his arm as he tried to drive the stinging insects away. Could it be spiders that had attacked them? But the strands were tougher than any cobweb Theron had ever felt. As he snapped one, he felt another wrap around him, then another and another. Still, there was no sign of whatever had attacked him except more stings blossoming painfully on his legs and arms. Theron roared in pain, trying desperately to break free from whatever was binding him. He could hear the boy screeching only a short distance away, and it encouraged him to fight harder. He managed to break through several of the clinging strands long enough to stumble out into the middle of the clearing, away from any of the houses. His employer, the hooded pilgrim, was nowhere to be seen. Theron swiped at his own stinging, aching face and wasted a moment cursing the fellow's cowardice. Something came off in his hand as he rubbed at himself. He looked down to see, not a dying insect, but a tiny arrow or an even tinier spear, its sharp tip still bloodied, lying broken in his palm.

Theron looked up in wonderment and saw the eaves beneath the nearest house boiling with tiny manlike creatures. The boy had managed to snap the cords that had caught him and had fallen to the ground, but from his shrieking and writhing he was still clearly badly beset. Theron could not even curse now—his superstitious terror was too great. He hesitated for a moment, knowing that this might be his only chance to run and make his own escape from the demonic little creatures that were even now swarming by the dozens down tiny ropes, climbing over the boy to wind him with heavier cords and bind him for good. Only the gods could guess what they would do with the poor child when they had him . . . !

Theron glimpsed the depths of his own cowardice but could not go there, could not leave the boy to such a fate. Shouting, he ran barehanded toward Lorgan and tried to pick him up. Tiny men stabbed at his hands as he rolled the boy over, flinging many of them off and crushing others. An attack of sudden pinpricks up and down his neck and the side of his face made Theron shriek in pain. As he slapped at the wounds, several of the invisible strands wrapped around him, binding his hand to the side of his head so that the sudden imbalance made him wobble and then fall across the boy. For a moment, as he lay helpless in the grass, he could see the tiny men come leaping through the undergrowth toward him, little horrors with grotesque faces like festival masks, squealing and buzzing in a tongue almost too high-pitched to hear. Then they were on him, dozens at first, then hundreds. He tried to swat them away as they swarmed over him, but he had only one hand free, and a moment later they had wrapped his other wrist with their bindings as well. Lorgan whimpered and squirmed helplessly beneath him.

Then something smashed into him, knocking him off the boy and sending him rolling through the undergrowth and up against the nearest cottage. At first Theron could see only the eaves above him and the monstrous little men swarming down from their strange nests. One of his hands was still tied to his face, and he had a sudden horror that the tiny creatures would fall into his mouth and choke him. He rolled over and climbed awkwardly to his knees just in time to see the nameless pilgrim swinging a tree branch almost as long as he himself was tall, smashing the hanging nests under the eaves so that the pulpy, barklike material dropped to the ground in great chunks, along with dozens of little, kicking bodies.

The hooded man now began to use the massive branch as a hammer, pounding at the tiny shapes as they darted through the grass, macerating the pieces of the creatures' nests, crushing as many of the little men as he could reach. Theron could sense rather than hear the change of tone in the little men's shrill voices, aggression and anger now taking a sharp upward turn into terror as the nameless pilgrim began to attack all the nests in earnest.

Theron finally tore his hand free of the binding strings—he could see them now, dangling from his fingers, miniature ropes not much thicker than spiderwebs—and got back onto his feet, grunting as he continued to be struck by the occasional invisible dart. He kept himself as low as he could and made his way to the boy Lorgan, then lifted him up and carried him away from the cursed village as quickly as he could go. He stepped on several of the tiny men as he went and did not regret it.

Theron grabbed as much of their baggage as he could hold, dragging it behind him as he stumbled back down the path and away from the houses. Only when he had put the bend in the river behind him and could no longer see any of the cottages did he finally set the boy down and let himself slump to the ground as well, gasping for breath.

By the time the hooded man returned, Theron had found a slightly more sheltered spot and had dug out his flints to start a fire. The nameless pilgrim did not speak, but only settled down beside the blaze so gingerly that Theron could never have guessed less than an hour earlier the man had been slaughtering the tiny little goblins by the dozens. The strange figure accepted a bit of dried meat, taking it in his bandaged hands, which were now stained with new blood. Theron did not think much of it was the man's own.

Lorgan was feverish during the evening, and Theron feared some of the minuscule arrows might have been poisoned, but he himself felt nothing worse than the great lethargy that follows a fight for one's safety. Lorgan moaned and thrashed a long time, but near middle-night seemed to pass through the worst, and from that point on slept quietly.

The boy appeared much better in the morning light, to Theron's great relief. Lorgan's face and hands and arms were covered with welts and pinpoint wounds, many with part or even all of the doll-sized arrows still in them, and Theron had to spend a good part of the early light cleaning the boy's injuries as best he could before he saw to his own. It was clear to him that the time to turn back had come earlier than he had previously thought, but there was no way he was going to risk himself or the boy traveling any deeper into a land that was clearly overrun with madness and the worst sorts of black magic.

As Theron put the last bits of the evening's camp back into his pack, the boy finished talking in whispers with the hooded man and turned toward Theron.

"He wants to know when we will reach Southmarch. He thinks we must be close."

"We?" Theron snorted. "We? We are not going to reach Southmarch. We are turning back."

The boy looked at him strangely, but turned obediently to hear what his master had to say. "He says it is not far—a few days' walk at most, he feels sure. And the gods do not truly oppose our journey, or they would have sent worse than that."

Now Theron laughed, astounded. "Ah! So if we continue we may be allowed to discover what the gods consider worse than being stabbed by a thousand needles and likely roasted and eaten by little goblins? A shame to miss it, but still, I think I will pass."

After another near-silent colloquy the boy asked, "Will you leave us, then?"

"If you mean will I leave *you*, child, no. I am not the best man who ever lived, and often I have forgotten that it is love of the gods itself which has given me my livelihood, but no, I will not leave you to follow this madman into danger and death. Either he lets you go with me or he will have to fight me." But he had seen the hooded man fight now, if only for a few moments, and it was daunting to think of going against him.

Now the boy stared at him for a long time before turning to hear the words of the hooded man. As the child listened, Theron dug into his jerkin and pulled out his purse. A strange feeling was on him, but he felt as though the time had come to do what was right and do nothing else. Strange things were afoot, both in the wide world and right here between himself and this mysterious man. By nearly taking his life the gods had reminded Theron that they were always present. He would not forget again.

"Here, boy," he said. "Come and take the purse."

"He says to you . . ." Lorgan began.

"I do not care. I've not done all that I promised—I haven't taken him as far as Southmarch-town—so I do not deserve his money. It does not matter. He paid me more than generously with the first gold coin, back when he joined the pilgrimage. If he permits it, I will take one more for the trouble and expense of bringing him so far, and if he is mad enough to continue without us, I will swear to find a good home for you, boy, if I do not give you one myself. But we go no farther."

Lorgan's eyes were wide. The boy looked as though he might cry, but it was hard to tell with a face that had already been so dirt-streaked, and was now swollen and blood-smeared as well. He took the purse and conveyed it slowly, as in some ritual, to the hooded man, who accepted it with equal solemnity.

The three of them stood that way for a long succession of heartbeats. The silence was breached at last by the ratcheting call of a jay, which seemed to break the spell.

The nameless man rose, still looking down at the ground as he generally did. After a month of traveling together, Theron had still never properly seen his face, or any of his skin. He murmured something that Theron could not hear, but the boy did.

"He says it does not matter," Lorgan repeated. "He does not need living companions any longer. He thanks you for your honesty. When you die and are judged, as he was, he thinks the judgment will be a merciful one."

Then the man in the battered, dirty robe dropped the purse to the ground and turned away, walking north along the track, back toward the village where they had all nearly died, headed toward Southmarch where it must lie beyond the valley and the hills.

The boy was crying quietly. After the man had vanished into the trees, Theron shook his head and took a few steps forward. He hesitated, then picked up the purse and tucked its jingling weight into his jerkin again. It did not seem important now—nothing much seemed important just at this moment—but the day would come when he would be glad of it again. And at least he could be certain that the boy Lorgan no longer had to live as a beggar on the streets of Oscastle or anywhere else.

Still, it wasn't until the jay squawked again and something answered it from the depths of the trees—some bird or other creature he didn't recognize—that Theron the Pilgrimer shook off his strange lethargy and he and the boy turned south, back toward lands where things made sense.

"No, you fool, put your hand flat against the wood. Now spread your fingers."

Tinwright did as he was told, but it was hard with his arm trembling so.

"Open your eyes, poet." Hendon Tolly made it clear this was not a request. "It takes all the joy out of the thing if your eyes are squeezed shut and teary like a little boy waiting for the clyster pipe." He drew the knife back by his ear.

Other than the lord protector's guards, they were alone in the room known as the King's Counting House, which had for years been the office of the royal exchequer. The walls, paneled in golden fir, were stained with food that the lord protector had thrown against them and pockmarked with ominous, dagger-blade holes.

"Now, watch," Tolly said, and flicked the knife. Despite a slight flinch from Tinwright, it did not harm him, but buried itself nearly two inches deep between the tips of his right index and middle fingers.

Hendon Tolly drew another knife, seemingly out of thin air. "Stay . . . !"

This blade smacked into the wood only a few inches away from the first and stood quivering, almost touching the web of Matt Tinwright's thumb.

Tolly smirked. "By the Knot of Kernios, look at you! Pale as death and shaking like a leaf! What does a poet need all his fingers for, anyway?"

Tinwright swallowed. Hendon Tolly expected to be answered. "For writing . . . ? Remember, you wanted me to write about . . . about your triumph, my lord."

"Triumph, yes. Except that crocodile-swiving autarch is trying to steal it out from under me." A third dagger suddenly flashed through the air so close to Matt Tinwright's face that he could feel the breath of its passage. As it shuddered in the wall beside the poet's head, Hendon Tolly stood up. "He believed I had this . . . what was it called? This 'Godstone.' So perhaps it truly is necessary to the whole enterprise." He pointed at Tinwright. "You . . . you will find it for me."

Matt Tinwright was completely muddled. His hand stung where he had brushed the skin of his thumb against the blade of the lord protector's knife. "Me, Lord? I don't understand."

Tolly looked at the guards along the far wall, who were grimly doing their best to seem attentive to their duty while never looking directly at Hendon Tolly for fear he would notice them; bad things happened to people the lord protector noticed. "You will examine Okros' books and scrolls and find out about this Godstone the autarch needs. You will get it for me."

"But, my lord, I know nothing about such things . . . !"

"And I do?" Tolly glared at him. "Get on your knees, poet. I grow weary of you."

"My lord . . . ?"

"Down!"

Matt Tinwright pushed his forehead against the cold stones of the King's Counting Room. He heard the lord protector's footsteps getting closer, then the sound of one of the knives being yanked out of the wooden paneling. A moment later something cold and sharp slowly traced the spot where his left ear connected to his head.

"It would be the easiest thing in the world to take your ear, poet," said Tolly sweetly, almost as though he were soothing a small child. "Or both of them. What kind of poet would you be then? A deaf one?"

Matt Tinwright didn't bother to point out that he might still be able to hear even with his ears cut off. In fact, he didn't even breathe as the knife tickled his tender skin.

"I have other things I need to do, poet. You can read and you are not the dullest man in my kingdom. I'm sure you can make sense out of all those old, learned fools rabbiting on and on. Find out what the autarch meant. Then find out where the stone is." For a moment the blade of the knife pierced the skin and Tinwright had to struggle not to cry out. "Or bad things will happen—and not just to you. Lest you think you can simply flee my employ and hide from me, you should know that I have a watch on your sister's house. Your mother is living there, too, I believe. It would be sad for them both to be burned for witchcraft in Market Square." Tolly suddenly laughed. "No, I suppose we will have to burn them somewhere in the inner keep, won't we? Too many cannonballs landing on Market Square these days. Wouldn't want the autarch doing our work for us . . ."

Matt Tinwright was struck dumb with horror, not so much at the idea of his mother and sister being burned as witches—although his sister, at least, had done nothing to deserve such a fate—as the thought that if Lord Tolly's men entered the house, they would find Elan M'Cory there, and that would certainly be the end, both for her and Tinwright.

"Of course, Lord," he managed to say at last. "I will do just as you ask. You needn't worry about me or my family."

"Good man." The cold, sharp thing was no longer against his head. Hendon Tolly had turned and was walking back to his chair, allowing Tinwright to breathe freely again. "In a while I will show you to Okros' chambers—I think his books are still there. But first, I have had a thought. Put your hand against the wall again." He settled into the chair, pulled a kerchief from his pocket and draped it over his face. "I think I can do this without being able to see you, but you'd better talk, just to be on the safe side—that will help me aim. Recite something, poet." He lifted the knife.

This time Matt Tinwight did close his eyes. If the lord protector couldn't see, he didn't want to either.

An hour later Tinwright was waiting outside Avin Brone's cabinet, through some miracle still in possession of all his fingers. He could not help feeling impatient. He was off Tolly's leash for the first time in over a tennight and he had many things to do, visiting Avin Brone only the first.

Tinwright had seen no one either following him or watching for him when he left Hendon Tolly, but just to be cautious, he had left and then come back into the residence through a minor gate, then promptly lost himself in the warren of tiny rooms that had been made in the past two centuries out of what had once been the broad heights and expanse of the old King's Chapel on the ground floor. More recently, it had been a school for the sons (and a few daughters) of nobility. Now the siege had driven all the castle's defenders back to the inner keep, and the boxy maze was serving as the lord constable's chambers, crowded with pages and soldiers. Brone, in exile only a month or so before, had been given his own small suite of rooms.

The men in Eddon livery guarding Brone looked very serious—Tinwright could tell this was no sleepy backwater. However much Brone infuriated and terrified him, he had to admit that the man was formidable. Only a few months ago he had been all but imprisoned in his house at Landsend and roundly mocked at court. Now he was back in the thick of things again, his chambers right next to those of Berkan Hood—the man who had replaced him! Brone had outmaneuvered them all. With Olin gone and so many of the March Kingdoms' best dying in battle during the last year, no one else commanded near the loyalty Brone still did—certainly not Hendon Tolly.

"By the three benevolent brothers, where have *you* been, little Tinwright?" said the big man when the poet was finally allowed in. "I've got Perch and Chaffy looking for you with the aim of breaking your legs."

"Hendon Tolly has kept me at his side for the last tennight and more."

Brone only snorted at this and didn't even offer Tinwright a drink (he never did), but underneath the usual bluster, he seemed fairly pleased to see the young man alive and well.

"I'll keep the guards out a bit longer, then, eh?" said the count. He took a comfortable listening position with his sore foot on a hassock. "Tell me everything you have seen and heard, poet. Give me something useful and there's gold in it for you."

Gold? I'll be grateful just to get out of all this alive, Tinwright thought, but of course he didn't say it—he could certainly find use for a few coins of any metal. He did his best to tell Brone everything that had happened, starting with the strange scene in the cemetery and Okros' corpse in the Eddon family crypt, continuing through everything he could remember of his days of personal service to Hendon Tolly. He was only halfway through, and had just finished telling Brone in a slightly stumbling fashion about the lord protector's meeting with the autarch, when the older man did something that astonished him. Brone lifted his hand to silence Tinwright in mid-sentence, then shouted for a page.

"Oyler, bring some food for Master Tinwright," he told the dirty-faced boy when he came in. "And nothing cold and nasty, you little devil. Make sure you take something that's been on the fire."

The boy scuttled out. Then, as Tinwright was already wondering if he'd fallen asleep and was dreaming, Brone lifted a jug of wine out from behind his chair—not without a great deal of grunting and cursing—and poured a cup for himself and also one for Tinwright. Unprecedented!

"When you've had something to eat—you look terrible, lad, by the by—you'll tell me all that autarch bit again, and slowly, so I can write it down. Go on, drink up." Brone frowned at Tinwright for a moment, as if it was the poet who was playing out of character instead of Brone himself. "In the meantime, while you're eating, tell me everything else that's happened since then." He shook his head. "So that was what truly happened to Okros, was it? His wound never looked much like he had been caught under a wall—the Three alone know how many walls we've seen knocked down since those cannons started booming, and how many dead and dying we've pulled out from under the stones. Not to mention that there was no arm to be found. No, I couldn't make sense of it, myself—murder, certainly, but taking an arm off like that, neat as a butcher . . . ?"

Tinwright stayed with Brone for what must have been at least another hour and was likely more. Brone kept asking him questions, which sometimes made him change what he had said before, which Brone would then cross out from the parchment with a great many sulfurous curses before laboriously writing down the new version.

When the questioning was over, Lord Brone told Tinwright some ways he could get a letter to him in sudden need. Then, to make the topsy-turvy evening complete, he offered Tinwright a handclasp of farewell. "You've done well," the large man said. "This is much and much to think about. Try to stay alive. It would mean a loss of useful information if Tolly put a knife in your throat."

This last was much more like the Brone he knew, and in a way it made everything that had come before seem even more impressive. The man hadn't gone mad: Tinwright must have actually pleased him.

After leaving Brone, he had an overwhelming urge to go and see Elan, but if Hendon knew about his sister's house as he had claimed, then the worst thing Tinwright could do would be to draw further attention by actually going there. Since for once he wasn't hungry, he decided to take advantage of this unusual feeling of well being and have a start at the work he was supposed to be doing.

Okros' rooms were also in the residence, only a few corridors away from the old royal chambers that Hendon Tolly had commandeered for his own. The sour-faced guard waiting in front of Okros' doorway wore the key on a chain around his neck, but when he saw the message bearing Hendon Tolly's seal, he sprang to attention. After unlocking the door, he clearly intended to follow Matt Tinwright inside, but the poet told him, "I need to be on my own here. *'It is not enough to see with the eyes of my body,'*" he added, quoting from the Kracian bard Tyron. "*'I must see with my soul as well, or I am no better than blind.'*"

The guard gave him a look that suggested speaking Kracian poetry was a suspicious thing to do even at the best of times, but reluctantly agreed to remain outside.

Tolly had told him that Dioketian Okros' rooms had been left more or less as they had been when he died. If so, Tinwright decided, the physician must have been something less than tidy. The place was in chaos, books and papers piled on every surface, as well as what looked like entire baskets of documents dumped out and scattered across the floor. Tinwright suspected however that some of the havoc had been caused since the scholar's death and that more than a few people had likely rummaged through this chamber in search of any secrets or wealth Okros might have harbored, perhaps even the guard standing outside this moment. Tinwright knew that Hendon Tolly had taken many of the physician's books and artifacts himself on the night Okros died; he would not be able to examine those without Tolly watching over him. This was his one chance to see if Okros had left anything else.

What remained seemed to be divided between the most ordinary and the most esoteric sorts of texts, mostly to do with history and the divinatory arts. The only thing that caught his attention was a volume entitled *The Agony of Truth Forsworn*, which he had never seen nor heard of, but whose author, Rhantys of Kalebria, he seemed to remember having once heard something strange about. Tinwright pulled it from the shelf and then began to look in less obvious places, testing the dead scholar's furniture for secret drawers, even examining the backs of all the cabinets for hidden compartments, but with no luck. While Tinwright was pushing the last of them back against the wall, he did notice something quite extraordinary. On the corner of the top of the cabinet, on a surface otherwise covered in a thick fall of dust, were several strange marks which looked almost exactly like the prints of tiny human feet.

It had to be some trick of the eye, he decided—probably they were only the marks of someone's fingers who had, like Tinwright, been moving the cabinet. Still, it was impossible to look at the half dozen small marks, obscured though they were by subsequent larger and less specific marks, and not imagine a human the size of a clothes peg leaving them behind in the dust like tracks in the snow.

To his great irritation, Tinwright then had to spend long moments quibbling with the guard as to whether he was permitted to remove something from the room, but he relied on his temporary power as Lord Protector Hendon Tolly's envoy and the guard, grumbling, finally gave up.

While he had this unwonted freedom, Matt Tinwright had no desire at all to go anywhere near Hendon Tolly himself, so instead he made his way back across the residence and out to the servants' dormitory near the kitchens where he and Puzzle had for so long shared sleeping quarters.

The jester was half asleep on the cot, a little the worse for drink, but began to move over to make room for Tinwright.

"No, I'll sit up," he told the old man. "I have reading to do."

"I haven't seen you lately," Puzzle said. "I worried about you."

"I've been waiting on the lord protector."

Puzzle sat up now, his eyes wide. "Truly? What good luck!"

Tinwright rolled his eyes, but it was foolish to expect the old man to understand the truth. "I suppose. I do not mean to disturb you, though. I just needed a place to read in quiet."

The jester would not take the hint. "Did you know that Lady M'Ardall asked me to come to their house in Helmingsea and entertain her friends and family? As soon as the siege has ended, they will take me in their coach and all!"

"That's wonderful." Tinwright opened Rhantys' book, trying to ignore the jester, who had apparently decided against sleeping and had begun to rattle off all the interesting things that had happened to him of late—interesting to Puzzle, in any case.

". . . And of course Berkan Hood said he didn't approve of talk about leaving, because, after all, we *are* at war. Have you seen the lord constable lately, Matty? He has been at it less than a year—how long was Brone the constable, a dozen years?—but he already looks like a man who can hear the Black Hound at night, quite pale and drawn and years older . . ."

"I'm sorry, Puzzle, but I truly need to read this." Tinwright had been staring for some time and had not recognized a single word, although it was in reasonably modern Hierosoline. "You should get to sleep now, and we'll catch up in the morning."

"Oh! Oh, of . . . of course." Puzzle gave him a look like a child slapped for some other child's misdeed. "I'll just keep silent. While you're working."

"It's just that Lord Tolly will have my head if I don't . . ."

"Of course." Puzzle waved his gnarled fingers. "It's of no account. I'll just sleep." But when he lay back, he was rigid as a plank.

Tinwright sighed. He knew when he had been defeated—his mother had been the supreme mistress of disappointment used as a weapon. "Oh, very well," he said. "I'll go find a butt-end of something to drink in the kitchen, and we'll catch up."

The old jester clapped his hands and bounced back upright, as pleased as if he'd found the Orphan's coin and sweetmeats in his shoe.

* * *

Hours later, when Puzzle had at last fallen asleep and was happily, drunkenly snoring, Tinwright picked up *The Agony of Truth Forsworn* and began to look through it again. It was hard going—a series of cranky disquisitions on the great errors of history, as far as he could tell, many of which surrounded events of which he had never heard, like the apparently controversial Third Hierarchical Conclave. It was only as his cursory exploration reached the last part of the book that he discovered something which caught his attention, a heretical sect called the Hypnologues who had maintained that the gods did not merely communicate with mortal oracles during sleep, but were asleep themselves. This sect had been persecuted by the Trigonate Church all through the eighth and ninth centuries, and all but wiped out before the arrival of the year 1000, although some related groups had appeared during the madness of the Great Death when many folk in Eion lost faith in the Trigonate Church and other authorities completely.

But what was interesting was that Rhantys, writing in the early 1200s, seemed in no hurry to join in the condemnation of the Hypnologues. He even quoted from many of the Oniri and from passages in the *Book of the Trigon* itself in a way that suggested the heretics might be correct—that the gods might truly be asleep and taking a less active role in the lives of men than had been true in the days when the texts of the *Book of the Trigon* were first being assembled.

Some of this, Tinwright thought, sounded more than a bit like what Tolly said all the time. More importantly, it sounded like what the terrifying autarch had said as well. If two powerful men from different ends of the world both believed in sleeping gods who longed to wake and escape back into the world, maybe there was indeed something to it.

Then his flagging, weary attention was caught again, and this time what he read made his skin itch and his hackles rise.

"The Hypnologues had at the center of their beliefs a tenet that was stranger still—that the center of the religious world lay not in the southern lands or Great Hierosol itself, or even in Tessis, the more recent capital of the Trigonate faith, but rather in the northern territories sometimes called Anglin's Land or the March Kingdoms, and specifically in the keep of Southmarch, the royal seat of those kingdoms. Their faith maintained that the entrances to the domains of the sleeping gods were to be found there, and that, in fact, the very struggle which had led to the gods' insensibility took place there, back in the depths of time.

"Trigonarch Gerasimos, a man who had seen the Korykidons burned alive for pretending to have found the Orphan's birthplace and making it a shrine, was not one to take a challenge to the church lightly, and he anathematized the Hypnologues in his Proclamation of 714 T.E. This did not end the heresy, of course—it would last until the plague era and beyond—but it marked the end of any public speculation about whether the gods were truly watching over mankind . . ."

So it wasn't just Hendon Tolly and the autarch, Tinwright thought, it was an entire movement that the church had tried to destroy. And they didn't just claim the gods were sleeping, but also that this very city—Southmarch, of all places!—had been the site of the kingdom of Heaven. Or something like that.

But how could something so mad be true, even if Hendon Tolly and some maniacal southern king agreed?

Then again, why had the Qar attacked Southmarch even before the autarch did? Why *was* everybody so determined to lay hold of this minor northern kingdom when all of Eion was in play? Clearly, whether he actually meant to help Hendon Tolly or not, there was much more that Matt Tinwright needed to learn.

He fell asleep that night with a hundred strange new ideas spinning in his head, and dreamed of himself tiptoeing through forests of twisted trees in near darkness, with giant slumbering shapes looming up on all sides and no one awake but himself in all the world.

16
A Cage for a King

"With the hidden aid of Erivor they came to shore at last beside a village called Tessideme at the snowy northern end of great Strivothos . . ."

—from "A Child's Book of the Orphan, and His Life and Death and Reward in Heaven"

"YOU CANNOT DO IT, Princess Briony." Eneas could not stop pacing. Perhaps it was easier than looking at her. "I cannot let you throw your life away on such madness—it would be a crime against your people. I am sorry, but I must forbid you to go in search of King Olin."

"And I am sorry too," she told him, "but it's you who don't understand, Highness. You cannot forbid me. I am going to do it. I have not spoken to my father in a year. I will risk anything to see him."

"No!" He turned to her, distraught. "I will not let you!"

"And how will you stop me, my dear friend?" She fought to keep her voice low and calm—she did not want him to think it was some womanly frailty on her part. "Will you imprison me? Will you force your men to listen to me screaming night and day that you have betrayed me?"

"What?" Eneas looked her up and down in something very close to astonishment. "You would not do such a thing." He did not sound entirely certain.

"Oh, I most certainly would. I know it is dangerous, but I must go to him."

The prince threw himself down on a stool opposite her. He looked so miserable that it was all she could do not to take his hand. Eneas was a good man, a very good man, but, like most men, he believed he was responsible for the well-being of every woman who drew breath in his vicinity. "You truly mean it, don't you, Princess? You truly mean to do this."

"I do."

He sucked air through his teeth and sat thinking, toying with his ring. Helkis, his captain, stood near the wall of the tent trying to keep all expression from his unshaven face. "You say I must either imprison you or simply let you go," Eneas said at last. "But there is another possibility."

"Oh?" She tried to sound calm but she hadn't foreseen any third way.

"I can help you not to get caught. I will send some of my best warriors with you . . ."

"No." She shook her head firmly. "That will do no good. I'm not going to fight my way in, Eneas. There are thousands of Xixian soldiers there, but there are also hundreds of local people, Marchlanders, who go in and out of the camp peddling food and drink and trinkets to the autarch's men. And there are other women visiting the camp. I think we all know what they are selling."

Eneas was staring at her with eyes wide. "Are you saying you will masquerade as a . . . as a woman . . . one of those . . ."

"As a whore?" She laughed. "Blessed Zoria, Eneas, look at you! Did you think I didn't know the word? I will not masquerade as anything in particular. I will dress in shabby clothes and let anyone who sees me draw his own conclusion."

"But your safety . . . !" he said, appalled.

She extended her hand. Her Yisti knife was already there, as if by magic. "I can protect myself—Shaso dan-Heza taught me well. Besides, there is no other way. Do any of your men speak Xixian?"

He darted a helpless look at Lord Helkis. "No, I think not. A few words, perhaps . . ."

"Nor do I, so we are not going to fool them that way. It would be stretching the point to try to pass an entire troop of soldiers off as farmers come to sell their onions. No soldiers, Eneas. I will go myself. No one will suspect I am anything but a local girl."

"As if that guaranteed your safety." He gave her a hard look. "I think you have been traveling with the players too long, Princess. You have fallen in love with legends and pretense. Just remember, such things are meant to entertain, not to instruct. In our time, great Hiliometes would have eaten the famous bull, not carried him up the mountain." He frowned. "Very well, then all I can offer you is a distraction. I will not risk my men's lives in a full assault, but there is a deserted village on Millwheel Road just to the southeast of the autarch's camp that his men use as a sentry garrison. If we attack it with substantial force and then withdraw I think we will draw attention and make it easier for you to slip into the camp."

Briony realized how quickly Eneas had shifted his thinking, and she was again impressed. Was there a cleverer prince anywhere in Eion? "You would do that for me?"

"I would do much more, Princess," he said seriously. "If only you would let me."

As the afternoon wore on and Briony prepared, she began to wonder if Eneas had been right: was she really too much in love with old stories? Had she taken the example of Zoria or even her own great-great grandmother Lily Eddon too much to heart? Outside her tent she could hear the men readying themselves for the attack on the Millwheel Road garrison and knew that despite the prince's best intentions some of them might not come back alive. It reminded her of a favorite saying of her father's, "Until you've worn a crown, you have no idea how heavy it is." The thought of Olin sent a pang through her, not just missing him, but thinking about the fierce impossibility of ever living up to his example. Did she really want to put men's lives at risk to satisfy her own need to reach her father?

But what if I never have another chance to see him again? Worse, what if I could have saved him but failed to try? How could I live with that?

She owed it to her people as much as to herself, she decided. The best thing for Southmarch would be King Olin free again.

Still, it continued to trouble her as she used the little hand mirror Feival had once given her and leaned close to the candle. She carefully rubbed wet dirt onto her face, a thin wash to darken and roughen all her features, but she laid it more thickly around her eyes and in the hollows of her cheeks to make her face appear gaunter. She needed to look much older and much less healthy if she wanted to escape anything but cursory inspection. Even here in the camp of the Temple Dogs, where she was protected by the power of the prince himself, men stared at her when they did not think she was looking—even sometimes when they knew she was. A woman in an army camp always attracted attention, unless she was *very* unappetizing. Briony had been thinking all day about what she could do to make herself less interesting and she had a few ideas.

"By the Three, what is that on your face?" Eneas drew back. "Are you hurt?"

She laughed, although she was not feeling very cheerful: the sight of the prince in full battle array had reminded her that she was not going to be the only one taking risks. "It is a wound made from mud and a little berry juice. Never fear, it is not real blood."

"I hope that is the only such thing I see today," he said. "On you or any of these others."

"We may bloody a few Xixies," Lord Helkis suggested with a harsh laugh. "Or even a few fairies."

Eneas shook his head. "No. I will not make that mistake twice, Miron. Until we know better what these . . . Qar are doing, we will treat them as we would treat Marchlanders and will not show harm to them unless we must."

He was a good man. Why could she not feel more for him? "May the gods grant you and your men all come back safe, Prince Eneas," she said.

"And what will help *you* to come back safely, Briony?"

"My disguise," she said, pointing at her face, trying to speak lightly. "And my cunning."

"I pray to the Three Brothers that it will be so." He reached and took her hand before she could think about it, then brought it his lips. "Take care, Princess."

The closer she got to the autarch's camp the more terrified she became. It did not help that the scout who led her over the hills was a taciturn southern Syannese whose thick dialect she could barely understand.

What if I'm captured? I do not fear for myself so much—although she did, of course, how could she not? The autarch's cruelty was legendary—*but what about my people? Do I have the right to risk myself?*

But of course she could not judge that, not from here. She assumed that they needed her or her father back—that the people would be miserable without an Eddon on the Southmarch throne, but perhaps it wasn't true. Perhaps they were even happy with Hendon Tolly!

Still, they're under attack, she reminded herself. *They can't be happy about that.*

As they got closer to the top of the hills, the distant rumbles, which she had barely noticed, became louder; Briony suddenly realized that the noise was not thunder in the cloudy distance but the drumroll of the autarch's cannons—cannons being fired at Briony's home.

She and the Syannese scout were on a deer track at the crest of the hill when the treeline dropped away down the hillside and she could see the broad, gray-green sweep of Brenn's Bay for the first time in months and the mainland city looking surprisingly ordinary with wisps of gray curling from its chimneys. In the distance, through the haze of smoke and low clouds, she could see Southmarch Castle itself.

The smoke was not from chimneys at all, she saw a moment later, but from the cannons the autarch's army had set up atop the mainland seawall and in emplacements along the shore. The long guns boomed over and over, a succession of muffled crashes like irregular drumbeats. The beach where the causeway once joined the Mount to the mainland was a seething mass of tiny shapes, so many of the autarch's soldiers moving there that it looked as if someone had kicked an anthill, but Briony saw little sign of the camp itself but for tents erected in the public squares, as well as in clusters across the open farmlands between the city and the hills. She suspected many more of the autarch's soldiers were sheltering in the city itself, but even just the number of tents was astounding.

All of that? She felt her heart grow heavy and cold. *Sweet Zoria, the southerner has brought an entire nation to our doorstep.* The impossible magnitude of the forces arrayed against Southmarch made her feel sick. The little March Kingdoms could not defeat such a horde even if her father were still on the throne and they had not lost all those men at Kolkan's Field . . . !

Struggling with despair, Briony sent the scout back to Eneas' camp and began to make her way down the hillside.

The sun was gone and the air suddenly turning cold when she reached the outskirts of the camp in the fields. She watched for a moment from a hedgerow and saw that there were still people walking in and out along the makeshift roads the troops had built, but far more were coming out than going in. She did not have much time if she wanted to be unnoticed. Briony joined a small group of peddlers a hundred paces from the guard post, doing her best to walk like an older, frailer woman as Feival had taught her—back and neck bent, head well forward, steps small and careful. The camp was too big to be fenced but four or five sentry posts stood within Briony's view, each staffed with bearded soldiers in pointed helmets, all of them armed with spears or curved swords. She did her best not to hurry as she trudged past the observing gazes of the nearest guards, leaning her weight on the stick she used as a cane, holding her breath in fear that she would be called back, but no one seemed to pay her any attention.

She waited until she was out of sight of the original sentries before speeding her pace a little. The tents spread out on all sides of her, and now she could smell food cooking, spicy scents like nothing she had experienced since she had been driven out of Effir dan-Mozan's house. The soldiers, as far as she could tell without making her staring too obvious, seemed to be of many different types, most (but not all of them) much darker-skinned than she was. Many wore a sort of uniform of baggy breeches and leather harnesses, but she saw other kinds of costumes as well, long, loose white robes that reminded her of the Tuani folk, colorful arrangements of scarves and brass ornaments that looked like something a jester might wear, and even one tall, pale-skinned man wearing black with a snarling white dog as his insignia; except for his pointed Xandian battle-helmet and diamond-shaped shield, he could have been a Marchlander.

The pale soldier, who was talking to a group of smaller, darker Xixian soldiers, noticed Briony watching him and stared back at her. She quickly dropped her gaze and walked on, so flustered that she remembered to limp only after she had taken her first few steps, but when she stole an anxious glance back at him he was talking to the Xixians again.

"He's a bad one," a voice said just beside her, startling Briony so that she almost stumbled and fell. "A Perikali fighting for the autarch, can you imagine? And do you think he'd throw me a copper crab for pity? Not only didn't he, he kicked me, too." The voice came from a small, hunched shape warming its hands over a tiny oil lamp. Briony thought it best to ignore whoever it was and walk on, but the figure called after her, even louder. "Wait! You didn't rub my head. You don't even have to give me any money. We have to stick together, our kind! Wait!"

Every impulse told her to hurry on, but the big, pale-faced soldier was looking in her direction again, as were the Xixians beside him. Briony stopped, then bent with careful gravity, pretending to pick something up from the ground before turning back to the small shape.

"Why are you shouting at me?" she asked, keeping her voice low.

"Because you didn't rub my head, dearie duck. I can tell you're not one of those Xixies, are you?"

Briony had no idea what that meant. She was trying to watch the soldiers without being obvious, but they were still glancing over from time to time, although laughing now. She hoped that was all they wanted out of her, a little amusement. She squatted down beside the small figure as though they knew each other and were passing the time. "Why?" she asked. "What would the Xixies want with you, anyway?"

For answer, the bundle rolled back the saggy hood that had obscured most of its head, revealing a little round face that looked like a child's, but wasn't. "They like to touch my head. They think dwarfs are good luck."

Briony was surprised and spoke before she could think about it. "You're a Funderling!"

The little woman looked surprised. "Well, if I didn't know you weren't a Xixy from the way you talk, I'd know it now," she said. "Usually folk out in the country only know the old stories, but they don't truly know any of us. Did you live in the city, my pigeon?"

"I . . . once, yes." Briony risked a glance. The soldiers were still there. She considered just walking on. It was almost dark now, which meant that the hour for sunset prayer was almost here, the planned moment for Eneas' attack on the garrison.

"He's one of them White Hounds," the woman told her. "That big fellow there in black. Captured and raised by the autarch as children, they are. He breeds them and trains them like hunting dogs. Said they're the cruelest soldiers in his whole army."

Briony wanted nothing to do with the White Hound or any other Xixian soldiers, and the longer she stayed here, the greater the chance that something would happen. "I have to go," she said, bracing herself on her stick as she stood, doing her best to look like an old woman with aching legs.

"You're not from around here," the Funderling woman said, "—and now that I see you close, you're no one's gammer, either. I don't know what your kinch is, mortlet, but it's not worth it, you know. Cheap?

These southerners can squeeze a silver swan until it quacks. I've been here three days, and all I've made is this." She pulled over a cap with a half dozen coppers in it. "See? Tight as Perin's bung, the lot of them."

Briony laughed at the blasphemy despite herself. "What's your name?" she asked.

"I'm called Little Molly."

"That's not a Funderling name."

"No, it's not." She gave Briony another sharp, inquisitive look. "What's yours?"

"Just by a rare chance, they call me Little Molly, too."

Now it was the small woman who laughed. "Well, from now on they'll have to call you Big Molly. But you'll have to find another pitch, dear. This is my spot. See that? That's the beer tent, over there, and they gamble there, too. They'll come and throw in a copper and rub my head to keep the dice rolling."

Briony had an idea. "Can you walk?"

"Good as you!" Little Molly was indignant. "Just not fast. Legs are too short, and . . . and I'm a bit lame."

"Then come with me and I'll give you . . ." she thought about what she had brought with her," . . . say, five coppers. How's that?"

Now the Funderling woman looked suspicious. "What do you want from me? And where did you get so much money?"

So much money! Briony almost wept. Little Molly, despite her cheeky attitude, was very thin and pale, as if she had not eaten well in some time. "Never you mind. Just come with me—I'm tired of those soldiers standing so close."

The Funderling lifted herself to her feet and together they walked down the main track. The little woman went gingerly, as though she were showing Briony how it truly looked to have fragile, weak legs. "Broke them when I was little and they never healed right," she explained. "That's why everyone mistakes me for a dwarf."

"What else can you tell me about the camp?" Briony asked. "Are all the men here or in the middle of Southmarch city? How long have they been firing on the castle?"

"A tennight, more or less," Little Molly said. "But they were here for days before that." She looked around, although at the moment they were in the open and more or less on their own. "They say that the autarch, he met with that Linden Tolly fellow in secret, face-to-face. Some sort of deal they were making, but it fell apart. Then the cannons started firing." She shrugged. "Do you know what you want to know yet? I need to sit for a bit."

"Sit, then." Briony crouched down beside her. Across the bay, the last daylight had lit the top of Wolfstooth Spire as though it were a candle. "I have heard tales that the autarch is holding King Olin prisoner."

"Oh, we've all heard that. Don't know if it's true. Why would he? What would the southerners want with our king?"

Yes, what indeed? Briony wondered. *And we might also ask what game Hendon Tolly is playing—does he want to ransom my father for some reason of his own?* "So you don't know anything about where the king might be kept if they had him?"

Little Molly gave her a hard look. "You ask some strange questions for a beggar-girl. Where's my coppers? I won't say another word until you give them to me, not another word . . . !"

Briony produced a silver coin from the purse hidden under her ragged clothes. "Here. That's worth a dozen crabs at least. Now answer the question, please. Where might King Olin be?" Even as she spoke, she heard a strange, blatting horn call rise above the camp, a signal for evening prayer or else an alarm call—perhaps even the alarm about Eneas' attack. Time was slipping away. "Tell me!"

Little Molly looked around in worried surprise; Briony could hear some of the men shouting to each other. Many others were hurrying in all directions across the camp, perhaps to get weapons or armor they had left in their tents. Eneas had made good his word. Now it was up to her.

"How would I know such a thing?" the little woman moaned. "Who are you? Why do you want to know such things?"

"You would not believe me if I told you, Molly., but I have given you what I promised—now earn it. Where would they keep an important prisoner?"

"But I don't know! The mayor's house in town, maybe. They used to keep prisoners there, I've heard, although maybe that's when the goblins were here. Oh, and the Xixies have built a great pen on the city green for something—animals, everyone thinks. I heard some of the traders talking about it who brought in the metal—twenty wagonloads of iron bars just to make it! Can you imagine?"

Briony rose to her feet. "Keep the silver, Little Molly. May Zoria bless you."

She left the Funderling woman looking after her in astonishment.

The fast-darkening evening was alive now with figures rushing past, with torches waving nearby and in the distance, and men's loud, excited voices. She prayed that Eneas and his men would do as they said, striking only long enough to force the garrison to call for reinforcements before they fled back over the hills. The autarch's troops would never follow them in the dark, and with luck would not send more than a token force to search for them the next day, assuming them to be local bandits or a surprise counterstrike by Hendon Tolly.

What was the purpose of Tolly's parley with the autarch, if that had been more than just gossip—simply the southern monarch demanding the city's surrender? But Hendon would never attend such a humiliation in person. Had he been trying to ransom Olin for some purpose of his own? A chill ran through her. What if the autarch no longer held her father? What if he was in Hendon Tolly's hands now?

Briony had followed the track now all the way to Market Road, where the farmhouses and open land gave way to the true city. Buildings were packed in side by side here and the streets were narrow, which made avoiding soldiers more difficult, but evening had fallen and the encampment's torches were too infrequently spaced to shed much light, which made her disguise better.

Even here, where the soldiers did not seem to be responding directly to the alarm horn, Briony could hear urgency in the voices of the passing men. Some leaned out of upper windows and called to Briony in Xixian; a few even came down to the doors and beckoned her in, but she only waved her hand in thanks and limped along as fast as she dared. Long-legged Dowan Birch had taught her how to keep her sinews loose even as she held a demanding pose which would otherwise quickly exhaust her, so she could continue this awkward, halting gait for a while more, but the constant ache of it was beginning to weary her badly.

She hurried over Grasshill Bridge and past the burned husk of a temple. When she was almost to the green Briony stepped off the main road, doing her best to make sure she wasn't followed. Even in ordinary times the streets around Shoremarket after dark were a haunt of thieves and worse. She made her way a little distance south of the square, then onto the green, walking slowly toward the torches. Their light made the wide thing seem to glow, a sickly pale light like a mushroom crouching at night in the undergrowth.

The tent was a hundred paces across but only a dozen high at the center, guyed by dozens of ropes, a vast, peaked expanse of white that took up much of the center of the green where the city's sheep had always been grazed. Torches blazed all around it, and several solders guarded not only its front entrance but the sides and doubtless the back as well. Briony was a little relieved to see there wasn't much light beyond the ring of torches. As long as she kept a good distance away, she wouldn't be seen while she tried to decide what to do.

She moved as quickly as she could along the edge of the green, staying in the shadows of trees or in the doorways of empty houses, of which there were more than a few. As she had feared, there were guard posts on each side, but the distance between them was large and the corners of the tent kept them from seeing each other. Shaso would have scoffed at whoever set out the sentries, she decided. The fool had made sure a spy would only have to avoid the eyes of one sentry post when approaching the building, which made the guards vulnerable to misdirection, among other things.

Briony did not need misdirection, though, because even as she watched from behind a well at one end of the green, a group of armored horsemen rode past with a great drumroll of hooves and clanging of weapons on shields, headed no doubt toward Millwheel Road and the besieged garrison—reinforcements. The jaws of the trap would close on Eneas soon if he didn't put space between his company and this pack of hounds.

Merciful Zoria, help them find their way out in time! Eneas was a good man—a wonderful, brave man. She cared for him, she had to admit, more than she sometimes realized. A thought struck her. *And help me, too, sweet goddess, please!* She had almost forgotten to pray for herself. She wondered if Zoria could be bribed and decided it couldn't hurt to try. *If the Eddons regain the throne, I will build you a beautiful temple, Mistress!*

As the reinforcing Xixians thundered by the men at the tent's nearest guard post stepped out to watch them. Realizing that she would never have a better moment, Briony ran down the length of the green, waiting until the reinforcing troops had almost passed the tent. Then, with the guards now facing almost completely away from the nearest corner of the great tent, she broke from the trees along the edge and sprinted across the green, head held so low she had to fight against stumbling all the way. But perhaps Zoria had decided to accept her offered bargain. No one raised an alarm, and a few long moments later Briony was crouched near the corner of the tent where the light from the torches was dim, breathing far harder than she should have been just from running. She was terrified, but did not have enough time to consider that fact: she scrabbled at the bottom of the tent and found, as she had hoped, that there were bars beneath. She slid herself under the heavy fabric of the tent until she was squeezed between the canvas and the cold iron bars like a bed warmer slid between coverlet and mattress. There were some small lights at the far end of the tent, but it was otherwise dark beyond the bars, and the air stank of unwashed bodies so badly that Briony, who had been living among soldiers, still nearly squeezed herself back out of the tent again, despite the risk of being spotted.

As her breathing and the tripping of her heart slowed, Briony heard a sound very close by, a woman or a child quietly weeping. A moment later her breath caught at what sounded like murmured words in her own tongue. What prisoners were these? Was it some kind of brothel of captured Marchlander women? For a moment she entertained a feverish fantasy of waiting for the autarch here and stabbing him when he came to ravish another victim, but she knew even as the anger burned through her that it was a foolish and useless idea—the kind of scene that Nevin Hewney would have written after drinking too much.

"Who's that crying?" she asked quietly. "Can you understand me?"

The weeping abruptly stopped.

"Where are you from?" she asked. She had given herself away now; she couldn't turn back. If only it wasn't so wretchedly dark! She had no idea how this prison tent might be set out—was it one big cage? Or were many separate cells grouped here under the ghostly tent? "Won't anyone answer me?"

"Frightened," a small voice told her from somewhere nearby. "Want to go home."

"What's your name?" she asked. "Why are you here?"

"Men took us. We'n been doin' nought wrong. Came into village and took us, uns did."

"Where did they take you from?"

"Mam?" said another voice, slightly older. "Did you come for us? Will you take us out from here?"

Zoria's heart! Why had the autarch stolen Brennish children? "And you're all prisoners?" Her heart seemed clenched like a fist. "Are there any grown-ups in here? An older man?" Would they know who her father was? "A king?"

"No king," the small voice said, sniffling again. "Just us littl'uns."

Before she could ask more questions, a sudden light flared on the other side of the pitch-black tent: someone had pulled back the flap and now stood in the opening with a torch. Briony crouched. More torches, more silhouetted figures—then the light dazzled her, and she had to look away. Briony stayed very still until she heard voices and the clang of an iron door opening and closing on the other side of the huge structure. The torches withdrew and the flap dropped, leaving the interior of the great tent pitch black again. Could the guards be looking for her?

"Can anyone else tell me if they know anything about why you're prisoners, or whether the king of the Marchlands is one of the prisoners?"

When there was no reply Briony began to make her slow way around the exterior of the cage, still beneath the tent. She had to cross one doorway, but to her relief the flap was down and, judging by the voices of the guards, none of them were even looking back at the tent they were guarding. At last she reached the place where she judged the torches had been, the main entrance, but stopped short of the doorway.

She took a breath, but there was no sense hesitating, nor did she have the time—the guards might be coming back any moment. "Hello? Who's here? Can anyone hear me?"

The voice, when it came, made her skin prickle all over. "What . . . ? Meriel?"

"Praise Zoria! Father, is that you?" She pushed herself as close to the bars as she could. It was all she could do not to shout. "Father? It's me! Oh, the gods are kind! Father!"

Suddenly, she could feel his presence. His hand came through the bars and found her face, which was already wet with tears. "By all the gods . . . ! Briony? Is that truly you?" Olin's voice was hoarse, but it was undeniably his voice. "This is a miracle beyond belief! I was almost asleep . . . I thought . . . your voice; I thought it was your mother. Am I truly awake?"

"Yes, Father, yes! It's me!" She clutched at him—he was so thin! Still, it was really her father, after all that time, clearly and plainly *him*. "I never thought I'd see you again!" She laughed through her tears. "I mean . . . I still can't see you . . . !"

He was also laughing. "Are you well? What are you doing here? Gods, child, this makes no sense at all! Are you here by yourself?"

"I heard the autarch was holding you. I came to . . ." She couldn't bear to waste time talking about it. "It's a long story. But we have to get you out of here!"

"No, it is you who must get away from here, my lamb. They will be back soon to return me to my usual prison. They only put me here because someone attacked an outpost, and Vash feared it might be an attempt to rescue me. The autarch is out of the camp this evening and his minister is terrified something might go wrong while he's away."

"All the more reason to get you out now," she said.

"It's not possible, Briony. This is not simply a barred enclosure—it's a cage, with bars on top and bars on the bottom that are sunk in the earth." He kept his voice low, but she could hear stirring among some of the other captives. "I do not know exactly what the autarch plans, but he is obsessed with Southmarch and thinks somehow if he can take the castle he can awaken a god. Are you with Shaso or Brone? Can you tell them that?"

Briony laughed, but it was painful. "Shaso is dead," she said. "I'm sorry, Father, but he was burned in a fire in Marrinswalk. Brone is either a prisoner in the castle or a traitor—maybe both. Hendon Tolly is holding the place, but I hear he has been bargaining with the autarch about something."

"Then how did you get here? Are you with Barrick?"

"Never mind. We have to get you free." But suddenly Barrick's name was working in her like a spark slowly growing into a flame.

"You can't! It's too late for me, my dear one. But you must not be caught. Get away! Get away before the guards come back."

"No." And now it was burning inside her, a fire she had kept banked for months. "Why did you lie to me? Why did you do that, Father?"

He sounded surprised but not shocked. "What do you mean?"

"You never told me about . . . your curse. About Barrick. About what happened that night his arm was broken." She bit her lip, fighting the tears again. "Why did you lie to me?"

Long moments passed. Her father had been holding her arms, but now he let go and even took a half step back from the bars. "I'm . . . sorry."

"But why? Why didn't you tell me? Why didn't you tell us?"

"I was ashamed, girl! Can't you understand? Ashamed that I passed my tainted blood to those I loved most in the world. Ashamed that I almost killed my own son!" His whisper was hoarse. "And now it is beginning again."

"What is beginning?"

"The poison! The poison in my veins—I can feel it again. Oh, merciful gods, Briony, I might have been a prisoner for much of the last year but I at least I was free of my cursed blood! Can you understand? For the first time the madness that used to afflict me nearly every moon did not touch me. But as we drew closer and closer to the castle—to my own home!—the affliction returned. Even now I can feel the gall boiling in my veins . . ."

"But I would have helped you! You should have told me! We could have found a way to cure it—Chaven would have found something . . . !"

"You cannot cure someone of their own blood," the king told her in a bitter murmur. "Not unless you slit their throat and hang them up like a slaughtered pig."

Briony began crying again. "Then it's my curse, too, Father. You had no right to keep it from us."

"Don't you see?" He came back to the bars then, caught her shoulders, and pulled her against the cold metal so that he could put his cheek against hers. "I would have done anything I could to keep it from you. You and Kendrick showed no signs of it."

"But what is it? Why us? Why the Eddons?"

"Because of love," he said. "Because of treachery and death, too. But mostly because of love." And then he told her a tale so astounding that for a few moments Briony forgot everything else and thought of nothing but her father's pained voice.

"We have . . . fairy blood?" she asked when he had fallen silent at last. "The Eddons . . . ?"

"The Qar claim it is the blood of a god," Olin said. "That is what the autarch believes as well. That is why he keeps me, he says . . ."

"To do what?"

Her father tried to explain, but at last shook his head—she could feel it moving violently against her hand. "I do not understand it all for certain, but remember—we have only until the midnight at the end of Midsummer's Day to prevent him—he has told me that hour is when this will all take place. It's only a scant few days away now." He hesitated; she could feel him deciding not to frighten her more than he had to. Had he always been so transparent to her? Or was it Briony herself who had changed? "Quickly," he said, "while we still have time, tell me all your news about . . ." But he never finished the sentence. Voices were approaching the tent from somewhere behind her. Olin quickly stepped away.

"Hide," he muttered. "Quickly!"

She had barely an instant to back away from the spot and hide before the tent flap flew back and a guard stood in the opening with a torch. As Olin turned toward the light, she saw her father for the first time and her heart flooded over with love for him. He was so thin! A group of children were ranged behind him, almost a dozen in all, sitting or lying down on the straw piled at the bottom of the cage.

Briony watched a tall, thin old man in a minutely decorated robe step in beside the guard. He gestured and another guard began unlocking the bars. "Tell your young friends that if any of them come too close to the bars, they will be killed," the old man said. "I want no trouble, King Olin. It is time for you to go back. Whoever those bandits were, they have fled. The White Hounds are after them and will make short work of them."

"I prefer not to go back now," said her father, his voice pitched a little louder than it needed to be. "I like it here with the other prisoners. They are but children, you know—no one has showed them any kindness at all. I thought better of you, Vash."

"I do the autarch's work, King Olin. And I credit you for your sympathetic heart. but that is all the more reason you must go back—I do not want you fomenting revolts among the children." He said something in Xixian to the guards. The lock clanked and the door creaked, and Olin let himself be led out by a guard at each arm.

"Very well," her father called back over his shoulder, as if to the other prisoners. "Just remember, I love you all. Have courage—there's hope as long as you remember who you are!"

Briony was weeping as the flap fell back. The guards were long gone before she dared to move or speak again. A few quiet conversations proved that the child-captives could tell her nothing interesting. She felt terrible leaving them to their unknown fate, but there was nothing else she could do. At the next distraction she slipped out of the tent.

I love you, too, Father. Briony hurried across the darkened green. With luck, she would be back in Eneas' camp by midnight and they could think of a way to save King Olin. *If love has cursed our family, perhaps it can save us as well.*

17
Defending the Mystery

"The village was in mourning because so many of the young men of the town had died during the Great War between the gods, which the church calls the Theomachy. The castaways were welcomed with great kindness . . .

—from "A Child's Book of the Orphan, and His Life and Death and Reward in Heaven"

"THEY ARE TOO MANY!" the young Funderling shrieked as he rushed past. His face was dirty and flecked with blood, and he had dropped his weapon and shield somewhere. "The autarch's army has overrun Moonless Reach . . . ! Run!"

Ferras Vansen turned to grab him, but Malachite Copper was equally determined not to let the soldier's panic affect anyone else. He caught the fellow's arm first and hit him hard with a flat hand on the side of the face. The Funderling soldier stared at Copper in surprise, took a wobbly step, then crumpled and fell to his knees.

"Now get up, man, and show that there's some mortar where your stones don't fit true. What's going on?"

"Forgive me, Master Copper . . . !" The young fellow was terrified—it was clear that all he wanted to do was to keep running.

"Give us your news," Copper said, "like the sworn apprentice to the Stonecutter's Guild that you are."

The soldier's lip trembled, but he did his best to harden his expression; it was a less than perfect show. "They've broken down the last barrier, and they're driving Jasper and the rest back like sand fleas, Master Copper. It was terrible." He turned to Ferras Vansen and the others as if they had disagreed. "Terrible! Flames and something like burning oil all over—people screaming . . . and the smell, Masters, the smell . . . !"

"What could that be, Physician?" Vansen asked. "Chaven, did you hear?"

"Ah, ah, what are we discussing? Yes, the flames, that would be some blend of naptha and resin." The physician appeared slightly befuddled, as though he had only been half-listening. "War Fire, as they used to call it in Hierosol." He turned to Vansen. "There is nothing you can do against it except try to douse the flames, but they burn cruelly hot."

"I do not believe that," Vansen said. "There is a defense against any weapon—Murroy used to tell me that."

"Who?" The physician looked surprised.

"Never mind." He turned to the frightened soldier, who had calmed a little. "Do you bring any message from Sledge Jasper? Does he live?"

"I . . . I do not know, C-Captain." The Funderling looked frightened of Vansen now, finally realizing how badly he had acted. "When the guardhouse came down . . . and then we were attacked . . . I should have . . ."

"But you thought you were the only one who could carry the news," said Cinnabar Quicksilver, who had been silent thus far. "We understand, son. Was Dolomite still holding his section when you went past? Think. He was? Good—now go and find the quartermaster's fire, and he'll give you something to drink and a place to lie down. We'll get help to Jasper and the rest."

"Th-thank you, Magister."

As the young soldier limped off, Malachite Copper had already begun finding reinforcements to help Sledge Jasper and the rest keep their withdrawal back to Ocher Bar from turning into a rout.

"I wish you had not done that, Magister," Vansen quietly told Cinnabar. "He deserted his fellows. He did not even wait to see if his commanding officer had survived . . ."

"These are not true soldiers, Captain," Cinnabar reminded him. "They are brave men, but they have not learned the ways of an army. I don't think they will, either—we just don't have the time. But I will do my best in the future to let you discipline them as you see fit."

Now Vansen felt a little ashamed. He was not a Funderling so he could not understand them—was that what Cinnabar was trying to tell him? Ferras Vansen swallowed his resentment. This was not the time.

As more of Jasper and Dolomite's troops arrived, they told a story much the same as the first frightened warder's, but with an unexpected ending.

"The autarch's men did not follow us or press their advantage as we fell back," the survivors reported. "They did not even follow us down the passages toward Ocher Bar and try to keep us from reaching the rest of you here!"

Vansen could make little sense of it. "They had the perfect chance to destroy almost half our force as we retreated. Why not?"

When Dolomite and Sledge Jasper at last returned, limping and bloody but more or less whole, they confirmed what the others had been saying. They stood with Vansen and the rest looking over the maps Chert had made, trying to understand the southerners' intention.

"See, they have come under the bay from the mainland on Stormstone's secret road, the Great Delve," Malachite Copper said, making a few quick strokes on the map with a piece of charcoal. "But if they wish to move on Funderling Town and then continue up to the castle, why should they turn down through Iron Reach? That way leads nowhere except into the depths."

Cinnabar frowned. "They will not even be able to circle around behind us without a great effort and much engineering. They would have to go miles through the narrowest of tunnels to come at the temple any other way!"

Vansen's eyes grew wide. "Perin's Hammer!" he swore. "So it's true—the autarch is headed for the Mysteries themselves!"

"Which leaves us little time to make a terrible decision," said Cinnabar. "Leaves *me* little time, to be frank, since I carry the Astion here for the Guild." He frowned in dismay. "Another few hours and the autarch's men may have driven down past us here in Ocher Bar. After that we will be unable to accomplish anything more than harrying them from behind." He hung his head and stared hopelessly at the maps. "What other choices do we have? Captain, where are these fairies who claimed they were our allies?"

Vansen knew enough of Cinnabar now to know how agonizing this responsibility was to him, and also how few men of any height he would rather have trusted to make the judgment. "The Qar have sent no word yet of what they plan, but I'll send another messenger to them. Then we can only wait," Vansen told them. "But in the meantime, Magister, you must decide what your people will do next. Let the autarch go by, and concede them the Mysteries while we retreat to defend Funderling Town?" He raised his hand as Cinnabar and Jasper both groaned aloud. "I know that cuts you to the heart."

"It is the Funderlings' Mount Xandos," said Chaven suddenly and loudly. "Their holiest place."

"I know," Vansen told him. "Let me finish, Chaven Makaros. We can let them go and save our small force to protect Funderling Town, or we can make a stand below Five Arches and try to keep them out of the Mysteries. We would at least have the advantage of knowing the terrain."

"But with the numbers and weapons they have, they will overwhelm us at last," said Malachite Copper. "No matter how well we fight, they will push us back—that is inevitable."

"Yes, and when they push us, we will give way," Vansen said, "— but slowly, and we will kill as many as we can. If we cannot win," and suddenly he thought of his family, nearly all lost now, and the princess who had been lost to him from the moment of his humble birth, "well, then, I would just as soon die here with you lot as with any others."

"You honor us, Captain Vansen," Cinnabar told him with a sad smile, "but are those truly our only choices? Give up our most sacred place or resist and be massacred? That is grim." He reached into his pocket and withdrew a shining circle of black stone, reverently touching it to his chest before setting it down on the table. "You see that I have taken out the Astion—the seal of the Guild is now on all our talk. Let us hear more about each choice . . . and do not hold back your opinions! I won't sleep well no matter which I choose, but like anything painful that can't be avoided, I say the sooner broken the sooner mended. By the Elders! I wish Chert Blue Quart was here, since we also have that mad proposal of his to consider." Cinnabar sighed. "Ah, well, nothing to do but make cement with the sand we have. Tell me all so I can decide how we should die."

Ash Nitre was the younger brother of Sulphur, the temple's most ancient monk, but that certainly didn't make him young: Chert thought he looked a bit like one of those dessicated frogs sometimes found in a pocket of metamorphic stone. Brother Ash's mind seemed lively, though, and his movements were, if not graceful, at least purposeful. This was important because he was in charge of an operation that would kill scores of Funderlings if it went wrong.

"I don't understand you, boy," Nitre said—the first time Chert had been called that in as long as he could remember. The monk wore eye shields of thick mica crystal—his eyes seemed big as silver coins. "What do you want with more blasting powder?" He gestured to the open area behind him where at least a dozen temple brothers were busily engaged. "I've already got my workers making as much as they can for bombards. . . ."

"But we need more."

"How much?" Nitre asked.

Chert had made calculations, but he did not trust them very far. The problem was, blasting powder had never quite been used this way, so it was very hard to guess how much was necessary. Chert would have liked Chaven's help—the physician knew a lot about many different things—but he was hard to find these days: Chert assumed he was busy helping Captain Vansen.

"Well, Blue Quartz? I do have work to do, you know." Nitre and the temple brothers he employed were in charge of the dangerous task of crafting the blasting powder in careful allotments, because it was dangerous to store—too dry and any spark might set it off, too damp and all the labor of mining the materials and making the deadly black powder had been ruined. Already, with the need to store large quantities to make into weapons, the Funderlings had moved into unknown territory. They were about to move farther in that direction.

"Perhaps . . . two hundred barrels?"

Nitre's eyes went so wide behind the eye shields that his lids and lashes disappeared. "Two *hundred*? Did you say 'two hundred'? Are you mad? I am laboring to produce half that much—you cannot simply shovel these powders together, you know! Have you ever seen a rocket like the ones the upgrounders shoot into the sky during the Zosimia festivals? Imagine something hundreds of times that strong, in our confined spaces down here. . . ."

"Yes, yes, I know." Chert took a deep breath and produced Cinnabar's letter with the imprint of the Astion prominently displayed. "Nevertheless, I need as much as you can make for me, as quickly as you can make it."

"Ridiculous. Sorry, Blue Quartz, but it simply can't be done. You tell the Guild they would have to send me another two dozen workers just to sift powders. And I know, because of my own requests that they cannot do that—they do not have even a man to spare."

Chert sat for a long moment in silence. It had been a very strange idea in the first place, a last-ditch sort of thing. He could not expect to pull workers away from making powder for the fighting, especially when the situation seemed to be growing more desperate by the hour. As the monk had said, there simply weren't enough workers.

"I have a question, Brother Nitre," Chert suddenly said. "Is there any reason blasting powder has to be made by men . . . ?"

"I fear this decision," said Cinnabar Quicksilver. "No matter what we do, something will be broken beyond mending."

Brother Nickel made an unhappy noise, a cross between a sniff and a grunt. He had been summoned from the temple, which had not pleased him, but the discovery of what was being decided pleased him even less. "Seems to me," he said now, "that we Metamorphic Brothers have already seen our lives and peace broken beyond mending, and we have not complained."

"By the Elders, Nickel, you have done nothing *but* complain," said Malachite Copper. "And now that the decision is on us you want to complain again before you have even heard it!"

"Peace, you two," said Cinnabar. "You are not making this any easier. Chaven, you have said almost nothing the whole time we have discussed this. Have you nothing to offer?"

The physician blew out air. "I wish I did, Magister Quicksilver. Either way, we will all do what we must."

Cinnabar clapped his hands. "Then as the bearer of the Astion, speaking on behalf of our sovereign Stonecutter's Guild, I feel we have no choice—we have to fight them and fight them now. We must try to keep them from the Mysteries.

"I know that the odds are terrible—if I were a wagering man, I would feel a fool to put a single copper chip on our chances. But everything we have heard says that the autarch has a fascination with our sacred depths, and priests and wizards with him who have filled his head with ideas about gods and black magic. We cannot take the chance there is truth to their ideas. And, more than anything else, we cannot give up our holiest places without a fight. The Elders in their stony beds would curse and condemn us, and who could blame them?

"No, we must resist them as best we can. We are only a thousand, perhaps two with the men still coming, but we will have the Qar beside us—I think you have all seen their mettle." He lowered his head for a moment, picked up the Astion and stared at it, then tucked it back into his shirt. "We defend the Mysteries. That is my decision."

"So the temple is to be abandoned . . . ?" said Brother Nickel, but he sounded more resigned than angry.

"We will leave some token force," Cinnabar told him. "But if the autarch behaves as the Qar say he will, he'll show little interest in the temple or even in Funderling Town."

"This underground invasion is not meant to deliver the castle," said Vansen. "We can see now that it's the thing Sulepis came here to do. He broke great Hierosol in a matter of weeks. I find it hard to believe he could not do the same with Southmarch itself, at which point everything beneath it would be his as well, and he could starve us all out. So there is clearly some hurry to what he does, as Yasammez and the Qar suggested, something which drives him swiftly forward when there might be easier ways to reach his goal."

Copper turned to Vansen. "Why aren't the Qar here at this council, Captain?"

"I can't tell you." Vansen stood. "The Qar—as always, I suspect—will come in their own time. What is important is that we now have Magister Cinnabar's decision. If you'll pardon me, I have much to do and time is short—the southerners will be moving again soon." He turned to the others. "We will meet here after the hour of the evening meal. May the gods protect us and protect Southmarch. And Funderling Town," he added quickly.

"We will certainly need help from somewhere," said Chaven.

"The Qar must come," Vansen said quietly, almost to himself. "We will fail without them."

18
Exiles and Firstborn

"Old Aristas was soon celebrated in Tessideme for his wisdom and little Adis for his piety. They lived together in a hut beneath a vast, leafless oak tree, and the village folk often came to them and asked them to speak of the gods' ways."

—from "A Child's Book of the Orphan, and His Life and Death and Reward in Heaven"

THE BOAT LIFTED AND SAGGED on the waves of Brenn's Bay, and the silhouette of the castle grew ever larger against the moon. Barrick's vision seemed much sharper than he remembered, even from the previous night. The very stones of the castle's seawalls seemed to glow; not with light but with intensity of color and detail he could see even in the evening dark from hundreds of ells away. And as his eyes moved across every crack in every stone he could feel the history of the place breathing out at him from the depths, amazing true tales of the gods and their servants that sprang from his deepest memory as if they had grown there in the dark like mushrooms.

Ancient stories told that Hiliometes himself had entered here once, tasked by Mesiya the moon goddess to steal the golden hawk that watched over her and kept her a virtual prisoner of her husband Kernios. And in an earlier day, before mortals had even come to the land, Erivor had fought the monstrous serpent-bull Androphagas here and stabbed it to the heart with his barbed spear. Some claimed that the body of Androphagas had become Midlan's Mount, but the Elementals declared that the Mount had been here always.

The Last Hour of the Ancestor, as the Qar called Southmarch, was a place that only a few of the Twilight folk had visited in recent centuries, but it was old and strong in their lore. Their knowledge of it—as well as their fear of it, and their fierce, painful longing for it—enfolded everything Barrick saw like a heavy mist, but with Ynnir's largely silent help, he was learning ways to live with it. Back in Qul-na-Qar he had stopped thinking almost entirely so that he could cope with the strangeness of these new memories; now Barrick Eddon was beginning to take his first cautious steps toward letting the Fireflower become a true part of him.

As he stared at the shadowy walls and the jumbled granite boulders of the shoreline, wondering how they would enter a castle under siege, Barrick suddenly realized where they were going—it all but bloomed in his head. "The Sea Postern," he said out loud.

Saqri turned to look at him and then returned her serene gaze to the water. The moonlight behind her made her look as still as a painted wooden figurehead.

The walls now loomed high above them. Rafe carefully began to bring the pitching boat in close to the boulders of the breakfront, which were stacked in haphazard piles like the telling-stones of giants. As the side of the boat scraped on granite, Rafe reached out one long arm and found something beneath the water, then tied his boat to it. A moment later he had clambered up onto the piled rocks, a dim, tall shape that began to turn into stories of the entire Skimmer race if Barrick stared too long and too incautiously. Rafe climbed a short distance and then grabbed a wide, irregular chunk of stone that looked a little like a juggler's tenpin, bigger near the water than at the top, bottom hidden in the splashing waves. The young Skimmer reached around behind it and popped something loose—a hidden latch that protected it against being moved by tides and storms.

"Hold tight, all you," Rafe said. " 'Be a splash."

He swung his weight against it, and the stone began to tip downward. Barrick knew what was going to happen but it was still astonishing to see. The stone toppled slowly toward the water, but with the slow precision of one of the bronze Funderlings on the great Market Square clock swinging his bronze hammer. The stone itself was only the visible half; a stone counterweight of almost exactly the same weight lay underneath the water on the other end of the ancient lever, so that a single strong man or woman could open the Sea Postern if they only knew where the latch was hidden.

The stone tipped down into the bay heavily enough to make the boat bob like a curl of bark. Rafe made his way back to his craft, untied it, and steered it through the opening. Before they had drifted more than a few yards past the opening the young Skimmer tied the boat up again, then caught a rope that hung down from the darkness above and swung easily onto a stone in the middle of the narrow watercourse. His weight on it pushed it beneath the water, which brought the other stone back up to cover the entrance, and suddenly all light was gone but for a tiny gleam trickling down from above. Other than the black watercourse beneath them, they were entirely surrounded by stone.

Rafe got back into the boat and lit and hung a lantern in the bow, then used one of his oars as a pole to move them through the narrow crevice. Barrick felt completely encased, as though the stone that surrounded him were the body of a living thing, a sleeping ogre or dragon.

But Southmarch *was* a living thing, he realized for the first time. It was not the Qar voices that told him so, because to Fireflower phantoms everything in the world was as alive or dead as everything else—being "dead" or "alive" was, they seemed to feel, a largely meaningless distinction. Barrick didn't know why he suddenly knew it, too, or why it seemed so significant, but Southmarch was indeed alive, and in a way that almost nothing else was. It was alive because it was full of doorways, and it was full of doorways because it was curiously, even uniquely alive. The gods, the Qar, even the late-coming humans, had not *made* this place the heart of so many happenings. They had all come here because the place itself was as vital as a beating heart.

How had he lived here all his life and never known that? How had his own ancestors lived here for so many centuries and not recognized it? Because they could see only the colors they had been given to see. But now that had changed, at least for him.

Barrick could see it now, at least a little, but could he make sense of it? And would it make any difference if he could?

The short trip along the watercourse was a dreamlike inversion of their trip from M'Helan's Rock, but the waves that rose above them this time were not made of water but of dark granite sprinkled with white limestone foam. They followed their own lantern light through a tunnel of naked rock until they found themselves at last prevented from going forward by a heavy iron grille set in a wall of dressed stones. On all sides, stone-and-clay water pipes opened out of the walls, although in this season they all seemed dry.

Rafe gestured toward the heavy grille, thick with rust and mud. "Beyond lie the backwaters of the castle, under the Lagoonside houses and suchnot. Then comes the lagoon. But you'll not be going there. Far too dangerous for such as you, Your Majesty." He looked at Barrick and frowned in confusion. "Your Majesties, I should say, Egye-Var's pardon on me."

"And so . . . ?" Barrick asked him.

"We wait." Rafe seemed pleased to be able to announce this. He sat back in the bow with his long, thin arms crossed. The Rooftoppers in their box murmured in anxious voices to each other, so that Barrick felt as though he sat beside a hive of sighing bees. "Some are coming to lead us the rest of the way."

They did not wait long. Barrick heard their approach even before Rafe did, and saw them as they approached the end of the pipe, their little torches glowing; none brighter than an Orphan's Day taper. It was another crowd of Rooftoppers—hundreds, as far as he could tell, crowding up against the lip of the pipe.

Rafe stood up abruptly, which made the small boat rock, then lifted out the box and its surprised passengers. He put it down carefully on the brick ledge beside the canal and opened the door along its bottom. The first Rooftopper guards filed out, looking around warily, followed shortly by the impressive if slightly rumpled figure of Duke Kettlehouse.

A squadron of Rooftopper engineers, as if prepared, dropped a ramp into place to bridge the difference of height between the end of the pipe and the brick ledge, then the rest of the Rooftoppers made their way down it, most on foot, but a few dozen seated on hopping birds. The last one to hop forward was the most decorated, and its passenger wore a tremendous headdress on top of her curly red hair. A tiny man stepped out in front of her and held up an equally tiny speaking-trumpet. "Greetings, Saqri of the Fireflower, great Queen. Her Uproarious Highness Queen Upsteeplebat of Rooftop, Wainscoting, and Rooftop-Over-Sea bids you welcome back to your home, Saqri of the Ancient Song."

Welcome *back*? wondered Barrick, but then a moment later he saw it as if he had been there himself—which something that was now part of him had, he realized—the young Saqri, slim as a birch tree, hair dark as the space between stars, walking along an ancient passage that wound down into the depths beneath Southmarch . . . Beyond this image, like a succession of mirrors looking on the reflections of other mirrors, the daughters of Crooked's blood, all the queens of Qul-na-Qar, stretched back along those same stairs, each one individual, but also part of a single, many-legged thing that spread forward and backward through time . . . or at least backward.

Because there may never be another, said a voice in his head, a clear, familiar voice. *It ends with her . . .*

Ynnir? he asked, if one could truly ask anything of another part of one's own heart and thoughts. But the blind king's presence was gone again.

"You are kind, sister," Saqri said in her calm, quiet voice. Far below her, Upsteeplebat smiled as Saqri continued: "It has been too long since our two peoples met in concord."

The gathered Rooftoppers, even Kettlehouse's people, made little murmurs of approval and contentment. Barrick could only guess how important it was to such small creatures to be treated as equals.

The little queen took the speaking-trumpet from her herald. "We have much to speak about," Upsteeplebat said to Saqri. "But first we have other business, if you will forgive us."

"Of course." Saqri nodded.

"Duke Kettlehouse—my dear uncle, you are most welcome back!" said the Rooftopper's queen.

Kettlehouse stepped toward her as her grooms helped her down from her beautiful gray dove. She waited for him as he approached, then watched as he at last knelt before her. "I thank the Lord of the Peak heartily for this happy day."

The little queen bent and threw her arms around the bearded man's neck, encouraging him to stand, then kept her grip on him for a long moment. "Too long have the tides splashed between us," she said. "Now our family is whole again."

A great cheer went up from the assembled Rooftoppers—Old Duke Kettlehouse even seemed to be weeping, but he waved his arms and shouted, "So be it! Huzzah for the Wainscoting! Huzzah for the Great Green Drapery! We are one again!"

"Come, then," said Queen Upsteeplebat when the shouting had died down, remounting her dove. "We have prepared a place for all of you in the tunnels beneath the castle. We will settle you and feed you, then we shall talk of how we can aid you, great Queen of the People." She turned to smile at Barrick as well. "You and the other noble guardian of the Fireflower." She waved and the entire contingent of Rooftoppers, mounted and afoot, men at arms, women, children, and old people mounted back up their ramp and into the circle of the great clay pipe. The engineers stayed behind to dismantle their ramp, but even they finished and left in what felt like a very short time.

"Where did they go?" Barrick said.

"We will see Upsteeplebat again, and soon," Saqri told him.

"But why didn't they . . . why aren't we . . . ?"

"Didn't say we were waiting for *them*, did I?" said Rafe, who had hung back during the meeting. "Just said we were waiting."

"So who are we waiting for, then?" Barrick asked, but Saqri did not answer.

Rafe spoke in her place. "Somebody else," he said, grinning. "Oh, aye, somebody *well* else."

❧

The farmer's wife was reluctant to let Qinnitan go. "Are you certain, child? If you stay, you can eat with us again tonight."

Qinnitan wished she spoke the language better. "No. But thanking. And for the carrying, thanking, too." She clambered down out of the wagon. She had encountered this Blueshore farming family on the road and had bartered the dead priest's donkey to them for lodging, food, and clothes during the time it had taken them all to reach this town on the eastern edge of Brenn's Bay. The farmer, who was asking a port reeve where in Onir Beccan's fish market the wagon could be set up, nodded to her. Three of the family's four children were asleep after the long day's ride, but the oldest shyly waved farewell.

She walked through the center of the town but passed by the market, continuing instead until she reached the town walls and could look down at the port, which stretched away north for a little distance along the intricate coast of the wide bay. Surely somewhere in this muddle of ships, she could hire someone with the money she'd stolen from Daikonas Vo who would take her away from here without asking questions. If Vo had been carrying her to the autarch's camp at Southmarch then she would be happy to get on almost anything going in the opposite direction. But what after that? She could never set foot in Xis again—to do so would almost certainly mean death. But Hierosol, the only other city she knew, was also in the autarch's power. Where else could she go?

Qinnitan stared across the bay toward the sunset skies over Southmarch Castle. Every now and then a dim thump flew to her on the wind—it had only just occurred to her that she was hearing cannons firing. Those must be the autarch's guns, the same ones Sulepis had used to level the walls of Hierosol. And here she stood, separated from him only by the width of the water! She flinched a little and took a step back, as though he might suddenly reach out all the way from the farther shore.

Anywhere but here, she told herself. *Anywhere but this close.*

The Onir Beccan Market was the best and biggest fish market in all of Blueshore, and the healthy portion it took from all the catches sold there by fishermen from all the cities along Brenn's Bay had been enriching the ruling Aldritch family for at least two centuries. It was a bustling, successful place, oddly no less so now even with war on its doorstep, and it was the first real city she had seen since Agamid. As Qinnitan walked through the marketplace between arguing Blueshoremen, hurrying cooks, ostlers and innkeepers and drunken Marrinswalk sailors, she was reminded of the seafront in Great Xis, a place she seen only once since she was a child, on the night of her escape from the Seclusion. Perhaps it would not seem so impressive now, but as she remembered the port's mad crush of people and the sights and sounds and smells that could exist together nowhere else on earth, she felt a terrible pang of homesickness for the places where she had grown up and the people she had known as a child. But her parents had all but sold her, she reminded herself, and her childhood friend Jeddin had nearly gotten her killed, so what exactly was she missing?

Still, she had certainly been happy at the docks. She remembered one time she had gone with her father when he had to speak about a job for her older brother. While he was talking to the dock factor, little Qinnitan had wandered off and spent a blissful time alone in a world of dreams and miracles and mysteries. She had seen a man selling monkeys and another selling parrots, and then one of the monkeys had got loose and climbed up among the parrots and what screaming and shouting there had been!

She had also seen a real witch, a woman being carried along the waterfront on a litter by two bearers, an old, cruel woman weighted down with necklaces of gold, with a face like a sea turtle, and everywhere she passed, the people behind her turned away and made the pass-evil sign, or spat on the ground.

Qinnitan had also seen a man dancing on crutches even though he had no legs, and another who could set his skin on fire and then blow it out again, both performing for coppers. She saw children singing and dancing, too, and many of them did not seem to have parents. Young as she was, she had still been a little envious of them.

Now, ten or more years later, far away from her home or even any thought of having a home, she again touched the feeling from that long-ago day, being alone but not lonely, of being solitary and yet sufficient. Because what else was there to . . . ?

Qinnitan banged into something and suddenly found herself tangled in a heavy cloak or cloth. Her arms caught, she lost her balance and fell, and something large stumbled over her, driving her knee and elbow into the stony cobbles so that she cried out in pain and even cursed a little.

It was only when the man yanked his cloak away from her, almost knocking her over again, that she realized she had collided with a soldier and made him fall. His friends, three more soldiers, helped him up.

She was confused and frightened by the way they all stared at her, but it was only when one of the soldiers said, "She curses in the name of Nushash!" in perfect Xixian that she realized she must have said something in her native language.

Before she could even begin to guess what four Xixian soldiers were doing in a fish market in Blueshore, they had surrounded her.

"What a funny thing to find in the middle of nowhere," another soldier said, also in flawless Xixian, accented ever so slightly with the vowel sounds of the southern desert. "A sweet little girl from home. She could be your sister, Paka."

"Watch your tongue," growled the one who must have been Paka. "This little whore is no sister of mine." He grabbed Qinnitan's arm and began to hurry her across the wide market. "But she does have a few questions to answer. Don't you fools remember? We're supposed to have our eyes out for girls this age who speak Xixian—that's straight from the Golden One's minister. If you'd let her go, we'd have been facing the torture-priests."

The other guards, trotting after him now, lowered their heads and muttered in shamefaced piety at the mention of the autarch's name.

Qinnitan could not believe her ill luck. Panicked, she tried to break away, but Paka the sergeant had her tight.

"No use struggling," he told her. "You'll just get hurt."

When they came out of the darkness at last it was not in martial procession like the Rooftoppers, but in a small group—Yasammez, dark as a crow's wing, her chief eremite Aesi'uah (the name drifted into Barrick's thoughts like an echo), and two hulking shapes—*Deep Ettins*, the Fireflower whispered to Barrick, the largest of them no less important a figure than Hammerfoot of Firstdeeps.

For a moment Saqri and her many-times-great-aunt only stood looking at each other, then Saqri stepped toward her and extended her hands to Yasammez. Their fingers met and they both stopped again, but what passed between them was deeper than any embrace. It went on and on, a river of meaning passing silently between them.

Barrick watched, unmoving. Rafe the Skimmer caught his eye and grinned as if this momentous reunion were some kind of surprise the Skimmer youth had arranged all by himself. The giant Hammerfoot's expression was harder to read, even with the whispers of insight that flooded Barrick's skull, but it was not hard to see dislike and distrust in the creature's deep-sunken eyes and sour expression.

Saqri and Yasammez finally stepped away from each other, so Barrick could compare them side-by-side. The family resemblance was unmistakable, but so were the differences: although at first glance neither of them looked to be out of the prime of womanhood, Saqri had a softer, more rounded face. Yasammez had the look of a predator, her nose strong, her cheekbones high and sharp, her eyes tilted up at the outer corners as if she stood in a perpetual wind. Her black armor—she wore every piece except a helmet—added to her dangerous appearance.

Now she looked Barrick up and down. "I could not have believed that the Book could contain such a strange chapter, yet here you are again." Yasammez spoke aloud, each word like the chime of cold steel. "I had meant only to show Ynnir what the sacred Fireflower had come to in the veins of mortal murderers, but he has bested me again. The Lord of Winds and Thought must be the cleverest coward who ever lived."

"He is no coward," Saqri said calmly, "and it is too soon to assess what he has done, but it seems premature to judge his actions."

"You always had a soft spot for your brother," Yasammez said. "Even when I told you he would bring destruction on all our line. Can you pretend I was wrong?"

"As I said, it seems too early to judge." Saqri bowed her head for a moment. "But I would prefer not to argue with you in any case, my great and beloved. Let us see what we have and what we may yet do. Later there will be time to talk of who was right and who was wrong."

Yasammez could not have made her distaste for this more plain, but still her pale face remained as expressionless as a mask beneath her tangle of dark hair. "Later there may be time only to die," Yasammez said. "However, that is not the way to greet kin, and not the way I wish to greet you, my only heart." And without saying anything more she turned and walked away into the shadows. After a moment, Saqri and Barrick followed.

"I'll just go and tell my folk that it's all begun, shall I?" Rafe called after them. "Tell them to send folks as like to flap lips to join the war council."

Barrick didn't know what to say, and none of the Qar seemed to feel a need to reply.

"Right, so," said the Skimmer cheerfully. "I'll get to it, then."

They were beneath Southmarch—beneath even Funderling Town! Barrick had never suspected there was anything beneath the Funderlings' underground city except stone. Surely they must be in the very roots of the earth now!

As Barrick sat on cushions on the floor of Yasammez' tent, with Saqri and the tent's mistress again locked in deep, silent communication, he could feel the whole history of the place, or at least as much history as was known to the last Qar who walked the same earth as the gods did. He knew that Kernios—Earth Father—had met his end here at the hands of Crooked, the clever god whom mortals called Kupilas. He knew that the cavern in which this tent stood, surrounded by the Qar camp, had once been known as "Glittering Delights," and had served as the garden of Immon, the gatekeeper, although that version of the cavern was no longer visible (or at least only appeared at extremely irregular intervals.)

Saqri sat up straighter. She had put on something more martial, a less spiny version of the armor Yasammez wore, its cream-colored plates trimmed with different shades of gray and blue. "I do not know why you still keep so much hidden from me," Saqri said, and the fact that Barrick heard her say it was evidence that she wanted it heard.

"Because you are not yet yourself." Yasammez' tone was stern but Barrick's deepened understanding could also detect a note of unhappy need—almost a plea.

"May I know the subject?" he asked. "Perhaps Lady Yasammez—to whom I am grateful for having my life spared, of course—now thinks I would have been better off as a dead example than as a live prince. But I am here, and for better or worse your Fireflower now burns in my veins—*mine*, Lady. So please, talk to me if you value my goodwill. I grow tired of wondering what's afoot."

Saqri actually smiled, although it might have been purely perfunctory. "Wait only a few moments more—talking, in large part for your benefit, Barrick Eddon, is just what we are about to do. . . ."

Even as she said it, folk began filing into the large tent, silent and watchful as deer, although with some the silence was distinctly more threatening. Elementals swathed in runecloths but still leaking radiance, bright-eyed Tricksters, Changers, Stone Circle People (each of whom might have been the twin of little Harsar back in Qul-na-Qar) goblins and drows and Mountain Korbols all entered in groups of two or three and spread themselves along the perimeter of the tent. They were followed by a contingent of Skimmers. Rafe was one of them, and he was carrying the box from his boat. Although the light in the tent was dim, Barrick could see at least a dozen Rooftoppers standing at the rail of the box like passengers on a ship watching for the approaching shore.

But where are the Funderlings? he wondered.

"Hear me!" a loud, clear voice said from behind them in the ordinary tongue of Southmarch mortals. It was Aesi'uah, Yasammez's chief eremite, but her mistress did not even look up as the counselor spoke. "On behalf of my lady Yasammez, I bid you lay down your weapons and your feuds—all peaceful folk have safe welcome in this house." The words echoed in Barrick's mind, a time-lost traditional greeting, a memory of more warlike days that now seemed to have come again.

"The Autarch Sulepis' army is outside the castle walls," Aesi'uah continued. "He has brought machines the world has not seen since the gods' day, great guns that smash the stone like a hammer. He has bred monsters. He has even bred living children of the Exile to use like beasts, all so that he can raise the god he thinks is Whitefire—Sulepis calls him Nushash—from eternal sleep and force him to wield his matchless strength on the autarch's behalf." She bowed her head for a moment. "He has studied and prepared carefully. We believe he has the power to do just what he intends."

"But how could he command a god even if he could wake one?" said a Skimmer man, standing up. "Egye-var speaks to us through the sisters and the Scale, but we could no more tame him than we could tame the watery ocean itself."

"The southerner believes he has a way to force the god to do his bidding," said Saqri, speaking up from her seat beside Yasammez. "The ripples of his exploration—with apologies to Turley Longfingers and his beloved ocean—could be felt in the Deep Library, and even by some of the more sensitive still among the living." She paused in an odd way, and Barrick suddenly sensed that she spoke of herself—that her own long, long sleep and the dreams that had come with it had not always been peaceful or pleasant. "We do not know how this mortal plans to control a god, but we believe after everything else he has done, it would be foolish to assume he cannot accomplish it."

"So, if it pleases my fellow monarchs," little Queen Upsteeplebat called out through her speaking-trumpet, "what is the point of our all being here? The autarch has already plunged down past these halls and is moving in the deeps with his men, forcing his way downward to the Funderlings' sacred place—to the Shining Man."

"It is *not* only the Funderlings' sacred place," said Saqri. "No matter which gods we chose to follow, he who is prisoned in the Shining Man saved us all from continuing enslavement. Without him, the gods would yet rule us."

"Would that have been so bad, Mistress?" asked Turley the Skimmer. "Our god speaks often-like to us and it's done us naught but good."

"It could be that you misremember what it was like when the sea god could take a more active interest in things," Saqri said. "But I will grant that he was always the most peaceful of the brothers—his power came not just from his strength but also from his wisdom. In any case, it is not the return of the gods we fear, though it is something worth fearing, as much as the more frightful idea of a mortal madman controlling an immortal's power."

Aesi'uah spoke again, relating things Barrick had already heard but with new details which had clearly been learned only recently, like the story of the autarch's visit to M'Helan's Rock and conversation with Hendon Tolly, which the Dreamless woman now reported word for word in her calm, clear voice. She, and occasionally Saqri, also spoke of things Barrick had not heard, or had heard only imperfectly, retelling the tale of Crooked and his destruction of the gods in such a way that it seemed almost entirely different from the version the raven Skurn had told him, full of strange details which raised quiet Fireflower echoes in his thoughts.

From time to time the Skimmers and the tiny people called Rooftoppers chimed in as well, and Barrick began to grasp how little he had truly known about his father's kingdom, especially its capitol, when he lived in Southmarch.

"A question occurs to us," Queen Upsteeplebat said at last. "Where are the Funderlings? Where are the stonecutters? The children of Egye-Var are here, as are those of us who worship the Lord of the Peak. . . ." She gestured to her Rooftoppers. "But where are the minions of old Karisnovois, King of the Mud and the Rock?"

Aesi'uah turned to look at her mistress, Yasammez, but it was Saqri the queen who spoke instead.

"That is part of the reason we are here," Saqri told her. "The Funderlings are at this moment far below us, fighting to protect the deep place they call the Mysteries from the autarch and his thousands—the place we call Ancestor's Blood."

"What do you mean, fighting? Below us?" Barrick didn't like the sound of that at all. "We sit here talking when this autarch is already in the depths?"

Yasammez stirred. "Too late to pretend innocence, last bearer," she told Barrick coldly. "Come out and speak or hold your peace." After this cryptic remark, she stared at him for a long moment, then lowered her dark, dark eyes once more.

"We would hear the answer that this young man seeks," said Upsteeplebat. "But first we would know his name."

It was bizarre for Barrick to realize he could be in a meeting of nearly a hundred souls in his own castle—or at least beneath it—but not be recognized. He bowed toward the tiny, handsome woman. "I am Barrick Eddon, son of King Olin, Majesty. I am a prince . . . now the only prince . . . of Southmarch."

The murmur of surprise that rose seemed laced with more than a few angry mutters. Most of the latter seemed to be coming from the Skimmers. Turley, their leader, turned to Barrick with a worried look.

"Your pardon that we didn't recognize you, Prince Barrick. My daughter speaks well of your family—especially your sister, whom she helped leave the castle."

"My sister? Briony?" It had taken a moment for his sister's name to come to him. Briony seemed . . . *diminished* now, somehow, her place in his memory and thoughts smaller than it had been in the past, as though a mist had flowed between them. "Is she truly here?"

"She lives," said Saqri. "But I cannot discover where she is. These days the restlessness of the sleeping gods disrupts all the gifts of Grandmother Void, but what have become most difficult are far-seeing and far-talking." She spread her hands—*The Sea is Calm.* "Later I will tell you all I know . . . but right now we have more pressing matters than even sisters and brothers." She looked at Yasammez as though she would say something to her ancestor, but then turned back to the rest of those watching. "The Funderlings and the men who fight with them are far below us in the place they call the Maze, making a stand against Sulepis and all his men and monsters. The hour is fast dying when we can still help them directly. Thus we come to what we think will be the final struggle."

"But that is why we have joined together," said Upsteeplebat through her speaking-trumpet. The tent quieted so everyone could hear her. "The Exiles and the Firstborn, the commoners and the high ones of the Fireflower—we have joined together to fight for our home. Why do we waste time talking?" She pulled a tiny streak of silver from a sheath and lifted it high. "I pledge my sword as a token of my people's willingness to risk their lives in the service of this goal."

The roar of shrill cheers from the box was drowned out by Turley Longfingers, who rose yet again to say, "All well and good, but why should we? What benefits *our* clans when we could be away before the next tide and find elsewhere to fish and ply our crafts?"

"There is more to a decision to fight with us . . ." Saqri began, but Yasammez abruptly rose to her feet beside her, swift and ominous as a black cloud scudding in from the horizon.

"The water-man is right that this is no fight for his people," Yassamez declared, "but he is wrong about the reason." She looked around the room from her thicket of armored spikes, her anger almost visible. Some of the mortals actually cringed as her gaze touched them. "The reason the Skimmers should not fight—that *none* of you should fight—is because there is no point. Victory cannot be snatched from the jaws of this failure because these are the final moments of the Long Defeat. Ancient apologies should be made and accepted by those . . ." she looked directly at Saqri," . . . who believe in such things. But the rest of you might just as well return to your families to spend your last hours with them. There is no cure for this disease. There is nothing ahead of us but death." Her long pale fingers rose to the ember-red stone on her breast. "So I declare as holder of the Seal of War." She said this not in anger, but with calm and horrifying certainty. "Those who ignore me will learn soon enough that I speak the truth."

And then Yasammez turned and walked from the tent, leaving open mouths and silence behind her.

19
Mummery

"The north was almost empty of men in those days because of the great cold that had followed the Theomachy, after Zmeos, the jealous god of the sun's fire, was defeated by his three brothers, Perin, Erivor, and Kernios . . ."

—from "A Child's Book of the Orphan, and His Life and Death and Reward in Heaven"

FERRAS VANSEN COULD BARELY sit still. "Where are they? Where are the Qar? I thought we had an understanding!" The fearsome Yasammez was beyond anyone's understanding, of course, but her councillor Aesi'uah had as much as promised Vansen that the Qar would fight side side by side with Vansen and the Funderlings—after all, what else could the Twilight folk do?

"I do not mind waiting a little while longer for them," Cinnabar said. "It will give me time enough time to put on my armor. Where is my son, Calomel? He was going to help me with it." The magister shook his head mournfully. "I have not worn armor since my youthful days in the warders. Even if it will still fit me, I fear I misremember which strap goes to which buckle . . . Calomel? Where are you, boy?" When the Funderling youth appeared, his father said, "Go and get it all for me, son. It's time." Calomel trotted off.

The guards brought the Qar's messenger to Vansen and the other commanders.

"Spelter?" said Malachite Copper. "They sent you?"

Vansen glanced up in surprise as the drow entered the makeshift command post. He liked Spelter, but why should the Qar use a humble military scout as their envoy when so many others like Aesi'uah could speak the mortal tongue just as well?

The bearded man bowed, a quick downward flick of his chin. His inscrutable, vulpine face seemed even more blank than usual. "Magisters, Captain—I bring you greetings from Lady Yasammez."

"I am glad to have her greetings," Vansen said, "but what I need is to know what's in her mind. She gave me to understand the autarch was her enemy, too. He is not stopping, and we are falling back to protect the Mysteries."

"Yes, we know," said Spelter, nodding once.

"Well, then? Is she coming? Will your mistress stand beside us as she all but promised?"

For a brief moment Vansen glimpsed the unhappiness that had been hidden in Spelter's dark eyes, perhaps even the twist of a frown in the drow's beard, and his heart went cold.

"No, Captain," said Spelter. "She is not."

"What?" Cinnabar stumbled forward, his vambraces dragging on the floor. "Not coming? But we gave your mistress sanctuary in our own tunnels—we gave you *all* sanctuary when the autarch came! And this is how she pays us back? Leaving us to fight alone?"

"I am sorry, Magister." Spelter turned to Vansen and nodded a salute. "Captain." He kept his back rigid and his eyes staring ahead, even when there was nothing before him to stare at; a soldier was a soldier, it seemed, even among the Qar. "I regret bearing this news. You are brave allies. I can say no more. Good luck."

Vansen watched the drow walk back across the chaos of the breaking camp. A few of the Funderlings watched him with superstitious fear. Only half a year ago the drows and the Qar had been stories to excite and frighten young children. Now they were real.

Real, but cowardly, Vansen thought in sudden rage. He should have known that Lady Porcupine was too proud and spiteful to be able to overcome her hatred of mortals—he should have known! Now it was he who had betrayed his allies by promising them help that would not come. . . .

"Balls of the Brothers!" he spat, full of fury and shame. "Cinnabar, I've failed. I'm prepared to hand the command to Copper right now if you'll let me."

"You'll do nothing like it," said a startled Malachite Copper, coughing up some of the water he'd been drinking.

"He's right," said Cinnabar. "You'll do nothing like, Captain. We hung you on the marshal's hoist because you're the best for the task." He reached out blindly to take another piece of armor from his son Calomel, but his hands were shaking. "You've done nothing to show otherwise. By the Elders, Captain Vansen, do you blame yourself for the Qar not coming? If you had not risked your life to make treaty with them, we'd still be fighting them as well as the filthy, fracturing autarch!" Cinnabar looked upset. "Sorry, lad. Don't tell your mother I said that in front of you."

Young Calomel brightened considerably.

Vansen shook his head. "Do not be so quick to exonerate me, Magister. Perhaps the Qar and the autarch would now be fighting each other if I hadn't interfered."

"Still and all," said Copper, "don't be foolish. No one else would have done differently, but you were the only one who *could* do it, in any case."

"Once more our old friend Copper speaks the truth," Cinnabar agreed, waving his hand. "Enough. Except to say that not only won't we let you out of your responsibilities, Captain Vansen, my people will long remember what you did for us." A moment later, he added, "If the Elders decree that my people survive, that is."

Vansen, who had already been mulling his own version of this, nodded. "A wise soldier never presumes that the gods will reward good intentions." He felt about to drown in his own misery. "Well, if the fairies aren't coming, I suppose we need wait no longer. Anything else left to finish here?"

"Me." Cinnabar, tongue between his teeth, was busy with his high-collared chest plate.

Calomel reached up and helped his father tie the knots. "He's almost ready, Captain."

"And he looks very handsome, our Cinnabar," Malachite Copper said almost cheerfully, as if they had not just been told they were fighting alone. "Not in the least like a fat townsman who has forgotten everything he learned in the warders."

"Yes, I'm sure one sight of me and the autarch's men will all run," said Cinnabar, but no one had the heart to laugh.

He had become an animal, a thing of rough, matted hair and sharp teeth. He could smell her. He knew that the soldiers had taken her across the water—he had her scent and it told him everything. He could even smell the warm blood that would gush forth when he caught her and began to bite and tear . . .

Daikonas Vo shuddered and blinked. No. He was not an animal. He was a man, even if it was getting harder to remember that sometimes. He looked at the crowd of people around him. Some of them were staring. He could only guess what he looked like. But what was he trying to remember . . . ?

It came back. The girl. The girl from the Seclusion. He didn't smell her, that was only his madness speaking, but he had seen the soldiers take her and march her onto a boat headed back across the bay toward Southmarch. He knew where she was going—to the *autarch*, the wonderful, powerful, treacherous, murderous autarch . . .

It was important to remember the truth and defend against madness. If Vo lost control, he knew he would become an animal in truth—a dead one, as forgotten as any cur left to rot by the roadside. But there were moments he did feel he could smell the girl, no matter how far away she was—he could almost picture her scent wafting behind her as she ran, trailing in the air like a broken spiderweb, dissolving slowly but lingering just long enough to coil about him like mist, leading him on . . .

He stopped himself just before he began howling. The sun was bright, and his head felt as though it had been split by a stoneworker's chisel. The people around him had drawn back, and many were staring at him in apprehension—he must be talking to himself again.

Vo put his head down and began to walk.

She had tried to kill him. That memory helped to keep him going when the pain almost became too much. It was not the worst thing she had done, of course—in fact it was scarcely important at all except as a reminder of how slack he had been. But in trying to murder him she had poured all his sweet black medicine away, the one thing that had quieted the gnawing monstrosity the autarch had left in Vo's guts. Now the agony grew in him by the hour. Vo had tried other remedies since he had lost his boat, wild simples he had picked in the forest and eaten, and later, when he had reached villages and small towns again, things he could get from apothecaries and healers, simply stealing when he could, killing without hesitation when he had to. But even the most learned of these country healers knew little more than the name of Malamenas Kimir's healing liquid—they certainly did not have any. If he had not been certain beyond doubt he would be dead before he reached Agamid and Kimir's shop he would have started back there already; instead he had only one chance to end the burning pain in his guts: he might still be able to convince Sulepis of his usefulness and be released from this endless torture.

So Daikonas Vo walked across the waterfront of Onir Beccan toward the place the ships docked, ignoring the local apothecaries because he could not afford the time or distraction. Every hour it seemed to become harder to think. Sometimes his mind was nothing but a black cave of screeching bats. Sometimes his legs cramped so badly that he dropped helplessly to the ground, but he always got up again.

Somebody was making strange noises. Growling and wheezing, mumbled words.

It was Vo himself, of course. He laughed a little through the pain. It was strange being mad, but he had been through worse.

Vo had been trying to ignore the pain that burned in his gut like a blazing coal while he watched the small ship he planned to board. A crane swung barrels of supplies up onto the deck as half-naked men pulled the ropes and shouted at each other. Could he manage? It seemed unlikely: to judge by the number of Xixian soldiers on the deck the autarch's army had commandeered the Blueshore cog outright, which would make it hard for Vo to slip aboard unnoticed, especially in his present condition.

It was only after he had reluctantly decided to wait for another ship that he suddenly remembered the parchments that old Vash had given him—the autarch's writ. The whole memory seemed strange, as though it had happened to someone else, but the documents had served him well when he commandeered the first ship in Hierosol, and could do so again . . . if he still had them. . . .

Fortunately, Daikonas Vo had not had the wit for most of the last month even to remember the oilskin pouch hidden behind his belt, so it was still there. The documents were still there, too, although a bit smeared and hard to read after his unexpected swim from Vilas' boat to the Brennish shore. Still, the falcon glyph of Sulepis III was unmistakable, and the bright vermilion ink showed that it was no mere copy but a document approved by the autarch himself. With the waterlogged parchments clutched tight in his fist he headed toward the cog, reminding himself not to howl no matter how hot the sun felt or how his gut burned him.

The *mulasim*, the officer who came down when the guards at the top of the gangplank called him, was one of those old hands Vo had seen a thousand times. While the *mulasim* looked skeptically at Vo's documents, the soldiers behind him stared at Vo himself. He couldn't even imagine what he looked like, but the part of him that could think through the pain knew it must be bad. They might not doubt the documents themselves, but they were bound to wonder if he had stolen these from the real messenger.

"Hear me," he said, summoning what felt like a great deal of strength to speak calm, sensible words. "I have taken tremendous injury in the autarch's service. I have critical information to give him which he needs *this moment.* I have sworn my complete loyalty to the Golden One. If you refuse to take me to his camp, I will have no choice but to kill you all, then eat your hearts and livers so that I have the strength to swim across Brenn's Bay."

Something about the way he said it must have been convincing. When the ship left Onir Beccan on the evening tide, Vo was on board, with a great deal of the deck to himself.

Despite the dangers—and they were many—Matt Tinwright felt exhilarated to be out of the royal residence at night and on his own. Of course as bad as the inner keep had become it was still was nothing like the outer keep, which was so crammed with hungry, terrified people that walking across it at night would be taking your life in your hands even were it not for the destruction being rained down by the autarch's cannons and the dangerous ruins left in the wake of the cannon fire.

Two days of freedom in a row! Tinwright prayed that Hendon Tolly would continue to be distracted just a bit longer.

He had considered waiting until late to try to sneak into his sister's house, but the inner keep was almost as crowded with refugees as the outer; if he went during waking hours the noise from the camps would be good cover. He went through an empty shop and climbed out an upstairs window, then clambered across and dropped into a knacker's yard, also deserted. From there, he made his way into that building and then climbed the stairs to the room at the top that his mother shared with Elan. He watched the street for some time, but could see no one obviously keeping an eye on the place.

To Tinwright's disappointment, it was his mother who answered his discreet rap at the shutter. She had her triskelion clutched tightly against her stomacher until the shutter was halfway up, then she thrust a fist holding the chain through the gap so suddenly that she hit Tinwright in the chin as he was about to speak.

"The Brothers abjure you, foul demon!" cried Anamesiya Tinwright, then struck him on the ear with the triskelion.

"Sweet Zosim Salamandros, woman, what are you doing?" He tried to keep his voice down, but it still came out in a muffled shriek. "You've bloodied my nose! Let me in."

"Matthias, is that you?" His mother stepped back as he half-clambered, half-fell through the window. "What are you doing at the window, you fool? I thought you were a demon!"

He sat on the floor collecting himself for a moment. "I am not. Do we agree on that? Or would you prefer to hit me again?"

"Matthias?" It was Elan this time, calling not from the bed but from a stool by the table where the single lamp burned. She had been sewing, and she looked so pretty in his sister's simple clothes that it took him a moment to realize what she had called him. Not Matt, or even Matty, but Matthias. What his mother called him.

"Yes, it's me." He got up and dusted himself off, wiped a few drops of blood from his upper lip, then walked over to give Elan's hand a kiss. "I've come to . . ."

"Do you have my money?" his mother asked. "It was the tennight three days ago."

It was all Tinwright could do not to shout. He had to remind himself that there might very well be spies, even armed soldiers, watching the building. "I have been more or less Hendon Tolly's prisoner, Mother, kept at his side morning and night."

"Oh, so you truly are coming up in the world." His mother smiled with pleasure. "We heard, but we were not sure . . ."

"You poor man," said Elan. "Can you bear it? Is he cruel?"

"I don't want to talk about it." He sat down cross-legged beside her. "How are you, my lady? Is it too hard for you living in these . . ." he looked at his mother," . . . rough circumstances?"

She laughed. "With what is going on around us? Did you know that the Erilonian shrine just one street over was blown into firewood by a cannonball? I am fortunate to have a place to live and people to help me." She smiled teasingly. "Your mother has been very kind."

"Oh, I have been filling Lady Elan's head with the wonders of the temple and the stories of the gods' kindness. She is all but signed and dismembered to become a Trigonate Sister."

"Signed and delivered," he said offhandedly. "I see now that I am not the only one suffering. You do not have to listen to her, Elan. She is used to her speeches being ignored."

This time, the young woman's smile was calmer, more genuine. "No. I like to hear of it. I think I might indeed find some peace, someday, in holy orders . . ." She saw the stricken look on Tinwright's face and misunderstood it. "No, truly, I do not say it simply to please your mother."

Anamesiya Tinwright nodded happily. "Lady Elan knows that the gods punish wickedness, and that the only way to avoid punishment is to do what the gods wish. . . ."

"But you have told us nothing of what brings you," Elan said, cutting across his mother's preamble. "Tell us your news, Matthias."

"Ah!" He sat up. "You have reminded me—I brought you something." He dug into the pocket of his doublet, where he had been carrying it next to his heart. "Here. It is a book of prayer with images of the life of Zoria." He handed it to her. "It once belonged to Princess Briony. I found it in the chapel."

Elan looked at it carefully, but she seemed less than ecstatic with the gift. "It is very beautiful, Matthias. Look at the paintings! Such skill!" She turned the pages slowly, then handed it back. "But I cannot accept such a gift. It belongs to the princess and if she comes back, she will want this lovely thing again."

He was surprised and confused. "But . . . surely she would not begrudge it to someone who . . . who has suffered as you have suffered . . ."

"No, thank you. It is a kind thought and a lovely thing, but I can't accept it." She would not quite meet his eyes. "It belongs to someone else."

"But what am *I* to do with it?"

She shook her head. "I do not know, Matthias."

He was so disappointed that for a moment he considered leaving it there and walking out, but his mother was watching him with such a poorly-hidden expression of satisfaction that he changed his mind and put it back in his breast pocket again. "I will think of something, then. Perhaps I'll offer it at the Zorian shrine."

"Have you any other news to share?" Elan asked. He had the distinct feeling now that his presence was being endured rather than enjoyed.

"Nothing much," he said, and stood. "In fact, I am on an errand to the Erivor Chapel for Hendon Tolly even now and should be on my way. Things at the residence are . . . well, they are bad, to speak truthfully. Tolly is full of strange notions and doesn't seem to have any desire to withstand the autarch's siege—he can hardly be bothered to speak to Berkan Hood or Avin Brone. . . ."

"Our poor lord protector has forgotten that the gods do not give any of us burdens too great to bear," Tinwright's mother said piously. "He will recover his faith. He is a good man."

Even the newly religious Elan couldn't quite go along with this. "We must pray for Lord Hood and Lord Brone, Anamesiya. They will need the gods' help, too."

Anamesiya! She was even calling his mother by her first name! What next?

He had never thought he would make up excuses to leave the company of Elan M'Cory, but now he found himself doing exactly that.

Alone among the thousands of people crowded into Southmarch Castle, Father Uwin did not seem to realize that a war was going on, let alone that its result might be the end of the world.

"Yes, yes, of course, with pleasure—we get so few visitors these days!" the spritely old man said as he led Tinwright into the chapel's library, which was in the King's South Cabinet, a room for prayer and meditation that doubled as the chaplain's office. It had been less than a year since he had replaced Father Timoid, who had been the Eddon family priest for years. "What does Lord Tolly want? What can we do for him?"

Tinwright tried to tell Father Uwin what he had learned to this point, a confusing jumble of happenstances, rumors, and strange ideas. He had spent all of the past two days (traveling only in daylight, of course) in the great Trigonate Temple in the outer keep to study the books there. "I was trying to find out why some of the Hypnologues thought Southmarch was such a significant place, you see."

"Hypnologues?" The priest cocked his small head. With his tuft of white hair waving atop his head he looked like a startled chicken. "That heretic sect from the old days? The ones who thought the gods were asleep? Why should Lord Tolly care about them?"

Tinwright wanted to end this particular discussion before it ever began. "That is for him to say, Father. It is only for me to do his bidding."

"Of course, of course." Uwin rubbed dust from his eyeglass lenses, which hung on a scissor-shaped holder around his neck, then lifted them to his squinting eyes. "Here is Clemon—he wrote on them, I think, although only briefly. But you must have seen that already in the great temple library."

"Yes, I have. I came here because there was a rumor mentioned about a sacred stone that the Hypnologues believed came from the gods themselves, and on which they based much of their beliefs. Rhantys thought that the stone was lost somewhere below the earth here in Southmarch. But another book said that very stone was displayed here during King Kyril's reign—right here in the Erivor Chapel! Do you know anything about that, Father?"

"A stone sacred to heretics, here in the chapel?" He shuddered and ostentatiously made the sign of the Three. "I find it hard to believe—I have certainly never heard of any such thing. Perhaps you could find Father Timoid and ask him. I've heard he's living at the university on the far side of the bay. . . ."

Uwin obviously wasn't considering the difficulties of visiting Eastmarch on the other side of the autarch's besieging forces, even if the university hadn't already been burned down by one of the occupying armies. "I'm sure that won't be necessary, Father. But I would like to look through the books here if I could. Especially if there are records kept by your predecessors."

Uwin gave him a skeptical look. "The bond between the Erivor chaplains and the royal family is not for outsiders to scrutinize, and their conversations are not meant . . ."

Tinwright held up his hand. "I'm only interested in the daybook, or whatever it would be called here. Records, purchases, things like that."

The little priest led him down to a row of heavy, leather-bound volumes. "These are the charter books for Kyril's reign. Good luck with your search."

When Uwin had left him alone, Matt Tinwright pulled a stack of thick books from the shelf and sat down on the floor. He had not told Uwin everything, and one of the most significant facts he had left out was the strange thing he had read about how the statue came to be in the chapel. Kyril, the king, had taken the stone from the Funderlings as part of some dispute and then had dedicated it to Erivor. But why? And why did the Hypnologues and other believers think it was something to do with the gods in the first place?

Most importantly, though, could this statue truly be the Godstone that Hendon Tolly and the autarch were looking for? The thought made Tinwright's skin go cold. Could he truly have found the key to the war that raged all around?

Father Uwin came back about an hour later. "And how do you, Master Tinwright? Any fortune?"

"I think so, Father. See here." He pointed at a passage in the charter book and read aloud. " *'Given to the chapel, by His Majesty, King Kyril, a statue of a god made from some unknown stone or gem, taken from an altar of the Funderlings beneath the castle, dedicated by the king to great Erivor . . .'* So you see, that might be it. But I could find no other mention of it . . ."

"We have no such thing in the chapel now," Uwin said with certainty. "I would have seen it."

"You didn't let me finish, Father. I found no other mention of it for fifty years, until Father Timoid spoke of it in his own charter book—here, a bit less than ten years ago: 'The statue of Kernios given to the chapel by Kyril has been stolen. I have informed King Olin and begun a search through the castle. I suspect a servant.' Later he mentions that several servants were questioned and some were beaten, but no sign of it was ever found."

"Beat the wrong servants, perhaps," Uwin said cheerfully. "Might not have needed to, anyway. Surely you know the famous tale of the thief who stole a gold chalice from one of Perin's shrines and it began to burn in his pocket as though it was molten . . ."

"Well, if it burned somebody up, this . . . 'statue of Kernios,' it is not recorded. But the real question is, *where did it go*?"

"Ten years past?" Uwin shook his head. "Somebody took the statue ten years ago, with people going in and out of the castle by the hundreds every day, and scores of ships coming and going . . . ? It is lost, young man, whatever it was. Comfort yourself and the lord protector that it could not have been worth much, to be so little discussed even after it was stolen."

"I do not think that will bring much comfort to Hendon Tolly," Tinwright said as he bade the priest farewell. "But I will tell him."

As he made his way back, Tinwright wondered precisely what news he could give to the lord protector. There had been a statue, but it had disappeared years ago. Not the kind of news that Hendon Tolly would enjoy.

It was only as four men stepped out of the shadows below the Lagoon Bridge that the idea came to him.

"Please, fellows, I'm in a hurry," he said. "I have no money . . ."

"You look like you might be worth something, though," said the leader, a fellow with only one eye but very broad shoulders and an equally broad gut. "At the very least, we'll have those fine clothes off you, my lord."

Tinwright certainly had a few things they would like, like the prayer book he had tried to give Elan, but as the other three moved in behind their leader, Tinwright suddenly realized that these men might not stop at robbing him. But if they killed him, he'd never learn whether the Kernios statue really was Hendon's Godstone!

He raised his hands. "Let me make something clear." He reached slowly into his doublet and produced the letter of safe-conduct Tolly had given him. "I am on a personal mission for Lord Protector Hendon Tolly. If you think your lives are misery now, just slow me one long moment in my work for him and you'll find out what true suffering is."

One of the men looked at him, then turned to One-Eye. "He works for Tolly."

"He says he does!" the leader said, but the others were already turning away.

"That'd be my balls in the lagoon and my head in after it," said one. "Let's go find somewhat else to bother."

So it was that only a short time later Tinwright was back in his old room in the back of the residence, shaking Puzzle awake.

"Come on, old man, get up!" he called. "I need you to tell me what you remember about a statue of Kernios being stolen out of the Erivor Chapel."

And despite his initial fear at being awakened so suddenly, and his subsequent pettishness, Puzzle told him everything he remembered.

"By the silent footfalls of Zoria herself," Tinwright said when the old jester had finished, "this just gets madder and madder." He got up, pacing as he tried to make sense of what Puzzle had suggested. "Is there no end to this mystery?" he finally groaned. "What should I do now?"

But the jester was already asleep again.

20
Words from the Burned Land

"The great god Perin destroyed Khors Moonlord, his daughter's ravisher, after Khors himself slew the war god Volios. With the death of these two great gods, the fighting ended . . ."

—from "A Child's Book of the Orphan, and His Life and Death and Reward in Heaven"

BRIONY FOUND PRINCE ENEAS IN HIS TENT, stripped to the waist as one of the troop barbers bandaged his wounds. "You're hurt!" she cried. The skin of his flat belly was covered with cuts just beginning to bleed again after having been wiped clean.

He shook his head. "Nothing. I fell from my horse and was dragged a bit—these are scars made by my own mail." Eneas had put aside his plate armor for the raid, preferring the lightness and flexibility of a coat of rings.

Briony knew that being unhorsed in the middle of a fight was no small thing, but she had also learned that Eneas preferred to make light of injuries. "And your soldiers?"

"We had a few spites but lost not a man—but I am even more relieved to see you, Briony. I almost dare not ask—did you find your father?"

She told him the story, or at least the bare bones, since many of the things that had passed between her and Olin were for the family's ears alone. The prince listened carefully.

"It is splendid news that you found him, and that his spirit is still strong," he said when she had finished. "Splendid—but I wonder at what he says about Midsummer. Does the autarch really believe in his superstitions so strongly that he would risk an attack when the siege itself would do his work in a matter of a few weeks or less?"

"My father heard it from the autarch himself. Everyone says this Sulepis is quite mad!"

Eneas frowned. "I suppose. But it gives us very little time. Have you rested?"

"I'm well, yes." The scout had brought her back to camp just before sunrise, and Briony had promptly fallen directly into a dark, deep sleep, so that now the whole evening, especially speaking to her father, felt like a dream.

"But what will we do?" she asked. "We have so little time, and I saw the Xixian camp—they are so many! Close to ten thousand men camped on the mainland, more than half of them fighters. And from what I heard, many more have already gone into the tunnels. I think they plan to attack the castle from below, through Funderling Town."

"Funderling . . . ?" He looked at her blankly for a moment, then nodded. "Ah, yes, the Kallikan settlement. I have heard of it—the fabled ceiling, is that right? Your father must be correct. There could be no other reason for the autarch to be in such haste—Hendon Tolly is barely fighting back at all and the autarch's ships rule the bay. I would guess the castle might even surrender in a matter of days if the Xixians simply kept knocking down the walls with their cannons."

Briony felt a flare of anger. "Tolly is a monster, but there are still men in Southmarch—and women, too!—who will not give in so easily."

"I believe you, Princess." Eneas smiled; it was approving, not mocking. "I have seen the stuff the country's royal family is made of, so why would I doubt their subjects? Still, we cannot make any decisions until tomorrow at the earliest. That is when the first of the spies we have sent into the camp will begin to report back on the autarch's full strength and perhaps even something of his plans. . . ."

"No!" She realized she had shouted: everyone in the tent was staring at her. "I mean . . . my father . . . I do not want to wait before we free him. I've thought of a way to do it, but if we wait longer they may take him somewhere beyond our reach!"

It took Briony a moment to realize that the prince was looking at her strangely, as was his lieutenant and several others. "You do not know?" he asked.

"Know what?" But already she had that vertiginous feeling, what had seemed solid crumbling away beneath her. "Tell me!"

Eneas sighed. "Your father has already been moved," he said. "Some of our spies say that an armed party of more than a hundred men escorted a prisoner to the tunnels in the rocky hills along the bay." He reached out a hand to her, but Briony pulled back. "I am sorry, Princess, but it was your father, King Olin. He is no longer within our reach—at least not for the present."

The tears which she had held back ever since the night before suddenly filled her eyes; Briony knew she could not hold them in. She turned sharply and walked out of the tent, desperate to find a place where Eneas and the rest could not hear her when she began to weep in earnest.

"It will do no good to argue with her," Saqri warned, but Barrick had grown weary of being told what to do and what to think by the Qar in all their manifestations. He followed the retreating forms of Yasammez and her small troop of bodyguards as they walked back through the passageways toward the cavern where they were camped.

The fearsome dark lady of the fairies had already disappeared into her tent when he arrived. The Elemental before the doorway did not want to let him in, but Barrick simply stood, ignoring the thing's gestures and even the silent, resentful threats the thing offered him, thought to thought. The Fireflower suggested that he had standing among these folk and he was determined to use it. The flickering of the Elemental's Profound Light through the gaps in the shrouding cloth grew brighter and more agitated, but Barrick Eddon was not going to let himself be treated like a servant. He might be a fool, he might be a *mortal* fool, but he had survived impossible hardships to be here—Yasammez would not escape him so easily.

At last the half-hidden fires guttered and diminished. The Elemental stepped aside, but not without a last flare of protest as Barrick walked past.

Yasammez was alone in the tent, without even her counselors or guards; Barrick couldn't help wondering whether that meant she trusted him or simply counted him as no possible threat. The angry confidence that had sent him after her began to melt as soon as he saw her sitting cross-legged and as still as stone, her pale hands resting on her knees.

"And what do you want, little blood-jar?" Yasammez asked.

He had become so used to his new and strange ways of hearing and seeing that for a moment he could not tell if her words had been silent or spoken out loud, but after a moment he realized he could feel a tiny reverberation lingering in the close air of the tent. He decided that he would speak out loud as she had. Perhaps she thought she could anger him by speaking in air and echoes as if he were any mortal, but if she did, she did not know how Barrick Eddon had changed. "I wish to speak with you, Great-Aunt."

"I am not your great-aunt. The blood that is in you gives you no rights with me, any more than pilfering a royal signet ring would make you fit to issue orders in the king's name. That blood—our family's sacred blood, gift of our patron god—was stolen."

Now he truly was angry, but he held it in. "Don't speak to me of signet rings and royalty, Lady Yasammez. My family may not be as old as yours—or at least our throne may not be—but I know a great deal about the rights of kings and queens. Those rights have a price, and part of that price is doing what is best for your people. Do you really think refusing to fight for Southmarch is what's best for yours?"

She cocked her head like a heron watching a fish. "Ha! I am being lectured by a spring toadlet, newly hatched and still wet from the pond." She showed her teeth, but it was not a smile. "I have told my people the truth. It is too late to win by force of arms. Better to accept what is written, to run and perhaps live a little longer or stay and accept that the final hour of the Long Defeat has come at last."

"So you're giving up?" He stared at her and the voices in his head murmured a thousand different things, a storm of confusion, secrets, old tales, half-forgotten histories, battlefield incidents, all with the black, shadowy form of Lady Porcupine standing at their center like a witch from a nursery tale. "No. I don't believe that. You never surrender. Everyone knows you would fight for your people to the last drop of blood, so why should you counsel them to do what you would never do yourself? What do I not understand, Lady Yasammez?"

This time the wolfish grin pulled her lips back so that she looked as though she might be thinking about the skin on his throat. "You are a very annoying mortal, Barrick Eddon. What makes you so certain of yourself? Look at you! You are a scarecrow, cobbled together from other people's odds and remnants—the immortal blood of your betters runs in your veins, you have been bespelled by senile Dreamers and gifted with the Fireflower, though you cannot possibly understand it. Why should I even give you the courtesy of an audience? Why should anyone treat with you at all, a mere child who has taken everything that makes him exceptional from someone else?"

She was right, which made it even more important that Barrick not lose his temper. The question she asked was deceptive, because what lay behind it was true—there was no reason she should be speaking to him, should even bother to defend herself.

"Why, then?" he asked. "Why do you speak to me at all?" Barrick moved a step closer. Her strength was palpable. Within him the Fireflower sang of woe and defeat and courage. "You remind me of someone, Lady Yasammez."

One thin spiderweb of eyebrow rose. "Do I? A mortal?"

"I have not known many immortals until the last few days." Unbidden, he seated himself cross-legged before her. "Yes, a mortal. My teacher, Shaso dan-Heza. He was the greatest warrior of his people, I'm told, just as you are. But he lost his purpose."

The predatory smile appeared again. "I have not lost my purpose."

"So Shaso thought, too—but he had. You see, my father captured him and took him away from his own people. And although he taught us, and eventually became Southmarch's master of arms, a part of him never left Tuan, never left Xand—never left the old days."

"So you think I am trapped in the past? Is that your considered judgment, O wise princeling?"

"I think you are crippled just as he was—by distance. In Shaso, it was distance from Tuan, which was always more real to him than Southmarch, although he never went back. But with you I suspect it's the distance between *then* and *now*—between a time that made sense for you and these strange modern days, when, to fight a greater evil, you must ally yourself with those you see as traitors and enemies . . . with mortals."

"I do what is best for the People," the dark lady said, but for the first time a little of her ease had gone. "You could carry the Fireflower for centuries and still not be worthy to judge me . . ."

"Then tell me—when Ynnir presented you with the Pact of the Glass, what did you say?" The Fireflower had already brought him the answer on wings of murmurous near-memory.

Yasammez cocked her head again. It was said that the Autarchs of Xis held the falcon as their token—well, here was a true hunting bird, bright-eyed and remorseless. "I told him that the People's enemies must not be allowed to hasten the Long Defeat. That we no longer had a choice, and must fight or surrender."

"But now you all but demand we surrender. Queen Saqri has returned! The autarch means to wake the gods—even you said this would be disaster for us all! Why won't you fight, Yasammez?"

He could feel the misty tendrils of her thought pulling at him as she silently considered. "I will not fight because there is no longer a point," she told him at last. "The end of the Long Defeat is here—I see that now. The People . . . *my* people," and here she gave him a look so fierce he could almost feel his lashes smoldering, "have done all they could. With only a handful of troops we have defeated your armies of ten times that number. But the king of Xis has a hundred times that number or more, and priests and mages whose handiwork we have not even seen yet. There is no victory over such a force."

"So you would leave the mortal men of Southmarch—not just my people, but the Funderlings, too—to fight and die while your army sits by and does nothing? That is how you would write the last pages of the Long Defeat? With cowardice and callousness?"

"Grace and cowardice are two different things, child of men."

"Then let your people fight if they wish to! You can watch gracefully while the rest of us pretend we have a chance." He was angry now, and the incomprehensible differences of age and experience between them suddenly seemed unimportant. "Saqri came here to fight at your side. I don't believe she came here to watch others being slaughtered without lifting a finger."

Yasammez looked different now, like a wounded creature that still might strike. For a long moment she did not look at Barrick at all, but he could feel her anger, cold and strong. When she did rise abruptly to her feet and reached into the chestplate of her armor, he even raised his hand, fearing a thrown dagger. Instead, she drew out something that dangled on a black chain, a light glinting red as molten iron, and held it out to him. Her thoughts were like a roiling thundercloud, but although he could feel her anger and despair, most of it was hidden from him. Something else lurked there, too, something deep and terrifying, but he could not tell what it was.

"Take the Seal of War," she said. "Take it and give it to Saqri. Keep it yourself if you wish. I care not. If I am no longer fit to judge, then I am no longer fit to command."

He stared at the dangling glow. "But . . ."

"Take it!"

He did, reaching toward her with as much caution as toward a poisonous serpent. She stared at him as he let the heavy gem rest on his hand, and he swore he saw hatred in her eyes, although he was not entirely certain why.

"Because I am a mortal?" he asked. "Because my family stole the Fireflower?"

She understood him. "All of it," she said. "And more. Fight if you wish. It will only make the end harder. And what if the cosmos spins a-widdershins and you are victorious? The People are still doomed. The Fireflower will find no more bearers—the royal line of the Qar is dead and only Saqri remains. So go, little mortal, and tell the others how you taunted Lady Porcupine and lived. It will be a pretty tale to while away the hours before death takes us all."

So fierce was the heat behind her words, so furious her stare that Barrick suddenly could not speak. He turned, the Seal of War dangling from his fist, and stumbled out of the tent.

Briony was not so foolish as to go far from the perimeter of the camp but she could not simply spend the day sitting, as Eneas and his Temple Dogs seemed perfectly content to do. Too much anger and too much frustration were inside her. She had to move.

She found a little hill overlooking the camp and in sight of the sentries, then set off to climb it. The day was gray, but patches of sunny sky slid by overhead, and the way up was just difficult enough to engage her mind. By the time she reached the top about midday, she felt better. Still, she dared not think about her father too much. To have been so close to him after all this time, and then to lose him again . . . !

Prince Eneas and his captains were planning swift, unexpected raids to harry Sulepis' mainland troops, and to prevent supplies from reaching the autarch's army. This last was largely pointless as long as the autarch still controlled Brenn's Bay, but at the very least Eneas meant to make the autarch aware that he had enemies behind him as well as in front of him.

But although Briony didn't really expect the Syannese prince and his troops to do anything else, she could not escape the bitter idea of her father being taken away into the depths. But why should he be taken down into the tunnels under the castle? What lunacy did the southern king have planned?

Her father had also told her that his old, bad feelings were coming back to him as he returned to the castle. Perhaps that had something to do with why the autarch had brought him here. And gods? Her father had said something about gods, too, and Midsummer's Night, which was far less than a tennight away.

If only I had a longer time to talk with him. If only I could see him again, embrace him again . . . The tears were coming back.

Briony pulled out Lisiya's charm and turned it over and over in her hand, trying to find some kind of peace. So many questions, and none of them likely to be answered soon, or at all. And meanwhile, the sun slid by overhead, in and out of the clouds, on its remorseless passage toward Midsummer's Day.

Despite her climb, she lay awake for a long time that night listening to the soldiers talking and singing quietly and playing dice. The scouts the autarch had sent out to search for the raiders had long since returned to their encampment along Brenn's Bay, so the men were enjoying the relative security.

Briony was still clutching the charm in her fist. *Please, dear Lisiya,* she prayed, *help me to sleep. I feel like I will go mad if I do not get to sleep tonight!* But when sleep came at last in the deep watches of the night, Briony did not immediately recognize it for what it was. . . .

She was walking through what had once been a forest, something deep and green and quiet—but that had been before the fire. Now it was a scorched wasteland, pocked with the blackened remains of trees both standing and fallen, the grasses and undergrowth burned away, even the earth itself blackened. It was hard to tell what time of day it was because of the pall of smoke that lay over her and made the gray, hot sky seem shallow as a bowl. Smaller wisps still rose from the ground, as though the flames had stopped burning only a short while before.

It was as she crunched through the burned stubble that she realized she was still holding Lisiya's charm tight against her breast.

Briony found the demigoddess at the base of what had been a great silver oak tree, but was now little more than a tortured sculpture made of charcoal. Lisiya was leaning on a staff, frail and gray as a dandelion puff. She looked half her previous size, as though the hot winds had leached all the moisture from her, leaving only skin and bones.

"Somebody is angry at me," she said with a weary grin.

"Who did this?" Briony asked. The demigoddess looked so delicate that she almost didn't dare approach her.

"I cannot say. I am being watched." Lisiya lifted a clawlike hand. "The sky itself listens."

"Is this because of me?" Briony asked, sinking to her knees on the scorched earth. "Because you helped me?"

"Possibly." Lisiya shrugged. The demigoddess had previously seemed inexhaustible, but now moved as though she was afraid any effort might snap her brittle bones. "It does not do to speculate, child. The gods are asleep and that makes it hard to understand them, or even to recognize them . . ."

Briony didn't understand. "Is there something I can do to help you?"

The specter of a smile crept across the gaunt, wrinkled face. "Listen. I will tell you what I can. I am . . . limited, though." She sagged a little, then pulled herself upright on her staff again. "The hour is coming. It is almost here. The hour when the world we know will end."

"But . . . do you mean it's too late?"

"It is too late to turn things back to the way they once were," Lisiya said. "It is too late for the world that was. What kind of world will come—that you may yet be able to influence."

"Influence? How?"

"That is not for me to say. But you have only a little time."

"Do you mean Midsummer Night? My father said . . ."

"Men call it Midsummer, but here in the place of the gods and their dreams, it marks the moment when the sun begins to die. And every year since time itself began, since Rud the Daystar first mounted the firmament, the battle rages. Mortal men celebrate Midsummer as if it is a victory, but it has always been the opposite—the moment when the sun, when light itself, begins to lose its battle. It is an ill-omened day." She shook her head.

"But what can we do? It's almost upon us!"

Now the frustration showed on Lisiya's bony face. "I do not know! I am only a small thing, when it comes to it—a servant, an errand-runner—and I am out of my depths. But I called to you, or you called to me, so there must be something I can give you, some word . . ." The old woman closed her eyes, making Briony wonder what was happening: Lisiya seemed so tired she could barely breathe, swaying in place like a long stalk of grass. At last, she opened her eyes.

"*Omphalos*," the demigoddess said faintly. "Look for the omphalos, that which connects the past to the womb and the womb to the future—that which is the center of the spinning universe."

"What does that mean?"

Lisiya waved her clawlike hand. "I have told you what I can!" she said angrily. "Even now my words have attracted attention."

"But I don't understand . . . !"

"You must, because there is nothing else I can . . ." She broke off suddenly as red light flickered across the sky, flaring like blood against the gray smoke. "Go," Lisiya said. "There is nothing more I can do. Farewell, Briony Eddon. If you survive, build me a shrine!"

Briony tried to ask her another question, but thunder was rattling the burned trees and making the parched ground shudder, and the harsh red light seemed to be growing by the moment.

Fire, Briony realized. *The fire is coming back . . . !*

And then the sky exploded with bloody, glaring scarlet, so bright and hot that Briony screamed in terror and woke up panting in her tent in the Syannese camp, her fist pressed hard against her breast. When she opened her hand, she saw the charm was blackened and shriveled as if it had been burned.

❧

Barrick did not speak a word as he walked to Saqri's tent. Hundreds of eyes watched him crossing the great chamber, and all of them must have seen the blood-red stone dangling from his hand. Others, more familiar with mortals, might have recognized the expression of surprise and growing wonder on his face.

She gave it to me, he marveled. *I told the oldest, strongest woman in the world that she was wrong, and so she resigned the leadership of the Qar armies.*

But was it really as simple and straightforward as that? Something about the exchange still troubled him, although at the moment he was too stunned to ponder it much.

The guards did not lift a hand to stop him as he walked past them into Saqri's tent. She looked up from a silent conversation with two fairy creatures he did not recognize. Her eyes widened a fraction when she saw what dangled from his hand.

"I felt her, but I did not know what I was feeling," was all she said. "Is that for me or for you?"

Barrick laughed. It had not even occurred to him that he might keep it himself. He did not understand enough—he might *never* understand enough. "For you. And then you must decide what your people are going to do."

"We will fight, of course," she said, reaching out with slim fingers and letting the gem nestle in her hand. "Crooked was my grandfather's longest grandfather, as we say—the father of the Fireflower. We cannot let him be used by this mad king. If the Long Defeat finally claims our kind, most of us will embrace it, for who would want to live in a world without the beauty of accident?" She stood looking down at the gem for a moment, then carefully lifted the chain over her dark hair and let the Seal of War rest on her white breastplate.

"Call them all from their camps—water children, air children, and all of the People who follow the Seal of War. Tell them we are making last choices now. The end of the Godwar has come."

And so the Qar and their ancient allies, Rooftoppers and Skimmers, came from all the places they had been waiting and met in a great cavern near the Funderling temple, a wide, low-roofed chamber filled with limestone columns. Saqri sat beside a small, shallow pool in the middle of the cavern and all the others ranged themselves around it like the knights of Lander's famous court, except instead of a table they gathered around a liquid mirror which reflected the lights of their torches and lanterns. Upsteeplebat's people stood in their miniature lines near Saqri, with headman Turley and his Skimmers beside them. The leaders of the Qar seated themselves around the rest of the pond, their peoples crowded in behind them. Even the chief eremite Aesi'uah, the woman with the dark eyes, was there. Only Yasammez herself was absent. It was strange for Barrick to think of Lady Porcupine wandering alone and bitter somewhere beneath his old home, but he thought he understood her. She was not the type to surrender, but she had done so. She would not want to watch decisions being made without her.

"Once we were one people!" Saqri's voice sounded as hard and sweet as the ring of a stone temple bell. "Once we were one song. Now we are dozens of different melodies, but today we join together to bring our songs into harmony once more. The Children of Black Earth—the Funderlings, as they are named here—have gone before us to fight the enemy, but to us they are drows and they have always been family, however estranged. The Skimmers are here with us. We call them Ocean's Children, and although some have tried to make them follow this leader or that over the centuries, like the ocean they have remained free. We are proud they return to fight alongside us.

"And Thunder's Children, who are the smallest of all, except in courage. Their kindred, the Tine Fay, live on in the shadowlands, some in the wilds, some in the towns and cities. Perhaps one day you will be reunited with them. Perhaps not. Nothing is easy to see or understand this close to the collapse of things.

"And we will fight beside humans, too, those we once called 'stone apes' before we learned to respect their strength and fear their intolerance. I would not be alive today without them. Barrick Eddon, the heir to this castle's throne, brought me back the essence of my life, and he also stands with us in this fight. If there was any doubt about the days we live in they will be answered when I tell you that the Fireflower now blooms in his veins. Yes, think on that—the king my husband is dead, but his essence, and that of all his predecessors, is alive in the blood of a mortal man."

A flock of whispers came from the gathered Qar, and many turned to stare at Barrick, eyes of almost every imaginable shape and size widening as they gazed at him.

"Mortal men also fight along with the Funderlings below us," Saqri continued, "and thousands more have fought and died in the castle above, protecting the god who saved us all, though they did not know what they did or what it meant. Nevertheless, all debts will be paid by this last battle," Saqri declared. "Whether we succeed or fail, live or die, our invasion of mortal lands is over."

Somewhere Lady Yasammez heard that, and the clutch of anger and sorrow that came back, the feeling of being forced into dishonor, was so strong in his thoughts that Barrick almost fell over.

"Now we must plan," Saqri said. "The ritual this autarch wants to perform in the Last Hour of the Ancestor must take place at Midsummer, and that is only days away. If we can somehow help the Funderlings to hold him back, he will miss his opportunity, and then have to hold his gains for a year before he can try again. Anything might happen in that time. Make no mistake—his army is vast and fierce, and he will sacrifice them to the last man if necessary to reach his goal, because once he has the powers of Heaven at his command he will no longer need an army. He will be unvanquishable."

Only days, Barrick thought, looking around the cavern. Even counting those who were invisible in the shadows, they had only a few hundred fighters and not much more than a thousand Qar all together. Aesi'uah had told them that the Funderlings numbered perhaps two thousand, but likely much fewer.

"We will make our numbers felt," said Saqri as if she had heard his thoughts. "But not down here—not at first. To make ourselves feared by the men in the earth, we must first strike in the open air. The southerners are used to seeing their own soldiers disappear into the tunnels. They will not be prepared for what comes out of them."

"What do you mean, Mistress?" asked old Turley, his hairless face wrinkled in puzzlement. "The Xixies are digging down into the earth like worms."

"Yes," said Saqri. "But more than half their soldiers, their supplies, and ships remain on the surface. So we are not going down—we are going up."

Barrick thought the idea was bizarre. Surely they did not have time to waste fighting on the beaches of Brenn's Bay! And what hope did they have in any case—a few hundred fairies, fishermen, and creatures no bigger than mice? Either the Xixians' cold steel or the coming of Midsummer would destroy them all. He felt cold and withdrawn at the thought. Saqri's plan seemed nonsense.

And you will see it all, a voice sighed inside him, rising up from his thoughts like a single wisp of smoke. *You will see many die.*

Ynnir? Lord, is that you?

Yes, but you will lose me again. This I can see . . . The voice barely whispered in his thoughts, like a priest relating an old tale of outrage, one whose purpose had long since become obscure. *I fear you are to lose everything, manchild. Everything . . .*

By the time he returned to his tent in the Qar camp, Barrick found someone had laid out a suit of fine Qar armor for him made of a type of pearly gray plate he had never seen before, as well as a high helm with a crest in the shape of laurel leaves. The armor was not new—it had many tiny scratches that had not been entirely polished away—and he could tell by the buzzing in his head that the Fireflower voices recognized it. Still, at the moment Ynnir or some other agency was keeping the Fireflower thoughts from Barrick himself, so the only memories it awakened in him were distant and unclear.

The armor was beautifully made and he knew he would need it, but something about the gift remained hidden from his understanding and that troubled him.

21
Call of the Cuttlehorn

Zmeos, whom many named the Horned Serpent, retreated into mourning in his brother's castle and thereafter kept the sun's light to himself. For years the northern lands remained lost in winter.

—from "A Child's Book of the Orphan, and His Life and Death and Reward in Heaven"

"WHEN THEY COME AGAINST YOU," his sergeant Donal Murroy had told him, "you'll think at first they're endless and all the same, like waves breaking against the causeway. Don't let that fool you."

It had been one of Ferras Vansen's first nights alone on sentry duty with the old soldier. He could still remember every word.

"Did you really fight them?"

Murroy had spit over the edge of the wall, then ducked back when the wind changed. "The Xixies? Aye, lad. Two years fighting for King Olin when he was a young man—and I was, too! Siege of Hierosol. That old bastard, Parak. He was autarch then. Parnad's his son."

Now it was Parnad's son, Sulepis, that Vansen in turn had to face. The names changed, but the aggression of the Xixian army seemed to go on and on.

"What do you mean, don't let that fool you?" the young Vansen had asked.

"They're not all the same. Our armies here in the north, we pull them together when we need them. We're lucky if we can run a few kerns with spears out first to trouble the other side's horses. The autarch keeps a hundred thousand men under arms at all times. He has to, to keep down all those Xandian countries he's conquered. Biggest army since the great days of Hierosol itself, and each soldier has a different place in it. By the balls of Volios, boy, did you know there's an entire company that does nothing but feed and water the autarch's elephants?"

Vansen had never even seen an elephant. "Truly?"

"Truly. Pray you never have to come up against those beasts, lad. Big as a house and they can take arrows like a miner's mouse. I've seen them pluck up a grown man and throw him a hundred feet through the air, like Bram Stoneboots in the old stories. They are demons to fight." Murroy had paused to spit again. "Here was how the autarch's army came at us at Hierosol." Unlike most soldiers, old Murroy had believed in knowing his enemies well, something he had done his best to teach Vansen. "First were the Naked, as they're called—infantry, armed with spears and shields. Most of them are from the subject countries, Sania, Zan-Kartuum, Tuan, Iyar, but their officers are all Xixies. They come like the waves on Brenn's Bay—the autarch will throw them at the enemy for hour upon hour. Behind them were the Hakka Slingers, the gunners, and the Great Thunder, his cavalry—desert riders on horses fast as the wind. When they charge, all you can do is wait and trust your spears and your shield-wall.

"And of course," the sergeant had continued, spitting over the side once more as if to rid himself of the memory of waiting for the Great Thunder to strike, "the gods-cursed autarch has his special troops as well, his White Hounds, who are captured Trigonates from the north, and his Leopards, his personal riflemen and bodyguards. Each trained Leopard guard, they say, is worth a full rank of lesser soldiers."

"If the autarch's army is so vast and so powerful, then how did Olin defeat him?"

"He didn't, not truly," Murroy had admitted. "The siege failed, but only because the walls of Hierosol are so strong. If the day comes when Hierosol falls to Xis—well, I hope I am not alive to see what happens to the rest of Eion."

"They're bringing back the fire!" bellowed Sledge Jasper as he pushed against Vansen's belly, tumbling him backward. The cry was still echoing past the rest of the Funderling defenders as the advance guard tried to squeeze themselves back into the tunnel at the same time as the men with the fire shields were trying to push forward. "Hurry!" Jasper screeched.

The shield-troop got there only moments before the Xixian artillery dragged their fire-cannons into place, weird, octopuslike arrangements of bellows and plastered barrels and flexible piping that more closely resembled the instruments played by Settland hillmen than weapons of war. Still, it was only the swift erection of the Funderling fire wall, each recurved shield nearly twice a Funderling's height and covered with a fiber they called "rock wool," that saved the lives of those behind them because the passage into which they had fallen back was too narrow to allow a swift retreat. The liquid Xixian fire, ignited as it leaped from the gunlike pipes, washed over the shields. Some drops got through and splattered on the troops cowering behind the shield bearers, causing men to scream in terrible pain; even several rows back from the front, the heat made Vansen's hair and eyelashes crackle.

"Crossbows!" Vansen would have given everything he owned for a single company of Kertish longbowmen, but no one had given him one, so he was making do with the dozen or so old crossbows the warders had owned since King Ustin's time. Still, he had to admit the warders had acquitted themselves well.

As the first casks of Xixian fire emptied and the flames reached their greatest strength then began to fall off, Vansen hurried his crossbowmen down the crowded passage and had them stand behind the protective shields. As the Xixians rushed to replace the spent casks with full ones the Funderling shield bearers lowered their great curved shields and crouched so that the archers could fire over their shoulders. Screams and a great gout of fire from a burst bladder on one of the fire-cannons gave Vansen the courage to call for a charge.

The Funderlings poured out of the narrow passage and into the cavern like rats out of a hole, their axes and hammers swinging as they shouted, "The Guild!" and "Earth Elders!" They fell on the dozen Xixian firemakers and their guards in a moment and curses and shouts and the ring of steel on steel filled the small chamber. But the rest of the Xixians, hundreds of well-armed infantry—"the Naked"—surged forward.

"Grab that fire-cannon and fall back!" Vansen shouted.

As his men stumbled back into the passageway he made them drop the cannon in a heap of bent and scorched parts at the place where the passage opened to the main chamber. He found the matchlock and trigger for the fire-cannon and spiked the end of the smoldering match on a stray crossbow bolt. He grabbed a bow from one of his retreating archers and then scrambled with them back up the passageway. When Vansen saw the Xixian infantry beginning to shove their way into the passage, he took careful aim and put the sparking match into one of the fire-cannon's larger bladders.

The gust of hot wind and flame and the terrible screams of the Xixians drew cheers from the retreating Funderlings.

"Back to Pilgrim's Reach," Vansen called. "They won't soon get past the Midsummer bonfire we've made for them here!"

"We haven't even dug in," said Jasper. "They struck so quickly they must have known we were here. But we should be able to hold them here for a long time."

"We can't afford to," said Vansen. He pointed to the uppermost of Chert's maps. "Look. If we choke off Pilgrim's Reach here, then they will just go around us. They'll likely find their way down by one of the spur tunnels. See, this laborer's passage doesn't even have a name, but it's certainly wide enough for the Xixians to use."

"Chert's maps are more useful than I had thought," said Cinnabar, breathing heavily as his son helped him take off his helmet. "I did not know there were so many unknown passages."

"He studied the library in the temple, but he has also been down here himself, remember?" Vansen shuffled through the pile until he found the map of the level below them. "All the way to the island in the Sea in the Depths."

Sledge Jasper, who had all but appointed himself Vansen's personal bodyguard, let out a low whistle. "That Blue Quartz fellow was on the island? With the Shining Man himself?" He shook his head. "Never would have thought it of him."

"Don't underestimate him," said Cinnabar, drinking water from a moleskin bag. "Chert is a rare and clever fellow. I hear more good sense spoken at his and his wife's table than I do in the Highwardens' chambers, and I don't care who hears me say it."

"But where is he?" asked Sledge. "I thought he stayed back in the temple with the priests and the others who can't fight . . . or won't fight." His face told what he thought about those who would not take up weapons for Funderling Town.

"Don't underestimate our allies, either, friend Jasper." Vansen told him. "We have an entire platoon of monks standing bravely with us even though they have little training for it. By the gods, man, most of them have no better weapon than hoes and hammers and walking sticks!"

"Sorry, Captain. I meant no insult. I just wondered why he wasn't here."

"I know, Jasper. Chert Blue Quartz has a plan—an idea of his own, a big and desperate one—and we've told him to make what he can of it. It won't help us, but if we fail it might at least help to save the rest of Funderling Town."

"What's he doing, Captain?"

Vansen shook his head. "I'm sorry, but I can't speak any more about it. The Guild seal is on it—is that spoken aright, Cinnabar?"

The magister nodded and sighed. "That's it, exactly. It's Guild business now, mad as it is."

"You sound as though you think it will fail," said Jasper.

"I do." Cinnabar, with his young son Calomel's help, lowered his armored back end onto a rock. "But I agreed to it, promised I would help, and I've done so. Now enough of this. We can do nothing more to help Chert, so let us think about what we can do here."

Vansen pulled the map around. "As everyone knows, we'll give ground as slowly as we can manage, but we will have to give ground. From the Counting Room and on down the tunnels. We'll hold them for a long time in the Cavern of Winds, I hope, but our real stand will be in the Maze, I think. We'll make then earn every inch there."

"But they have their own miners, not to mention those weird little creatures covered in tortoiseshell." Malachite Copper had joined them after seeing to his men. "Surely the southerners can find other ways around us?"

"Eventually, no doubt," Vansen agreed. "But whenever they seem frustrated, we're going to give a little. We'll keep sentries in the other tunnels, so we'll know if they find any of those routes. But if we fight as hard as we can and seem to give back only when we have to, then the autarch will keep his patience, and we'll draw him downward as nicely as can be."

"But that way we'll lead him right into the Mysteries!" protested Sledge Jasper.

"We can't beat them, Sledge. I know it sounds mad, but the fairies swear that what the autarch wants is to be there on the night of Midsummer's Day to perform some black magic. That's what we have to stop."

"Well, you're right, Captain." Sledge Jasper nodded. "It does sound mad. But you've led us right so far, even in the beginning when I thought you'd have us all killed. Me and my men will do what you say."

Vansen smiled. "We couldn't manage it without you." He turned to the others present, Cinnabar and Copper and the other Funderlings, some of them hereditary leaders of their own troops, some selected from the ranks of the warders by Vansen and Jasper. "This is a fight to the death . . . but it is also a dance. We must learn our partners' movements and mood as well as we know our own."

Jasper's confidence disappeared in an instant. "A . . . dance? My men don't dance, Captain."

"Then think of it as a story being performed. Do you Funderlings have plays and players?"

Cinnabar frowned. "Of a sort. Some of the Metamorphic Brothers who conduct special rituals . . ." he hesitated for a moment," . . . in the Mysteries, they are players of a sort."

"Well and good," said Vansen. "Think of it that way, then. It is up to us to put on a good show of resistance, but the only way we can do that is to fight and perhaps lose. And then, even if we manage to hold off a much greater force, when they begin to tire, we must give ground, however weary we are ourselves, and however good the position we must abandon." Ferras Vansen spread his hands to show that he had nothing else to give. "That is our task, gentlemen. Perhaps the most difficult thing fighting men could be asked to do, and we must work this miracle with untrained troops and many new commanders. Could the odds be longer?" He turned to Jasper. "So don't fear, friend Sledge. We may die in obscurity but there are many worse ways to do it—and many worse reasons."

"It will be an honor to break my spade in obscurity with you, Captain." Jasper sounded as though he was ready to run out and throw himself on a Xixian spear this very moment.

"Just the same," Vansen said, "it is an honor I would have been happy to turn down."

Pinimmon Vash was terrified by how much stone now lay above his head, of how far beneath the sky—and even beneath the sea!—he had come. It was all that he could do not to leap out of his litter this moment and force his way back past the soldiers in their strung-out camps until he had fought his way back to the surface. It wasn't the knowledge of the permanent and fatal humiliation that would bring that kept him in place. Even the idea of losing face wasn't enough to overcome the horror of these miles of stone weighing down upon his thoughts and feelings. Instead it was the face of the autarch himself, staring at him across the smoke of the ceremonial brazier, that kept Vash seated and smiling vapidly when he felt as though any moment his skin might yank itself free from his bones and run away without him.

Sulepis could go nowhere without the brazier, because it represented the fire of his godly ancestor, Nushash. It was the kind of thing Vash himself approved of: ancient, orderly, ceremonial, respectable—and exactly the sort of things his young master was emphatically not.

"Your face seems sour to me, Paramount Minister," said Sulepis. "Has your keen eye spotted some weak spot in our assault?"

He hated it when the autarch made light of him in front of the soldiers, but even the polemarchs knew better than to show too much amusement. Whatever they might think of him in private, they all knew that Pinimmon Vash's reach was second only to the Golden One's. More officers than were gathered here today had incurred the paramount minister's ire, and all of them were gone now, the luckiest in ignoble retirement.

Vash did his best to smile. "Sour, Golden One? How could anyone be sour in the midst of such a splendid adventure? I but reflected on worries of my own."

"Ah, did you? How selfish you are, old man. All those concerns and you would not share a single one?" Sulepis turned to his prisoner. "Come, Olin, wouldn't you like to hear what is worrying my good servant?"

To Vash's eyes the northern king looked even paler than usual. His brow was damp, as if a fever were coming upon him. "I beg pardon," Olin said. "I did not hear."

"Never mind. Tell us why you are worried, Minster Vash."

Vash took a breath, held it a moment. "I worry about you, O Golden One, that is all. I fear for your safety so far below the ground, in such a dark and treacherous place, and with such uncanny enemies."

"But you told me only yesterday that I would triumph against any odds—that Heaven had ordained my victory, so how can you doubt me today? Do you doubt me, Minister?" The autarch was smiling, but the yellow lights of his eyes seemed as deep as the vast fires in the temple of Nushash.

He's angry about something, Vash suddenly realized. *Not me, but I was fool enough to let him notice an expression on my face.* "I am sorry, Golden One. I try never to doubt your victory, but your enemies are so treacherous, so wicked . . . !"

Olin turned with a look of clammy disbelief on his face. "What? My poor people, wicked? Is it not enough to kill innocents without slandering them, too?"

"He does not mean them, Olin," said the autarch, his mobile face suddenly full of noble feeling. "Although nobody who allows that Tolly creature to rule them can be truly innocent. Old Vash refers to my real enemies—the gods. And, yes, they are strong and cruel, but they do not have what I have . . . the blood of humanity flowing in my veins!"

The northern king, who unlike Vash himself seemed to have no reason to fear aggravating the autarch, asked, "What do you mean, humanity? It's the blood of gods you're always talking about—the blood that supposedly runs in my veins."

Sulepis smiled with pleasure. "Ah, but that is just the point. The blood of the gods has grown thin and tired, but it is still the key that will unlock the door I need to open . . . and when the door is open, power will come through it. That power—the might of Heaven itself—will be mine. But my blood may be entirely mortal, or if Nushash is indeed my ancestor, it may have become an even thinner soup over the years than your own. What's important about me is that I have the blood of human conquerors running in my veins—hard, silent men of the desert who seized what they wanted and held it by wits and bravery and nothing more. Who else would even think to snatch Heaven's power? I am the closest thing this world has to a god, and it is exactly because of my mortal ancestors that the circle will be closed and I will inherit the greatest power imaginable."

Olin looked at him for a long time. "Every time I think I have plumbed the uttermost depths of your madness, Sulepis, you surprise me yet again."

"Excellent news!" The autarch was pleased. "Now come with me while I inspect the troops, Olin. They do not like this sunless place, and who can blame them? But I am their sun and I must shine upon them a little."

"But I don't shine," Olin said quietly. "I only burn."

"Ah." Sulepis peered at him. "That is right, my friend, you suffer as you grow closer to your old home, do you not? Bad dreams, a racing heart, a pounding head? What an irony is there!" The autarch shook his head in dignified disapproval, like a grandfather watching the carryings-on of disrespectful youth. Vash could not help wondering how his master had managed to become even stranger than usual: Sulepis seemed to be trying on different ways of being, as though character could be changed like a priest's ritual mask. "Is your suffering great?"

The look Olin gave him should have immediately set the young autarch aflame. "I persist. I survive."

"Which is, after all, the highest to which most mortals can aspire, is it not?" The autarch laughed and stood. Half a dozen body servants rushed forward to unroll the sacred blue Bishakh carpet in whatever direction he chose to walk: Sulepis was still under the stricture of the priests not to touch the ground. Vash thought it strange that a man who was willing to kill kings and rob the gods themselves should be so scrupulous about religious ritual. "Now come along," the autarch told his captive. "You will keep me company while I bring the sun's brightness to my languishing soldiers."

As his guards helped the northerner to his feet, Olin stumbled and took a lurching step toward Vash, then caught at the older man's robes to keep from falling—or so it seemed; but as his sudden grab bent the paramount minister almost double, Olin leaned close to Vash's ear.

"I know you are no fool," the king whispered quickly. "If you wish to survive, go to Prusus. You will find him a good listener."

For a moment Vash thought his own command of Eion's common tongue had failed him—that Olin had muttered a curse and he had misheard it in a ludicrous, impossible way. But the quick look of significance the northerner gave him before allowing himself to be led away made the old minister's heart, already beating swiftly, begin to rattle like a festival noisemaker.

Is he mad? Does he think for a moment I would betray the autarch?

But a second, guiltier thought followed quickly. *What did he see in me? Is it in my face? Can everyone see my doubts?*

A moment later came the third and most horrifying idea of all: Olin must have heard something. *He's telling me that the Golden One already plans to have me removed and executed. Sulepis only toys with me, like a cat with a granary rat.*

Vash watched as the autarch was carried across the great stone chamber, bobbing on his litter with lanterns hung at each corner, and suddenly felt his treacherous thoughts must be leaking out like blood through a bandage, or like the fever-sweat on Olin's face. Perhaps everyone knew!

Badly frightened by the words of a condemned foreign enemy, the Paramount Minister of Xis hurried to his tent, seeking shadows and a chance to think.

"I can scarcely see anything," Vansen whispered to the young warder Dolomite as he stared out into the blackness of the vast, low chamber. He had been told there was enough light from glowing fungus on the walls in most parts of the Mysteries for the Funderlings to see at least a bit, but Ferras Vansen thought he might as well have a bucket over his head. "I'm blind here!"

"That's because you are an upgrounder, Captain Vansen."

"Fortunately for us, then, Warder, so are our enemies."

A moment later Dolomite whispered, "I think the southerners are breaking through the last of the rubble we stacked. Some have shuttered lanterns—even you could see them if they were a little closer, Captain!"

But Vansen had chosen this place at the opposite end of the wide Counting Room quite deliberately for his command post. The cavern floor was covered with broad, tablelike mounds of stone, and the cover they provided was why Vansen had decided to contest this cavern as fiercely as he could. He knew he would eventually have to give ground, but first he planned to make this stone room deadly for the Xixians. "Save your breath for the facts," he told the young warder, making his voice harsh. "Jasper sent you to me to help me. If I have to argue with you, I'll get another messenger and you'll be making your explanations to Jasper."

"Sorry, Captain." The young fellow was clearly surprised, his voice unsteady. "Won't . . . I won't do it again."

"No, you won't. And speak more quietly. I may be an upgrounder, but even I know that sound travels strangely in caves."

"You're right, Captain. I beg your pardon."

"Withheld, for now. Get on with it." Doubtless the young warder was only trying to keep fear at bay. Still, it was distracting.

"Sir," Dolomite said after another sustained silence, "a troop of southerners have formed up and look like . . . yes, they are moving forward. But these don't look like Xixians!"

"Their emblem? Can you see one?"

"A wolf or a dog, Captain . . ."

"The autarch's White Hounds," Vansen said. "I wondered when we would see them. They are northerners—from Perikal, or at least their fathers were. Fierce as a wounded bear in a fight. How many?"

"Looks like one lantern for every ten or twelve, Captain. I can see . . . perhaps twenty lantern in the first mass of troops."

"So many? And Jasper and the others?"

"Crouched out of sight. The Hound-men are still coming forward, but slowly. The ones in front have spears, but there are bowmen just behind them."

"Can't let them get too close. Tell me when they are halfway between the rest of their troop and Jasper's rocks."

Dolomite squinted. In the silence Vansen could hear his own blood throbbing in his temples. *The White Hounds may be a couple of hundred trained soldiers,* he told himself, *but they're the ones on unfamiliar ground. My men are fighting in their own fields.* Still, he could not help thinking of the vast line of Xixians snaking back up the tunnels behind these ten or twelve score, swelling to fill the larger chambers with armed men, several thousand in all, their ranks eventually leading up to the encampment on the surface where twice that many soldiers waited. The Funderlings talked a great deal about rockslides, and this would be a rockslide of murderous humanity; no matter what heroics they performed or good fortune they might have, they would never overcome such odds.

"Those Hounds are almost halfway, Captain," whispered Dolomite, startling Vansen out of his unkind thoughts. "Almost . . . almost . . ."

"Then give the signal!" Vansen said. "Here!" He handed up the lantern; the warder lifted its shutter and stood to hold it in the air above his head.

"Jasper's seen it!"

"Then get down, man!" Vansen reached up and yanked hard, toppling him backward. As the lamp spun away, spattering burning oil as it bounced down the shallow slope, three arrows splintered against the stones just in front of them.

"Sorry, Captain . . ."

"Don't apologize, Warder, just get back to work. They won't be shooting at us again now that we're dark. Tell me what you see. Are our crossbowmen taking any of them down?"

"Some, but there are many more arrows stuck in shields."

"We could aim lower if the cursed floor wasn't covered in lumps of stone. You Funderlings need to keep things a bit more tidy."

"Captain?"

"Never mind, Dolomite. Tell me more."

"They're down low, those White Hound men, and they're going forward only a little at a time, when their archers are firing. And . . ." He stopped, suddenly. "By the Elders," he said then in a strangled voice, "that was Chrysolite. I know him!"

Vansen let him have a moment, but only that. "Many good men will fall. We need to make sure we take down more of theirs—many more. Report."

"The Hounds have almost reached the place where our men wait. Ah! And now they come together, they come together . . . ! Oh, no, stop them! Don't . . . !"

The cries of men fighting and dying now echoed so densely that Vansen could hardly hear what the Funderling was saying. "Dolomite, I need you to tell me what you see!"

"The southerners, the White Hounds, they've reached the rocks and they're trying to push out Jasper and the others. They're using spears. Oh, Elders, it is terrible to see!"

"Don't see it, then, just tell me what's in front of you. As if it were a picture in a book."

"The . . . the southerners and ours are fighting very fiercely in the rocks. In some places, the Big Folk have pushed in between the stones and are fighting with our people in the open spaces. In others Jasper's men have fallen back. Ah, there is Cinnabar bringing men to help them—they are all holding near the back of the rocks . . ." He stopped to lean even farther, so that Vansen reached up and grabbed the little man's collar to prevent him from tumbling off the rock. "Oh, no, Captain! The southerners are getting past!"

"What does it look like?"

"Sorry, sir. Some of the White Hounds have found a way past along the edge of the cavern—they're slipping by while the rest are fighting in the middle. They'll be behind Jasper's men in a moment . . . ah! Ah!"

"Keep talking, boy."

"It's bad now, sir! The White Hounds have gotten past on both sides of our soldiers. They're surrounded, our men are surrounded; they'll be overwhelmed . . . ! Let me go help!"

"No! Stay here. Curse this dark place!" Vansen fumbled in his pack. "How I wish I could see. Tell me things that are happening, Dolomite, not what you think might be happening. Are the White Hounds all around our men now?"

"Yes, sir. Almost as thick on this side as on the other. It's a ring of torches all the way around . . . !"

"Good." Vansen held something up. "Do you know what this is?"

He felt certain that the young warder was staring at him as though he had gone utterly mad. "It's . . . it's a cuttlehorn, sir. One of those stony seashells. Like the one the Brothers blow to call the monks to prayer."

"Would you like the honor of blowing it, then?"

"Sir?"

He put it in the warder's hands. "Blow it. Loud as you can. It is time to call those White Hound bastards to temple."

After a long moment, a rasping, breathy note rose beside him, growing louder and louder until its triumphant clamor set echoes bouncing all over the Counting Room. In the shuddering aftermath of the horn's call came a sudden roar from Malachite Copper's Funderling troop, who had been hidden in the rocky slope above the place where the autarch's soldiers had first entered the cavern, and now came streaming down onto the backs of the nearest White Hounds.

"There are Funderlings—Copper's men!" said Dolomite excitedly. "They are attacking the upgrounders!"

"I know."

"The killing is terrible, but they are forcing the White Hounds forward into the rocks! Some of Copper's men are shooting crossbows into the entrance, keeping the other southerners out of the Counting Room."

Vansen nodded. "It is time to sound the horn again, Warder Dolomite. You haven't lost it, have you?"

"No, Captain!"

"Good. Then let them hear it once more. Let Sulepis himself hear it, somewhere back up the tunnel—let's hope it makes his skin crawl!"

"Yes, Captain!" A moment later the mournful call rose again, louder than the first time, so loud that Vansen felt pleasantly sure that the Xixians who survived were going to remember it with fear.

"Those Hounds know they're in a fight now!" Dolomite called a few moments later, having quite forgotten about silence. "And their other troops can't get in to help them! Look, the autarch's men are turning into hedgehogs, all spiked with arrows! Oh, Earth Elders, but they are still fighting." His voice faltered a little. "So much blood!"

Vansen decided it was time for his next trick. He sent Dolomite down the slope to Corundum's engineers to make certain they were ready, and while he waited for the young warder's return, he hefted the weighty cuttlehorn in his hand. Brother Antimony, who had given it to him, had told him it was made from a creature of the ancient days that had turned into stone.

Turned to stone—just like the greedy merchant in that old story. Can even a mute creature offend the gods? Vansen didn't know whether he understood all that Chaven and the others had told him, but he knew from his own experience that the gods' power was everywhere and it was dangerous. He knew enough of the gods to fear them more than he had ever feared anything else, even failure and ridicule.

"Corundum says they're ready," Dolomite reported, his sudden, quiet approach making Vansen jump. It was harder than he had thought to sit in the empty black, to rely on the eyes of others, but he knew darkness was their greatest advantage over the autarch's soldiers.

"Then we will fall back now while they are reeling." He lifted the horn himself this time, and its call soared once more through the great stone chamber. The White Hounds flinched and crouched a little lower, waiting for whatever would follow this time. They did not seem to realize for long moments that their enemies were stealing quietly away from them toward the passage at the back end of the Counting Room. Vansen and Dolomite joined the retreating group.

The White Hounds finally let out a shout as they realized that the last horn call had signaled retreat. The autarch's fiercest soldiers leaped forward, and with Malachite Copper's crossbowmen gone, for the first time their comrades trapped in the entranceway could finally join them. Together, the invaders surged like a wave across the uneven cavern floor, ducking as an occasional bolt snapped invisibly past, their cries for revenge growing louder and more savage as they sensed that they at last had these surprising little men on the retreat.

"Let the first half dozen lantern-bearers through," Vansen told the engineers as he and the others hurried out of the tunnel into Ocher Bar, the long cavern below the Counting Room.

So it was that when the first few dozen of the autarch's men came out of the passage in a half-crouch, holding their shields up and their torches even higher to see what was before them, no horn had to be blown. The commander of the engineers waved his arm and his minions threw their weight against the great iron wedge the Funderlings had brought down from the quarry for just this purpose. Wedge-staves bent, the wood groaning and the men groaning louder, and for an instant it seemed they would fail. Then, even as the first of the White Hounds below them realized what was happening and began looking up into the darkness for something to aim an arrow at, the slab of stone shivered loose and slid down onto the men just below so suddenly that only the wounded survivors had a chance to scream. They did not scream long.

The passage between Ocher Bar and the Counting Room was now sealed, at least for a few hours. Copper's crossbowmen loosed the rest of their bolts into the autarch's soldiers, mostly White Hounds, who were trapped on the near side of the rockfall, then the rest of the Funderlings hurried forward to finish the job, dispatching even the helpless wounded before Vansen could stop them. He had not guessed there'd be such reserves of ferocity in the little folk.

Ferras Vansen came forward as the first lanterns were lit. He stood over the bodies of the autarch's White Hounds, their armor so beautifully made and their beards so carefully braided. "Look at them," he said. "They must have thought Death invited them to a wedding instead of a funeral."

They came to a land they did not know, he thought, *to kill people they did not know, simply because a madman told them to do it.* He shoved them over with his foot, turning the nearest faces to the ground. *Yes, they were soldiers too, like me. I feel for them—but I do not feel sorry.*

The guards at the scotarch's tent stepped aside, their eyes so firmly downcast that Paramount Minister Vash thought it a wonder they'd been able to see and identify him in the first place. The scotarch's body servant, a eunuch almost as old as Pinimmon Vash, had the door open before Vash could even clear his throat.

"Come in, Paramount Minister," the Favored said. "I will tell the Desert Kite that you are here. No doubt he will graciously offer you audience."

Yes, thought Vash, *he no doubt will, seeing as I can walk in when I want and Prusus can do nothing about it except to wag his head and make noises like a dying calf.* "That is well," was all he said aloud. What was the eunuch's name? It was a curse to grow old. "And when you have announced me, and he has graciously agreed to the audience, perhaps you will be so good as to leave us alone for a space—the merest quarter of an hour."

Vash would not have seen greater suspicion in the Favored's face if he had announced he planned to put the scotarch in a sack and take him for a walk in the sun. "Great one, I do not understand," was all the body servant came up with.

"No, you don't. Come back after a short while, as I said. You shall find your master quite unharmed."

The smooth-faced man looked very undecided, but at last bowed again and went into the larger part of the tent, which had been separated from the rest by screens showing silk pictures of sand larks guarding their nests at the base of some of desert shrub Vash could not identify. No one in his family had actually seen the deep desert for several generations. Of course he hadn't ever wanted to be deep beneath the earth either, yet here he was.

The eunuch pulled back one of the inner screens and gestured him through with an appropriate amount of bowing, then ostentatiously let himself out of the tent, making enough noise that even if blindfolded Vash still could not have missed him leaving.

Vash walked to where Prusus sat, or rather leaned, in his traveling throne. It was a mark of how bizarre the autarch's choice had been that Prusus had no attendants beyond the single eunuch, and only a handful of guards. Previous scotarchs had commanded retinues only outstripped by those of the autarch himself.

But previous scotarchs, even the worst of them, had been able to talk and had possessed at least a little wit. Their heads had not lolled on their shoulders like overcooked mushrooms. Still, if poor crippled Prusus was like a mushroom, then he must feel comfortable here, down in the depths where such things thrived.

"Good afternoon, Chosen One, if it is indeed still afternoon." Vash bowed. "Please do not let me disturb you. I have come only to look for something." He gazed at the empty, rolling eyes, wondering if he would see any recognition there. "King Olin said I should listen to you." He could not help smiling and, in fact, almost laughed. "Which is, of course, a sort of code, since you don't actually speak. But I believe I may have underestimated you—as have many others. I believe you are not as addled as we thought. So tell me with your eyes, if you understand me. Did he leave something for me? Did Olin leave something for me?"

For a moment, as if his task could be accomplished only with a supreme effort of will, Prusus stopped shaking. He stretched forward his head as though trying to fall out of his chair—as though terror had gripped him and he sought escape. Vash fought back anger of his own. Why should he be forced to sully himself treating with a mismade creature like this? Then he realized that Prusus was looking fixedly in one direction, toward his own lap, and that he might have been trying to use his head to point the way.

Vash leaned in. There, clutched in the scotarch's bony fist, was a wisp of white—a piece of parchment.

"Ah," said Vash. " 'Look to the scotarch for help,' he said. Very clever." He reached out and fastidiously wiggled loose the folded scrap of parchment without touching the skin of the scotarch's hand. "And what treason against our beloved Golden One does the enemy king propose?" He said this for the benefit of any listeners, who always had to be assumed in the court of Sulepis, as in the courts of the autarch's father and grandfathers.

The parchment was unsigned, and from the clumsiness of the letters been written in a hurry.

"It is not too late to save yourself. Get word to Avin Brone inside the castle. Tell him what you know. Otherwise, both Southmarch and Xis will be destroyed. The madman S. has no allies. Everything that lives is his enemy."

Just looking at such a thing made Vash feel as if he stood in an icy wind, that he held a restless, angry viper in his hand. He knew he must destroy it, and quickly. Whether he remembered the words written in it or not, whether he let himself think about them or not, he would have to make sure nobody ever saw this piece of paper. Avin Brone indeed! Pinimmon Vash looked around, suddenly feeling like a thief forced to walk slowly down the street with stolen goods bulging in his pocket. Did he dare carry it all the way back to his own tent where he could burn it in his brazier?

Something made a bubbly, sighing noise nearby. Vash, his thoughts racing so fast he could barely move, looked absently at the scotarch, whose mouth was already moving again. This time Vash realized that the eerie noise, a nasal moan punctuated by wet sloshes of consonants, was actually somebody speaking words, and that with a little concentration he could even understand what was being said.

"Parsshhhmen isssh . . . shmalll . . ." Prusus repeated, his hand clenching and wriggling in the air as though it had its own life, its own secret joys and sorrows. "Jushh eaddd iddd . . ."

The parchment is small, he was saying. *Just eat it.*

Astonished, Vash did. It almost stuck in his throat, but he got it down at last.

22
Damnation Gate

". . . And the village of Tessideme, like most of its neighbors, suffered beneath year-round snow, icy wind, and frozen fields. The animals wasted and died, and the crops turned black and perished in the earth . . ."

—from "A Child's Book of the Orphan, and His Life and Death and Reward in Heaven"

THE SUN HAD BURNED THE FOG off the bay and Southmarch Castle's tall towers glinted in the sun from behind the great outer walls as they stretched toward heaven, each a different color, each with its own peculiarities of design. In ordinary circumstances it would have been an impressive sight, but to Qinnitan, a prisoner being taken to the one man on earth she was most terrified of seeing again, the sight meant nothing except failure and horror and the power of inescapable Fate: the gods were clearly bent on humbling her for trying to avoid the destiny they had assigned her.

As Qinnitan watched the approaching castle, she suddenly felt something she hadn't experienced for months, the sensation that had swept through her when the high priest Panhyssir had force-fed her his terrible potions: the world was not solid. It was as fragile as a bubble, and *things* waited beneath it. She could feel one of those things this moment. It was alive to her presence and unfazed by distance, because even though it lay more than a mile away across the cold waters of Brenn's Bay and buried beneath hundreds of feet of stone, it was also beside her, even *inside* her.

Qinnitan could sense its interest—it felt her just as strongly as she felt it. Couldn't any of the other people on the deck of the troop ship feel its ghastly, intrusive presence as she did?

Why did you leave me, Barrick? Why did you stop talking to me? I'm so frightened . . . !

But it was pointless to mourn. Wherever he was, Barrick was only a mortal. In fact, like Qinnitan herself he was little more than a child: he couldn't do anything to save her from Sulepis, let alone from the gods themselves.

The sun was far too bright. Daikonas Vo knew it must be Hexamene now, almost summer, but the light still seemed too strong, a glare all around him as though he walked over a bank of blazing, white-hot coals.

"*First rays, Nushash praise,*" he said out loud. When he was a child, his mother had always said that when she got out of bed in the morning, although she didn't say it much as he got older. Strange—he hadn't thought about the bitch in what seemed like years. Fitting that excruciating pain should bring his memories of her back.

As they rode a light tide into the docks in mainland Southmarch, the little cog stuffed with traders and their goods slipped between half a dozen Xixian warships lying at anchor or being escorted into harbor. The sailors on these other ships, unless they were in the middle of some task, watched Daikonas Vo and the others crowded on the cog's deck. He was still the object of much attention from the crew—a ragged beggar who had somehow commanded a place on a vessel the autarch had commandeered—but Vo did not intend stealth. If the girl from the Seclusion was being taken to Sulepis, perhaps had reached him already, it was far too late for stealth.

The deeper Vo walked into the camp the more eyes followed him. Men began calling to him, shouting at him to stop and tell who he was, did he think beggars could simply walk in among the tents of the famous White Hounds? Vo knew a few of his old comrades were following him. Ordinarily, he would have thought nothing of turning and confronting them. None of the White Hounds were cowards, but Vo had a way of looking at people, even very strong, very fierce people, that seemed to remind them that there were still things they wanted to do in life. But he dared not waste time.

He grunted and had to stop for a moment, bending double with his arms clutching hard across his belly, trying to keep his jaws clenched, to keep in the scream fighting so hard to get out. It was like a hot coal with legs crawling back and forth in his guts.

None of his old troop had recognized him yet; he must look like a beggar indeed. He finally managed to fight down the pain and straightened up before any of the soldiers confronted him. His goal was only a few dozen paces away, so he set off toward it, trying not to stagger, trying not to show any weakness that would make them hurry after him again, that might prompt them to pull him down like jackals on a wounded lion. Or to try, at any rate: Daikonas Vo knew he would kill them all first if he had to—fingers in eyes, kicking even as he heard bones snapping, all his weight pushing his hard forearm down until the other man's throat collapsed. . . .

Vo could taste blood in his mouth. He spun around, arms up, ready to protect himself, but the soldiers who had been watching him had not followed. They were laughing among themselves, watching him stagger and twitch and talk to himself. Vo was full of shame. How bad was he? Had he pissed himself, too?

Shuddering, his guts like knotted, burning rags, he turned back and stumbled toward the quartermaster's tent.

Vasil Zeru looked up as he entered but clearly did not recognize his face: he curled his lip at Vo's appearance and turned back to scolding one of his underlings.

"Zeru, it's me, Vo," he said, leaning in the doorway. "Daikonas Vo."

It still took a moment more for the look of recognition to come. "By the fiery boots of the Lord, is that truly you? You look like you caught fire and someone put you out with a Thunderman's saber."

"I am . . ." he clenched his teeth again, waited for the spasm to pass, "I am in need of your help. And your private counsel."

The quartermaster understood. He sent the underlings away. "We have all wondered about . . . about your mission."

"Yes. I am in the Golden One's service," Vo told him, "on a special mission. I must reach him as quickly as I can. But there are enemies, traitorous, high-ranking enemies who wish to stop me. . . . I have information the autarch must see!" He swayed, and that was entirely genuine, but it seemed to impress the quartermaster as well. Vasil Zeru was a hard man, but unlike most of the other officers his cruelty was impartial and meant as discipline. He had no wife, no son. The White Hounds were the closest he had to family, and he took his responsibilities very seriously. Vo, who had always made the other White Hounds uneasy, was exactly what Zeru liked in his unit—a clean-living, quiet and able professional soldier. So he believed, at least; Daikonas Vo's other pastimes were unknown to him.

"I will help you, of course," Vasil Zeru told him. "God's blazing blood, of course I will! Is it that old pantaloon, Vash? There is a devil who never lifted a blade or a bow himself, but would be quick to have someone else done in." He shook his head. "The kind that thinks nothing of sending soldiers to do every filthy task. . . ."

"May Nushash bless you!" Vo was able to make it sound convincing because of the relief he was feeling; the pain in his gut had suddenly lessened. "I will tell the autarch of your service to him, of how you helped when others would not."

Old Zeru actually looked a little flushed with sentiment. "It is nothing," he said, but he seemed pleased. "What any good soldier would do for our great Falcon!"

"Do you have some water?" Vo asked suddenly. The retreating agony had left his throat ash-dry and his head as light as smoke. "To drink?" His voice sounded far away.

Then he fainted.

"By my ancestors!" said the young priest as he looked Qinnitan up and down. "What am I supposed to do with her?"

"Take her off our hands, Brother," the soldier on her left said. "Captain said if we even had a bit of fun with her, they'd have our heads. She's to go to the Golden One, or to His Radiance, the high priest."

"Panhyssir himself?" The young, shaven-headed priest straightened as if that almost incomprehensible presence had just entered the room. "And the Golden One? Well, of course. That is, someone should take responsibility for this." He swallowed, half-smiling, looking at Qinnitan but no longer seeing her. After her time in the Seclusion, she knew the look of all-conquering ambition. This creature wouldn't let her out of his sight until he had made certain everyone had seen him deliver her to the highest circle he could reach.

Qinnitan slumped between the two guards; her chains rattled. In truth the irons were too big for her—the Xixian military generally expected most prisoners to be larger than a girl her age—and were scraping her skin raw. She could have slipped out of them easily, but a reflex told her not to give that away yet. Still, the guards themselves had not seemed very worried about her causing trouble.

The young priest was called Brother Gunis. He wasn't just an under-priest of the War Chariot of Nushash, he explained as she slumped on the floor against the wall of the shrine-tent: he had already been chosen to become a true priest, but after he brought her to Panhyssir—or even to the Golden One himself, *praises to his name, may the Falcon of Bishakh forever fly*—he would almost certainly become a speaking-priest, a high honor indeed.

"But I have done nothing wrong," she protested. "I am a priestess of Nushash myself—I was part of the Hive. I'm still a virgin. Do you understand that I will be tortured if you do this, Brother Gunis? That I'll be killed?"

He paused for a moment and then his mouth set in a line, as if he was frightened something might get out . . . or in. "If you are a prisoner, then you should repent your crimes," he said. "Everyone knows that the Golden One is generous beyond other men, forgiving beyond even the gods themselves!" He nodded. "Yes, give me your hand, girl. Let us pray for your forgiveness together."

She did not have the strength to fight him. Qinnitan let Brother Gunis clutch her hand tightly in his own moist, warm grasp. The young priest had a gleam in his eyes that had nothing to do with her, or at least not with her fleshly presence: he was seeing the glory that might be in his future. Qinnitan winced as he began to pray aloud. It was the New Catechism, the one the young autarch himself had written. This Gunis was either very ambitious, or he was a true believer. Either way, he would do nothing to help her.

Gunis took a pair of guards with him, sullen Hakka Slingers who looked as though they'd rather be drinking fermented milk than dealing with a priest and—as they had clearly decided after looking her up and down in an unimpressed manner—a scrawny girl not even worth the effort of rape. They straightened up when they heard that she was bound for the Golden One himself, but clearly did not expect to get far up the chain of command before being relieved of the duty: ordinary soldiers did not get to meet the Master of the Great Tent.

The soldiers led her and Gunis across the camp and out toward the southwestern edge of the harbor, where the city ended in rocky beaches and a few piers used by some of the poorer Southmarch fishermen. Here the hills that ringed the side of the bay came down almost to the water, and wind-carved chunks of standing stone marched down even beyond the edge of the hills, so that some of them stuck up from the bay itself like crooked teeth. The rocky sides of the hills that loomed above the beach as though they had been sliced with a great carving knife were white and soft pigeon-gray with tracings of greenery at the top, but it was the black holes along the beach that caught her eye and held it. She knew she had no choice, but it was still all she could do to make one foot follow the other toward those dark, ominous openings.

Once, when she was a child, Qinnitan's family had gone out to the coast of Xis for her great-grandmother's funeral. Afterward, while the adults had been singing songs and drinking, some of her relatives had taken her and her siblings down to the ocean to look at the tidal flats. It had been a strange place, especially for someone like Qinnitan, used to being surrounded on all sides by buildings and people. One of her cousins had tried to pull her into the mouth of one of the bigger caves, but she had refused to go, even when her younger brothers had agreed. She had remained on the rocks instead, splashing in the shallow waters of the ocean pools, waiting for what seemed like hours. At last the rest of the children had come back and, although she had felt bad for being afraid, Qinnitan had not been sorry to miss the adventure. The dark holes had reminded her of what her father used to tell her about Xergal the Earth-lord, one of the enemies of great Nushash: *"He lives in the ground, do you see? So far down that the sun can't reach, and it's cold, so cold. And he hates it there, and he hates Nushash and the rest of the Ugeni tribe for banishing him. And so he wants nothing more than to get his hands on bad little children who don't love Nushash, and keep them for himself."*

He had been talking about wicked Xergal stealing those children's spirits and keeping them in his harsh, dark underworld for all eternity, but it had been easy for Qinnitan to see that if you went under the ground, especially in a place as fearful-looking as those caves, you were as much as offering yourself to the cold, dark, angry lord of the earth.

Thus it was that when she should already have been as frightened as she could be, Qinnitan discovered that she had reserves of terror untapped until now. By the time they reached the elaborate guard post built at the entrance to the central cavern, she was fighting back tears of exhaustion and fright. Although the opening in the cliff wall stretched far above her head, she stared down at her feet as the guards, after an exchange with the young priest, ushered them past the gate and inside. Both guards took torches from the pile and lit them in the brazier by the gate. Within moments the doorway and the actual light of the sky were behind her and Qinnitan was being led down into immense, flickering darkness.

The autarch's troops had made a road of sorts through the main cavern—carved flat and wide where it had been too narrow for the wheels of small supply wagons, scratched and covered with gravel where the limestone was too slippery, until it almost looked like one of the supply roads leading in and out of the massive camp outside. But this was no ordinary road; it led through a strange fairyland of stone pillars, most of them on the floor of the outer cavern, whose shadows stretched and gyrated on the cavern walls as the guards walked past with their torches. Then at the edge of the cavernous anteroom the road tilted down and began its back and forth progress into the depths, lit by the occasional torch wedged into a pile of rocks by the road. From time to time they passed another guard station or an empty supply wagon heading back to the surface, but otherwise the only people Qinnitan saw were the three accompanying her, eager Brother Gunis and the two bored guards, who spent much of their time talking quietly to each other.

Some hundred feet below the earth, the torchlight revealed a trickle of water dripping from the slabs that made up the walls, and Qinnitan realized they must now be underneath the bay itself. The water dripped through in several places from above, creating little ponds on the rock floor that overtopped and flowed away down the cracks into darkness.

As they passed out of that cavern into a larger one, Qinnitan could suddenly see a long distance downward as the track wound around the outside of a huge open cavern at least a hundred feet deep. The stone track had been replaced by huge wooden structures like bridges that seemed to be hung directly on the side of the cavern and which together made a single continuous road winding all the way to the bottom. The cavern was full of torches; dozens of soldiers, maybe hundreds, were moving in and out of various holes at the base of the wall, presumably a series of tunnels leading off in different directions like the spokes of a wagon's wheel. From this height the soldiers looked like ants, and Qinnitan had the sudden, unpleasant sensation that she was being led deeper and deeper into something that was not actually a human thing at all.

"It is wonderful, what our autarch has done here," Gunis said to the guards. "Have you men dug this all out in such a short time?"

The soldiers shared a look. "The caves run all through here and also underneath the bay and the island," one of them said. "The miners didn't have to do much, to tell the truth."

"Still, it is wonderful." Gunis clasped his hands together on his breast and offered an ostentatious prayer of thanks to Nushash.

Qinnitan hardly noticed him. As they walked down the inclined walkway, their footfalls now booming on wood instead of swishing through gravel, something had reached up from below, something invisible but incredibly strong, and fastened itself around her like a cold hand, making it suddenly hard to draw breath.

It knew she was here. She could feel it turning her over in its thoughts. It knew she was here . . . and it was very hungry.

❧

I've seen this before, Daikonas Vo thought as he faced the cliff and the great uneven black door. *It's the Damnation Gate.* It was something else his mother had spoken of—in fact, the night his father had killed her she had spat at him and said that evil spirits were going to drag him down to the Damnation Gate so that Xergal's servants could flay off his skin. Vo's father had not liked that, and in the course of expressing his displeasure he had broken Vo's mother's neck.

But this, he thought, this was not mere words: this was the thing itself. Yermun the Gatekeeper must be watching from inside, wearing his skin backward as he was said to do. Yermun, the brother of Xergal—"Immon" and "Kernios" to the northerners—was a bit of a hero to the White Hounds, who considered themselves to be lifelong prisoners in a foreign land just as Immon himself, powerful though he might be, was a prisoner in Kernios' dread realm.

Brothers in Hell, the old White Hounds' song ran, *come running to the fight, and Heaven take the slowest!*

With his clean new armor and his beard trimmed to something resembling Xixian military standard, Vo walked into the mouth of shadow. The pain in his gut was beginning again, that feeling like dirty claws scratching at the tenderest parts of him; it was all he could do to walk straight instead of stumbling like a daytime drunk. The guards at their post outside the huge hill entrance stopped him for a moment, perhaps troubled by something strange in his eyes, but Zeru had given him the code of the day and so they let him pass.

The pain became even stronger as Vo walked down into the great tunnel.

I am cursed. I have lost my wager. I took service with the autarch's Hounds because it gave me license to do as I pleased, but I could not let well enough be. Because I wanted something more, I won a place in the autarch's special service, and now that "something more" is killing me. I have lost a wager and the autarch, as he always does, has won. Someone else will get credit for my hard labor and I will die like a gutted animal.

He could not think about it. It did not make the pain in Daikonas Vo's body worse but it made his very mind hurt, spread a red, glaring fog in his mind that confused him, and made him fear he might stumble off the path into some deep place.

Vo saw her at last from the top of the great cavern the Xixian soldiers called "Xergal's Tent." He knew it was the autarch's whore even though she was far below him at the bottom of the chamber, knew her as if she were family, and although he could see scarcely anything from his vantage point except her black hair as she walked captive between two soldiers, he knew her shape and posture as a lover would. Her big, dark eyes would be half-shut, her thin face quietly mournful and her thoughts turned inward into one of those great, long silences that had impressed even Vo. He had never met a woman who could stay such a time in her own thoughts, except a whore he had bought once whose tongue had been cut out by a previous client.

He hurried down the creaking ramp that wound its way around the cavern wall. The girl and her captors were still standing in the middle of the moving crowd, facing a wall with several tunnel mouths of several sizes, when the thing in his middle grabbed at both his gut and his heart at the same time. Vo staggered, gasping, feeling as though some terrible fire had burst through the walls of his belly and would consume him entirely. For a moment the next torch down the path shrank to a spark and he could not get any air into his lungs, but then after a little blackness, Vo discovered that although he had fallen onto his hands and knees, he could breathe—and think—once more. He got up and began to stagger downward again, but could no longer see the girl and her guards below. They had chosen one of the tunnels.

By the time he reached the bottom, the pain had let up enough for him to talk.

"Which? Which way for the high officers' compound?" he demanded of a Naked infantryman.

The man seemed to recognize the White Hound badge, if not Vo himself, so he replied respectfully. "The officers' tents—go to that one, there." He pointed to one side. "That's your fastest way."

Vo let him go and hurried toward the opening, staggering as he went. He knew there was little chance that he would recover the girl even if he caught up with her—how could he kill two guards without anyone knowing? The girl herself would give him away, just to see him tortured and executed. His work, his suffering, had all been for nothing. He had truly walked of his own will through the Damnation Gate.

He followed the path downward for what seemed most of an hour, in places having to shoulder through men clustered around some half-done task or other. The autarch's engineers and their slaves were still working in the tunnels even after the strange subterranean invasion had begun, widening and strengthening them. Vo could half-imagine that by the time they were finished the caverns would have become a replica of the Orchard Palace, all high ceilings and white stone facing. In fact, if the autarch stayed true to his youthful direction, perhaps the entire world would become a single Orchard Palace, and everyone in it either one of the autarch's soldiers or whores or slaves.

It should have been me. But he is clever. He can see things as clearly as I can, almost, and he was born into power and riches. I never had a chance—but it should have been me. This should have been mine; the world should have been mine, not an Orchard Palace but a Palace of Vo as wide as the world . . . !

He wandered along the narrowing path, his mind filled with the thoughts of his world-palace and what each room would contain, until the complexity of the instruments he would need and the number of victims his schemes would require made his head whirl, and he suddenly stopped. For a moment, he thought the terrible gut-pain was coming back—it was just such a nervous stab that generally alerted him—then he slowly realized what it was that had stopped him.

The road had come to an end.

Daikonas Vo looked down at the blackness, the sudden, violent falling away of the earth. He had almost walked into empty air.

He turned and made his way carefully back up the path, only noticing now that it was very narrow indeed, that he had not been following a proper Xixian military road for some time. Had he turned somewhere? Several tunnels had crossed his track earlier, but they had all been smaller than the empty space through which he walked and he had passed them all by. What had happened?

Vo made his way back up the track, following it along the side of a deep drop that gradually grew shallower until the echoes all but stopped. He was circling a deep cavern on a path around its rim, and must be getting closer to the bottom with each circuit, but nothing he could find seemed anything like the wide road that had brought him here. It was not a small chamber: it took him the better part of an hour to go all the way around, just to make sure.

Still, after another long climb up another featureless stone track between two long, leaning slabs, with only an occasional army torch stuck in crevices on the wall to supplement the light he carried, Vo had to admit that this did not look much like anything he remembered from before. Some of it didn't look like it was Xixian work at all. He wondered if they had foreign engineers and workers down here as well.

Whatever had happened, Vo had clearly lost his chance of catching up with the girl, at least by any conventional pursuit. Ah, gods, and now the pain was coming back again, he realized, the gnawing in his guts.

For a moment he could only stand, his shadow fluttering out behind him like a king's coronation train. It hurt so badly! He tasted blood. Everything in him told him to escape it, but there was no escape . . . unless he tore it out . . . tore out his entire belly. . . .

A sudden movement made Vo go still as a statue, his killer's instincts strong enough to overcome even the fire in his guts, if only for a moment. Someone was crossing the path a few dozen yards below him, crossing from one hidden passage to another on the far side of the path. Vo shrank back into shadow and watched with bated breath.

It was a boy—a northern boy, several years short of man's age and height, with hair that even in this dark place seemed to gleam like palest gold, and he moved through the tunnel as though he felt comfortable there. It was like looking at one of his mother's woodcut pictures of the Orphan. What could a child be doing in such a place by himself? What did it mean?

A sudden thought occurred to him—could it be the work of the gods? Had they decided at last to show Daikonas Vo their favor, after all his misery? To lead him to the girl so that he would receive the rewards he so richly deserved?

Vo made himself move forward. He had already passed through the Damnation Gate, through which Vo's mother had always told him there was no return save the Orphan's—and now, as if out of his mother's rambling tales, here came the child, in a place no child should be. Could it truly be a sign? Vo decided he would be a fool to think otherwise: he would follow the pale-haired boy.

A perfect vessel of despair, a perfect agent of chaos, Daikonas Vo straightened his back and followed the golden child down into deeper darkness.

"She's a skinny one. Do you think she's really going to the autarch?"

"Maybe he likes them like that."

"But they say his first wife has a rump like a prize mare."

Qinnitan curled her lip and tried to ignore the guards, even though they were walking just behind her and not talking quietly at all.

"Still, look at her—scarcely more than a child."

"She's got that red witch-streak. They say that's a sign of a temper—that they're like cats, you try to have your way with one and they'll scratch you into sandal straps."

"Ho! That makes her sound much more interesting."

Brother Gunis, the young priest, finally intervened. "Here, now," he said, turning on the soldiers. "You are talking about the Golden One's prisoner, which is bad enough, but if I had been listening to your filthy tongues wagging, I would have heard you insult Queen Arimone, too, and that could send you both to the royal strangler."

The guards murmured an apology. Gunis turned around, his head held high.

"Prig," she heard one guard say quietly.

"Never touched a woman, that one," the other muttered. "No stones left."

Some of the tunnels were narrow enough that Qinnitan and her captors had to back up if a cart was coming the other way so that the vehicle could get by. Most of the carts were loaded with dirt and chunks of ore coming back up from places where the engineers were still working, but others carried more disturbing cargo, corpses loosely wrapped in the soldiers' own cloaks, bare feet protruding because their boots, which they themselves might have received from another dead man, had been passed on to another soldier.

What more proof did any of these men need, Qinnitan wondered, that they were nothing to their master Sulepis but murderous toys? When the life was out of one it was stripped of anything useful and then thrown on a midden heap.

The number of shrouded corpses that passed them moved Qinnitan in conflicting ways. She had long since given up hope of ultimate escape for herself, but she was heartened to see that these northerners were resisting the autarch. Still, every one of these shapes bouncing lifelessly past on the wagons was a young man of Xis or its dependent countries, no different from her own brothers or even poor, mad Jeddin.

But if the autarch won here, or did whatever it was he had come for, so far away from Great Xis, then it seemed soon the entire world would be nothing more than food for his greed and cruelty. Soon even the oceans would not offer escape from his rule—he would hold all lands everywhere in his grip. Sulepis was young enough and powerful enough, and he was certainly mad enough, to make that horror real.

They had reached the edge of the military's subterranean camp. They were still far above any fighting, although Qinnitan could hear traces of it for the first time, faint, distant shouts and the occasional boom of something that almost sounded like cannons. The guards who stopped them now seemed much more intent and cautious than the others they'd seen so far, and certainly more so than the ragtag soldiers who had accompanied them down from the surface. A *mulasim* had even come out to question them, an officer wearing the infantry crest of the Naked.

"If she is bound to the Golden One, then we will take her to him," the officer said. "Or rather, we will take her to the Leopards, who will take her to the minister in charge, who will decide what happens next."

"But *I* must . . ." Gunis began.

"With all respect, Brother," the captain said, "you must do nothing except what you are told. If the prisoner is so important, why did you bring her without even the seal of your superior?"

"The seal?" Gunis seemed dazzled and confused by the mere idea. "Do you mean I should take her all the way back to the high chaplain?"

"I'm not saying anything." The *mulasim* was a squat, grizzled man with the skeptical face of a market peddler but the arms of a wrestler. Now he stepped up until he was face-to-face with the young priest; the soldier was no taller, but a great deal bigger. "I'm saying that this is a problem, and you haven't helped me any by showing up." He scowled fiercely and looked around. "I'll need at least two men to take her forward, and the gods know, I've none to spare."

"But I *have* two guards . . . !"

The captain laughed. "These?" he said, gesturing at the soldiers who had accompanied them from the surface. "These two pricklepigs? Fat lot of good they'd have been if you'd run into a pack of those Yisti devils coming up out of the ground! No, you two can turn and hurry back to your important work guarding the dung pits. Go on with you, or I'll have you in irons just like this little girl!"

The guards did not need another warning. They were already a dozen hurrying steps away when Gunis finally found his breath. "What about me? I . . . I was entrusted with this girl. I must be the one to accompany her."

"Entrusted?" The officer looked from Qinnitan to the monk. "By slavers?" He turned back to Qinnitan. "Do you speak any of our tongue, child?"

For a moment Qinnitan was too surprised to have been addressed to say anything. "Yes. I am Xixian. Please, do not send me to the Golden One! I was taken by mistake from the Hive. . . ."

The captain glared. "I asked you a question, not to sing all the verses of the Morning Prayer. In a million, million years I would not interfere with something that was a matter for the Golden One, or at least those around him, to decide." He turned back to survey the men in his vicinity. "Now, who to send . . . ?"

Somebody shouted, then there was a loud crash. Everyone around Qinnitan turned. A cartload overstacked with stones had run one of its wheels off the track on the level just above and the cart was wobbling precariously, half off the edge. A moment later it overtipped and several of the stones fell, sending the men staring up at it from below jumping hurriedly out of the way. The cart wobbled and then the whole mass slowly toppled over and broke into pieces on the stony ground below, sending rocks bounding in all directions.

Qinnitan did not need to be invited: she ran, shaking the loose shackles off her wrists as she went. She did not have time to think, but simply chose the nearest passage leading out of the wide chamber and sprinted toward it, sharp stones poking through the flimsy Marchland shoes the farmer's wife had given her to wear.

Darkness punctuated with the glow of torches. Men's faces turning toward her as she ran, some with their mouths open like masks of roaring demons, shouting questions at her. Qinnitan knew her one chance was to get out of sight of any witnesses and then hide.

A soldier snatched at her as she dashed past, and although he could not hold her, his brief grasp made her stumble. As she wobbled, trying to get her weary legs back beneath her, somebody else stuck out a foot, and she tripped and fell hard on the stony ground.

"What's this?" someone demanded in a harsh desert accent as she lay whimpering and trying to catch her breath. "A spy?"

She did not get up, or at least did not remember getting up. A moment later something hit her hard on the back of her head and drove the rest of the thoughts away.

It was the bees. She knew that buzzing, had felt it deep in her bones and guts many times. On a day when the bees were said to be happy they could be marked throughout the Hive, a sturdy rumble so low it was felt, not heard.

It had all been a dream, then—just a dreadful dream. Duny was in the next bed and soon they would be up, washing their hair together in cold water. She would tell her friend the silly dream she'd had and they would laugh—as if little Qinnitan, who scarcely had grown breasts, would ever be chosen as a wife of the great autarch! All the girls would laugh, but Qinnitan didn't mind. She was happy to be in her home, and safe—watched over by the bees, and by the priestesses, and even by great Father Nushash himself.

But why did the buzzing of the sacred Bees of Nushash have words . . . ?

". . . is Panhyssir? You summoned . . . hour . . ."

". . . too much. The high priest would . . . than he . . ."

Her head hurt. Her knees hurt. Her arm hurt badly. She wondered if it might be broken. What had happened?

"Enough, Vash, you are tiring me, walking around flapping your hands like an old woman. Besides, she is awake." The friendly warmth, the feeling of safety, both vanished in an instant. Qinnitan knew that voice.

"Awake?"

"Can't you tell? Her breathing has changed. She is lying there, bent like a bow, trying not to be noticed. And she succeeded—at least with you!" The laugh, high-pitched and musical, only made her guts churn. It was like listening to music made with instruments of human bone and skin.

Someone bent over her—even through closed lids she could see the shadow. Whoever he was, he smelled like fruit pomanders and scented oil. "Are you sure, Golden One?"

She wanted to throw up. She wanted to cry out.

"More than sure." Another laugh. "Give her a little love-pat on the cheek. Open up your eyes, my frightened bride! You have returned to your rightful master at last."

She did not want to see. She did not want to know. The worst had finally happened.

"Open your eyes, or I will have them opened in a way you won't like." Still, he spoke sweetly, reasonably. Qinnitan gave up and looked at him, feeling empty and deathly cold inside.

Sulepis was unchanged, taller than any man she knew, handsome and golden-skinned as he reclined on a mound of cushions that covered most of the floor of a large, lamplit tent hung with costly fabrics and mirrors. The autarch wore his golden falcon helmet, golden finger-stalls, and golden sandals, but nothing else. His brown flesh appeared smoother than any mere human skin, as though he had been carved from soapstone.

He raised his hand toward her, spreading his long fingers as though he could stretch them out from a dozen feet away and wrap them around her. "Your blood flows true, priest's daughter. Your heritage feels the nearness of destiny, of the great change coming to this world, and draws you to me. You have returned just in time." He smiled, a brilliant slash of white across his narrow face that in someone else would have looked joyous, but which was inhuman as a crocodile's smirk. The autarch had her—for all her frantic labors, she had failed and it had all come to nothing.

He pointed a long, gold-tipped finger. "You are a rare one, child, and that should be rewarded. I promise you will die last so you can see it all—yes, you will see me put on glory like a cloak of peacock feathers. . . ."

23
A Storm of Wings

"Little Adis began to dream nightly about a flock of martlets that flew around his head. The little birds told him they could not land because the ground was too cold. They were doomed forever to remain in the air . . ."

—from "A Child's Book of the Orphan, and His Life and Death and Reward in Heaven"

THE NAMES AND THE VISIONS crowded in on Barrick like beggars—the moment just before the charge, repeated over and over again throughout the People's history like a nightmarish ritual . . .

The Ghostwood, where the Dreamless waited in their shrouds, invisible in the twilight, all their handpicked stratimancers whispering death-songs at the same moment so that the whole forest rustled, though no wind was blowing . . .

. . . Shivering Plain, where Yasammez fought her enemies in armor that glowed scarlet like sword-iron in a forge . . .

. . . the screams around Giant's Cairn and the horrors that had waited for the first riders to top Blue Wolf Ridge . . .

All those terrible moments crowded in on him, or at least the Fireflower's memories of those moments, all the times the People had fought with their very survival at stake, all those dull, painful martyrdoms that together were called the Long Defeat. Even with his eyes closed, the phantoms still surrounded Barrick, a thousand different voices from a hundred different ages, all that the Fireflower had seen and heard and thought now swept through him like crackling sparks.

We have always fought and we have always lost—even when we won . . . Winding through it all came a faint, dry thought he could scarcely pick out from the cloud of memory and lamentation—a whiff of humor dry as dust. *Perhaps someday we should try to win by losing . . .*

Ynnir, my lord! Will you stay with me?

But that intimate stranger's voice had already trailed away into silence.

Barrick's Qar armor felt no heavier than another layer of skin and the laurel helm fit him just as comfortably. But the thing he wore most lightly was his own self, which seemed no more substantial—a fraction of the weighty whole, a flame to its candle. Barrick felt utterly careless, even fearless: to die would only be to lose his body and float away as all the thoughts and memories that had been Barrick Eddon scattered like dandelion fluff. *And the Qar memories inside me, the Fireflower kings . . . they would be scattered, too . . . ?*

Saqri came toward him in her white-and-blue war armor. She looked Barrick up and down and did not say anything, but he knew her well enough to see the single mote of disquiet—the subtle, tiny trace which was recognizable to the Fireflower only because of generations of experience with the women of Crooked's descent. "The last of the Xixian column has just passed on their way down from the surface," she announced quietly. "Be ready." She turned and walked away.

"She is not like Yasammez," said a deep, rumbling voice beside him. "She does not like killing, even when she must."

Barrick turned to discover massive Lord Hammerfoot standing near him—and not just Hammerfoot, but a spectral blur of all the Ettins that the custodians of the Fireflower had ever known, so many memories that, if Barrick did not concentrate, they fogged his mind like winter glass. The master of the Ettins stared back at him, the burning coals of his eyes barely visible beneath the helmet that further shadowed his great, ugly face. "I will watch out for you, Barrick of the Eddons, fear not." The creature's voice was so deep that Barrick could scarcely understand him. Hammerfoot slapped at his ax, a monstrous thing with a blade half the size of a small table. "Give me a lot of room when I start swinging Chastiser here. He's a big lad, needs a lot of room when he gets playful." He patted the massive ax. "You may soon notice, Barrick Eddon, that unlike Saqri, I enjoy killing men. Do not take it amiss."

"You . . . you speak my tongue . . . our—what do you call us, sunlanders?" Barrick asked. "You speak our sunlander tongue very well."

"Used to hunt your folk and eat them, to tell it square," Hammerfoot admitted. "Means I had to live close enough to get to know them." The Ettin didn't seem to be joking now. He shook his broad head. "Who would ever have thought . . . ?"

Barrick could not easily of summon anything to say to that.

A silent signal from Saqri sent the drows forward at last, scuttling down the uneven passage in almost complete silence. Hammerfoot stepped out after them, his footfalls so heavy Barrick could feel them through his own bones. "Stay with me, human," Hammerfoot growled. "Even better, stay behind me. A'nd do everything I tell you."

The Fireflower specters were singing excitedly in Barrick's head and the drows were running, and a few moments later they all burst out of the passageway and into the wider corridor known as the Great Delve, which led ultimately under the bay and up to the Xixian camp on the far side of the water—Saqri's goal. The troops who had marched past on their way to join the autarch below had already vanished.

The drows and Hammerfoot did not hesitate, turning in the opposite direction and hurrying up the wide track toward the world above. Barrick sped to a trot, grateful for the solid but featherweight Qar armor. He had just looked back to see Saqri and the others pouring out of the branch-tunnel behind him when a roar from Hammerfoot made him stumble and almost fall.

Just ahead, a Xixian platoon had appeared around a bend of the passage. They shouted in alarm at the sight of the approaching Qar and quickly ranged themselves across the road, raising their shields to head height and leveling their spears in bristling formation, but even in the dim light of the tunnel's torches Barrick could see the southerners' eyes widen in terror as Hammerfoot bellowed even louder and thundered toward them, Chastiser spinning above his head. Every single one of the Xixians lifted their shields, but that did those who were in front of Hammerfoot no good: the gigantic ax fell with a swift, savage *crunch*. The shrieking of those crushed beneath the weapon and their own crumpled shields was horrible to hear.

The Xixians a little farther back escaped the giant's first onslaught but were caught with their shields up as the drows running behind Hammerfoot quickly reached them and began ripping at the soldiers' legs and feet with the hooks on the base of their short spears, tumbling dozens of the dark, bearded men to the gravel track.

Then the Ettin bellowed a word the drows seemed to recognize. The little men dropped to the stone; Hammerfoot snatched up Barrick, then turned and threw himself to the floor as well. A moment later a swarm of arrows snapped out of the Qar ranks and feathered the first row of Xixian soldiers. The wounded and dying sagged back and tangled the men behind them.

Barrick dimly heard Saqri's voice, although he could not say whether in his ears or in his head, since the battle was already casting a thousand shadows in his mind, and it was all he could do simply to understand what he saw before him.

Saqri's deadliest hand-to-hand fighters, Tricksters and Changing People, now leaped out. Within moments they were in among the Xixians and drawing blood with blade and talon so quickly that armored, bearded men appeared to fall untouched to their red-soaked knees, worshiping swift shadows. But the autarch's soldiers were no cowards—these men had fought many enemies, if not any stranger ones—and within moments had begun to recover from the initial surprise and retaliate. A few clashing, shouting knots began to form in the chaos, and in places the Qar were being pushed back. When somebody fell against a wall and knocked down a torch, it was quickly stamped into sparks and the hallway became even darker.

Like hired fighters performing in the halls of Kernios, he thought wildly.

Earth Lord, the voices sang to him. *We are in the Earth Lord's house. His vengeance will be terrible—if we fail, we lose more than our lives . . . !*

We fought him and his brothers on Silvergleam's walls cried others, flung this way and that in Barrick's thoughts like leaves in a gale. *Do not catch Death's cold eye! Do not let him freeze your heart as he did Lord Silvergleam's . . .*

For Whitefire! For the Children of Breeze!

No. Find yourself, said Ynnir's voice, closer than the rest. *Find yourself only. Let the rest go.*

Barrick grabbed at the elusive thought, struggled to push the rest away.

Find yourself.

And suddenly, like a child learning the trick of walking for the first time, Barrick reached out toward himself and stepped out of the noise. What was happening was still all around him, but it slowed and grew more and more insubstantial until it seemed no more distracting than a pleasant breeze.

You are needed.

And suddenly he could see everything, clear as the finest glass, like something Chaven had ground for himself, and time lurched forward again, pulling Barrick as though with a string. A short distance away across the broad, dark space he could see Saqri's red stone glowing, bouncing like a floating spark as she faced a half dozen Xixian soldiers. Six foes, but a hundred queens, a hundred ancestors, were in her, Barrick could feel it. He could sense her hot furies and cold joys as she fought, could even perceive a little of the chorus of battle-queens of which Saqri herself was only a part, a music of thought so complicated and bizarre that he could barely hear it, let alone understand it, even though it filled his head.

"Whitefire!" It came to his thoughts and his lips at the same moment—Whitefire the sun god, the brother of doomed Silvergleam. And Whitefire, the god's sword, carried so long by Yasammez in the defense of the People. It felt right. "Whitefire!" Barrick shouted again, and suddenly saw—no, not just saw, but for a moment truly lived—that god's last doomed charge against the monsters who had killed his brother Silvergleam, his hated rivals and stepbrothers, the Children of Moisture. Barrick hurried forward and the battle surrounded him like roaring water. All the battles surrounded him. A song of war that was many songs and many sounds filled his head, so many voices singing it that he could no longer tell which thoughts were his own, though that did not matter to him. Like a salmon breasting the crash of the river, Barrick Eddon swam into the dark and the blood and all the sounds of death run wild in a small place.

❧

Briony thought she had plumbed the depths of surprise during this year of impossible strangeness, but she had not expected to wake up to find a man smaller than the stub of last night's candle standing beside her head. She gasped and sat up. She closed her eyes and opened them again, but the tiny man was no dream.

"I am searching the leader of this lot," he called up to her. "I carry important news for un." He bowed to her. "Beetledown the Bowman am I. Beest tha the princess Briony, good Olin's daughter?"

A hundred different responses came to her lips, but what came out at last was a startled giggle. "Merciful Zoria," she said. "I am. What are *you*?"

"Telled tha oncet already." She could see his little face frown in irritation, then suddenly go wide-eyed. "Oh, beg pardon, Majestic Highness! Forgive us our rough scout's manner."

Briony really didn't think she could still be sleeping, but couldn't help wondering whether she might have lost her wits somewhere. "You said you're . . . Beetledown?" She shook her head. "But what *are* you, Beetledown?" The first light of dawn was creeping past the flap of her tent. She could hear men moving outside, the sound of the day beginning, and could smell the fires that had only recently been lit. In the midst of everything else the smell of burning wood made her stomach twitch with hunger.

"I'll take you to Prince Eneas," she said at last. "These are his men. But I'd better carry you." She stared at him. "How did you get here? Did you simply . . . drop out of the sky?"

His smile was no bigger than an eyelash, but still quite charming. "After a manner of saying . . . yes, mum. I came as a courier. My feathersteed waits on a branch."

"Your what where? Feathersteed . . . ?"

He looked at her in surprise. "My bird, Your Heightsome Majesty." He was worried now that she might be making fun of him. "I prefer to fly a flittermouse, in truth, but with the sun up, I left 'em to their sleep and came by pigeon."

"I can promise no more," the tiny man told Prince Eneas and his captains. Beetledown was doing his best to stand still in the platform of Briony's outstretched hand, but every time he shifted his balance it made her palm tickle. "Just that my queen and the queen of the Fay both say to you and your soldiers that if you come to look on the autarch's camp you might see something that will interest you. They advise to come in force."

"*Might* see something?" Lord Helkis looked at the little man with disgust and something that might have been fear. "Are we so foolish that we are meant to fall for a trap like this? Simply march out to be destroyed on the word of some magical creatures out of a story? This . . . roof rat?"

"Rooftopper," said Beetledown with affronted dignity. "Your kind know my kind well enough, tall man—used to put out bowls of milk and pieces of bread for us, to ask our favor and blessings on the house."

"The night-elves of your nurse's stories have come to visit us, Miron!" The prince was laughing, but more at his angry lieutenant than at the tiny messenger. "Perhaps you should look to your shoes to see if any of them need mending."

But Lord Helkis was not to be so easily convinced. "Do you not understand, Highness? These are Blue Caps. Speak of the old tales? They are creatures of the twilight, the shadows. We cannot trust them."

"If you remember," Briony pointed out, "that is who this small gentlemen and his friends are fighting. Would we make the same mistake again, attacking allies and helping enemies?"

The tiny man looked puzzled by this. Briony quietly explained what had happened.

"Those must have been Akutrir's lot," he told her. "Lady Porcupine sent them out, but they had not returned when I left," he said. "We did not know you had found each other."

Eneas scowled; he had heard. "We shall speak more of *that* shame later. For now, we must hear all of what your mistress has to say. Queen Saqri, is it? Is she the one who has terrified the north—the dark lady?"

Beetledown shook his head. "Nay, but un's that Lady Porcupine's daughter—or granddaughter . . . I am not certain. But dark lady has stepped down and Saqri commands the Qar now, and says that if tha hurry toward the mainland city of Southmarch on the bay shore tha might see something of interest." He turned toward Briony. "You, too, Princess, although the queen didn't speak or send 'ee any message. By the Peak, tha and thy family have been away a long time!"

She nodded. "We have."

"What else can you tell us?" demanded Eneas. "What exactly will we find on the shore of Brenn's Bay, besides a vast camp of Xixian soldiers?"

Beetledown moved a little, trying to keep his balance on Briony's unsteady hand. "I do not know for my personal self, Prince. I tell 'ee only what was given to me to tell—I know nought else. But Queen Saqri sent this message knowing tha wert here when none of the rest of us knew, so I think tha would do well to listen."

Lord Helkis snorted. "A mannekin no bigger than a whisker bids us trust his fairy-mistress. How could that possibly have an unhappy ending?"

"Your mockery is duly noted, Helkis." Eneas frowned at him. "It does not help me decide what to do next."

"Ah, tha minds me of another part of my message," said little Beetledown. "Tha should be on top of the hills above the bay by sundown."

It was only after Barrick had defended himself through a dozen struggles and bloodied his sword several times—first on a fallen Xixian who tried to stab him from the ground, next on another southern soldier surprised to have missed his spear thrust, who did not get a chance to thrust again—that he tumbled out of his exalted state and began to feel like an ordinary mortal prince again. The Qar were now pushing back the autarch's men without much resistance, so he let the battle eddy past him while he leaned against the wall and tried to get air back into his burning lungs. Every muscle in his body throbbed. He remembered every moment of what had happened, but at the same time it seemed so distant that it might have happened to someone else.

Even when I can subdue them, the Fireflower voices are too strong for me to silence for long. But Ynnir's words had given him an idea, a first taste of how it might feel to harness the Fireflower like a battle charger and put all that strength to work.

What can I become, he wondered. *What will I become? I understand the speech of the fairies,* he thought. *My crippled arm is healed. There is nothing of the old Barrick left. It has all been burned clean away.*

If Hammerfoot was protecting him, it was in a very distant sort of way. The jut-browed giant was currently somewhere in the middle of the autarch's men, roaring as he used a soldier from the Sanian hills as a club until he could pick up his ax again, which had become stuck in the shattered carcass of a supply wagon. Barrick's safety did not appear to be uppermost in his mind.

Barrick reached again for the trick of thought that would allow him to muffle the voices and dim the shadows that the Fireflower made in his thoughts—a trick like squinting inside his own head. It was hard to hold it, easy to be distracted, and he knew it would avail him nothing if he were pushed to his limits.

Let it move through you, Ynnir's quiet voice told him. *You cannot make it happen. You cannot make it anything. It is.*

The Xixians were fighting desperately now, retreating back up the wide tunnel but grudging every step, and even without the benefit of a hundred Qar kings and warriors Barrick would have known why. Many thousand of the autarch's men were camped just above. These troops had undoubtedly sent messengers for reinforcements already. But didn't these fools wonder why? Did they not question why the Qar would attack such a large army and in such a strange way—from beneath?

Perhaps this autarch is too used to having his own way. Or perhaps he has simply underestimated the People.

A huge, one-eyed man with a beard crashed through the Qar just in front of Barrick. The attacker thrust a spear all the way through a slender, pale-skinned Qar warrior so that the creature dangled like a broken puppet, then knocked aside two more with his hide-covered shield before immediately turning on Barrick, who tangled his sword with one of the other Qar's blades and lost it as he tried to spin out of the way. The one-eyed man's spear snapped out and missed Barrick's gut only by the width of a finger or two. The tip scratched its way up the chestplate before slipping past his helmet. Barrick brought his shield up in time to repel a second thrust, but the Xixian giant swung his own shield, big and heavy as a door, and knocked Barrick onto his back.

The Xixian giant grinned as he stood over him, showing teeth and also the places teeth were not. He kicked Barrick's shield out of the way, almost wrenching his arm out of its socket, then lifted his spear up over Barrick's chest.

Things changed so abruptly that for a moment Barrick couldn't tell what was different. Only when blood fountained out of the ruin of the man's neck and splashed down onto him did Barrick realize that the giant's head was gone. Someone had cut it off—no, knocked it off and sent it flying as a child might decapitate a daisy with a stick.

"Time to get up, young master," growled Hammerfoot. "You will miss seeing the Elementals at work, otherwise." The massive lower lip jutted like a granite cliff as he looked Barrick up and down where he lay. "You are covered with blood. Well done."

"Most of it just sprayed on me when you took his head off." Barrick got up slowly, aching as though he had fallen down two flights of stairs. "But I thank you."

Hammerfoot nodded and licked at the red smeared on his fingers. His eyes glinted deep in the black pits on either side of his flat nose. "It was my pleasure."

Briony could not fail to be impressed. All of the Syannese nobles had been given a chance to speak their hearts. Many had felt it was too soon to be going anywhere near the autarch's legions, that it must almost certainly be a trap, however bizarre its methods. Then, when they all had finished, Eneas gave his decision; they would ride. After that they had readied themselves for battle as calmly as if they had not argued against it.

"Nothing can be harmed by listening," her father had always said, and here was proof: the prince's soldiers, especially the sons of proud old Syannese families, wished to be heard. Briony decided there was nothing for a good king (or queen) to fear in letting their subjects speak and even object to the ruler's desire as long as they would join in wholeheartedly afterward, as the Temple Dogs were doing despite not winning the point. Briony sometimes felt that despite all the wisdom her father had shared with her, she had learned more about governing people in the days since she had left Southmarch Castle than in all the years she had lived as a princess of the ruling family.

The sun was just past noon and they were already high up into the coastal hills, making good time. The day was warm and dry, the dust rising around the horses' hooves, and the larks were singing. It seemed unthinkable to Briony that so fair a world could have so much dread in it.

"Tomorrow is Midsummer's Eve," she told Eneas as they watered the horses. "My father said the autarch planned to raise a god. What do you think he meant? What will happen two days from now? The autarch must believe in it, at least. He hasn't even conquered Hierosol, yet he left his siege and sailed all this way."

Eneas was listening to her, but he was also watching every rider who went by, every foot soldier. The prince of Syan had been born to command men, she decided, in a way her father had not been, for all his virtues. Some things about the task of leadership had always filled Olin with dismay or sadness. Kendrick had often teased that, "Father is too kind to be king. He should be in a cave out in the Kracian hills with the other hermits and oracles." Barrick had never thought this was funny, though the idea had sent Briony and Kendrick into gales of laughter, but only now did she understand why. *How could that man I spoke to in the dark be the same monster Barrick hates and fears? How was it that after all the years of kindness their father had shown him, her twin only remembered his moments of cruelty, his madness . . . ?*

"I cannot tell you what the autarch thinks," said Eneas, breaking her reverie. "But I am afraid."

At first she thought she hadn't heard him correctly. "You are *what,* Highness?"

"I fear the Autarch of Xis as I fear no other man—as I fear nothing but the ultimate judgment of Heaven." He solemnly made the sign of the Three. "I have fought against him, you remember—or at least his men—and I have heard of his deeds all these last two years as the flotsam of the armies that tried to stand against him landed on the shores of Eion. He is mad as a wounded snake but as clever as Kupilas himself, and has an entire terrified and terrifying empire struggling to fulfill his every whim." He still watched his men file past, but now his handsome face was troubled. "But what *are* his whims? No one can say, Briony. We can only guess, and wait, and . . . and fear."

Before she could think of anything to say, Lord Helkis came racing toward them down the forested slope, swinging his charger back and forth between the trees, clearly bearing some kind of important news.

"My good Miron, is all well?" Eneas asked. "No, do not bow, speak to me! Why such haste?"

"Highness, you must come. The forward scouts are calling that the camp is under attack!"

"What camp?" demanded the prince even as Briony's heart leaped into a swifter rhythm.

"The *Xixian* camp, Highness. The autarch's men! They're under attack!"

"By whom? From where?"

"Come and talk to Weasel and the other scouts," Helkis urged.

Eneas was already clambering into his saddle, not even waiting for help from his groom, as though his coat of chain armor were no more substantial than linen. Briony realized she was staring and hastened to get back into the saddle herself; unlike the prince, she was grateful for the groom who sprang to aid her. "The scouts can talk as we ride," Eneas declared as he pulled on his helmet. "I wish to see this for myself!"

They found a place where they could see down past the last curve of the foothills to the vast Xixian encampment sprawling beside the bay and throughout the city itself, the round tents seeming as numerous as grains of sand. The autarch's men were fighting, that was clear, but with whom seemed considerably less so. After staring through it himself for a few moments, Eneas passed his silver spyglass to Briony. She had to push and pull at the tube for a moment, then suddenly, as if she had flown down upon the scene as swiftly as a hawk, she could clearly see the camp and the fighting.

"Zoria's mercy—some of those are giants!" It was like a dream, seeing what happened so clearly but soundlessly. "That one—I swear it is a monster! Is it some devilry of the autarch that has rebounded on him?"

"I think those are Qar," said Eneas. "We know the fairy folk were here at Southmarch. Those who attacked the merchant wagons had to come from somewhere."

"But where? I thought they had retreated." Briony could make no sense of this unexpected fairy army, their shields and armor a hundred different colors, their shapes almost as varied. She swung the glass toward the place where the fighting was thickest, along the edge of the camp nearest the rocky hills that came down almost to the shore of Brenn's Bay. "They're coming out of the rocks," she announced. "No, out of the caves! The fairies are coming out of the caves and they're trying to get into the autarch's camp. Some of them have, but most of them can't get past the fighting along the wall." She winced and handed the spyglass back to Eneas. "The fighting is terrible. They are dying by scores at the wall of the camp."

The prince had a strange look in his eyes, a gleam she had not seen before. "Then let us try to give them a moment's help. I suppose it is pointless to ask you to stay behind?"

She laughed despite sudden, breath-stealing fear and nodded her head vigorously because it was taking her a moment to speak. "Pointless!"

Eneas frowned. "So be it. Come, then, and may the gods watch over us all. We chose the wrong side once. Not again!"

At the prince's signal the horns called the assembly. The Temple Dogs who had dismounted scrambled back into their saddles; those who were drinking took a last swallow and wiped their mouths. The horses stamped and capered as Eneas stood in his stirrups.

"Anglin came to save my ancestors!" he shouted, holding his sword high. "Now we will pay back a little of that blood debt! Drive these southern dogs into the sea!" He waved and spurred his horse along the crest, following the scouts down the hill toward the camp. "For Syan and Southmarch!" he cried. "For King Enander and King Olin!"

All Briony had time for was the briefest of prayers . . .

Kind Zoria, bring us through this danger safely . . .

. . . And then she was riding too; they were all riding, plunging down the dry hills with a noise like summer thunder.

The Xixians had been arrogant, Barrick decided: they had not truly expected an attack, and certainly not out of the very depths where the autarch had been using his own huge army like a hammer, pounding away on his outnumbered enemies. His generals had made mistakes and they had also been profligate with the blood of their soldiers, confident they had the numbers to shrug off most mistakes . . . and they were right. The Xixians were fierce, stubborn foes who still had the fairies grossly outnumbered. The Qar had not reached the surface in their initial surge, and now it was beginning to look like they might never reach it.

Saqri's troops had managed to break through the first wall of Naked infantry—spearmen with shields, their sheer numbers and weight meant to force the Qar backward—and had also managed to destroy two of the autarch's war-fire wagons before they could be used against them: even now the wreckage burned so hot that no one could come within a dozen yards.

A pitched battle up the slope had followed, which finally gave the Trickster archers a chance to work, and Xixian bodies were soon tumbling from the heights. When the Qar reached the top of the passage at last they slowly fought their way up the ramps that spiraled around the high-ceilinged rock chamber, then up onto the rocky beach. A cannonball exploded near them and killed three of the Ettins and a score of smaller Qar. The autarch's men had not been as stupid as Barrick had first thought. Instead of assuming they would hold the smaller Qar force in the tunnels, the Xixians had brought up reinforcements . . . and more:

they had killed several of their own horses in the hurry, but had succeeded in turning around one of their own half-cannons. The first cannonball had missed the fairies but had dug a huge hole into the hillside; they were loading now to fire again.

A squadron of Xixian archers hurried down the beach to help defend the camp, still buckling on their gear and stopping to pull strings onto their bows: others were firing arrows of their own even as they ran toward the massive cannon, clearly intent on setting up a new main line of defense. The Tricksters clambered up into the rocks beside the cave mouth, trying to reach a vantage point where they did not have to shoot past their own allies.

Barrick, for the moment in the relative safety of Hammerfoot's massive shadow, could only stare helplessly out at this scene of madness. *We will be trapped here in the caves,* he thought. *Then, if the autarch sends troops back out of the tunnels, we will be caught and broken like a walnut in a blacksmith's tongs.*

Another thunderous blast and a cannonball struck beside the mouth of the cavern, sending large stones bouncing away in all directions. As the echoes died away, Saqri inclined her head and a squadron of Changing tribe warriors rushed out of the cave mouth, shrilling a war cry, their bodies dropping to all fours and blurring into metamorphosis even as they raced across the uneven, rocky hillside down toward the cannoneers. Some of the Xixian archers simply turned and fled from this horrifying sight, but the swiftest of the Changing tribe veered aside from the main emplacement and quickly caught up to them, singing as they shed mortal blood again.

Xixian arrows flew toward them from all directions. Three of the Changing tribe fell like dropped grain sacks, and another beast-man arched his back and stumbled with a shriek of agony—a cry like something wild having its heart ripped out that made Barrick flinch badly, though he was nowhere close.

Suddenly the world broke apart around him, or seemed to, as if it had been smashed like a plate thrown against the hearth. Barrick's ears seemed to have been pierced by white-hot needles; when he could think again he could hear nothing but a high-pitched hum and the faint murmur of Hammerfoot. The giant crouched only a short distance away, but to Barrick's ears the creature's powerful voice seemed as small as a mouse's, scarcely to be heard above the thumping of the cannons.

Hammerfoot brushed dirt and chips of stone from his skin. "Earth's blood—the Xixy-men are bringing up two more of their cursed guns." The Deep Ettin seemed more annoyed by this than fearful. "They will just keep setting sparks to them until they smash us into powder. . . ."

Another huge thump of sound and the cavern shook again, hard. Debris rained down from the ceiling, and rocks rattled harshly on Barrick's helmet as though a bullying hand smacked him over and over. Dizzy, spitting blood and wet dust, he shoved himself back against the cavern wall and watched the last stones patter down onto the ground in front of him. He was frightened but not much surprised by this world of ringing silence. Every song the People sang was about defeat and honorable death; now they had earned what they sought, what they believed in. And whether he was one of them or not, he seemed to have earned the same thing.

The world convulsed again. This time, darkness followed.

In all the years that her father and Shaso had talked about it, in all the courtly tales she had read about of bravery and daring, nothing had prepared Briony Eddon for the truth of war. All was chaos—shouting, flying arrows, blood splashing like water—and if both armies had been human, there would have been no way to pick out friend from foe. As it was, even before she struck a blow, Briony was already struggling to remember that the creatures who appeared to be the stuff of nightmares were her allies, or at least were fighting against the same enemy, the warriors of Xis. Things that crouched and snarled like apes or bears but wore armor, others that leaped like insects, crossing a dozen yards in a single bound to strike with slender, needle-sharp spears, some creatures wrapped so thoroughly in flapping, dark cloth that she could see nothing of them but a glint like fire where their faces should be—it was as though the painted margins of Father Timoid's ancient prayer books had come to life, spilling demons and monstrosities out into the air of the world.

The Temple Dogs' initial charge had cut deep into the Xixians as they rushed to keep the rest of the invading Qar trapped in the cave just south of the camp. Shortly, though, their resistance had stiffened and now Briony could see that Eneas' troops would have to fight their way back out of a crowd of southerners, who surrounded them almost completely.

More Xixians were on their way as well, fumbling themselves into their battle gear as they hurried to the fight. Three of the Xixian cannons had now been turned away from the walls of Southmarch and trained instead on the cavern entrance where the Qar had emerged. The big guns boomed and spat fire, each shot smashing more of the base of the hill around that cavern entrance into rubble and smoke and dust.

At the moment, Briony was in comparatively less danger, as long as she kept her head down—in the center of Eneas' men, surrounded on all sides by able riders who had fallen back into close formation and with their spears and shields were contesting the Xixians, who were mostly on foot. Only Eneas and a few others at the outer edge of the fighting had discarded spears in favor of their swords or axes. Briony watched Eneas defeat two foot soldiers in a matter of moments, using his shield to deflect the spear thrust of one before staving in the man's helmet with a sword blow, then stabbing the second in his gorge. As the man fell, blood already sheeting onto his chest, Briony had to look away—not because of the Xixian, but because watching Eneas risking his life was almost as painful as finding her father and being helpless to free him.

One of the Temple Dogs near her was in trouble. His foot had slipped from the stirrup; as he struggled to stay in the saddle, a pair of Xixians were trying to pull him down. Briony spurred forward. Growing up, she had tilted more than a few times at the quintain—it was one of the first times her father took her side in a dispute with Shaso over what she should be allowed to do—but the short spear that the Syannese armorer had given her was nothing like a tilting-lance. It was so light that she almost felt she should swing it like one of the bulrush swords of her childhood duels with Barrick; as she reached the struggle, she jabbed it hard at the nearest man and caught him just at the juncture of his armpit and chest. It sank in several inches, mostly because of the power of her horse, and the screaming man spun away from her Syannese ally. An instant later, the horse of another mounted Temple Dog trampled the wounded Xixian into silence.

The second southerner had been distracted by the screamer's fate; when Briony reined her horse up and then spurred back toward him, his eyes widened. He let go of the Syannese knight's arm and mail shirt, flung up his shield to take Briony's spear, and narrowly missed stabbing her in turn as she went past him. The knight she had come to help found his stirrup and, once righted, was soon belaboring the man with heavy sword blows. Another Temple Dog rode up and hacked at the base of the Xixian's neck before he even saw the new threat. The man fell heavily to the ground in a pool of blood and mud, his head only partially attached to his body.

It was fighting. Real fighting, bloody, dreadful fighting, the kind that Shaso had taught her about but she had never actually known. It was terrifying. It was astounding, too, but mostly it was terrifying. She had been a fool to join in, and now she could not escape it. This was not a song, not a poem; it was blood and shit and shrieking men and screaming horses.

Heart hammering, wild as a rabbit in a trap, Briony Eddon concentrated every bit of her thought and skill on staying alive.

A man was on top of her, his knee pressing her sword back toward her chest. She didn't quite remember how it had happened—something striking her from behind, a stumble, a slip, then this fellow out of nowhere—but it didn't matter: in another few moments he was going to get his dagger out of his belt and he was going to kill her, and she wasn't strong enough to stop him. Nothing in her life so far—not her family, not her royal blood or her princely protector, not even the demigoddess—could save her. Briony struggled to push back on the sword, to keep the man's hands busy, although it felt like her arms were breaking. The Xixian hung over her in bizarre intimacy, mumbling words she could not understand, sweat dripping from his face onto hers. His gritted teeth, the mustaches like two horsetails, the huge whites of his bulging eyes, made his face a Zosimia demon-mask.

Something swooped past her head, a flicker of shadow as though someone had waved a hand in front of the sun. The pressure on her chest suddenly changed as the man rocked back, clapping his hand to his face. A moment later, he let out a strange grunt and slid limply off her.

Briony rolled over, gasping as she fought to get her breath back, then remembered her vulnerability, unhorsed in the middle of a battle. As she struggled onto her hands and knees, she caught sight of the body of the Xixian who had been trying to kill her, his tongue half out of his mouth and already swollen. An entire garden of slender needles protruded from his eyes. Needles with feathers on them.

Not needles, she realized in astonishment—*arrows. Very small arrows.*

People were screaming on all sides now, many of them in terror. Another shadow flickered over, then another. Briony looked up into the deepening twilight, squinting at the small shapes that swept past. Birds. Hundreds of birds were flitting through the knots of fighting men, and every time one of the birds dived and pulled up, a Xixian fell back holding his face or throat. Many of the southerners were running away without concern for direction, hands over their heads as if angry bees were attacking them.

The little man's folk, she thought as she watched the madness. *Beetlewhattsit. He said they rode birds.*

Many of the Xixians were already racing madly back toward the shelter of the camp. Those remaining on the beach were rapidly finding themselves outnumbered. For the first time, Briony felt she might live to see the sun rise the next day.

Another bird snapped by, brushing her face with its wing, so close that she heard the shrill battle cry of its rider: *"For the queens! For the queens!"* And still more followed that one, a storm of wings dropping down in dark clouds, gliding in and out among the desperately fleeing Xixians, making them stumble and fall.

Zoria's mercy! Briony climbed to her feet. *If I live through this, I'll remember this moment all my life . . .*

24
Disobedient Soldiers

"In another dream, Adis climbed the oak tree high into the sky. As he reached the upper branches, he found he could touch the stars themselves, which sang to him, begging him to bring back their father . . ."

—from "A Child's Book of the Orphan, and His Life and Death and Reward in Heaven"

A COUPLE OF DOZEN REFUGEES from the outer keep were living in the middle of the stairwell that led to the Anglin Parlor, its walls painted in frescoes of the Connordic Mountains and scenes of the first king's life. The folk crowding the stair were just as uninterested in the pictures on the walls as they were in making room for Matt Tinwright to get past.

He was angry to have to step over people, but he kept his feelings hidden. Some of the men were looking at his fine clothes with interest, doubtless wondering what they might fetch at one of the impromptu markets held on the green in front of the royal residence. It was shocking, of course, to be weighed for robbery by squatters right inside the king's house, but these were not ordinary times.

One of the women reached up as he tried to get past her and ran her fingers over his sleeve. "Ooh, a pretty one in pretty clothes, aren't you?" Tinwright pulled his arm back quickly.

One of the men took notice of his worried haste. "Hoy, are you bothering my woman?" The man started to rise. Another squatter moved a little farther into Tinwright's path on the steps above him. "Did you hear? I asked you . . ."

He made his voice as hard as he could. "If you touch me, you will weep for it. I am on Hendon Tolly's business. Do you mean to trifle with the lord protector's servant?"

The man on the step above him exchanged a look with the other man, then sidled back a step toward the wall.

"Even his lordship can't have it his own way forever," said the first man, but he too was already in retreat. Tinwright recognized the tone of the squatters' murmuring. They were still afraid of Tolly, but his hold on them was slipping. Half the outer keep had been leveled by the autarch's cannons, and the lord protector had shown little interest in fighting back.

Tinwright made his way up the stairs as quickly as he dared, going just slowly enough to show that he thought himself safe. In an hour like the one that had fallen on Southmarch, he reflected, people slowly began to change into something else—something simpler, something frightened and angry enough to kill.

Hendon Tolly was standing at the narrow windows of the chamber looking down on the small, unhappy city covering the spot that had once been the royal green and all the space inside the walls of the keep to the base of Wolfstooth Spire, and if the base of the great tower had not been full of armed soldiers, Tinwright felt certain they would be squatting there as well.

"Ah, here is my pet poet," Tolly said without looking away from the window, as though he could see what was behind him as well as before. "It has been a dreary afternoon. The day after tomorrow is Midsummer, you know. Speak some poetry for me."

"What . . . what do you mean, Lord?" Tinwright swatted away a fly. The room seemed to be unusually full of them, even for summer.

"By the bleeding, vengeful gods, fool, you are the rhymer, not me. If you don't know what poetry is, then I fear for the art."

"But I bring news, my lord . . ."

Tolly finally turned. He was pale as a drowned earthworm, eyes deep sunken and shadowed with blue, his fine, high brow covered with sweat. His clothes and hair were in such disarray that Tinwright could half believe the dandyish Tolly had just fought his way through the same crowd that had accosted him on the stairs. But it was Hendon Tolly's eyes that were most disturbing. Something bright and shiny but unknowable burned there—a monstrous secret, perhaps, or a vast, subtle joke that Tolly alone of all living creatures could understand.

The lord protector bent a little, as if he was bowing. His sword was in his hand so quickly Tinwright did not see the movement until the point was quivering a handsbreadth from his chest. "I do not want news . . . yet," Tolly said carefully. "I want verse. So speak, poet, or I will hand you your heart."

". . . For if your ear
Shall once a heavenly music hear,"

Tinwright recited, nearing the end of one of Hewney's bits of doggerel,

"Such as neither gods nor men
But from that voice shall hear again,
That, that is she, oh, Heaven's grace,
'Tis she steals sweet Siveda's place . . ."

"Enough." Tolly made a quick gesture like a man shaking warmth back into cold fingers; when he had finished, his sword was in its scabbard again. "Now pour me a cup of wine—you may have one yourself if you feel a need. There is a middling Perikal on the table. You will know it because it is the only jug still upright. Then you may give me your report on the Godstone."

Tinwright picked the wine out from among the empty casualties that littered the table. As he did so, he noticed for the first time an odd bundle of clothes in the corner of the room, a bundle from which a single bare man's foot protruded. Tinwright felt his stomach rise into his throat, choked it down, then leaned on the table for a moment with eyes closed, regaining control.

"What's taking you so long?" Tolly turned. "Ah, him. Yes, that pig of a butler will never again tell me that we have no red wine." He laughed suddenly. "As the blood was running out of him onto the floor, I said, 'What do you think? Does it need to air a bit?' He didn't laugh."

Trying his hardest not to look at the silent thing in the corner, Tinwright delivered the wine and quickly downed his own.

Tolly took a long, savoring sip. "Now, speak."

Matt Tinwright did his best to make his days and nights of reading into something easily understood, but it was not an easy chore. He explained to Tolly, who did not appear to be listening very closely, how the *Hypnologos* sect had believed that the gods were not awake, but only touched humans in dreams, and that the scene of the gods' downfall had played out right here, in Southmarch Castle—or at least somewhere nearby.

"The stone was here. It was in the Erivor Chapel and had been made into a statue of Kernios."

"That old cuckold," said Tolly with an angry laugh. "You see, even here old Kernios tries to keep her prisoner. But he cannot. No, I don't care for any magical stone. If the autarch can open the gate to the land of the gods without it, so can I! We have proved you can speak the words to open the mirror just as well as Okros! Better, in fact, since you still have your life and both arms!"

"My lord?" Tinwright suddenly wondered if Tolly had heard a word he was saying. "I don't understand any of . . ."

"Of course you don't, so shut your mouth and listen. I spent months with Okros, learning the truth that hides behind other truths. The *Hypnologoi* have a sign they use to know each other—Okros was one himself! Their learning is secret and shared only among themselves . . . and certain others, such as me, who sponsor their inquiries.

"It's the *land of the gods* we're talking about, poet—the very place you prating verse-spouters are always on about. The place where they sleep and dream. The autarch seeks to open it up and take the power for his own. But I know how to do it just as well as he—Okros was ready, it had been the study of his life, you see?—and I have all the things I will need to do it. The stone . . . that is something else, something foolish, a mere precaution that Okros already told me was likely not needed. We have a mirror that will serve the task perfectly well, whether the southerner has one of his own or not. But what we need, ah, what we need now . . . is the *blood*."

Tinwright was caught by surprise. He took a step back, heart beating very fast. "But, Lord Tolly, I have worked so hard for you . . ."

Tolly laughed even louder. "Do you think I mean you? Do you think any immortal is going to smell the mud that runs in your veins and come running, especially when she's been asleep for a thousand years and more?" He threw back his head and laughed even louder, an edge of madness in it. "Ah, I have not felt so cheerful all day! *Your* blood! Fool of a poet!" He turned and slapped Matt Tinwright across the face so hard that Tinwright fell to his knees, stunned. "Do not ever presume," the lord protector said, his voice suddenly a snarl, "that you are like me. The blood that runs in the Eddon family's veins and also runs in mine is the holy ichor of Mount Xandos—the blood of the gods themselves! But to open the proper doorway, that blood must be spilled from a living heart, and I assure you it won't be mine." He laughed again, but this time it was a distracted growl. "No, we must find a proper sacrifice. Almost all the Eddons are gone from here . . . but there is still one left who carries the sacred blood."

Matt Tinwright was confused and frightened. He had not heard Tolly talk this way before, as if he believed the maddest of the old tales and meant to act on them. "Eddon blood . . . ?" Who could Tolly mean—old Duchess Merolanna? But she was from somewhere else, wasn't she? Not of the Eddon bloodline, whatever that truly meant—she had only married an Eddon, like Queen Anissa . . .

Anissa. He had almost forgotten about her. Tolly had been manipulating her for quite some time, long before Tinwright himself had become the lord protector's unwilling servant. Anissa, who had married the king and had given birth to King Olin's last . . .

". . . Child?" Tinwright had been frightened before, but now he felt sickened as well. "You . . . you don't mean the child, do you? Anissa's child?"

Tolly nodded. "Young Alessandros, indeed. He is exactly what I need. Take soldiers and fetch him to me. Do not harm Anissa, though—I may still have some need of her." He stood looking out the window again, staring down at the lights of campfires.

Tinwright wanted it not to be true; he wanted to have misunderstood. "You want me to steal the queen's baby—the king's son?"

"If you are too craven just to take it, you may tell Anissa whatever you like," said Tolly, waving his hand as if stealing a woman's only child was an everyday sort of task. "Tell her that I mean to have the priests give him a special blessing or something like that. No, then she will wish to come along. I don't care, poet—time is short! Just bring the child back to me here. Take two guards along. Three of you should be able to deal with a single small Devonisian woman. Now go, curse you. Make haste!"

Child stealer. Tinwright stumbled out of the protector's chamber, wondering how he had been consigned to the darkest, cruelest pits of the afterlife without ever noticing his own death.

Ash Nitre's apprentice looked as though he didn't quite believe Chert. "Are you certain you only want two donkeys?"

"Just enough to pull the cart, yes." Chert nodded toward the line of waiting men, mostly stonecutters now too old for daily work but willing to do what they could to save Funderling Town. He wondered what they would say if they knew what he planned, but he also knew he could not afford to tell them until they were well away from the temple, on the site, isolated from the temptation to let a word or two slip. "The rest will be carried on foot. We've got narrow paths ahead of us. We may have to lift the donkeys over in a few places!"

"Problems enough of my own," the apprentice said. "Cinnabar and the rest of those unbraced Guildsmen now expect us to make five more barrels a day—five!"

Here, in this quiet part of the sheltering earth, it was doubtless hard to remember sometimes what was going on only a short distance away. Still, Chert thought, Nitre and his helpers might benefit by leaving their blasting-powder mill for a day and visiting the far end of the temple estate, where the healers were hard at work all hours of the day and even the men who had not suffered badly in the fighting had faces that looked as though they came from poorly made dolls, their eyes staring blank as buttons.

"It is a war, you know," was all Chert said.

"Oh, the Elders know I know *that*. Even after we go to all the work of making it, we still have to lower it down five hundred ells of rope. Do you know how long it takes to splice that much rope together well?" The apprentice shook his head. "I know it's a war. It had *better* be a war, to wear me out like this."

Flint, back today after another of his mysterious disappearances had driven Opal almost to distraction, clambered up onto the narrow seat of the wagon. Chert made certain the sacks of different ingredients were all tied before flapping the reins against the donkey's hindquarters to start the procession. He knew enough about the making of blasting powder now that he wasn't worried the saltpeter might catch fire and burst and kill them if it fell. Instead, he was worrying about what would happen if he had an accident on one of the steeper tracks and lost one of the large sacks completely, or—Elders forbid it!—the entire load. They had very little of anything to waste.

It was madness, of course, Chert knew. The whole idea was mad. Even if it worked correctly it might kill them all . . . but there was very little chance it would work correctly.

A worker walking in front of the cart slowed as others slowed before him, then at last had to set his barrow down. Chert pulled back on the reins while the road ahead was cleared of some minor blockage. He worried that he might have exaggerated the chances of success of this venture to Captain Vansen and the others.

"Papa Chert?"

He started. As was often the case, Flint had been silent so long he had forgotten he was there. "What, lad?"

The boy frowned as if trying to find the words to put across some particularly difficult notion. "I don't feel well."

"What's wrong? Is it your middle? Are you hungry?"

Flint shook his pale head. As always, he was as solemn as a Metamorphic Brother at prayer. "No. I feel strange. Something is starting up. Coming awake." He closed his eyes for a moment. "No. Not coming awake. Still asleep . . . but coming *closer.*" He wrapped his slender arms around his chest as though suddenly cold. "It gets stronger. In my sleep every night I hear the singing. It's my fault. That's what it says. It's my fault and it's going to get out."

Chert opened his mouth and then shut it. He knew that what he had been about to say, whatever it might have been—*Don't worry, lad, all will be well,* or *They're just bad dreams*—would have been a lie. And one thing about Flint was, it didn't do any good to lie to him. He always seemed to know. Since the moment he had entered their lives, since the moment Opal had fed him and he had attached himself to them like a stray cat, Chert had always felt that the boy knew more than Chert did himself. And, often enough to be disturbing, Flint had proved that it was true.

"Is there anything I can do?" he asked instead.

Flint looked up at him, and there was enough of the frightened child in him still, of a true frightened innocent, that Chert's heart felt as though it would break in his breast. "I don't know," the boy said quietly. "I don't think so. But sometimes I feel that I shouldn't be here—that I should go away. Far away."

"You can't do that, lad. Your mother would throw a strut and dump a load wall. No, if you're really worried about things then you should stay close to her. There's nothing on this earth, whether goblin or southron, that wouldn't be scared of Opal."

Flint actually smiled, a tiny, shy twitch of the lips that Chert had seen only twice or thrice all told. "You always say that, but you're not really afraid of her."

"Oh, but I am, lad. That woman is a terror, and I am more frightened than you can guess."

Flint looked at him closely, not certain whether he was joking or not. Chert wasn't quite certain, either. "Frightened of what?"

"That I'll disappoint her. That I'll let her down. That she'll finally decide she shouldn't have married me—that she should have accepted my brother's offer, instead. Oh, he fancied her, your uncle Nodule did. But she thought he was a blockhead." He laughed. "Blockhead—that's what she said! A wise woman, your mother."

He found Opal, Vermilion Cinnabar, and the rest of the women sitting in the deserted courtyard of what had once been the old way station between the Great Delve and the temple, talking and enjoying the cool, moist air. The way station was not only near the place Chert had chosen for his undertaking, but the air came down to it from vents above sea level, so it was always a bit cooler than the rest of the temple's lands. That was one of the reasons they had chosen it as a spot to mix gunflour: even mill dust could burn and explode if the weather was too hot and dry, so how much more dangerous would the mixture they were making be?

Opal and Vermilion had explained to the others most of what was to be done, the need for careful separation of the saltpeter from the other sands (it would be added at the last moment) and crafting the blasting powder into little balls the size of peppercorns, which according to Nitre made it burn hotter, faster, and more evenly.

"We will come only two times a day to carry back the blasting powder you ladies have made," Chert explained. "That way we can apply ourselves to our own tasks and you can do yours without too much interference."

"Too much interference from men, you mean," said Pebble Jasper, Wardthane Sledge's wife, who had her husband's delicate touch with a joke. "Men trying to interfere with us women, is what *I* mean."

"Since when do you run away from that?" another called. "We've heard you down on Gem Street, mooing like a lost cow outside the guildhall—'*Sledge! Sledger, my beauty! Come home to your Dolly! I'm a-lonely!*' "

Several of the women laughed so loud Chert thought they'd hurt themselves. He felt a bit awkward to have the boy hearing this, although of the two of them, only Chert was blushing. "Enough, good ladies. We all need to get to our work. Opal, a moment?"

She looked well—good color, as though she had been out in the upground sun. It was clear she had been working hard as well as talking and laughing. "So you're off, are you?" she asked.

"Have to, my old darling. We'll be back by suppertime to see how you ladies are doing and take away what you've made so far. Did Nitre show you all the tricks?"

"It's not a lot different from making a stew," she said dismissively. "We've got it written down—Vermilion writes a beautiful hand. Like something you'd see here in the temple, in a book." Her frown of preoccupation abruptly softened and she looked straight into his eyes. "Oh, my old man, you are so full of mad ideas! Do you really mean to bring down so much stone with this blasting powder? What if the whole world caves in? You frighten me, sometimes. You always have."

"What does that mean?" He had to admit it was mildly pleasing to be thought of as full of mad ideas. Certainly it was better than being Magister Nodule Blue Quartz's less-successful brother.

She looked around as if others might be listening in, but the women were busy overseeing Chert's men as they unloaded the various powders from the cart and their barrows, making certain each was delivered to its proper place and taking the opportunity to show off the innovations they had thought of, which of course set the men to arguing with them.

"You are my husband," she said, so quietly it might have been a secret. "I love you dearly, old fool, whatever you have got us into in the past—and I do not even wish to think what you might have done to us this time." She laughed, but her eyes blinked, and Chert realized to his surprise that they were full of tears. "You remember that as you dash about with your . . . strategies and wars." She made them both sound like playthings for errant boys. "Come back to me safe. I *demand* it of you. Do you promise?"

He looked at her face, her adored, familiar old face. "I do—at least I will do my best . . ."

"No. Promise." She had his hands tightly. "Don't go without saying it. Say you'll come back safe."

He looked at her, felt once more what he had felt other times—that she wanted something important from him, but he could not understand what it was and she could not tell him. "I promise," he said at last. "I'll come home safe."

"Good." She let go of his hand and swiped her sleeve roughly across her eyes. "Go on then. We'll be fine. We're Funderling women—we'll get the job done."

"I know." He leaned in and kissed her on the lips. "The boy should stay here with you. I do not want to have to keep an eye on him out where I'll be. Too many cross-passages, too many places to fall."

She nodded. "Fine. Go on, before I start blubbing again."

Lightened of its load of blast powder makings, the cart bounced over every stone as they wound along toward the Stormstone Roads, and Chert bounced with it. He reflected that it would probably be more comfortable to be walking and pushing an empty barrow like the others, but somebody had to make certain the donkeys didn't roll the cart into a pit.

Where are the others now? he worried. *Vansen, Cinnabar, all of them—are they still alive? Fighting for their lives down there?* His hours in the Maze and beside the Sea in the Depths were never far from his memory, a foreboding he could not shake off, like a terrifying dream. *How will I even know if they want me to go through with the plan? I suppose I could send down a message with Nitre's gunflour, wait for them to send one back up the same way.*

But what if they didn't reply? What if they couldn't? Who would make the decision then? Chert could not imagine making it himself. Chasing his adopted son through the Mysteries had been bad enough, but this was a responsibility that might horrify the Earth Elders themselves.

Ferras Vansen could no longer even guess at what day it was. Time itself had been smeared into a succession of hours with very little difference between them. They might have as many as three days before Midsummer's Eve, but Vansen had no precise idea and was far too busy fighting for his life to find out.

The Metamorphic Brothers' temple was only a distant memory now, far behind them and far above them: the autarch's superior force had driven them downward along the twisting passages between Five Arches and the Cavern of Winds, then out of that vast cavern and all the way down to the beginning of the dark Maze, the place where the Funderlings took their initiates.

Vansen's troops had slowed the autarch's progress considerably, but they continued to pay a high price for their resistance: the Funderlings had numbered less than two thousand at their greatest strength, when they had first entered the tunnels near Five Arches, but now they were less than a thousand and had stacked their dead three and four deep in the side tunnels as they gave ground—too many bodies to give any of them more than a cursory death-blessing before leaving them behind.

It was the grimmest struggle Vansen had ever seen, his undersized defenders hungry, exhausted, slippery with sweat, and forced to fight for hours beside the unburied bodies of their friends and kin. But what made it worst of all was the knowledge that their ending was already assured. This defense, however heroic, could only end in death for all of them, and what followed might even be worse for the survivors they would leave behind—their families and their neighbors.

Exhausted though he was, Ferras Vansen was finding it nearly impossible to sleep. The war was always on his mind, and he stayed awake long past his comrades trying to puzzle out impossible chances because he already knew that none of the possible chances would allow them to survive. When he did manage to fall into a shallow, uneasy slumber, he would be startled awake again by the feeling that all the stones in the world were tumbling down on top of him.

He was near the bottom, and the bottom was growing closer by the hour.

"Gods, but your men have fought well, Magister," he told Cinnabar. "I do not mean to sound surprised—I expected no less—but I am even more impressed by their bravery since you have no tradition of war."

"War isn't the only forge of bravery." Cinnabar reached over and ran his hand through his son's hair, but the boy didn't look up. Young Calomel had been kept out of the worst of the fighting but had still seen more than any child his age should have to see. He had gone from being the mascot and delight of the makeshift army to only another silent, weary, terrified young Funderling whose stare made Vansen's heart ache. "But make no mistake, Vansen, we Funderlings were warriors once upon a time."

"I have never heard it."

"Then you have never studied the history of Eion, sir." Cinnabar spoke sharply, but Vansen thought it was more from fatigue than any real animosity. "We fought in the greatest war of all, just to name one—against our own kin, the Qar."

"The Godwar?"

"Yes, but we fought in the wars of men, too. We were miners and sappers in all the great empires, Hierosol and the Kracian States and Syan and even here, in Anglin's day. Who do you think secured these caverns again after the Qar invaded? That was Funderling work and almost as bloody as this. Say what you will against the Qar but they are fierce, fierce fighters—thousands of our folk died taking these caverns and tunnels back. We called that time the 'Kinwar,' and we still have an expression, 'Lonely as a Kinwar maid,' because there were so few men to be husbands." He shook his head sadly. "If our people survive this, there will be far too many widows and unmarried girls again in the years ahead."

"If only the Qar had stood with us." That betrayal troubled him far more than any of his own wounds. He had misjudged the Twilight People badly, and now the whole Funderling tribe was paying for Ferras Vansen's stupidity. "I still can't believe . . . !"

"Don't torture yourself, Captain." Sledge Jasper looked up from his whetstone. The Funderling sharpened his knife so frequently that the blade was growing hard to see. "The Earth Elders have a plan for us—no mortal can claim to know as much as the gods."

"But this time it's the gods we must fight, or so it seemed from what the Qar told us."

Cinnabar snorted. "Me, I take nothing the Qar say on trust, but it doesn't matter. Whatever the truth, this southern king, this autarch . . . *he* thinks he can free the gods, and he's battering his way into our holiest of holies. That's reason enough to stand our lives on the balance. That you fight alongside us, Captain Vansen, is more than anyone could ask. Don't waste your strength on regrets."

Vansen wished it were so easy, that he could command his feelings like soldiers; but that army was far less obedient than these brave Funderlings.

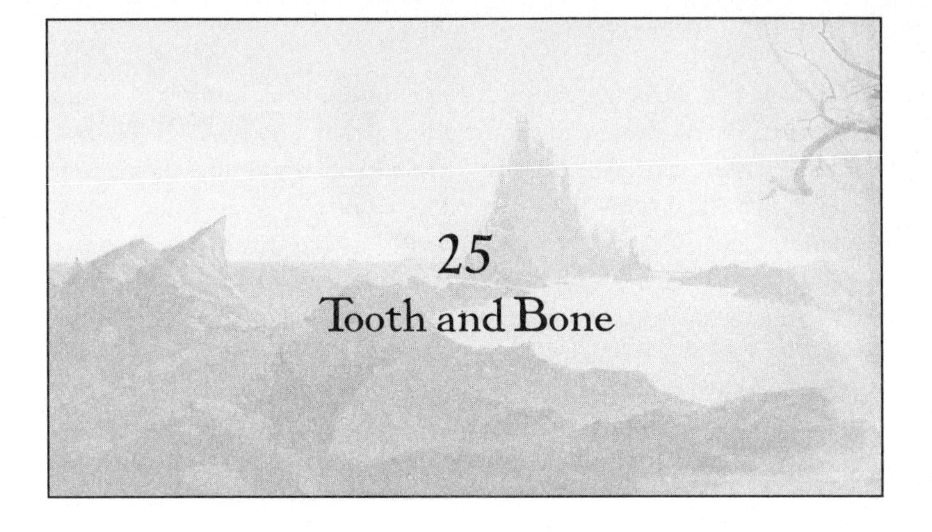

25
Tooth and Bone

"Blind Aristas told the boy that his dreams had been given to him by the gods, and that the meaning of them was that an innocent must go to the house of the angry god Zmeos Whitefire and find the lost sun."

—from "A Child's Book of the Orphan, and His Life and Death and Reward in Heaven"

HE AWAKENED SLOWLY, as if swimming up from Erivor's pounding depths.

"Why do you hide from the battle, Barrick Eddon?" One of the Trickster Qar grinned down at him like a fox. "There is still much to do."

"Yes," said another smiling nightmare. "You should not sleep so late."

But even as they taunted him, these long-limbed Tricksters—three of them, as far as he could see, in different downy shades of gray or brown and with angular faces like laughing demons out of the *Book of the Trigon*—had been clearing away the dirt and stones that had engulfed him when the wall of the cave collapsed. He could still hear the sounds of strenuous fighting outside the cavern, but at least the cannons had fallen silent. Barrick wanted very much to get out in the open before they began firing again.

As he staggered to his feet and began to knock the worst of the clumped dirt from his armor, the first Trickster handed him his sword, hilt-first. "Perhaps you would like to go out and stick some other sunlanders with that," the creature suggested.

"Perhaps I would." He examined the strong, slim Qar blade, which was scratched and dented in a few places but not too badly damaged. "And since you helped dig me out, perhaps you would like to keep me company while I do so."

"It would be a pleasure, Barrick Eddon," said the creature, its gray face shiny as ancient leather. "Oh, yes, we all know *your* name. I am Longscratch. These are Riddletongue and Blackspine, my quarterling cousins. We came here to kill sunlanders, but if it is now the southern sort we kill instead of your sort . . . well, let it be so."

The Qar had already made clear how they felt about his people; Barrick was undaunted. "Very well, then, you feathered bandits," he said. "Show me what you can do."

They dashed out of the cavern. The sun had mostly set, though a bit of it was still spread on the horizon like melted butter, and the sky had begun to show its first stars. It would be full dark soon, which would help the Qar, but even so, what chance could they have against the autarch's vastly larger force?

Barrick was surprised to see that the cannons facing the hillside had been abandoned, but only when a flight of a dozen or so birds swept past him and the shrill voices of their riders floated to him on the wind did he begin to understand some of what had happened. Birds were swooping down without warning all over the near side of the beach and at the edge of the picket around the Xixian camp, but attacking only southerners. That was because little men were *riding* on the birds—Queen Upsteeplebat's Rooftoppers, he realized. Thick leather and Mihanni plate didn't protect the soldiers' eyes and throats from the tiny darts the little men were firing at them. All around him, Xixians were running madly, hands clapped over their faces; many more lay unmoving on the sand, a-bristle with miniature arrows.

Barrick looked back to the cavern they had just quitted, but there was no sign of more troops coming. "Where is the queen?" he asked the Tricksters. "Where are the rest of our troops?"

"We are the end of the line," Longscratch said. "Our army is all in the field."

The flying Rooftoppers had only managed to drive the nearest Xixians back toward camp, but the attack from the air had given the rest of the Qar a chance to escape the hill caves without being blown to pieces by the autarch's cannons. But the Xixians were hardened fighters and had discovered that, as astonishing as little men on birds might be, they were not impossible to fight; some of the southerners had grabbed burning brands from their campfires and swung them through the air like rippling banners of flame.

Longscratch and his cousins finished scavenging up loose arrows, stuffing as many as they could find into their quivers, which, other than their arm-shields, seemed the only thing they wore.

"We must find Saqri and the others," Barrick called. "Follow me!"

He sprinted across the sand and then leaped over the ring-pit the southerners had dug around their camp. Some of the wooden barricade still lay on the ground, smoldering. A great knot of men and horses were caught up in a whirlpool of battle a few hundred paces away along the broken fence. Hundreds more of the autarch's men were running across the camp to join the struggle, some of them covering their heads with tent cloth against the claws and arrows of the bird-men. The Xixians were clearly beginning to regroup.

Barrick and the three Tricksters reached the rest of the Qar, who were trying to hold their newly won position against an ever-widening force of Xixian soldiers, but every time a southerner fell, another stepped up into his place. The rest of the autarch's troops, just arriving from the farther parts of the camp, were organizing themselves for a counterattack; in moments they would swoop down and wipe the few hundred Qar away like a storm wind threshing sea foam to oblivion.

Barrick could not pause to think about the worsening odds. The fighting was all around him now, spears leaping out at him like striking serpents, the bearded Xixians yelping and growling like dogs around a midden. His Qar armor was so light he hardly felt as if he was wearing it, but it was becoming cruelly hard work simply to stay alive on the ground, and now even more enemies were rushing toward them, many of them mounted. As if awakened by all this chaos, the Fireflower voices were threatening to overwhelm his thoughts.

Crying Hill, and the Gray Ones advancing . . .

Ah! My queen, my sister, take the children and flee . . . !

Stand and face us, soul-drinker . . .

Moments Barrick Eddon had never himself experienced washed over him and he found himself slowing, stunned by so many new ideas. A Xixian spear slipped past his shield and dug into the joint between his sword arm and the shoulder of his armor. He stumbled and almost dropped his blade as a line of fire burned across his skin and sinew. One of the Tricksters—the darkest one, Riddletongue—jumped forward into the breach and caught a second Xixian stab on his arm-shield, little more than a padded tube of bone too large to come from any creature Barrick knew. The Trickster then jabbed at the attacker with his own spear, an ivory-white needle only a few handspans longer than a sword.

Rasha, something in his memories whispered. *The tooth.*

The Trickster flung his arm up and let another attack scrape off his arm-shield. *Omuro-nah,* the Fireflower voices murmured. *The bone.*

Rasha-sha, omuro-nah, rasha-sha, omuro-nah! chanted ghosts from a hundred different battlefields in a hundred different centuries. *Tooth and bone, tooth and bone!* They had sung it in victory many times, but they had sung it even more frequently as their allies had died beside them and as they themselves had formed the ring in which they would postpone defeat as long as possible.

You will not see us because we hide in the night. You will not feel us until it is too late. You will not defeat us because we will die with our fangs in your throat—tooth and bone, tooth and bone . . . !

Barrick scrambled forward to fight beside these anciently familiar yet barely known allies, trying to remember all that Shaso had taught him. Each moment that unfolded was so full of sharp blades and screaming faces that for a while even the singing of the Fireflower rolled off him, as unremarked as a light rain.

He stopped at last to rest, lungs burning, sweat stinging his eyes, dozens of small and large cuts stinging him too. He was amazed by his own strength and stamina; even the Tricksters could not keep up with him.

They woke your blood, a voice sighed in words he could just separate from the din around him.

Ynnir? Speak to me! Dizzily, he looked around. The southerners were giving ground, but Xixian arrows still fell all around him, appearing suddenly and quivering in the churned ground of the city's bayside commons like some odd crop. *They are so many, Lord! What can I do to help Saqri?*

You can make haste, the voice told him. *Midsummer comes with the morning. If the southern king can keep you here until tomorrow, he has won—he has already nearly reached his prize.*

Make haste? How?

Tell my sister-wife that you and the rest of the People have served your purpose here. You must find a way down into the depths before it is too late . . . too late . . . ! The king's voice, already faint, trailed into silence.

Barrick could not find Saqri. The sun had set behind the hills, but that was not the reason. He could see much better than he should have been able to, so that the night seemed no darker than late afternoon. Catlike, his eyes made use of light he had never noticed before, light which gave edges and colors to things that ordinarily would have been obscure and gray. And his muscles and sinews seemed already to have recovered enough to begin fighting again. It was as though the power and experience of all the kings inside him were plaited like the fibers of a rope, strengthening all that he was, making him a newer, stronger thing.

Godlike. That was the word—there were moments he felt almost godlike. The Fireflower was like molten silver in his veins, strengthening him, filling him with heat and weight. Even with all Shaso's careful training, he would only have been a crippled boy of sixteen years who would never have survived this fight, but instead he had killed at least half a dozen men and wounded a dozen more, his blade finding its way through the Xixians' defenses time after time, like a stroke of lightning.

As he hurried toward the nearest fighting, some of the Xixians turned and saw him. They shouted with dismay. Something hot and gleeful rose up in Barrick Eddon's chest, like hands of fire cupping his heart.

They fear me!

As he reached the edge of the nearest skirmish, he finally saw Saqri and Hammerfoot and the others who had led the way. The queen and her friends were trapped in a swirling melee near the center of the Xixian camp. The moon had crept above the horizon, and its bony gleam was enough for him to see color, detail . . . everything. He could even make out the terrified faces of the men Saqri was fighting—or destroying, rather, because if Barrick's own blade had been like lightning, the queen's spear was something even swifter and more deadly, perhaps the heavenly thunderbolts that had once flickered around the peak of Mount Xandos itself.

But the Xixians had so many more soldiers that they could bury Saqri and the Ettins in bodies. Cavalrymen from the farther reaches of the embattled camp were now galloping toward the Qar in great numbers, and these newest arrivals, unlike the earliest defenders, were fully armored. Battle standards waved from the backs of their saddles in the colors of half a dozen Xixian companies, horsetails flapping, leather straps jangling with coins.

As Barrick watched, three of the riders split off and headed toward him. Good sense should have made him drop back to the security of the rest of the Qar forces, but something in Barrick was afire and would not let him do the sensible thing.

I've been running for years. No more. My banner is my blood—if they want it, let them come take it!

"For Whitefire! For Kupilas!" he shouted, and leaped forward so that he would be better spaced between the approaching riders. Something black flew at him, and he let his momentum carry him onto his side in the dirt as the arrow hissed by. "For Crooked!" he shouted, climbing to his feet again.

Something boomed on the bay behind him, but Barrick had no time to look. The first of the riders was upon him, leaning half out of the saddle and swinging a long, metal-headed club. Barrick took the blow on his shield and managed a cut at the rider's back, but his own blow only bounced harmlessly from the Xixian's armor. As the rider wheeled past, Barrick confronted the other two horsemen, both carrying long, small-headed axes. Instead of retreating, he ran forward, forcing them to mistime their swings. He feinted toward one, then shoved his blade into the other Xixian's chest just below his armpit. The Xixian clung to his saddle and did not fall, but he was shouting in pain and bleeding badly.

More thundering noises, and from the corner of his eye Barrick saw a huge burst of fire and smoke and flying dirt in the midst of the Qar, and bodies spinning through the air. The ships in the harbor! The autarch's men were firing their deck guns, but in their eagerness to destroy the Qar, they were firing into the mass of their own men as well!

The horsemen who were after Barrick had turned and were coming at him again, slower this time, to take better advantage of having him outnumbered.

Surprise them, the voices urged. A thousand different invisible maps of things he could do came to him, as if he could read every page of a book at the same time. He took a few steps, then suddenly sprinted forward and rolled beneath the middle rider's swinging mace. He grabbed at the man's wrist as he passed, something he could never have done with his arm crippled as it had been, then held on, digging his heels into the earth so that the horse's own force was enough to yank the man out of his saddle.

The soldier fell only halfway and dangled with his foot caught in the stirrup, thrashing helplessly until Barrick caught up. He vaulted into the saddle, then turned and hacked away at the screaming man's trapped ankle until it parted company with his foot and both parts of the Xixian soldier fell to the bloody sand.

As soon as Barrick had his own feet in the stirrups and the horse under his control, he made a point of riding after the wounded man he had already stabbed, not because the noises the man was making bothered him, but because a certain cold implacability was growing in him and he wanted to leave no loose ends, but before Barrick caught him the wounded horseman grabbed at his throat and fell from his horse, pierced by a Qar arrow. The last rider, now confronting a very different kind of fight, abruptly turned and spurred back toward the greater safety of the Xixian ranks at the edge of the camp.

Mounted now, the experience of a dozen kings helping him to calm the Xixian horse, he caught sight of the Tricksters fighting a group of southerners.

"Longscratch, Riddletongue, Blackspine—here!"

As he waited for them, Barrick could see a group of Xixians running away from the fight, but not with the desperate haste of men trying to flee the field of battle: they seemed to be under the control of an officer and were headed toward a large tent near the center of the camp, out between the edge of the city and the bay—the quarters of the autarch himself or some other high-ranking Xixian? Or perhaps something more directly of use in the battle, like one of their huge cannons? Or it might even hold important prisoners. "Hurry!" he shouted at the Qar. "Those Xixies are hiding something. We have to catch them!"

By the time the three Tricksters reached him, the fighting had surrounded him and Barrick was battling for his life again. As he and the Qar fought their way free, Barrick could see that something was happening on the hillside just outside the edge of the city and the camp. A great force of men was riding down out of the heights, singing and shouting. Were they enemies—or unexpected allies? Who could it be? They sounded like northerners! For a moment Barrick could almost believe the Fireflower was showing him some long-buried memory of Coldgray Moor, some vision of men and fairies at war, but it was no ancient Qar battle, it was here and now.

They fought their way out of the worst of the battle. Blackspine found a horse that had lost its rider and clambered into the saddle, soothing the frightened beast with a few whispered, hissing words, then extended a slender arm to help Riddletongue up behind him. Longscratch had found a mount of his own; the previous owner's severed hand was still tangled in the reins, bouncing against the horse's shoulder.

"They are hardy, these sunlanders," said Longscratch with a nod toward the dangling hand, "but the fighting does not have much savor. I liked them better in the old days, when they fought one at a time like proper warriors."

"And one had time to suck their marrow when they were dead," added Blackspine wistfully.

Barrick pointed with his bloodied sword. "Look! Those southerners have fallen back to guard that tent. Let's go have a look at what they don't want us to see." He spurred toward it, and the Tricksters followed, laughing and singing wordlessly.

Even as the Xixian horse hit full stride beneath him, its brute strength flowing as smoothly as oil from a flask, something darted past Barrick's face, passing so close that he ducked down against his stolen mount's neck. The men guarding the tent had seen them coming and were loosing arrows as fast as they could, but they did not flee. What was it they were willing to give their lives to guard? Barrick's heart began to pump even faster. Could they truly be so lucky as to have caught the autarch himself on the field?

Several of the guards disappeared into the tent. Barrick and the Tricksters came down on the rest and scattered them. Riddletongue killed one with a swift lunge and a thrust through the eye while his cousins occupied the others, and Barrick swung down from the saddle and forced his way in through the tent flap.

Half a dozen men were backed into the corner of the lavish tent, which was so full of lamps the interior seemed bright as day. Behind them, mostly hidden by the guards, stood a smaller figure with dark hair. Barrick could feel the blood racing in his veins—holy blood, god's blood. He leveled his sword calmly, as though he could pierce all the guards with one thrust, which at that heady moment did not feel impossible.

Careful—you will overstep . . . warned Ynnir's quiet voice, but Barrick could hardly hear it through the roaring triumph of his thoughts. *Find yourself, manchild.*

Oh, but I have found myself, he thought. *And I have found our enemy.* "Step out, Sulepis, you coward!" he shouted at the shape half-hidden behind the guards. "You have thrown men's lives at us like they were stones. Will you test your own arm?"

The one who stepped out was not the man Barrick expected. In fact, it was not a man at all, but a woman, strongly built and with her black hair cut short. She was clearly a Xixian but broader than any of the guards. She had a brutish look in her small eyes.

"Who you, little flea?" she demanded, her accent thick, her voice deep and hoarse.

"The autarch's death—and yours if you are hiding him, woman."

The woman laughed, showing discolored teeth. "I not autarch's wife! I am Tanyssa—I am Royal Strangler of Seclusion!" She lifted her surprisingly large hands to show she held a long knife in one and dangled a red silken cord from the other. "Come. I send you to hell."

The old Barrick would have wasted time on foolish doubts about fighting a woman, but this Barrick leaped forward, sword swinging. The guards bunched together in front of him—apparently the strangler's life was more valuable than theirs—and he suddenly realized he had set himself a problem that might be beyond even the skills the Fireflower had brought him. He managed to kill two of them, but the other four had him surrounded and the strangler Tanyssa was doing her best to reach his unprotected side with her blade when three dark shapes slipped into the tent, yellow eyes aglow.

"Do you require any help, Barrick Eddon?" Longscratch asked.

Barrick deflected a blow meant to take his head off and then spun away from the woman's long knife. "I would accept some, yes."

A moment later, the Tricksters were among the guards, ivory *rashayi* digging into flesh and even through Xixian armor. Barrick leaped over a newly fallen corpse toward the muscular woman. She spun to pull something from a golden chest.

"Where is the autarch?" Barrick demanded, his blade only a quivering inch from her back. Where is he?"

She turned around slowly to reveal she was holding a small piece of clouded crystal in her fingers and grinning like a castle gargoyle. "This to protect Golden One," the strangler said with a note of satisfaction. "Golden One gone now—I use to kill *you*!" And as Barrick stared in astonishment, Tanyssa popped the murky gem into her mouth like a sweetmeat.

Sand sprang into the air as if from every corner of the tent, a whirling cloud that blinded Barrick, but the sand rushed past him as though the strangler were its target, flowing over her, covering her body in tiny particles of stone. In the rush of air and sand, most of the lanterns blew out. The guards, suddenly uninterested in Barrick and the Qar, broke away and ran shouting in terror toward the tent door.

The thing that had been Tanyssa seemed to be getting larger but also more shapeless, no woman anymore but only a vague figure, big as an Ettin and growing bigger, with clublike hands that sprouted spiky claws. It had eyes like stars behind fog and a mouth that seemed a pit leading down into darkness. An unlucky guard that had not escaped was caught and shoved toward it by one of the Tricksters; the thing snatched up the screaming Xixian with talons that clacked like broken bricks, then lifted him to its gaping hole of a mouth, *swallowed* the hapless southerner to the shoulders and bit down. As the rest of the guard's still-twitching body fell to the monster's feet one of the Tricksters flung a lamp, but it bounced off the demon's stony skin and spread gobbets of fire along the tent wall.

"Run!" Longscratch shouted as he scrambled for the door. "We cannot kill a Stone Swallower!"

Flames ran everywhere. Barrick pushed his way through the smoke and followed the Tricksters outside. A moment later, with a bellow like a hamstrung bull, the thing that had been Tanyssa burst through the blazing silk in a shower of sparks.

Who do I pray to now? Barrick wondered as he dragged himself to his feet once more. *The gods are asleep!* Arrows whipcracked past him. The other Qar were hurrying toward the scene, but although a dozen arrows hit the demon, they bounced away and the thing hardly seemed to notice. Even the Fireflower voices had gone quiet in confusion or fear.

"Turn and run, Barrick Eddon!" Longscratch shouted. "There is no killing a beast like that. It is too strong . . . !"

"No! It will kill dozens of our warriors if we let it go!" he shouted back. The thing had caught Blackspine's horse and although the Trickster leaped off and escaped, the Stone Swallower was tearing the still living animal into pieces. Shouting as loud as he could, as much to keep out the terrible sound of the horse's death as to steel himself, Barrick picked up his sword and ran forward, then slashed at the thing's arm. It was like attacking a stone wall; the monster scarcely seemed to feel it. Other Qar joined him, jabbing at the thing with spears but achieving no more than

Barrick had. The Stone Swallower caught those who came too close and tore them apart with horrifying speed and strength. Barrick picked up a spear and threw it, but it bounced off uselessly. The inhuman silhouette stood stark against the burning tent, a victim in each hand. Barrick couldn't tell if the ruined corpses were horses or Qar.

The beast's bloody, scraping hand closed on him and this time all Barrick could do was hack at it over and over until the demon flung him to the ground like a man harried by biting flies. The fall dashed the air out of his lungs; for a moment blackness flowed over him as though he had tumbled into a cold, lightless river. He felt the Fireflower folding around him as if to ease him into the waiting dark, but then he heard one of the Tricksters screeching in agony, and Barrick swam back toward the light and the world.

As he tried to struggle to his feet, a huge, icy hand curled around him. He smelled breath that stank like molten iron as the Stone Swallower lifted him toward its gaping mouth. Most of the strength had run from Barrick's body as if he were a stuffed doll that had lost its sawdust. From the corner of his eye he could see flames, but now they had sprouted in a most unexpected place—out on the water of the Bay, great flaming banners rippling above the autarch's ships. He could not understand what that meant and, dying, did not much care. A voice drifted up from his memory—not the Fireflower, but old Shaso, berating him: *"You always ask to be given quarter when you tire, but your enemies will not care!"*

This thing thinks it's already killed me . . . !

The black maw stretched wide just before him. He knew he would have only one chance. He braced himself in the monster's grip, then shoved his sword as far as he could into the thing's mouth.

His blade vanished, ripped from his grasp by the violence of the creature's convulsion. It dropped him, then reared up over him with a horrible gurgling howl so loud it seemed the sky itself had torn loose from its vault, a seemingly unending howl of fury and pain. It gasped and coughed and gurgled wetly. A bloody, smoke-colored stone fell to the sand beside Barrick. Then the sky, or something just as big and dark, crashed down on top of him and stole the world away.

26
By the Light of Burning Ships

"The villagers of Tessideme did not want the boy to go on such a perilous quest, for he was much loved, but Adis the Orphan knew this was the task for which the gods had marked him."

—from "A Child's Book of the Orphan, and His Life and Death and Reward in Heaven"

BRIONY'S MOMENT OF HOPE was short-lived. As the Xixians on the waterfront fled from the attack of the airborne Rooftoppers and their birds, a force of the autarch's cavalry burst out from the town and came thundering down Market Road toward the harbor.

Briony joined Eneas and his remaining soldiers as they wheeled to face this new and deadly charge; all the nearby Qar quickly joined them. Some of the fairies were mounted on horses as beautiful and slender as the sticklike creatures she had seen in ancient mosaics, and the riders were even stranger than their mounts. Some of these new allies weren't even people, but foxes and wolves and wild forest cats whose very presence made the Syannese horses skittish.

"Do not lose heart!" Eneas cried to his men, who had begun to scatter in fear as the alien Qar came among them. "These are allies! Together we will bring the southern Falcon down!"

They met the charging Xixians at the place where Market Road crossed the dock road. As the two troops crashed together, the clamor of steel on steel and the screaming of both horses and men was so heartbreaking that Briony, still a dozen yards back from the fighting, wanted to clap her hands over her ears until the dreadful noise stopped.

Why was I so stubborn? Why did I think I should ride to war like a man? She was terrified.

But even the bravest of these knights must be frightened, she suddenly thought. *Even Eneas himself.* It didn't matter why she was here—she was here.

Briony had little time after that to think about anything except staying alive, dealing enough blows to defend herself, or to help an ally in need—she saved a bulky, bearlike creature from a mounted spearman by hammering the Xixian's helmet with her sword and knocking him out of the saddle. The bear-thing did not stop to thank her, but only hurried off to another part of the fray.

She stayed back from the thickest fighting where her smaller size and reach would be a disadvantage, striking only when she had to. If the southerners managed to push past on just one side, Briony's company and their allies would be caught between two halves of the autarch's forces and quickly squeezed to death. Torches were streaming toward Market Road from the fields and the town—hundreds, maybe thousands more of the autarch's foot soldiers still making their way to the battle. Eneas was too deep in the battle to see it, fighting for his life—without a miracle, there would be no escape from this nightmare except death.

Then the bay behind her exploded into flame.

No, not the bay, Briony saw as she struggled to turn her startled horse. Tongues of fire ran up the mast and along the furled sails of the nearest Xixian ship; as she stared, a dozen more vessels, large and small, kindled one after another. The flames seemed to leap across the bay like living things, two or three southern ships catching fire at a time until dozens were ablaze and the wavering red light of their burning fell across the battlefield as brightly as if the setting sun had returned. All around her, voices called out in surprise, wonder, and horror.

In the midst of this apparent world's ending, both sides again flung themselves at each other in the scarlet glow. With their means of escape now gone, the Xixians fought with growing desperation. The line of battle moved like a living thing. One moment the Qar and Syannese seemed poised to overrun the Xixians and drive them out of their own camp, then a few moments later the shape of the struggle convulsed again and the Syannese and the Qar became the desperate ones as they were forced back to the edge of Brenn's Bay.

A crackling arc of fire leaped out from behind Briony and set one of the nearest Xixian tents ablaze. A dozen more fiery streaks followed and several struck buildings along the waterfront, setting flames in their rafters and roofs. A few even reached the town's watchtower and within moments it, too, was blazing like a great torch.

Fire arrows! Where was this attack coming from? The water? The bay was black and shiny as pitch, ships and water both striped with smears of shuddering, blazing light. The autarch's ships were all on fire now, the survivors swimming for their lives—who could be shooting arrows?

Her answer came a moment later as long, dark shapes began to slide up onto the beach, dozens of long, low boats pushed through the shallows by dark figures who whooped and shouted as they dropped the boats and came running up from the water, some already loosing more fiery arrows into the Xixian camp. Why were they helping? Who were they?

Skimmers! she realized in astonishment as the first of the long-armed newcomers came sprinting up the beach and threw themselves onto the nearest Xixians.

"Egye-Var!" they screamed, jabbing with their fishing spears and slashing with strange swords as short and heavy bladed as butcher's cleavers. The southerners staggered back in dismay at this latest and most unexpected assault.

Briony felt a cry well up in her own throat. "Erivor—and Eddon!" she screamed, spurring her horse back into the thick of the fighting.

Barrick watched the girl crawling through the maze as though he were a bird hovering high above her, distant and detached. He could see how hopelessly far she was from the way out, but he could not find his voice to tell her and was not even certain he should bother. The black-haired girl looked familiar but he could not summon her name. That disappointed him, although he did not know why.

She is precious, a voice told him. *More precious than even you know.* It was the blind king speaking, he knew, but he did not understand why this nameless young woman should mean anything to him.

First of the last, the king told him. *Last of the first.*

What did that mean? Why was it so hard to think?

Do not forsake her, the king said.

He tried to ask, *What do you mean?* But nothing would pass his lips. He might have been some mute creature, a bird, a horse, watching things far beyond its understanding.

First of the last, the voice said, quieter this time, farther away. *Last of the first. Marriage of the dead. Hope for the living . . .*

What does it mean? But still he could not speak; the words were only in his own head, only in his own lonely, friendless thoughts.

No, Barrick Eddon.

The voice sounded different this time, closer—and it was a woman's voice. Could it be the dark-haired girl? Was she aware of him at last?

Come back to us, Barrick Eddon. Come back. It is not time for this journey yet. The roads are wrong. The darkness began to slip away like sand through an hourglass and a different, brighter world began to appear behind it.

"No!" Barrick cried, finding his voice at last. "She'll be lost! She'll be lost . . ."

"She still has a chance," someone said to him—another female voice, this one deeper and also more familiar than the first. "Do not give up hope."

A face was looking down at him, a pale oval with black eyes and an expression so calmly patient it might have been carved in marble—Saqri, the queen of the Fay.

"Hope . . . ?" he asked. He felt light-headed, but at the same time his body ached badly. A shadow, he remembered—a great shadow had fallen over him and pushed him into the darkness. "So dark . . . !"

"It is all one thing," Saqri said. "What you saw, what you fear, what you fought. All one thing concealed in a thousand, thousand guises. And that one thing is *oblivion*. Remember that, Barrick Eddon. The worst that can happen is that you cease to exist. Is that so bad?" Saqri had shed her battle armor and now wore a robe of shining white silk. A smaller Qar woman stood beside her, her angular features and animal eyes making her seem both less human and less frightening than the queen. "This is Sunset Pearl," Saqri said. "She is a healer."

Urayanu, the Fireflower voices murmured. *She of the Strengthening Touch.*

"What happened?" Something was missing. How had he come here?

"You destroyed the Stone Swallower, then you fell."

"That thing, that woman or . . . monster. . . . Who was she?"

Saqri shook her head. "Some minion of the autarch's. But the stone she had from her master—that was a great weapon indeed. A broken bit of tile, a small piece of Silvergleam's ruined moon-palace—a *kulik Khors*, as some mortals named them. As the greater Tiles can open a door across the roads of Grandmother Void, so too can one of those bits of stone. But it only opens doors to a very unpleasant place, and when the way is open, one of the things that lives there comes through to inhabit the body of the Stone Swallower. That is what you saw. That is what you fought." She turned to the other Qar woman. "How are the manchild's wounds?"

"The worst was that the thing fell on him in its death throes," the small woman said. "He will survive, my lady, but he needs rest."

"And that he will have. Thank you, Sunset Pearl." Saqri reached down and touched her cool fingers to Barrick's brow. "You did a brave thing, manchild. You set yourself against a terrible, pitiless foe who would have killed many. . . ."

He suddenly remembered what had been happening before his encounter with the Stone Swallower. "The autarch—all those soldiers—what happened? Did we beat him?"

"The southern king is no longer in the camp by the bay," Saqri told him. "But I think you guessed that already. He has taken his strongest forces and gone into the depths, so the danger is as great as ever. We and our unexpected mortal allies only had to fight troops he left behind, though even those were many times our number." She told him of the success of their plan, how the bird-mounted archers and the Skimmers with their flaming arrows and their small, silent boats had astonished the Xixians. "Only the surprise of our cousins' attacks saved us," Saqri finished. "The southerners broke and the survivors fled into the hills, so for the moment we are safe." She shook her head so gently her glossy black hair barely moved. "My husband was right. He often told me that one day we would fight beside our sundered kin again. I was certain he was only hoping for something that could never be."

"And you?" Barrick asked. He was tired and in pain, but he felt a stronger connection to the queen than ever before. "Are you well, Saqri? Have you rested?"

"I have just risen from a hundred years spent in unwilling sleep, Barrick Eddon. I will not need to rest again until my race is run." She touched her fingers together to form *Spider's Sleep*, which announced a moment of change. "Time is important to us now . . . and time is short. I am going now to meet with the mortal soldiers who aided us and talk with them of what will come next. I would be glad to have you with me." She looked at him for a long moment. "But I think Sunset Pearl would be angry with me if I brought you out. You have been near the edge and are only just back." She hesitated, something he did not remember seeing from her. "Unless it is that you miss the chance to speak with your own kind?"

Barrick shook his head. Just the thought was exhausting. "I scarcely remember speaking with my own kind, and I don't feel any strong urge to do it again. Who are they, anyway? Do you know yet?"

Again Saqri seemed to consider. "They are commanded by a prince of Syan. I am told his name is Eneas."

"Enander's son? I know of him. He is said to be a good man." Barrick let his head sag back down onto the cushion. "If I am truly needed, I'll manage. I'll come. . . ."

"You have convinced me," said the queen. "Stay. Rest and grow stronger." She bent and kissed his forehead with a touch dry as paper.

When Saqri had gone the healer named Sunset Pearl came back to Barrick's bedside with a cup in her hand. "Drink this," she said. "I think it will do you no harm, and it may do you much good."

He stared at her. He was feeling truly tired now, struggling to keep his eyes open. "You *think* it will do me no harm?"

She looked back at him sourly. There was something catlike about her, but it was a cat that had seen many years and many disappointments. "I have never plied my craft on a mortal man. Content yourself that if you die in terrible agony I will at least know what not to do with the next mortal."

He laughed a bit despite himself. "And who do you think will recommend any other mortals come to you if you kill me?" He lifted the cup to his lips, closing his eyes to try to make sense out of the unexpected but not wholly unpleasant flavors.

"You did not come to me by choice, Barrick Eddon," the healer said, "and I doubt the others needing my help in days ahead will be any different." Her look was less amused than resigned. "In truth, I expect to see more than a few dead and dying mortals here. Now drink up, Redling."

The name and its hint of the familiar puzzled him for a moment. He lay back and closed his eyes. "Strange," he told the healer, if she was still there. "I'm certain someone used to call me that . . . but I can't remember who . . ."

The Xixian carrack, or what remained of it, had been driven far onto the sand by the tide, but the big ship still blazed like a Zosimia bonfire, outshining the smaller but still sizable campfire that the Syannese soldiers had made near the water's edge.

Southmarch Castle lay just across the water. Briony could not quite accustom herself to that thought after so much time away—her *home* waited just across the bay. Just as the burning ship dwarfed the fire Briony shared with Eneas and his commanders, so the torches on the castle's battlements shone much brighter than the stars above the smoke-shrouded bay.

"Are you warm enough, Princess?" Eneas asked.

She almost laughed. Only a couple of hours before, men had been trying to murder her with spears and swords. "I am quite well, thank you. When are they coming?"

"The messenger said . . ." Eneas paused. "Look. They come."

A strange procession was making its way along the strand toward them by the light of burning Xixian ships that still smoldered on the bay. Some of the Syannese soldiers camped around their own small fires got up and scrambled away, although the Qar did not come close to any of them. Briony could understand their alarm. No one could see so many weird shapes and gaits go past or meet the gaze of those glowing eyes—orange, yellow, green as a will-o'-the-wisp—without feeling that something had changed forever, and not necessarily for the best.

The newcomers slipped up to the edge of the prince's fire and then stopped. At first Briony wondered why, but then a slender figure dressed in white stepped forward.

"May we share your fire?" The woman's voice had a strange music—Briony did not understand her words until a moment after she had finished. "I am Saqri, mistress of Qul-na-Qar. You would call me the queen of these folk."

"Of course, Majesty," Eneas said. "You are welcome here."

Saqri beckoned a small group of her own people to accompany her to the fire; the rest, perhaps two or three dozen at the most, promptly sat down on the ground. Relieved, the prince's soldiers went back to eating their well-earned meals and bandaging their wounds. They had already buried their dead. The Syannese had lost many men, but the Xixians had lost far more.

The fairy queen was not quite what Briony had expected. She was beautiful, of course, with skin as translucent as snow and eyes so wide and black that Briony was frightened to look into them for more than an instant. But although Saqri's beauty, preternatural stillness, and calm bearing lifted her above any mortal monarch, she was not tall. Briony was at least half a span taller. And even the Qar-woman's grace did not entirely hide the fact that she was sore and weary.

Eneas offered wine, and to Briony's surprise Saqri and most of her companions accepted it, although some of them had trouble drinking from cups. When they had been served, Eneas cleared his throat.

"So, Queen Saqri," he said, "we are grateful for your help today fighting the Xixians, but before we talk of anything else, I must know something. Are we still at war, your people and mine?"

The fairy queen's mouth pulled tight for a moment in what might have been a smile. "You ask a good question." For a brief moment the Qar woman's penetrating gaze left him and turned to Briony, who could not face it and looked away; instantly, she was angry with herself. "The answer, Prince Eneas," Saqri told him, "is that we are what we make of ourselves tonight, at this fire. But know this . . . ! Even though we may continue as allies, we will never be friends." She was looking at Briony again. "Your people—and particularly those who live in this castle—have taken things from me that cannot be replaced or forgiven." The fairy queen spoke with such feeling that Briony sensed the Syannese knights around her growing wary. "But I am not Yasammez, the dark lady you have already met and whom you already fear," Saqri told them, her voice turning measured once more. "She is the one who warred on Southmarch . . . although I admit I did not discourage her. Her bitterness toward your kind will never heal. But on this matter I have broken from her, and the People follow me." Saqri spread her hands. "So, Prince of Syan, our peoples are at peace as long as we fight together. There will be no treachery. Not from my folk, at least."

Eneas nodded. "Nor mine, I swear. So then, let us put the past aside and talk only of things that matter now. What do you plan? Has the autarch truly gone down into the ground under the castle, as I hear?"

"Tomorrow's sun brings Midsummer's Eve," Saqri said. "The day after is Midsummer, and when Midsummer ends, the hour we fear will be upon us. The year begins to die. The sun begins its slow journey away from the earth and the spirits of discord rejoice." She raised her hand as if in warning. "If the southern king, Sulepis the Autarch, defeats the few Funderlings who still resist him and reaches his goal in the depths beneath the castle by midnight of Midsummer's Day, he will be able to perform the ritual. He will open the gate of dream and free the gods."

"I have never heard of such a thing, not even in old tales," said Eneas. "Why would he do it?"

"It is said the southern king wishes to command a god . . . but this Sulepis may not wield as much power as he thinks." The Qar woman spoke quietly, but everyone at the fire strained to hear. "He may open a door that cannot be shut again. And there is nothing . . . nothing . . . to give us promise that the gods who come through will be awake and sane." Saqri made an odd gesture, hands spread on either side of her face. "In any case, though, it is certain that if the way to the gods is opened, it is this world—*our* world—that will suffer."

"Then we will help you, of course," said Eneas. "Strange as it all still seems, I have seen much to convince me today. We must fight with you to keep the autarch from his goal."

"Yes, you must fight with us," Saqri said. "But not *beside* us, I think. Your knights are not best suited for the battle beneath the castle . . ."

"Why this slander?" Lord Helkis demanded. "Our good men of Syan have held a wooden guard tower against a Xixian army ten times their number—you saw them on the field today! They fear nothing!"

"You misunderstand me." Saqri held the Syannese noble's stare for a moment until he dropped his head in a mixture of fury and shame. "I did not say they were not capable or brave, I said they were *not best suited*. Can they see in near-darkness like our Changing tribe? Can they make their own light in the depths like the Elementals? Can they break stone with their fingers like the Deep Ettins?" She extended her own hand, palm up. "Your men are brave, but the best of them are horsemen. In the steep black depths they would quickly become less than their best. Here beneath the sky, in Southmarch itself, they can make certain that Tolly the Protector does not throw in his forces on the side of the autarch."

"Surely no northerner, no matter how corrupt, would do such a thing," protested Eneas.

"But he already has." She said it with such calm that Briony knew even Eneas would believe her. "Our luck was good, though, and the two of them fell out over something. But when a creature like Hendon Tolly sees how things are going, he will fight fiercely to preserve his own life. If he attacks us from behind, that alone could slow us enough to allow the autarch the time he needs . . ."

"But how do you know so much about the plans and doings of mortals?" Briony asked. "About Tolly and the Xixians?"

"I know much about you, too, Briony Eddon," said the fairy queen. "Do not forget, until this moment our peoples have been at war. You may know little of the Qar, but it does not follow that the Qar also know little of you. We have long had . . ." She trailed off.

"Spies?" Briony demanded. "So—you, too? Is there anyone in this failing world who has *not* made my family's business their own? And why should I trust you, madam, to decide how my own castle is to be defended?"

"Trust? I have told you nothing that you cannot see for yourself. Prince Eneas, your men are horsemen—they would be wasted in the dark, cramped tunnels. Go to the castle. Find Tolly and kill him or imprison him. If you can do that, then feel free to send help to us through the gate to Funderling Town."

Briony turned to Eneas. "Don't do it!" The look on his face made her want to shout. Surely he could not so easily trust these fairies, who only weeks before had tried to throw down Southmarch and had killed so many of its citizens!

"Wait, I begin to understand," said the fairy queen. "It is your father, is it not, child? He is the true matter we discuss." Saqri pinned her with her gaze, and this time Briony could not escape it. "You want to march with us into the depths because your father is there—because you hope to save him from the autarch's clutches."

"No!" Briony said, although the fairy woman was absolutely right. "You know nothing about him . . . !"

"On the contrary—I know more about your father than I know of almost any other mortal. But that is not the point." Saqri reached out and clutched her arm. Briony tried to shake herself free but felt suddenly weak as an infant. The fairy woman's voice took on a harsher edge. "Look at me, child! Your family is at the center of many things, but I can tell you this—it is not held for you to save your father. I am not one of my people's Gray Egrets—I cannot peer through the future's veil—but I feel strongly and clearly enough *how things must be* to tell you that. Do not waste your warriors' lives on a selfish gamble, Briony Eddon. It could be that we Qar will find him and free him, but his fate will come to him whether you are beside him or not."

Tears filled Briony's eyes; she blinked, then wiped them away. Saqri's voice grew quieter now, almost kind. "I cannot say I feel sorry for you—not after what your family has done to mine—but I do know something of loss, and I also know something of confusion. For a long time I did not know whether to hate or forget. I have come now to believe hate is useless . . . but so is forgetting. Those who forget too easily are the toys of fate."

Briony's tears threatened to overspill again. "But what should I *do*?" she asked, and was not even certain to whom she spoke.

"Live, Briony Eddon," the fairy queen told her. "Live and remember. Remember and *learn*."

The dark-haired girl was running from him now. No matter how he tried to call out to her, to calm her, she wouldn't stop, as if he himself had become the thing she feared. He didn't immediately know where they were—at first he was not certain it *was* a place—but as he pursued her, he began to recognize the walls and stone floors of Southmarch.

He was in the Portrait Hall now, in front of the picture of Queen Sanasu that had so often caught his attention. Now, as he looked into his ancestor's dark eyes, he saw for the first time that her expression was not the distant, superior thing he had always thought, but a combination of many things—loss, fear, anger, and perhaps a little hope; even stranger, though, the portrait was moving, rippling as though something behind it was struggling to emerge.

He stretched out his hands toward the red-haired queen and began to scrape away what lay on the surface. It was not a picture at all, he realized—it was dirt, only dirt, but the more he scraped, the more dirt he found. He could still feel the movement just below his hands, so he doubled his effort, digging faster and faster until his fingers curled around something small and hard and cool to the touch. He pulled it out of the clinging earth and found he was holding a stone statue of the dark-haired girl, her face frozen in a look of terror. But even as he stared at it, the statue fell apart into a clump of shiny beetles that tumbled from his hands and began to crawl and fly away like a handful of spilled jewels. He cried out and tried to catch them, but within moments they had all vanished into the earth once more.

"Time grows short, Eneas Karallios," the queen of the fairies said. The light of the burning ships made the shadows of those gathered jump and caper like demons. "Have you come to a decision?"

"Please, do not trust them so easily, Eneas!" Briony pleaded.

"I am sorry, Princess," he said. "Truly sorry, you must believe me, but I must consider the safety of my own men first and, ultimately, my own country. That means I must also trust my own instincts, and those tell me that the fairy folk are right . . ." He raised his voice. "We will do as you say, Queen Saqri."

"Good. Then we have done all we can do here," Saqri said. "The rest of the southerners are scattered through the hills. They will not come back soon."

Briony did not trust herself to speak. They were going to leave her father's fate to the fairies. For a moment she entertained several wild schemes of how she could search for him by herself, but Briony knew she couldn't leave Eneas and his Syannese soldiers to free her home without her. Dull resignation set in.

"But when they see how small our numbers are, the Xixies now hiding in the hills will come back," Eneas said to Saqri. "What then?"

"You will be across the water and beyond their reach," the queen assured him. "Our allies will see to that . . ."

"Allies?" Eneas asked. "What allies are those . . . ?"

Briony would have sooner blinded herself than let the Qar woman see her fighting back tears of anger, but as she turned to leave this foolish, misbegotten council behind, she was distracted by a tall figure staggering up the beach from the Qar's tiny settlement of tents, headed toward the bonfire. At first she thought from its stiff-legged movements that it must be one of the Qar, but as it came closer she saw that, other than the odd, hobbling gait, the slender figure looked quite human. Its hair seemed to have the reddish color of the fire itself.

How strange, she thought—so much like Barrick's . . .

She stood, thunderstruck, as her brother limped past her and made his way toward the fairy queen. Barrick wore loose-fitting clothes, shirt and breeches of white cloth only a little darker than his skin, which seemed paler than she remembered, and he was a full head taller than Barrick had been the last time she saw him. Still, there could be no doubt it was her brother.

"Saqri!" he cried as he reached the queen, "Saqri, I understand now!" He noticed the others staring at him, although he had not yet seen Briony, and made a gesture she did not recognize. "Pardon." He turned back to the queen. "Qinnitan! The girl named Qinnitan—she is here! She is here, and I think she must be under the castle! I forgot her for the longest time—but how could that be? How could I forget someone so important?"

Saqri did not have a chance to respond before Briony pushed through the strange creatures ranged on the Qar side of the fire and stepped in front of him. "Barrick? Is that really you?" But it was—there could be no mistake. She threw herself at him, arms wide. "Barrick!"

To her astonishment, he did not respond at all; it was as though she embraced a stone oracle in a temple. "Who is this?" he asked, stepping back and pushing her arms away.

She stared at him in amazement. It was without doubt the face she had looked into like a mirror all her life—her brother, her twin. "Barrick, it's me, Briony! Your *sister*! Don't you recognize me?" She was stunned. Had she changed so much?

And then something came into his eyes . . . but it was not what she had expected, not at all. She saw a gleam of memory, but also mistrust and even irritation. "Ah. Of course—Briony. And have you been well, sister? It has been a very long time."

"Well?" She stepped back as though he had slapped her. "Barrick Eddon, what's happened to you? Why do you treat me this way? I have feared for you and suffered for your sake every day since we were separated. Do you tell me you have not thought of me at all?"

Instead of answering, he turned to the queen of the Fay with a helpless look on his face, as though asking for aid.

"Much has happened since you saw each other last," Saqri said. "Doubtless, you will find much to talk to your sister about when all this is over, Barrick Eddon. But now our time is short."

Barrick nodded as though that summed everything up perfectly. "I wish you well, Briony," he said, then nodded in Eneas' direction as well.

"And of course our other mortal allies, too. Saqri, I must speak to you when you return. I can feel Qinnitan's presence. She is *here*—I'm certain the autarch has her." He paused as if he might say more, then turned and limped back down the beach toward the Qar camp.

Briony stared after him, aching inside as though she had swallowed a handful of freezing stones. Within a few moments her brother had vanished into the dark once more.

27
Full of the Stuff

"Old Aristas was too feeble to accompany him now, so Adis set out on a white horse the villagers gave to him, with only a servant named Moros for companionship."

—from "A Child's Book of the Orphan, and His Life and Death and Reward in Heaven"

THE GOBLINS WERE BUSY DISMANTLING Yasammez's tent, but when the Elementals shivered into view they hopped out of the way, nimble as crickets, before returning to their chores. Neither Yasammez's chief eremite Aesi'uah or any of the others paid them any further attention. Goblins, especially those who labored in the larger houses, were legendarily discreet.

Only a few dozen other creatures remained in the large cavern known as Sandsilver's Dancing Room, most of them engaged like the goblins in removing all remnants of the camp that wouldn't dissolve or disappear on their own. The chamber was full of unusual scents and sounds; some of the rendering powders smelled like burning flowers; some of the laborers sang or rubbed their wings instead of speaking.

The newly arrived Elementals stood before Yasammez. "Hail, Great Lady," said Stone of the Unwilling, courteously diffusing the glare of his presence. "You called, we came."

"Is that true?" The dark lady pitched her voice in the tone that the Elementals could see as a cold blue light. "Because there are other times

I have called you but did not receive such a swift answer. In fact, I received no answer at all."

Stone of the Unwilling shifted, flickered. "My lady?"

"You have always been faithful to your people's old promises," Yasammez said, "both to me and to the Fireflower."

"Of course, Lady. And I am still faithful."

"Perhaps. But I would have hoped you would have brought me a clanswoman who would be as faithful in friendship and courage as you are . . . instead of this one."

The smaller Elemental's glow jittered a bilious yellow for a moment before she spoke. "Mistress, do you doubt my loyalty to the People?"

"I make no accusations, Shadow's Cauldron, but I do ask why you have not responded to my call. Three times I summoned you, and three times the void in which your people swim like fishes sent me back no word of you."

Yellow-green flashed again. "And does that make me a traitor, Mistress?"

"Clanswoman!" It was easy to see that Stone of the Unwilling was agitated; his light jiggled like wind-whipped fire beneath his wrappings. "That is no way to speak to the Daughter."

"Not even a demigoddess can call me traitor."

Watching this bizarre confrontation, the councillor Aesi'uah felt a shadow of superstitious terror fall over her. The Elementals were the last and fiercest of the races to join in the confederation of the People; some said they wielded powers that even the Fireflower dynasty feared. Stone of the Unwilling's people would make terrible enemies.

"Why so much anger, Shadow's Cauldron?" the eremite asked aloud, framing her hands in a carefully chosen gesture of supplication. "That does not seem best for people surrounded by enemies, as we are."

"But we begin to wonder whether it is Lady Yasammez herself who is no longer as firmly in service to her people as she would have us believe," said the smaller Elemental.

"Clanswoman, I do not understand you," said Stone of the Unwilling. "Clearly, we must go somewhere where the winds and lights of our words can play unhindered, so you can explain this outrageous behavior to me." He turned to Yasammez, his robes billowing in his discontent. "Forgive us, Mistress. Forgive my clanswoman."

The lights glared from Shadow's Cauldron's hood, and her arms stretched as though she might reach all the way to the high ceiling of the cavern, but she was only reshaping herself; when she had finished, she made herself into a strange replica of Yasammez, but she had let slip the ribbons covering her face and what hung before them was a terrible, empty glare. "Why did you give up the Seal of War?" she said. "Tell us why, Lady."

"It is hardly your place to demand answers." Her thoughts were as cold as stinging sleet. "I did what was best for the People."

"You gave both your blessing and your army to Saqri, wife and sister of the mortals' greatest friend in Qul-na-Qar, that traitor Ynnir!" Shadow's Cauldron's thoughts were sharp and comfortless. "If you needed any more proof, she has already brought a mortal into our midst and all but shares her power with him! A *mortal*! Together, they will throw away lives by the handful, when there is only one weapon we need to destroy this southern upstart and his plans." She flourished her gloved hand and the gleaming sphere that was the Fever Egg appeared there. "Do not try to take it from me," she warned. "It is an image, no more. But it has been given to the Elementals and we will make certain it is well-used."

"This goes too far . . ." began Stone of the Unwilling.

"It is powerfully close to the very treachery you deny," said Aesi'uah.

"Who are you, eremite?" spat Shadow's Cauldron. "A creature of bones and mud. Not to mention one of the Dreamless—an entire country of traitors . . . !"

"*Enough*." The voice of Yasammez was like a whipcrack in all their thoughts. Though she made no audible sound, the goblins carrying her tent across the other side of the cavern fell to the floor, clutching their heads in terror. "Silence—all of you. Do you know to whom you speak, woman of the Elementals? Has no one told you?" Yasammez took a step forward, and although the movement was slight, the Elementals' robes billowed as though a great wind had come. "I am Yasammez of the Wanderwind Mountains, the daughter of Crooked himself! You dare to hold your judgment up to mine?"

"You have given up the Seal of War . . . !"

"I have given the Seal of War to Saqri, the last in my family's line—the hearth of the Fireflower! It was she and her husband-brother who gave the Seal to me in the first place." She closed her outstretched hand and the image of the Fever Egg was suddenly gone from Shadow's Cauldron's hand. "Now I will tell you what will happen. You will listen and understand. If you do not obey me, the void will not recognize you and the wind will not carry you nor the darkness hide you."

"Since we swore our loyalty to the Fireflower, we have always been its strongest and most determined allies," declared a fretful, flickering Stone of the Unwilling. "This is only a small dispute, Mistress—a confusion created by the fires and shadows of war."

Yasammez gave him a cold look and went on as though he had not spoken. "I do not know what will happen in these final days. I do not know what my own role will be. I *do* know what yours will be, Shadow's Cauldron. You will keep the Fever Egg safe and unbroken until I say otherwise. Do you understand?"

The flicker of the Elemental's fire was purplish and sullen. "I will never . . ."

Yasammez opened her hand, and this time Shadow's Cauldron rose into the air and grew smaller and smaller until she was little bigger than the Egg itself, a small black bundle leaking light.

"The Egg must not be shattered unless I tell you to do so." Yasammez's words were like precise hammer blows. "Under no other circumstances will it be employed. Thus I bind you and command you by the fire that is in us all. *Do you understand*?"

The purplish glow guttered and then grew again, this time suffused with a deep, leavening blue. "I understand," Shadow's Cauldron said at last.

"And agree?"

Blue deepened into violet. "Yes. I agree."

Yasammez dropped her hand and allowed the Elemental to unfold into more ordinary proportions. "Furthermore, the next time I summon you, you will come like the biting winds of the Between are blowing you. Do you understand and agree?"

"Agree."

"That is enough, then. I have other matters to attend to." Yasammez stepped back, and the pressure that had made the cavern seem to be shrinking around them suddenly diminished. "These may be the last days of the People. Do not let your petty schemes and hatreds betray you—or us."

And then she turned and walked from the cavern. Aesi'uah followed, more than a little alarmed.

* * *

Stone of the Unwilling, so discomfited that his light flickered, found his voice at last. *"What were you thinking, Clanswoman? You challenged the dark lady!"*

"She will betray us all if we let her. I feel it. Many in the clan feel it. You are too old, too trusting. When the mortals are gone . . . yes, and when the mortal-loving Fireflower dynasty is ended . . . the earth and all its colors and sounds will be ours!"

"You can call me what you want, foolish young one. If you meddle with Yasammez, she will destroy you without a second thought. She is the daughter of a god!"

"She is stronger than I supposed," Shadow's Cauldron admitted. *"But she has given us the greatest weapon of all."*

"Do not think to use it against her!" Stone of the Unwilling was clearly disturbed. *"That is folly beyond any I have ever seen. She will know, and she will destroy you—perhaps destroy all our clan!"*

"We are the Elementals," his clanswoman told him. *"We should never have let ourselves become the lackeys of the Fireflower. I am not such a fool as to challenge Yasammez again, not without my swarm-sisters and swarm-brothers present, so for now she has the whip hand. But nothing lasts forever."*

And with that she was gone back into the void, leaving Stone of the Unwilling to follow, cursing the young and their foolishness.

The Cavern of Winds was as broad as many of the larger chambers in the lightless depths, and despite their superior numbers the autarch's troops had not found it easy to conquer; they had only driven out the Funderling defenders a few hours earlier. While the vanguard of the army pushed deeper, Pinimmon Vash and the rest of the moving city prepared the camp.

The great cavern was a strange place, with wind skirling noisily through rifts in the ceiling, droning so continuously that it sometimes seemed to Vash they had stopped to rest inside a hurdy-gurdy. Now that the fighting was over and they could bring in torches, the Xixians had discovered that a great crevice ran along one side of the cavern, a place where part of the massive slab of limestone that made up the floor of most of the room had broken off and tumbled into the depths, leaving only a ragged edge and beyond that, unknown darkness.

Pinimmon Vash's mood should have been improved by the knowledge that he was surrounded by thousands of Xixian fighting men, but it made little difference except that in his nightmares of collapsing earth, he was now accompanied into crushing, smothering death by many other men, all as helpless as he was.

Still, he was glad for a moment to be in a space that did not make him feel as though he had to crawl under a table just to cross from one side of it to the other. The lights of the fires—still not too many, of course, because of the smoke in the confined space—reflected warmly from the jagged heights of the high ceiling, and altogether the place had a delicate beauty unlike even other larger chambers they had traversed.

But I would still give one of my limbs to be aboveground again for good.

The royal prisoner was waiting for him when he emerged from his tent, so Pinimmon Vash shooed away the two boys still meddling with the hem of his robe. He had only been allowed to bring a single pair and felt very inhibited, afraid to give either of them the beatings they deserved for fear of being left with only one healthy servant—or none!

"Is there something I can do for you, King Olin?" he asked, praying silently that the man would not start babbling about the scotarch again. Vash was still considering what he had learned about Prusus.

The northern monarch did not look well. He hadn't seemed entirely healthy since they had reached Southmarch, but had taken a sharp turn for the worse since the autarch had brought him beneath the ground in their relentless march downward to only-Nushash-and-the-other-gods-knew-where. "Yes, Lord Vash, you can." Olin smiled, but he looked pale and ill. "You can tell me if the autarch plans to join us today?"

There was something odd about the question—generally the northern king did everything he could to avoid the Golden One—but Vash had not had even one cup of tea yet this morning and his head hurt. "That is not for me to say, King Olin. If we are fortunate, the Golden One may gift us with his presence later. Why?"

Olin mopped sweat from his forehead. He managed a sickly, but still angry, smile. "After all, I do not have much longer to satisfy my curiosity, do I?"

Vash squirmed a little. He cared nothing for the northerner, but was uncomfortable with the amount of time he was being forced to spend with a man whom everyone knew would soon be killed. It seemed to reduce his own importance, for one thing, but there were moments when it bothered him even more than that, in ways Vash could not quite express. He had known many a man who had later been executed, but he had never been asked to sit and talk with the fellow after the sentence had been passed and make sure he was comfortable, in fact to treat him like an honored guest in all ways except one—the manner of his leaving. The fact he should have to do so now was awkward and unfair.

King Olin turned and walked a little distance away; his guards stayed close beside him. For a moment Vash wondered if the northerner had some trickery in mind, but dismissed it. Olin had ample reasons to behave strangely. Perhaps like Vash himself, the knowledge of so much stone and dirt above his head was enough to make the northern king unwell. In any case, even if it was shamming, it scarcely mattered: Olin was now under the constant guard of three of the autarch's Leopards, all of them armed with matchlock rifles. Still, it did no good to be overconfident—the man truly looked unwell. Vash decided he should ask the guards how Olin was eating. If he died before the Golden One was ready for him it would be a catastrophe.

A skirl of flutes rose and echoed through the cavern; scented smoke billowed from the door of the autarch's massive tent as it opened. The Nushash priests came out on their hands and knees; even by lamplight Vash could see them struggling to speak their prayers without coughing. The men who filed out after them each carried a length of carved and polished and painted wood—the walk boards, as they were called. With the quickness of a team of acrobats honed by long practice, they dropped onto the ground, arranged themselves on their backs, and then held the boards on top of themselves, steadying them with foreheads, hands, and feet to make a pathway for the autarch to walk upon. Vash knew that the Golden One did not like to use the walk boards for more than a short distance because the men from one end hurrying forward with the heavy boards to throw themselves down in front of him disturbed the serenity of the monarch's thoughts.

"What think you?" Sulepis was dressed, not in his battle armor as on most days, but in the high, scalloped hat and scarlet robes of a Nushash priest, and his face was striped with ash. He struck a pose and intoned, *"May the darkness pass you by."* It was a ritual greeting: today was the Xixian Day of Fires, the day the northern infidels called Midsummer's Eve. Tomorrow the sun would begin to die.

"And may it pass you by as well, Golden One." Vash remembered how fearful the holiday had seemed when he was small, especially the evening, the darkness full of mourning cries and the chants of the ash-covered priests. Then, in the middle of the night, crowds of wild women and men (or so it seemed to him then; the child Pinimmon had not recognized that they were simply ordinary people who had been drinking and dancing for hours) would charge through the streets, lighting bonfires and demanding that those in their houses come out and join them in making noise to frighten away the dreadful Deathlord Xergal, who was trying to steal the moon from Nushash's brother, Xosh. When the sun finally rose the following morning, known as the Day of Smoke, the celebrants would slink back inside to sleep off their excesses. That day the streets were always deserted except for children; Vash could still remember the feeling that he and his younger brothers walked through a city of the dead.

"Yes, Vash, it is strange and wonderful to pass a Day of Fires here beneath the earth, unable even to see the sun." Despite his words, the autarch did not seem unduly disturbed. He turned to Olin. "I heard you speak my name." He took a few steps down the line of walk-board slaves. Each slap of his sandal was met with a small grunt as the man beneath took his weight; the autarch was not bulky, but he was very tall. "You seem glum, King Olin," Sulepis said to the northerner, bending over him like a concerned parent. "Is our hospitality lacking? Is there something more you wish of me, King Olin?"

Olin nodded and even made and held a long bow, which seemed odd—he had always gone out of his way to avoid showing Sulepis any but the broadest social courtesies. "Yes. Yes, I do. I wish you . . . *dead*!"

To Vash's utter horror, the northern king abruptly straightened and leaped at the autarch, far more swiftly than the paramount minister would have imagined a man Olin's age could move. The guards were caught completely by surprise as the northerner drove whatever he held in his hand into the autarch's belly. The weapon shattered.

Olin fell back, holding the broken end of a long, jagged shard of stone in his hand. For a moment Vash was terrified to see blood around the northerner's fist where he clutched the broken stone blade, but then realized with relief that the dripping darkness came from King Olin's own hand.

Olin cursed in a broken voice and staggered back. All three of the guards had their weapons out and aimed now, two with rifles, one with a matchlock pistol that only the autarch's most senior guards were allowed to carry. More guards hurried up and likely would have beaten the northerner to death on the spot, but Sulepis stopped them.

"Do not harm him. I am well," the autarch announced. He pulled aside a fold of his robe to display the padded, sleeveless shirt beneath. "It is a pity you did not study our people more carefully, Olin." Sulepis appeared unmoved, even amused, as though a jagged piece of stone had not just been driven into his midsection. "On the Day of Fire, the autarch must dress like a high priest of Nushash, which means he must wear all the vestments, outer and inner." He chortled with childlike glee. "I will not complain about having to wear such hot undergarments again!"

Olin dropped the piece of broken stone, then turned and ran toward the place where the cavern floor dropped away into darkness. The Leopard guard with the pistol took aim at his back but again the autarch stopped him.

"He can go nowhere. He knows that. Let him have his moment of freedom."

The guard reluctantly dropped the weapon to his side, and they all watched as the king of Southmarch halted at the edge of the abyss. He looked down for a long moment, then turned back to the Golden One and the guards. "You have a demon's luck, Sulepis. I have waited long for that chance, but your god must be watching you."

"Oh, he is watching," the autarch said again, still laughing. "But he is watching because he fears me!" He gestured toward Olin. "And now, little king, what will you do next?"

"The one thing you cannot prevent." The northerner was disheveled, pale, and sweating, all his recent ill-health plain on his face and in his labored breathing. "I am going to take my own life. I need only step back one pace. Then you will see how far your plans go without any of Sanasu's blood to make your filthy charms with!"

Vash did not doubt from the look on Olin's face that he would carry through on his threat. He felt a moment of unexpected hope. *If Olin Eddon dies, then perhaps our master will give up this mad plan of his. Perhaps we will be able to return to Xand—to a life worth living.*

But the autarch seemed quite undisturbed. "Oh, Olin, this is a fine comedy. Like something played here during your Zosimia festivals, is it not?"

"I am no longer listening to you and your madness and your tricks." The northerner was at the very edge of the pit—he did not even need to step back again to fall, only lean too far. Nobody would be able to prevent it.

"No trick. Rather, just like your comic tales, it is all a matter of timing. If you had made this threat yesterday or the day before, you would have posed a serious problem for me. But today . . ." Sulepis chuckled again and shook his head. "Oh, wait until you see how your own gods have cursed and betrayed you!"

"What are you talking about?"

Sulepis turned and whispered something to one of the half dozen guards hovering nearby. The man turned and went back to the autarch's magnificent, gold-stitched tent. "You have made one small misjudgment, Olin. That is no mean tally, but it is one more than you could afford to make. You see, it is not particularly the blood of Sanasu the Weeping Queen I must have, it is the blood of her ancestor, the god Habbili—the one you northerners know as Kupilas the Crooked." The autarch smiled at the king's growing look of dismay. "The god spread his seed a bit more widely than only among the Qar, you see. For one thing, he lived long on Mount Xandos among his enemies, and in that time fathered a child or two upon mortal women. Or perhaps it was upon goddesses or demigoddesses, and they in turn mated with mortals—it does not matter. In Xand we have always heard tales of the survival of Habbili's bloodline. My priests and I eventually proved those rumors right . . . and that is why, since last night, you are no longer the only key that will open Heaven's door. Look!"

The guard was returning with the girl, who had been dressed like one of the Brides from the Seclusion. He brought her to Sulepis and pushed her roughly to her knees beside the walk-board slaves.

"You will remember Qinnitan of the Hive, I think, King Olin," the autarch said, as if introducing them to each other at a state banquet. "You see her now as we first saw her, with the mark of her bloodline visible in her hair." He bent and reached out a long arm to pull the girl's hair back; a streak of fiery orange-red ran through the shining fall of black like a wound. "So you see, you may throw yourself to your death if you wish, Olin Eddon. I will miss these last hours of your conversation, but now that I have her, I no longer need you or your blood."

The northern king looked from the triumphantly grinning autarch to the dull-eyed girl. "Ah, it's you, child," Olin said. "I was right—there *was* something about you, after all."

She only looked at him and then back to the autarch, face full of sullen terror.

After a moment Olin lifted his hands. "I surrender. You can do with me what you will, Sulepis. I ask you a boon, however. I will go to my death without struggle if you promise you will spare the girl. She is only a child!"

"A child with very, very old blood," said the autarch. "But you are in no position to make demands, Olin."

The girl looked up, and for the first time seemed to understand what was going on. Her eyes, already large and dark, widened as she saw Olin on the precipice. "Go!" she shouted, and then, as if to make it clear she did know what was happening, added, "Go, die! Be free!"

But instead of heartening him, these words seemed to take the last strength out of Olin Eddon. He sagged to his knees, letting the broken piece of stone fall from his hand, and did not move as the guards dragged him away from the edge and then quickly tied his hands behind his back.

"Do not harm him, but put him back under lock and key." The autarch smiled at Vash. "We cannot reward him for bad behavior, of course."

"Is there nothing to which you will not stoop?" Olin asked the autarch as they marched him past. "To hide behind a child . . . !"

"I would murder a million children to reach what is mine," Sulepis said calmly. "That is why I will be a god when you and your countrymen have disappeared into the dust of the past." Vash must have betrayed something with his expression, because the autarch pointed at the old courtier as if to drive the lesson home. "A million children, my old friend—ten million! It makes no difference. I would destroy everything that lived without a second thought, if it brought me my heart's desire."

Vash invented an errand and left soon after. The autarch, who was discussing the push into the depths beneath the castle with his officers, did not seem to notice his departure.

Matt Tinwright had thought he could sink no lower—that his days living at Hendon Tolly's side, kept at the lord protector's beck and call, forced to watch and even participate in some of Tolly's more disturbing pastimes, had pulled him down so far nothing could ever shock him again. He had been wrong.

It was bad enough he had to carry young Prince Alessandros, who had been squirming and crying all the way across the residence; Tinwright could not imagine what he would have done if he had been forced to keep Queen Anissa restrained, a task that had fallen to the two guards after they had taken the child. She fought and shrieked in their arms, but the upper floors of the residence might as well have been deserted: as the group made its way down the hall no one even opened a door to look out at what was happening. Tinwright could only guess that they had become familiar with the sound of distressed women being dragged across the residence at night.

But why am I helping this monster? he thought. *Nobody knows better than I do what a mad beast he is. I should find a way to kill him, even if I die myself making it happen.*

But that was just the problem: Matthias Tinwright did not want to die. Not even to rid the world of a murderous piece of offal like Hendon Tolly. In fact, he was so terrified of the lord protector that he couldn't convince himself he would succeed even if he somehow steeled himself to do it. Tolly would survive, somehow, and he would go out of his way to make Tinwright's death long and painful.

So instead you'll go along with him? he asked himself. *By Zosim's lyre, what kind of man are you?*

A coward. There was no reason to lie—Tinwright was talking only to Tinwright, after all. *A coward who wants to live. Besides if I die, who will take care of Elan? Who will keep her from falling back into Tolly's clutches?*

But it wasn't really Elan, he knew. Coward—that was the true shape of it. No sense in pretending otherwise.

Queen Anissa was struggling with the guards again, trying to reach Tinwright and the child. "Sir!" she cried to Tinwright, "Sir, I know you not, but you have a kind face. Will you let at least me carry him? Please, sir! He is frightened, the poor, dear little lamb." She strained toward the red-faced, weeping baby. "Let his mama hold! Let me . . . !"

Matt Tinwright felt as if he might be ill. What could the harm be, after all? Why shouldn't Anissa hold the baby?

Because she might kill the child instead of letting Tolly have him, he told himself, and was horrified not only to be able to conceive of such a thing, but to know it was true and he had to act on it. *Come now,* he told himself, as if another member of the crowd of Matt Tinwrights had shouldered forward to have a say. *If you hold onto the baby, you can keep it safe. No telling what this hysterical woman might do.*

"Please, sir, please!" Her tone changed, grew louder and more desperate as they approached Tolly's chambers. "Oh, by the gods, by the holy Three," she began to screech, "and our lady Zoria and all the demons in the deeps, curse this monster for stealing my baby! Curse him!"

And the worst thing was that he did not know which monster she meant, Hendon Tolly or himself, and he could not find much difference between the two.

"Why do you act like this, my queen? Why do you make such a clamor? No one will hurt your baby. Go back to your rooms." Hendon was smoother and more composed than the last time Tinwright had seen him. He had bathed and put on a clean doublet and hose; except for a certain feral quality in his stare and his ceaseless pacing and gesticulating, he almost seemed the old Hendon Tolly again.

Anissa was trying her hardest to believe the lies he was telling her, but she was not finding it easy. "Why take him from me, Lord Tolly? Why such treating of me, who always gives you kind words and . . . kind help?" Her accent, thick at the best of times, had become nearly impenetrable. "Just give back him and I bring when you need him."

"But I need him now, sweet Anissa." Hendon smiled, but he was clearly out of patience with her. He held the baby awkwardly, like a fastidious scholar who had been handed a mud-spattered pig. "Enough talk, now. Go back to your chambers and I promise I will soon bring him to you, safe and sound."

"But why do you take him? For what?" She tried to smile back, but it was agonizing to see how poorly she did it. "You cannot need such a little one!"

"Ah, but I do, my queen, and you must trust me. Have I not helped you since your husband was taken from you? Have I not guided you during these most difficult times, and sworn to you that Alessandros here would follow in his father's footsteps?"

"But why do you need my baby?" She pulled free of the guard who held her arm and threw herself down onto her knees in front of Hendon

Tolly. It was painful to watch, like a sick drunkard begging for a last cup.

"Enough. I do not have time to explain everything. Go back to your rooms, Anissa." Tolly's already scant tolerance was fraying fast. The imposture—his attempt to seem ordinary and composed—was already falling apart.

"No!" She crawled rapidly toward him and threw her arms about his legs. "Please, Hendon! I beg you! Not this thing! Not my Sandros!"

"For the love of all the gods, will you simpletons get this woman off me!" Tolly shoved her away with his foot, fighting to keep a grip on the young child, who was squirming and crying again. He managed to get his heel against the queen's shoulder and kept her at bay that way, although she wept and tried to get to him. At last the guards pried her loose and dragged her to her feet, then had to hang on as she shrieked and fought to get to Tolly again.

"Take her away," he said. "Lock her in her rooms—no, she will raise a fuss there that will put the cat amongst the mice for certain. Lock her in the strongroom on the next floor. Feed her and see that she is tended to—she may have one maid, a young one—but I do not want to see her again until I call for her."

The guards dragged the queen out of the room. It was not easy, even though Anissa was a small, slender woman, because she fought them every step of the way, and even with Tolly's orders, the guards still could not bring themselves to be rough with the king's wife.

When they were gone and the echoes of the woman's wretched cries had finally faded, Tolly set the child down on his bed where it kicked and wailed.

"Do you know anything about changing a child's smallclothes?" Tolly asked him suddenly.

"Sire?" Tinwright had not been expecting this.

"The creature stinks. I am sure it needs cleaning. We shall have to find a woman who can do it." The lord protector shook his head in disgust. "My library is small—I am not going to share it with that ghastly stench."

"Library, my lord?"

"We have incantations to speak, potions to prepare and serve to this little beast," Tolly said with a look of distaste toward young Alessandros Eddon. "Okros explained it to me, although I do not remember everything he said. No matter! You are a scholar too . . . of sorts. We have all his books and papers. We have a day or so before the autarch's bloody Midsummer Night—plenty of time. The magical royal blood is already there, after all." He gave a sudden laugh—long, loud, and harsh. "Yes, the little beast is simply full of the stuff!"

28
Better Than Expected

"The Orphan's journey north was a long one. He and Moros were menaced by robbers, heathens, cruel demons, and spiteful fairies . . ."

—from "A Child's Book of the Orphan, and His Life and Death and Reward in Heaven"

THE FIGHTING AS THE FUNDERLINGS were forced back through the Maze was as bad as anything Ferras Vansen had ever experienced. He had been terrified facing the Qar, he had been confused and despairing almost his entire time behind the Shadowline, and of course his earliest fighting, raids that his old commander Donal Murroy had led against bandit chieftains in the Southmarch countryside, had been terrifying precisely because they were the first time he had faced opponents trying to kill him—but this was different than all of them. Most of it was siege work, breast against breast, shield against shield, a sweaty, slippery, exhausting struggle where a moment's loss of concentration could cost your life. In some spots the ranks were so tightly packed that men were killed next to him but could not fall down until he and his Funderlings finally retreated; other times Vansen and his comrades remained tangled with the very Xixian soldiers they had killed and could not shove the bodies away until the southerners fell back. It was a disturbingly intimate war: because of the darkness and close quarters archers became almost entirely useless, so most of the struggle was with men you could touch and smell and see . . . if not see well. The bearded, desert-browned faces of the Xixians, their conical helmets and armor of overlapping plates, began to seem almost as familiar as those of the little men who fought beside him. Together, the two sides moved deeper and deeper into the earth, twined like courtiers engaged in a complicated dance. The defenders gave ground, and the attackers pressed them, so that sometimes it seemed to Vansen the entire struggle was only some complicated way of worshiping great Kernios, lord of death and darkness.

Has ever a stranger war been fought? he wondered to himself. *And by more bewildered combatants?*

After hours of bloody fighting, Vansen's men were able to use their dwindling supply of blasting powder to drop a large section at the front of the Maze onto the autarch's army, utterly blocking the central chamber known as the Initiation Hall with the rubble of collapsed walls, and thus closing the only route through the Maze. After retreating a safe distance, the defenders were able to snatch some much-needed rest as the Xixians labored to dig their way through the shattered stone that barred their path.

"But I need to know more!" Vansen told Brother Flowstone, one of the monks who had come to fight with the other Funderlings. With many of the Maze's corridors now cracked and in danger of collapse, he had pulled his men all the way back to a wide, low chamber called the Revelation Hall where the young Funderlings spent the end of their vigil before finally being given a sight of the Shining Man. "Why can't you tell me the names of these tunnels?" Vansen continued. "It's the one thing Chert didn't put on his map. With so many different ways to choose, we might even be able to attack the southerners from behind or from the side!"

"Because these tunnels do not have names!" A broken nose and several long cuts disfigured Flowstone's youthful face. "I told you, Captain, we Brothers only learn the steps of the maze by heart so that we can pass through it and lead the celebrants. We do not learn the names of each back-around and blind pass. Don't you understand, Captain? *We Funderlings didn't build this place.*"

Vansen was astounded. "You didn't? Then who did?"

Flowstone shrugged. "Perhaps the Qar. Perhaps your gods—the same gods that this mad southern king wishes to bring back to life. In a way, we are *all* strangers here."

Ferras Vansen tried to rest, but as had happened so many times on this retreat, he got up after a short, ragged sleep and wandered through the makeshift camp, watching over his men and wishing he could do more for them. Too many dead had been left behind; here too many were wounded and in need of care. For a while Vansen lingered to watch some of the Funderlings building walls across the narrower end of the broad chamber so they would have some cover when the time came to retreat from the Revelation Hall—if any men were still left to retreat.

His heart heavy, Vansen wandered back to his own fire. "Gods! This will drive me mad!" he said. "We have used all but the last of our blasting powder. When they dig through this fall of rubble, we will have no other way to hold them back but our sinews and blades. Why did we say yes to Chert's cursed plan—how much blasting powder will be wasted up above . . . ?"

"Might as well calm yourself, Captain," Jasper told him. "What the Elders decree the rest of us will see."

"But we need only hold them back for a day or two more, and it will be too late for the autarch's lunatic scheme!" Vansen was nearly beside himself with frustration. "Am I wrong about the day, Copper?"

"We may not have had enough water to drink," said Malachite Copper said, "but we have kept the water-clock damp as a ferret's nose." He shook his head sadly. "Up in Funderling Town they will be lifting a cup to Midsummer's Eve."

"Gods bite me. What do people who live in a dark cave care about summer?" Vansen asked pettishly.

At that moment, Cinnabar's son Calomel came running through the camp. He was a great favorite, but the men were so weary and downhearted that few of them even bothered to look up as he passed. If they had, they would have seen his dirty face streaked with tears.

"Captain! Come quick!" he cried. "Hurry! Bring men! My father needs you at Initiation Hall!"

"What?" Vansen jumped to his feet. "But he only went back to look after the ones pushing rubble into the tunnel . . ."

"The Xixies have used blasting powder of their own!" Calomel said, tugging Vansen back across the camp. "They have knocked down an entire wall of the Maze and they have trapped my tada!"

"Perin's beard!" Vansen said, "I feared this. The autarch has finally decided he is tired of making his way inch by inch! Copper—bring your men. Sledge, you and Dolomite get the rest up and moving after us . . ."

"Hurry!" shouted the boy. "Hurry—oh, they will kill him! They will kill my tada!"

Vansen could think of no words to console the child. He had hoped the southerners would not break through until at least tomorrow. Was this the end, then? Had the Funderlings fought so long and hard for nothing? *Cinnabar deserves a better death than to die alone, whatever else happens,* he thought. *If we must go down, let it be with our hands filled by our sword hilts.* He was fearful for his comrade, but also felt a wild sort of optimism that had nothing to do with the truth of things. *Let be what will be,* he thought as he raced after little Calomel. *The gods alone know a man's end.* If it had not been for the terrified boy, he would have shouted it out loud. *As my father used to say about his ancestors . . . if you're not a coward, a good death beats a bad life any time!*

❧

Briony had captured perhaps an hour of hard-earned sleep, but the shock of seeing her brother still dizzied her as she pulled her boots back on and staggered to her feet. What could have happened to him? How could Barrick simply walk away from her as though they meant nothing to each other—as though their lives growing up together in Southmarch had never happened? She felt as though her heart had been pierced by one of the battle's arrows, that she had been murdered but no one had told her to lie down.

It was still dark out, but all around her the Temple Dogs and their followers were hastily tearing down what little camp they had bothered to raise. The beach was covered with torches. At least one seemed to be pushed into the sand beside every one of the long, low boats that had been grounded along the shore of the bay, so that Briony felt as though she passed through a forest of light. Dozens of Skimmer men waited beside the boats, many of them in armor made (as far as she could tell) of pungent dried fish skin, carrying bows and long forks and spears—weapons that she thought looked better suited for spearing sharks.

But these Skimmers had done more than their share, she realized, and far more than simply killing a few southern soldiers. The firing of the autarch's fleet, some of which still burned out on Brenn's Bay, little left above the waterline but charred, sparking hulks, was a deed that might mean everything in the hours ahead.

Eneas strode across the sand. "I have had men scouring the city. I feel certain now that the rest of the Xixies truly have retreated into the hills. Not a sniff of them to be found anywhere . . ." He reached her side. "You look unwell, Briony."

"How could I feel otherwise? You saw my brother act as if we did not know each other."

The prince looked as though he didn't know what to do. *He doesn't like problems he can't solve,* she thought, although she suspected she was being unfair. Still, just now she didn't care. "I have seen men badly taken by war in the past, Princess . . ."

"He is not mad. It is not war that has done this to him; it is that Qar woman, Saqri. She's put a spell on my brother." She looked around. "Where are they?"

"Gone," said Eneas. "Back into the caves in the hills. Back into the ground beneath the castle."

For a moment the lights of the torches and Eneas' face and even the few stars blinking miserably behind the smoke all blurred as tears came to her eyes yet again. She dragged her fist across her lids. "No more," she said. "No more talk. Let us get on with what we must do."

"All is nearly ready," he said. "I have only a few matters yet to see to . . ."

"Then see to them," she said. "Don't fear for me, Eneas. I will not run into the bay and drown myself. I am made of sterner stuff."

"But I never . . ."

"Go on." She turned her back on him and walked toward the waiting boats without looking back. When she reached the nearest she turned along the strand and began walking from torch to torch, trying to ignore the angry, miserable thoughts that swarmed through her weary mind like bees. The Skimmers watched her pass, eyes bulging and faces expressionless.

"Princess Briony?"

She turned and found herself before one of the armored Skimmers, although something about the fellow's hairless face was not quite right. A moment later Briony realized that the *he* was in fact a *she.*

"Do I know you . . . ?" She squinted in the dim light. "Zoria's mercy, is that you? Aren't you Ena, the headman's daughter?"

The girl nodded. "I am pleased you remember me, Highness. It was only a night or so that we spent in each other's company."

"The most frightening of my life—at least up until then." Briony shook her head. "But what are you doing wearing armor and fighting with the menfolk?"

Ena laughed. "I might ask you the same! It seems we both wished to play a greater part in these final days."

"Final?"

The Skimmer girl shrugged. "One way or another. Egye-Var has made that clear." With her helmet off she was much more recognizable, her solemn, heavy-lidded eyes and her high brow reminding Briony of things and times she would have rather forgotten. "And how is Lord Shaso?" Ena asked.

That was the memory Briony had been trying to keep at bay. "Dead, may the gods rest him. He was a good man. He was killed in a fire in Landers Port, when our house was attacked." At the will of Hendon Tolly, she felt sure; someone had to have put the local lord up to the attack. Briony was furious with Prince Eneas' decision to let the Qar queen Saqri have her way, but at least now there was a chance Briony would meet Tolly the traitor again, preferably with them both free to settle things. She owed him something on behalf of the entire Eddon family, not to mention her own honor—she could think of no other word for it.

"I am very sorry, my lady," Ena said. "Lord Shaso was a brave old man and always a friend to the Ocean Children."

"To be honest, I'm surprised your people knew him so well. When he walked into your father's longhouse it seemed as if they were old friends."

"There are many stories to be shared, that is certain," the girl said. "But not now, I think. We must cross the bay before dawn. At the very least, that will stop the Xixians firing on us with the guns that they were able to drag back into the hills. Do me the honor of letting me be the one to bring you back to your home."

"Thank you, Ena. Let me go and gather up my belongings."

Briony made her way back across the shingle to the temporary camp where Eneas and his men were making the last arrangements with the Skimmers. She supposed she should have remained—she was certainly one of Eneas' advisers, if nothing else—but she found it too painful. The tall player Dowan Birch had told her she would speak to her father at least one more time, and she had. Could that hour in the prison tent have been the last time? And now she had found Barrick, and he had turned his back on her. Seeing the two of them again was all that had kept her going through her darkest days. Now she was near them both but could not have them. The pain threatened to overwhelm her.

I must believe I will see them again—that Heaven means for it all to come right. What else can I do?

But Briony had not convinced herself. *You can go on pretending you're living in a story, with gods and spirits watching over you*, she told herself, *or you can accept that you're living in a much different sort of world—that the gods are dead or hateful, that someone else will have to save your father, and that nobody, least of all you, knows how this story will end.*

Chert hurried up the narrow path, angry and frightened in equal measure. He and his workers were already hard-pressed to the point it seemed impossible that his undertaking would ever be ready, but now an urgent message had arrived from Brother Antimony insisting he come at once to the site of the digging. Half a day would be lost—more if they were unlucky.

He passed at least a dozen other Funderlings coming down from the dig, most of them pushing barrows of soil, but others on missions whose purpose he could not easily discern, and Chert began to feel a little better; at least things were still happening. At least Antimony had not let this urgent matter stop work entirely. Still, as he searched for Antimony, he took a good look around the site to make certain things were as they should be. The Funderling workers moved past, mostly in two crowded lines, one going to the site and one coming back. All of those moving away had barrows full of rock and earth to be dumped. Many of those who had already emptied their loads were returning to the nearest site carrying the newest sacks of blasting powder.

He found Antimony at the center of the workings, near the first and largest tunnel which would connect to the broad crevice leading down into the Sea in the Depths—"Chert's Chimney," as some of the workers had mockingly dubbed it—the Pit, as he thought of it. The End of the World. The tall monk looked harried beyond his years, but it was the identity of the two Funderlings who stood with him that hit Chert like a body blow. One was Nickel, the abbot-to-be of the Metamorphic Brothers' temple, a humorless fellow Chert had disliked from their first encounter, but the other . . . the other was Chert's own brother Nodule, magister of the Blue Quartz clan, and one of the few people in the world he could honestly say he liked less than Brother Nickel.

"Well, well, and well," said Nodule as Chert walked up, "how fortunate it is that our father is dead. He would have been furious to see how you have scratched and marred the family name."

"A pleasure to see you, too, brother." Chert nodded to Brother Nickel, who only scowled back, then turned to Antimony. "I am here at your call, Brother, but I can wait if you have business with these two . . . worthy fellows."

"In truth . . ." Antimony began.

"We are here because of you," Nickel said. "Or rather, because of what you are up to. What you are doing here is dangerous, and it is especially a danger to the temple. If you bring down so much stone, you will kill us all. I have decided I will not allow it. It must stop today."

For a moment Chert could only stare at him. "What . . . what do you mean? Stop? Stop what?"

"This. All this." Nickel waved at the men rolling barrows of stone and dirt. "You may not undertake such a risky project so close to the temple."

Chert almost grabbed the man by the collar of his robe. "But . . . but you know why we are doing this!" Or did he? Was Chert himself going mad? He could have sworn that Nickel had sat through all the discussions, arguing bitterly against it but having to agree with Cinnabar's decision in the end. "It may be our only chance to save ourselves! Cinnabar has put the Guild's seal on it . . . !"

"Has he?" Nickel smiled unpleasantly. "I do not remember such a thing. I vaguely recall that you had some farfetched plan for using blasting powder to knock down stone and defeat our enemy, but I do not believe that Magister Cinnabar would ever agree to such madness."

"You . . . you *liar*! You were there! You heard it all and you heard and saw Cinnabar and Vansen agree!"

"Here now!" said Nodule, his broad jaw working in indignation. "You cannot speak to Brother Nickel that way. He is an important fellow. You shame me again, Chert."

Chert had wanted to hit his brother in the eye for years, and for a moment felt certain this was the time, but he decided that the risks were too great, the work here too important. "Others were there. Malachite Copper—he is a well-known and honorable man! And some of the other commanders."

"Are they here now?" Nickel spread his hands. "I don't see them. If you claim to be doing the Guild's business, and with Cinnabar's permission, where is the Astion?"

Chert was dumbfounded. A replica of the Astion, the star-shaped sigil of the Stonecutter's Guild, was the ultimate arbiter of who served Funderling Town . . . but Nickel was right. He didn't have one. "Cinnabar and the rest had to fall back and protect the Mysteries before he could give it to me—you know that!"

"I know nothing of the sort." Nickel shook his head. "At the moment there is only your word for it, and the risk is far too great to trust one man's word."

"Especially a man like my brother," Nodule said officiously, "who has already been called up in front of the Highwardens once for his foolish, risky behavior." He nodded. "But since Cinnabar is not here, *I* am the highest-ranking Guildsman, and I rule that Nickel's complaint is valid. No work will be done here until an Astion is produced." He smirked. "Good luck, Chert."

"Please, let me take you back to the temple, Magister," Nickel said. "We are grateful to have you here, but you have had a long journey. I have a very nice old mushroom jack in my cupboard—we call it by the old name here, *mykomel*. You must share a cup with me."

"It would be an honor." Nodule's round face flushed with pleasure. "I love a good jack! But my brother cannot join us, I'm afraid. He will have too much work to do closing down the job here." He looked sternly at his younger brother. "But I will return, and if even one apprentice sweeper is at work here, the full weight of the Guild's power will fall on you, Chert!"

When the monk and the magister had gone, Chert sank to the ground and put his hands on his head. "That cursed fool, my brother! And Nickel—what is he doing? He knows what we are doing here and why we are doing it! Elders know we pray it isn't needed, but it might be our only hope." He looked at the workers milling around in confusion and distress. "Still, it will be a terrible, mortal tragedy even if it succeeds." He blinked. "Fracture and fissure! I cannot believe Nickel would be so short-sighted."

Antimony sighed and sat next to him. "He is not shortsighted, I can tell you that. Nickel is the cleverest of all the Brothers. That is why, despite being young, he is going to be the abbot soon." He chewed on his lip for a moment. "I think he doesn't believe that Vansen and the others can win, but he doesn't want you to succeed, either. He may be gambling that he can make some kind of peace with the invaders. . . ."

"Or that Hendon Tolly will." Chert frowned. "I cannot help wondering just how much of a liar he is. Enough to turn traitor?"

"Nickel?" Antimony was clearly surprised. "Selfish and dishonest, yes, but anything more seems hard to believe . . ."

"Enough." Chert shook his head in disgust. "There is no use trying to puzzle it out this way. We must get the Astion from Cinnabar, or my brother will shut down the work, just as he said, and then even this faint hope is lost to us. The Guildsmen have all scattered to their homes since the siege began. I could never round them up in time to have them vote a new Astion! Cinnabar is our only powerful protector, and his younger supporters are mostly fighting with him and Vansen, but my brother and his faction are not the kind to join in any war unless their own houses are threatened." He made a growling noise in his throat. "And by the time that happens, it will be too late!" He stood up. "I'll have to get the Astion from Cinnabar, somehow . . ."

"But if you can't round up the Guild in time, there's no possible way you can reach Cinnabar," Antimony said sadly. "He's at least as far away, and there are thousands of the autarch's soldiers between him and us."

Chert felt like an overloaded arch; one small crack and the whole thing would tumble. "How is the work here? Would we have succeeded?"

"In what, two more days? Three?"

"According to Vansen, it might be as little as one."

Antimony snorted. "No offense, Master Chert, but I doubt we'd have managed it. We still have several more yards of stone to cut and move in Mudstone Reach before we can lay the charges, and twice that in Last Reach. Too bad we couldn't use blasting powder to open the holes to put in the blasting powder . . ." He chuckled.

Chert's gloom turned to a moment of pure terror. "By the Elders, Antimony, don't even jest! If we knocked down the walls at Last Reach before we were ready . . ."

"I know, I know." The young monk rubbed his big hands together. "But I wouldn't mind if we did it and forgot to tell Brother Nickel, I'll confess. Does that make me a bad Metamorphic Brother, do you think?" He laughed again, but it had a morose tone. "And how are your wife and the other ladies doing?"

"Very well, actually. They surprise me." Chert knew he should get up and try to solve some of his many problems, but he felt weak and brittle, as if all his supporting struts had burned away. "I do not think we will have corned sixty barrels worth of blasting powder by tonight, but we will be close to it. That Vermilion is at least as much of a general as her husband, if not quite so sweet-natured. She and Opal have not just the other women jumping to their drumbeat, but Ash Nitre and his men, too. Do you remember when part of the guildhall fell down a few years ago, how the men stood in lines passing stone hand to hand all through the first night? That's what it looks like down by the ladies' camp. Never doubt that women can sweat, Antimony."

"I never did," the monk said. "I come from a big family. Our mum had nine to feed, but she still always had a hand free to give me a clout on the head if she thought I was out of line."

Chert smiled. "Ah, well. I have sat here like a lump of flint in a limestone bed for long enough. We'd better make sure things are safely secured here while I think of what to do next. Where's Salt?" Although Antimony was Chert's eyes and ears, Salt Nitre, Ash and Sulphur's nephew, was the job's foreman. "And for that matter, where's Chaven?"

Antimony looked at him strangely. "What do you mean? Isn't Chaven back in Powder Camp with you and the women?"

"No." Chert felt a clutch in his chest. "Of course not. He said he was coming here to give you what help he could—told me he was too big and clumsy and would only be in the way among all those nimble little ladies. You know how he talks. Didn't he come here?"

"Never." Antimony shook his head emphatically. "We have fewer than a hundred men here, all of them retired Guildsmen. We take our meals together here and we sleep each night back at the temple. I've seen no sign of Chaven either place and he's hard to miss, being twice as tall as the rest of us. He's been gone since the Xixians invaded our tunnels."

"By the Elders," Chert groaned. "He is wandering lost down in the depths somewhere, with the autarch's men all around, and those horrible clawed monsters, and . . . and . . ."

A sudden, even more frightening thought occurred to him: Chaven had been acting strangely since he had come to Funderling Town—perhaps his obsession with the mirror had turned him traitor. Perhaps the physician had sold his allegiance to the one man who could help him get the mirror back, the mirror that he yearned for like a drunkard craved mossbrew. Perhaps even now he was taking news of Vansen's and Cinnabar's plans—and even of Chert's own farfetched scheme—to their greatest foe, the Autarch of Xis. . . .

"He wouldn't do that . . ." Chert said quietly, mostly to convince himself.

"What did you say, Master Blue Quartz?" Antimony asked. "You don't look well. Should I get you something to drink?"

"No, no." Chert's skin was cold with sudden fear. "Nothing for me. I don't think I could keep anything down."

❧

"The southern mortals will come down from the hills with the morning's light," Saqri said when she returned to Barrick's tent. "They have numbers and powerful guns, and they fear their master too much to do otherwise. Most of all, they fear what he will do to them if he is victorious below but they have lost everything above."

Barrick tried to heave himself out of the cot, but the walk down the beach had overwhelmed him. He settled for sitting upright, which made him feel less of an invalid. "What does that mean, Saqri? We fight them again?"

"It means we must not be here. Otherwise, we will be fighting a pointless battle for nothing more important than the honor of the Xixians when the true danger is below. How is your strength?"

"I can walk if I go slowly." He paused, troubled. "My sister. That was my sister."

"I saw her, yes."

He didn't remember how he had once felt, that was the problem, but he knew he did not have those feelings anymore. "She was unhappy with me. Why?"

"Perhaps because you are no longer the child she remembered and that frightens her. Perhaps because you have found newer and greater responsibilities, or have changed in other ways she cannot understand." Saqri's dispassion was so complete it almost looked studied. "Who can say?"

"It bothers me, and I don't know why. I feel as though I've lost something important. Left something behind . . ."

The minute downturn of her lips was a frown. "Do not waste your thought on it, Barrick Eddon. We have more than enough to do. The southerners have a long lead on us—in fact, they have almost reached the deepest place, the very Last Hour of the Ancestor."

He did his best to shake off the mood brought on by seeing his sister. What could it matter now, when the People's last moments were at hand? "But it seems so hopeless—you told me that the ritual, the spell, whatever foul thing it is that the autarch seeks to do, is meant to happen tomorrow . . ."

"One moment after midnight," Saqri said. "When the year begins to die."

"How can we possibly stop him before then? He has thousands of men in the caverns. You sent our only allies away, my sister and those Syannese, to fight in the castle against other mortals. Why? What chance will we have now?"

"No chance at all, of course." Still the impassive mask. "But we have many other important things to concern us. I myself must choose what to do with my death."

For a moment he thought he had not heard her. When he spoke, his skin was prickling. "Your . . . death?"

"It is hard to explain, but I think there will be no small power in the death of half the Fireflower. Perhaps not enough to change the outcome of such an uneven fight, but perhaps at least enough to thwart the autarch in some way. But if I am not there to employ it, my death will avail nothing."

He swallowed. "And me . . . ? Do I have this . . . death to give, too?"

She made the gesture *The Book is Closed*, a Qar equivalent of a shrug. "What I speak of has never happened before. Always when one of my ancestors died in battle their heirs were primed to take the Fireflower. Now, who knows? I die with no living issue. As for you . . . ?" Saqri shrugged. "Nothing like you has ever been heard of, not by the Fireflower, not even among those of the Deep Library." Her smile looked like the bared teeth of a wolf. "Still, I would advise you not to sell your own passing lightly, either."

He nodded, pushing away the mote of disquiet which meeting his sister had left in him. "So we fight. And we almost certainly die." It seemed so simple and so final—but also so terrifying. "Not knowing if we have won or lost. Not knowing what happened to Qinnitan."

"It is possible we will find your southern girl before the end." Saqri did not quite seem to approve. "As for the rest, we will lose, of course—that is certain. In the whole of our world there is no longer enough Qar . . . *magic* left, as you would call it, to save us. But you and I still have work of our own to do. For better or for worse, my husband chose you to carry the Fireflower of the kings into this final battle. That is why I gave you the armor that once belonged to my son, Janniya. It did not save him. He died here in Southmarch at the hands of your ancestor, but to me he was noble and lovely beyond even the gods themselves." She put her hand upon his. "Will you fight with me, Barrick Eddon?"

Barrick felt strangely empty, like a pottery vessel cleansed by fire. All the things he had worried about for so long, loved so hopelessly, now seemed to have vanished; he could scarcely remember them.

He nodded slowly. "I'll fight with you, Saqri, yes. You're all the family I have, now. And when the time comes, I'll die with you, too, if the gods grant it." He did his best to smile, but it had become an unfamiliar exercise. "After all, it will be a better ending than what I've always expected."

PART THREE
THE OWL

29
A Little Man of Stone

"After more than a year's journey they reached the grim castle known as the Siege of Always-Winter, but Moros was too frightened to go farther and so he deserted the Orphan at the threshold."

—from "A Child's Book of the Orphan, and His Life and Death and Reward in Heaven"

THE FIRES BURNING in the mainland city and the Xixian ships still smoldering on the water made the night almost as bright as dawn. Some of the ships had burned to the waterline, unrecognizable hulks that still hissed steam and spat sparks into the dark sky.

I never dreamed I would come back like this, Briony thought, watching the mainland recede as Ena plied the oars. All around her boats slid toward the castle like water beetles converging at one end of a pond. Eneas and his men had been loaded onto wherries in twos and threes, the horses onto barges, and now almost twenty score small Skimmer craft were making their way back across the bay to Southmarch.

Neither Briony nor Ena were much interested in conversation; the short journey passed in silence until the first of the boats neared the ruins of the causeway, now nothing more than a short spit of land between the great outer gate and the edge of Midlan's Mount. Briony let Ena help her out onto the slippery stones.

"But where do we go?" Briony asked. The huge Basilisk Gate looked down on them like a frowning giant. She had never thought about how it felt to come to this place and see such a daunting thing—always before it had been one of the last signs that she was returning home. "How do we get inside?"

"Not the way we Skimmers go, my lady," said Ena, smiling. "That's our secret, and in times like these it'll remain our secret. But you have no need for secrets, Highness! You have come back to your own house!"

"Not everyone here will be so glad to see me," Briony said, but Ena was already pushing her boat back from the rocks and into safer waters.

"Take care, Queen Briony! We will meet again!" the Skimmer girl called.

She wanted to shout, "I'm only a princess," but thought better of making so much noise. The other Skimmers swooped in to deliver their passengers to the causeway; then, when all Eneas' troops were unloaded, they swung back into the open water. A song rose up among them, deep and barely audible above the crash of the ocean against the rocks. It was in no language Briony knew, and she only guessed it was a song because it had a sort of tune that went up and down like the waves themselves. Who were the Skimmers, really? That Saqri creature had said something about them being the kin of the Qar, but that seemed impossible. The water people were part of Southmarch and had been so for centuries, long before and long after the Qar had been driven into exile beyond the Shadowline.

Eneas appeared out of the evening mist, so tall and stern that for a startled moment she thought he was her father. "Princess, are you well?"

"I am, sir, thank you." Dawn was still hours away; they had no light but the glare of ships burning on the bay and fires on the distant mainland. "This seems a rather uncomfortable spot to make our camp." She gestured to the mighty walls jutting out above them, the gate itself as tall as a tall tree all carved in the stony coils of its namesake. "Do you have a plan to get us inside?"

"Well, we are a little late to the inn, but perhaps we can wake the porter." Eneas called to one of his men, and a moment later a trumpeter had taken out his horn. At a second word from the prince, he began to blow a brazen battle call. Startled, Briony could only put her hands over her ears and shrink away.

Moments later a head appeared atop the gate, then three or four more, helmeted guards crouching so low they were scarcely more than bumps above the battlements like a baby's teeth nudging through its gums.

"Who goes there?" one of them called, so high above them atop the wall that the wind almost tore his words away. "One of the autarch's men, hoping for a dram of water to put out your fires? We'll send it down to you, but not in a way you'll like!"

"No Xixians, we!" cried Eneas. "We are allies! Let us in!"

"Allies! Not likely!" the man shouted back. "Just blew in on the wind and landed in front of the Old Lizard, did you? Think we'll let you in? Then you're a madman, that's what you are."

"A madman *and* a madwoman!" the prince shouted back. "Here is one who thinks himself the rightful heir of Syan, and another who believes herself mistress of this very castle!"

"For the love of the gods!" Briony told him in a horrified whisper. "Eneas, are you mad? These are Tolly's men!"

"Perhaps," he said cheerfully. "But perhaps not. Let us find out."

"What foolery are you at, man?" demanded the fellow on the wall. "Mistress? Your mistress is likely a slattern and you are certainly a drunk fool, fisherman. Get back in your boat and go away before we feather you and your lady properly!"

One of the Syannese soldiers already had an arrow on his string and was preparing to dispatch the guard when Eneas held out his hand. "Leave him be," he said quietly.

"But, Highness . . . !" the soldier protested. "Did you hear . . . ?"

"I heard." Eneas raised his voice. "It is you who is feeling the breath of Old Knot on the back of his neck, fellow. I am Prince Eneas of Syan. Open the gate! We are allies of your true king!" He turned and said quietly to Briony, "That should start some interesting conversations!"

More heads popped up along the top of the massive gate, and several men held up torches, peering down into the darkness below for a look at the visitors. Briony could only hold her breath and pray for Zoria's continued protection. The gatehouse above it, and the monstrous towers on either side probably housed a pentecount of men or more. Eneas might have far more men than that, but they had no protection and nowhere to go if the archers began firing on them. The Skimmers were gone and there was no other way off the narrow piece of land in front of the gate.

"That *is* the Syannese prince!" one man atop the gate shouted. "I've seen his banner! That's him!"

"Liar!" another screamed. "Or traitor!"

"Open the gates!" someone called. "Let them in! They sank them Otarch ships!"

"I'll kill the first man who goes near that windlass . . . !" a man cried, and then many voices began shouting at once, and even the figures lined up atop the gate suddenly dissolved into chaos. To Briony's horror, a figure came flying off the top of the gatehouse, ten times a man's height in the air, and hit the ground in front of Eneas and his men with a horrible moist thump.

Flames rippled across the top of the gate and in the narrow slits in the towers on either side as men with torches ran in and out. One of the Basilisk Gate's huge bells began to ring out an alarm, then fell silent again almost immediately, as though the bell ringer had met a sudden, violent end. Torches began appearing along nearby sections of the wall as the struggle at the main gate caught the attention of the other guard posts.

"Form up!" Eneas told his men. "Shields up—the arrows may begin flying any moment!"

Briony was only too happy to lift her shield over her head, although it was not long before her arms were aching so badly she would almost have preferred being shot. A few arrows did come sailing down, but more or less randomly, and not from atop the gate itself, as though a few scared soldiers on the walls were merely firing out into the darkness.

At last silence fell, then the great gate creaked open; Eneas held his men back when they would have surged through. The portcullis shuddered and rose, and a handful of figures with torches stepped into the cobbled opening, a space wide enough for a dozen men to ride through.

"Is it truly you, Prince Eneas?" one of the torchbearers asked, taking a limping step forward and holding up his torch, which rippled as the breeze from the bay whipped through the open gate.

"It is. Do I know you?" Eneas strode forward. Briony hurried to stay with him—his confidence, at that moment, seemed better protection than any Syannese shield.

"No, sire. You wouldn't. But we true Southmarchers are happy to see you. Was it you burned the Xixy ships?"

A crowd of guardsmen quickly surrounded Eneas and his men, but to Briony's relief the mood was more festive than combative. Several dozen were climbing down from the nearest guardhouses to see what was happening, but most of the fighting was already over. At least a dozen men sat sullenly on the ground with their backs to the wall, being guarded by men with spears. Half a dozen more lay nearby and did not need to be watched, as their contorted limbs and the blood on their tabards made clear.

The soldier who had spoken saw Eneas and his men looking at the dead. "They were Tolly's men, those scum. One of them tried to ring the bells. The rest would have been off to warn the Protector and his bullyboys—they've all gone to ground in the royal residence. What is happening, Sire? Have you come to chase the damned Summerfielders out? May the gods bless you if you have, Highness." He peered out past Eneas and the others, squinting as if he could make out what was happening on the far shore. "What about that autarch? What happened to his ships?"

"These are long stories," Eneas said. "And my men will need food and drink and a place to sleep."

"Of course, Prince Eneas . . ." the leader began, but then Briony stepped out of the shadow of the wall and into the torchlight.

"I will not enter my own home in secret," she said. "You men have done more than open the gates for the Syannese—you've let the Eddons back in as well." She pulled off her helmet and hoped they could still recognize her with her hair cut short.

The men around her heard a woman's voice and turned, staring. The leader, the man with the limp, lowered himself to one knee. "Praise the Three," he said. "It's King Olin's daughter."

Murmuring, the other men, who had been gathering around her, began to get down on their knees.

"Do not bow," she said. "Look at me—please don't bow! I don't want to make my presence known yet. Not until we learn how things fare here and decide what to do next." She would have preferred that they had remembered her name as well as her father's, but the hope and even happiness on the faces of most of the men she could see was reward enough. "All of you who can hear me, come now. Let no one leave. Set some men to watch the gate again while you others follow Prince Eneas and me."

"The inner keep is Hendon Tolly's armed camp, Highness," one of the guards said. "You're safe here in the outer keep, but most of Tolly's supporters are with him in the residence. They have at least as many men as your Syannese, Princess, and they also hold many of our women and children."

"All the more reason that we should move slowly and not make a great parade," Briony said. "Take us to a place where our soldiers can rest."

Several of the Southmarch guards let out a cheer, but the others silenced them. The limping man who had welcomed them looked up at Briony.

"Is it truly you, Princess?" he asked.

"It is. And my father is alive, too. The Eddons have not given up their throne—or their people."

"And will it all be well, then? Things will be well again?"

She looked at him and suddenly the weight of who she was, and what she still had to do pressed against her like a great stone on her chest, so that for a moment she could not speak. "That is beyond my power to say," she managed at last. "But I will do everything I can to make it so."

Something about seeing his sister still troubled Barrick, although he could not say exactly what that something was. It was not emotion—at least not the sort of confused, ill-defined feelings that had been so common in him before the gift of the Fireflower—but it made it hard to concentrate on what Saqri was saying about Lady Yasammez.

". . . So she will meet us in the Great Delve."

"But I don't understand. Why didn't Yasammez come up with us to fight the Xixians? She lives for war!"

Saqri's thoughts had something of both unhappiness and anger in them, but those she chose to express were straightforward. "I imagine she wished to see what I would do with the command and the Seal. Perhaps she had matters of her own to deal with as well."

"Like what?" A swirl of Fireflower memories tantalized him but he was learning how to do what Ynnir had taught him; to simply *be* and let them swim around him like fish.

"Dissension among her close advisers, I suspect. You know about the disagreement between Yasammez and my husband. What you may not know, or may not have been able to sift from what the Fireflower has given you, is that the distinctions are not so simple as to be divided into two camps only."

"Tell me." But what he said was closer to *"Bring me to your thought."* He found that in his own head he was now using Qar ideas nearly as frequently as his native tongue.

"From the first, great Yasammez warned that we should sweep the mortals from the land before it was too late. But her great age and long experience have changed her, and her hatred of your kind is no longer as deadly as it once was. However, there are still many others of our people, some of the wilder folk, Tricksters and Elementals, who would happily see your kind vanish from the earth forever. . . ."

"But then why did Yasammez send me to King Ynnir?" Barrick asked. "Does that mean she's changed her mind about my people somehow? Or that she thought keeping me alive could . . . could help the Qar?"

Saqri let him feel a blank, cloudy thought, another kind of shrug. "I do not know. I have tried to sense her mind on this but she keeps it hidden, even from me." And now she let him feel a little of the pain that caused her. "So much has changed. Once Yasammez was more to me than my own mother . . ."

She did not finish the thought, and Barrick did not press for it. Too much hurt and confusion was there, things he could not understand, feelings so naked and private in a being of such immense composure that he did not want to go farther.

"So we face our final hours, Barrick," Saqri finished at last, "and all that was once certain has become uncertain. Except for defeat. That, as always, is the end of all our stories."

The dark lady met them in a place the Funderlings called the Old Baryte Span, her vanguard carrying torches that made the veins of quartz in the walls flash like lightning. Barrick could not help wondering if this great show of light was for him, since most of the Qar saw as well in dark passages as the little people who usually walked here.

As Yasammez stepped down from the crude rock stairway onto the cavern floor, Saqri raised her hands in greeting. "We are together again."

"Yes. We are together again." Yasammez turned her somber face toward Barrick. "You have had to fight against your own people now. Do you still wish to stand with us?"

"My own people?" It took him a moment to understand she was talking about the Xixians, the autarch's soldiers. "They are nothing to me—invaders. Intruders. If I could kill them all with one swing of my sword, I would."

Yasammez looked at him for a long moment, silent and calculating. "Time is short," was all she said.

The council was surprisingly brief. Barrick had grown used to the Qar taking days to decide or do anything, but it seemed the passing of the Seal of War to Saqri had brought a great change: Yasammez offered little in the way of advice and objected to almost nothing, letting Saqri make the decisions and give the orders.

"We must try to beat the southerners to the Last Hour of the Ancestor in the uttermost deeps," Saqri said when she had heard from all her lieutenants. "But they are too many for us to stop them by main strength. Even if Vansen and his drows are still alive and we could attack the southerners from both sides, the autarch has too many soldiers. Fighting is beside the point, anyway. *Time* is what is important now, and they are already deep below us, at the doorway to the depths."

Fireflower thoughts and memories swirled in Barrick's head, but the silent presence that had been Ynnir led him to those that mattered, each as delicately precise as a note picked out on a lute. He began to understand. "But Crooked . . . is dead." He shook a little at the storm that realization raised inside him—all the meanings, the memories, the ancient hopes and miseries. It was hard even to say it. The god whose blood ran in him and in Saqri was dead. The god who had fathered Yasammez, and whose own parentage had started the Godwar . . . Barrick ignored a cold wind of irritation from Yasammez and some of the others. "He pushed the old gods through and then sealed the way behind them. But the autarch wants to release them again!"

Saqri nodded. "And like most mortals, he has no idea of how dire many of these . . . beings are, how long they have waited outside the walls of nightmare . . ."

"And how fiercely and greedily they are watching for their chance." Yasammez stood, her black armor covering her like a shadow, so that for a moment it seemed her face rose in darkness like the moon. "Whatever sins mortal men have committed, I would not wish such horrors on the earth itself, which is blameless. It is time. We can wait no longer. What is your wish, granddaughter?"

Saqri paused as if the Porcupine's abruptness had caught her by surprise. "We need a better way." She turned to the Ettins. "Singscrape, you and others have been working here while the rest of us fought the southerners. What have you found?"

Hammerfoot's son spoke in a rumbling voice like a slow avalanche. "Tunnels that will lead us down to the naked wound of Crooked's last and greatest effort, and from there to the ultimate depths, Mistress. Some of the way must still be cleared, and we will have to fight when our way crosses the autarch's line of descent, but if we strike swiftly and work tirelessly, we may yet beat the humans to the Last Hour of the Ancestor."

"Let it be so, then." Saqri let out a breath, the closest thing to a sigh Barrick had ever heard from her. "Tomorrow is the last day—perhaps the last day that ever will be. Let none of us say that he or she could have given more."

Daikonas Vo watched the parade of monsters with dull fascination. He had been stumbling in darkness for so long that the glare of their torches made him blink and shy away. What did they want? Were these truly *pariki* as the Xixians called them—the fairies of his own mother tongue? What were they doing here beneath the castle? He had thought the autarch had driven them all away . . .

Vo shook his head to clear away some of the confusion. Did it matter? He had been wandering in darkness for so long he could scarcely remember who he was. Only the hot pain that had spread from his gut and now ran through his entire body like poison reminded him of what had happened to him, why he still breathed and walked when everything inside him urged him to lie down and accept the sweet relief of death.

If even death would be a relief, that was. Because in the dark, lost hours Vo had begun to hear his mother's voice again, whispering the stories of the gods to him, warning him of the serpents and other shadowy demons that would hunt him after he died and keep him from the bosom of Grandfather Nushash, the sun.

And weren't these grotesques marching below him through the underground caverns proof that such things could and did exist even in life? Bat-winged, hyena-headed, some covered with rough scales like the lowest desert snake . . . and their eyes! Glittering, glowing eyes that burned like coals. Surely they could see him even in his stony hiding place high on the cavern wall where the narrow trail he had been following had suddenly ended, a hundred feet above the cavern floor. So many times he had almost fallen to his death in this dark, ancient hell—there must be a reason he still lived! The gods existed and had taken pity on Daikonas Vo. There could be no other explanation. And when he completed his task they would honor him. No beasts would hunt him in the dark lands of death. No serpents would devour him.

The things below had been still for a long while, immersed in some silent ritual. At last, though, they roused themselves and began to make their way farther into the depths, toward what must be the same ultimate goal as Daikonas Vo's. He would follow them, he decided. To one who had been wandering so long in darkness even the distant light of their torches would be enough to lead him, their stealthy passage loud enough to guide him without his coming too close and being discovered.

As if to remind him what the penalty for such clumsiness would be, a burning pain made him grimace and bend himself double so that he almost tumbled from the ledge. The agony did not pass for long moments.

The girl with the red streak in her hair, the girl who had tried to murder him, was waiting in the depths. Great Sulepis was waiting there, too. Even the gods were waiting there for Daikonas Vo. He could not disappoint them.

As the pain ebbed and the last of the immortal monsters passed out of the cavern he began to climb carefully and quietly down from his high place.

After traveling for so long by dark, narrow ways that Barrick fell into a waking dream, Saqri at last signaled that it was time to make camp. For a while now they had been following a ledge around the lip of a great, nearly circular chasm that seemed only a little less wide than the old inner walls of Southmarch, and which fell away far beyond the light of any torches.

"This is the wound," Saqri said as she stood watching her householders preparing the camp. "This is the scar of Crooked's last struggle."

"This? This hole?" It did not match with the Fireflower memories that drifted up through his thoughts like bubbles. "We are there . . . ?"

"No." She moved closer to the edge. "If you dropped a stone, it would drop for long, long moments still before it rattled to the bottom. But far down, past many twists and turns of this great rift, that low place waits—the Last Hour of the Ancestor. So this is the beginning of the last part of our journey. When we have prepared, we will begin the climb down."

"All the way to the bottom?" Barrick thought of the stone dropping and dropping through darkness and could not imagine descending such a distance. "There aren't ropes long enough for that in the whole world!"

Saqri allowed herself a tiny smile. "We will go down a little way to the next tunnels, then use them. Later we will return to the wound again. It will take time, but at last we will reach the place where our enemies . . . and our allies . . . are gathering." She made another gesture with her palm facing down—*Water Enters Soil.* "You have some little time now, manchild, so rest. I will send for you when we are ready to move on."

He did his best to follow Saqri's advice, but his own disquiet and the continuous murmur of the Fireflower voices made him too restless. He rose and walked among the Qar, watching them work, marveling at their different shapes and types despite the Fireflower chorus assuring him that all was ordinary and familiar. He did not speak unless one of the Qar spoke to him, still uncertain of his place among these strange and ancient people. He thought he saw resentment on many of their inhuman faces, curiosity on some others, and it occurred to him that his presence was at least as disturbing to them as it was strange to Barrick himself.

What am I? I'm certainly not their prince, but I'm no ordinary subject, either. I have the blood and the memories of all their kings inside me, but I know less about them than I know about the peasants in far-off Xis.

He made his way at last to the edge of the rift and stood a long while in silence, trying to make sense of such a great hole in the earth. How could his family have ruled this place for generations and know so little about it? Or was it only Barrick himself, hung and smoked in his own misery, who had been oblivious?

"Master?" someone asked. It was a Qar term of carefully chosen resonance—it meant not so much a leader or superior as a foreigner whose status was not yet known. Barrick turned and found a trio of goblins standing behind him, looking up with solemn, shining eyes.

"Yes?"

"We have been in the side tunnels, doing the bidding of the queen in white. While there, we smelled a man. A human man."

For a moment he thought they were insulting him obliquely, perhaps suggesting that he bathe: the Qar were much more interested in cleanliness than Barrick's own people, he had noticed already. "A man . . . ?"

"Yes, Lord. Like you, but different." The goblins nudged and glared at each other, then the one who had been chosen as spokesman tried again. "Older. A little smaller. Will you come and see?"

Barrick let himself be led away from the lip of the great chasm. "What have you done to him? Is he a captive?"

The goblins looked shocked. "No, Lord!" said the spokesman. "We would do nothing without your word . . ."

"The queen was busy," said one of the others, earning a glare from the one who had been talking. "And we are frightened of the dark lady."

"Quiet, fool," muttered the third, but it was unclear to whom she was speaking. Only the whispered knowledge of the Fireflower allowed him to discern which goblins were male and which female.

They led him up a winding path through the Qar forces until they were just beyond the camp. Here at the edge of things, where the light of the torches was dim and the shadows long, Barrick was reminded again of how little he had seen of the sun since he had first set out on this blighted adventure.

I should have stayed under the open sky as long as I could. . . .

His thoughts were interrupted by a memory of Briony and himself as children, running along the bright hillside of M'Helan's Rock, knee-deep in white meadowqueen blossoms as the sea boomed and hissed below. The thought was as painful as a dagger, a cold stab in his heart. He felt the Fireflower memories swarm up and cover it like butterflies alighting on a bush, but for the briefest moment he had a twinge of doubt. Was the Fireflower keeping things from him, somehow? Separating him from his own life?

A moment later all such speculation vanished as another group of barefoot goblin soldiers appeared, half a dozen at least, prodding diffidently with their slender, sharp spears at a man twice their small size. For half a moment Barrick thought it might be one of the Xixian soldiers who had become separated from his troop, but the man's round face was as pale as Barrick's own . . .

Barrick stared. The man stared back at him.

"My prince . . . ?" the man said at last. "Are you . . . do you . . . ? Is that truly you, Prince Barrick?"

It took longer for Barrick to remember. "Chaven," he said at last, speaking the name out loud. His voice was dry and ragged from disuse. "What are you doing here, physician?"

"Prince Barrick—it *is* you!" The man stared as though newly awake;

a moment later, as if something had slipped inside him and his feelings could now move freely, he suddenly lurched toward Barrick with arms wide. Barrick stepped back from the embrace. "But you are so tall, Highness!" Chaven said. "Ah, I suppose it has been almost a year . . ." He shook his head. "Listen to me babble. How do you come to be here? How did you survive the war with the fairies?" He gestured to the goblins, who were watching the exchange with deep suspicion. "Are you a prisoner? No, you have made them *your* prisoners somehow . . ."

Barrick found himself increasingly impatient with this stocky little man who would not stop talking. "I asked you what you are doing here. You are in the middle of a Qar camp and we are at war. You do not belong here."

Chaven stared at him. "Why so cold, Highness? Why so angry? I have done nothing but good for your family in your absence—I helped to save your sister's life!"

Barrick was awash in confusing ideas, the voices of the Fireflower and his own memories. He did not even know himself why he was angry with the physician. "I will ask you one last time, Chaven— why are you here, sneaking around on the outskirts of our camp?"

"Sneaking? I . . ." The scholar shook his head, then fell silent. "I will be honest, Prince Barrick—I do not know. I . . . I confess that I am a little confused. I seem to be lost, too." He looked around him slowly. "Yes, where am I? Last I remember I was with Chert and the others . . ."

The name meant nothing to Barrick. He was about to turn his back on the man when one of the goblins pulled at his sleeve. "He is hiding something, Master. We saw it when he approached—there, under his robe. It is a little man of stone. 'Ware lest he try to hit you with it . . ."

"What? Nonsense!" Chaven cried, but he seemed more baffled than offended. He wrapped his arms around his middle as if he meant to protect his belly against an attack.

"What are they talking about, Chaven? Show it to me."

"But . . . it's not . . ." Frightened by the look in Barrick's eyes, Chaven reached into his robe and lifted out the thing he had been hiding. It was a small statue of a man with an owl crouched on his shoulder, crudely carved in crystal that was streaked with pale pink and gray and blue. The Fireflower voices sang loud and harsh in his head, as full of confusion as Barrick himself.

"I've . . . I've seen that statue before, somewhere." He stared at it, then glanced up to Chaven, who still looked half awake but fearful, like a man dragged out of bed into a completely unexpected situation. Then it came to him, like a fire racing through dry kindling. "It was in the Erivor Chapel at home. Someone stole it." Barrick's face felt as if it was someone else's—he had no idea what expression he wore. "*I* stole it. And Briony and I threw it into the ocean. How could you possibly have it?"

"I don't know, Highness!" The physician shook his head violently. "No, I do know—of course I know! The Skimmers brought it to me. Some of their oyster divers found it and . . . and they thought I might tell them if it was worth anything. I bought it from them." He looked up at Barrick, his face full of calculation but also something deeper and stranger, a kind of animal terror. "I had never seen anything like it—an image of Kernios Olognothas, the all-seeing Earth Lord. I . . . I wanted it so very much."

"You wanted this heavy statue of the dour god of death so much that you carry it around with you through these depths? What are you doing here under the castle at all, man? What are you hiding?"

Chaven cringed a little. "My prince, you are frightening me. I will tell you everything, I promise! Answer all your questions, yes. Just take me into your camp and give me some water to drink. I find that I am very dry. I'm not certain how long I've been lost in these lonely tunnels . . ."

"You will do more than come back to the camp," Barrick said. "You will meet Saqri, the queen of the fairies, and answer her questions as well. And if you are *very* unlucky you will also meet Yasammez. Some of them call her Lady Porcupine. She will likely make you wet yourself."

Barrick stared hard at the physician for a moment, then thanked the goblin sentries and dismissed them. When they had scuttled away, he turned back to Chaven. "But first . . ."

The physician's mouth was hanging open. "You spoke to them—but you did not say a word that I could hear. How did you do that?"

"That doesn't matter." Barrick waved his hand. "First, before we go back to the camp, you will leave the statue in my tent for now. I don't think I want Saqri and the others to know about it just yet." He took Chaven by the elbow and directed him back along the rocky path that circled the great hole at the center of the cavern.

"I . . . I don't understand, Highness," said Chaven.

"No, you don't." Barrick gave him a little push to speed him up. "That's because you don't have the blood of gods and monsters running in your veins like some of us do."

30
Slipping on Blood

"The moment he made his way inside the castle, the Orphan was discovered by the goddess Zuriyal, the sister of Zmeos the Horned Serpent. She felt pity for the child because of his youth and innocent kindness . . ."

—from "A Child's Book of the Orphan, and His Life and Death and Reward in Heaven"

"THE LAST HOURS are truly upon us now," said Malachite Copper. The high-ranking Funderling was looking less handsome every hour, his armor dented and dusty, his hair wild and scorched short on one side where a flare of Xixian war fire had burned him. "When the southerners dig through all that rock we dropped in the middle of the Maze, we'll have to make a stand. We've slowed them badly these last days, but once they push through here, there'll be nowhere else we can hope to stop them."

Vansen took a tiny sip from his waterskin. The blasting powder the Funderlings had used to block the autarch's march as they slowly gave ground through the Maze had also cracked the stone of the ancient building's aqueduct; they no longer had fresh water or any notion of when they would get some again. "How much longer do we need to hold them?"

"Not long" Copper said. "I looked in on the monks carrying the hour-candle a short while ago to learn the time. Midsummer's Eve is over now, Captain. Upground, Midsummer's Day has already dawned. Today, we will live or die, succeed or fail."

"I wish it *were* such an even thing—a toss of the coin, live or die." Vansen frowned; it made his jaw hurt where one of the Xixians had knocked his helmet off his head with a spear thrust, but he had been fortunate not to lose his eye. "But I think the chances we live to see the day *after* today are much smaller than that, friend Copper."

A short distance away Cinnabar Quicksilver was tossing and murmuring in shallow sleep. He had been felled by one of the Xixians' powder blasts in the Initiation Hall at the center of the Maze. A dozen other Funderlings had died but Vansen and Sledge Jasper had reached the wounded magister in time to drag him and a handful of other survivors out alive. The fever that had come with Cinnabar's wounds had been the greatest danger but it seemed finally to have broken. Now he lay on a makeshift litter here in Revelation Hall, the last roofed section of the Maze. Only the open Balcony lay behind them, then below it and beyond stretched the great open spaces of the cavern that contained the Sea in the Depths and the island of the Shining Man.

Wardthane Sledge Jasper limped over and lowered himself to the floor beside them. His face was a mask of dried blood and dirt, his hairless head crisscrossed with cuts and dappled with bruises: Vansen thought that he looked like he had been trying to knock down walls using nothing but his own hard skull.

"It's a short walk to the end of the road," Jasper said matter-of-factly. "I just came back."

"The Balcony?" Vansen asked. "I know, I've seen it . . ."

"We'll be able to hold them less than an hour or two after they break through into this hall . . . and our spies say they're coming *soon*. Hundreds and hundreds." Jasper looked to where a group of weary Funderlings was piling stones for the last of the defensive barriers they were building across Revelation Hall. "At least we won't have to go far when we *do* retreat again."

"Vansen . . . ?" Cinnabar was awake on his litter and stretching out his hand. "Captain Vansen . . . ?"

"I'm here." He crouched down beside the Funderling magister. One of Cinnabar's legs was badly broken. Vansen thought that even if some miracle saved him from death at the hands of the Xixies, there was little chance the Funderling would keep the damaged limb.

"Where is . . . my boy?" Cinnabar asked.

"Calomel is well." Vansen leaned forward and took his small, rough hand. "We just made him get some rest and something to eat. He's been at your side all day."

"Truly? Truly he is well?" Cinnabar's eyes swam with tears. "You are not telling me this only to keep a dying man happy?"

Vansen shook his head. "You're not dying, Magister. The fever has broken and the worst is behind you. And I swear on my soldier's honor that Calomel is in good health—well, as good as any of us on short rations and short rest. He's a fine, brave little lad and he will be angry we sent him away just before you woke up again."

Cinnabar at last let himself be convinced. He lay back; soon he was sleeping again.

"And what *will* happen at the end?" asked Malachite Copper suddenly. "I have never thought much of such things before. Will we lie in darkness for a thousand years, as some say, or will we immediately be raised up again to stand before the throne of the Lord himself?"

Vansen could only shake his head, angry again. If the stinking Qar had held to their bargain, it might never have come to this. He felt a scalding surge of hatred toward the fairies—that creature Aesi'uah, for all her seeming kindness, had looked him straight in the eye and told him that the Qar would not desert their allies!

But I suppose in a way she told the truth, Ferras Vansen decided. *After all, how can you desert what you never truly joined?*

"I'm going to put my head down now," he said heavily. "Grab a few moments' sleep. One of you be good enough to wake me if some of the autarch's men happen by, will you?"

Olin Eddon groaned. His pale face was dappled with sweat.

Pinimmon Vash bowed respectfully to the walking dead man. "If there is anything else you need, Majesty, you have only to ask."

"Other than having my arms untied, you mean." Olin had lost weight rapidly in the last days and his cheeks were hollow, blue-shadowed above the tangle of his unkempt beard. His eyes, though, were still so bright that Vash found it discomforting to meet the man's gaze.

"There is no one to blame for that but yourself, King Olin." Vash realized even as he said it that he must sound like some old Favored of the

Seclusion scolding one of the lesser princes. "Surely you cannot expect to walk free after trying to kill the Golden One."

Olin laughed bitterly. "If you had any wit, you and the rest of these Xixian sheep would have helped me. The monster might be dead now."

Vash could not help feeling a thrill of relief at the mere notion but could not show anything of it, of course. "You are a fool, King Olin. He is the sun of our sky. Every Xixian thanks heaven for the health of our autarch every day."

"While making plans for what will happen when someone finally achieves what I failed to do. Speaking of that, how *is* the scotarch?"

For a moment, Vash thought his old heart would crack like an egg. His gaze darted wildly, but none of the soldiers or royal functionaries except Olin's guards were close enough to have heard. Still, who was to say that in his anger the northern king might not spew such fatal nonsense again in front of the Golden One? In his terror, Paramount Minister Vash began to give serious thought to how he could kill the autarch's prisoner without anyone knowing.

"Did you speak to him as I suggested?" Olin pressed.

All gods curse this man! His persistence was insane! "Do not even talk to me, Majesty. Do you seek to make my master distrust me? It will not work. He knows my loyalty is complete."

"It can't be." Olin was smiling now. He was proud of his smile: the guards had knocked out one of his teeth. "You are too clever a man for that, Vash. Why would someone who has lived as long as you yoke his fortune to a madman like Sulepis? I am certain you have done what I said, and I am certain that your mind is full of new ideas . . ."

Vash looked around frantically. Would this horror never end? Of course he had spoken with Prusus, the crippled scotarch, a man nobody had even suspected had the power of speech. Olin was right in one thing, of course: Pinimmon Vash had not lived so long by being a fool, and if there were things he did not know about the man who might replace Sulepis Am-Bishakh then Vash needed to know them. And he had learned much that surprised him . . . but he was not so stupid as to discuss any of it with this walking corpse.

"I know nothing of what you say," he told Olin. "And I do not wish to know anything of it, either. Ah!" He had finally seen someone of high enough status to be recognized. "There is High Priest Panhyssir—someone whose conversation makes sense."

"As you say," said Olin. "Dig your hole, then, Minister Vash. I hope you dig it deep, because there will be much killing when the end comes and few enough places to hide."

Vash was tired of holes and he was tired of Olin Eddon. He turned his back on the northerner. "Panhyssir! A moment of your time . . ."

"I'm sorry, good Lord Vash," said the priest as he marched by with a small entourage of robed followers. He waved a thick hand. "I cannot stop to talk. Very important work for the autarch is before me, and the time grows short."

The ass. At that moment, Vash nearly broke his staff across the high priest's ugly, self-satisfied head. He stood for a moment composing himself, then hurried after Panhyssir, saying: "I will walk with you, old friend, and leave Olin to the pleasant company of his guards."

Vash generally found getting around difficult, especially in the first stiff, aching hour after he rose in the morning, but fortunately the high priest Panhyssir was fat and no faster than a Mihanni tortoise. Vash caught up to him only a short distance away, then immediately had to duck his head under the low lintel of a doorway leading into one of the side passages. These were ceremonial precincts, that much was clear, so the doors and ceilings of this maze were not as low as they might have been—Vash could only shudder when he thought about what it must be like to live among these terrible little creatures in their horrid, dark, cramped little city. A man his size would be forever on his knees . . .

But soon enough it will be over and we will go back to Xis and I will never have to see these miserable, dank places and ugly creatures again, he reassured himself.

Panhyssir had slowed a little. The tone of his voice suggested this was a great sacrifice. "What did you want, Vash, my friend?"

"Simply to ask you a question, good Panhyssir, but I would rather . . ." Vash paused to duck under a low place in the passage which the quartermaster corps had marked with a splash of paint," . . . talk to you in private somewhere, instead of gasping for breath here among the common herd."

"Ah, so you do not find it as invigorating as the rest of us do, being on the front lines of battle with our Golden One?"

Vash scowled at Panhyssir's wide back. The fat, self-righteous fool! Vash had heard the priest complaining many times during this ill-omened voyage, fulminating about the absence of his regular cook or the danger to his health from damp and chilly northern airs. Once, Vash had even heard the high priest claim that the weeping of the captive children in the hold disturbed his afternoon nap. Invigorating, indeed! "I do not have your wonderful constitution and boundless joy in adventure, old friend, that's true," he told the priest. "But my reluctance is more to do with matters I would not air among our inferiors."

"Oh, well then, follow me. I shall have a few moments to speak when we reach the Sanctuary."

Pinimmon Vash almost groaned out loud. The chamber the priests had chosen for a Sanctuary was two floors up, a walk of several minutes. "You are too kind," he said. The new Sanctuary had been one of the larger chambers of the maze complex, this one near the top of the front end of the rabbit warren the northern Yisti had built for themselves and which the autarch's troops had only liberated a few days earlier. He gritted his teeth and hobbled along behind the priests.

Vash was interested to discover that the Golden One's latest prisoner had a position of honor in the Sanctuary second only to that of Nushash himself: her cage was in the center of the room, not far from the draped cabinet that held the ancient gilded wooden effigy of the god. The girl—Kinten, Kwinten, her name did not matter, she was only the daughter of a minor priest—was kneeling in the straw in the middle of the cage with her wrists tied behind her and her black hair hanging over her face—sulking, no doubt. Still, Vash knew it was her because of the streak of violent, unruly red in her hair.

"You will pardon me for a moment, Minister Vash," said Panhyssir, all formality now. "This must be punctual. Every day, at dawn, midday, and again at evening." He laughed. "Although, of course, sunrise and sunset are purely intellectual experiences here in these caves."

Caves, thought Vash with a shiver. As if anyone could call something as vast and ancient and strange as this underground world by the mere name of caves! Had Panhyssir seen nothing of these bedeviling depths, with their huge, echoing spaces, their monstrous painted shapes and carved spells? Caves were shallow niches in the ocean rocks near the Vash family summer home. This was an entire world.

The girl's cage was unlocked, but she did not move. One of the young priests brought a steaming bowl to Panhyssir. The high priest passed it beneath his nose for a moment, taking the merest sniff of the rising vapors, then nodded with his usual grandiosity and handed it back. The younger man carried it to the cage and held it out for the girl, then went through a little dumbshow pantomime when she would not take it, as if he could not be bothered to speak to such a creature.

Panhyssir moved over beside Vash. "As usual, we will have to threaten to kill one of the other captives if she doesn't cooperate. She wishes to protect the children the Golden One has gathered, so she will give in after a short while. It is the same every time." He laughed. "Ah, but no service is too aggravating when it is a service for the Great Tent himself, am I right, Minister?"

"Of course, of course," said Vash, watching the girl. She did not look like the whole thing was merely a daily ritual: she looked desperate and badly frightened. In truth, Vash did not like having to harm children, at least not any more than was absolutely needed for proper correction. This whole business of the Golden One's mysterious plan was becoming more distasteful by the day.

Vash shook his head, annoyed by his own woolgathering. "The thing is, High Priest Panhyssir, I was wondering whether you had been experiencing any of the same . . . communication problems that I have?"

The other man looked back at him, eyes flat, expression carefully smoothed. "What exactly do you mean, Paramount Minister Vash?"

"Every day I send my letters back to the main military camp on the surface, giving orders to my subordinates, answering questions of protocol from those wishing to communicate with the Great Tent himself in some way. I am sure you do much the same."

Panhyssir shrugged. "Most of my priests are here," he said, sweeping his broad hand around the Sanctuary, which had been so filled with candles and ornaments and religious statuary now that it did look little different from one of the great Nushash temples back home. "There are priests of the Great God ministering to the troops of course, but they only rarely need guidance from me."

"Perhaps it has not been as apparent to you, then, as it has to me."

"What hasn't been?"

"That my letters are not being answered. It's almost two days now since I've had a reply from the main camp. I inquired of the courier corps and they said their men have set out for the surface the last two days but haven't yet returned, and that no one else has come down from above, either."

Panhyssir's face was still carefully neutral, but Vash thought he saw a flicker of apprehension. "Ah. Still, I am sure it is nothing. A confusion of duties, perhaps, or even a mere physical impediment like a rockslide . . ."

"Then why haven't our messengers come back to say the way was blocked?"

"I couldn't say. And it is something to be aware of, Brother Pinimmon. But not, I would say, something to fret about overmuch."

The girl was weeping now, and Vash was distracted. The young priest was bent over her, whispering angrily. Now that his eyes were used to the light in the Sanctuary, Vash could see that not all the methods of persuasion used on her had been mere threats. She had bruises on her face and upper arms as well, and doubtless others hidden by her shapeless robes.

"I . . . I'm not certain I agree, High Priest Panhyssir. It could just as equally be . . ." Vash was still staring at the unhappy girl. "Why does she make such a fuss?"

"What? Oh, because the Sun's Blood potion tastes foul, I suspect. We do not have the leisure of giving it to her in smaller amounts because time is short."

Vash shook his head. "I do not understand. Sun's Blood . . . ?"

"In case she must be used in the ritual in place of the northern king. He is of the direct bloodline of the gods, only a few generations displaced." Panhyssir nodded his head gravely. "She is of mongrel stock and the blood of Habbili in her is much thinned, so we must bring it back to a point of concentration, and quickly." The girl groaned, a noise of true distress. Panhyssir smiled a little. "Good. She has drunk the potion. You do not want to be here when the visions take her. It can be a little upsetting for a layman. Screaming, thrashing, you can imagine."

Vash, who had presided over dozens of tortures and executions (not particularly by choice but by the requirements of his position) raised an eyebrow. "Oh, yes, it sounds dreadful. Thank you for sparing me. But I still would like to finish speaking of that other matter . . ."

"Other . . . ? Oh, yes. And this problem with communication between the camp aboveground and our forces here worries you? Perhaps you should talk to the antipolemarch. Surely he would be aware of any difficulty."

Vash nodded. "Yes, that is a good idea. Because I can think of more sinister reasons the messengers might not be getting through . . ."

Now it was the high priest who raised an eyebrow. "Sinister? Truly? Such as what?"

"There might be hard fighting on the surface. Or a force might have come down from the castle through the Yisti city, and has now cut our supply lines."

Panhyssir stared at him for a moment. When he laughed, it was as sudden and loud as a cannon shot, and everyone in the room except the gagging, weeping girl turned to look at him. "Cut our supply lines! What, that force of tiny soldiers? With what, toy swords and broomstick horses to ride?" He grabbed at his stomach as if it hurt. "Oh, Vash, my distinguished friend, I hope you will forgive me when I say that it is clear you have very little knowledge of war. We have crushed the resistance here so thoroughly that they will be trying to surrender to every stranger who passes for years after we are gone!"

Angry and ashamed, but as usual showing nothing, Pinimmon Vash bowed and thanked Panhyssir for sharing his wisdom. As he went out, he could still hear the girl coughing and sobbing in her cage.

Vansen scrubbed himself as well as he could with sand before he put his armor back on. It was a soldier's habit he had learned from Donal Murroy, his old captain—take any opportunity to get clean that you can find. Most of the others hadn't bothered, and Ferras Vansen didn't like that. It wasn't the smell of sweat and blood and less pleasant things that bothered him—a soldier quickly became used to the stink of many men together, especially in confined places like the Maze—but he feared that it meant his untrained Funderling soldiers, who had fought so long and so bravely against hopeless odds, had nearly given up.

Ferras Vansen didn't blame any of them. Sledge Jasper had lost nearly half his original troop of warders, men he had trained himself. Malachite Copper's household guard had been halved as well, and among those dead were Copper's own brother-in-law, hacked to death on his back as he screamed for help; if Copper survived, he would still have to give his wife that dreadful news. Many of the other Funderlings were monks who had never expected to leave the temple again in their lives, let alone be forced into a war against Big Folk, and the rest were volunteers, young Funderling men who had not even joined the Stonecutter's Guild yet.

Vansen watched a pair of monks as they carefully strapped Cinnabar to his litter under the watchful eye of the magister's son Calomel. The past days had taught the Funderlings that retreats were often sudden, uncalculated affairs, even with Vansen's experienced leadership, and since retreat was the only thing guaranteed in this campaign, they did their best to prepare for it ahead of time. The monk Flowstone was crouched near them, leading a few of the other Metamorphic Brothers in prayer; when he had finished, Ferras Vansen called him over.

"I am sorry if I have treated you more harshly than you deserve," he told the young monk. "In truth, you have done well. I'm sorry you and your brothers have to go through this."

Flowstone tried to smile bravely, but it didn't entirely work. "Our faith teaches us that the past and present are nearest each other at moments like this, and so of course it is painful to be one of those caught in the folds of history. That is when we are closest to the scorching flames of the Eternal."

Vansen wasn't at all sure what that meant. His ideas about the gods had never led him much beyond what the priests had told him, coupled with a certain doubt about the good sense of any complicated hierarchy, even a heavenly one. He nodded, which was the best thing he could think of to do, and changed the subject. "We can only defend the last chamber—the Revelation Hall as you call it—then we will be forced out of the Maze entirely."

"Captain!" One of Dolomite's men trotted up, sweating. "They are breaking through the last of the rubble! The sentries say they will be on us soon."

Vansen felt it like the last note of a triad—something he had been expecting, almost needing. Soon he would not have to fear his own mistakes any longer. Soon he would not have to watch good men die. He had given everything he had. There could be no shame in that . . . could there?

"Everybody to the back of the hall!" he said, pitching his voice to be heard by as many as possible. As the farthest who could hear him called to those who could not, Vansen added, "Douse any torches and get everyone behind the first barricade. We'll make our stand there."

Jasper grinned tightly and looked at the monk Flowstone, who appeared more than a little queasy at the prospect. "We will indeed," the wardthane said. "We'll give 'em something they'll be talking about in Funderling Town and Xis itself for many a year!"

Fear ran through the hall like a ripple on a pool, but no one hesitated; within only moments they were moving in a ragged but orderly way toward the foremost barricade.

Flowstone looked up at Vansen, and his mouth trembled. "We're all going to die in this hall, aren't we?" he said quietly. "The same place where I was initiated—the place where I became a man."

"Nobody knows when their time has come or what the gods plan." Vansen shrugged. "Least of all now, when even the gods seem baffled. A year ago I thought I'd certainly die behind the Shadowline. That didn't happen. Who knows what comes next, Brother Flowstone? Only the Sisters of Fate. Tighten your helmet strap and have a sip of water. You probably won't have a chance at another for a while."

Pinimmon Vash had no idea what to expect of the event. It seemed like one of his master's typical whims—some sort of ceremony, apparently religious, but with a full slate of the autarch's Leopard guards in attendance. Vash made certain that Panhyssir was informed so that the sanctuary would be ready.

To Vash's inestimable relief, the northern king for once was nowhere to be seen. The girl with the red streak had been removed from the chamber as well, so that only the shrine of Nushash remained of things that might steal attention from the autarch—not that anything could truly compete with Sulepis. In his ceremonial golden armor and high-crested falcon helmet the tall ruler indeed seemed something far beyond a mere man. The autarch's eyes even seemed to catch and reflect back something of the smoldering torches, shining almost orange beneath his crown's golden beak. Two dozen of the autarch's Leopards stood before, beside, and behind him, making a sort of human cage that briefly gave Vash a bizarre glimpse of the autarch imprisoned. Yet Sulepis stood nearly a head taller than even the biggest of them: the cage of men seemed scarcely enough to contain him.

Vash didn't know himself what the autarch was planning. He had fulfilled all that was expected of him, and now waited with ragged nerves to discover it. He sometimes thought it must be the same to be a bird as to serve a capricious, deadly master like Sulepis. The winds shifted, a warm updraft became a downdraft that hurled you toward the earth, and all you could do was fight to keep your wings out and pray you would level out once more.

The autarch called out to the Leopard guard officer. "Did you bring them, as I bade you? Are they here?"

He bowed, shaved head gleaming with oil. "Waiting outside, Golden One."

"Good. Send them in to me now."

Two Leopards went out. The rest of the guards did their best to remain at strict attention, but they were clearly curious as to who might be such a risk that so many guards were present at once. Soon, three large women were led into the sanctuary. They were all Xixian, by appearance, and each woman was as tall and heavyset as almost any of the Leopards; also, all three were hard-eyed and sullen. The guards' eyes grew wide to see them. Some of them must have wondered whether the autarch planned one of his strange jokes.

Sulepis waved his long, gold-tipped fingers and the desert priest A'lat appeared bearing a box of carved ivory. At a nod from Sulepis and despite his blind appearance, the priest walked directly to each of the women in turn and gave her something from the box. As the priest returned to the autarch's side, Vash saw that each of the muscular women now held something that looked like a piece of dull crystal about the same size as a honey-sweet.

"You are Khobana the Wolf, are you not?" the autarch asked the tallest woman, whose hair was chopped shorter than that of most men. "The one who was sentenced to execution for killing her husband and family?"

A sort of sneer curled her lip. "Yes, Golden One."

"I remember you. With your bare hands, yes?" He nodded, pleased. "Now, you three each hold a great gift—one that will make you as fearsome a fighter as one of the gods themselves, as powerful as Xosh the moon god who slew Okhuz, the god of war. And if you survive to return it . . . it will also buy your freedom."

The women stared at him, mistrustful as wild animals. Vash was unsure of what was happening, but he could not help remembering that as powerful as Xosh Silvergleam had been, he had been slain in turn by another, stronger god. It was something Pinimmon Vash thought about more and more, these days: the servants of the powerful often came to a bad end—and nobody mourned them. . . .

The autarch had continued. ". . . And although in ordinary times such weak resistance would mean nothing—less than nothing—because I now have need of haste I cannot allow these mongrel Yisti and their Marchman general to balk me any longer. That is why you hold those kulikos stones in your hands."

Kulikos? Vash shivered. He had heard enough of the old stories to know such powerful magicks would bring death to many—and eventually, to their bearers as well.

As he warmed to his subject, the autarch's voice rose and echoed. "With the stones and the spells A'lat has taught you, you will be *true* she-demons! You will tear my enemies apart as if they were mice and rabbits, and they will run weeping before you. You will leave nothing in your wake but blood, and when the sun has passed through the sky one more time in the world above, I will stand before the god himself and make his power mine. And you three will be among my most honored servants!"

Khobana the Wolf was the first of the women to drop to her knees. "Hail, Sulepis!" she said. "Hail, Golden One!" The other two echoed her cry.

"Hail, indeed!" the autarch said, laughing.

31
The Gate to Funderling Town

". . . Zuriyal told her brother Zmeos that the strange smell in the great house was only that of a mouse that had snuck in to get out of the cold."

—from "A Child's Book of the Orphan, and His Life and Death and Reward in Heaven"

"IT'S FOOLISH and I won't let you do it," Brother Antimony told him. "With all respect, Master Chert, I can't. Cinnabar and the rest would never forgive me." He blanched. "Oh, Elders, and think of what Mistress Opal would do! She'd have my hide for a cleaning rag!"

"Unless you're planning to tie me up and sit on me, young man, you can't stop me." He scowled. "Don't make it harder. Do you think I'm not terrified?"

"But . . . but it's a war up there!"

"It's a war down here, too. Our friends are fighting and probably dying this moment. I owe it to them to do what I can."

"But what makes you think Brother Nickel will listen to you anyway? He is stubborn, Chert, and he hates you."

"He won't listen to me—but he'll listen to the Astion." He finished tying his pack closed and stood up, slinging it over his shoulders. "Nickel is a nasty piece of work, but he is not a traitor. Neither is my brother, much as I dislike him. And they have Guild Law on their side." It still galled, though, the way his older brother Nodule, the clan magister, had walked in and immediately taken Nickel's side. "No, if we want to be ready to save our people, we will have to do it the correct way, the Funderling way—with all permits correctly chopped and filed." He patted the big youth on the arm. "Keep the work going any way you can, Antimony. Work in secret if you can. They will likely not bother you if I'm gone, and I'll make sure they hear about it."

"But what about your wife and son . . . ?"

"I'll deal with them, lad. Cinnabar and the others are down in the depths facing certain death. I can at least have the courage to tell Opal what I plan to do, face-to-face."

Antimony clasped Chert's hand with the worried look of someone sending a friend off to nearly certain death.

"You *what*? Of course you will not! In fact you will have to walk over me to get out this door." Opal threw herself across the doorway of her temporary quarters beside the gunflour-works. The women who shared it with her had all slipped out when they heard the first of Chert's words, sensing the storm that was brewing—even the redoubtable Vermilion Quicksilver. Chert wished he could have followed them.

"It's no good, my old darling," he said with a stern resolve he did not feel. "I have no choice. I've told you why. If I wait any longer, it will be too late."

"All the more reason. It was a wild, dangerous plan to begin with, so why risk your life for it?" She folded her arms across her breast. She wasn't going to budge without a fight, that was clear. In that moment he loved her for it even as he began to wonder whether he would have to knock her senseless to escape.

"Just listen to me, my love," he begged.

"No and no and *no* . . . !" She broke off, distracted. Flint had wandered out of the back of the cavern rubbing his eyes, his hair still mussed from sleep. "Oh, child, were we shouting?" she said in a completely different tone. "Go back to sleep. Mama will be in soon. I'm just having a little discussion with your wicked, wicked Papa."

"Let him go, Mama Opal. I . . . I dreamed about it. The Shining Man was on fire—it was hot as the sun! Everybody was screaming. Let him go."

"What nonsense is this?" Opal frowned and tried to turn him around. "You had a bad dream, child. Back to bed."

"No." He held firm. He was bigger than Chert now, almost the size of the young giant Antimony, and could not be so easily moved. "Papa Chert has to go."

Chert took a few steps forward and touched Opal's arms. "The boy has been right before . . . about many things."

Her expression was not of anger but naked terror. "No! Not again! I won't let you go off again. Do you know what it's like for me . . . ?"

Chert shook his head. "I can only guess. But I know that you miss me like I miss you." He took another step, put his arms around her even though she stiffened in his embrace and turned her face away. "Please, my only love, don't make this so hard for me. I would not do it if I didn't feel I had to, but lives and more depend on me—perhaps all of Funderling Town!"

She pulled herself away but kept her back to him. "Then just . . . just go. But do not expect me to weep quietly and wave farewell like some dutiful wife out of a story. Go and be cursed!"

"No!" The thought horrified him. "Don't send me away with that on my head, Opal."

"Get out." She shrugged off his embrace, slapped at his hands when he tried to touch her again, and still would not meet his eye. "Go!"

He kissed the boy on the forehead, ran his hand through the child's flaxen hair, then left the makeshift dwelling and turned toward Funderling Town. Opal was right about one thing—it would be a long and dangerous trip, with the Earth Elders only knew what kind of monsters and enemies between him and his destination. He felt as if he waded through chest-deep water, his feet sticking and sliding on a muddy bottom.

"Wait! Chert, wait!"

He turned to see Opal leaping up the path behind him, the hem of her skirt clutched in her hands so she didn't trip. Before he could say a word, she reached him and threw her arms around him, squeezing her small, compact body against his so tightly that for a moment he lost his breath.

"I take it back, I take it all back," she said through tears. "I take back what I said! You are my man, Blue Quartz, and I love you. But if you let something happen to you then I *will* put a curse on you that will make you hop and jump like a rat with fleas even as you stand in front of the Elders themselves! I swear it!"

He did not waste breath trying to come up with anything to say to that, but only held her for a long time. After they finally kissed and murmured their good-byes Opal turned and went back down the path without looking at him again.

Any hopes Briony might have had of a swift conquest of her family home did not survive the first hours of their incursion. Hendon Tolly's loyalists, caught by surprise when Briony and Eneas arrived at the outer wall in the middle of the burning of the autarch's ships, quickly dropped back to the inner keep. Berkan Hood and his soldiers pressed hundreds of castle folk into involuntary service, forcing them to hoist cannons rescued from the Qar's attack up to the top of the inner keep's walls, and by the time the sun rose on Briony's first morning back in Southmarch, those guns had begun to boom from the towers of Raven's Gate.

"We have our own demi-cannons atop Basilisk Gate and the outer walls," Eneas said as they sheltered with his lieutenants in a merchant's tall house on the North Lagoon. From the window of the uppermost room they could see the smoke of the guns curling along the top of Raven's Gate, but at the moment Hood and his defenders didn't seem to know where their enemies were and were firing wildly. The morning air off the ocean was warm and damp and salty as blood; the weather seemed to have changed from spring to late summer in a day. "We could leave some of them in place against a return by the autarch's troops and have the rest brought to bear on the inner keep by tonight."

Briony shook her head. "Tolly has surrounded himself with innocents. I won't fire on my own people."

Eneas nodded. "I sympathize, Princess. Perhaps I even agree, but I am not certain you can afford too much care. If what your father told you is correct, we have only until midnight tomorrow before the autarch . . . well before he does whatever it is he plans."

"But the autarch is deep beneath the castle. That witch Saqri told us."

He shrugged, a pragmatic warrior out of his depths. "I am certain you remember what the fairy queen said better than I do, but I remember that she told us, 'Every battle here matters.' She said there were strands of danger everywhere, like a spider's web, and that no one could know for certain which strand touched which."

Briony loosened and retied the strip of cloth meant to keep the sweat out of her eyes. The mere thought of being ruled by the fairy queen, the creature who had stolen her brother, filled her with fury. "I don't care. I will not turn the guns on my own people unless they have taken up arms for Tolly. But from the distance a cannon shot will travel, that's impossible to know."

Lord Helkis, the prince's friend and chief commander, cleared his throat. "I beg your pardon, Princess Briony, but this is no ordinary siege. We cannot wait them out. From what we are told, Tolly has been stocking the residence with supplies for months. Do you think we can make them surrender by wagging our fingers at them?"

"Miron," said Eneas warningly.

"No, Your Highness, it must be said." The young nobleman turned to Briony again. "I will speak what my liege cannot, either because of his feelings or his courtesy. If the fairies are right, Princess, then you will doom your own people by this faintheartedness."

"Miron! You go too far . . . !"

"No, Eneas." Briony lifted her hand. "He is giving you what any good councillor should—the truth as he sees it." She turned to Helkis. "Yes, my lord, it is a dilemma. But I will not let anyone fire willy-nilly into the heart of my castle. Tolly has gathered many of my subjects around him. Even among the soldiers, a large number of those fighting probably believe they are defending the keep against the autarch or the fairies or some other foreign invader. No, I will not return to my home and spill any blood that I needn't spill." She frowned at a sudden thought. How many times had her father said, *"Even a good king will always have blood on his hands . . ."*? More than she could count. Briony had thought he meant simply that wars could not be avoided, but now she was learning the truth: Olin had been saying that almost every decision a monarch made would cause suffering for someone. "Please, let me consider this problem for a short time, if you would be so good," she said when Lord Helkis would have spoken again.

"Would you like a moment to yourself?" asked Eneas.

"That is exactly what I would like, Your Highness," she said gratefully. "But I will not evict you from your own rooms. I will walk a little."

"But not beyond the yard of this house . . . !"

"Of course not, Prince Eneas. You have my promise."

She made her way downstairs past the sentries and other soldiers, bemused as always not by the way they evaporated from in front of her—

Briony had been born into a royal family; she was used to deference—as by the way they steadfastly avoided meeting her eyes. This was a new thing. Only the most fearful or guilty had looked away from her before, and ever since she had reached womanhood, she had become used to men sizing her up with the unconscious insolence of horse-traders. So what had changed?

These are Eneas' men, she realized. *And they think I belong to their prince.*

It was a realization that disturbed her more than it should have.

She reached the ground floor and made her way across the crowded courtyard to the gate. The merchant who owned this house had been a wealthy man—Briony believed she had met him at a few court functions, although she didn't remember his face—and his property was large, more than adequate for Eneas and his command staff. She made her way up the stairs of the small gatehouse.

It was beyond strange seeing what had become of the outer keep in her absence, horrifying as any nightmare. The Qar's brief invasion had all but emptied it, and though a few residents had filtered back out after the fairies had withdrawn, they had quickly found themselves under fire from the autarch's huge cannons and so had fled back to the inner keep again.

The outer keep had once been as pretty and thriving a city as any north of Tessis, but now it seemed lifeless as a pile of charred bones. Entire buildings had toppled into spars and brickwork or burned away until only their chimneys remained, solitary as grave markers. Scarcely any of the tallest buildings still stood, and those that remained upright were blackened and deserted. Briony could not look at the wreckage without her eyes filling with tears.

But that will do you no good, woman, she told herself. *Keep your thoughts on what you need to do. Concentrate!*

The problem was clear. From here on White Bank Road, she could not see much of the old walls of the inner keep, although she could see the towers of Raven's Gate clearly enough and the shapes of soldiers atop it, scurrying like ants on a garden wall. But the inner keep's walls were high and nowhere could they be quickly breached. Whether traitor or not, Avin Brone had always been a useful tyrant about keeping them in good condition and the gates and guard towers well staffed.

Briony couldn't help but wonder where Brone was at that moment, and what he would do if he knew she lived. How deep did his treachery run? Had he made common cause with Tolly, or would he at least support her to get the castle back into Eddon hands? That was something to think about, if they managed to breach the walls of the inner keep: Brone didn't know that Finn Teodoros had spilled his secrets. He didn't know that Briony knew all about him.

But it did her no good now unless she could get word to Brone on the other side of the walls and he really would support her. After all, he might just as easily lead her and Eneas into a trap. Might Tolly have some kind of hold over him? It was so hard to know, because Brone himself was so full of shadow. *"He is the man who does what I cannot,"* her father had sometimes said, but never told her or her brothers exactly what he meant. Now Briony Eddon was beginning to suspect.

Thinking of Brone and his countless subterfuges reminded her of something—a night long ago, or so it seemed now, after Kendrick's death but before everything had gone completely wrong, when he had summoned Briony and her brother to his chambers. It had been the same night Finn Teodoros had read Brone's plans to have her family imprisoned and destroyed, but that was not what had sparked in her memory.

Father's letter . . . ! A page of that letter had been stolen, and that night Brone had given it back to them, saying he found it among his own papers and claiming his innocence. Briony doubted that innocence now, but it was the letter itself she remembered. It had said something about protecting the drains of the inner keep because Olin feared vulnerability there. Could that help her now?

Her heart fell as she remembered that Brone had resolved the problem the king feared, covering the drains with massive iron grates whose holes were too small for even the slenderest child or slipperiest Skimmer to pass through. In fact, the Skimmers themselves had sworn to her only hours earlier that there was no way they could enter the inner keep. Her beloved father had unwittingly made certain her only chance at rescuing his throne was prevented.

Another idea came to her then—an odd idea, the sort of thing that would have Eneas frowning and doubtful, but thinking about the Skimmer-folk had brought it to her and the more she considered it the more it seemed her only chance.

She turned her back on the gate so suddenly that she bumped into one of the Syannese knights, who dropped to a knee, full of apologies. "None of that," she said. "What's your name?"

"Sir Stephanas, Your Highness." Like the others, he wouldn't look directly at her. It irritated her.

"Well, go find me half a dozen of your brave fellows and tell them all to put on ordinary clothes—the deserted houses must be full of them. Then meet me here in an hour's time."

"Clothes . . . ? Houses . . . ?"

"Oh, dear, Sir Stephanas, I hope it is my accent that is at fault and not your brains. Yes, put on the clothing of ordinary people—but bring your swords. In the meantime, I'll tell your master the prince that I'm sending you on a little errand."

Chert made his way carefully around the temple. It wasn't so much that he was afraid of having to confront his brother or Nickel again—or at least so he told himself—but rather because he had no time to waste on conversation and the sort of small-minded niggling he felt sure he would get from the temple's guardians. So he snuck through the great fungus gardens in front of the temple, then around the kitchen side where the smells from the malt house, especially the smoke of the oasting fires where the brewmoss was still being dried even in these terrible times, gave him a sharp pang of regret. When was the last time he had sat down and simply raised a cup with friends? When was the last time he had done anything except struggle to keep his family alive and to help out Vansen and the others fighting this terrible war? A man should not have to live like this.

But when gods and demigods fight, Chert reminded himself, *an ordinary man is lucky if he can stay alive at all.* He said a prayer to the Earth Elders and struck out for the grounds behind the temple and the path to the Cascade Stair.

It took him the better part of the morning to make his way up the long, circuitous route to the Silk Door and the outskirts of Funderling Town. The roads were quite deserted. He walked down the broad expanse of Ore Street and saw not a single worker returning from a job in the outer tunnels, no women coming back from the drying caverns or peddlers with handcarts trying to find a last customer before the midday meal. Were all his neighbors really so frightened? Chert thought that was strange when the fighting itself was so far away.

He stopped at the Salt Pool to have a look around but saw no one, not even little Boulder, and he began to wonder if he even wanted to travel through Funderling Town itself. What was going on here? From what Opal had told him, a tennight or so ago things had been mostly unchanged, the numbers reduced but the life of the town going on much as normal.

He found a lamplighter asleep sitting up in a back alley off Gem Street on the outskirts of the guildhall district. Chert shook him awake.

"What goes here?" he asked as the fellow sputtered his excuses. "Quiet! I don't care what you were doing! What goes here? Where is everybody?"

The lamplighter, who had by now realized he was in no immediate danger, beckoned Chert down beside him. "The question is, what are *you* doing, mate? Have you got permission? A Guild pass to be out at this time of the day?"

"What are you talking about?"

"Since the Big Folk came—didn't you know? Nobody can be in the streets of the town unless they have permission from the Guild."

"Hold on! The Big Folk? *What* Big Folk?"

The man did not much want to talk, but he also clearly didn't want Chert making a loud fuss, either. He explained quickly that when the southerners' boats had caught fire in the bay (the first of this astonishing news Chert had heard) and newly arrived Syannese soldiers had unexpectedly conquered the outer keep, some of Hendon Tolly's still-loyal soldiers, led by Durstin Crowel, had forced their way in through the Funderling Gate. When the Highwardens and other Funderling leaders had protested they had been imprisoned in their own guildhall.

Chert's plan to find a sympathetic Highwarden who would grant him the Astion to complete his project had just become immeasurably harder, if not absolutely impossible. There was only one other way to achieve his aims, one he had briefly considered and then discarded as too dangerous, but he saw little choice now.

As Chert sat considering this wretched news, the lamplighter seized the chance to make his escape. Chert didn't try to stop him—he had far too much to consider already. Should he try to find someone trustworthy among his own folk, navigate his way through all the inevitable fear and mistrust under very the nose of Durstin Crowel and his bullies? Or should he try to make his way out the gate of Funderling Town into the aboveground castle in search of another very particular kind of help? But even if he found his way out, the second idea would still be a long shot.

It seems I have become the master of unlikely schemes, he reflected.

It hurt to think and Chert had already spent many hours walking. He was exhausted and hungry; if he was going to be killed, he decided, it might as well happen now when he already felt wretched. He got up and made his way down Gem Street as inconspicuously as he could. The stone trees and their many carved residents looked down on him from the famous ceiling as he made his way toward the Funderling Gate.

The familiar outlines of the gate looked very different now, even from a distance. Certainly, the array of guards, their tent, and the barricades of broken stone they had put up made it clear that the purpose of the gate had become less that of ceremonial transition and more that of keeping some people out and other people in.

At least a dozen guards from the castle waited there, dug in well back from the opening to the outer keep. Chert could hear the reason for their caution—cannon fire, not frequent, but enough to make him wonder whether he shouldn't turn around and go back. But who was firing at whom? Was it the Xixians, still trying to break the defenders' spirits? Or maybe those same defenders were shooting back at the Xixians, or maybe even at some Qar, if any of the fairy folk had ventured back aboveground.

It is a play, he thought. *But not a comedy like the sort Chaven has told me about, with disguised princesses and runaway lovers. This is one of those great epics of disaster that he likes so much, with shouting and bloody bandages and kettledrums for gunfire. The kind you're always grateful are happening to someone else.*

Chert crept a little closer to the gate. Despite the noises of destruction from beyond the cavern's mouth, the guards were still going about their business of denying exit to the ragtag crowd of Funderlings begging for their attention.

"I *told* you little rats, only Guild work gangs go through," growled one of the guards, a man whose greasy face and bad temper suggested he had been interrupted in the middle of his meal. "Nobody else."

"But two of our folk came back injured from working on the old walls this morning," shouted a man at the back. "They will need replacements."

"Then they will choose them when they come back tonight," the shiny-faced guard declared. "What are you in such haste about? Don't you like living in New Graylock?" He laughed and looked around to share the joke with his comrades. "New Graylock, eh?" He turned back to the supplicants. "Now piss off, or we'll give you little naturals a spanking you won't like."

The crowd of Funderlings groaned and grumbled but showed no immediate signs of dispersing. Chert felt like groaning, too. How was he to get past this guard post? It was as hopeless as trying to find a sympathetic Highwarden who still had the authority to grant him an Astion.

Outside the cannons began to bark again. Chert was about to retreat to a safer spot and consider what he might do next when something abruptly smashed against the outside of the cavern with a crash so thunderously loud that it made his earlier thought of kettledrums seem childish. Half the opening came down in a moment, huge shards of stone flattening the makeshift guard post, crushing the tent and anyone still inside. Fragments spun through the air, knocking down other soldiers and Funderlings. Those of Chert's people who had not been badly harmed immediately picked themselves up and fled deeper into the safety of the cavern entrance. Clouds of dust hung in the air, but Chert could see the guard who had spoken only a moment before, now bloodied and lying in a strew of rubble, twitching feebly.

Now or never, he thought. *The Elders have shown me the way, I hope.*

Of course, it could also have been that the Elders were showing him which way *not* to go: the devastation was astounding. The front of the gateway cavern had become a chaos of broken stone and swirling dust, and the cannons were still crashing outside.

Chert ducked his head and ran forward, stumbling over loose rocks. He had to step over a body buried under shattered stone, pale skin smeared with dirt and blood. He could not even tell if it was a Funderling or one of Durstin Crowel's guards.

When he got out into the open, he kept his head down. The cannonball had struck the facing of the ancient cliff above the entrance to Funderling Town, just beneath the high, pale wall of the inner keep. The dust thrown up by the bombardment was nearly as thick here as inside the gate, but Chert was still struck by the sudden immensity of having sky over his head again for the first time since he and Flint had gone to the Drying Shed.

I can only pray to the Elders that the Rooftoppers will . . .

His thought went unfinished.

"Here he is!" cried a loud, unfamiliar voice, then someone pushed him to the ground from behind and yanked off his pack. "Got him." A moment later, with Chert still pressed facedown against the stones, his captor pulled something like a sack over him. A few jerks as it was made tight, then a moment later he was lifted up and carried away at a fast, bouncing pace.

"Let me go!" he said. "You don't understand! I have something important to do—lives are at stake . . . !"

"Shut your mouth and keep it shut," growled his captor, and thumped the sack so hard against something that the little man's teeth rattled. Chert didn't try to speak again.

32
A Coin to Pay the Passage

"After Zmeos ate his eggs and porridge, he sat back in his chair. The Orphan quietly played his flute until the god fell asleep, still holding the great disk of the sun in his lap . . ."

—from "A Child's Book of the Orphan, and His Life and Death and Reward in Heaven"

RAFE COULD NOT HAVE been happier. His seventeenth Year-Moot had finally come and his father, the headman of the Hull-Scrapes-the-Sand clan, had given him beautiful black *Sealskin* to be his own. Rafe had long dreamed of this day—the day he could finally earn the necklace of a man! No longer would even his most impressive feats be undercut by the scornful words, "He still paddles his father's boat."

He had already made a name for himself, not just as a fisherman but also as a warrior. Had he not been one of the first to take fire to the ships of the southerners? Had he not braved the terrors of the Old Ones more than once, landing right on the Porcupine's doorstep as he conveyed nobility back and forth from the Mount? Now *Sealskin* was his at last. All the years of his childhood, he had dreamed of this day, keeping her always waterproof and slippery as an eel by painting and repainting her hull with pitch. And most important, all that he earned now would no longer go into his father's great jar. He would have his own jar, and soon enough his own house. Then he would take Ena away from her brute of a father and make her his wife. When they had enough money, they would marry and he would never again have to listen to any voice except hers and the ocean's.

He slipped out through the secret way that led from the Western Lagoon and out to the sea road to Egye-Var's Shoulder—M'Helan's Rock as the drylanders called it—but Rafe did not plan to go anywhere near the Drying Shed nor any other part of the island. Clan curfew was an hour gone, and the last thing Rafe needed was to get into trouble again his first night as a man. He didn't think his father Mackel would go so far as to take *Sealskin* back—he would be reluctant to shame the clan that badly in front of his rival Turley Longfingers and the Sunset-Tide folk at the Little Moot—but Rafe knew the old man would probably be very rigorous with whatever punishment he chose instead, which almost certainly meant a beating. Rafe didn't want another beating. So although his heart felt as full as a bellied sail, he would not be singing or cutting capers on this, his first voyage with his own boat.

The southern ships had stopped burning, although many of the floating wrecks still leaked smoke into the dawn sky. Rafe swung widely around one of them, trying to decide whether it was one of those onto which he himself had thrown spears wrapped in flaming rags. He had never done anything more exciting in his life (except perhaps for some of the things he and Ena had got up to) and still could not quite believe he had even been allowed to do such a thing. But the Skimmer clan leaders, those stodgy old fellows like Turley Back-on-Next-Year's-Tide, had suddenly changed: a single mysterious audience with some of the Old Ones and they had become warriors. Who would ever have guessed? Rafe had asked his father several times what had changed things so, but all Mackel would tell him was: "They have reached out a hand. We are forgiven." When he asked, "Forgiven of what?" his father had told him to shut his blowhole and go catch some fish.

But what did such things matter anyway? No matter who won this war, it meant nothing to Rafe. If he had to, he would pack up all his belongings, set Ena on *Sealskin*'s bench, and together they would paddle away somewhere else, upcoast or down. Perhaps it was time for the Ocean Lord's folk to return to the Vuttish Islands? He and his sweetheart could surely find a deserted skerry and live out their lives there in happy solitude . . .

Musing on this and other fantasies, Rafe guided his boat in and out among the flotsam of the burned ships, looking for things to salvage. He had discovered a floating cask of southern honey this way the night before, the wood only lightly singed and the insides still protected by wax and cotton cloth, a find that had delighted his father who said he could get several silver coins for it at the least. In fact, Rafe felt sure that the goodwill caused by that discovery was why Mackel had finally told him the boat was his. Reminded of his good fortune, he patted *Sealskin*'s strong but delicate frame. The next cask of honey would be for Rafe himself to sell. Perhaps he could buy Ena a wedding necklace.

He passed through the ghost fleet and made a wide swing along the coast below the Marrinswalk headlands. The sun was coming up soon, and he knew he should not be staying out so long. Daylight would make it harder to sneak back in. He supposed he could pretend to have fallen asleep in the boat shed while cleaning *Sealskin*. He had certainly done it enough times in his youth.

Rafe's planning was interrupted by something moving on the shore. He stared, trying to make sense of what he was seeing—something tall that stood almost at the waterline and was shrouded in cloth that whipped fitfully in the freshening breeze. What was it? Some bit of useful wreckage that had floated ashore and that another scavenger had found and might be coming back for? Was that why it was covered by that tattered cloak? Did someone really think that was enough to claim it as their own?

Rafe swung his bow toward the shallows until he could not get any closer and still remain in the boat. The thing standing where the water splashed up onto the rocky strand was man-shaped, although still motionless but for the ragged, windblown cloth that covered it. Was it a statue? Or had some lonely wanderer died here, so slowly that he had remained standing? Rafe had found corpses on the beach before, most of them drowned, but others as unmarked as though they had come to such a lonely spot just to die. He had never found one still standing. A superstitious shiver went through him.

Then the figure turned.

Rafe gasped and paddled the boat back from the shore. It had been the movement of something that lived—something that stood on this lonely stretch of shore by choice.

Even as he stared, the figure slowly lifted one hand and beckoned to him. Rafe could only stare. The thing raised its arm higher and made a gesture that was broader but still stiff, as though the creature in the billowing cloak was very old or very weak. There was no question that it was gesturing at him.

"What do you want?" Rafe called. "If you value your life, don't you meddle with me! I'll break your pate for a laugh!"

The figure only beckoned to him again. Rafe's curiosity began to get the better of him. He plied his oar deftly and shot closer. As his boat bobbed beneath him, he examined this apparition, or at least what little he could see of it. The stranger wore a dark, hooded robe, ragged on the edges, which covered his face, and his hands appeared to be bandaged in old, dirty bits of linen so that no skin showed. Again, a shiver of dislike passed through Rafe. The boom of the surf died down for a moment, and he could finally hear the stranger's voice, or at least a rasp of loud breathing. It was a disturbing sound, but it proved that the creature was no ghost.

"What do you want of me?" he asked again.

Rafe could only see the faint gleam of the stranger's eyes as he pointed to Rafe's boat, then slowly extended his bandaged hand toward the castle in the middle of the bay. The meaning was quite clear.

"You want me . . . to take you there?" He laughed and hoped it sounded braver to the stranger than it did to him. "Are you joking, man? Why should I take you across the water? If you are a spy for the southerners, you can't be a very good one, with your bandages and your gloomy looks—like something out of a Kerneia parade!"

The man only pointed again.

"I asked you why? Why should I?"

The hooded stranger lowered his hand. After a moment he began to fumble with the knot of his robe. Rafe decided he did not want to see what was under this creature's cloak and began to back-paddle his boat to put a little more distance between them, but the specter was having trouble getting the robe untied. Rafe stopped and floated, paddle dripping in the air. What was this absurd creature doing?

The stranger finally succeeded in opening the knot of his cloth belt, but instead of stripping off the cloak he only pulled something out of the knot and held it up in the thin but growing dawn light, pushing it in Rafe's direction as if to hand it to him across the distance. Rafe could only stare. It was a gold piece as big as a bull squid's eye.

"You're saying you want to give me that," he said at last. Even to his own ears, he sounded a bit breathless. "To take you over to the castle.

Over there." He pointed. The cloaked figure did not nod or say anything, but thrust the coin toward him again. "Very well then, if you say so. But, remember—I have a knife!" He reached down and lifted his fish-gutter. "So don't try anything or you'll regret it."

It took no little time to get the stranger into the boat. The man was crippled or at least he moved that way, with limbs that seemed stiff and brittle as icicles, but Rafe managed to get him seated on the bench at last and then took the gold. The man's bandaged hands were filthy, but the coin itself was shiny, real, and very beautiful. Payment made, the stranger promptly lowered his chin to his chest so that his hood covered his head completely, and then seemed to sleep.

Rafe paddled hard, trying to get back before the sun rose too high above the hills. He would have to find a place to let off this rich madman, then hurry home. Of course, even if his father found out and gave him a whipping, Rafe didn't much care—he was rich himself now. He could buy Ena not only a necklace but also the grandest dress the lagoon had ever seen, with more shells on it than there were stars in the night sky.

It was strange how the hours crawled past when your freedom had been taken. Qinnitan was realizing that she had been some sort of prisoner for much of her life, first in the Hive, although they had treated her kindly, then in the Seclusion. Finally, after one brief, heady taste of freedom in Hierosol, she had been recaptured by the monster Daikonas Vo. She had then managed to escape even him, but it seemed the gods themselves did not want her to be free, so here she sat, despite all her efforts, bravery, and sacrifice, the doomed prisoner of the world's most dangerous madman.

She shifted, trying to find a less painful position. With her arms tied behind her back, there was no such thing as comfortable. Around her, the High Priest's lackeys came and went, paying no more attention to Qinnitan in her cage than if she was a piece of furniture or the remains of a meal.

No, she thought, *like a sacrificial animal.* The knowledge of her suffering was far less important to them than her place in the upcoming ritual.

But *what* upcoming ritual? What did the autarch plan for her and for poor Olin, the northern king? She had listened carefully to every word uttered in her vicinity, especially by that bloated old monster Panhyssir, but she still had no real idea what the autarch planned.

Despite her determination to say nothing, she couldn't help letting out a moan of despair as the priests' potion began to act. Oh, sweet honey of Nushash, here it came again—that horrible burning crackle running from her head to her tail, like a bolt of slow lightning. In her memory the stuff Panyhyssir called "Sun's Blood" had become only another indignity of her time in the Seclusion, but now she was forced to experience again how truly vile it made her feel, the terrible thoughts it put into her head. She could feel her mouth force itself open in a silent scream, feel her fingers curling and cramping until she could no longer keep her tattered robe wrapped around her. Qinnitan perceived herself crumpling to the floor as if she observed it from a great distance, then she watched the world turn sideways and disappear into the blackness of her closed lids.

Boom. Boom. Boom.

It was the slow throb of her own blood, the hot red river that, thanks to the priests' potions, now mimicked the god's own holy ichor. She could feel it moving sluggishly through her body, filling her as melted silver might fill an intricate mold, until everything that was Qinnitan-shaped had grown turgid and trembling, poured full of the deadly, exalted Sun's Blood.

And now something in the darkness became aware of her. It did not rise up so much as it uncloaked itself, and that cloak was the darkness in which the thing lived, just as a great whalefish lived in water or a monstrous thunderstorm lived in the sky. It was too big to live—it didn't make sense!—but at the same time she felt she understood it, almost *was* it. . . .

But the more Qinnitan felt of its monstrous, cold interest, the more terrified she became. It drew nearer, and its very presence made her ripple and spread like an oil stain—any closer and she would surely come apart! But it did come closer, and suddenly Qinnitan understood that the god-thing wanted something from her—something she had not felt before. Always, she had sensed its predatory interest as just that, as something hunting, with herself as the hapless prey, trussed and left to the mercies of this merciless thing. Now, she realized with a quite different sort of horror that it didn't want to devour her, not in any ordinary sense. This impossible thing wanted to *use* her, to inhabit her so that it could cross the void and return to the land of the waking and the living.

Qinnitan knew she would never survive sharing her place in the world with something so powerful and uncaring—every moment it lived inside her would burn part of the real Qinnitan away. But that was exactly why they fed her the Sun's Blood, she realized: to prepare her as a vessel for the god, to make her a more hospitable home for this hideous presence which had not walked the earth for thousands of years. And she could do nothing to stop it. When midnight came, either she or King Olin would be offered up as a shell for this dreadful thing to inhabit.

Shrieking without sound, Qinnitan began to swim up through the blackness, desperate to escape. Patient as death itself, the thing let her go; after all, it only had a short time to wait before it would get everything it wanted.

Hands quickly but efficiently tied behind his back and a sack pulled over his head, Chert now was hurried across uneven ground. Cannon fire still boomed above his head but it was growing a little fainter. From the sound of the sea, he guessed he was being forced toward the North Lagoon. The men who had captured him spoke little among themselves, and although they did not spare him any kindness, they were no rougher than they needed to be, which made him decide with a sinking heart that they must be soldiers. That meant they were Tollys' men, and the swiftness with which they had grabbed and captured him suggested he had been recognized.

He staggered and nearly fell again as he understood that he might never see Opal again, or Flint, or Funderling Town. If he was to be executed, he might never see anything again but the inside of this noisome sack. . . .

Chert stopped and planted his feet. "I won't go any farther until you tell me where you're taking me," he said, ashamed to hear how his voice quavered. "If I'm to be killed, at least tell me why. At least tell me who my murderers are."

"Keep moving, half-size," growled one of the men and gave him a shove in the back that sent Chert staggering forward once more. The man had an accent Chert couldn't place—perhaps he was a Kracian mercenary. Chert had heard rumors Hendon Tolly had been looking for help abroad since it became clear the Qar were headed toward Southmarch.

At last he was pushed into a doorway, feet crunching across a floor made of strewn rushes, then rough hands grabbed his shoulders and forced him down onto a stool. An instant later the sack was yanked from him. When he had finished blinking, he looked at the strange figure in the chair opposite. At first the armor made him think it was a man, a young one from the look of his face, but he realized a moment later it was a woman looking him up and down with calm interest, her golden hair cut short and her serious face smeared with dirt in what Chert could not help thinking was a most unfeminine way.

"Only one?" the woman asked. Chert was certain he had seen her before somewhere. "All that time and you only brought back one? What if he doesn't know?"

"None were coming out!" protested one of the men, whose accent was less pronounced than the others'. "You saw it, High . . . I mean, my lady. Tolly's men have it sewed up tight, and they were keeping them all inside today. But just now someone dropped a cannonball on the Kallikans' front porch and this one hurried out, so we grabbed him."

"Funderlings. Here, in Southmarch, they are called 'Funderlings,' Stephanas, not 'Kallikans.'" She turned back to examine Chert once more. "Don't be afraid," she said. "I hope they didn't treat you roughly. They are rough men, but I told them to be careful."

"They did not hurt me . . . but I can't say I was given much choice about coming."

"No, you weren't. Because I need your help and I need it badly."

And then he knew her, at once and in a rush, and the words came out without any further thought from him. "Fracture and Fissure! Whatever you want, Princess Briony. I am at your service. It is good to see you back in your home again."

Her eyes narrowed. "It is not my home again—not yet. Who are you?"

"Chert of the Blue Quartz. We met once before, on the day your brother killed the wyvern. You . . . you nearly ran me over with your horse."

"Merciful Zoria, I remember! That was you?" She laughed, and for an instant was once more the young girl he had seen that day. "Do you really mean that you will help me?"

He shrugged. "Of course. Your father is our king, Highness. Is he coming back, too?"

The girl's mouth set in a grim line. "If I have any say about it. But just now he is somewhere beneath our feet, a prisoner of the Xixians."

Chert's stomach lurched, and he had to suppress a groan. "I know too much about the Xixians already, Highness! They have pushed down past Funderling Town and are chewing their way into our sacred Mysteries like worms through an apple. I will be happy to help strike a blow at those southerners—just tell me what I can do for you." But even as he spoke these brave words, he could hear Opal's voice in his head: *"Stop showing off for the Big Folk, Chert Blue Quartz. You have work of your own to do and time is dripping away!"*

"Well, these men and I are not fighting the Xixians just yet. . . ." The princess looked as though she wished it was otherwise. "My enemy is closer to hand—Hendon Tolly. But the prince of Syan and I cannot get our soldiers into the inner keep because the walls are too strong. I am kept at bay by my family's own castle!" Her laugh was sour.

"And what can I do?" he asked, but he was beginning to see the shape of things.

"I wanted a Funderling, Chert—any Funderling. I did not know it would be you. I need a way to get into the inner keep, and quickly." She fixed him with a surprisingly sharp, hard stare. "You see, I've learned things. I am not such a simple creature as I was when last I lived here. I met the Kallikans of Tessis, your relatives, and found that they keep secrets from their monarchs. I'm sure your folk have secrets they have kept from my family, too."

"Secrets . . . ?"

"Passages beneath the castle, perhaps. Tunnels. Hidden doors? Things that the Big Folk—isn't that what you call us—that the Big Folk aren't supposed to know about? But now I *need* to know, Chert of the Blue Quartz. How can I get enough men into the inner keep to open that gate and let the rest of our soldiers through?"

He had reached a moment of decision, that much was clear. She was asking about the Stormstone Roads, even if she didn't know them by name. Everything in him that was conservative and cautious warned that this was not a decision he should make himself. After the hundreds of years his people had kept those passages secret from the Southmarch royal family, even the present extraordinary situation did not give him the authority to make such a decision. But he had his own mission, and there was no longer any way he could get back in time to try something else.

"Will you give my people back their Funderling Town if you succeed? Tolly's men have occupied it."

Briony smiled. "Without a moment's hesitation. You have my word on it as an Eddon."

"Then I'll do my best to help you. You have *my* word as a Blue Quartz on that."

Her smile grew a little wistful. "It seems we both have weighty family names to live up to, Master Chert."

It was full dark when they reached the spot between the new walls and the castle's great outwall, a warren of small alleys between the ends of the East and West Lagoons where only the poorest lived because the walls loomed so high on either side that the sun only reached the streets for an hour or two each day, even in summer. Chaven's observatory was out of sight on the far side of the new walls, but the Tower of Spring stretched high above their heads. Chert imagined Tolly had a watch posted on its uppermost floor, but felt reasonably sure they were too close to the tower's base to be seen from there.

"Still," he whispered to Briony, "your men should keep their voices down. Sound bounces off stone in unexpected ways."

He led them down a tiny street and into a deserted house at one end of it, praying that he had remembered the location correctly, a hidden passage he had occasionally used when he wanted to depart Chaven's house without leaving the upground castle entirely. He was gratified by the surprise on Briony's face as he revealed the trapdoor hidden in what looked like a room piled with builder's trash.

Chert led the princess and her soldiers down a stairwell to a passage. A short while later they reached the basement door of the observatory where one of the soldiers slipped the latch with his dagger, then they were inside.

Chert looked around at the hangings and remembered when he had hidden here with Chaven from Hendon Tolly and Brother Okros. That seemed so long ago! Briony looked as though she had memories of her own. "And this is truly part of Chaven's house?" she whispered. "Incredible!"

"The last time I was here, there were guards," Chert warned her.

There were guards still. One of them, probably returning from a trip to the jakes, stumbled on the Syannese soldiers as they emerged from the stairs onto a ground-floor landing. The guard lunged at Chert with his spear, almost spitting the Funderling like a suckling pig, but Princess

Briony's Syannese soldiers surrounded the guard and cut him down before he could call out.

"Tolly livery," she said quietly, prodding the dead man with her shoe. "An ugly sight. I have seen it everywhere since I returned."

They encountered no one else as they made their way through the observatory. Chert did not take Briony and her soldiers out the front door, but led them out from a lower floor and along one of the other secrets of the observatory, a narrow passage that opened into the basement of a small building within the walls of the inner keep some distance from the physician's house. "Even Chaven himself isn't aware that I know of this one," Chert said. He didn't mention that it was actually Flint who had discovered it on one of their earlier visits.

"Our entire keep is riddled with tunnels like a rabbit warren!" Briony said in astonishment. "Not meaning any offense, Master Blue Quartz, but I thought I could not be surprised by anything else."

"We aren't rabbits," Chert said. "But we are small and we like to dig."

"Don't misunderstand me," she replied. "Just now, I am very happy with my Funderling subjects and their delving!"

The streets of the inner keep were all but empty, which was especially strange so close to Midsummer, when ordinarily the streets would have been full of revelers, but soldiers stood in numbers atop each of the cardinal towers and even in the shattered upper stories of Wolfstooth Spire.

"Now I must go, Highness, with your leave," Chert said as they stood in the shadows of the passage from the observatory. Briony's men had extinguished their torches and waited for her on the stairs just below.

"Go? I had hoped for more of your help, Chert Blue Quartz." The princess did not sound pleased, and he feared her anger because he truly had no time to waste.

"And I would gladly give it, Highness, but I have an errand of my own—one just as important as yours, if I do not overreach myself to say so, perhaps even *more* important. An errand for your people as well as mine. But time grows short."

She considered his words. "Yes, time grows short—it doesn't take the wisdom of the gods to know that. Do what you must. I hope if we both survive we can have a proper talk someday about this night's doings, Chert of the Funderlings, because I still have many unanswered questions. For one thing, you seem very familiar with the plan of the royal physician's house . . ."

"I . . . have been there before. A time or two."

"I thought so. Will you promise me that talk, then?"

"I'd be honored, Highness. But as you said, it can only happen if we both survive. Be careful, Princess. Your people do not want to lose you so soon after your return."

She laughed quietly. "And I feel sure your people would want you to be careful, also. Go with Zoria's blessing."

"And the Earth Elders protect you, Highness."

A moment later she had trotted down the stairs, quiet as a cat, leaving Chert alone on Chaven's doorstep.

The moon was high in the sky, mostly full, a lopsided white grape that shed so much light, sharp-eyed Chert felt quite conspicuous as he made his way across the inner keep in the shadow of the walls. The crashing of the cannons had finally ended, but he could still hear the sentries atop the walls shouting insults down at the Syannese in the outer keep.

The castle was quite different than he remembered—so much damage in such a small time! Rubble lay everywhere, and the once-beautiful greens had disappeared beneath dozens of refugee encampments, but the makeshift village abruptly ended at the hill on which the royal residence sat, enforced by a ring of armed sentries, an arrangement which made it plain that Hendon Tolly did not welcome peasants setting up housekeeping on his front doorstep.

Staying to the shadows, freezing at every unfamiliar sound or movement as though he really were a rabbit, Chert made his careful way across the inner keep beneath the rising moon, its great yellow bulk becoming smaller and colder as it climbed the sky. A lone bell in a residence tower was chiming midnight when he reached the Eddon family's ivy-covered chapel on one corner of the Throne hall. It was the only place he could think of to come for what he needed. But even after almost being blown to flinders by a cannonball and being thrown in a sack and kidnapped, the worst part of his day's work was still ahead. He had to climb to the roof.

Puffing so hard he saw little flashes before his eyes, so damp with sweat that even the cool night air could not ease it, Chert at last managed to pull himself over the wide, leaded gutter and onto the roof tiles. For long moments he could only lie on his back gasping for air. At last he was able to sit up again, wiping his forehead with his hands. The rooftop was empty but for the billowed moon perched between two chimneys as though someone had washed it and hung it out to dry.

He raised his voice as loud as he dared and called, "People of the rooftop! Subjects of Queen Upsteeplebat, it's Chert of the Funderlings—a friend! I need you!"

Nothing happened. He tried again, certain that down in the darkness of the courtyards or across the narrow streets someone must be listening, perhaps even hurrying off to report what they heard to Tolly's soldiers, but there seemed to be no movement on the rooftop. At last, just when he thought he might lie down and rest for a while and then try again when the moon had dropped behind the nearest tower, he heard a rustling sound and looked up to see a tiny shape crouching atop the roofline above his head, silhouetted against the parchment-colored moon.

"What be your business with Her Exquisite and Unforgotten Majesty?" demanded the tiny fellow. Chert crawled a few yards up the roof before answering so that he could keep his voice low. The little man watched him with what Chert imagined was amusement at how this monstrously large and clumsy creature kept its belly pressed against the roof as though a stray wind might sweep it up and blow it away.

The Rooftopper was a Gutter-Scout, but not one Chert had met before. Still, he seemed to know the Funderling's name. After listening to what Chert had to say he just nodded his head, said, "Tha must be waiting," and then dropped down the far side of the roofline out of Chert's sight.

Chert sighed and settled back, taking out the bit of bread and fungus he'd packed for himself. *Tha must be waiting, Blue Quartz*, he told himself, mimicking the little man's calm words. *Tha must. After all, we wouldn't want to hurry just ourselves because it's the end of the world, now would we?*

33
Spearpoint

"When the god was snoring the Orphan stole a little piece of the sun, but it was too hot for his mortal hands to hold . . . He hid it in one of the eggshells from Zmeos' plate . . . and escaped the great castle."

—from "A Child's Book of the Orphan, and His Life and Death and Reward in Heaven"

"WE CANNOT WASTE TIME fighting the autarch's troops from behind," Yasammez declared. Her thoughts were weighty, hard and cold as metal. "Time is short. This is no ordinary siege. We have already broken their chain of supply, but the southern emperor does not care."

"Then our only hope is to continue downward as we have planned." Saqri spread her fingers. "With good luck we might slip past to the Last Hour of the Ancestor before them."

"Where we'll still be outnumbered," Barrick pointed out.

Yasammez barely glanced at him. "We do not fear mortals in any numbers."

"Still, speed is our only hope now," said Saqri. "And our way down requires us to cross the Xixians' main path of descent below the Cavern of Winds. If the defenders are still holding back the southerners farther down, then that main tunnel will be full of Xixian soldiers and we will have to fight our way through the junction. It is a wide space, less than ideal for our purposes, but if we can cut our way through them we can make our way to the great pit itself where we can descend much more quickly."

"We will slice through them, never fear," Yasammez said. "We will be hard as a spear's point. The Fire of the Book has tempered us."

Even as the Fireflower filled his head with memories of the *Book of the Fire in Void* and ideas about the Always Fire that had caused it to be written, as well as a thousand other things as dear to the Qar as their own names, Barrick realized that Yasammez had reminded him again of his old tutor Shaso dan-Heza. What she had said about making their army into a spear's point was almost exactly the same as something Shaso had told him more than once.

"An army is a tool, boy. A good army is a very useful tool indeed. It can be hard and heavy where it needs to be, as difficult to breach as a piece of well-made armor. But it can make itself sharp as a spear's sharpened tip so that it can pierce another army just as a spear can pierce a breastplate, no matter how strong. When you narrow the force, you make the force greater where it strikes, you see . . ."

It was an odd thing to find Shaso looking back at him from the chilling, ageless eyes of Yasammez, but that did not make it any less true. Both warriors would have died before they would do something they considered dishonorable, but both could make mistakes because they were so certain of their own truths.

Which meant that Shaso had probably been innocent of Kendrick's death all along, and he, Barrick, had been wrong. It had been just as Briony had said after all. For the first time he wished he had spoken to his sister, really spoken to her. A pang of something he didn't recognize at first bloomed inside him, an ache of loss so sudden and powerful that it took his breath away.

Homesickness. Barrick was astonished. At this late hour? After he had changed so much? This place was not his home, nor had it ever truly been so, he was certain of that. The castle, the people—he felt nothing for them. So where did this strange yearning come from?

"We should stop talking and go," he said out loud, earning a look of chilly annoyance from Yasammez. "Time is short. Nothing would be worse than looking back on wasted time and mistakes we didn't need to make."

"Ah, friend Chert," called the tiny man on the white rat as he appeared over the crest of the roof. "Told Her Majesty, I did, 'Not seen the last of 'un, I haven't.' And here tha be."

"Beetledown." Chert couldn't help smiling. "You look well. That's a very handsome rat."

"Un's from the queen's own stable," he said proudly. "A reward, like."

"I'm glad to see you've been treated as you deserve. Would the queen let you do one more thing for me?"

The little fellow tilted his head. The rat began to groom. "Tell me what tha needst. I will go to my queen and ask." He straightened a little. "We Rooftoppers fight alongside of the Old Ones for the first time in many hundred years, you know. After all this time!" He began to explain some of his recent deeds of heroism, but Chert cut him off.

"It's good to hear the Qar have finally decided to take a stand, but what I'm asking of you may be the most important task of all." He quickly explained his need to Beetledown, who seemed less than enthused. "And then bring the Astion back to me at the place I've drawn on this map, quick as you can." He handed the little slip of parchment to Beetledown. "If I'm not there yet, give it to Brother Antimony."

"So important, truly?"

"Truly."

Beetledown did not look entirely convinced, but was polite enough not to say so. "Then so will it be, friend Chert. I can do nothing without queen's permission, so let us go."

"Of course. Lead the way. Just remember that I'm not a very good climber."

"Not very good?" Beetledown laughed. "Like a dog with one leg, to put truth to it."

A man who needs a favor, Chert reminded himself as he inched his way across the treacherous tiles, *should under no circumstances squeeze the little fellow who will do that favor into a jelly, no matter the provocation.*

❦

The Qar's attack took the Xixian soldiers by surprise, fairies pouring without warning out of what must have seemed just one more side tunnel out of the hundreds the southerners had passed on their way down into the depths, a crevice scarcely large enough for the bulky Ettins to squeeze through. In fact, it was Hammerfoot and his cousins who burst out first, roaring and waving their weapons, inspiring such fright that some of the startled southerners fell down with stopped hearts. After that it was blade on blade as the Qar fought to keep the much larger Xixian force split so the fairies could forge a path through to the other side of the large passage and the cross-tunnel waiting there.

For a time the blood flowed like rainwater in gutters as the desert warriors and the most warlike of the fairies, the Ettins, the Unforgiven, and the Changing tribe, hacked and ripped at each other in near-darkness. Although a few of the Ettins fell, swarmed by soldiers as a beetle might fall to attacking ants, the giants still dealt terrible casualties among the southerners until a Xixian commander, or at least the highest ranking of their soldiers in that cavern, pulled most of his men back to the far side of the passage. He had brought up archers and now they sent flights of arrows hissing toward the Qar, who fell back behind the gigantic shields and rocky hides of the Ettins, still unable to cross the broad passage.

Barrick, still trapped in the side tunnel but close enough now to see what was happening, wondered how they could possibly survive this. Unless they fought their way through to the other side, the Qar were trapped between the Xixians who had already passed this spot and those above who were on their way down. No matter how many of the southerners Saqri's fighters killed more would just flow back into this place until the Qar were finally overwhelmed and destroyed.

Why didn't Saqri let Yasammez lead the way? The dark lady's name was a byword for destruction; even without the Fireflower, Barrick knew the stories told by the survivors of her destructive advance across the March Kingdoms, how she had singlehandedly unhorsed and slaughtered the defenders of all the towns in her way, sometimes fighting half a dozen or more by herself and killing each and every one. But the Fireflower told him more—much more. Its voices sang to him triumphantly of Yasammez Aflame, the Scourge of Shivering Plains, the daughter of a god! And in images of so distant a past that even the memory of the Fireflower had dimmed a little, he saw the Yasammez of the elder days, glowing with green fire that hung about her head as she fought, so that she breathed it and spewed it out again in little streaks and sparks. In the stark instant of the lightning's flash at Silvergleam's hall, when all the field of war, men and Qar and even the gods themselves seemed to be frozen together as one thing, she had stood twisted in a spray of blood, the headless bodies of her enemies flung tumbling away by the force of her blow. That was the weapon that Saqri kept sheathed. Why?

Barrick could not begin to guess, but he knew as well as he knew his own name that the women of the Qar's highest house, and especially those who took the Fireflower, were no less subtle than their husbands. It was better simply to trust the queen of the Fay . . .

But feel free to ask questions, a sly thought suggested to him. It might have been Ynnir, faint as a bird chirping at the top of a tall tree. *Just be prepared to defend yourself afterward—a queen does not like to be second-guessed!*

And then the first wave of Xixian arrows had spent itself. In the moment that followed Saqri's troop leaped forward toward the center of the passage, into the flail of shadows and torchlight. Barrick was among them this time, caught up in the remembered glories of the Fireflower, shouting out things that even he did not understand.

Contorted faces, blades, the clank of metal on armor, or sometimes the weirdly thrilling *chunk* of an edge biting flesh—Barrick was terrified, but at the same time he felt hard as stone, cold and clear as diamond. The memories of a hundred kings were in him, some as warlike as Yasammez herself. Their ghostly voices sang with joy and their blood seized and pulled in Barrick's veins. He did not resist these spirits, but let them lead him in a complicated series of strikes and defenses that his thoughts could not at first keep up with. He used *Hawk's Tail* to catch a falling blade in the crossed metal of his sword and dagger, then kicked out and crushed the knee of the Xixian soldier. Even as the man toppled and Barrick whirled past, he dragged his blade backhanded across the man's throat, then tightened his grip on the suddenly blood-slick hilt, ducked the strike of a second man, and came up under his chin with the dagger—*Spiked Fist*—so near the man's face that he could hear the southerner gasp and then feel the man's dying breath leap from his body.

Spin, sweep with his sword to catch an enemy's hamstring, step on the man's throat as he went down, and then direct the spear thrust of another away with his arm-shield. Barrick found himself shifting deeper and deeper into an unthinking dance, as if he were nothing but a line of heat passing through the cavern in a complicated filigree of motion, like the mark a burning brand swirling through the night air could leave on the eyes for moments after the torch itself had passed. But although he nearly lost himself in the wash of sensation, the rush of memory, and the demanding movements, he could not ignore the fact that as many of the enemy as he killed or disabled, and as many of them as his comrades destroyed, still more were always coming, flowing into the passage from either direction like the immense weight of seawater that must surround the land beyond these stony depths.

Might as well try to kill the sea itself. *Saqri, where are you?*

Here, manchild. Behind you and nearer to the southerners who had already passed through the cavern, but now have come back to join the entertainment. There was a wicked joy to her thoughts he had not sensed before—war agreed with her, it seemed.

They are too many! For each one we kill three more come to take his place!

They have always been too many for us, the humans. Your people outbred us long ago. With the gods gone, you see, your folk have no predators . . .

He had no idea what she meant. *But what do we do?*

We persevere. It wasn't words but a feeling, the immensity of Qar suffering and the immensity of Qar stubbornness encapsulated in a single impression of resigned struggle. *But remember, we do not need to defeat all these men; we only need to cross the cavern and enter the far passage. Then we will leave them behind to toil down the tunnels like ants while we drop from the sky upon their leaders!*

She's mad, Barrick thought as he fought for his life. *This place has driven her mad.* His loneliness, so much a part of him that he seldom noticed it anymore, rose up and threatened to choke him. Only the urging of the Fireflower voices reminded him that life still continued—a life that the two southern soldiers rushing toward him wanted to end.

Shark's Fin. Catch the attack on the hilt of his sword. Spin into a two-handed slash, driving one man back long enough for Barrick to get his arm-shield up in the other's face. Rip with the dagger. Spin and block.

Shaso would have loved this, he thought. *Hopeless odds. No choice but fight or die. And no time to argue . . .*

He let himself step back into the dance again. After all, there was nothing else he could do. Several of the Xixian torches had fallen, and the shadows in the passage were widening, deepening.

Soon enough, Barrick thought, *we'll be fighting in utter darkness, like dead men struggling in their graves . . .*

It was all Utta could do to hold the frail older woman down. Still in the grip of the dream, Merolanna struggled so determinedly that she almost threw the Zorian Sister across the room. *"No no no no . . . !"* the duchess moaned, slurring her words so that it was more like an animal sound than the voice of a dignified noblewoman. *"Let go they let go . . . !"*

"Merolanna!" Utta leaned close to the duchess' face so the woman could hear her even in the depths of whatever dream had seized her. "Merolanna! You're having a nightmare! Wake up!"

"Don't go! You can't trust . . . he won't . . ." Her voice trailed off. For a moment she sat hunched in the bed, eyes closed as though she listened to some distant but important sound. Utta took the opportunity to pull the coverlet back up over Merolanna's pale legs. "You can't . . . !" the old woman said again, but this time with the confused sound of someone beginning to wake.

"All is well." Utta let go of her and sat up, taking Merolanna's cold hand in her own. "You have had a bad dream, Duchess. Wake up now and see that everything is well."

"But it's not." Merolanna's eyes fluttered open. She fixed Utta with a stare that was frightened but not the least bit groggy. "It's not well. Nothing is well. He is coming for them."

"He? Coming for . . . ?" Utta shook her head. "It was just a bad dream, dear. I told you. You were kicking like an angry horse." She raised her hand to the side of her face, which was beginning to ache now. "Throwing your elbows around freely, too."

"I am sorry." But Merolanna looked as though Utta's sore cheek was the last thing on her mind. "It was . . . it was not just a dream. It was too real. The gods sent it to me!"

Utta took a deep breath. "Do you want to tell me?"

"I . . . I'm not sure I can. It was so frightening, that's what I remember most."

Utta couldn't help thinking the duchess actually looked better than she had in weeks; perhaps the excitement of the renewed fighting had actually revived her spirits a bit. Utta had seen it in older women who had seemed ready to die, but responded to conflict—not war, but a struggle of some other kind, family or money troubles. Some people turned their backs at such times and death quickly took them, but others—and perhaps Merolanna was one of them—seemed to come back like a flower saved by unseasonal rain.

"Just try." Utta was awake now herself. *After midnight,* she thought. Outside, the cannons had finally stopped firing and the shouting had ended, at least until dawn when it would no doubt start again. Midsummer itself would clearly be another holy feast day spoiled by this endless war.

"It was Kerneia," Merolanna said suddenly, as if she had been thinking about holy days, too. "That was it. It must have been, because the people were in the street, all dressed in black and waving bones. But it was the cart, the great holy cart that frightened me so. It was closed, as it always was, but there was something inside it. Something alive, hidden inside that great black wooden box that sits atop the cart. All up and down the street the ropes were being pulled tight to get the cart moving, but I was the only one that knew something was wrong—that it wasn't just the god inside, but something worse, something . . . worse." For a moment, it truly seemed to come back to her and Merolanna's face twisted in a grimace of fear, but her gaze was distant: she was not seeing Utta or her own bedroom at all. "And all the children . . . there were children in the street! Little ones, I don't think they even knew what was happening, you know how they are when they're young. Just . . . excited. And the ropes creaked and the wheels creaked and that big black cart began to roll . . . The Kernios priests were all over the cart, sitting on top of it, hanging off the sides, but none of them saw the children! I was the only one who saw them!" Suddenly her eyes reddened and filled with tears. "I tried to tell them . . . ! I tried to say, 'No, don't, there are children in the way,' but nobody could hear me!"

Now Utta took Merolanna's other hand, too, and warmed them between hers while the woman snuffled quietly. "There. It's all well. It was only a dream."

"But it w-wasn't . . . !" said Merolanna. "That's the problem! It was too real, too . . . it wasn't just a dream."

"What do you mean, dear?" Utta wanted to go back to bed. In another few hours the fighting would start again, and she would spend another day waiting for a cannonball to collapse their small corner of the residence. She wasn't even certain who was fighting whom anymore, and it was nearly impossible these days to find anyone who knew any more than she did. "You really should go back to sleep . . ."

"It wasn't a dream, Utta. It was a vision—the sort the oracles have. I know it. The children are in danger. *All* the children. The gods want me to save them!"

It was all Utta could do at this point to keep her temper. It was one thing to humor a sick old woman, or even to be her unpaid companion, another thing entirely to have to sit exhausted at her bedside in the middle of the night and listen to her comparing herself to the Blessed Zoria. "It sounds terrible, dear Merolanna. We'll certainly talk about it in the morning. The gods know you need some sleep. . . ."

And only the gods would be able to say whether the dowager duchess got any. In the early morning, when the return of daylight brought the first crash of gunfire and shouting, Sister Utta awoke to discover that sometime after she herself had fallen asleep again, Merolanna had got up, dressed herself, and vanished from the residence.

It seemed to Barrick he was fighting a hundred battles at once, battles of memory and battles of very present danger all pressed together into one head-splitting mass. He and the Qar survived surge after surge of Xixian troops, which kept pouring inward from either end of the main passage as though a river of soldiers had flooded its banks.

He found the queen resting for a moment, which showed how long they had been fighting. He had never seen the Qar anything but tireless, although he knew from the Fireflower voices that they could indeed grow weary. She was protected by Hammerfoot's huge son, who had reddish, bumpy skin like crumbled bricks. The Ettin turned at Barrick's approach and nearly took his head off with a swipe of his rocky hand.

"Peace, Singscrape," Saqri told him. "It is the manchild."

"What makes you think I didn't know that?" asked the giant.

"Why doesn't Yasammez fight?" Barrick demanded. "And where are the Elementals? They could paint this whole cavern with fire and we'd drive these southern animals out in a moment."

"The Elementals . . . are not under my control at the moment."

Shocked as he was, Barrick could also feel a history of discontent and wounded fellowship, but Saqri was hiding her darkest thoughts from him. The Fireflower had fallen almost entirely silent. "And Yasammez . . . ?"

"She is too important to waste here, long before our greatest need. No, I need her strong."

"But if we can't get across this passage . . . !"

"We will. I have been waiting for the moment when our foes are most precariously balanced. Even as we speak, a confusion has fallen among the southerners coming down from behind. The Tricksters have distracted them. The Xixian archers in this room have also nearly run out of shafts. We have a short time to do what we must."

And before Barrick could ask any more questions, Saqri sang out a single high-pitched note. Simultaneously, he could feel her in his thoughts, as did every other Qar creature in that part of the deeps. *"Now strike for the far side!"*

From that moment on, Barrick Eddon had no more time to think. The Qar surged forward in what looked at first like a ragged and uncoordinated mass, but by the time the Xandian troops realized that it was very well coordinated indeed, the fairies had stabbed into the southerners on the far side of the cavern like a well-honed spear, with the monstrous Ettins and corpse-white Unforgiven at the forefront, spreading terror. The Xixians did their best to hold, their sergeants shrieking at them to dig in and not give up a step, but no pair or even trio of ordinary men could stand up against one of the Deep Ettins hand to hand, and now the giants were crashing through the Xixian lines together, their massive clubs and axes flailing. With each blow, one or two southerners were smashed to the cavern floor or tossed into the air, helpless as rabbits caught by a mastiff; those who fell were cut down by the Unforgiven or swarmed by the glowing Children of the Emerald Fire, who slit throats as easily as if they murdered oblivious, sleeping men.

Still, it was a near thing. Once the southerners had absorbed the shock of the new attack, they rushed back in from the sides even faster in an attempt to block the opposite passage with their own bodies and thus keep the Qar bottled in the main tunnel.

Barrick was fighting only a few paces behind Saqri now, doing his best to guard the queen's back. She moved forward in perfect balance, blocking and then attacking with the precision of a temple priest enacting an ancient ritual, and the Fireflower voices inside him rejoiced and yet also fretted to see this queen, who to them was all queens, matching herself against warriors twice her bulk and still succeeding. Barrick could not watch her for longer than a moment or two without risk to his own life, but Saqri moved like a white flame, slipping in and out of the deepest shadows so swiftly and so brightly that at moments he thought he could see her swan form flickering about her.

Only a last few defenders still blocked the entrance to the far cross-passage. At a word in their heads from Saqri, the Ettins fell on them and within moments cleared an opening. The last of the Qar force now hurried across the main passage and followed the rest into the cross-tunnel, the physician Chaven and the less warlike Qar near the back. Yasammez and her black-clad guards came last. The god's daughter did not even look at Barrick when she passed, her cloak pulled up around her neck and head, her face like a thunderstorm.

When everyone was in, Yasammez's guards turned to hold the doorway—the Xixians had regrouped outside and were now trying to push their way into the passage. "We cannot have them behind us." Saqri's voice echoed in Barrick's skull. "Hammerfoot, my friend, are you badly wounded?"

The giant took a few steps forward, forcing others to flatten themselves against the corridor walls. The edge of his great shield was hacked and pitted, as was his helmet, though his eyes still gleamed beneath the visor. His rough skin was shiny with dark blood from a dozen or more deep wounds. "Passing well, my queen."

"It is for you and your kin to hold this passage now. We cannot do what we must do if the southerners are behind us. I need time, Hammerfoot, prince of the deeps."

"Daughter of the First Flower, my sons and I will give you as much as our last breaths can buy," he said. "Come, Deeplings!" he bellowed, and several of the great Ettins moved up to join him, Singscrape and a half dozen more; in a moment they had taken the place of Yasammez's guards, their big bodies filling the tunnel as though they had rolled there in some ancient avalanche. "Go, now," Hammerfoot rumbled, even his thoughts so deep and strong that they made the bones of Barrick's head quiver.

Saqri turned away. Her eyes were dry. "Forward," was all she said to the rest.

Barrick looked back at the Ettins. Hammerfoot was sharpening his great ax blade against a stone. He saw Barrick and lifted a massive pointing finger in a sort of salute.

"Keep the queen alive as long as you can, manchild," the giant rumbled. "Do not waste our deaths!"

Barrick turned to follow the rest of the Qar down into the hot depths.

34
Coming Home

"The treacherous servant Moros had run away with the shining white horse . . . The Orphan had to walk all the way back to Syan (as it is now called) carrying a piece of the burning sun in an eggshell . . ."

—from "A Child's Book of the Orphan, and His Life and Death and Reward in Heaven"

MIDSUMMER'S EVE WAS OVER and the morning sun of fateful Midsummer's Day was high in the sky, but the castle was still not theirs, and only the gods knew what was happening in the depths beneath their feet.

Briony and Eneas hurried the rest of the Temple Dogs in from the outer keep through Chert's secret way and fast-marched them through the empty streets behind Raven's Gate, deserted since the cannon fire had resumed. Briony half expected an ambush to erupt from the Throne hall but the damaged building remained as silent as the immense graveyard beside it. Was Hendon Tolly really so certain he could defend the royal residence against all comers? Or did he plan to use her subjects as hostages and stall her until he could escape? Briony had no doubt that Hendon Tolly knew an Eddon rode with the Syannese soldiers. It must be clear to him that his reign was over, but he was waiting for some final throw of the dice. She had imagined every way the coming confrontation might play out, from the dramatic foolishness of challenging the usurper to single combat to simply having him filled with arrows the first time he showed himself, even under a flag of parley, but the more she considered, the more she doubted she'd have the restraint to deal with Hendon face-to-face. The thought of his satisfied smirk had haunted her dreams for months.

Briony, Eneas, and the Temple Dogs, their numbers swelled now by Southmarch soldiers, crossed the edge of the great commons and halted by the small, mostly empty lake to assess the defenses. It was strange to see the royal residence caparisoned for war—almost pathetic, like some ancient nobleman forced into armor at a point when he was long past it. The great lawns and gardens were gone, and only torn, naked earth remained; the lower floor had been covered in boards and piled stone to protect the windows, and the turrets at each corner of the vast, square building had been turned into cannon nests. Briony wondered how long the guns would stay silent. Several hundred of Eneas' soldiers were still fit for battle, but if they had to take the residence under cannon fire and arrows from the guard posts on the roof this would be a long, difficult siege, the last thing Briony wanted. Still, she could see no other choice.

"We must give them a chance to surrender," Eneas said in a low voice.

"No. Hendon will only parley to buy time. He is a devil. We will have to take the residence. That is the only way."

"And I say we will not." Eneas' voice rose a little. "My lady, I do not doubt that you know this Tolly fellow well, but I cannot risk my men's lives without giving the defenders a chance to surrender. You said it yourself. The innocent must be spared. If you fear to see Tolly himself, stay back with Helkis and the others."

She felt her cheeks go hot with blood. "I don't fear to see him, Eneas, but if you parley with the dog who stole our kingdom, I can't promise I won't put this blade right through his grinning face."

"You will not do that under my flag of truce," he said, his voice hard. "You will not, Lady."

Her teeth were clenched so hard her jaws hurt. "Very well. I will stand back and stay silent. Call for your parley."

To her surprise, the man who came out of the front door of the residence under a white banner made from a bedcover was Sisel, the Hierarch of Southmarch. The old man had not aged well since Briony saw him last, his face so thin and his cheeks so shadowed that she wondered if he had been ill.

"I come under your safe-conduct," he said as he approached. "Prince Eneas, I believe? I have news for you." As he came closer, his eyes lit on Briony and widened, but he did not say anything to her.

"Do you speak for Hendon, Eminence?" the prince asked. "I have terms for his surrender. Surely he knows there is no chance for him. This is Her Royal Highness Princess Briony. She has returned to claim her family's throne."

"To claim it for my father, who still lives," she said as loudly and clearly as she could, so that anyone listening from atop the residence walls would hear—especially any Tollys.

"Blessed Brothers, it *is* you, Princess!" Sisel seemed not just surprised but frightened, as though simply by surviving this year of war he had done something wrong. "My eyes . . . It will be a great joy to your people to know you live . . . !"

"Enough," she said. "There will be time for such things later, Hierarch. Tell us what the traitor Tolly has to say. Will he surrender and spare innocent lives?"

"But . . . but that is just it," said Sisel. "He is not here!"

"The pig!" Briony could scarcely contain her anger and disappointment. "Where has he gone?"

"I am still a lord of the church, whatever else has happened," Sisel said stiffly. "To insult my position is to insult the Trigon itself."

"My apologies, Eminence," Briony said, cursing inwardly. "Please forgive me."

He gave a little nod of satisfaction. "No one in the residence has seen him since yesterday, Highness. It could be he's hiding somewhere, or has disguised himself in hopes of escaping unnoticed—many strangers and refugees are living in the great hall these days. He may even have left the castle entirely. . . ."

"Gone?"

Eneas held up his hand. "Then who rules here, Eminence? What of Tolly's lieutenants?"

"Lord Constable Hood fled less than an hour ago. He has likely headed to the southernmost side of the keep, near the Tower of Summer. He took scaling ladders. He and his men may mean to climb out and join Durstin Crowel in Funderling Town."

Eneas promptly sent two pentecounts of his men at speed around the residence to try to stop Hood from escaping. He and Briony and a small troop of men then followed the Hierarch back into the residence, wary lest somehow, against all seeming, the Trigonarch's chosen might lead them into a trap, but the welcoming crowd that spilled out was real enough, courtiers and even a few Southmarch soldiers, all dirty and thin with hunger, all anxious to greet their rescuers, and all doubly pleased when they learned of Briony's presence. She and Eneas had not gone more than a few paces through the loud and growing throng when a small woman shoved her way through, wailing like a death-spirit, ignoring Briony entirely to cast herself at the feet of the Syannese prince.

"He has taken my baby!" the creature howled. "Locked me in! Stole my little beauty, Alessandro! Stop him!"

Briony stared. "Anissa . . . ?"

If the princess was astounded, her stepmother was no less so, jumping at the sound of Briony's voice as though at the howl of a ghost. "Br-Briony? Is that truly you? We . . . we thought . . ."

"I am sure you did. What do you mean, he took your baby?"

"My baby Alessandro! Olin's beautiful son! Hendon Tolly has stolen him! Oh, gods, someone please help!"

Now others of the residence folk began calling out their own tales of woe, voice after voice until Briony could scarcely think. "Quiet!" she shouted. "All of you! Anissa, tell me what happened—tell me everything."

"He took my baby. He said there was blood—that Alessandros' blood was magical, I don't know. To summon the god. I didn't understand him!" She began to weep loudly and would not stop until Briony shook her violently.

"What are you doing?" demanded Eneas. "Don't hurt her."

"She will do this for an hour, and we have no time for her blubbering." She turned to the queen. "Anissa, look at me. If you want me to save your child you must tell me where Hendon's gone!"

"But I do not know!" the queen wailed. "He locked me in my rooms!"

"He has left the residence," said another, equally familiar voice.

Briony turned to find the big man standing just behind her, courtiers and soldiers having made way for him. "Lord Brone," she said. "So, you live."

"You do not seem very glad of that, Princess Briony, though I am glad enough to see you." The old noble was even fatter than he had been, and looked flushed simply from the exercise of making his way down the stairs. His skin had a yellow hue that spoke to her of ill health. "Still, we have no time to argue. One of my men heard Tolly talking about taking the child to summon a god, just as Queen Anissa says. Tolly and some guards left the residence hours ago. . . ."

"We saw no sign of him, and our men on the Basilisk Gate have been told to let no one out of the castle," Briony said. "He must still be here. Eneas, give me some of your men—Sir Stephanas served me well before and I would be glad to employ him again. I will find Tolly."

"I will go with you," Eneas said. "In fact, it would make more sense for me to chase the usurper and you to restore order here in your father's castle . . ."

"There will be no order until Hendon Tolly is captured and the king's son is safe. It is the Eddons who must bring the traitor to justice—and I am the only Eddon here."

"But that's foolish, Briony! I couldn't let you . . ."

"No, curse it!" She took a step toward him. "No! You are the prince of Syan, but you are not my husband, my brother, or my father. I'll take good men with me—I'm not a fool, Eneas. But Hendon is *mine*."

His face was tight with anger, but he did not speak until he had mastered it. "Take Helkis, too. I fear this choice of yours, Princess."

"So do I. Sir Stephanas, you men, come—we must hurry." But as she turned away, she saw Avin Brone move toward Eneas, the old man so tall that he had to bend even to whisper in the prince's ear, a bulky shape like a vicious bear trying to pass as human. Briony's stomach lurched.

"I have changed my mind," she told Helkis quietly. "You must stay, Miron. You will do more good here than with me."

The Syannese noble was puzzled and angry. "What do you mean, Princess? I am ordered by my prince to go with you."

"For once, disobey Eneas and serve him better," she said. "Do not leave him with Brone—the man is not trustworthy. It might be so subtle a thing as bad advice on whom to let go and whom to keep, but it might be something else . . . something much worse." But could that really be, she wondered? Would Brone risk trying to strike down Eneas in the middle of his own soldiers? Briony wasn't certain, but she knew she couldn't overlook someone who had planned the death of the entire Eddon family. This might be Brone's last chance ever to strike for power, if that was what the count of Landsend craved. "Just . . . stay with your prince, my lord. Watch over him carefully. If he discovers and protests that you're not with me, tell him I overruled you."

Lord Helkis frowned. "Very well." He did not stay any longer, but hurried to keep Eneas and Brone in sight.

Briony swiftly led Stephanas and the other soldiers out of the residence. She had an idea where Tolly might have gone: the gate to Funderling Town was still defended by his own men, and if there was room enough in the warren of caverns beneath the castle for thousands of fairies and Xixies, there was room enough for Tolly to hide there, too. But that was precisely the problem—how could she hope to find Tolly in all those dark deeps? And what chance was there she could catch him and still find her father, too?

Tolly. The name was a curse on her tongue, foul as black bile. Would he doom her family even in the throes of his defeat? But even through all her anger and hatred a worm of fear gnawed at her: these were deadly times and she had been very lucky so far. Her enemy would never give up and would bite even at the last. Just knowing Hendon Tolly still lived cast a cold shadow over her.

An immense silence hung over the Qar encampment by the side of the great chasm, not only because so many of them shared their thoughts without words, but because so many of them had been killed winning their way here. Saqri was conferring with a few of her advisers, but it seemed a desultory meeting, more an excuse for a moment's rest, and Barrick had not remained with them long. The feeling among the Qar, and even from the Fireflower voices inside him, seemed one of quiet contemplation and preparation for the unavoidable disaster to come.

"May I speak with you, Barrick Eddon?"

He looked up, startled by the sound of actual speech, and found the chief eremite, Aesi'uah. *It is not necessary to use words with me,* he told her.

"I know," she said quietly. "But sometimes it is well not to remind others of what you can and cannot do, Prince Barrick. Then they are more likely to forget and give themselves away if they mean you harm."

He smiled. "You are clever, Aesi'uah."

"I would not be the chief adviser of Lady Yasammez otherwise," she said. "In truth, it is about her I would speak—and one other thing."

He looked around. He had wanted solitude, so they were far from any others, even the sharp ears of the Changing tribe. It seemed safe to continue. "Go on."

Aesi'uah took a breath and hesitated as if unsure whether to continue. She would have been beautiful even by human standards were it not for the lifeless, leaden tint to her skin and the deep, almost frightening glow of her blue eyes. "My lady is troubled."

He almost laughed, despite the gloom that lay over the cavern. The small number of flickering fires only seemed to emphasize the greater darkness. "What does that mean? We fight a hopeless battle against ridiculous odds. Your lady's father, the god, has *died*, and we shall all of us probably be dead tomorrow, which will be the end of the Fireflower she's guarded for so long. Is there truly anything to be cheerful about?"

Another woman might have flushed or stammered or even grown angry at his harsh words, but the eremite was a deep well; she waited for him to finish. "My lady has been preparing all of her stretching life for this—it is not by chance that we refer to our war with your folk as the Long Defeat. But something has changed. She is not just troubled, but . . ." Here she leaned forward and lowered her voice, a gesture of such ordinary humanity that for an instant Barrick saw the truth of what he had been told, that human and Qar shared the same ancestors. ". . . My mistress is confused, Barrick Eddon. I have never felt such things as long as I have served her, and though I am young by her score, I have been with her since your father's grandfather was a child."

"Confused? How so? And why do you tell this to me instead of to Saqri, the queen?"

"Because I do not know what it means—that is why it frightens me. At a time when Yasammez should be most set in her purpose, most determined in her course, I can feel her thoughts darting like startled birds."

"Is she frightened? Frightened of the end?"

Aesi'uah laughed, a hollow, disturbing noise. "It seems that even one who bears the Fireflower can ask a foolish question. No, she is not frightened for herself and she is not frightened for her people. All her years she has been preparing for this death." The eremite closed her eyes for a moment. When she opened them, something subtly different had come into her expression. "As to Saqri—she knows. Her thoughts and Yasammez's thoughts twine together like two trees that have grown side by side. If she finds it disturbing, Saqri gives no sign. Perhaps she is right. Perhaps it is wrong to doubt such a power as Lady Yasammez. But I am not so calm or so wise as that."

Barrick could think of nothing to say. Even with the Fireflower, his understanding of the Qar still barely broke the surface. If he lived, he would be years learning anything real about them. "And what would you have me do, faithful servant Aesi'uah?"

"I cannot say, Barrick Eddon. I do not think at this moment there is anything to be done. But I am relieved that someone else knows."

And that, too, was so human that Barrick could only sit, wondering at the strange world into which he had fallen.

"You said there was something else."

"Two things, in truth, one small, one large. The first is a question—have you seen Kayyin?"

"I don't know the name."

"He is a . . . relative of Yasammez. He was with us for a long time, all through the siege. Now he is gone. Yasammez and Saqri show no concern, but it seems strange to me."

"I can't help, I'm afraid." He dimly remembered the fellow now, a sort of half-Qar, half-human, or at least so he had appeared, who was often seen near Yasammez, but Barrick could not remember speaking with him.

"Ah. Well, perhaps I will have better luck with my other question. How well do you know this Chaven Ulosian whom you brought to join us?"

Barrick's heart sped, and he was certain that the eremite must sense the difference in him. "Why? I didn't really bring him. I found him wandering around near the edge of our camp. But I know him well from the old days. He was the royal physician of Southmarch." Chaven was also in possession of a strange, familiar statue that he now carried in a spare bedroll, thanks to Barrick's feeling the object should be kept hidden, but he didn't mention that to the chief eremite.

"I think he is more than any mere physician. As with you, I can feel the presence of more than one in him."

"What does that mean?"

"You carry the Fireflower. You no longer seem like a single thing to me, but like a blur of different things. It is hard to explain in mere words." For a moment she lapsed back into silent communication and he caught something of his own shimmering, refracted nature as it came to Aesi'uah. *Just so*, she told him. *The physician is different, but still more than a single thing—or perhaps less.* And now Barrick caught a glimpse of her perception of Chaven, who seemed to carry something shadowy inside him like a second silhouette. Could it be the mere presence of the statue, Barrick wondered? What was the thing? Had he made a terrible mistake keeping it hidden from his allies?

In that instant he almost told Aesi'uah, but he was too ashamed of his deception and his own fascination with the thing; his greed to keep it near him until he could understand his feelings. Instead, he asked her, "Will you tell Saqri about this?"

"I do not know." Aesi'uah rose, crossed her slender gray hands across her breast, and bowed. "There is little time left. I wonder if I am catching at small things because I am too frightened to look at the large. It will be strange to die, knowing my entire people die with me, that no one will ever again dance on the slopes of M'aarenol or sing at midwinter in the caves above the Cold Sea. Fare you well in the hours ahead, Barrick Eddon. May your death be a swift one."

And then she was gone, graceful and silent as a phantom drifting through a forgotten churchyard.

In the end, Briony took seven of Eneas' Temple Dogs with her: Sir Stephanas, another knight named Gennadas, and five foot soldiers. Stephanas seemed pleased to have been asked to accompany her; Briony thought he might be imagining himself as the captor of Duke Hendon, one of the few deeds in this confusing, frightening struggle that would be understood and talked about back home.

The Midsummer's Day sun had long since crested the sky and was heading down toward the western walls by the time they left the residence. Cannons still boomed and their missiles still crashed into walls and towers, some so close that Briony could hear the whicker of stone fragments flying past overhead, but she could not puzzle out who was firing now. Was it Durstin Crowel's men in Funderling Town, firing into the inner keep because they knew the Syannese had taken the residence? Or was it one of the two or three damaged Xixian ships still afloat out in Brenn's Bay, firing at the castle out of general hatred?

A more important question, though, was where was Hendon Tolly? She had assumed that he had escaped the inner keep the day before, when it became clear that the Syannese were not going to be easily turned away, but none of the Eddon supporters at the Raven's Gate or the Basilisk Gate had seen him go. Which meant Hendon might have escaped in disguise or might still be somewhere inside the inner keep itself, waiting for a moment to sneak out in the confusion. But, as Chert the Funderling had just demonstrated, there were other ways in and out of the castle, ways she had never even guessed. Briony knew that even if she somehow survived and won back the family's throne, she would never sleep securely again until someone had charted each and every tunnel.

The inner keep was still packed with refugees, homeless subjects from the surrounding countryside, from mainland Southmarch, and from the castle's outer keep as well; everywhere they went they had to force their way through the stink and gabble of frightened people. Some recognized her, or thought they did—Briony did not stay to confirm their beliefs—and after a while she began wearing a cloth wrapped around her face. She did not want a vulnerable procession of well-wishers and curiosity-seekers following her in her search for Hendon.

She still could not understand why Hendon had taken the infant, Alessandros. Briony's frightened stepmother had said something about summoning a god, and about magical blood. Her father had said something about it, too. Was Hendon Tolly a victim of the same madness as the Autarch of Xis? Worse, was it something other than madness?

Stupid woman. Stop it. All she was doing was frightening herself. She needed to find Hendon Tolly; she needed no magical terrors to give her reasons to hurry.

Several hours had passed and the light was all but gone from the sky above Southmarch. As Briony, Stephanas, and the others finished a fruitless search of the residence gardens and turned back toward the center of the keep, the wind from the ocean grew stronger. The evening was warm, but the clouds had closed in and darkened the sky. The air was as damp as if a storm was sweeping in.

The cannons were still roaring as they crossed the colonnade and stepped out into the nest of narrow streets between the armory and the Throne hall. Briony's attention was caught by something stuck in the branches of one of the tall trees near the corner of the hall that contained the Erivor Chapel—a pale shape, reaching and fluttering as though it struggled for the housetops and freedom. She doubted it was anything significant—the castle was full of blowing scraps—but she was still squinting at it in the dying light when the cannonball struck. A slower, louder round had just passed over their heads, shrieking like one of the skeletal daughters of Kernios and disappearing into the commons behind them. A moment later, the wall of the Throne hall burst into pieces as big as hay wagons, crushing Sir Gennadas and three of Briony's Syannese foot soldiers and spilling bodies out of the building along with the flying rubble.

Stephanas and Briony and the other two soldiers did their best to dig the men out but it quickly became clear it was hopeless. A bedraggled priest, one of the crowd of homeless refugees, came forward and began to pray over the bodies. Others worked by lamplight, trying to dig out the other victims who had either been inside or beneath the walls of the great Throne hall when the cannonball smashed it open.

Overwhelmed by the dust and the smell of blood, Briony at last wandered away to catch her breath. One of the sections of the wall had fallen only an arm's length from her, taking Gennadas but sparing Briony. She had imagined her death would be a personal thing, something she could face bravely, like a true Eddon. She had never thought of death being so swift and uncaring, an event that could obliterate not just her but also several strangers at the same time.

Briony realized she had wandered away from the destruction, and she was shaking as though the weather had suddenly turned freezing. That wouldn't do—she was a princess, after all. These were her people, and she had no right to walk away and leave them, however frightened she might be.

As she turned she saw something flapping just to one side—the pale thing in the tree that had caught her attention earlier. Shocked loose by the crash of the cannonball into the Throne hall, it had floated down a short way before catching in the branches again. It was a shawl or something similar, doubtless once some woman's admired possession, lost now as so many other things had been. She walked toward it and yanked it down, only half looking, marveling that something so delicate and finely made should have survived in the midst of this destructive madness when the great stone walls themselves could not.

Perhaps there is something to be learned here . . . she thought absently, staring at the fine texture of the cloth. If it was a woolen shawl, it was a small one and its owners' initials had been worked into the design of flowers and birds. No, it wasn't a shawl at all, it was a Naming blanket, the kind children were wrapped in for the important religious ceremonies, and this one had four initials on it, which seemed unusual: OABE.

Her heart fluttered and threatened to stop entirely. She gasped for breath. Could it be? Who else but a royal child would have four names? And what would make more sense than for little Alessandros to have his father's name, too—Olin. And Anissa's father had been named Benediktos . . .

Olin Alessandros Benediktos Eddon. It was baby Alessandros' blanket.

"Sir Stephanas!" Briony shouted. "Come here!"

The tone of her voice was such that Stephanas and the other two soldiers did not hesitate, but left the death rites of their comrades and ran to her side. She showed them the blanket, then turned and looked past the ruined wall to the dark slopes beyond, a place of tangled old trees and few lights. Even the homeless might hesitate to make their camp in such a place.

"The graveyard?" asked Stephanas. He did not sound as if he liked the idea.

"It makes sense. There are more than a few tombs there big enough to hide in—some of them go very deep." This thought chimed strangely, but she pushed it aside. "I would bet my life that Hendon is hiding in there somewhere with my half brother." She turned to one of the two surviving infantrymen. "Hurry back to the residence. Tell Prince Eneas where we're going—ask him to send more men."

"Where we are going?" Stephanas was still staring out into the dismal shadows of the temple yard. "Why don't we wait for the prince?"

"Because it might be hours. Because we might be wrong, and if Hendon's not here, we need to know so we can look elsewhere. Don't you understand—he has one of my family as a hostage!" She turned back to the newly appointed messenger. "Go! Swiftly!"

He hurried off. Briony turned to her remaining two companions. "Stay close to me. I know the place better than you do."

"We will need torches," said Sir Stephanas.

"That's the last thing we need," she told him. "No light to give us away! And we will have to be quiet, too. Don't you know anything about Hendon Tolly? He's like a serpent—he will always try to bite."

As they reached the ancient, leaning gate, she held her finger to her lips to remind them to remain silent, then guided the reluctant soldiers through into the land of the dead.

35
His Dearie-Dove

"As he passed through the great Marches, the shell of the egg became so hot that it crumbled to ash and fell away . . ."

—from "A Child's Book of the Orphan, and His Life and Death and Reward in Heaven"

IT WAS THE LAST CONVERSATION Ferras Vansen would have expected to have.

"Moping, then, Captain?" someone asked him as he sharpened the blade of his ax. "Got a dearie-dove back home you wish you could see once more?" It was Sledge Jasper, cheerful despite a face that looked like a burned roast. His thickset right-hand man, Dolomite, squatted beside him.

"A what? A dearie-dove?" Vansen couldn't help laughing a little. The hopelessness of his choice on that front mirrored the likelihood of him having picked the winning side in the war. He had been the gods' fool for so long he could barely remember the time before his hopeless love had settled over him like a storm cloud.

"A sweetheart, Captain," said Jasper with an offended tone. "You know what I mean."

If I survive, I will tell her, Vansen decided suddenly. *I will have to leave Southmarch—if they do not have my head first for my presumption. But it will be worth it. I'll be an empty man, hollowed out and ready for something else to be poured in. Or at least prepared for an empty life afterward.* "Nothing much to tell about," he said out loud. "What's the hour?"

"The timekeeper puts it about an hour until midday," Jasper told him.

"Ah." Vansen nodded. "So Midsummer's Day is still young." It was a bleak piece of news, since they needed to hold off the Xixians until past midnight. "As to ladies, how about you, friend Jasper? An accomplished fellow like yourself, a Wardthane, you must have someone waiting."

Sledge Jasper made a face. "A wife. Does that count?"

Dolomite grinned. "Your Pebble would have your knackers for that, Sledge."

"And you, Dolomite?" Vansen asked, grasping at anything that might lead the men to think of something other than what lay ahead. "Have you a dearie-dove, as Jasper calls it?"

The little man frowned. "None of the town girls understand me, Captain, to be frank. They don't see a man like me can have ideas beyond knocking heads. In truth, I'd like to start a tavern. Save up a few copper chips for a nest egg and then go to the next Guild Market when they start having them again, find myself a girl who hasn't already made her mind up about me. Maybe a Westcliff lass. They're not so handsome, the Settland Funderlings, but I've heard they're sensible . . ."

Jasper and Dolomite went back to their men as Brother Flowstone returned and crouched beside Vansen.

"I am afraid, Captain," the young monk admitted. "I thought I would be honored, even exalted, when the Elders called for me, but I am only frightened. I don't want to die."

"You would be a strange young man in the prime of your life if you did."

"I had many . . . I thought things would be . . . different . . ."

Vansen reached over and patted the monk's shoulder. "Don't despair—you may yet live! But whether today or fifty years from now, we will all stand before Immon's Gate . . ."

"We call him *Nozh-la*," Flowstone told him.

". . . We will all stand before Nozh-la's gate," Vansen continued, "waiting for the kind attentions of his master, the lord of death."

"You are a poet, Captain." The monk seemed amused despite the quaver in his voice.

Vansen, however, had been seized even as he spoke by a sudden vision, a memory so powerful that it shook him like a rat in a terrier's jaws, and for a long moment he could barely breathe. *Immon's Gate.* He had been there, or at least he could see it in his mind's eye as clearly as if he had, the great ornate portal of black stone, tall as a mountain, part of the featureless stone of the House of the Lord of the Underworld. And all around it lay the sullen, red lights and tall, deep shadows of the City of Death. Could it be? Had he actually seen it? But when? This phantom of his mind seemed so real!

It doesn't matter when. Or even if it was a dream. I've seen it. I know it. I have been to the very gates of Death's own castle and returned. If the gods were trying to speak to him, Ferras Vansen was listening. He could almost hear rising voices like a temple choir, something bigger than himself lifting him, and for a moment he no longer feared anything.

No matter what happens to me now or later, I have not had a small life!

Something thumped at the far end of the great hall, a muffled crash that nearly extinguished the torches and sent stones rolling from the pile of rubble blocking the far entrance. Another thump, louder this time, forceful enough to slap both Ferras Vansen's ears and deafen him for a moment, shattered his thoughts into pieces. The far end of the chamber was full of dust and skittering stone. Shapes moved where only moments earlier a thousandweight and more of rubble had been piled.

Vansen could see immediately that the autarch had not sent his ordinary foot soldiers, the Naked; instead, behind the swirl of dust and smoke, the cleared entrance was full of tall, pale shields, wedged together like the scales of a snake, an armored mass that bristled with spears like a hedgehog's quills as it advanced slowly into the room. The men were huge and their shields were painted with the ugly, snarling head of a dog—the autarch's most feared killers were leading the attack.

With a roar that to Vansen's damaged hearing seemed scarcely more than a loud moan, the White Hounds surged forward into the Initiation Hall.

The afternoon went by like a thunderstorm that lasted years. Vansen and his men held the first barricade of skillfully piled stone as long as they could, but despite the protection of the high wall at least a dozen Funderlings fell. In lulls between skirmishes the bodies were dragged away and their armor and weapons redistributed. Vansen noted with grim amusement that finally, from sheer attrition, nearly all of his men were properly armed. At last, when the warders holding the far right side of the barricade had been so badly overwhelmed that the Xixians were clambering over the wall in numbers, Vansen called the retreat and the Funderlings dropped back to the second barrier.

"Now hold them here!" he shouted. "Spears up, Guildsmen, spears up!"

They held the second wall as long as they could. Time passed in a blur and the shouting became a smear of noise like the roaring ocean somewhere above their heads.

Sky and sea, thought Vansen—*oh, to see them both once more! And Briony Eddon's face!* If you could love a god or goddess who would never know you, why not a princess? Was the love any the less because it couldn't come back to you?

More Funderlings fell, even brave little Dolomite, Jasper's sergeant; more sprang forward to fill the places of the fallen, including monks who had only ministered to the wounded. Three Metamorphic Brothers, freshly come to the front line, were set on fire by an oil lamp the autarch's men shoved over the top of a barrier. As they ran screaming past their fellows, Vansen could feel despair welling up in the Funderling troops like a poisonous venom, stealing their strength; he knew that any instant they might all break and run for the great balcony and the whole force would be overwhelmed and slaughtered. Vansen leaned out and grabbed one of the blazing monks as he went past, burning his hand, and then threw himself on top of the shrieking man, doing his best to smother the flames with dirt and his own body. Vansen sat up to see the other Funderlings watching him in numb surprise.

"Stop staring!" he bellowed. "Help these men! Call the healers. And protect your barricades!"

Startled back to something like sense, the Funderlings dug in afresh. Others caught the burning monks and wrestled them to the ground to extinguish the flames, then dragged them to the back of the hall. When the Funderlings did give way some time later and fell back to the third barricade, it was under discipline and at Vansen's command.

They could not hold the third barricade for long, nor the smaller fourth. The Xixians continued to swarm into the huge chamber, and as they cleared the stones from between the columns, they were able to bring more and more soldiers against the Funderling positions. The southerners could use arrows now, too, and although these did little damage against those who crouched behind the barricades, it was different for the Funderlings at the rear of the chamber. Young Calomel, Cinnabar's son, was shot in the back as he tried to drag his father's litter to a safer spot. As the monks carried off the wounded youth, Vansen and the others could only tell the sick and fretful Cinnabar over and over again that his boy would be well, though none of them truly believed it.

Soon the ground was slick with blood, the ancient stone flags as treacherous as ice. At least a half dozen more Funderlings died defending the fourth wall, many of them from the ranks of the warders, Vansen's most experienced fighters. The little men were fighting bravely and the terrain was to their advantage, but the autarch's officers could bring up wave after wave of soldiers who were not only trained and equipped, but fresh to the fight as well.

As the doomed afternoon and evening wore on, Vansen pondered the increasingly grim arithmetic of their defense. He had known they could never hope to do more than slow the Xixians, but it was plain now that without a miracle they couldn't hope to hold even an hour longer. At this pace, he and his Funderlings would lie dead to a man long before midnight.

"Fall back!" he shouted. "Back to the last barricade!"

He and several warders stayed to protect the retreat. Funderlings tumbled past him as they scrambled for the rear, their faces pale and haunted. Scaffolders, quarrymen, carvers, not a one of them had been a soldier, but here they were, giving everything they had to defend their tiny piece of country, and everything was indeed being taken from them. It was all Ferras Vansen could do to keep his rage and sorrow from overwhelming him.

As Vansen and a few others fell back to join their comrades, a Xixian arrow caught Sledge Jasper in the back of a leg. He stumbled, falling behind the rest, and in that moment one of the Xixian soldiers saw his chance: the southerner sprang out into the no-man's-land between the two walls and drove his spear into Sledge Jasper's back as easily as skewering a fish in a drying pond, then leaped back with a shout of delight as Jasper took a step, crumpled, and fell.

Before he could think about what he was doing Vansen had clambered back over the wall and rushed to his fallen comrade, meeting the surprised Xixian's defensive thrust with contempt. He yanked the man's spear out of his hands so hard that the Xixian took a helpless couple of steps toward him, which let Vansen bring his ward-ax around in a great sweep to crush the man's helmet and the head beneath.

More Xixians were scrambling toward him now, ducking the rocks being thrown by Vansen's men from behind the last barricade. Vansen scooped up Jasper, whose small, stocky body was heavier than he expected as well as slippery with blood, and ran to the barricade. He delivered the wardthane into waiting hands, then dragged himself over to momentary safety as a flurry of arrows snapped against the stones all around him.

He bent to the wounded man but it was too late: Jasper had stopped breathing. His eyes were open but saw nothing. Vansen felt a cold hatred seize his guts and squeeze them.

"The Elders' blessings on you, Sledge," he said quietly.

The Xixians had not attacked again, but he knew they soon would. Vansen turned to the other Funderlings, who watched him with wide-eyed fear or exhausted despair. This last wall had been built smaller and higher than the others in this narrowest part of the cavern, with the hall's only exit behind it. He made a quick estimate of how many men he still had—perhaps two or three hundred able to fight, no more. Even so, most of them were wounded, and Vansen himself was covered in blood too, much of it his own. He thought of several things to say, discarded them all.

"Sit up straight, men," he told them finally. "Be pleased, not ashamed. We have nothing else left to do today except make a brave death. We have already made certain that these southerners, twice your size and ten times your numbers, will never be able to speak the name of the Funderlings or of Revelation Hall without sorrow at their losses and surprise at who caused them."

A small murmur ran through the huddled men, including what might have been a ragged cheer or two.

"Enough of this talking," Vansen told them. "Cinnabar is still here—he's just a little under the weather, but he still breathes. And Malachite Copper? He's here in his best suit—aren't you, Master Copper?"

The Funderling cleared his throat. "Here indeed, Captain."

"And Wardthane Jasper will be in the line outside Nozh-la's Gate with the rest of our friends who've gone ahead, watching to see what you do in the next hour. So don't disappoint them! Up, men, up!"

As they struggled wearily to their feet, Vansen raised his voice to make sure even those in the back could hear him. "Put your shoulders against each other and lift your spears, men. Those who still have shields, keep them up and locked with your fellows'. Don't give ground except back toward the doorway . . . and whatever you do, *do not break unless you hear me calling the retreat.* More than our own lives depend on it."

"'Ware the wall!" someone shouted. The Xixians had brought up a ram and had begun trying to knock down the barricade. Suddenly, the Funderlings were all up and hurrying into place as if the moment of quiet had never happened. Vansen saw a face appear near the top of the wall and took a swing at it with his ward-ax. The Xixian soldier dropped away unscathed and went looking for a spot where the defenders were not so tall. After that, Vansen had little time to do anything except avoid being killed.

Something bad had happened to Ferras Vansen's left arm; he could no longer lift it above his shoulder. Something else bad had happened to his leg. He could still stand on it, but every time he shifted his weight he felt weakness and pain pierce his knee like a hot needle.

Xixian rams had knocked holes in their last barricade in several places; beyond, Vansen could see manlike shapes and the flicker of torches. Another part of the barricade now shivered as more stones worked loose and tumbled to the floor, one of them crushing an already wounded man's leg. The fighting had grown too fierce even to pull the injured out of harm's way. Vansen had never been so exhausted in his life, not even in the lost months behind the Shadowline—it took all his strength simply to remember where he was and what was happening around him. Still, the ladders coming over the top of the barricades at either end were no dream, and the men climbing them were as real as Death itself.

Nearby, several of the Naked warriors leaped down from the top of the barricade, swinging their curved swords and hand-axes. He realized he was staring like a drunkard while men died—*his* brave, brave men.

"It's time!" Vansen shouted. "Back through the door! We'll make our stand on the Balcony. Fall back!"

This time the distance was short. Vansen actually grabbed men and tugged them back from the fighting, but many others had been waiting for this moment and were already hurrying toward the doorway at the back of Revelation Hall in a retreat so ragged that some fell and others stepped on them. More and more Xixians were swarming over the final barricade.

"Hurry!" Vansen picked up someone's spear from the flagstones and used it to keep the attackers at bay as the last of the Funderlings extricated themselves. He had taken so many wounds today that at any other time he would be with the other injured being cared for, but as the biggest man among his troops he knew that he was always being watched: Vansen remaining upright through all the waves of attack had done much to keep his own men in fighting spirit. But Vansen also knew that the time had come when strategy meant nothing. Each man must now sell his life for as brave a price as he could, but they would never know whether it had been enough.

Vansen and Malachite Copper and a few of Copper's household troops were the last to retreat through the doorway and out onto the great slab of stone the Funderlings called the Balcony, which stood on the edge of the stony cliff that held the Maze. A hundred feet or more below the Balcony spread the gigantic underground chamber of the Sea in the Depths, although to call that immensity a chamber was like calling Three Brothers Temple a shack, or mighty Hierosol a village. The cavern was almost as wide as the inner keep itself, and its height was unknown. If the great cave had a ceiling, it was lost in darkness above them and could not be seen even from the high balcony of the Maze.

And at the center of the cavern lay the shining, still surface of the Sea in the Depths—"the Silver," as he had sometimes heard the Qar name it. Veins of glowing stone threading through the walls of the massive chamber gave a faint but steady light, so that even from the Balcony, Vansen could see the thing that the autarch apparently sought and had already killed so many to reach, the gleaming crystalline monument called the Shining Man, standing on its island in the middle of the silvery underground sea.

"Look out, Captain—here they come!" shouted Malachite Copper. Vansen sighed and turned his back to the stone railing, then stepped forward so he couldn't easily be pushed over. Some of his men would probably choose that way out by the end, he knew, rather than die on a Xixian spear. He couldn't blame them, but that way would not be his.

Smoke billowed from the doorway of the Revelation Hall onto the balcony. For a few moments, Vansen thought it was dust again, that the Xixians had knocked over the entire barrier, but even so it seemed too big a cloud. Several figures stepped out of the rolling murk, their dark silhouettes somehow magnified by the smoke so that they seemed monsters, not men.

But it *was* a monster, he saw a moment later with sinking heart, or at least it was no longer anything human. Big and getting bigger every instant, the thing was a writhing shadow, uneven and unstable.

It growled out something that almost sounded like words, a horrid deep rasp. Two more just as terrifying stepped up beside it, one of them still with a hand to its mouth as though it were eating something. All three seemed man-shaped whirlwinds, as if the dust and debris of the chamber were being drawn up to spin through the air and circle them, covering the creatures like moss growing on a stone but a thousand times more swift. The shapes grew wider and even taller. As Vansen stared, dumbfounded, he heard Funderlings shrieking in terror behind him.

"Curse their Xixian devilry!" Vansen groaned. "Copper? Where are you? I need your men and their spears!"

He did not wait, but hurled his own ward-ax at the nearest of the creatures. The weapon only bounced off the swirling, shadowy mass, as ineffectual as a snowball against a siege tower. Vansen tore a spear from the hand of a staring, dumbfounded Funderling and advanced toward the things, jabbing at them as at an angry boar, but the demons did not give ground. The three shapes had grown huge now, bulky and irregular, but they still walked on two legs as they waded forward, swiping at the defenders with clawed hands big as serving platters. They moved surprisingly quickly, too—the first nearly beheaded Vansen with one swipe.

"Help the captain, you sons of the Guild!" called out Malachite Copper. "The Elders are watching you—don't let him fight alone!"

And then other Funderlings began to push their way in beside him, jabbing bravely at the things and ducking blows from the stony talons if they were lucky; but several were sliced in half as they stood, and another was thrown into Ferras Vansen by a backhanded swipe of a malformed hand with such violence that it knocked him spinning. Vansen struck his head against the base of the Balcony's stone railing and when he tried to sit up so he could rise and fight, all around him seemed to waver as if seen through fathoms of water.

A tiny white shape dropped down from out of the darkness above, but Vansen could make nothing of it, any more than he could of the weird, liquid roar of the devil creatures as they mowed through the shrieking Funderlings. An instant later, he realized he was staring at a small, slender woman dressed all in white armor who stood just in front of him, the rope down which she had climbed still dangling beside her.

"We of the People have served you poorly, Ferras Vansen," she said in a voice so sweetly calm he was half-certain he must be dreaming it all. "Now we will try to make up for that, at least in some measure."

She was Qar, that was obvious, but he had never seen her before. He wondered again if he might be dreaming . . . or dying. "Who . . . who are you?"

"My name is Saqri. I must go now."

Other shapes were falling down out of the darkness all around him, many figures sliding down on ropes and jumping to the Balcony before swiftly springing forward to attack the clawed demons. Vansen tried to get up, but the world spun so briskly that he fell back and did not try again to rise; it was all he could do just to lie on the stone and listen to the weirdly musical sounds of desperate battle, the clang of stony claws on smooth Qar armor. Flashes of light made the carved walls of the Maze jump out in sharp relief and revealed dozens—no, hundreds!—more Qar as they dropped down onto the Balcony like graceful spiders.

One of the demon creatures died with a Qar arrow in its eye all the way to the feathers. It thrashed and gurgled wetly for a long time until the life finally leaked out of it. Another stumbled as it charged and was then jabbed with fairy-spears until it went mad and tumbled over the railing—it roared like receding thunder all the way down. The last, as far as Vansen could tell, was set on fire somehow from within and died in a smoking mass in the middle of the balcony, leaving a corpse that looked like a chimney hit by lightning.

Vansen sat up, his arm and leg throbbing horribly, trying to make sense out of what was happening. Where were the rest of the autarch's soldiers? Why had they stopped attacking? Had his Funderlings actually defeated the Xixians with the last-moment help of the Qar?

A tall warrior in gray Qar armor came toward him across the balcony. "Ferras Vansen," this newcomer said, crouching at his side. "By the gods, I never thought I'd see you again. Never." The stranger took off his helmet and for a moment Ferras Vansen could only stare at the shock of red hair in aching bemusement.

"Barrick . . . ?" he said at last. "Prince Barrick? Is it really you?"

The prince gave him a cold, serious gaze. He looked ten years older. "Yes, it's me, Captain. How are your wounds? Will you survive?"

"I . . . I expect so . . ." Vansen shook his head in amazement. "But how do you come here? How did you escape from the shadowlands?"

A human expression, a little smile, twisted Barrick Eddon's lips. "I'm sure we both have many stories to tell . . ." he began, then another Qar woman hastened up, one Vansen recognized. It was Yasammez' gray-skinned adviser, Aesi'uah.

"Captain Vansen," she said. "It is good to find you alive." She turned to Barrick. "Saqri says we cannot delay. It is a feint, as she feared. They are already gone."

"What?" Vansen struggled to get up. He hated this feeling of weakness. "Who is already gone?"

"The southerners," Aesi'uah said. "This last attack by the autarch's Stone Swallowers was meant to destroy you and your men, but he was not waiting for you to die. There are long stairways back in the Maze which lead far down, then cross under the Sea in the Depths to the island where gods fought and died—the place where the Shining Man stands. The autarch and his priests and soldiers stealthily went that way while we fought. They have slipped past beneath us.

"Despite all your bravery and all our haste, Captain Vansen, we have lost."

36
When the Knife Falls

"The poor Orphan had to wrap the piece of the sun in oak leaves, but at last these also burned away and he had no other choice but to carry it in his soft hands."

—from "A Child's Book of the Orphan, and His Life and Death and Reward in Heaven"

"IT IS A HANDSOME THING, is it not?" Hendon Tolly held it up so Matt Tinwright could see it; but in fact Tinwright could see almost nothing else: the blade was so close and its presence so alarming that his eyes nearly crossed. The knife was as long as Tinwright's forearm and palm, its slender jade handle inlaid with unfamiliar golden symbols, as was the even slenderer blade. "It is Yisti work, I was told, from the southern part of Xand," Tolly said. "A *ghostmaker*, it is called. We will see if it is also a godmaker." He laughed, but it seemed perfunctory. Tolly was pale and sweating, as if, despite his usual air of confidence, the events of the last few days had shaken him very deeply. "Just think, poet! A thousand years or more it lay in a Hierosoline tomb, and you will be the first to wield it again in all that time. That is something worth making a rhyme about!"

The knife was so close that Matt Tinwright was beginning to think Hendon Tolly might be about to test it on him, despite his promises. Tinwright looked to the soldiers, three hardened men in Summerfield colors, Tolly's handpicked guards, but they would not even meet his eye.

The protector's madness was as clear as a large livid bruise on pale skin. No one wanted to endanger himself by catching Tolly's attention.

"What do you w-want me to do . . . ?" Tinwright didn't even want to touch the knife. The green handle and the tomb-patina made it look envenomed.

"Follow me, of course." Tolly lowered the knife and pointed to the steps leading down into the Eddon family vault. The sun was well behind the hills now and the opening seemed a gateway to the void itself, the naked emptiness that came before the gods. "We have work to do, fool, and midnight is only hours away. If we are to beat that brown dog Sulepis to the prize, we cannot wait any longer." He turned to one of the guards. "When Buckle arrives, send him down to me at once."

The guard nodded. Tolly turned back to Matt Tinwright. "Come, now. Bring the child. Haste!"

His stomach roiling so he feared he might vomit, his head full of confused and fearful thoughts, Tinwright wrapped the blankets a little tighter around the squirming royal heir and followed Hendon Tolly down into the tomb.

Tolly led them to the old vault, which lay behind the first outermost chamber where Okros Dioketian had died and Tinwright himself had been caught by a returning Hendon Tolly. The old vault was larger and higher than the front chamber, a hollow, six-sided mountain of stone, each of the six walls honeycombed with niches, and each niche holding its own stone or lead box. Most of the old coffins bore no images of the dead, and few even had inscriptions; those who slumbered inside, many of them kings and queens of Southmarch, had now become nameless and faceless.

"No one has been buried in this room for hundreds of years," Tolly said, walking slowly around the hexagonal chamber with his hands behind his back like an idler out for a stroll. "Kellick built the outer chamber, it is said, which means that great Anglin himself must be here, crumbling in one of these hidey-holes." He looked up to see whether he had shocked Tinwright with his blasphemy. "But nobody knows which!" Tolly laughed. "No matter how famous in life, when you are dead, you are nameless clay!" The baby in Tinwright's arms was beginning to cry steadily now, the hitching sobs becoming a single wail. "By Perin's beard, poet, will you give that cursed child a shake?" Tolly said, frowning. "Make it be quiet."

Matt Tinwright held the small creature gingerly. What did someone like him know about comforting an infant? "Does he have to be here, Lord?"

"What are you babbling about? Of *course* he has to be here—we cannot perform the ritual without him! Might as well try to have a dinner with no roast!" Tolly closed his eyes as if he could bear no more, but he kept them closed for longer than Tinwright would have expected, and when he opened them, they had a perilous cast. "I said, silence that child."

Tinwright could think of nothing else to do except to give the tiny creature his finger to suck. It was a trick he had seen Brigid use on her sister's child to quiet it. Little Alessandros continued to hitch and sob for a while even with the finger in his mouth, but gradually grew silent.

Tolly thrust out his hand, and one of the guards handed over a sack he had been carrying. "Where is that other fool? He should have been here by now."

"My lord . . . ?"

"Shut your mouth, poet, I am not talking to you. Well?"

The guard who had handed him the sack squirmed beneath his master's bright, disturbing glare. "Buckle? I'm sure he'll be here right quickly, Lord Tolly. . . ."

Tolly silenced him with a mere movement of his hand. "Enough. Go and wait outside for him, both of you. I would talk with Master Tinwright."

The guards, only too willing to leave the Old Vault, hustled away. Tinwright heard their footsteps going up from the new vault to the surface. When they died away he became uncomfortably aware that he was trapped far beneath the ground—in a tomb, no less!—with a dangerous madman.

"It's almost time," Hendon Tolly said after some moments had passed. "Did you hear the bell as we came down? That would have been ten of the clock. The Syannese must have taken the residence by now—much good it will do them!" The lord protector laughed. Of late he had stopped trimming his beard and paying close attention to his clothing. Now, ragged and almost untended, Hendon Tolly no longer looked like the mirror of Tessian court fashion. "They will strut and imagine themselves as conquerors, just as that Xixian dog beneath our feet dreams himself to be the chosen of the gods—but they will both be wrong! Because I will beat them to the post. The goddess' favor will be mine!"

Tinwright could no longer keep track of what his fearsome master planned to achieve with his dreadful sacrifice. Sometimes he talked as though the goddess Zoria would serve him personally, other times as though he himself would become a god. Tinwright might have marked it all as the ravings of one moonstruck, but he had felt the cruel power that lurked in Tolly's mirror, had felt it stalking him like a hungry wolf. He didn't want to feel it again and he certainly did not want to hurt a child, royal or not. But what else could he do? Run? Even if he got away from Tolly, the sentries were just outside.

Better to let Tolly kill him, perhaps. If they fought, at least his death might be swift. He could go to the gods with the knowledge that he had refused to do an inexcusable thing.

He squeezed the baby tightly against him, which made the infant burst out crying again.

"My lord," Tinwright began, "I can't . . . I won't . . ." but even as the words came out of his mouth—and admittedly, they were not loud to begin with—Hendon Tolly silenced him with an imperious hand.

"Quiet. Do you hear that?" He cocked his head. "There. That fool Buckle has finally arrived. You will enjoy this, poet. A little surprise planned just for you."

"F-For me . . . ?" But now he could hear it, too, a commotion in the other vault, the sound of people moving, of boots on stone and a woman's voice, protesting, pleading . . .

Oh, gods, has the monster brought Queen Anissa to watch what happens to her child? Was there no limit to Tolly's depravity?

The soldiers dragged the struggling woman into the room. When he saw who it was, Tinwright's knees almost buckled beneath him.

"Ah, and here is that last member of our convocation," said Tolly cheerfully. "Lady Elan, how I have missed you. You were a cruel, fickle girl to let me think you had run away."

Elan M'Cory stopped fighting against the guards who held her arms. "You're a monster, Hendon—a goblin! A demon!"

Tinwright could only stare. The world seemed to be falling in on top of him.

"Nonsense, my dear." Hendon was at her side in a moment, then pressed her cheek with the blade of the jade-handled knife as the guards held her. He pushed a little too hard and a thread of shining red appeared. "Our friend the poet will do everything I say because he will not want to see harm come to a single hair on your lovely head. Did he not go to great lengths already to hide you from me?"

Tinwright felt as though his insides had turned to sand and cold water. "Oh, gods help us, how . . . how did you find her?"

"Oh, the gods will be helping you soon enough, never fear." Hendon Tolly's glee was mounting by the instant. "I have had you followed every time you left the castle, little poet. You may have thought yourself clever with your twisting courses, but all you have done is make my soldiers tired and angry—you fooled no one. Honestly, did you really think to hide a noblewoman of Summerfield in your sister's hovel?"

Tinwright turned to catch Elan's eye. "I'm sorry. I never thought . . ."

"Enough." Tolly lingered a moment to sniff at her hair and face like a cat at a fleck of carrion. "Ah, I hope he does what he says, my dear," he whispered loud enough for Matt Tinwright to hear. "I pray no harm must come to you. I want you back, you see. I have missed marking your white skin and I have missed the sounds of your suffering. It is like a sickness, this longing of mine. . . ."

"Do nothing that he wants, Matt!" Elan called to Tinwright. "I was already a dead woman when we met—I was a corpse from the first time he touched me . . . !"

"But our poet is not made of such cruel stuff," Tolly said. "He will do what he is told. He will help me perform the ritual in place of poor, foolish old Brother Okros. He will sacrifice the child." Tolly came to Tinwright then and touched the king's child on the forehead with his dusty white finger, leaving a mark. "Because if he does not, he will watch me take the skin off his beloved Elan before he dies."

She heard something moving around in the dark—a dark too deep for even her strong Funderling eyes—and sat up.

"The Tortoise . . ." a small voice was whispering. *"Then the Knot . . . and the Owl . . . the Last Hour of the Ancestor, which deep in the ancient days was the door to his house . . . the signs are so clear that surely even a fool could see them . . . but why . . . ?"*

"Who's there?" Opal cried.

A moment of silence passed before the answer came. *"It's me, Mama Opal."*

"Flint? What are you doing, boy?" She elbowed herself up out of the narrow cot and felt for the warmstone. When it was in her hand it began to glow a faint pink, enough to let her see around the room. To her dismay, Flint stood before her dressed not in his nightshirt but in daytime clothes and boots, a cloth sack in his hands.

"What in the name of stone and stonecutting are you doing? What is that sack for?"

"I was only putting some food in it. Some bread and a few dried winter mushrooms."

"What . . . ? Oh, I see—you're going somewhere, or at least you think you are." She sprang out of bed and put herself between him and the door to the monks' dormitory where they slept. "But I won't let you."

Flint looked at her, his expression calm but solemn. "I have to, Mama Opal. Please let me go."

"Go *where*? Why do you do this to us, boy? To me? Haven't we been good to you?"

He flinched as if something hurt him, surprising her. "Yes. You have been better to me than anyone else ever has! I'm not running away, Mama Opal, or getting into trouble. I've just realized that there's something I must do. It . . . came to me."

"What came to you?"

"I . . . I can't tell you. Because I don't entirely know. But I know where it starts, and this is it. I must go."

Opal was close to despair, her anger melting away as fear supplanted it. "But where? This is foolishness, child! Where could you go? There's a war outside! The southerners might come down on us any moment with swords and spears. You'll be killed!" She came toward him, her hands now clasped before her breast. "Don't say such things, my rabbit. You're not going anywhere. Come back to bed. Sleep—it will all look different in the morning. You had a dream, that's all, and it seems very real."

"No." His voice was not cold, but neither was it comforting. "No, Mama Opal. *This* is the dream. And I am beginning to wake."

"Why couldn't Chert be here . . . ?" Flint was taller than she was now, but it didn't matter: the thought of trying to restrain him had never seriously crossed her mind. She threw her arms around him. "Please, my sweet boy, my son, don't do it. Don't go. I've already had to see your . . . to see my husband off on another bootless errand. . . ." Tears spilled down her cheeks.

The boy put his arms around her in an awkward embrace. "I'm sorry, Mama Opal, but I have to."

She leaned back a little and looked keenly, sufferingly at his face. "You're not like anyone else, are you? It's no use trying to make you something you're not." She laughed, a bitter, heartbroken sound. "I'll never see you again. The Elders gave you to me only to snatch you away again—a sort of joke."

"You will see me again." The confusion had left his voice. "I promise that. And you have done so much more than you know. You have saved me."

She stepped away from the door. "Go on, then. I've never been able to stop either you or Chert from doing what you must. Can you really not tell me where you go?"

He shook his head. "I don't know. Not yet. But I will know soon. Be brave, Mama."

She had long ago set down the warmstone; deprived of her hand and its coursing blood, its light had by now all but faded. Only the faintest rosy glow touched Flint as he opened the door into the hallway and stepped out into the echoing darkness.

Through the last several days Qinnitan had heard the fighting only distantly, as though somewhere in the endless, rocky deeps two ghost armies were fighting and re-fighting some ancient battle. When they passed through large caverns, the screams and shouts came to her unexpectedly, carried on the confused currents of air that drifted through the labyrinthine tunnels, and for a terrifying moment it seemed that soldiers were dying only yards away, around the next bend. She could not help thinking of the covered colonnades around the marketplace where she had run as a child, where in certain places you could hear the whispered bickering of merchants halfway around the square.

How had that little girl—barefoot and laughing, chasing her neighbors through the bazaar—become this pathetic thing, a caged creature that would never again see the sunlight, like the birds the copper miners carried down into the darkness with them?

The gods are punishing me—but I did nothing. It filled her with fury. *I am innocent of any wrong and so was poor Pigeon! It is the gods themselves who have done this to me!*

Qinnitan moved closer to the hardwood bars of her prison and pressed her face against them. She could dimly see the northern king's cage a few yards away, swaying on the shoulders of a half dozen bearers just as hers did. The feet of the men carrying the cages crunched on the path of broken stone the autarch's slaves had prepared. Sulepis had commanded a wider road be built down into the earth despite all his haste, simply so that he and his men could travel more comfortably. Qinnitan had seen some of the tons and tons of stone being carried out past her. It numbed her thoughts, this willingness to put a thousand men to work for days, killing dozens in the process, for a path that would be used once.

"Do you like our road, King Olin?" she called out.

"Is that you, Mistress Qinnitan?" They had talked a few times, whenever their cages were near enough. Her command of the northern tongue had improved during her time in Hierosol. She was embarrassed by how wordless she had been at their first meeting.

"Who else?"

She heard him laugh a little. Some of his bearers looked up at her, their faces full of resentment that the prisoners should talk and joke while they worked so hard.

But I think you would not really change places. Out loud she said, "The Golden One makes a big road down into this mountain. Doesn't he fear the mountain will fall on him?"

"He doesn't seem to fear anything," said Olin. "In another man I might admire that, but I think your Golden One does not believe anything *can* happen except that which he desires."

"Not *my* Golden One," she said. "He is a pig—a mad pig!" She repeated it even louder in Xixian for the benefit of the bearers. Several of them stumbled in frightened surprise.

"I wish you would not do that," Olin said.

"Why? What can Sulepis do?" And at that moment she truly did not fear him or any tortures he might use on her. "We are as good as dead. Even the autarch cannot kill us more than once!"

"It's not that. Whatever you said made the men carrying me almost drop me down this ravine. You likely cannot see it from where you are. In any case, I would prefer not to die that way."

Because you are afraid you would be leaving me to be the sacrificial goat in the Golden One's ritual. That was what he meant, she knew. But she only said, "I apologizing, King Olin. I try not to do it again."

They bumped along for a little while before she said, "Once you say I remind you of your . . . daughter? Is that the word? Your girl-son?"

He laughed again. She could not quite see him now. The nearest torch was behind him, and his face was in shadow. "My girl-son. It is funny you say that, because she has never liked having to wear women's clothes."

"Truly? She is like a man?"

"Only in that she wants to use her own wits instead of relying on a man to think for her." Olin's voice warmed. "You would like her. From what you have told me you two are much alike. Like you, she has escaped from her enemies again and again."

"You have pride of her."

"Yes, I do. And of her brother, too, although I haven't told you about him. He was given more to bear than any grown man should carry when he was only a child." The king went silent for a little time. "I have done him wrong, Qinnitan. That is my greatest sadness. I don't fear death, but I hate that I will not see them again."

"Until Heaven."

"Of course. Until Heaven."

Qinnitan woke from a thin sleep when the bearers set down the heavy cage, groaning and mumbling like oxen given the tongues of men. The torchlight showed they were in a strange, narrow passage, the roof only a few arm's lengths above Qinnitan's head. The paramount minister himself, Pinimmon Vash, as old and shriveled as a piece of sandal leather lost in the desert, was giving out orders to the soldiers guarding her and the northern king.

"I apologize, King Olin." Vash spoke the northern tongue as though he had been raised with it. "But here we must descend many steps and move through many narrow spaces. The cage and its bearers will not fit. I fear you must walk."

"But I will still be bound," Olin said.

"Regrettably, yes, your hands will be tied. After the recent incident . . . well, you understand." Outwardly Vash seemed bored and formal, but there was something else in his manner as well, an odd brittleness. Was he afraid of these crushing deeps, so far beneath the sunlit surface, or was there something else? Although Vash hid it well, Qinnitan, who had been well schooled in the constant smiling deceptions of the Seclusion, thought Paramount Minister Vash seemed almost to be afraid of Olin. But why would that be? Clearly, despite his one attempt on the autarch's life, the king was no longer a threat, any more than she was.

"Of course," Olin said, and there was something subtle beneath his words as well. "What else can you do? None of you wish to see anything happen to the Golden One."

He was goading the old man, she could tell—but why? Over what?

They took her out first as a hostage against Olin's good behavior. Occasionally she could hear the dull roar of men fighting nearby, louder than the ghost murmurs that sometimes floated to them. So the battle was close, Qinnitan thought; that meant that enemies of the autarch were also close by. Was there any chance she could escape? She would gladly take her chances in the dangerous confusion of the fighting.

But such a chance was not to be. The soldiers handled her as though she were a captured killer: they tied her hands firmly behind her back and looped a cord around her neck before bringing her out of the cage. When they had her surrounded with soldiers, one holding each arm and one behind her, they just as carefully removed Olin from his cage.

"I feel like Brann's white bull," he said. "Fed and cozened all year only to have his throat slit on Orphan's Day." His face was ashen. "May Lord Erivor's mercy cover us all."

A chill passed through Qinnitan, and it was all she could do to keep upright as the soldiers led her into the narrow passage and down the ancient, rounded steps into a darkness even the torches could not fully illumine.

❦

"Chew, man, chew! Curse you, I told you this must be done." Tolly shoved another piece of the gritty black bread at Tinwright. "Swallow it and take more. Blood of the Brothers, are you *weeping*?"

Matt Tinwright wasn't precisely weeping. Tears had welled in his eyes because he was choking and he could barely breathe. The black bread, tinted with cuttlefish ink and baked without salt or leavening, was foul and dry, and his mouth was so full of it that when he coughed pieces flew out like cinders from a fire.

"Just be grateful I couldn't find a black dog," Hendon Tolly said, "or I would give you a meal that would make you weep for true. Now pull on those grave rags—Okros said the summoners must dress thusly to speak to the dead lands beyond."

But Okros died like a mouse half-eaten by a cat, Tinwright thought miserably. There was no escape from this. Any way he turned, bleak horror waited. Elan stood swaying between two guards with her face a shuttered window, so pale she might have been one of the newly dead herself, evicted from one of the coffins that lined the vault's six walls. The infant prince Alessandros, destined for sacrifice, was sleeping restlessly in Tinwright's arms, exhausted by his own tears.

Matt Tinwright was trapped as no one, not even the sacred Orphan himself, had ever been so utterly trapped, and no bright goddess would step in to save his soul as Zoria had rescued the Orphan's. Tears? The ocean itself did not contain enough salt and water for all the tears Matt Tinwright ached to shed.

The garments one of the guards now pulled out of a bag stank so badly of decay that he dared not guess where they had been obtained. As Tinwright dragged them on, rotted fabric tearing at each pull, Hendon Tolly wrapped himself in a much more presentable black cloak, although it, too, gleamed with pale mold and smelled of the grave. Tinwright could not bear to think of what was about to happen. He finished wrapping the cerements around him and stood, hopeless and miserable, waiting dumbly for Tolly's next order.

"Bring me one of the coffins out of the wall," the lord protector told the soldiers. "There—one of the old ones. That will be our altar."

His guards went to the dusty box he had chosen and extricated it from its niche, then carried it to the center of the vault with a marked lack of enthusiasm. Elan M'Cory didn't speak, but her mouth tightened at the sight of it and she turned her face away. Tolly took the baby from Tinwright and laid him on his back atop the featureless lid with as little care as if the child were a sack of meal. Alessandros whimpered but remained asleep. Hendon Tolly then commanded one of the other soldiers to remove the mirror from its wrappings and place it on the stone floor beside the makeshift altar.

"Now read from the book, poet!" Tolly said. "The page is marked by a ribbon. Read!"

If he only looked at the page of the book Hendon Tolly had given him,

Tinwright decided, if he only read the words that marched across the page, though they squirmed before his eyes like insects, he would almost be able to pretend that all was well. If he did not look at the hideous demons and monsters cavorting in the margins of the pages, drawn with too much gleeful indulgence to be the work of any gods-fearing scribe, if he looked at nothing but the words themselves and ignored the death that was all around him and the madness in Hendon Tolly's every word and, worst of all, the knowledge that in mere moments he would be forced to do something so unspeakable that his soul would be damned to the deepest, darkest pits of Kernios' gray realm for as long as time itself existed . . . well, then he could almost pretend that what he was doing made sense. . . .

"Curse you, you crawling peasant scum!" Tolly was almost jumping up and down with rage; a little bubble of white spittle had appeared at the corner of his mouth. "Read, curse you! Read it *aloud*! It is an invocation. It is meant to open the way to the land of the gods! *Read!*"

Tinwright swallowed. It felt as though something as large as a fir cone had lodged in his throat.

"The sky is heavy, it is raining stars.
The arches of the sky are cracking; the bones of the earthgod tremble;
The Seven Gray Birds are struck dumb by the sight of me,
As I rise toward the sky, I am transfigured into a god,
Who throws down his father and eats his mother!
I am the bull of the sky. My heart lives off the divine beings.
I devour their intestines where their bodies are charged with magic . . . !"

He gained a little strength as he went, not because his heart had grown any less leaden, but because the rhythm of the words themselves caught him up, a cadence as powerful as the pace of a marching army.

"I eat men and gods! I swallow their magic power! I relish their glory!
The large ones are my morning meal
The middling I eat at noon
The small I save for supper, and those who are too old I burn for my incense!
I appear in the sky and I am crowned as Lord of the Horizon . . ."

When he had reached the end of the passage, Tinwright stumbled on without realizing it, reading a few more words before Hendon Tolly angrily struck him on the side of the head, a stinging blow that almost made Tinwright drop the ancient book.

"Dog! Now take up the knife, and when I say it is time, make the sacrifice. The mirror must be smeared with the blood—that is what Okros said. But do not slit the creature's throat until I say the proper words!" Tolly thrust the dagger into Tinwright's unwilling hand. "Take it and hold it close. We are drawing near the hour when that cursed Xixian dog will be performing his own ritual. We must bargain with the gods before he does!" Tolly's voice suddenly rose in a peal of laughter that was as frightening as anything else that had happened so far—a note of pure madness. "Oh! Oh! Can you imagine the autarch's rage when he finds that I have broken into Heaven first—that I have stolen everything he coveted?"

"Don't do it, Matt!" Elan's voice was as ragged as Tinwright's stinking grave-clothes. "Not the child! My life, your life—nothing is worth such a crime . . . !"

He could not bear to listen to her. Each word felt like the sting of a whip. He lowered the knife until it touched the baby's throat. At the feel of the cold metal, little Alessandros woke and began to cry again and Tinwright hurriedly lifted it so he didn't accidentally cut the infant's soft skin. He could not bear to look at the squirming baby, so he closed his eyes.

Nothing, he told himself. *Nothing I can do. Nothing. It might as well not be happening. I could be asleep. All a dream.* He groped for the child's heaving chest until he found it, let the fingers of his free hand rest gently upon it. *Nothing.*

Hendon Tolly was reading now, more words from before history, last uttered in the days of the unmourned Shadow Lords or chanted over a rock tomb in the southern forests when Hierosol itself was yet to be.

"Those I meet are swallowed raw!
I have broken the joints of gods;
Their spines and necks;
I have taken away their hearts . . ."

It was more than an invocation they had been reading, Tinwright dimly realized, it was a challenge—a challenge to the gods themselves, the death-song of some heathen king who claimed that the grave would not hold him, that the gods themselves would not be able to restrain him.

He could hear something else behind Tolly's words, a soft sound that nevertheless was coming from all around him, quiet bumping, scratching, as though in every box in the great vault something was stirring into movement.

"I have swallowed the great crown!
I have swallowed the scepter of rule!
I have consumed the heart of every god!
My life will not end!
My limit is unknown and unspoken . . ."

Matt Tinwright opened his eyes. He could see nothing except the flickering of the torches, which bent in a sudden draft, but the soldiers were staring around wildly. The scraping grew louder, as though rats were gnawing their way out of the walls. Two of the guards suddenly bolted for the next chamber. Hendon Tolly watched them go, his eyes bulging with rage, but his chant was growing louder and it seemed he did not dare to stop.

"Give me the eyes of He Who Stares!
Give me the bones of He Who Builds!
Give me the heart of He Who Rules!
Give me the wisdom of He Who Defines!
And give me She Who is Most Beautiful to be my woman . . . !"

And now Tinwright could feel something more than merely the restlessness of ancient kings disturbed in their moldering slumber. A hatefully familiar presence lurked somewhere just beyond the edges of what the poet could see and smell and hear, the same thing that had stalked him in the mirror. It was as close as it had ever been; he could feel its attention pinioning him as if he were an insect on a tabletop. It was old and strong and had as little interest in Tinwright's mortal thoughts and feelings as he did in the hopes and cares of a stone. And it was drawing closer. . . .

"Bow down to me! I do not fear you! I have eaten your organs and stolen your courage!"

★ ★ ★

. . . said Hendon Tolly, his voice rising to a pitch that might have meant terror or exultation—or a grotesque combination of the two.

"I command the darkness not to hide you!
I command the light to seek you out and reveal you!
All Heaven is my hostage and the gods are my slaves. The hour is mine . . . !"

Tinwright's gaze flicked helplessly back and forth between the ivory throat of the child and the flushed, pop-eyed face of Hendon Tolly, as apoplectically caught up in his own words as any wandering madman. A few yards away Elan M'Cory had slumped silently in a faint, but the remaining guards still held her tightly, their own faces gray with fear.

"Now!" Tolly shrieked. "Now, you wretch, lift the knife while I speak the final words! Then spill the blood and wash the mirror in it!"

Matt Tinwright's arm rose as if it was not attached to his own body any longer, and hung above the restless child. The flames of the torches were sucked first this way, then another. Shadows capered across the walls. The rustling all around him became loud cries and stamping sounds—were the dead rising all at once? Would the living all be pulled down into darkness this day?

He could not make his arm move. He knew Tolly would kill him if he didn't, but he just could not harm the child. *Please, all you kind gods, help me . . . !*

Something struck Tinwright so hard that at first he thought Hendon Tolly had hit him with the heavy grimoire. He stumbled back a step and the knife slipped from his suddenly strengthless fingers and clattered to the stone flags.

Tinwright stared in horror at the arrow quivering in his own chest, so close to his face that only the feathers on the end told him what it was that had struck him. He could feel warm blood running down his belly and soaking into his foul, muddy garments. Then everything spun away and Matt Tinwright's world went dark.

37
The Blood of a God

". . . By the time he reached Tessideme, with all the beasts of the field and the birds of the air in his train, the oak leaves had also burned away so that the weeping Orphan carried the sun's flame in his naked hands . . ."

—from "A Child's Book of the Orphan, and His Life and Death and Reward in Heaven"

GREENJAY, leader of the Qar's Trickster tribe, climbed back out of the door in the stone flags with little of her usual grace. Fury sparked in her eyes. "A hundred paces below us the stairs are crammed with southern soldiers. This autarch has stolen a trick from the drows—we will have to win each yard forward with blood. We will not catch him this way, may the wind eat his name as well as his footprints!"

"He leaves us no choice," Saqri said to Barrick. "Come, manchild—the ropes must be ready now. They will have to be our way down. Haste!"

Barrick followed Saqri back through the Maze, its passages still littered with rubble and the corpses of men and Funderlings. Saqri's soldiers had prepared ropes so her troops could quickly descend to the bottom of the cavern and the Sea in the Depths; those who were too heavy, or simply not built for climbing, would make their way down the narrow trails that crisscrossed the rocky cliff.

Aesi'uah was waiting for them, several rope-ends in her hand like a bouquet of silvery catkins. "Most of the southerners have already made their way out of the tunnels and up onto the surface of the island," she told them.

Barrick, whose vision was not as sharp as Saqri's, squinted into the distance, trying to make out the dark forms across the island in the middle of the silvery sea. Behind it loomed the silhouette of the colossal Shining Man.

"Some of the autarch's men are building boats," said Saqri. "They have brought what they needed with them." She frowned; it was strange to see even such a small show of emotion on her smooth face. "We have underestimated him—even Yasammez has. This Sulepis knows the ground as well as if he had scouted it himself."

"But why boats?" Barrick asked. "He and his soldiers are already on the island."

"Because he knows that with his men holding the tunnels he used to get past us, we will be forced to attack him from this side of the Sea in the Depths. He wants to send troops across to keep us at bay." Saqri made the gesture *Unwilling Blindness.* "We can waste no more time in talk. Grab a rope, Barrick Eddon! Every heartbeat brings us closer to catastrophe."

And that catastrophe, he could not help understanding, would be nothing like the Great Defeat that Saqri and her kin had been awaiting all these centuries as a lover anticipates the return of the beloved. This end would be something much different—dark, wild, and pointless.

The ropes creaked, but despite their astounding slenderness, they held. Every now and then one or the other of Barrick's feet slipped and his body spun away from the cliff face, and in those perilous, nauseating intervals he could see boats pushing off from the island onto the odd, metallic sea. And each boat, he knew, was full of Xixian soldiers, men ready to paint over their own fear—which now, in this strange place, must be great indeed—with the blood of as many Qar and Funderlings as they could destroy.

He looked back up to the clifftop where Ferras Vansen and the Funderlings were finishing up their own slower, more cautious rigging, preparing to descend and join the Qar in what Barrick could not help feeling would be at best a glorious shared suicide.

"Remember Greatdeeps!" he shouted to Vansen, and his voice echoed from the cavern's distant walls. The guard captain raised one hand in a salute.

Barrick had surprised himself. Why should he do such a thing? There was nobody more human than Vansen, with his stolid goodwill and his unthinking loyalty, and there was no mortal less human than Barrick Eddon had become, the Fireflower smoldering in his heart and thoughts. What did he care for mortals and mortal things?

Pinimmon Vash had seen many strange places, from the secret water dungeons underneath the Orchard Palace to the infamous crypts of the Mihannid Blue Kings, and even the autarch's own family tomb, the legendary Aeyrie of the Bishakh which stood out against the sky as if it had grown from the very stone of Mount Gowkha . . . but he had never seen anything quite like this.

The cavern itself—well, it seemed foolish even to call it a cavern. This immense chamber deep in the earth appeared to Vash to be almost a quarter the size of the entire Orchard Palace in Xis with all its grounds. Veins of dimly shining stone and knobs of glittering crystal in the cavern's arching walls made it seem some kind of celestial model built to grace a god's table, but in the middle, almost directly above Vash's head, stretched only darkness. Any roof to the great cavern was much higher above their heads than the feeble light of the Xixian torches could reach. The sensation, Vash thought, was that of looking up from the bottom of a deep well.

He stood, with the rest of the autarch's army, on the island at the center of the Sea in the Depths, but it was the Shining Man—the mountainous, man-shaped lump of dull stone at the heart of the island—that truly dumbfounded and oppressed Vash. It wasn't a statue. No hands, human or otherwise, had crafted it as a replica of some actual being. Instead, it had the look of something cruder, as if someone had poured molten gemstones into the impression a man had made falling headlong into mud. But there was more to it than that. Although at the moment it glimmered only with the reflected, refracted light of the chamber itself, Vash had seen a stronger glow throb briefly within it, like a candle guttering behind old glass, and his hairs had stood up on his neck and arms. The paramount minister had no wish to see it again, that pulse like a huge, diseased heart beating.

All around him, the rocky island swarmed with Xixian soldiers doing their best to ignore the ominous surroundings as they finished tying together the reed boats. Vash noted that he and the antipolemarch seemed to have correctly planned how many bundles of reeds the men would have to carry down from the surface, and he felt a moment's relief before he realized how foolish that was: what difference did it make that Vash had done his duty, that the autarch could find no fault with his arrangements? In a moment, they might all be dead, or the autarch himself might gain the strength of Heaven. Either way, nothing would ever be the same again.

"Where is my trusted paramount minister?" the Golden One called. Vash felt his hackles rising again.

"Here, O Great Tent." He hobbled across the sliding, rounded stones until he reached the place where Sulepis stood tall and slender in his golden armor, a glorious vision even in this inconstant light. "How may I serve you, Master?"

"Are the boats finished?"

Vash took a breath but hid his frustration. It was plain to see that they were. The soldiers stood lined up along the shoreline beside the completed boats, massive rafts with the bundled reeds pulled together at each end to make a bow and stern. "Of course, Golden One," Vash said. It had been an immensely difficult task to transport so many river reeds from Hierosol on such short notice, to keep them dry and safe from mold, but there had been no way of knowing whether they would be able to find the proper materials in this godsforsaken northern wasteland, and the Golden One did not respond well to failure.

Sulepis will become a god while I will probably die and receive a makeshift grave here in this wet northern hellhole, Vash thought, *without even a priest left behind to pray for me. But there stand the boats. I have again done what is mine to do.* Out loud, he said, "All the boats are ready. What else does the Golden One desire?"

"The prisoners, of course. All of them."

Vash blinked. "All of them?"

Sulepis stared at Vash as though from a huge height, as though he himself were the Shining Man. "Yes. The king, the Hive girl, and the northern children. Does that suit you, Minister Vash? Or should I ask someone who has nothing better to do?"

Vash felt a cold shock down his spine. "Forgive my stupidity, Golden

One, I did not understand. Of course they are all being brought. Panhyssir's priests are getting the children, and the others are there." He pointed to a small procession of soldiers coming forward from the tunnel they had followed under the silver sea and onto the island, surrounding the prisoners, King Olin and the girl with their hands tied behind their backs. The priest A'lat capered at the front of the procession, walking backward with a smoking bowl in each hand, wreathing the prisoners in fumes. When he turned, Vash saw with a twist in his stomach that the desert priest wore a mask that appeared to be made from the skin of someone else's face.

"Good, good." Sulepis peeled the gold stalls off his fingertips and dropped them to the carpet. One of the slaves stared for a moment, then quickly gathered them. "I must feel this with my own skin. Look, Vash." His long arm swept up, indicating the cavern, the Shining Man, and perhaps other things that only Sulepis himself could see. "Be aware of everything around you—smells, sounds, sights—for within the next hour the world changes forever."

"Of course, Golden One. Of course." Vash was desperate for the whole sordid horror to end so that he could find some way of accommodating whatever followed, if such were even possible. "You haven't told me what else I can do to aid your . . . ritual. Do you need an altar . . . ?"

"An altar?" Sulepis found this very amusing. "Don't you understand, Vash? This entire place is an altar, a place where the heavens were once made to shake—and will be again! This spot is sanctified by the blood and screams of the gods themselves!" The autarch's voice had grown so loud that soldiers and functionaries all across the island stopped, trembling in fear because they thought the autarch had lost his temper. "No, my altar is the earth itself, this silver sea and the scar that Habbili left when he sealed the way back to this world with his own dying spirit." He waved at the Shining Man, which loomed above them like the spire of a great temple. "Do you not know what that thing truly is? That is where Habbili the Crooked tore open the very flesh of the world so that he could banish the gods! Then, mortally injured himself, he closed the hole with his own being to keep them prisoned—and it has remained that way ever since, hiding here in the earth for thousands of years, worshiped by primitives as though it were a living thing." He bent toward Vash as if to share a secret. "But now Habbili's wounds have killed him at last. The priests and prophets have felt it. They have told me! Habbili's strength will no longer hold shut that wound in the world. Anyone who has the power or knowledge can reach out across the great void . . . or reach *in*." He straightened up to his full height, leaving Vash to stare up at him like a man watching an approaching thunderstorm. "So bring on the children! Let their blood open the door and then let the gods themselves beware! Sulepis will be the master even of the immortals themselves!"

Barrick had only just alighted on the cavern's rocky floor when he saw Yasammez standing nearby looking out across the cavern toward the dark, distant shape of the Shining Man. She was alone for once, wrapped in a vast black cloak, her eyes half-closed so that she seemed as calm and remote as a cat lying in the sun. Her hair had pulled loose from its elaborate knots during her descent and hung around her head like thorny branches.

The Lady of Weeping, the voices whispered inside him in a kind of superstitious awe. *The Scourge. Exile of Wanderwind.*

Barrick approached her but did not kneel or bow. "My lady, will you not fight beside us? This is the last day, the last hour—the moment when we write the final page in the *Book of Regret*."

Her eyes slowly turned toward him. "That page was written long ago, before your kind had even entered the world."

He felt the sting of that but would not be drawn. "But I am also your kind now, Lady Yasammez, whether you or I wish it to be so . . . and you are our greatest warrior. If you do not fight for us now, when will you take the field? When the rest of the People lie dead?" For a moment, the shocked clamor of his Fireflower ghosts, their outrage at his disrespect, filled him with anger. "Is that your form of self-slaughter, Lady? To wait until there is no one left to see your fall so you spare yourself the shame of defeat?"

"The shame of defeat?" In cold anger she threw back her cloak to show her black armor and the naked blade of Whitefire that she leaned on like a cane; its gleam leaped to his eye like a tongue of lightning. "Child of men, I *am* the defeat of our people in the breathing flesh. I have lived with the foreknowledge of my own death since your people gnawed uncooked bones in the forest. I will not survive this day and I know it, but I will not have such as *you* questioning me. Begone, child of a stolen heritage, and do what you will with the end of your own life."

The black murk of her cloak and the dark spikiness of her armor framed her pale, fierce face like storm clouds around the moon. For a moment Barrick saw things in her bottomless eyes he had never seen before, or perhaps in that strange place and time he merely dreamed them, but to his utter astonishment he felt a tear overspill his lid and trickle down his cheek.

"If I have wronged you, Lady, then I ask your forgiveness." He bowed and turned away.

Saqri was waiting for him, her hair strayed from its diadem and fluttering in the strange winds of this deep place like black spidersilk. "Here is the bearer of the Fireflower," she said and the Qar around her stirred and turned away from their enemies on the far side of the cavern. "Now our strength is complete." She looked from Barrick back to Yasammez, who still stood by the base of the cliff. "Did she have a word for you?"

"Yes. Several." He pulled on his helmet. "Lead us, Saqri. I need to smell blood in the air. That will make me stop thinking."

Unexpectedly, she laughed. "Come, then!" she called to the surrounding Qar, who banged spears and swords against their shields or threw back their heads and bayed up at the cavern's ceiling and the moon hidden so far above it, the moon that was in their blood as the Fireflower was in Barrick's. "The hour is upon us! The last of the old years begins to die tonight! Let us show this presumptuous mortal king how the People dance at Midsummer!"

With a shout the Qar leaped forward and raced across the cavern toward the southerners stepping off their boats along the near shore, soldiers as numerous as ants. The Xixians were already nocking arrows and bending bows, waiting for the Qar to come in range.

"Midsummer!" cried Barrick, and the voices within him wept and exulted.

Ferras Vansen had been in battles both fierce and frightening. He had stood with his master Donal Murroy against both bandits and rebels. While scouting he had hidden in a tree for half an agonizing day, knowing that even the slightest noise or movement could bring death because a troop of mercenaries had camped almost directly beneath him. He had disarmed a maddened Southmarch guardsman who had killed his own wife and their four children, wrestling with the man in the smeared blood of his dead family. He had fought the Qar themselves on battlefields as strange as nightmares—but nothing had prepared him for this final deadly struggle deep beneath Southmarch.

By the time Vansen and those Funderlings still able to fight made their way down the cliff, the Qar and their small, silent queen had already flung themselves at the first of the autarch's men to land on the shore. Vansen could not see well enough to guess who was getting the best of things because the light in the monstrous chamber had begun to flicker and gleam as colors he could scarcely recognize pulsed in the depths of the Shining Man the way red heat rippled in the embers of a fire.

"Double-fast, men!" Vansen shouted. "Otherwise the fairies may not leave us any!"

"Ha!" Malachite Copper was gasping along beside him. "I knew the Old Ones to be uncanny—I didn't know they were greedy, too!" Copper's leg had been injured in the final melee in the Initiation Hall but he was limping along gamely, doing his best to keep up. He had cursed when Vansen suggested he stay behind and tend his wound. "Well, Captain, we will just have to take what they leave us."

Vansen looked back. The Funderlings following were wide-eyed with something more than fright, a look that seemed to search beyond the moment and perhaps even beyond their own short mortal lives. Weighted down with weapons and armor, none of them much more than half Ferras Vansen's size, they still hurried to keep up with him, as if after all they had suffered they remained intent on proving themselves. "Sledge Jasper would be proud of you," he called to them now. "He is watching!"

"Make your Wardthane proud, boys!" gasped Malachite Copper, stumbling for a moment in his weariness. They had reached the outskirts of the fighting, a twilight world of unsteady shapes locked in struggle as the stones overhead glowed and then darkened, glowed and then darkened.

"At them!" Vansen's heart was strangely full here at the end, despite all that he had lost, all that he had never had. "At them, my brave men!"

To Beetledown's astonishment, the queen of the Rooftoppers herself was waiting for him when he reached the stables in the ruins of Wolfstooth Spire. His favorite mount Muckle Brown had been saddled and was scratching impatiently—a fine, strong young female flittermouse, dark as sweet ale and almost as large as a pigeon—but Beetledown had eyes only for his mistress.

"Majesty." He bowed as low as he could. "You do us too thickish an honor."

"Nonsense." Upsteeplebat smiled. "You are the best of my scouts, Beetledown. Still, we must not waste time in talk. If the Funderling Chert Blue Quartz says that the hour grows short, then you must fly now into the depths to find this man Cinnabar. Are you ready?"

"Directly, Ma'am," he said. "I had but my oilcloth to fasten tight—some of the ways lie through curtains of water tall as one of the castle doors!"

"I wish I had seen it as you have, brave Beetledown."

"If . . . if all goes well," he said, "perhaps Your Majesty would do me the honor of letting me be your guide. I wot well that my friend Chert and un's kind would be only too proud to show you the great caverns."

The queen's pretty face grew solemn. "And I would love to be shown them. It is a promise, then. If all goes well, you will show me some of these places you have seen, my brave scout."

He feared he would burst out singing at the honor. "Too kind you are, Exquisite Majesty." He finished lashing the oilcloth cloak close around him—it would not do to have anything dangling when he flew through those tight, dark spaces—and then moved toward Muckle Brown, who hunched between her folded wings and stared at the Rooftopper with the cross, bleary expression of a child awakened too early from a nap. Beetledown climbed onto her lushly furred back and sat patiently as the grooms tied him into the saddle and put the rein-rings in his hand.

"Ah!" said Queen Upsteeplebat suddenly. "Do not forget your blade, brave Beetledown!"

"Blade?" He shook his head. "I fear you mistake me for another, Majesty. I have never . . ."

"Never until now. But you have shown yourself not just a brave Gutter-Scout but a queen's paladin as well, and the traditional gift is . . . a sword." She clapped her hands and a small page came forward, carrying the sword as if it were made of precious jewels—which, in a way, it was.

The silver thing was as slender as a cat's whisker and sharper than a bee's curved barb, its hilt wrapped in golden thread. "This is the needle of Queen Sanasu herself, dropped beneath her chair in the Long Ago. Take it, Beetledown. Serve your friend Chert well, and you will serve us all well."

He knew if he spoke much more he would say something foolish. He leaned down and took the sword from her dainty hand, then thrust it through the strap over his shoulder so that the hilt bobbed near his head and the pointy end did not trouble the flittermouse. "Thank you, Majesty." He signaled to the grooms who undid the bat's fetters and stepped away sharply to avoid being nipped. The big mounts were notoriously ill-tempered when kept from flying at night, and sundown had passed hours ago. Feeling her freedom, Muckle Brown leaped out through the arched window of the belfry and into the black sky.

Beetledown prodded his mount with his heels; the bat turned up her wing and swept toward the wall of the inner keep, then over it, swimming through the air in brisk strokes followed by long, gliding moments where nothing moved but the air rushing past. He gave the bat a little more heel and then pulled on the rein. She swung high up into the air, banked so that for a moment it seemed even the moon was below them, then dropped down like a stone, spreading her wings only as the ground rushed so close that Beetledown held his breath.

A moment later they were through the gates of Funderling Town and skimming beneath the carved ceiling that was as lively as an upside-down world. Beetledown only knew one route into the Mysteries, the long and dangerous one Chert had shown him. He could only pray to the Lord of the Peak that he could do what had been asked of him in time.

Ferras Vansen felt as though he were nothing but an eye—as if none of his own sinew and bone remained except that organ of sight. Even the sounds of combat had become so unrelenting that they dulled almost to silence; faces slid past him like the faces of ghosts in a dream, angry, frightened, some even familiar, but he had no time for ordinary thought. He was in the middle of a storm of injury and death and could consider little beyond survival.

The Xixians on the far side of the Sea in the Depths had lined up their archers, and as the first of their manufactured boats reached the shore where Ferras Vansen, the Funderlings, and the Qar hurried forward, arrows hissed through the air, nearly invisible in the unsteady light. One of the Funderlings just in front of Vansen dropped with a shaft in his neck; another went down with one in the meaty part of his thigh. The first man was dead already, but Vansen dropped to the rocky cavern floor beside the second man and removed the arrow as carefully as he could, then tied the man's belt around his leg to stop the bleeding before hurrying forward to rejoin the charge.

With his longer legs, Vansen caught up to the vanguard just as they reached the first wave of Xixian irregulars, many of whom were still clambering out of their boats, doing their best to avoid touching the strange silver liquid of the underground ocean or lake. Some of them looked almost like children trying to keep their feet dry as they leaped from the prows of the unsteady boats to the stony beach. It gave Vansen an idea.

"Shove those nearest to the shiny sea back into it!" he shouted. "They are afraid of it!" It only occurred to him a moment later that the Funderlings might be just as frightened. After all, wasn't this the heart of their religious mysteries?

The Xixian soldiers seemed to be endless, as if the autarch possessed the harvest god Erilo's magic sack and could simply pour out whatever he wanted. Vansen, Malachite Copper, and half a dozen more Funderlings cut their way into the center of a group of Sanian infantrymen, each of whom carried two spears and small arm-shields that were little more than oversized gauntlets of metal and leather. These nearly unencumbered desert fighters were fast and a difficult match for the Funderlings, who got no particular advantage from being close to the ground. One of the little warriors died when a Saniaman threw one of his spears before the groups had even clashed; moments later a belch of fire on the far side of the Sea in the Depths was followed by a vast eruption of dirt and stone as the cannonball struck the ground near Malachite Copper. Two Funderlings were flung through the air, broken and bleeding; Copper himself was lucky to get away with a dozen new cuts made by flying shards of stone.

The Funderlings had been fighting for hours, first in the Initiation Hall, now here in the glittering semidark. Vansen was exhausted, and he knew his troops were, too. Most of the Xixian soldiers here hadn't even taken part in the battle for the hall. Not only were there ten times as many of them, they were all rested.

Unless we can find another way, we've lost, Vansen thought desperately as he gave ground against a tall, grinning Saniaman whose face was a mass of dark tattoos and who used his twin spears so cleverly that it was like fighting two men. Vansen had to make certain there was no one behind him while he concentrated on this nimble enemy, so he backed away from Copper and the others, trying to find an open spot. *Even if we are in the last hours of Midsummer, it doesn't matter—the autarch must already be on that island and he's almost certainly begun whatever he means to do.* The thought spread through him like a poison, distracting him so that a sudden lunge by the half-naked Sanian soldier nearly caught him in the belly. He quickly brought up his shield and gave a little more ground.

Vansen saw that he was being forced too far from his fellows: even if he managed to kill his man, he would have a hard time finding his way back to the relative safety of numbers. The man lunged again, but it was a feint; a moment later, he swiped with his other short, flexible spear, trying to rattle Vansen's helmet or even knock it to the side a little to blind him, but Vansen managed to get the edge of his shield up and deflect it, then spun back out of the way of a second, more serious thrust.

The tattooed spearman laughed, a shrill, disturbing sound. Drunk, perhaps, or drugged. They said the Xixian priests gave their men potions to make them fearless. Some opponents found it terrifying, no doubt, but Vansen found it made him burn with anger. Was he a peasant, to be cowed by some giggling foreign savage while defending his own home?

An arrow snapped past the Saniaman and Vansen both, and in the instant's distraction, Vansen leaped forward, swinging his shield into the man's face while turning sideways to avoid the inevitable thrust of at least one of the spears. The spearhead darted out at him like a serpent, but he sucked in his belly and threw his weight behind the shield, bearing the man backward so that it was all the southerner could do to keep his feet, his arms helplessly flying out to either side for balance. In that moment Vansen kicked out and swept the man's nearest foot off the ground, then put his knee into the man's groin and fell on top of him, staying inside the circle of the reach of the two spears. Before the Saniaman could do more than try to grapple with the weight on top of him, Vansen let go of his shield and pulled his dagger from his belt. By the time the Sanian fighter had shoved the shield aside, Vansen had already struck him twice in the guts with the knife. The man's eyes widened and his mouth stretched as though he would scream, but Vansen kept pounding the blade into his middle and the man vomited blood instead.

Vansen climbed to his feet as the man still lay scraping with his fingers at the stony ground as though he might dig his way to safety. He stepped on the fellow's head and pressed down until he heard the man's jaw snap, then stood up and looked around.

A squad of the autarch's Leopards had set up on the far side of the silver sea and were beginning to fire their long rifles, each shot accompanied by a clot of smoke, so that within moments the men seemed to crouch beneath a tiny thunderstorm. The rifle balls traveled far too fast to be seen, but their handiwork was all too apparent: nearly every shot threw a Funderling to the ground or ripped into one of the Qar. Vansen even saw one of the few remaining Ettins fall back with half his head shot away. Had there been more Leopards, or had they been able to load their filigreed rifles faster, the battle would have ended quickly. Even so, the Leopards and their guns were keeping the Funderlings and Qar from outflanking the Xixian irregulars so that the allies would have to continue taking on the autarch's strength face-to-face.

Vansen had just begun to form an idea about how to attack this hopeless situation when Barrick Eddon came running to him across the uneven stones, the prince's pale face smeared with blood from some small wound, his helmet in his hand and his curly red hair flying, so that for a moment he looked to Vansen like some freakish, supernatural creature, an armored demon with his entire head on fire. It still startled Vansen how tall the boy had grown, how he seemed to have aged years in the matter of a single season.

"We are trapped here, Captain—the hour is almost on us!" Barrick shouted. Arrows sped past him but he did not seem to notice. "If we remain, we have lost!"

"But what else can we do, Highness?"

Barrick laughed, a harsh, wild sound. "I saw you look at the boats, Vansen. You were already thinking it! Come, while Saqri and the others can yet hold the center and distract them. She has told me that in a moment she will stage her play!"

Vansen had no idea what Barrick meant by that, but the prince was right. They had thought of the same thing. They could not fight their way through the Xixian defense by strength alone, but if someone reached the autarch and put a blade or an arrow in him the day might still be saved.

"Which one, Highness? The one on the end?" Vansen knew that they had to stay as far from the center of the fight as possible. If the riflemen on the far side noticed them floating unprotected, they would never reach the other shore. "I'll go—but for the love of the gods, put your helmet back on!"

Vansen and the prince hurried down the sloping shore in a prolonged and painful series of crouches—painful for Vansen, anyway. To his astonishment, Barrick Eddon had not only grown in size, he had grown in strength and grace as well, and even seemed to be freely using the arm Vansen had been told was forever crippled. What had happened to that sulking, red-faced child of a few months ago after Vansen himself had fallen into the dark in Greatdeeps?

He hunched as low as he could while a volley of arrows snapped overhead, the sound of their passing made almost inaudible by the clamor of voices and crash of guns in the great cavern. As he did so, a strange, unexpected thought came to him. Despite the terrible danger all around them, Barrick Eddon was alive and well and had returned to Southmarch. Which meant that Ferras Vansen had *not* failed Barrick's sister, Princess Briony, after all. He might not have carried the prince to Southmarch all by himself, but he had helped to keep him alive. If Vansen lived, unlikely as that was, one day she might release him from her scorn.

Suddenly his heart felt as light as the poets often claimed, light as a bit of down caught on the puff of someone's lips. He had not failed, although so many times he had been certain he had done so. However little Briony Eddon's curses and scorn of him might have meant to her, they had meant the world to Ferras Vansen, had lain upon him as heavily as stone. Now that weight was gone.

"Hurry," Barrick shouted. "Saqri has begun!"

A sound rose behind them, a weird and beautiful moan like the howl of a wolf given words. The queen of the fairies had climbed over the backs of her own soldiers to engage the enemy, her sword sparkling and darting like a hummingbird in a pool of sunlight. It was her voice that rose above the clamor of battle. Saqri had become the focus of nearly all eyes. Her long, slender blade struck and struck again. She danced through the Xixians like smoke, and for that moment they fell back from her in astonishment. Through it all, Saqri kept singing.

Vansen heard a noise and dragged his attention back to his own situation. Two Xixian soldiers left to guard the farthest boat were hurrying forward to intercept Vansen and the prince. He ducked a swipe from one guard's sword, stumbled and rolled, then came up to find the man coming back at him again. At that same moment Barrick Eddon dodged past his own man, snatched the rifle from the man's hands just as the Xixian was lowering it to shoot, and then whirled and hit him from behind with the gun hard enough that the man's chin snapped down against his chest. Before that man had even fallen to the ground, Barrick turned and threw the gun at the other guard like a short spear. It hit the southerner in the head and knocked him onto his back, bloodied and dying. Vansen gaped at the men Barrick Eddon had so effortlessly bested as the prince made his way to the grounded reed boat.

"Gods, it's big." Barrick lowered his shoulder against the bow and began to push. The boat gave a squishy creak but did not move. Vansen came up beside him and began to help him, but it felt like trying to slide a basket of wet clothes the size of a house; Vansen was certain that his own blood was going to burst from his ears before the thing moved even a fingernail's breadth.

At last the boat scraped forward, skidding a few heavy inches. Vansen clenched his teeth until they felt as if they might shatter and pushed harder; beside him he heard Barrick talking quietly to himself. The reed boat shuddered and began to slide, faster and faster until Vansen stumbled trying to keep up with it and found he was already knee high in the silver sea.

"Push a little farther to get it moving," Barrick said quietly. "And when you get in, stay low."

Vansen pushed, walking on his tiptoes, trying not to splash. He was chest high in the silvery liquid now. It was thicker than water but more slippery, shiny and heavy, but less so than actual metal. It was also disturbingly warm. "We're in it—the silver stuff!" It was all he could do to whisper, so strange did the substance feel where it touched his skin, almost . . . alive.

Barrick scrambled up into the boat, then turned and reached a hand down to help Vansen climb up also. Vansen threw himself down in the bottom of the boat, gasping for breath, and watched the silvery liquid run off him, slithering away into the crevices between the bundled reeds. "What is it? What is this lake made of?"

Barrick Eddon had stretched out, too, lying on his side near the far side of the boat. His eyes were half-open and fixed on nothing, as though he could see through the bundled reeds of the gunwales, and perhaps even through the stone of the cavern itself. "You ask, what is the sea made of, Captain? The very last remains of my oldest ancestor." He smiled a little, but it only made Vansen feel cold. "You've been splashing in the blood of a god."

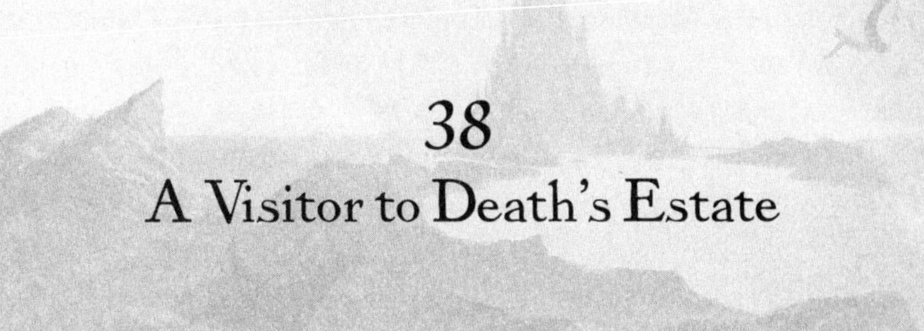

38
A Visitor to Death's Estate

"By the time the Orphan reached the house of Aristas the piece of the sun had burned his hands away to ash. He gave the piece of sun to his friend and then fell down dead at his feet."

—from "A Child's Book of the Orphan, and His Life and Death and Reward in Heaven"

EVERYTHING HAPPENED with astonishing swiftness.

Briony, the Temple Dog soldier, and the Syannese knight Stephanas were making their way silently across the hilly temple yard with nothing but the light of the three-quarter moon, which was just strong enough that Briony didn't notice the lesser light, a dim glow on the overhang at the front of the Eddon family tomb, until they were almost on top of it.

Both fear and fury surged through her. What was Hendon doing in her family's vault?

As she signaled to the Syannese to stay quiet, two soldiers in dark cloaks came up the steps of the tomb together locked in some kind of struggle.

"The dead . . . !" one of them gasped to the other even as he fought with him, so frightened he could barely speak. "He's trying to bring back . . . !" The terrified soldier at last broke free from the other, who seemed to have been trying to restrain him, and sprinted off across the cemetery grounds to disappear into darkness. The other soldier watched him go for a moment with wide eyes, but he must have heard something closer to hand. He lowered his spear and began inching toward the spot where Briony and Eneas' soldiers crouched behind a stone vault.

"Who is that?" he demanded in a quavering voice. "Step out, in the name of the lord protector . . . !"

One of Tolly's men, then. Briony nodded to the soldier with a bow, who stood up and loosed his arrow more or less in one motion. Hendon Tolly's sentry looked down at the slender wooden shaft shivering in his gut as though it were the most puzzling thing in the world, then he folded over and dropped noiselessly to the ground.

Briony led Stephanas and the other Syannese soldier down the stairs. To her surprise, the tomb's main vault, the place where her grandfather, mother, and brother had all been laid to rest, was empty except for the coffins that contained them and other recent Eddon ancestors, but she could hear voices—surprisingly loud voices—in the inner vault. She looked to Stephanas and the soldier, raising a finger to her lips.

"The child," she whispered. *"Remember—save the child at all costs."*

And then they stepped through the short passage between vaults. When they emerged with weapons raised into the light of the inner tomb, Briony saw several figures, the most startling a man with a long knife about to murder the infant prince on some sort of makeshift altar, but before she said a word her Syannese bowman shot the knife-wielder in the chest. The man spun in surprise and then toppled heavily to the floor, his long dagger clinking on the stones as it bounced away.

Hendon Tolly acted almost as swiftly as the archer. By the time the man with the knife touched the stone floor of the crypt, Tolly had thrown the heavy book he was holding at the bowman, knocking his weapon out of his hands. Hendon's sword hissed out of its scabbard. Briony drew hers, too, but Hendon had no intention of anything so civilized as fighting an armed enemy. His slender blade leaped forward like the tongue of a silver snake and hung, barely wavering, above tiny baby Alessandros, who had begun to cry, a strange, homely sound in the middle of such an unhomely place.

"Well, now," said Tolly, his eyes wide and bright in the light from the torches burning in the sconces. He moved a step closer to the infant prince, all the time keeping his blade within a few inches of the child's eyes. "What an interesting evening this has turned out to be!"

"Don't listen to talk," Shaso had always told Briony, usually after dis-

tracting her into dropping her guard. *"It is either foolishness on the part of your opponent, or it is meant to distract. Know where you are."* Briony did her best to follow that advice, though the sight of Hendon Tolly's smirking face only a couple of yards away made her hand tighten on the hilt of her sword until it ached.

Briony had never been inside this inner vault, with its six walls and narrow shelves and dark, deep corners—a chamber that now seemed full to bursting even without the ancient coffins. Besides herself and the two Syannese, the only ones still standing were Hendon and one of his guards and what appeared to be a hostage, a dark-haired woman Briony recognized after a moment as the Summerfield noblewoman Elan M'Cory, the one who had been so miserable about Gailon Tolly's death. Tolly's other minion, the knife-wielder, was lying facedown on the floor in a small pool of blood. But Hendon's sword so near the young prince's throat trumped any advantage Briony had in numbers.

And it was clear that Hendon knew that. "Retreat, Briony, or I will kill the child. You will not take me without losing little Alessandros here. I would happily rob you of a brother as I go." He laughed.

"Is there nothing decent in you?" she asked.

He shook his head. "This is a pointless conversation. You could not understand me if you lived as long as the fairies do. Go slowly back, out of the tomb. If you let me get the door closed, as I should have been minded to do before, then you can do as you wish." He laughed again. "You can call for a battering ram if it pleases you!"

"No. Don't be a fool. I will not leave the child with you."

"I feared you would be stubborn. It is so like you self-satisfied Eddons." Hendon nodded slowly, letting his gaze slide to her guards. "I see you have brought the Syannese to Southmarch." Tolly raised a mocking eyebrow. "Which of course means that you have whored yourself out to young Eneas." His eyes widened at her expression. "No? Truly? Well, then, perhaps to the old man himself. Is that it? Did Olin's daughter give herself to the ancient king of Syan to save her people? How noble!"

It took every bit of strength she had to resist Hendon's goading, to stay where she was. The crying of baby Alessandros was beginning to make her head ache. "Sir Stephanas," she said. "Send your man to find Prince Eneas. Tell him we have Hendon Tolly trapped in my family's vault."

"No! If he even takes a step toward the outer vault," Hendon Tolly warned her, "I will take out this child's eye. The little prince will still be fit for my purposes, but he will scream all the louder."

"Dog! Is this your idea of honor? To threaten children?"

Hendon Tolly laughed so hard it could be nothing but genuine. "Honor? What whey-faced nonsense is that? Do you think I care for such things?"

"Gods! You are filth, Tolly. And even if you keep me here for hours, eventually Eneas will come looking for me. There is no way out of here."

He looked amused at this. "Truly? Well, that is sad."

Briony was desperate to shake him from his certainty, to get him away somehow from the child. "Yes, you are as good as on the headsman's block—and then he'll minister to your treacherous family, too. I will knock down Summerfield House myself and drag your brother and your mother out into the light of day like the creeping things they are. . . ."

Tolly nodded. "If you do, you'll probably find our mother still there, but it's rather a funny story about my brother, Caradon." He laughed. "It seems he's found himself a bit short lately. . . ."

"For the love of the Trigon, Highness!" said Sir Stephanas loudly. "Do not waste words on this coward any more. We have him outnumbered!"

"No, Stephanas . . ." Briony began.

"She's right, young fellow," said Tolly with a grin. "After all, it might *seem* like you have me outnumbered, but there are only two of you and a woman against me—a duo of Syannese, at that. There has never been a day that a few butter-eaters could beat a man from the March Kingdoms . . . !"

"Braggart!" To Briony's horror, Stephanas leaped toward Tolly, striking down at Tolly's sword with his own to sweep it away from the helpless infant, but Tolly only stepped aside and then his slim blade flicked out. Stephanas stumbled, then stood up straight and took another couple of halting steps, blocking Briony's view of Hendon Tolly. Stephanas let go of his sword, then his knees folded and he slumped to the ground, blood pulsing from the socket of his eye. Hendon lunged toward the baby again . . . but Alessandros was gone from the makeshift altar.

"What . . . ?" He saw Briony and stopped. His lips curled, but this time the smile was slow and reluctant. "Well played, girl. You are resilient, you Eddons, I will grant that. Now stop this foolery and give me the child."

Young Alessandros was surprisingly heavy, and squirming and crying on top of it. Briony raised her own sword and slowly pivoted, keeping herself not between Hendon Tolly and the door, but between him and the other Syannese soldier, who was looking at Stephanas' last, gasping moments with round, startled eyes.

"Take the child," she said to the young soldier. "Take him!"

"No!" Hendon moved forward but Briony took a step back, keeping distance between them. "Take the baby, curse you!" she snapped at the Temple Dog. "Take him and run back to the residence. This is the king's son! Get him to safety!"

The soldier reached out his hands, but stared at Hendon all the while like a rabbit watching an approaching snake. Briony pushed Alessandros toward him, then almost sighed with relief as the young soldier took the child. "Run, I said—run!"

Hendon looked as though he was about to say something, but then suddenly lunged forward with a stroke so long and vicious that if Briony's own blade had not been raised enough for her to bring it up with only a flick of the wrist and divert Tolly's attack, his thrust would have gone right through her. He struck and then struck again, so swiftly that it was all she could do to fall back and stay between Tolly and the door, shielding herself behind her own moving blade as he hammered at her.

"Run!" she screamed.

The Syannese soldier at last took the point. In an instant, Briony's last soldier had vanished from the inner vault carrying the infant in his arms. Only when Briony heard his feet scuffing on the stairs leading up from the outer vault did she take a breath. "The child's out of your reach now, Hendon."

"Bitch," said Tolly. He wasn't smiling anymore. "You'll die slowly for that. And, after all, your blood will serve as well as that child's for my sacrifice. . . ." He turned to his guard, who was still holding Elan M'Cory. "Forget that whore. Come and help me with this mannish princess."

A little unnecessary emphasis in his words warned her. Briony turned from Elan and the other guard just in time to save herself from another of Tolly's unexpected attacks.

He quickly forced her back, but instead of letting her get to the door of the inner vault, he kept her moving until he was backing her toward his own guard, but even as Briony realized this she heard a shout of surprise and pain. She risked a swift glance, enough to see that Elan M'Cory had leaped onto the soldier's back and was scratching at his face with her nails. The guard shouted and cursed as he tried to throw her off.

The distraction gave Briony time to avoid Hendon's thrust and keep backing past them, around the outside of the six-sided vault, doing her best to keep Hendon on the other side of the lead coffin that lay in the center of the room. Briony realized that he had forced her into a losing game, and that Elan M'Cory was about to be overpowered by the soldier in Tolly's boar-and-spears livery. Then the odds would be two to one. She feinted twice, then took a wild, swinging blow at Hendon's head that he dodged easily, but did not let herself be carried so far that his following stroke could find her unprotected belly. As Hendon took a step back to set himself once more, Briony suddenly turned and lunged in an unexpected direction herself, slashing Hendon's guardsman across his face. As he dropped his blade and reached up to his bleeding cheeks and mouth, she plucked her long Yisti dagger from her belt and stabbed at him, piercing his mail and sinking the slim blade deep into his belly.

The man stumbled, gurgling, then fell across the lead coffin.

"There's your bloody sacrifice or whatever you were planning, Hendon," she said, keeping the corpse between them as she circled and tried to catch her breath. "Now I'll be happy to send you off to Kernios after him."

Tolly's face was set hard. "You have learned a few things." He feinted, then lunged, then lunged again, the second one actually meant to strike her. It nearly did. She was weary already, but Hendon was not even breathing hard. He was not a big man, but he was very strong, with muscles like braided whipcord. "Was it Shaso who taught you so well, or your new lover, Eneas?" he asked. "I was the one who had Shaso killed, you know. It was by my order that nest of black traitors in Landers Port was burned to the ground. Too bad you weren't roasted with the other birds in that same oven. . . ."

Don't listen, she told herself even as she wanted to weep with rage. *Don't listen.* She dodged another one of his attacks, then a moment later caught a second one on her blade and just ducked under it, but she felt the sharp tip of Tolly's steel pierce her surcoat and for an instant even slide along her neck before she spun away. She was tiring badly; the effort made her lose her balance and almost fall. Hendon saw his advantage and leaped after her, raining strokes on her like a blacksmith hammering at his anvil, so that Briony could do nothing except try to keep her steel between Hendon's sword and her flesh.

But I can't. He's faster than me . . . stronger than me . . . and he always has been . . .

Suddenly Elan M'Cory screamed, a shriek of genuine terror that made even Hendon Tolly take a step back from Briony to look. A dark shape blocked the doorway between the vaults, and now took a shaky step forward into the inner vault.

At first, Briony thought one of the dead out of her family's tomb had risen to stand swaying on the edge of the darkness, its filthy, tattered cloak like a shroud, its deathly face hidden deep in a hood. It reached toward them with hands that looked like ragged claws in the flickering torchlight, still wrapped in the cerements of the grave.

It spoke, but its voice was an inaudible, scraping hiss. The hairs on Briony's neck rose and her heart, already speeding, threatened to burst from her breast.

"B-B-Brothers protect us!" Briony said.

The apparition tried again to speak, and at last words could be heard—ragged, gasping words nearly as painful to hear as they must have been to form. *"Briony . . . !"* the thing scraped. *"I have . . . come back . . . from Death's lands . . ."*

Her breath caught in her throat as the hooded shape took another staggering step into the vault. "Zoria's mercy," she gasped, "is that you, Shaso? Gods preserve us, is that *you*?" But even as she said it, even as superstitious terror gripped her, something seemed wrong.

Even stranger was Tolly's reaction: the lord protector's eyes bulged and his hands lifted as if in hopeless defense against this phantom, the sword he held in one fist all but forgotten. "You . . . ! But . . . but you're *dead*!"

And then Elan M'Cory came crawling across the ground, weeping and praying, and Briony was convinced that the chaotic air of Midsummer had driven everyone around her mad.

The bandaged hands came up and slowly tugged back the hood. At first Briony could make no sense of what she saw—the milky, damaged eyes and the oozing, pale skin worthy of any corpse, blotched all over with what looked like black earth. But then, as the ruined face turned slowly from her to Hendon Tolly, she suddenly knew what she was seeing—*who* she was seeing.

"Gailon," she breathed. "Gailon Tolly."

The thing pointed at Hendon. "*You*," it rasped, each word an agony. "You killed me."

"What is this madness?" But the bluster had gone from the lord protector's voice. "Is this some trick? You were dead, brother. Shot with a dozen arrows. But you are no ghost, that I would swear—you are flesh and blood . . ."

"Your men . . . shot me, brother, then . . . buried me with my servants and friends." Each word came a little easier now, but he still spoke with a halting and ruined voice. "They were not very good shots, as you can see." He bared his teeth in a terrible grin. "Hours, days, I lay wounded in the dark earth with the corpses of my companions, too weak to move . . . but unable to die. I was a stranger in Death's estate and Death did not want me. When I realized I was still alive, I dug my way out of what you meant to be my grave, Hendon, then came back to tell Briony of your treachery." He turned his nearly sightless eyes toward Briony. "But I see you learned too late what my brother is—the rottenest fruit of my father's loins. Now all I can do to atone for my mistake . . . is to end his life."

He took a few uneven steps toward Hendon, who seemed stunned by what was happening. Then the slender, dark shape of Elan M'Cory scrabbled across the ground and grabbed Gailon Tolly's legs.

"No!" she wept. "Don't leave me again, Gailon! Not again!"

"Let go, sweet Elan," the ragged figure said, his voice still the doomful scrape of an unquiet spirit, but he did not immediately pull away, and even seemed for the first time to show something like human emotion. "I cannot . . . I am no longer of your world. . . ."

"And I prefer to keep it that way!" cried Hendon Tolly, who leaped forward and drove his sword into his brother's stomach. Gailon grunted in pain, then he and the girl both tumbled to the floor, pulling the sword from Hendon's hand.

Briony saw her chance and dove toward Hendon Tolly, but he turned just in time to see her coming and managed to deflect her thrust with his hand so that her sword bloodied his palm but otherwise slid harmlessly past him. She stumbled and lost her balance; Hendon shoved her so that she took a couple of helpless steps and fell against the wall by the doorway. By the time she was able to right herself and turn around, sword at the ready, Hendon Tolly had vanished.

She was in the doorway leading to the outer vault, and Hendon hadn't gone past her. There was only one place he could have disappeared so swiftly, she realized, and that was into some deeper vault. She glanced briefly at Elan M'Cory as the woman wept and struggled to pull the blade out of Gailon.

"Get out of here now," she told Elan, then began examining the mossy walls where Hendon had disappeared. As she probed into one of the shadowy corners with her sword, the blade slid far deeper than she expected, encountering no resistance at all when it should have found unyielding stone. She stepped a little nearer and found an opening in the stone where two walls did not come directly together, a space wide enough for a slender man—or a woman—to slip through.

She considered waiting until Eneas arrived, but she had no idea when that might be. If this hidden passage led somewhere else in the castle—if, even worse, it was one of the tunnels made by Chert's Funderling people—Tolly could be out of their reach forever in a short time. The monster and murderer would escape . . .

She thrust her sword into the opening in the wall and poked wildly into the darkness beyond until she was assured no one hid there to ambush her. She wiped the blood off her dagger and slipped it into her belt, then went back and took a torch from the sconce.

Even more vaults waited behind the inner vault, or at least more underground chambers, half a dozen or more. As far as she could tell they had never been used for anything, let alone been finished like the family tomb: the walls were rough and the stone floors raw and uneven. But more worryingly, each new chamber led to another farther down.

Underneath us, behind us, everywhere around us . . . Briony had thought she lived on solid ground—what a bitter jest that had become! Seeing Gailon, whom she and everyone else had believed long dead, had shaken her badly, and finding these passages hidden below the family vault only made things worse. Nothing seemed entirely firm or real anymore.

After some little while spent carefully exploring each chamber in turn, she stepped out of the last one and found herself at the head of a path. The light of the torch revealed that on the path's far side the earth fell away into a dark abyss the torch couldn't illuminate past the first dozen yards. The path itself wound down and away for farther than she could see, with the chasm on one side and an unworked stone wall on the other, like the steps that spiraled around the inside of Wolfstooth Spire. How far down did this passage stretch? And where did it lead? For that matter, where had Hendon gone . . . ?

Just as she had that thought, Tolly dropped down on her from above, where he had been clinging to the wall like a spider. He almost shoved her off the path and into the black nothingness beside it, but Briony managed to twist and fall onto the stone of the edge. Then she struggled back toward the middle of the path, though she dropped the torch to the ground and lost her sword into the pit.

Hendon yanked Briony onto her back and knelt on top of her, his full weight on her arms as he set the cold length of his dagger against her throat.

"I have wasted a great deal of time on you, girl." Tolly's sweat dripped down onto her face. "So I'll just get on with slitting your throat."

He could hear almost nothing else but the soothing voice; its wordless approval, or sometimes disapproval, helped him to find his way, steering his steps through the dark. He felt as though he had been walking for days, but could that be? He struggled to remember where he had been before; it was slow in coming. Strange faces, strange smells, the murmur of unfamiliar tongues spoken by even more unfamiliar creatures. That was it—he had been among the fairy folk. But where was he now? And why was it so very difficult to think?

Chaven Makaros. That is my name. I am Chaven the physician . . . the royal physician . . . ! Those names and titles were all he had of himself, so why did they seem so unimportant?

The wordless voice urged him to go faster, a directive he could feel in his bones and organs. Faster, yes. He had to go faster. He was needed. Nothing could happen without him, and then he would be rewarded.

But why couldn't he remember what his reward was going to be? Or who it was that would reward him?

While the fighting had raged in the Maze, Chaven had made his escape. In truth, it had been a relief to leave Barrick and the bright-eyed Qar behind. Too many questions. Too many curious glances. They were not human, that was certain, and to be truthful, neither was Prince Barrick anymore. There were moments when Chaven had felt quite naked, certain that everyone who passed him could see straight through to his hidden allegiance.

It was strange to think that only a year ago or a little more his life had been ordinary. Then he had found the mirror during some trip to a faraway market, one of the trips he made several times a year, although he had no memory now of bringing it back. Over the following days, as he had cleaned it and wondered over it, his love for an interesting old thing had turned into something more. Chaven had begun to spend long stretches of time with it, polishing the bowed glass and staring into its alluring, sometimes slightly confusing depths. And although he could not remember it happening, one day he discovered he could see all the way though. To the *other side.*

And then . . . And then . . . And then he could not remember what had happened. Not all of it, anyway: sometimes life had still proceeded as normal, of course, the mirror nothing more than an uncomfortable shadow at the back of his thoughts, like a hidden stain. But other times it had made things . . . happen. He had found himself in strange places or situations with little memory of how he had gotten there. The Kernios statue had been one of those things that just happened. He had discovered it in the center of his table one day, and although a visit to the castle archives had helped him to discover what it was, he hadn't remembered anything of how it had made its way to him until that Skimmer man had come to his door asking for money—for the gold Chaven had promised him and his kin for bringing the statue up from the deep bay waters along the outwall near the East Lagoon. The Skimmer swore by his water god that Chaven himself had told them where to dive.

Frightened by this, the physician had sent the pop-eyed man away with a token payment and a promise of more, but then pushed it from his mind as something too disturbing to contemplate. Other gaps had begun to open in his waking life, more and more of them. Now he was trudging through the deeps with this cursed Kernios statue, not knowing where he was bound or why he was carrying it.

But Chaven could not turn back any more than he could leave his skin and become someone else. First the mirror, now the statue—whatever moved him to acquire these things had only tightened its hold, gripping him so surely now it did not even bother to fog his thoughts. He was a tool, he realized. A weapon. He belonged to someone and could no longer pretend otherwise, but he didn't know who his master was.

Chaven of the Makari trudged downward through the lonely spaces beneath the Maze, the sounds of distant battle wafting to him through the warm, dank air.

"Never think when you can feel what is happening," Shaso had told her many times. "*Thinking will get you killed.*"

But she *had* stopped to think, and just as the old man had warned, she was as good as dead now—as dead as Shaso himself. Her sword was gone, and Tolly was sitting on her chest and arms, his weight preventing her from pulling out the long Yisti dagger in her belt. Tolly's knife blade felt like a strip of ice against the skin of her neck. She felt him shift his weight to slash her throat, but at that instant something made a noise in the passage behind them. A footfall? Loose stone pattering down? Hendon Tolly hesitated for just a moment as he turned to look, but it was enough that a desperate Briony could free her hand to make a fist and drive it into the lord protector's crotch.

Hendon Tolly had given up his Tessian codpiece, she was grimly pleased to discover.

He groaned, gagged, and hunched forward, shifting his weight just enough that Briony could tug her other hand free. Before Tolly could get his knife back against her neck once more, she tugged her small Yisti dagger out of its sheath at her wrist and shoved it into the underside of his jaw. His eyes widened in surprise as he reached up to clutch his neck, the blood sheeting through his fingers, and as he stared down at her in astonishment, she yanked the dagger free and stabbed him again, this time in the eye. Hendon Tolly shrieked and clung to her even as his death throes took him; the two of them rolled toward the edge of the path, but Briony could not tear his slippery, bloody hands from her clothing. He would have pulled her with him as he slid over into blackness, but something caught at her belt and held her back from the brink. Tolly's fingers pulled free and for a single moment he turned his blinded eye toward her, the Yisti knife still lodged in the socket and a look of disappointment on his face, then he tumbled out of view.

"My lady . . . Princess Briony . . . are you alive?"

She looked down at the little man stretched on the ground beside her, still clinging to her belt. She could not help laughing a little at the strangeness of it all. "Chert," she said. "Praise Midsummer, you . . . you saved my life." Briony was shaking so badly now she could barely pull herself back into the center of the path. When she was safely away from the edge, she collapsed, panting and shivering, determined that whatever else might happen, she would not cry. "But I have taken back my family's throne—did you see? He's dead. Hendon's dead. I killed him like the mad dog he was."

The Funderling patted her back awkwardly, clearly uncertain of how to comfort a wounded, shaking princess.

At last Briony was able to sit up again. The torch still lay on the path a short distance away, burning fitfully. Chert wrapped a strip of his shirt around her wounded arm. "What's down there, Chert?" she asked. "What lies underneath my family's tomb?"

He looked at her, a little surprised. "Why . . . everything, Highness. This tunnel track leads down into the very depths of my people's sacred Mysteries."

"Where my brother and the Qar have gone." She dusted herself off and rose shakily to her feet. Every inch of her ached. "Where the autarch is. And my father as well." She bent and picked up the torch. "Eneas will take care of the rest. Will you lead me?"

"Lead you?" The Funderling got up too, staring at her as though she had suddenly begun speaking a different language. "You want to go . . . down there?"

"Yes. With you as my guide." She slid her knife into its sheath. "Unless you have something better to do, here on the last day of all."

"But . . . it will take us hours to reach the bottom. Everything will have ended down there long before. You will never reach it in time . . ." A thought occurred to him. "And there are dangers you do not know yet, Highness . . . !"

"Never say never to an Eddon, Master Blue Quartz. We are a stubborn family." And without waiting to see what he was going to do, Briony stepped past him and began to walk down into the depths.

39
The Very Old Thing

"Aristas took the piece of sun and, praising the Three Brothers, he threw it into the sky, where it hung and began to warm the northern lands. Soon the snow was melting from the tip of the Vuttish Isles southward to Krace as the land came back to life . . ."

—from "A Child's Book of the Orphan, and His Life and Death and Reward in Heaven"

THE AUTARCH AND HIS SOLDIERS had dragged the elements of a small city down into the depths and onto the strange island, tents and lumber and the makings of many reed boats. Now a legion of the Golden One's carpenters were laboring to build a great platform near the edge of the silver sea even as a battle raged only a few hundred paces away, so that the clatter of the builders almost drowned out the screams of the dying.

All along the shore blades gleamed and guns barked flame. From this distance Qinnitan could barely make out what was happening, but it looked as bloody and desperate as any of the fighting on the walls of Hierosol. Farther down the shore, the autarch's enemies had made their way in among the landed boats, and one of the small craft had even floated back out into the middle of the shining silver; Qinnitan yearned to be in that loose boat, drifting apart from the madness.

The monster of Xis himself, architect of all this confusion and suffering, sat atop his litter in his bright armor, shouting orders at men who were clearly already working as hard as they could. Several of them were bleeding only a little less than the soldiers in the fighting.

"The children!" Sulepis shrieked, standing up so suddenly that the twelve naked slaves holding his litter swayed and some of them had to struggle to keep their balance. "Where are they? Where are my prisoners?" One of the Nushash priests was leaping up and down beside the litter, trying to tell him something. "I don't care!" the autarch shouted. "Vash! Vash, where are you? By my father's tomb, where is Pinimmon Vash? Is he missing as well? I shall have him and the priest both torn to pieces!"

But before the paramount minister could be found and torn apart, High Priest Panhyssir appeared at the head of a procession of lesser clerics, soldiers, and children, thus distracting the Golden One. Qinnitan stared as the youngest prisoners trudged past the place where she and King Olin stood fettered to a large, deep-sunken post. Four or five dozen in all, the children had the look of northerners, their eyes hopeless and empty, their faces made even more wan by weeks spent in confinement on the autarch's ships. She wondered dully what he planned to do to them.

"Look away, Qinnitan," Olin told her. "Do you understand me? Look away."

But she could not. Here at the end she found herself greedy for every instant, no matter its horrors, because soon she would see nothing at all.

"Hurry them to their places," Sulepis called to the guards. "And you builders, away from the platform—all of you, away! It will serve as it is. The hour is nearly upon us."

The Xandian workmen began to scramble down off the platform, a simple wooden structure as crude and functional as a gallows. Sulepis' bearers carried him forward until he could step from his litter directly onto the wooden floor and look out across the silvery expanse of the Sea in the Depths. To the autarch's left, his soldiers were spread along the island's curved shoreline, many of them firing guns at the struggling armies on the far side of the silver sea, although even Qinnitan doubted they could tell friend from foe in the general confusion. Not that it mattered much. The leader of the attacking force, a slim figure in white armor, had just fallen, and the rest of the outmanned force was retreating. Now they fought just to stay alive against the autarch's superior numbers.

A pair of the autarch's Leopards came toward the post. They ignored

Qinnitan entirely as they unchained King Olin's iron shackles from the post.

"Don't be afraid, Qinnitan," he said. "I am not."

"I'll pray for you," she told him. "May the gods bring you peace, Olin Eddon . . . !"

The king's arms were still bound; the guards kept him upright as they led him away across the slippery stones, toward the platform and the waiting autarch. The Golden One looked back and forth between the reflective stillness of the Sea in the Depths and the massive, man-shaped stone outcrop at the island's center—the Shining Man. The stone seemed dark as black jade, but Qinnitan had seen gleams of color pulsing through it—almost furtively, as though whatever lived inside it did not yet wish to make itself known.

As Olin's guards led him up the crude stairs onto the autarch's platform, the other soldiers herded the captive children down to the shore of the island, then forced them down onto their knees at intervals along the water's edge. Panhyssir the high priest had appeared and had been helped up the steps so he could stand near the autarch. Several other priests were with him, and were already filling the air around the Golden One with incense and the sound of their prayers.

So this was how it ended, Qinnitan realized. All her struggles to escape, all her desperation, all of the times she had thought herself finally free . . . it all had come down to this. She was grateful she had saved Pigeon. But look! As if to prove how pointless rescuing a single child had been, now a hundred other children would be slaughtered here in front of her. Were the gods really so intent on showing her how worthless her efforts had been?

"Those awake cry to those who sleep,
'Here! Our door is open—come through, come through!
We have torn down the wall of thorns.
We have cleared the path of stinging nettles,'"

Panhyssir chanted in a version of Xixian so antique Qinnitan could barely understand it, the high priest's great beard bobbing up and down against his swollen chest. The soldiers around the edge of the island, each one standing by a kneeling prisoner, watched the platform intently.

"You have me," Olin shouted at the autarch. "Now let the girl go!"

Something was trying to get into Qinnitan's head.

"Thank you for reminding me," Sulepis said. "Guards! Bring the girl, too!" Another pair of soldiers hurried to unchain her from the pole and then shoved her stumbling toward the platform, but Qinnitan scarcely felt their rough hands.

Something else is watching us, she realized. The soldiers dragged her up the steps and dumped her beside Olin. Her heart, already beating fast, now began to pound against her ribs like a woodpecker's beak. *That monstrous thing I feel when the Sun's Blood is inside me . . . it's here.*

The cavern seemed to be getting darker, but Qinnitan somehow knew it was not the world but herself that was sliding deeper into shadow. The presence was all around her, yet it was *in* her too, scenting the world of daylight and air through her senses, waiting just on the other side of some incomprehensible door that had been closed against it thousands of years ago.

Here, she realized, her thoughts flailing in sudden terror. *This is where the door was shut, and it's been waiting here all this time . . . waiting to come back . . . !*

"Do not let the Immortal slow your coming!
Do not let the Whirlwind steal your footsteps!
We the dying say to you, the undying, 'Come through!'"

Panhyssir raised his arms in a dramatic gesture, unaware that as he did so an entire world of darkness held its breath like a cat crouching beside a mousehole, stone still but for the lashing of its tail.

"Step through the Gate of Bronze, which the Dragon of Reason guards.
Step through the Gate of Silver, which the Lion of False Belief guards.
Step through the Gate of Gold, where the dark things crouch in shadow, fearful of your bright light and majesty . . . !"

"Now!" The autarch's voice quivered with pleasure and excitement. "Ah, now! The blood!"

The soldiers along the shore grabbed their child captives by the hair and bent back their heads. As each raised a blade to a slender neck, Qinnitan knew that what was happening here was even worse than the murder of children—a hundred times worse! A thousand times! All along the island's coast the prisoners' reflections stared back in horror, a hundred children and then a hundred more mirrored in liquid silver. Qinnitan opened her mouth wide to scream out a warning—didn't they understand what the autarch was doing, the forces he was unleashing?—but the eager darkness was inside her as well as around her and would not let her make a noise.

The blades dipped, slid, and the children fell to the rocky ground as if they were sacks of meal—but to Qinnitan's astonishment the young prisoners were all unharmed, their flesh unmarked; the guards had only pretended to slit their throats. But the reflections of the children, unlike the real children, had been mortally slashed by the reflected guards. Blood fountained from their ruined throats in the reflecting waters of the Sea in the Depth, but in the real world the children still lived; yet a red stain had begun to spread through the silver.

"Do you see, Olin—it is the sacrifice in the mirror lands that matter!" the autarch laughed. Qinnitan could barely hear him through the hammering in her skull, the feeling that her head would split open like rotten fruit. "It only matters what happens there, on the far side—that the mirror is clouded with innocent sacrificial blood!" He spread his hands to take in the whole of the Sea in the Depths. The silver sea roiled with scarlet, a bright stain that was spreading swiftly now in all directions as if real blood had been spilled, gallons of it. "And this is the greatest mirror that ever was—a mirror made from Habbili's own godly essence!" He turned to his guards. "The children are no longer needed. The ritual has succeeded. You may dispatch the prisoners."

"But you accomplished what you wanted—you don't need to do that . . . !" Olin shouted in fury, then his voice choked off in a horrid, ragged sound like something tearing. And then, as the autarch's Leopard soldiers began to stab the helpless, shrieking children who still knelt at the edge of the silvery sea, and chase down any others foolish enough to think they could escape, something began to happen to the king of Southmarch.

Olin's guards held him up, but they did not find it easy: the northern king had begun to twist and moan like a terrified animal, eyes bulging as though something in his skull tried to force its way out through the sockets. All around him, screeching children were being caught up and slaughtered by Xixian soldiers, but Qinnitan could only stare in horror because the same thing that was clearly chewing its way into the northern king was pushing at her thoughts, as well—a very old, very terrible thing.

The surface of the Sea in the Depths was almost entirely scarlet now, and blood from the martyred children puddled in the low places of the stony island, but a hoarse shout from behind distracted Qinnitan even from this horrific scene. Far down the island shore, the loose reed boat had finally drifted across the Sea in the Depths and come to rest. Two men were climbing out of it even as the autarch's soldiers raced toward them. One of the two wore armor of ordinary battered metal, but the other wore plate that glowed a strange blue-gray, and his helmet was of the same unusual hue.

The Xixian soldiers reached the two fighters and fell upon them. Qinnitan was certain the newcomers were doomed, but a moment later the autarch's soldiers fell back, two of them tumbled aside like broken, bleeding toys. The tall one's helmet had come off; his hair was nearly as bright a red as the stain spreading across the silvery sea.

Qinnitan knew him at once, although she had never seen him in the flesh before, and a little strength came back to her. She could not die yet, and couldn't surrender to despair, either. Somehow she must stay alive at least a little longer.

Barrick had come for her.

The prince had hardly spoken as the boat drifted across the strange sea, and had moved only to lean over the side and give the boat an occasional paddle. Now, as the craft scraped over the stones near the shore, Barrick sat up and pulled his helmet on.

When the boat finally grounded he said only one word to Vansen—"Follow"—and then vaulted over the side and into the shallows. By the time the prince had waded to the shore, shiny liquid streaming down his legs until he might have been Perin himself walking through the clouds, dozens of Xixian soldiers were already hastening over the rocky beach toward them.

The first wave reached them just as Vansen caught up to the prince, but before Vansen could do more than lift his ward-ax to defend himself, Barrick had somehow caught several of the attackers and had thrown them all backward at once, as easily as a father wrestling with his children. Someone grabbed at Barrick's helmet and pulled it off, but instead of the sight of his unprotected head giving the enemy confidence they all flinched back from his fixed eyes and broad grin. The prince danced through them, sword flashing like glints of true sunlight; almost every time it withdrew, a Xixian soldier fell heavily to the ground and did not rise.

By the gods, what has happened to that boy? Vansen wondered. *What kind of magician has he become?*

But Ferras Vansen himself had no such magic, nor time to wonder at the transformation of the angry, crippled youth he had known: it was all he could do to defend himself from the Xixians who had instantly sized him up as the less dangerous of the two foes. To his shame, Vansen quickly realized that his best chance of remaining alive was to stay close to Barrick, so he bent himself to protecting the prince's back.

It truly did not seem as though Barrick Eddon needed much protecting. After the initial fury of his attack, the prince's pale face took on a distracted, almost exalted look, like the kind Vansen had seen on paintings of the great oracles in spoken congress with Heaven. But Barrick's actions were in the here and now. Every economical movement seemed to serve a purpose, and no blow was stronger than it needed to be. The prince could block a thrust on one side and still be balanced enough to turn the blade over and dispatch a man who had moved a step too near on the other.

Now Barrick began to fight his way up the beach toward the autarch, who stood a few hundred paces away atop some kind of viewing platform, but every thrust, every block, every body that Barrick kicked to the side also carried him farther into the jaws of the Xixian army.

Time, which for Ferras Vansen was already out of joint, now seemed to slow almost to a halt. Whether they fought their way up the beach for moments or hours, he honestly could not have said—earning each step forward seemed to take a lifetime. The faces of Xixian soldiers streamed past him like the waters of a river.

A rifle cracked nearby; Vansen could feel the hot wake of the ball. Somebody else managed to get a thrust past his defense and agony flared in his already wounded thigh. As he struggled to regain his balance, a heavy Xandian mace crashed against his shield so hard that one of the straps broke. Vansen threw it aside so it wouldn't drag him down, then employed the broad haft of his ward-ax in place of the lost shield.

He was no longer even trying to strike back at the enemy, but instead did his best to turn the closest and most dangerous strikes away from Barrick.

A shout came from the rear of the attacking soldiers. Others picked it up and repeated it, but Vansen couldn't understand the harsh Xixian tongue. Another mace struck his arm, and he almost dropped his ax. By the time he could lift it again, he had become separated from Prince Barrick by several steps, and half a dozen Xixian soldiers quickly forced their way into the gap. Vansen stumbled as they came at him. Someone grabbed his arm, then two men leaped onto his back. He managed to elbow one of them in the face hard enough to feel something break, but his ax was gone and others quickly pulled him down.

Farewell, Princess Briony, he thought as the last strength fled from his limbs and he was finally overwhelmed. *I gave everything for your brother . . . I pray I am forgiven . . .*

But to Vansen's astonishment, no final blow came, no quietus from a spear in the gut or slit throat. Instead, when he was disarmed, his captors dragged him to his feet, used rope to tie his arms roughly behind his back, then began to drag him up the slope toward the autarch's platform.

Perhaps the southern madman needs more blood for his spells . . .

Barrick was still on his feet. Vansen could see the knot of soldiers surrounding him, and for long moments it looked as though the prince might actually fight all the way to the autarch, but the prince's forward progress slowed and then finally stopped, only a dozen steps from where the autarch waited. The struggle went on for a little while, even so—men continued to stumble back weeping with pain, clutching ruined faces or the stumps of missing limbs—but at last the Xixians beat their enemy to the ground. Barrick's red head rose above them as the southerners lifted his unmoving form up onto their shoulders, handling him almost tenderly. He was carried to the platform and thrown onto the raw wooden floor, senseless and bloodied. Then Vansen was tossed unceremoniously onto the platform beside him.

"And what have we here?" asked a voice from high above him—a calm but somehow terrifying voice that spoke Vansen's own tongue nearly without accent. "I recognize you."

Ferras Vansen struggled until he could roll onto his back and look up at the unnaturally tall, brown-skinned youth in golden armor. This must be the autarch himself, he realized, but who would ever have guessed the monster to be so young?

The southern king's gaze flicked to Vansen and he frowned slightly. "Not you, northern dog. You are mud. But your companion—why, this must be one of the Eddon princes. Kendrick? No, he is dead, of course. But, ah, with that hair . . . of course. It is Barrick."

The prince might have heard his name, for he groaned. The autarch laughed. "Look, Olin—your son has come to watch you give yourself to the gods." He turned to a fat priest in a huge headdress. "It is time, now. The door is open. We must bring the god through to enter his chosen vessel."

King Olin? King Olin was here? Vansen did his best to lift his head and look around, and for a moment saw the back of what must be the king's head, but he was bent over and breathing hard, almost gasping, like a woman laboring through a painful delivery.

A boot on Vansen's back shoved him back down onto his face.

"Oh, no, Captain Marukh, let the peasant watch, too," said the autarch cheerfully to the guard captain. "Olin is his king, after all . . . and soon I will be his god!"

The pain was growing, there was no doubt about that. Every drop of Qinnitan's blood seemed to be getting hotter until she felt certain she would cook from the inside like a goat stuffed with hot stones. But it was more than just pain: the very air seemed to have become thicker, something as hard to breathe as water or the silvery stuff that surrounded this island at the bottom of creation. And cruelest of all, now Barrick had appeared before her at last, the one thing she had lived for during her miserable exile, and she was helpless to do anything about it.

Why have you done this to me? she demanded of Heaven. *Taken me from the Hive, dragged me across the known world, tormented me ceaselessly, just to show him to me in the moments before I die? I curse you, gods!*

But if the gods heard her, even at this moment when they seemed closer than ever, they clearly did not care. Barrick lay only a few steps from her but it might as well have been miles. He had been beaten so badly and was bleeding in so many places that she doubted he would ever awaken.

And Olin . . . ! What tortures had the uncaring gods condemned him to?

As the chants of the priests rose again, the northern king finally stopped shaking, but Qinnitan now could barely see him. Something terrifying was happening to her, as if with each moment that passed, her essence was boiling away. All that she was, all she knew and remembered, was beginning to evaporate.

"Groaner! Lifter! Bringer of Winter and Darkness!"

the priest intoned.

"Lord of the Gate
Isolator! Knot-maker! White Root in the Deepest Ground!
Step through to us! Show us Your face.
The door is open!
Step through to us! Show us Your fire!
Arise! Show us Your face!
Arise! Show us Your heart!
Arise!"

Each time the priest cried out that word, Qinnitan cried out too, and Olin made a sound without much humanity left in it. Qinnitan tried to roll toward the suffering king but she could not make herself move and could scarcely hold onto her thoughts.

"Arise!
"Arise!"

Suddenly Olin sat bolt upright, swaying like a hood snake, his mouth split in a clench-jawed grin of intense pain. His eyes had rolled up until only the whites showed.

"The door is open!"

It was so very near to her now—Qinnitan could feel the gap in the world that had been clawed open, and the huge, horrible presence that was forcing its way through. How could the priests go on chanting? How could Sulepis stand so straight, showing no more emotion than the weird half-smile on his face? The autarch, his soldiers, the priests—they all hardly seemed to notice the dreadful presence that was killing both her and the northern king.

Olin's breathing had grown even faster, a chain of rasping, percussive grunts. His arms rose up from his sides like the wings of a bird, as if he was being forced to embrace this terrible visitor. Blood started from his nose and his head rolled from side to side.

Qinnitan felt the thing thrusting itself into the body of the king, but somehow just by being near it burned into her as well. It was climbing into her world . . . into this very place . . . !

A stab of pain made her writhe and for a moment everything went black. When her sight came back, she saw that Olin had thrown back his head, his neck bent at a terrible angle as though he hung on a fishhook. The king's gasping breath had become a single, moaning cry of pain.

"Oh, gods, if you have any mercy, *help us . . . !*" she cried . . . but no god answered.

At the sound of her voice, Barrick's eyes opened. For just that instant, for perhaps the only instant Qinnitan would have again in this world, their gazes met . . . then the hot, remorseless blackness swept over her, swallowing her whole.

40
Fiery Laughter

"When he saw what had happened, Zmeos in fury left his castle behind. Because he could not undo what the Orphan had done, the Horned Serpent fled far into the cold north, to lands where ice and darkness still lived. And all the people of Eion rejoiced to see that the sun burned in the sky once more, and thanked the Three Brothers . . . "

—from "A Child's Book of the Orphan, and His Life and Death and Reward in Heaven"

THOSE WHO DIDN'T FLY THEM didn't know anything about it—flittermice and birds were just different. A bat didn't push as smooth as a bird, and the glide was shorter. A rider also had to cling close to the creature's furry body or else he'd wag from side to side and slow the bat's progress even more.

Beetledown the Bowman knew all this and more—he had been riding on bats since he had been big enough for his father to tie onto the saddle in front of him. People said nobody knew flyers better than old Beetle-wing had, and his son was proud of that legacy. What glory was to be found exploring the heights of the world on a docile rat, or on your own legs? A winged mount was the mark of a true Gutter-Scout.

But his command over Muckle Brown was more than a matter of pride, it was a matter of life and death—especially now. The farther into the depths he flew, the more the fetid air began to affect him as it had when Chert had first brought him down. He was already finding it hard to keep his mind on his journey, and each time his mount flew into a cold downdraft and dropped suddenly, or banked and turned him upside down in a matter of a single pulse, Beetledown felt himself less and less in control of either the flittermouse or himself.

Tha hast promised, he kept telling himself. *Tha hast promised Chert the Funderling and thy queen. Beest tha the man thy father named!* But it had already taken him an hour and more simply to find his way across Funderling Town and through the dark passages beyond the Silk Door, as Chert had once shown him, and more time had passed since then. It was work to stay alert, work to stay balanced on Muckle Brown's velvety back, and Beetledown had already been wearied by days of constant riding and flying when the queen's order had come. As the flittermouse plunged deeper and deeper into the pestilent depths he was finding it very difficult to stay awake.

A new smell tickled his nose, distant but unmistakable, and with it came a gradually swelling murmur, like the sound of ocean that echoed deep in the Royal Spindle Shell. The murmur continued to get louder even as the air itself grew thicker, until the report of his addled senses began to make him think that he and his mount had somehow turned downside-up: surely a roar like that could only come from the great ocean itself! But how could that be? Could he have so badly lost his way?

No, he decided a moment later, *that be no smell of good and honest ocean.* He had encountered the thick, cloying scent before, if not the noise. *No proper sea that, but Chert's foul silvery pond in the earth's heart.*

But where did this scent and the sounds come from? He was still far from the Metamorphic Brothers' temple, let alone the distant deeps to which Chert had sent him—and his time to reach them was also dwindling, he had no doubt.

He hesitated for only a moment before pulling on the reins and leaning to bank the flittermouse hard. Beetledown and the bat sailed on, farther and farther away from the one path he knew. After passing through a long and intricate series of narrow places, one of which was a crevice too tight to fly through, so he had to get out and lead the balking Muckle Brown through it, he began to smell the odd salt-and-metal scent stronger than ever. The echoes changed, too, the murmur spreading to take up space in what was clearly a huge, wide cavern.

But if we are so far from the ocean still, why does it roar so?

He pushed down on the stirrups; the bat dipped her head and dove, spiraling down so quickly that Beetledown could feel the air press his ears until they ached. For what seemed a very long time they swept downward through the vast, vertical tunnel until, with no warning, they dropped out of extended darkness and into a massive cavern whose dimly glowing stones burst out before his dazzled eyes like the stars themselves. For a moment even Muckle Brown was disoriented: the bat hit a wall of cold air and suddenly tumbled into a dive. Only as they plummeted toward the surging, bellowing shapes beneath them—the source, he now realized, of the roar his clouded wits had mistaken for the sea—did he pull the flittermouse back into his control.

Beetledown skimmed the great cavern once, twice, thrice, trying to make sense of what he saw. Many men hurried like ants across an island in the middle of the silvery lake. Some of these appeared to be defending the island against a motley assortment of creatures, many of which looked to be Funderlings, or at least were of a size to be. These must be his quarry, Beetledown decided, but he could not simply drop into the middle of a deadly struggle and expect to survive.

He circled until he found a small group of Funderlings who were snatching a moment of rest on the outskirts of the fighting. He brought Muckle Brown down in their midst. One or two of them started back in surprise, but the rest of the bloodied, filthy little men barely even looked up at his sudden arrival.

"Have a message for Cinnabar, I do!" Beetledown shouted as loud as he could, hoping they could hear him and would not simply swat him or his mount dead. His flittermouse did not like to be surrounded by these giant shapes, and it was all Beetledown could do to hold her down; he could hear the bat's protests at the edge of his hearing, a shrill and angry squealing. But the Funderlings, overcome by exhaustion, only stared at him.

"I need Cinnabar the Magister!" he shouted. "Lord of the Peak blast your ears clean, can none of you hear me? Cinnabar! I am Beetledown the Bowman and I bring a message from Chert Blue Quartz!"

One of the Funderlings pointed back toward the stony cliffs at the edge of the great cavern. "Magister's with his boy," he said. "He's the one in armor. Look for him there."

"I thank 'ee, good sir." Beetledown touched the brim of his hat and kicked at Muckle Brown's ribs. They vaulted into the air. One swift circle to orient himself, then he turned the bat toward the base of the cliffs.

He found Cinnabar sitting propped against a large stone amid a dozen of his wounded comrades. An even smaller Funderling lay beside him, pale and motionless. Beetledown landed only a short distance away, but Cinnabar did not turn from his sorrowful contemplation of the silent child.

Beetledown stood in the stirrups and waved his hands.

"Hear me! I come from Chert Blue Quartz! Are you Cinnabar the Magister?"

The wounded Funderling nodded but did not look up. "I am . . . for a little while longer. Then the Elders will decide." He reached out his hand to touch the boy's slack face. "They have killed my son. They have killed my dear Calomel . . . !"

Beetledown shook his head. "May the Lord lift him up. I grieve your loss and beg pardon, Magister, but my errand cannot wait."

Cinnabar glanced at him without curiosity. "What can any errand matter now? Can't you see we've lost everything?"

"Mayhap. Mayhap not." Beetledown urged the bat nearer, and Muckle Brown reluctantly crawled toward Cinnabar. "But I am sworn to it. Now list. Chert says to tell 'ee that Brother Nickel has stopped un—that Chert cannot go forward to do what was planned."

Cinnabar looked at him for a moment, his eyes dull and his face weary. "It was a foolish hope, anyway. Did you truly come all that way just to tell me of this failure?"

"No!" Beetledown was feeling the press of time very strongly now. "The *Astion*, Chert said. Send the Astion and still there may be hope."

"Ah. Hope." Cinnabar's mouth twitched—the faint ghost of a smile. "The Astion, is it? Even at the end the Guild *will* have their rules followed." He reached to his belt and drew out a leather purse, then shook its contents onto the stone of the cavern floor. Beetledown waited impatiently, listening to the sounds of men fighting and dying on the other side of the massive cavern. The Funderling picked up a shiny circle of black stone etched with a six-pointed star and extended it toward Beetledown. "Can you carry it?"

"If tha canst put un in the pack on my back," the Rooftopper said, "then I can carry un."

"Go then . . . but it will not matter," said Cinnabar. "We are too few, the southerners too many, and we and the Qar spent too much of our strength on each other. Now we are all dead."

But Beetledown could no longer hear him: he and his mount were already rising toward the vast chimney and the upper levels of the Mysteries.

There was no time now to return the Astion to Chert on the surface. Beetledown the Bowman knew he would have to fly directly up the great chimney to Funderling Town and hope that he could use Chert's map to find Chert's friend Brother Antimony from there, and that Antimony himself would be able to do what must be done. But even as they flew, Beetledown was weighed down by grief. What he had seen in the great cavern beneath the earth stank of failure and defeat.

Last hours of all, mayhap, he thought. *For all of us. At least I must do my duty and make Lord of the Peak proud of me.*

As he soared upward toward the cleaner air, he didn't see the black shape detach itself from the perch where it had waited, brooding and patient. The great gray owl banked in gentle circles until Beetledown and the flittermouse had rounded a bend on their upward flight, then it flapped its wings and followed them, eyes glinting orange even in the near-darkness.

For just that moment their gazes met, then the dark-eyed, dark-haired girl called out Barrick's name, convulsed, and collapsed. The Fireflower chorus went quiet in his head. He could hear only one voice—hers.

Barrick . . . ! Wordless now, dwindling as though a harsh wind swept it away. *Barrick, it's . . . the fire . . .*

And then one more voice, his own, drifting up out of the new silence inside him like a forgotten prisoner in a deep cell. *Qinnitan . . . !*

For just an instant he felt what she did—her terrible fear as the end came, the desperate spark of her bravery. And for just that instant, he felt the ice inside him melt away, the hardness that had separated him from his own heart. He was free again, naked of everything, even the Fireflower, but it was a freedom that felt like terrible weakness.

No. Not now. I cannot go back to being that useless thing again . . . ! Barrick forced himself to lift his throbbing head. *Strong. Strong . . . !* Qinnitan lay a short distance away, senseless, perhaps even dead. Blood trickled from her nose; one small drop hung poised, ready to fall from her cheek to the rough boards. For a strange moment, he could not pull his eyes away from that drop of blood, imagined it growing and growing into a vast, shiny red sphere, a *world* of blood into which one could dive and then vanish in living scarlet. . . .

No. He closed his eyes. That was human blood, the same as the thin stuff in his own veins that tried to weaken him. He had to be Qar now.

Barrick tried to stand, but his legs and arms would not support his weight. The Fireflower voices murmured in dismay at his helplessness.

That is how the Dreamers changed me, he realized. *They took the old, weak Barrick away and buried him deep inside me. So I could reach Qul-na-Qar. So I could live with the Fireflower. They buried him and built a wall around my heart to keep it strong.* And in the midst of everything else—the fetid, bursting air and the chants of the priests and even a dim apprehension of the vast and terrible *something* lurking behind it all—Barrick felt the poisonous gift of the Dreamers flowing back again to protect him, to make him safe from his own humanity.

They need me—the People need me . . . !

He got his knees beneath him and did his best to rise, his bruised and bleeding limbs as wobbly as those of a newborn colt. A half dozen of the Xixian soldiers fell on him at once and began to push him back down on his face, but the autarch turned and lifted his hand.

"Stand back, Leopards. I will not make the mistake of underestimating you again, Olin's son. Clearly, your *pariki* friends have given you some sprinkling of their magicks. *Mokori*!"

A massive hand closed on the loose mail of Barrick's armored neck, cutting off his air as it jerked him onto his feet. An instant later, a golden wire thin as a silkworm's strand dropped over his head and he was pulled back against one of the largest bodies he had ever encountered. The autarch laughed and waved his hand again.

"Do not kill him, Mokori! Olin's son will play audience. I suspect he may be one of the few people who can understand what is happening." The autarch stepped back to reveal Barrick's father, twitching on the ground like a man in the grip of a killing fever.

"Look, Olin—if you still are Olin," the autarch crowed. "One of your sons has come to watch you play host to Xergal, the god of death and the underworld."

Each time Barrick moved, the wire tightened around his neck. He didn't think that in his battered condition he could have fought free anyway—the strangler Mokori was almost as big as Hammerfoot the Ettin—but the sight of his father's suffering, even through the Dreamers' deadening spell or whatever they had done to him, made him squirm and struggle despite the noose around his neck.

"Father?" he cried. "Father, can you hear me?" But Olin did not seem even to see him, let alone recognize him. Now Barrick began to feel the greedy joy of the invisible watcher. It fed on misery, somehow—on deceit and shame. That was how it had kept itself alive all these centuries in the dreaming lands . . . alive, perhaps, but not sane.

Suddenly Olin doubled over and fell onto his face, legs kicking like a hanged man's. The sound that came from the king's throat was so desperate and horrible that Barrick's eyes filled with hot tears. Despite all his grievances, despite any wall around his heart, at that moment Barrick would have given his life to save his father from such suffering.

"Midnight is upon us!" cried the autarch. "He comes—the god comes! He enters the vessel!"

"That vessel is a man, curse you to the lowest hells!" Barrick shouted. "He is a king!"

"Come to me, great god—Xergal, or Kernios, or whatever name you wish!" the autarch cried, louder by himself than all the chanting priests combined. "Come to me, Earth Lord—Isolator—Gray Owl—Ageless Pine! I summon you to cross the void! I have made a home for you here!" Both of the autarch's arms spread wide, as though he welcomed a lover. "Enter and be my servant forever—my slave!"

And then King Olin's grunts of pain abruptly stopped. Barrick's father rolled onto his back as though thrown there, and his limbs shot out straight; for a moment his entire body seemed to bulge and distort, rippling from his head to his extremities as though something hot had been poured into his skin.

Barrick heard a shout of misery and recognized it as his own. *I've failed you all*, he thought, battered by the confused and chaotic swell of the Fireflower voices. *Failed.*

Another cry came, this one from one of the Xixians, then more and more, voices of soldiers and even priests, all rising in fear. Olin's body rose from the ground like a puppet being lifted by its strings until he stood upright and motionless. All across the platform and on the ground nearby the autarch's men stumbled back, some making the sign of Nushash with spread fingers like the sun's rays, others openly weeping with terror, overcome by what was happening in this strange place so very far from home. Olin had become utterly motionless, as if he were some smaller replica of the Shining Man that still loomed over them all, the dark, man-shaped shadow at the center of the island.

"Speak to me, servant," said the autarch. "Are you indeed the god of the dark earth?" The thing, Barrick saw, did not look much like Olin anymore.

Thin end of the wedge, the awed voices whispered in his thoughts. *The crack in it all. The last . . . !*

The thing turned its head slowly toward the autarch, and Barrick gasped at how his father's eyes had changed; whatever looked out of them stared out from a crawling tangle of fiery lines that filled the eyes from lid to lid, a squirming glow that bathed even the king's brow and face . . . but it still did not speak.

"I said, who are you?" The autarch's voice had become a little shrill.

"I am he who commands the Owl," it said in a voice of such musical sweetness that for a moment Barrick almost felt glad that he had tasted so much horror, just to hear it. But even as the words faded, he felt the undertaste of boundless cruelty that was in it and it made his gorge rise. *"I am the master of the Knot and keeper of the Pine. I am the Crowfather."*

Sulepis clapped his hands together like a pleased child. "The God of Death—and he is my slave! You are my slave, are you not, Master of the Depths?"

"I am the slave of my summoner as long as he holds me in this world." Again that beautiful, horrible voice made Barrick want to throw himself at the thing's feet and beg forgiveness, or hurl himself into the silvery sea to drown. But the most dreadful thing of all was that it was his father's skin it wore, his father's face being awkwardly moved by those inhuman emotions. How could he have ever thought he truly hated Olin when seeing this wrenched at his heart so?

"Then you must do what I say! You must!" The autarch closed his eyes and went almost completely still as if captured by the transport of lovemaking or religious frenzy. Barrick had never seen such an expression of rapture on a human face.

"As long as I am held here, I will do what I am told," the dead-eyed thing said. *"I will burn this world to its foundations if you so direct me. I will suck the life from every plant and bird, everything that walks and breathes."* And saying

this it laughed, a noise of such melodious horror that the Fireflower voices inside Barrick were shocked into silence again.

This god is insane, he realized. *It has been locked away from the world too long. Like a dreamer who never wakes, it no longer knows the difference between what is outside itself and what is inside.*

And now it had been loosed on the world, its only keeper the madman in golden armor. The autarch had begun to laugh, too, a loud and excited sound that was nearly a shriek of triumph. "Yes! Yes! Mine mine mine!" It was hard to say which of the two sounded less human.

"Make me immortal," the autarch commanded when he had regained control of himself. In the new silence that blanketed the great cavern his voice carried far. "Make me immortal like you!"

"I will not," said the god that wore the face of Barrick's father.

"What?" Sulepis straightened and turned toward the motionless figure. The autarch was taller than the being that had been Olin, but for all his size and the flare of his armor and feathered ornaments, there was no way anyone could have thought the autarch the more powerful. The god burned inside of Olin, glowing so that from different angles the king's very veins and bones could be seen. The skull beneath the king's face might have been made from the same gleaming stone that dotted the great cavern's walls. "Do what I say, or I will destroy you!"

Barrick was still held fast. Some of his strength had returned, but not enough: he was bleeding from many wounds, and bones were broken inside the sheath of his flesh.

"But you cannot destroy me, Sulepis am-Bishakh," the god said in a reasonable tone. *"You and these other mortals have not the power. You cannot compel me."*

"What? Are you saying you *lied*?" The autarch's voice, instead of growing shriller, suddenly took on a tone at once silky and dangerous. "That the promises you sent to me through the great Seeing Glass of the Khau-r-Yisti were meaningless?" The autarch turned as if to address his soldiers, although most of them were cowering facedown on the stony ground, or had retreated to the farther reaches of the island. Only the autarch's household guards, some two dozen of the formidable Leopards, remained on the stand with him and the priests and the prisoners. "Do you think I would not be prepared for such tricks from one of those who have already been banished from the earth once for their treachery?" the autarch demanded. "I will force you in ways you will not like, Death God."

The face of Olin, its glow like the sickly shine of a mushroom in dark earth, curled its lips in a ghastly approximation of a smile. *"Tell me of these ways, little emperor. Or better, show me."*

"A'lat!" the autarch called. "A'lat! Bring the book!"

A small, dark-haired figure, wizened and as bent as an ape, limped quickly forward from the back of the platform, holding a brown, tattered scroll in its knobby fist. It lifted the scroll and began to read the words written there. The Fireflower voices heard the words and shouted their meaning into his aching head.

"Xergal, I name you and bind you!
Kernios, I name you and bind you!
Earthlord, I name you and bind you!
You cannot die but I steal your joy!
You cannot die but I set black ants upon you to bite you!
You cannot die but I set pebbles beneath your skin to itch you!
You cannot die but the wind will blow and disperse your thoughts!
The dogs will bark at your window!
Sleep will never soothe you!
Your bed will be as restless and lonely as a grave without offerings . . ."

As the desert priest intoned the words the wood of the platform began to sway and creak, as though some great weight had been set down upon it. Even the rocks of the cavern wall seemed to rumble in discomfort, shaking Barrick to his core. Beside him, Ferras Vansen began to stir to life, though Qinnitan remained as still as death.

But the thing that had been King Olin, the waxy, gleaming thing that was no longer anything like a man except in form, only listened, motionless and unperturbed.

"Deathlord, by your secret names I punish you!
Master of Worms!
Empty Box!
Iron Gloves!
By your secret names I curse you! You cannot do harm to me in turn!
Burned Foot!

Silver Beak!
King of the Red Windows!
Master and Slave of the Great Knot!
You have disobeyed my lawful summons.
Your heart is mine! Your happiness is mine!"

The priest finished in a howl of imprecations, but when he fell silent. the god still stood, unmoved, his essence burning deep inside Olin's waxy flesh.

"Did you truly think I would let you thwart me, after all I have done?" the autarch cried, his anger too great to let him show fear. "You are trapped, Kernios, trapped in that mortal body! Because as I name you, so I command you—and I know all your names, Skull Eater! And if I choose to destroy that vessel, it may be that you die, too—a true death that can come even to gods!"

"*You know so little.*" The god spread its arms wider. The air grew tighter all through the cavern, making Barrick's ears ache. On the ground beside him, Vansen groaned and grabbed at his head. *"True, you have named a name . . . but it is not mine."*

"Kill it!" the autarch cried. All around, the Leopards came scrambling forward. "Grab this thing and cast it into the fire—burn it like a candle . . . !"

"No." The god extended its hand, and the soldiers fell down clutching their chests as if they had been pierced by arrows, rifles and helmets clattering from their hands. *"You know so little. I am not here, in this pathetic skin. Even with your ceremony, only a token part of my being can pass through to inhabit this twice-usurped king. The rest of me remains trapped in the dreaming lands, where Crooked banished me . . . but now Crooked is dead."*

"But you are my *slave*, Xergal or Kernios or whatever name you choose, Deathgod!" the autarch shrieked. "Nothing you say or do can change that. I have spoken the words of power. I have prepared the way. You have come through and accepted what I set out for you—this mortal vessel with its ancient, holy blood! Now you are mine, curse you, *mine!*"

The god laughed again. It still sounded something like music, but a music that scraped and grated in Barrick's skull until he thought he might fall back to the ground, screaming.

"*Fool,*" said the thing in Olin's body. "*You cannot tame me because you cannot name me. Now look to the foot of the Shining Man and you will see the rest of the answer to my riddle."*

Barrick turned with everyone else. In such a dim place, it was likely he was the only person in the great chamber who recognized the small, portly figure shuffling across the stony island toward the monstrous outcrop. It was the physician, Chaven Makaros, with the stone statue of Kernios clutched in his hand and an expression on his blinking face like something caught in the light when it would have preferred darkness.

"Who is that?" demanded Sulepis, losing control again. "Who is that walking there . . . ?"

"It is my slave," said the thing that wore Olin. *"Do you see what he carries? That is the Godstone, as you call it—the thing you sought in vain. It is the last piece of the Shining Man, and it broke free long ago when Crooked sealed the way with his own life's essence. Ignorant humans made a fetish of it, a statue . . ."*

"Kill him!" the autarch shouted suddenly. "Archers! Kill that creature!"

Before Barrick could even take a breath, let alone try to struggle loose from his captors, a humming cloud of arrows flew toward Chaven a hundred paces away; but although the darts seemed to fly right at him, they landed in a great spatter of loose stones without even touching him. The autarch bellowed in rage and had them fire again, but these, too, could not seem to find Chaven.

"You cannot strike him!" The face of the possessed king looked bloated and inhuman, as if something pressed out from behind the skin. Barrick had seen something like it once, when a drowned man had been fished out of the East Lagoon, swollen into something far more grotesque than any mere dead body. *"I have misdirected the eyes of your soldiers!"*

"I am sorry, Father," Barrick whispered. "Sorry, sorry . . ."

Untouched by arrows, Chaven seemed nevertheless for the first time to be aware of what was around him. He slowed his already plodding pace, then stopped and turned to look back at the autarch's platform.

"Where . . . ?" He turned slowly from side to side but didn't seem to recognize anything he saw. "Why am I here?"

"You are where you should be, good and faithful servant," said the god shining out through Olin's skin. *"Take the Godstone to the Shining Man. Let them be joined again, so that the doorway is completed after all these centuries. . . ."*

"But . . . but why does it hurt so? You promised me bliss . . . !"

"And bliss you shall have. Only complete the doorway."

Barrick didn't understand what was happening, but he knew that the physician was being used somehow as a helpless catspaw and that neither of the monsters that stood on the platform, mortal or immortal, could be allowed to triumph. "Stop!" He struggled until the strangler's wire cut deep into his throat. "Chaven, don't do it! You are being tricked . . . !"

Something hard struck him—the butt of a Leopard guard's gun—and Barrick felt his legs turn limp so that he would have fallen but for the metal noose. A red haze washed over his sight. The physician turned as if he had not heard him and continued across the rocky island toward the huge base of the Shining Man, which had begun to glimmer and pulse.

"Hurry!" screeched the autarch. "Stop him!"

Guards tumbled down the steps of the platform to pursue Chaven, but as their feet touched the stones, they began to waver and stumble like drunken men, then straggled off in all directions as though struck blind.

"Their wits are broken," crowed the god in Olin's body. *"They will never find him. And once the Godstone has rejoined the rest of the Shining Man, you will see what you have truly done, little mortal king!"* It loosed the terrible music of its laughter again. *"Self-important mortals—do you even know what the Shining Man is? It is not a god, but the shadow of a god's last moment on this earth. It is the mark left on the world from the moment wounded, dying Crooked used his own essence to close the door between this world and the worlds beyond the void. But now Crooked is finally dead, and as soon as the Shining Man is whole once more, the essence he left behind will vanish, too . . . !"*

"Why do you do this to me?" Sulepis screamed. The autarch leaped at the god's throat but pulled back his hands with an outraged squeal of pain, waggling them as if they had been burned. "Beast! Liar! Why do you thwart me?"

"Because you are a presumptuous fool!" The spirit in Olin was laughing again. *"You planned for years—I prepared a hundred times longer! You thought to prison me in a body but did not bother to secure the Godstone, and without it, you have no power over me!"* Colors were now running up and down through the Shining Man as Chaven drew nearer to it, milky blues and streaks of dark but radiant purple, even little flashes of red flickering just beneath the surface like summer lightning, as though the great, man-shaped stone were stirring into life.

The strangler finally let Barrick drop to his knees. He gasped in air once more, and the red tide before his eyes began to recede.

Then a new figure stepped into view from a crevice near the foot of the massive Shining Man as though it had been waiting there all along, a strange man Barrick had never seen before, ragged and bearded like a desert oracle. Chaven himself was so deeply in the grip of compulsion that he did not even see the newcomer, but it did not matter—the newcomer saw him very well. The stranger stepped out in front of Chaven, and for a moment they both halted, staring at each other. Then the bearded apparition lifted a piece of very ordinary stone and smashed it down on the physician's head. Chaven slumped to the ground still clutching the Godstone, but the stranger only bent over and continued hitting him with the rock, over and over again until even in the midst of so many horrors Barrick had to turn away. When he turned back, the stranger was standing over the physician's body in triumph, the Godstone now clutched in his bloody hands.

"By all my ancestors," the autarch said in astonishment, " . . . that is Daikonas Vo!"

"Noooooo!" Now it was the turn of the thing in Olin's body to sound astonished and dismayed, its voice suddenly barely human as it bellowed and hissed. "*It cannot . . . ! No! It is not written . . . !*"

The bearded man lifted the gleaming statue over his head and began to stagger back toward the autarch's platform like the winner of some village festival carrying his prize. The guards the autarch had dispatched to stop Chaven were still wandering like madmen and did not even seem to see him. "Vo!" the autarch cried, his voice throbbing with relief and joy. "Daikonas Vo, my wonderful soldier! You shall have a thousand gifts for this! Gold, virgins, spices—anything you name!"

The one called Vo stopped, then lowered the thing in his hands and squinted at it as though he had only just realized he carried a heavy stone statue. He raised his dull gaze to Sulepis himself.

The thing in Olin's body squirmed in frustration and rage. *"Do not give it to him!"* it cried. "*Why will you not do my bidding?*"

Vo looked at the god curiously, but then turned and spoke to the autarch. "You put a thing inside me, Golden One. It is killing me." Vo looked down at his belly. "No, that is a lie. It has already killed me. I can feel it."

"No, that is not true!" The autarch waved his hands in a fretful way that made him for the first time look like the young man he was. "A'lat, come and tell him." He beckoned to the desert priest. "Tell him! Tell my good soldier that we can make him right again. We will cure you, Captain Vo. You have nothing to fear. You will rise high in my service—none will be higher! Do you wish to be master of all this northern land? My viceroy? Nothing easier! Where is Pinimmon Vash? Tell him to bring out the Bishakh charter and I will make it so. Vash? Burning Nushash curse that old stick, where has he gone . . . ?"

Vo staggered a little, and now Barrick could clearly see that the man could barely stand. "And the girl from the Hive . . . ?"

"Of course," said the autarch. "The girl. Do you want her for yourself? You shall have her, to do with as you wish. She is yours—she is no use to me now, in any case . . . !"

Daikonas Vo took a few more steps toward the men, lowering the statue as though it grew heavier by the moment. Some of the Xixian soldiers still on the platform had their arrows nocked, waiting for a command from the autarch to kill him.

"You did not need her," Vo said, so quietly it was hard to hear him.

"What?" The autarch's ears were clearly not as sharp as Barrick's. "What did he say? Do you want more, Vo? Name it!"

"You did not even need her." The bearded man spoke so softly that nearly everyone on the island fell silent to hear him. "You put a demon in my gut to make me deliver the girl to you . . . and you did not even need her for your little mummers' show." He sagged at the waist and the knees, bending until Barrick was certain he was about to collapse. Then he slowly straightened. "And now you want this, too," Vo murmured.

"Leopards . . . !" said the autarch quietly, but his voice was far from calm. "Be ready . . ."

"*But you shall not have it.*" Daikonas Vo turned sharply and heaved the statue back toward the Shining Man as hard as he could. As the autarch and the others watched in gape-mouthed astonishment, it spun through the air toward the suddenly darkened Shining Man; then, as the statue vanished into the rock's great black shadow, the entire stone mass erupted in blinding light. The Xixian soldiers closest to it stumbled back, clutching their eyes, weeping and shrieking, but the autarch let out only a single, agonized shout of despair.

Even as the dazzling glare spread, the cavern began to shiver as if something gigantic had picked it up and begun to shake it. The platform pitched, and those still standing there fought to keep their balance. The blaze that was the Shining Man grew brighter still until its harsh glare had driven away everything else, until it seemed as though the sun itself had been kindled in the great cave.

The Fireflower voices filled Barrick's head.

"Crooked is gone!"

"Woe! The way has finally been opened! Woe to all the earth!"

"The gods will be free again!"

The streaming white light suddenly faded to something duller, a swirl of violet and indigo like a bruise on the air, then even that began to die. The shaking of the cavern became less. For a moment only a tattered black hole remained in the air where the Shining Man had stood, then the body of Barrick's father fell to the ground beside him with a noise like a sack of wet meal. The hole in the air at the center of the island filled with hot, red light, then something stepped through it, bigger than a man and growing every moment, a banked white fire in the shape of a beautiful youth who wore rippling flames as a cloak.

"I MUST NOW DECLINE YOUR GIFT OF A MORTAL BODY," the god announced, towering over all their heads now and still growing. His voice was so sweet that Barrick wanted to impale himself on it and die pierced by its music. "FOR AS YOU CAN SEE, I CAN NOW CREATE MY OWN. . . ."

"No! You are mine, Deathgod!" shrieked the autarch.

The youth laughed, his hair floating around his head in tufts of pale flame. "I TOLD YOU THAT IF YOU COULD NOT NAME ME, YOU COULD NOT TAME ME. I AM NOT KERNIOS, WHO STILL SLUMBERS WITH THE REST OF THE GODS, ALTHOUGH PERHAPS ONE DAY I WILL WAKE MY FATHER TO SERVE ME WITH THE REST OF THE COURT. NO, YOU FOOLISH MORTAL! YOU TRIED TO ENSLAVE A GOD, BUT IT IS YOU WHO HAVE BEEN COZEND BY ME—THE TRICKSTER, AS THE MEWLING QAR NAMED ME. NOW ZOSIM SALAMANDROS IS FREE! AND YOUR MORTAL ARMIES AND YOUR IDIOT CURSES AND SPELLS MEAN NOTHING TO ME!"

I have met this thing before, in a dream in the city of Sleep, thought Barrick, despairing. *"Can you kill the darkness?" it taunted me. "Can you destroy the solid earth or murder flame . . . ?" And it's right. Now that Crooked is dead and the way is open, we can't stop it . . . !*

"COME TO ME NOW, LITTLE SOLDIER!" Zosim thundered. He

snatched up Daikonas Vo, the man who had freed him, and lifted him high into the air. "YOU HAVE SERVED ME WELL—SO I GIVE YOU A GIFT! YOU WILL BECOME PART OF A GOD!" He threw Vo into his flaming maw and crunched him up like a roasted chestnut. "BE PROUD!" Zosim laughed, belching out a cloud of fiery amusement. "NOW YOU ARE IMMORTAL!"

The monstrous figure grew, and the air burned hotter and hotter; men screamed and burst into flame even as they tried to flee him. Now a handsome youth as tall as a temple minaret, the god of poetry and deceit stared down at their helpless struggles and laughed until the very stones of the cavern trembled.

41
Snakes and Spiders

"Many devout people came to Tessideme to see the place where the sun had been returned to the sky, and also to bring an offering to the grave of the Orphan. So many came that, as the years passed Tessideme grew from a small place to a city of high walls, where many people lived, and they called it Tessis."

—from "A Child's Book of the Orphan, and His Life and Death and Reward in Heaven"

THE THING THAT HAD BEEN following him drew closer, and for the first time Beetledown could see it clearly when he turned. It was a gray devil owl, a huge bird with eyes that shone as brightly as lamps even in the near darkness.

Devil owls were night-sky hunters—he had never heard of one so far beneath the ground—but it was foolish to waste time wondering why it was here. The silent predator was right behind him, nimbly matching every swerve that Muckle Brown made and never falling behind more than a short distance. Beetledown could feel the bat laboring as she tried to stay ahead of the monstrous bird, but the owl seemed to glide almost without effort. Three times now it had come close enough to climb above Beetledown's head, ready to drop and strike. Only Muckle Brown's last-moment spins out from beneath it had saved him, and he was less than halfway back to the place Chert had told him to go. Owls could hunt in total darkness if they were familiar with the territory, and with their silent wings and keen hearing, they didn't need much light even in a strange place. Long before he reached his goal, the hunting bird would catch them in its sharp talons, and then both he and the flittermouse would be torn to pieces by that great, curved beak.

It was by far the most frightening journey of Beetledown's adventurous life. He clung tightly to the flittermouse's back, his belly pressed flat against her shoulders and neck to reduce the pull of the wind and to keep him close as she swung rapidly through the narrower spaces of these stony depths, but although there were points where the owl fell back a short way, he and Muckle Brown never got far ahead: the creature was strong, pursuing them with a relentlessness he had never seen in one of the great birds before, as though it had a Beetledown of its own strapped to its back and goading it along. He had already tried twice to hide in small spaces the owl couldn't reach, but it had waited so patiently that both times he had bolted back into flight—he simply didn't have the time to wait.

When he dared to, Beetledown swung back out into the great open spaces of the chimney that had led him in and out of the depths, then climbed as swiftly as he could to gain much-needed upward distance before the monster caught up with him and forced him into the narrower, safer side passages once more. That was also the only way he could keep moving in the right direction; at this frenetic pace, even his own excellent instincts could make no sense of the twists and turns of the smaller tunnels, and he was nearly as frightened of getting lost as he was of being caught and eaten straightaway.

But did it even matter? Hadn't the Funderling magister told him, *"It will not matter,"* or something like it? *"Now we are all dead,"* Cinnabar had said.

All? What did that mean, Beetledown wondered even as he clung to his careening mount. Did it mean the Rooftoppers, too? Could this be the end of his own people—had he no chance of success at all . . . ?

High Lord, do you truly wish nowt more for thy faithful folk . . . ?

His prayer was interrupted by a purr of air, just loud enough to be noticed. Beetledown did not hesitate or turn to look—he knew the sound of an owl's wings close by. He yanked the flittermouse's head to one side and they fell away just as the spread claws drove past, one of the rear talons raking Muckle Brown's wing, making the little creature squeak in pain and breathless fear.

Can't outfly un, he thought. *Can't outwait un, either. Only time afore it claps its foot on us and then it be back to the nest with supper.* Beetledown reached back to try to find the hilt of his sword, but it was hard to grab it as they whirled in and out between the stalactites that dangled from the ceiling of this long, narrow chamber, and which were the only things keeping the devil owl at bay. At last he found the scabbard, which had slipped almost all the way down to his back during the bouncing flight, and then managed to find the hilt; when the next moment of relatively straight flying came he braced himself and tugged out Queen Sanasu's sewing needle.

Never drew a royal sword afore now, he thought sadly. *Ah, well, at least un'll get some use 'fore the end . . .*

He dropped into the first side-branching hollow that appeared to extend more than a few yards, grateful to be riding a flittermouse, which was better by far in such places than any other steed. He did his best to keep close to the top of the tunnel—little more than a wide crack—but it was not always possible; as the bat dove to avoid a series of stone curtains ranged one behind the other, the owl attacked again. Beetledown whirled, almost tumbling from his saddle despite being tied in, then braced and lunged. He managed just to pink the owl's knobby foot behind the claw as it swept past. The bird let out a shrill squawk of pain and beat its wings hard, dropping behind them once more.

Un won't make yon mistake again, he thought. *But un'll come back, doubt it not.*

It was like his worst childhood nightmares. Young Beetledown had often dreamed of being hunted by owls and other birds, of running with helpless, weary legs across broad, open spaces with nowhere to hide as winged shadows grew closer overhead. This time, though, he would not awaken to the comfort of his brothers' and sisters' warm, sleeping forms around him.

Beetledown had now seen the bird several times. It was clearly not being guided by any rider, but wouldn't stop chasing him, either. Was the creature sickened? Mad? Any other owl would have given up long ago.

Twice more it came close enough for him to jab it with his blade, once more in the foot and once when its immense wingtip swept right past his face. Both times the bird let out a cry of rage and protest but did not abandon the chase.

Muckle Brown faltered, lost some height, then struggled to get back to the ceiling again, but the owl had taken advantage of the momentary lapse and had once more pulled above it. Beetledown knew he had only a few instants at the most, so he pulled the reins and turned the bat into the next crevice that led in the direction of the wide chimney, knowing it was his only chance: with the owl above them in this narrow space and his mount tiring so quickly, they would not survive the next strike.

To his exhausted relief, Beetledown had guessed correctly: a moment later they spun out into the wider, echoing darkness of the great chasm, but the owl was right behind them now and there was no way they could outfly it to the top of the chimney . . . if there even *was* a top to it. He banked toward the walls, hoping to find outcroppings along the side that would offer some protection as they flew, but they were still a long distance from the Funderlings' work camp and the bat was exhausted, barely able to keep its wings moving. Even without the owl following them, Muckle Brown would die soon unless she could rest.

Suddenly, a vast winged shape dropped down on him from one side, catching him completely by surprise—he had not known they were so exposed. Beetledown had only a moment to reach out with his blade but he missed his thrust. The owl's talons snapped shut, failing to close around the bat, but they caught Beetledown's saddle strap and tore him roughly from Muckle Brown's back. The bat screeched in pain and fear and tumbled down and away from him, but for a moment Beetledown himself continued to fly upward, as though he might somehow continue his desperate journey even without a mount. A moment later he reached the top of his rise and began to fall again, spinning helplessly through empty air, down, down, down . . .

"Why have I never been here?" the princess asked Chert as they made their way down along the narrow path that circled the immense hole he had come to think of as the Pit. "How could I be so ignorant of a path that climbs down deep into the earth from *my own family's tomb?*"

"This path was built even longer ago than the Stormstone Roads I took you through to reach the inner keep," Chert explained. The madness of these final hours made it almost seem no more than an ordinary confidence. "My ancestors of those oldest days were frightened that . . . that *your* ancestors planned to keep us trapped in Funderling Town, just as we feared it in Stormstone's time. We wanted our own ways of getting in and out."

"You did it so you could break a royal decree?"

"With respect, Highness, you would have done the same if the pick was in the other hand, as we say. Any people will try to protect themselves. That's why we built the Stormstone Roads, and this path, too."

"Explain to me."

Chert did, wondering all the time what the future would be for his folk, if there even was one. *If the Big Folk know everything about us, then we will be at their mercy. And I have done much to make it that way.*

"Because you feared us," she said flatly when he had finished. "All this work, all those workers injured and even dead, because you feared my family." She shook her head. "That is a grim legacy."

The way she said it gave him a little hope. "You are not to blame for what your ancestors did."

"On the contrary, our only claim to the throne is what our ancestors did! If history is meaningless, then so is the Eddon dynasty."

Chert shrugged. "Then perhaps each generation must earn its throne anew."

Her eyes widened a little. "You surprise me, Master Blue Quartz. That is a truly . . ."

Princess Briony never finished what she had begun to say. They had been making their way around an outcropping that forced them uncomfortably close to the inner edge of the path, but now the light of Chert's torch revealed a dark shape sprawled before them.

"By the Hot Lord!" Chert said, then felt a pang at using such blasphemy here of all places, only a short distance above the Mysteries and the Sea in the Depths. "It's the fellow you fought—the lord protector!"

Briony carefully nudged the figure with her boot. "He was no one's protector."

Hendon Tolly's one good eye flicked open. Chert gasped and jumped back, but the lord protector did not move. Tolly seemed to stare up at them, but it was hard to know whether he saw anything. Drying blood and the hilt of Briony's small dagger obscured his other eye.

"You tried to destroy everything I love," she said. "But you failed, Hendon. You will spend eternity with the rest of your kind, snakes and spiders, down there in the dark." She yanked the small dagger out of his eye socket, then before the wound even began to bleed again, she set her booted foot against his chest and shoved him over the side and down into the dark chasm.

Chert's footsteps were growing heavier and heavier with each yard they descended. "Highness," he said, slowing to a halt, "I really cannot let you go any deeper. We must have already reached the depth of Funderling Town—perhaps we could cross over somewhere and then go back that way."

"Where Durstin Crowel and many of Tolly's other murderous followers are preparing a last stand? Why would I want to do such a thing? Are you saying that we cannot get to my father and brother and the Qar going this way?" She turned on him. "Did you lie to me?"

"No, Mistress, no." Chert shook his head. He saw more than a little of Opal in this young woman (though it seemed presumptuous to say so.) Both of them had iron in their spines and neither of them seemed to expect much good out of him. "But every moment that passes brings us closer to some sort of disaster." Now that the moment had come, he did not want to tell her. Such a terrible decision—and the reigning monarch had to hear of it from the simple Guildsman who had made it in her place! "Will you simply trust me when I say we should go no farther? That the danger is too great?"

She still stared at him. He saw no softening at all. "Will I trust you, Chert Blue Quartz? Are you mad? What does that have to do with anything? Almost all who remain of my family are deep in the earth below me, fighting for their lives. Why under Heaven should I stop here?"

Chert saw that she would not budge, let alone turn back, and as he had learned from his life with another stern-minded woman, he also knew he had run out of choices.

"Stay just a few moments, then, Highness, and I will tell you why we should go no farther . . ."

When he had finished, the princess stared. Chert could not even count all the different humors on her face—fear, surprise, and anger were only the most obvious.

"Is this true?" she demanded. "You Funderlings will *bring it down*? Collapse the very stones beneath my family's home? With all who live in it still here? And my family down below at the heart of it all?" Her eyes narrowed. "And you say this was *your* plan?"

"Yes—but it was to happen only if there was no other hope, Princess. And it was more complicated than that—more subtle, I promise . . . !" He did not want to tell her that he thought it was too late for anything now anyway—too late to defeat the autarch, certainly, but too late for his own desperate idea as well. The strength was running out of him like a seam of dry sand. What did any of it matter? He had thought about and dreaded so many things for so long, but had never imagined he might find himself too far from all those he loved in this final hour even to die with them. Folly. It had all been folly.

Princess Briony blinked, nodded once, then turned and resumed walking down the path that wound around the Pit. Chert stirred. "Princess? Where are you going?"

"Where do you think I'm going, Funderling?" she called back over her shoulder. She did not sound as if she thought much of Chert Blue Quartz at this moment. "I'm going to die with my family. You may die as you choose."

"But, Highness, if the gunflour works and the rocks fall . . . !"

She turned on him, her face contorted with fury. For the first time Chert saw that more than just Princess Briony's clothes had changed since the first time they'd met. She had grown not just older, but . . . deeper, somehow. Stronger. And something he could see in her now but not recognize frightened him more than a little. "You have taken a risk that was not yours to take, Funderling," she said. "Now let me do what I must do."

"But it must already be too late . . . !"

"Quiet, you!" She took a step in his direction, and for a moment Chert was actually frightened she might harm him. "Until my father takes the throne again, I am the princess regent of this kingdom. All who live above and below, your folk and my folk, are mine to protect—but you and your fellow stonecutters have taken that from me. Now leave me alone . . . or if you will not do me that courtesy, at least be silent." She turned again and stalked off down the uneven trail into the dark, a knife clutched in each hand. Chert hesitated for a long moment, then hurried after her.

Aesi'uah waited for her mistress to return from the dreamlands. The daughter of ancient Sleep had waited patiently as Saqri and the others had sacrificed themselves, as the autarch's ritual had gone forward, even as the screams of terror echoed through the cavern when the strange, gleaming shape on the island began to grow, as if the Shining Man had taken on monstrous, immortal flesh. Aesi'uah did not mind waiting: she could do little else. She was not a warrior but an eremite and could only wait until her mistress should ask her for her help.

Yasammez's eyes flicked open, black and deep, but she remained where she was a long time, sitting cross-legged on the rocky ground at the foot of the cliff beneath the Maze. At last she rose.

"I am going to die now," she announced. "Take any others of the People you can find who still can walk. Tell them to carry my sweet Saqri and the other wounded and retreat toward the surface as swiftly as they can."

Aesi'uah felt quite sure that Saqri was beyond help, but she bowed to her mistress' request. "What of the Guard of Elementals? I can feel them pressing you for an answer."

Yasammez shook her head. "I have given them my answer, which is *no*—I will not use the Fever Egg. The mortal Barrick Eddon has taught me something."

"Truly, Mistress?"

Yasammez's smile was like a knife slash. In the distance Xixian soldiers were dying in flames at the hands of a jubilant god, their screeching like the far-off cries of birds. "Truly," she said. "Their short lives seem to mean as much to them as the endless spans of the gods themselves—more perhaps. What right do I have, after my own long, Heaven-granted span, to take that away? Perhaps they will even make some accommodation with the returning gods and write an ending I cannot foresee. Our folk have suffered the Great Defeat, but perhaps their story will be different."

Yasammez slid Whitefire from her belt. It glinted like white jade, like a fallen shard of the moon. She held it out and looked it up and down. "Long ago, this mighty blade was wielded by the sun god. It killed other gods." She nodded. "Longbeard himself fell to this blade, and he was said to be the Heaven's greatest warrior. We shall see if it has one last fight in it—if it can spill the blood of one more immortal. A pity that I do not have the sun god's strength as well."

She turned to Aesi'uah. "Approach me." Yasammez then bent and, to the eremite's amazement, gently kissed her brow. "You have been a good servant, Aesi'uah—one of the best I have ever known in all my uncounted years. I hope that when you find your death, it is a kind one. If my many-times-great-granddaughter lives beyond this hour, tell her the People died nobly today. I could have hoped for nothing better." Yasammez turned and began to walk away down the rocky slope toward the silver sea, which was beginning to steam with the Trickster god's spreading flames; after a few steps she stopped and turned. "If the manchild yet lives and you meet him, tell him that I remember his words. I have decided to let his people as well as my own find their ends in their own ways. I hope he understands the burden he must now carry."

And then Crooked's daughter went striding away once more, down to the misty, silvered sea, toward the god she had already faced once and had said she hoped never to see again. Her aspect grew around her as she went, swirling, spreading, dark and fierce as a thundercloud, a small, inky blot set against mounting fires.

❧

Beetledown plummeted through the air tumbling end over end, and in that hurtling instant knew that he had failed: even if he miraculously fell onto the narrow path instead of down into the abyss, even should he survive the cracked bones, he would never be able to make the trip all the way up to the Funderling camp on foot.

But then something caught him.

It folded around him, soft and warm but solid, and for a moment he thought he must have fallen against the owl that had attacked him—nothing else made sense. But a moment later he was lifted up high in the air and the hand that held him opened and he found himself staring into the glowing light of one of the Funderling corals, which shone from a lantern on the head of the pale-haired figure who stared down at him.

"Hello, Beetledown," said Flint. "I thought I'd find you here."

Beetledown could only stare at the familiar, unlikely face in astonishment. "But . . . Chert's son, th'art. What dost tha here?"

"I had a feeling I should be here," the boy said. "And I was right—the Trickster god guessed your task and sent the bird to stop you. But there is no time to talk now. You must be on your way—hurry! Brother Antimony is waiting."

Beetledown couldn't help wondering if he might in truth be lying somewhere stunned or even dead and dreaming this whole thing. "Can't. I've no way for getting there. Yon owl has killed my mount."

Flint lifted his other hand up into the glow of the coral lamp and uncurled his fingers to reveal the brown, furry shape of Muckle Brown. Startled, the bat tried to spread its wings to leap free, but Flint gently closed his fingers over it again. "No," he said. "I caught her, too."

Beetledown could not help himself—he whooped with laughter. "What miracle is this? Something the Lord of the Peak has done, as's not happened since the old days?"

"Perhaps," Flint said. "I'm not certain. But you'd better go."

"The owl . . . ?"

"It's gone. Once it knocked you out of the sky, it had done what it was set to do. It's been released now. I don't think you'll see it again."

"Then help me get back onto yon flittermouse. Perhaps someday, Chert's boy, tha willst be good enough to explain this all to me."

"Perhaps." Flint nodded slowly. "But that's something I can't see."

Muckle Brown was unmistakably weary, but with Beetledown back in the saddle and the owl gone, she seemed willing to try to fly again. "I'll go better slow," Beetledown said. "She's barely able to scrape air."

"Not too slow," Flint said, getting ready to fling bat and rider into the air once more. "Many are waiting on you. And when you see Mama Opal, tell her not to wait for me—she has to go with everyone else. But promise her she'll see me again."

Before Beetledown had time to make sense of all that, he was spinning up into the darkness in a whirl and crack of leathery wings.

42
The Pale Blade

" . . . At last the mourners' prayers reached Zoria, the most tenderhearted of all the goddesses. She appeared to the people of Tessis and asked them what they wished of her, and they told her of the Orphan and how he had given his life to bring back the sun . . . "

—from "A Child's Book of the Orphan, and His Life and Death and Reward in Heaven"

MUCKLE BROWN WAS BARELY ABLE to keep flapping her wings when he finally brought her spiraling down on the makeshift table where the Funderling monk Brother Antimony sat staring at a series of plans scratched on slate. The bat landed heavily and pulled her wings in close, interested only in breathing, careless of what might happen next. Beetledown rolled out of the saddle and scrambled down onto the flat stone.

"By the Elders!" said Antimony, startled. "What is this . . . ?

"I am Beetledown the Bowman, Brother—we have met before." He slipped off his pack and lifted out the Astion, his arms trembling at its weight. "This, from Cinnabar. Un says the stones must fall *now*—that the battle in the deeps be lost."

"But . . . but . . ." Antimony was clearly overwhelmed. "Lost? Is that true?"

"I was there but a short while. That's what un told me." The Astion passed on, Beetledown sagged. "Hast tha any water to drink? I will share it with my mount."

"What? Ah, of course." Antimony rose. "But first I must deliver this news. The men are waiting. They have been stalling so as not to tear everything down, hoping that Chert would succeed . . . !" He shook his head. "Elders! This is a terrible hour. But we must do what we promised . . . we must . . . !" The Funderling monk was still muttering to himself as he ran out to the main part of the cavern where the workers were gathered.

Beetledown crawled across the stone until he could lean against Muckle Brown, who still seemed interested only in regaining her breath. "Th'art good, leatherwing," he told the creature. "Hast done well. Hast done nobly." He patted her. "There be my good girl. And soon summat wet coming."

Soon the end of the world, too, or so it seemed. But at least they would both get a drink of water first.

God of poets, thieves and drunkards.
God of fires.
God of lies.

The names and tales flared in Barrick's mind like details picked out by lightning—Zosim the Trickster stealing the war chariot of Volios, Zosim covering himself in flowers so he could hide and watch Morna the goddess of winter bathe, after which he raped her. He had once disguised his voice to protect himself from the wrath of Perin Skylord, claiming to be Perin's father Sveros returned from the void; now Zosim had disguised himself again, pretending to be Kernios to fool the Autarch of Xis into releasing him back into the world.

The Trickster had returned and the Fireflower voices inside Barrick were horrified: in the old days only the greater powers of the other gods had held Zosim back and thwarted his cruelest whims. Now he was alone in the world, the last of the gods. He was unstoppable.

Only the autarch and the last of his select Leopard troops still stood before the terrifying menace of Zosim Salamandros unbound. Most of the autarch's ordinary soldiers had already fled in panic, many of them trying to wade through the silvery blood of Kupilas to escape the island, only to find themselves caught in its strangely viscous grip and pulled down. Zosim had picked out others for even harsher treatment: as he pointed at them they burst into flames with a noise like a muted thunderclap, their dying shrieks lost in the god's loud merriment.

On the far side of the silver sea, the remaining Qar and Vansen's Funderlings were also in full retreat. The Xixians they had been fighting only moments before ran with them, no longer interested in anything but saving their own lives. Men and fairies were already struggling with each other for the dangling climbing-ropes, desperate to get back up to the Maze and the tunnels beyond.

Barrick's strength was finally returning. He twisted until he could stretch his bonds as tightly as possible; after a few painful moments, the ropes snapped. The Fireflower ancestors, still stunned by the appearance of the Trickster god, were little more than a muddle of confused noise in his head. He found his sword where one of the panicked guards had dropped it and used it to cut Ferras Vansen's bonds, then carefully did the same for the motionless black-haired girl.

Vansen rose slowly and unsteadily to his feet. The girl did not.

"Qinnitan." Barrick knelt beside her, put his face so close he could smell the delicate saltiness of her skin. "Can you hear? Qinnitan, don't leave me!" But it was useless: if she still breathed he could not detect it. The god forcing his way through into the world had burned in Barrick's own thoughts like a glowing ember—how much worse must it have been for her, specially prepared to be a vessel of that god? He blinked rapidly, unable to look at her slack features any longer. Fate could not be so cruel—or could it?

Of course it could. It always has been.

He turned then to the other figure that lay beside her. His father's beard had far more gray than he remembered, but otherwise it was the face he knew so well, one he had loved and hated in almost equal measure. Olin, too, seemed dead, but Barrick could sense a tiny pulse still throbbing beneath his ear. Was there anything left of him inside this near-corpse, or had the god burned it away while he occupied him? Was anything left besides barely breathing meat . . . ?

A tremendous splash startled him from his confusion. The monstrous, beautiful youth had waded into the middle of the silver sea to snatch up a handful of Xixian soldiers who had been trying to swim to safety. The god held the tiny, thrashing figures close to his beaming face.

"DO YOU LIKE THE TASTE OF HEAVENLY BLOOD?" Zosim boomed. "IT IS A HEADY NECTAR FOR MORTALS. DO YOU HOPE IT WILL CHANGE YOU? LET US SEE!"

Even as he spoke, the shrieks of the terrified Xixians altered as they began to stretch and lose their human forms. Barbs of the silvery blood, stretching and growing inside them like thornbushes, began to pierce their flesh. Their eyes bulged with terror and their limbs flailed, but they could not escape what was already inside them. Tendrils of twining silver sprung out of them like vines, lifting them up into the air until they dangled on thorns of their own solidified and shiny blood, like the larder of a butcher bird.

Vansen stared helplessly at the dying Xixians as if he would never move again.

"You must get Qinnitan and my father away from here," Barrick told him. "Take the boat and cross. Lie still. Hope the god doesn't see you."

Now Ferras Vansen turned to look at him, his face pale, his eyes full of the horrors he had seen. "What will you do, Prince Barrick?"

"Whatever I must." He could not help laughing at the idiocy of his own words—what on earth could he do against a god? "Take the girl first—I'll protect my father. Go. Hurry!"

As Vansen staggered off with Qinnitan's limp body in his arms, a huge shadow passed over Barrick's head. He turned, raising his sword, but it was only the god stepping back onto the island. The Trickster was headed toward the autarch and his remaining men, who had just reached the makeshift camp where they had first come up onto the island.

"The cannon, curse you!" Sulepis shouted at his minions. "Kill that thing!"

"OH, YES, SHOW ME WHAT MEN HAVE LEARNED TO DO WHILE I SLEPT!" cried the god, laughing again. "CROOKED THE ARTIFICER SEEMS TO HAVE TAUGHT YOU CREATURES WELL!"

But even though the autarch's men tried to do as he ordered, their cannon had never been meant to fire so high in the air. At its greatest elevation it still did not point higher than the god's knee. Zosim had now grown taller than the famous statues of the Three Brothers in the center of the great Trigonate temple in Syan. The cannon roared, but because the god was moving, the great cannonball hissed past and crashed against the far cavern wall, sending a shower of stone down onto the fleeing Xixians, killing many of them.

The autarch and his guards ran toward the tunnel that led back from the island to the Maze, but before they could reach it, the gigantic Zosim stepped past them and snatched up the cannon that had just been fired. He crushed the great bronze gun into a shapeless mass and then shoved it into the crevice like a bung into a barrel, leaving the autarch and his soldiers with nowhere to go.

"SCATTER, ANTS!" Zosim called down to them, laughing, then began plucking up the nearest of the soldiers, deforming them into ghastly, inhuman shapes even as they screeched and wept in his hands.

Barrick raced across the rocky crest of the island toward the huge figure, his fairy sword gripped tightly in his hand. Vansen was shouting behind him, but he knew the god must be stopped here. In a short time, Zosim would run out of victims, and his thoughts would turn to the castle above.

"Just take my father and the girl!" Barrick called to Vansen. "There is nothing else you can do here."

"I can't leave you!"

"For the love of the gods, man, why not?"

"Your sister told me not to do it! And I promised!"

Vansen's words kindled something in Barrick, a small train of thoughts that nevertheless stopped him in mid-stride. *It's true . . . I am both. Qar and man. The blood in me . . . it is her blood, too. Briony. I remember . . . !*

His walk became a run, as though he could really make a difference—as if he, a mortal, could actually fight against a god.

A pair of unnatural shapes dropped from Zosim's gigantic hand and landed on the stony ground before him—two Xixian soldiers who had been squeezed by the god until they looked like crabs made of melted brown candle wax. They scuttled toward him. Most horrible of all were the helpless, miserable expressions Barrick could still see on their warped faces.

"AND WHERE ARE YOU, LITTLE AUTARCH?" crooned the god, sifting with his immense fingers through the pile of squirming, screaming Leopards and priests he had made. Zosim picked one up and examined it, but shook his massive, fiery head. The thrashing creature in his hand puffed into flames and began to melt and run through the god's fingers like warm grease. He picked up a particularly fat figure—it might have been the Xixian high priest—and popped it like a grape, then licked his blazing fingertips, grinning. "SPLENDID! IT TASTES LIKE WORSHIP!"

"Face one who is not afraid of you!" Barrick scrambled up the slope toward the monstrous being crouched beside a pile of shrieking captives. "Turn, Trickster. My ancestor defeated you and his blood still runs strong!"

But before Barrick could even swing his sword, Zosim darted out a hand like baking-hot marble and snatched him up. The pain was so fierce that it was all Barrick could do not to scream like a terrified child, but his skin didn't seem to burn: Zosim clearly did not want to lose this entertaining moment so quickly. Zosim lifted Barrick closer, his face as big as a house. "ANCESTOR, YOU SAY? AND WHO WAS THAT? SOME MORTAL WHO PISSED IN THE CORNER OF ONE OF MY TEMPLES? SOME VILLAGE LOUT WHO USED MY NAME AS A CURSE, THEN COWERED THE REST OF HIS LIFE IN TERROR I MIGHT HEAR OF IT?"

"No," Barrick said, struggling in the creature's grip. "No, you piece of filth. Kupilas was my ancestor—Crooked, who beat you and bound you!"

"TRULY?" Zosim seemed pleased. He lifted Barrick closer, took a deep sniff of him, each nostril as wide as an arrow port. "AH, YOU DO STINK OF HIM. HOW AMUSING! SO HIS BLOOD STILL CREEPS AND CRAWLS THE EARTH IN MORTAL FLESH! BUT CROOKED IS DEAD, AND I AM FREE. WHAT DO YOU THINK OF THAT, LITTLE ANT?"

"This!" said Barrick, and used both hands to thrust his sword as deep into the monster's hand as he could. With a rumble of surprise and discomfort, Zosim shook Barrick free and let him fall. The landing knocked the breath from him and for a moment Barrick could only lie on the stones, gasping, but he had the small satisfaction of knowing he had annoyed his gigantic enemy.

"THAT WAS A NASTY TRICK, LITTLE ANT. YES, THIS IS A REAL BODY MADE FROM THE DUST AND CLAY OF THIS WORLD. I CAN FEEL THINGS—AND I FELT THAT, YOU LITTLE MORTAL MOUSE TURD." Zosim lifted his foot, ready to crush him. Helpless, Barrick could only look up at the shadowy shape, big as boat being winched up into dry dock. "BUT SOON THE REST OF MY ESSENCE WILL HAVE CROSSED THE VOID AND FILLED THIS BODY," the god rumbled, swaying a little as he waited to bring his foot down. "WHEN THAT HAS HAPPENED, EVEN WHITEFIRE, THE SUN LORD HIMSELF, COULD NOT HURT ME . . ."

"I am not the sun god," a new voice cried; loud as a trumpet's call. *"But I carry his sword. Come and taste its edge!"*

As Zosim turned in surprise, Barrick rolled out from beneath the shadow of the god's great heel and dragged himself as far away as he could. Yasammez stood at the edge of the Sea in the Depths, her face the only clear thing in the murk of her black armor and cloak; her blade, a clean slice of white light, was in her hand.

"YOU WILL DIE, OLD WOMAN." The god sounded pleased, as though he had finally discovered something in this mortal world that interested him. "EVEN WITH UNCLE WHITEFIRE'S PALE PIG-STICKER, YOU CANNOT HOPE TO INCONVENIENCE ME!"

"Perhaps not," said Yasammez. "But perhaps as you said, that body is more vulnerable than you wish anyone to know, little earthbound god."

Laughing, Zosim threw back his beautiful head and the flames leaped higher, so that the stones of the cavern gleamed with yellow light far above him. "This weakness is a nice idea, old woman—but untrue. Come! Show me your mettle!" He held out his hand and a great golden sword appeared there.

Yasammez stepped into the underground sea. The thick, shining liquid flowed away from her like a retreating tide, but even as she neared the center of the Sea in the Depths Yasammez did not sink between the hovering waves; instead she appeared to be growing, so that by the time she reached the far side she was almost half Zosim's size. A cold breeze knifed through the sweltering cavern as she passed, so that Barrick, who had been trying to rise, fell shivering back to his hands and knees.

By the time she had reached the Trickster god, Yasammez was as tall as he was, but where he appeared as solid as stone, the fairy woman was thinner and less substantial, as though she had stretched herself far beyond what was ordinarily possible. Barrick could see almost nothing of her true shape—she seemed as ill-defined as smoke. Only the great, white blade had retained its brilliance and density. It gleamed through the dark lady's own essence like a slice of the full moon.

Barrick finally struggled back onto his feet as the two great swords clashed for the first time, meeting with a sound like a monstrous bell that made the entire cavern throb. He could hear the autarch shrieking somewhere on the island, demanding that his terrified men help him attack Zosim again. Barrick doubted he would find many volunteers. Above his head, the heavenly blades rose and clashed again, over and over until the ringing deafened him. Barrick hobbled toward the gigantic pair. The combatants now resembled some fantastic illusion at the center of the island, cloud-shapes whirling above a troubled sea, blades sweeping before them like the wisps of a growing storm. Zosim's bright flames rippled and stretched, but as if in answer Yasammez only grew darker, more contained.

Barrick dodged through the murk until he saw the great moving wall of Zosim's heel and limped toward it. He stabbed at it as hard as he could, shoving his sword into the weirdly liquid flesh to the hilt, but although he heard a dim rumble of discomfort, as he watched in dismay, the sword itself seemed to melt and vanish, so that only the hilt fell to the ground like the blossom of a broken flower. The vast foot moved suddenly and knocked him flying.

"Run, manchild!" Yasammez's face appeared from the haze above him, grimacing in agony as though she held the weight of all the world and could not put it down. *"You can do nothing here. Even I can do no more than steal his time for a few more moments."* Something crashed against her, and she swayed back, vanishing for a moment in the clouds of her own gigantic essence. The face appeared again like the sun struggling to pierce thick clouds. *"Go! Save those you can. I can give you nothing else . . ."*

Something struck her again, and she shuddered and fell away from him, the whole of her dark mass toppled like a collapsing tower. Her white blade lanced out as she fell, but the monstrous burning shape that was Zosim was too fast, too strong. He leaped atop her and yanked her back upright again, or at least that was what Barrick thought he saw—it was all too blurry, too strange, like a battle in the mud at the bottom of a deep lake. The god's own golden blade hacked at the dark apparition like a great tongue of fire, and Barrick heard the terrible sound of Yasammez screaming in pain, a hideous, wrenching cry that seemed to shake the very stone from the cavern walls.

Someone was pulling at his arm. Barrick turned slowly, as if in a dream, to find Ferras Vansen standing behind him, bloodied and dirty.

"You cannot help her—she said so!" Vansen shouted, struggling to be heard above the sounds of god and demigoddess tearing at each other. "Help me get the others to safety."

"There is no safety . . ." Barrick said, then a great, flaming hand swung down from above and knocked him spinning through the air.

All over . . . at last . . . was all he had time to think, and then blackness burst inside him.

The work crew hurried to place the last of the blasting powder beetles along the base of an immense stone wall that ran the length of Brewer's Store cavern—the "cold wall," as the monks called it. The cavern—a place Beetledown the Bowman had never seen before, and obviously would never see again—stank of sulfur and other, less familiar things, and lay perhaps a hundred feet or more beneath the temple itself. Because it was cooler than most of the other caves, the monks aged their mossbrew in rootwood barrels there, but the precious brew had all been carried away days ago. As far as Beetledown could tell, the beetles—wedge-shaped iron objects the size of a big person's shoe—were all meant to burst at the same time and take down the entire side of the cavern. How the Funderlings thought this would affect a battle taking place much farther below he could not guess.

Beetledown could not sit comfortably after his long time in the saddle, but instead walked back and forth across the raised slab of stone that served as Antimony's writing table, waiting while the monk sent messages up the line to the other, smaller caverns that were receiving similar treatment, each of his hastily-scratched missives sealed with clay and the imprint of the Astion.

The presence of so much blasting powder was making Beetledown very fretful. Since war had come to Southmarch, he had seen what the stuff could do. The roof of Wolfstooth Spire, a sacred Rooftopper spot for as long as anyone could remember, had been blown to flinders by one of the southern cannons, and pieces of all the cardinal towers, including most of the top of the Tower of Winter, lay scattered across the inner keep like a child's broken toys. Yes, the black powder frightened him—but the waiting was even worse.

"Cinnabar, un said that the need were hasty," Beetledown called up to Antimony, who was bent over his plans, sweat beading on his forehead and dripping onto the little slabs of clay on which he wrote. "Un said that t'were almost too late . . ."

"For the love of the Hot Lord, little man, please be silent!" Antimony wiped his face. "I know we need haste, I know Cinnabar and the rest said to hurry—I know, I know, I know! But if we have made an error . . ."

Beetledown didn't know for certain what was going to happen if the Funderling engineers had planned incorrectly, but it was clear it wouldn't be good for anyone. "Tha pardon, Brother. My family always said I had too much to say . . ." He caught Antimony's look of exasperation and fell silent.

"That's the last," said Antimony a few moments later, pressing the Astion into the clay and passing the pile of messages to the waiting courier. "Take the rest to the other works, boy, but this to Brother Salt—he'll check the sums and if they're right, he'll lay the train." The young messenger sped off. With so many men at war, nearly every remaining male worker was either a child or an elder.

Antimony sat back and wiped away more sweat. The young monk's hands, Beetledown could not help noticing, were trembling badly. "We'll have to set fire to the train on the next level—that's the place the powder trails join and can all be lit at the same time." Antimony looked up as someone hurried toward them. "Mistress Opal?" he said in surprise. "Why are you still here? Only the last few engineers remain."

"He's gone!" said Chert's wife. "I can't find him!"

"Your boy?" Now it was Antimony's turn to look fearful. "Flint? Spite him for a rascal, where has he gotten to now? He knows this is your husband's plan—Chert's plan. It's too dangerous for him to be wandering. By the Elders, what is he thinking?"

Beetledown walked to the edge of the slab. "Mistress Opal, I greet 'ee again, and have some happy news which had gone astray. I saw him, your son. It was un who saved both the leatherwing and your servant from yon hunting owl, and who bid me say all was well."

Opal stared at him, eyes wide, then turned helplessly to Antimony. "What is he saying? A bird told him my son was well?"

It took no little time before the Funderlings understood Beetledown's tale, but when he had finally gotten the gist of it across, Opal was a little relieved, though not particularly happy.

"Always, with that child, since the very first . . ." she muttered as if to someone else.

"Go, then, Mistress," said Antimony. "If the Elders will it, you, your brave husband, and your son will all be reunited. Make certain the camp is empty as you go—call out that it is time to make haste to higher ground."

"Come with me, Antimony," she said. "You don't want to wait too long yourself."

He shook his head, but Beetledown thought there was something strange in his face. "Not yet. Still I must wait on Salt Nitre and the last of our engineers and powder-trail men. You go, Mistress Opal. I will join you all presently."

After she had gone, and the rest of the Funderlings in Antimony's employ began to hurry past, Beetledown began to wonder if he shouldn't move on himself. These depths disturbed him at the best of times—after all, he was not just beneath the ground here but several levels beneath Funderling Town itself—but now there was also the little matter of two hundredweight or more of blasting powder, primed and ready, so even a spark might set it off. The very idea made him shiver.

When he began to make his farewells, though, Brother Antimony asked him to wait. "The last of them will be gone in a few more moments," said the monk. "Stay a little longer."

Again he saw that strange expression on the Funderling's face. Beetledown could not sit still, but did his best to pace calmly as the last few engineers hurried past and Antimony marked them off his list of workers. Last of all was Salt Nitre, nephew of Ash, who came down from the level above at a saunter, as if he were involved in something he did every day, which, from the way he talked to Antimony, might not have been too far from the truth.

"All set and primed," he said. "That fuse is miserable short, though. You'll have trouble getting far enough away. Why won't you let me make you a longer one?"

"No time," the monk told him. "If we use something that will burn for half a candle, it will be too late for those down below when it finally reaches the powder." He shook his head. "Perhaps it's too late already—it's taken us a terrible time to finish."

"That's the fault of that snake Nickel, not to mention Chert's idiot brother, the magister," Salt said with an engineer's traditional contempt for authority. "If they hadn't shut us down, we'd have been ready hours or more ago. It's a miracle we had things as close as we did."

"I know," Antimony said. "You and the rest did well, Brother Salt."

The older monk shrugged. "Well, lad, you'd better run like the wind as soon as the train's been lit. It will be a horrid close thing. . . ."

Antimony guided him to the crude steps leading upward toward Funderling Town. "I know, I know," he told the old monk. "Haste, now." As Salt Nitre hobbled up the stairway, Antimony turned toward Beetledown. "And you too, friend—it's time to . . ."

A clatter of footsteps made both Funderling and finger-high Rooftopper turn as Brother Nickel, the would-be abbot, appeared from the same stairwell, his face dark with anger. "By the Elders, Antimony, what madness is this? You have gone too far—I will see you driven from the Brotherhood for this!"

Antimony stared at him. "Why are you here, Brother? You and the rest have been ordered to clear the temple. . . ."

"Ordered?" Nickel shrieked. "Have you lost your mind? I saw that order—*your* order, a mere temple brother. What do you mean by all this? Who could possibly have given you the right to . . ."

"Have the others gone, then?" Antimony interrupted. "Is the temple emptied? You great clod, you haven't kept them there, have you?"

Nickel only stood in astonished rage, his mouth opening and shutting. At last he found his voice. "I will not only see you driven from the order, Antimony, I will see you dragged before the Judgment Chair of the Guild!"

Brother Antimony leaped forward, surprisingly quick for his size—he was the biggest Funderling Beetledown had ever seen—and grabbed Nickel by his collar, then slapped the older man across the face with the front of his hand and the back. "Answer me, fool! Is the temple emptied?"

"Yes, curse you!" Nickel was almost weeping with rage. "You and that meddling mole Chert Blue Quartz have undermined my authority so badly that no one would remain when the order came! I told them not to go, but even Chert's brother, that coward Nodule, has fled back to Funderling Town."

"All blessings on the Earth Elders!" Antimony shoved him away.

Nickel took a few stumbling steps and fell backward to the stone of the cavern floor. "You would have doomed them all if you'd had your way, you fool! Now go, or you will die along with your temple." Antimony grabbed his collar with one hand and lifted the struggling monk off the ground. "Don't you understand? I am going now to put fire to the powder train. We have used a great deal of blasting powder, so if you are still here or even close when that happens, you will be obliterated—your flesh, your bones, even your name. You will become a tiny seam of ash in a pile of collapsed stone, nothing more. Is that what you wish? Then stay and continue with your noise."

Antimony turned his back on Nickel and headed for the stairs. Nickel stared after him for a moment, eyes bulging with rage and fright, then hurried to catch up. After a moment, Beetledown nudged the bat into the air and followed them. They stepped out of the stairwell into another, smaller chamber. At the center, a star of blasting powder stretched its arms out in all directions, the trails of powder disappearing into various crevices and side passages.

Antimony crouched near the center of the star and pulled out his flint and steel. "Now keep going, Nickel, if you don't want your rump singed," he said. "And you might as well be on your way, too, good Beetledown."

This time Brother Nickel did not need to be told twice. The monk raced up the stairs with clumsy haste, but managed to climb only a short way before he slipped and tumbled back down, landing badly at the base of the steps.

"My leg!" he wailed in terror. "I've broken my leg! Ah, by the Pit, it hurts!"

"Blood of the Elders!" swore Antimony. "I can do nothing for you, Nickel. I am staying to make certain the powder trails stay lit."

"Nay, help un," Beetledown told him. Nickel looked like a frightened child now. "Carry un to safety. If tha build'st a little fire for me, I will wait 'ee clear and then light the train."

Antimony shook his head. "Someone must wait long enough to make certain the powder catches. Otherwise, all is lost. That's my task."

Finally Beetledown understood the monk's strange expressions: he had not expected to make it out. "Thy task no more." Beetledown petted Muckle Brown to calm her—the flittermouse was frightened of so much noise, of being on the ground for so long. "Un flies faster than you or any man can run—we'll get out safe. Go now and save yon fellow, Brother. Time does be short."

Antimony wanted to argue, but soon gave in and made a small fire. "Do not lose your life for Nickel," he said quietly. The monk was still sitting on the floor but weeping now as well as moaning. "He isn't worth it."

"But tha dost be, friend monk," Beetledown told him. "Fear not for Muckle Brown nor me. We'll get well clear."

Antimony lifted Nickel and tossed him over his shoulder. "Farewell, Beetledown!" he called at the last visible bend before the way curved up and out of sight. "Don't wait too long!"

Beetledown waved, already wishing he had not done such a stupid, brave thing. And with no one even to see him! Pure foolishness.

But it be what my queen would want me to do, he thought. *And nothing else am I if not her loyal Gutter-Scout.*

When he had counted all his toes and fingers ten times slowly, Beetledown slid out from Muckle Brown's saddle and lifted a bit of wood from the small fire Antimony had left for him. He took the small torch and set it squarely in the middle of the star, then, when the powder began to fizz and burn, he scrambled up into his saddle and urged the flittermouse into the air. They skimmed across the chamber and into the stairwell, and would have been gone to the upper levels, but Beetledown remembered his promise and turned back to make certain the powder train was burning.

Five of the trails had burned perfectly well, but the one that led back to Brewer's Store and the cold wall had sputtered out just halfway across the cavern. He guided Muckle Brown down and took another burning twig to relight it. He watched as it caught and began smoldering forward once more, but he could also see that the other trains had vanished from sight on their way to the other caverns. Then the Brewer's Store train went out again.

Un's got damp, he thought, his heart beating very fast. He could no longer see the other trains and had no idea how long they would burn before reaching the blasting powder. Did he dare to leave? What if the failure of one would mean the failure of all? Or worse, what if it changed the destruction in some way that would make it worse, perhaps even threatening the castle itself and the home of Beetledown's own people . . . ?

He hurried to pick a longer piece of burning stick. "Come, tha," he said to Muckle Brown, then steered her down toward the cavern below.

The trail of powder reached all the way across the floor of Brewer's Store. He chose a spot near the center of the cavern floor and touched it with the lit brand. It sparked, then caught and began to burn its way toward the powder-beetles packed along the cool wall, but even as he goaded the bat into the air once more the fire abruptly raced forward along the train, many times as fast as it had before.

Uphill, was all he had time to realize, *un burns faster uphill*!

He and Muckle Brown shot across the chamber and into the stairwell. He clung to the beast's back, his fingers wrapped so tightly in its fur that he couldn't believe it wasn't coming loose in his hands. The powerful wings beat and the muscles pulled beneath him, beat and beat again as they rushed up through empty darkness. All Beetledown could hear was a sliver of the creature's impossibly shrill voice as it sang for an open way home. Then hot air suddenly surrounded him, squeezing him like a brutal fist, and Beetledown the Bowman and Muckle Brown disappeared into noiseless red light.

43
Fever Egg

"When great Immon had turned away, abashed, Zoria entered the gate. Soon she stood before Kernios himself on his throne of black basalt, the Lord of the Dead, stern of face and cold of eye . . ."

—from "A Child's Book of the Orphan, and His Life and Death and Reward in Heaven"

PLEASE, GODS, do not let him notice me. Do not let him notice me!

It was foolish, Ferras Vansen knew, praying to absent gods to protect him from a god who was all too definitely present, but old habits died hard and he had never been so terrified in his life.

At Prince Barrick's shouted order, he had carried the black-haired girl to the nearest of the reed boats drawn up on the beach, and now he struggled with the even more daunting burden of King Olin's limp body. Madness and chaos were all around. Men who had been burned to death on their feet stood in brittle postures like scorched scarecrows; other corpses lay in smoking piles or bobbed facedown in the Silver only yards from the charred boats they would never reach. A few still lived, but in such horrible condition that Vansen could only pray their whimpering lives ended soon: not even their Xixian enemies deserved such deaths.

Vansen was a soldier. He had often risked his life in combat with other men. In the past year he had fought both the legendary Qar and the autarch's vast armies. He had stood before the monstrous Deep Ettins and even the demigod Jikuyin, the one-eyed giant. Each of them had been fearful, and Vansen had lost track of how many times he had given himself up for dead. This, though . . . this was different. Because what had stepped through into this cavern from somewhere else—someplace Vansen could not even imagine—was an actual god.

A mad god, he thought in rising panic. *And he is going to kill everything I know.*

The cavern was ablaze with Zosim's fiery light. It echoed to his booming, exulting voice. The beautiful, giant youth still struggled with Yasammez, but now with every passing moment he tore away and burned great pieces of the black stuff that made her, and with each attack, she grew a little smaller, a little less tangible. Vansen was astounded that she had fought so long and so fiercely—as terrifying as he had always found her, he would never have guessed she had such power. She truly was the daughter of a god, that was indisputable. But she was matched against another god, and this one was too strong for her.

"CAN YOU FEEL THAT, LITTLE COUSIN?" Zosim bellowed at Yasammez. "CAN YOU FEEL YOUR ESSENCE BEING BOILED INSIDE YOU? THE SALAMANDROS IS FAR BEYOND YOU. I WOULD HAVE BURNED YOUR FATHER TO ASH IF HE HAD FOUGHT ME FAIRLY . . . !"

From somewhere in the swirling, dark cloud Yasammez's face swam up, deformed like melting wax, full of rage and agony. *"You are Liar by name and nature,"* she cried, her voice distant as a fading thunderstorm on the horizon. "*If you had not struck from hiding . . . you would never have wounded him . . .*"

"WOUNDED? KILLED HIM! WITH MY FATHER'S SPEAR!" Zosim's fires blazed again, so that for a moment he became a pillar of white flame that seemed to stretch up through the roof of the great cavern. Hundreds of steps away, Vansen felt the hairs on his arms begin to smolder, his skin to dry and crack, until he stumbled and almost dropped the king's limp body. "YOUR RIDICULOUS, LIMPING FATHER IS FINALLY DEAD," Zosim bellowed, "AND IN A MOMENT, YOU WILL BE, TOO."

"It . . . matters not . . ." Yasammez said, each word its own painful breath, each more faint than the one before. "*I have . . . held you back . . . long enough . . .*"

What does she mean? Vansen wondered. *Long enough? What does she see—or has she lost her wits at the end? We are dying. We are utterly defeated . . .*

The laughter of Zosim was so loud and so gleeful that this time Vansen did stumble. Overbalanced, he fell to the loose stones; Olin's body tumbled from his arms and rolled away. Vansen could barely see through the tears that filled his eyes, tears of pain and exhaustion and the endless, blistering hot winds that raged through the cavern.

Zosim's voice rattled Vansen's skull. "AFTER YOU ARE DEAD, I WILL CLIMB OUT OF THIS STONY TOMB OF MY FATHER'S AND UP INTO THE AIR. EVERYTHING THAT LIVES WILL SERVE ME OR DIE!" Again came the laughter, gusting and crashing, as flame licked the walls all around Zosim's head.

Vansen crawled as fast as he could across the loose stones, praying again not to be noticed. He could tell by the waxing of the fiery light all around him that Yasammez was fading. He reached Olin where he lay, still unmoving and lifeless, then wrapped his arms around the king's chest and began to drag him. He reached the boat and tugged Olin clumsily over the side so that he rolled into the bottom beside the senseless dark-haired girl. The huge craft was mired in the loose stones of the shore; Vansen knew he would not have been able to drag it himself even if he had not been bruised and battered to within an inch of his life. Where was Barrick?

At last, as the great golden blade ripped the dark cloud that was Yasammez into tatters once more, Vansen spotted the blue gleam of the prince's armor. Barrick was not moving. Vansen hobbled toward him as fast as he could.

To his great relief, he could feel the prince's chest moving steadily up and down, though his armor was burned and blackened and the prince's usually pale face was bright red as if he had been dragged through a Midsummer's Bonfire.

Midsummer midnight, Vansen thought. *Who would have thought the world would end on such a day, in such a place . . . in such a manner?* Yasammez was all but defeated, shrunk now to a shape less than half Zosim's size, her great aspect curling further back on itself with each passing moment as the god in her was overwhelmed. Soon nothing would remain but what was mortal, and Zosim the Trickster would make short work of that.

"Prince Barrick! Can you hear me?" Vansen shook him again, but the prince did not wake. He began to drag him toward the boat, Barrick's heels furrowing the stony ground. Halfway there, Vansen had to set him down, gasping in the hot air, never daring to look away for long from the pillar of fire at the center of the cavern as it steadily burned away the resistance of the woman who had been the greatest of all the Qar who ever lived.

As he finally reached the boat, something grabbed at the neck of his armor coat, yanking him backward so that he overbalanced and the prince fell from his arms. A long, curved Xixian blade fell across his neck as he lay on the ground, an edge so sharp that he could feel it cutting his skin merely by resting against his throat.

"Those are *my* prisoners, I think," said the Autarch of Xis, showing all his teeth. Even as he spoke, the pressure grew on Vansen's throat until he could feel blood trickling down his neck. "I will have them back, now, peasant."

"Please, my lady!" Chert pulled at Briony's sleeve again. He couldn't help thinking that in other circumstances people might have their heads cut off for less. "Please, Princess, you can do nothing good for anyone by this course . . . !"

Briony would not even slow. "Sir, I'm sure you are accounted a mighty warrior among your kind, but I am the princess of Southmarch and I am twice your size. If you tug at me again, I will throw you off this path!"

Chert withdrew his hand. He knew even better than she did what a long way down that would be. "But you will be killed!"

"No, everyone I know will be killed if I do nothing!"

With her determined stride and her manly armor, Briony had the look of something out of one of the ancient tapestries—Queen Lily riding at the front of her armies, perhaps, facing the Mantis and his mercenary legions. That the sweet-mannered girl who had run him down in the hills should have grown to this . . . ! Chert could not help admiring her, which made him all the more reluctant to see her throw her life away.

And I'll throw my own life away, too, if I follow any farther . . .

"My lady, please! See sense! I told you what will happen . . . !"

"But it has not happened yet. Perhaps it never will—perhaps you have miscalculated, or your gunflour has got wet." She hurried down the path along the edge of the abyss, trotting when the way grew wide enough, slowing to a walk when it was narrow and the footing treacherous. "Then my family and my friends will need my help even more. No, you will not stop me, sir."

"Unshored, stubborn . . . !" he muttered, but Chert of all people knew stubborn women well. They did not change their ways simply because a man told them to.

I can go with her and die or turn back and perhaps live—if any live through this, that is—and hate myself because I deserted her. Earth Elders, why have you cursed me? Why can I never be master of my own life . . . ?

As if in answer, Chert heard the sound of footsteps rapidly approaching. He stopped. After another step or two, Briony also stopped, staring into the darkness before them, but as the sound grew louder, it became clear that whatever approached was behind them, coming down from the surface.

"Who . . . ?" was all Briony had time to say when a young, dark-haired woman appeared in the circle of torch glow, running fast though she herself carried no light. She scarcely seemed to notice Chert or Briony as she dodged around them and hurried on; a moment later she had vanished into the darkness below them. For a few more moments they could hear her rapid footfalls, but then even those faded.

"What in the name of all the gods is happening here?" Briony said, staring wide-eyed. "How could she see? And why should she run that way, headlong into the dark?"

"I . . . I know her," Chert said. "I know that girl."

Briony was on the move again, hurrying down the path once more. "What do you mean? That was no Funderling—she was almost as tall as me!"

"I have met her—spoken to her. Her name is Willow. She is touched, I think, but she once led me to one of the Qar. . . ."

"Willow? I know that girl, too. Captain Vansen brought her back from the western country—she had been lost behind the Shadowline, he said." She sped her pace a little. "But why would she be hurrying down into the deeps without even a word? And how can she see to run in the darkness?"

Chert couldn't answer. He didn't know why the girl was there. He didn't even know why he was still there himself.

This time they did not hear her until the last moment, when the girl called Willow burst out of the shadows in front of them, hurrying back toward Chert and the princess as though they had only now become visible to her. "Save him! They will hurt him! Please, they are too much for him!" She threw herself down in front of Briony without any care for her own body and wrapped her arms around the princess' booted ankles. "Save him—my Kayyin!"

"Wh-what? Who..?" Briony stammered, but the girl was already scrambling back onto her feet. She grabbed the princess' arm and tried to tug her forward.

"Come! Oh, come! The creatures of fire and wind will kill him!"

Briony allowed herself to be pulled forward into the dark. Chert hastened after them. He could hear the sound of voices before them, one more or less human but others that gusted and whistled like the wind.

They stumbled out into a place where the path widened and saw what at first looked like a tall, slender man in the grip of some terrible palsy, arms flailing above his head and body swaying like a sapling in a fierce breeze—but it was shadows he fought with, Chert saw a moment later, shadows who clutched at him with hands like torn, flapping curtains.

"Help him!" the girl screamed.

Briony only hesitated for a moment, then raced toward the strange struggle with a dagger in each hand. Chert could only stare, wondering again what had happened to the young girl he had seen at the funeral. When had she become this thing of rope and steel?

But it doesn't matter—those dark things will kill her. Then Chert, too, was running, waving his torch and trying to force a frightening bellow out of his pinched throat but not succeeding.

The half-elf was wrapped in a ragged mass of darkness that leaked light like a hooded lantern. As Briony approached, one of the creatures detached itself from Kayyin and floated toward her, billowing like a cloaked man in a high wind. Only its eyes had color, glinting like green garnets.

"Those are old blades you carry," it said as it neared her. The voice seemed to sigh from every corner of the darkness beyond Chert's torch. *"Metal of a tumbled star. They have even wounded some of us in the past, and it is not easy to spite us."* The eyes flared briefly. *"But wounding is not destroying—and you are no mighty warrior, girl."*

Briony had not stopped to listen, but was keeping her two blades before her as she moved in a broad arc, trying to draw the thing away from Kayyin and the other black shapes. "What you say is that you can be hurt, demon." Her voice was tight but surprisingly steady. "That is all I needed to hear. I just killed my vilest enemy with my own hands, so come, then—let's see who ends up the better!"

Briony crossed the knives in a quick flick as she lunged, like a single great pair of scissors. The apparition rippled away from her like smoke, then flowed back again and hooked at her with a ragged claw. Chert swung his torch at the thing's arm, but the brand only passed through; the shapeless thing turned toward him and the darkness of its face seemed to fill his eyes. Chert was thrown backward. He cracked his head against the wall on one side of the path. The torch flew from his fingers and bounced toward the edge, landing a pace short; the flames rippled and nearly died, then flared up again.

Chert tried to rise, but it was not only the unsteady flames that made things before him tilt and spin. His head felt like it was full of bees, and his legs had no feeling at all. *Earth Elders,* he thought, *I can't die, not like this, not at the edge of someone else's fight and away from Opal. . . .*

The flapping, flickering thing that had spoken before swirled around Briony like mist, then slid just out of reach again when she swung her blades, as if it mocked her.

"Come close enough for me to kill you, you coward!" she said, her breath coming in gasps. "Queen Saqri swore that your kind would be our allies!"

"*Saqri does not speak for us—and a mortal cannot kill an Elemental,*" the thing said in a gleeful tone. "*I am Shadow's Cauldron and my doom is written down in the Book for long after you will be dust. Besides, I only sought to amuse myself until our task could be completed. Sisters? Have you taken our prize back from the thief?*"

The other shadows lay stretched over the half-Qar Kayyin like black blankets, but at the sound of Shadow's Cauldron's voice they fluttered up into the air. Balanced in the overlap of their two darknesses was a large stone that gleamed yellow and roiled like muddy water. "*We have it,*" they declared, and it was their thoughts Briony understood, not their words.

"*Yasammez is his mother,*" one of the Elementals cried. "*She must have told him of the Egg!*"

"*No,*" said the other. "*He saw it in her thoughts.*"

"*Take it, then,*" cried the one called Shadow's Cauldron. "*How he learned of it does not matter!*" The Elemental waved a ragged appendage and

Briony was flung down, her knives clattering from her hands. Shadow's Cauldron then blew away like mist and re-formed a heartbeat later in midair above the abyss, flapping now like some great, fire-eyed bat. *"Now take the Egg and drop it onto hard stone, sisters. Crack it open and let death spill out for all these warm, fleshy creatures!"*

All the shadowy shapes flew up into the heights so quickly that they might have been blown there by a howling wind. Only the gleam of their watching eyes and the sickly sheen of the Egg showed Chert where they hovered.

"The bodiless thoughts of the Deep Library helped us create this, but they did not have the courage to use it! Neither did Yasammez—in the end she died as much a coward as even Ynnir the Traitor. But we are different—we are the Guard of Elementals!" The calm certainty in the thing's hissing voice grabbed at Chert's innards like an icy hand. *"We have nurtured it in our darkest garden and made it even more potent than Yasammez could have dreamed."*

"The Egg must not be broken," croaked a weak voice. Kayyin crawled shakily onto his feet, so close Chert could almost have touched him. "When the fevers hatch out they will not just destroy what is in the castle but will creep up and down the earth for years to come, until there is nothing left that breathes," the half-fairy said.

"Yes!" crowed Shadow's Cauldron. *"Our children will dance beneath the moon, with all the empty lands and seas to themselves. . . . !"* Its voice rose like a shrieking gale. *"Cast the Egg down, sisters, and scour this sullied earth clean again . . . !"*

"Those are *my* prisoners." Of all those in the cavern, dead or still clinging to life, the autarch alone looked as though he had walked in from somewhere else. Sulepis was free of burns and only lightly touched with ash, his golden armor gleaming with the reflected light of the flames all around. The autarch's falcon-crested helmet had been pushed high on his perspiring brow and his eyes bulged with an insane fury that Vansen had never seen before in any man. "And this boat is mine, too. What have you put there, dog—what else have you stolen from me? Ah, it is another Eddon, the fire-haired one. More ancient blood to be spilled, then, yes, more blood." Although his knife pushed ever harder against Vansen's neck, the autarch scarcely seemed to notice him. "Surely I can find another of Heaven's prisoners—another sleeping god who will bargain for his freedom and rid me of this turbulent, treacherous Trickster," Sulepis said. "No, the gods are not yet done with me—I will repay them for this slight. Who do they think they are?" His eyes turned back to Vansen. "I am the *Golden One*! I am the Living Sun!"

Vansen had to speak through clenched teeth. He fully expected these would be his last words. "You . . . are . . . only . . . another . . . fool."

"What?" The autarch leaned down, pressing a little harder on the knife, spreading his knees to hold down Vansen's shoulders and stop his struggling. "What are *you*? One of the Southmarch peasants?"

"I would rather . . ." Vansen's voice was barely a whisper; the autarch leaned closer. "I would rather be . . . the lowliest sheepherder in Southmarch . . . than you in your golden armor . . ." Vansen had not been struggling at all, but reaching for a stone; he grabbed it and smashed it as hard as he could against the autarch's gleaming falcon helmet.

Vansen had little strength left. The blow was only hard enough to surprise the Xixian god-king, but it allowed Vansen to throw him off. He did his best to crawl away, but Sulepis was on him in moments, stabbing with his blade so that Vansen could only throw out his hands to grab his enemy's arms. He did his best to keep the blade from his unprotected face and neck, but Ferras Vansen was weary beyond description and wounded in several places; Sulepis was taller, well-muscled, and rested. Vansen managed to roll on the autarch's wrist, forcing him to let go of his curved sword, but that was the guard captain's only victory. As they struggled, the autarch quickly overpowered him again and clambered atop Vansen's chest, then fastened his long, strong fingers around the northerner's throat and began to squeeze.

The blackness gathered and spread before his eyes. Vansen could hear nothing but the roaring in his ears, see nothing but the blur of the autarch's mad face, all eyes and bared teeth. Then a great flame seemed to fill the sky above them both, as though the glaring, blazing sun itself had fallen down into this deep place beneath the earth. An instant later, the weight of the autarch was lifted from Vansen's chest. He coughed, struggling painfully for the air that had been denied him.

When he could look up again, he saw the tiny golden figure of the autarch dangling from the blazing white fingers of Zosim, whose vast, youthful face wore a smile of triumph.

"AND WITH CROOKED'S DAUGHTER DEALT WITH," the

god purred in a deep rumble like an approaching storm, "THAT LEAVES ONLY YOU, MY LITTLE SUMMONER."

Sulepis struggled until the straps of his armor broke. He tumbled free, but as Vansen watched, the monstrous Zosim snatched him out of the air like a man catching a fly. "NO, I SHALL NOT LOSE YOU SO EASILY," the god said. "AFTER ALL, I OWE YOU SOMETHING. YOU INTENDED TO COMMAND ME AS IF I WERE ONE OF YOUR SLAVES." He laughed and the sound rolled and pounded through the massive cavern. He lifted the autarch until the struggling, shiny figure was just before his eyes. "I SEE YOU WEAR THE SUN LORD'S HAWK ON YOUR BROW, LITTLE MORTAL CREATURE. HOW HE WOULD LAUGH TO SEE THAT! BUT I LIKE THE IDEA. YES, YOU SHALL BE . . . MY CREST!"

And so saying, Zosim put his thumb in the middle of the autarch's breast to hold him, then tore off first one of his arms then the other, letting them fall to the ground. Then, as the autarch's thin shrieks filled the cavern, and his blood spurted and streamed over Zosim's hand, the god yanked off the Xixian's long legs as well. The autarch's mindless cries of agony rose until it seemed the very stars in the sky might be screaming in the invisible heights. The god lifted the autarch's writhing, limbless torso and head to his mighty forehead and affixed it there, so that the bloody golden lump seemed almost grown into the flesh . . . then it burst into flames. Sulepis still lived, burning but unconsumed, and screeching helplessly as he struggled against the god's flesh that now held him fast. Ferras Vansen could only lie gasping in the muck, half-mad with all he had seen.

"NOW YOU WILL GO WHERE I GO, LITTLE KING, SEE WHAT I SEE . . . FOR A WHILE." Zosim turned and stalked away across the island, each step making the ground shake as he headed toward the shore and waded into the Silver up to his marble thighs. With every step, the god seemed to glow brighter, hotter, and the flames that danced on his skin burned higher. By the time he had reached the far side of the Sea in the Depths, he blazed so brightly it was hard to see the form of the god within the fires.

Zosim reached up a massive hand and clutched at the cavern's stone wall. The rock smoked and cracked and crumbled outward. He reached up and made another handhold higher up, then dug his foot into the wall. The god was no longer even remotely human, but only a titanic manlike shape of almost pure fire. From such a distance Vansen could see nothing of the autarch, but he thought he could still hear thin screams through the roaring of the flame.

"AND SO I RETURN!" the god proclaimed, then began to mount the sheer cliff of smoking, melting stone, climbing steadily toward the surface.

44
The Screaming Stars

" . . . And so Kernios summoned the Orphan's shade, and said that if anyone in bleak Kerniou would weep for him, he could go . . . Zoria gave him hands of oak wood so he could play his flute."

—from "A Child's Book of the Orphan, and His Life and Death and Reward in Heaven"

SEE WHAT THEY HAVE DONE.

Barrick stirred, tried to open his eyes, but could not. The blackness simply was. *I can't see anything!*

You must see with the eyes of the Fireflower. Ynnir's voice. *This is the last time I can speak to you, I fear—it is harder and harder . . .*

Barrick began to move toward something—not light, but a lessening of the shadow, a shape that seemed to create itself by its resistance to the darkness. It stood calmly before him, waiting, its antlers a tangle that seemed to have no ending.

Am I dying now, too?

Not yet. The great stag lowered its head for a moment as if to crop at the grass. *But no one—not even the gods, it seems—will outlast the Book. And this will be one of its strangest pages. . . .* Suddenly, the beast lifted its head as though it heard something. *Come. Follow me. See what they have done . . . !*

The stag sprang away, and although Barrick could discern nothing of the ground on which it ran, it had the sound of a real place, of grass and leaves and twigs beneath the stag's hooves. Barrick sprang after it.

What who have done? he called.

The short-lived ones. Your kind—tall and small. See? See how they have found a way through the darkness . . . !

The two of them raced now through a black emptiness shot by streams of fire. The bursts of flame shot out, one after another, great blossoms of burning force that rolled and gleamed, spreading out in spumes of hot wind, until the very earth trembled and began to come apart.

What is this, Lord?

The mortals have unleashed fire to battle a fire god, Ynnir said as they watched the conflagration grow and spread, watched the stone splinter and the earth collapse. *Crooked's Fire, it is called. Do you see? The strength of Fire is the strength of Time itself, that ravages all things, but here the ravages of fiery Time have been shrunk to a single point, a moment of destruction that we now see in all its magnificence. Behold! With nothing but powdered earth the mortals have made flame and broken the earth apart.*

But why? Do they think to crush the Trickster and his flame?

Oh, no. They have a greater plan. They have called up the fire to crumble the earth, and when the earth crumbles—now, see!

And then, as the stones of Midlan's Mount broke and fell, as burst after burst of fire collapsed first one wall of the Funderling Mysteries then the next, the sea at last broke in.

The Water Lord may sleep, but he is still mighty! cried Ynnir. *What can destroy the fires of the Trickster god? The deep waters, manchild—the deep, cold waters of the great ocean . . . !*

The great burning god had scarcely climbed up the stone chimney and out of Ferras Vansen's sight when a roar like thunder rolled down out of the monstrous opening in the cavern's ceiling. For an instant Vansen thought it was the god shouting his rage and triumph again, his voice made even greater by the echoes of the great vertical tunnel, but this time the very earth shook as well, the rounded stones of the island slipping and bouncing and tumbling all around him.

Vansen struggled onto his hands and knees and then raised himself painfully to his feet. Stones were tumbling from the cavern's walls now, only pebbles at first, but chunks of rock as big as his head quickly followed, and then others larger still. A boulder the size of a goods wagon crashed down out of the heights into the Sea in the Depths and sent up a silver fountain as high as the castle outwall.

Somewhere, the gods must be laughing at us, Ferras Vansen thought. *Zosim the Trickster will climb to the surface while we mortals who remain behind will be crushed by falling stones, helpless to escape.*

The rumble grew louder. The ground shook harder. Vansen staggered as the island swayed beneath him like a rope bridge, but at last he reached Prince Barrick. He hoped the tremor would end soon, but instead the earth throbbed on and on—harder now if anything, as though he stood jouncing on the skin of a beaten drum. At the same time, the air around him was growing heavier and tighter, pressing on his eyes and making his ears ring.

"Highness! Barrick! I'm not . . . strong enough . . . to carry you . . . ! Wake up!"

Vansen dragged the prince a few steps toward the boat, but he could barely keep upright and his arms were numb. He felt Barrick stir a little beneath his hands.

"What . . . ?"

"It collapses around us, Highness—the entire cavern is falling down. Perhaps if we can reach one of the tunnels . . ."

Barrick fought his way out of Vansen's grip. "No!" He rolled over, then began to crawl across the stones, clumsy as a tortoise. "No, the . . . the boat. We must . . . get into the boat."

"Highness, that is madness," cried Vansen. "It will never protect us—some of the stones are big as houses . . . !"

"Vansen, I do not . . . command you as a prince, I . . . beg you as a friend. *Get into the boat!*"

Barrick clambered up over the bundled reeds and into the boat with what looked like the last of his strength, then lay stretched between King Olin and the black-haired girl, as pale and motionless as if his heart had stopped. Vansen crawled in beside him.

"No matter what happens, hold them," Barrick said, his eyes closed and his face as pale as his dead brother's had been on the night of his murder. "Hold my father tightly and do not let his body go. He deserves . . . to come home . . ."

And then the first great gush of seawater plunged down out of the heights and into the Last Hour of the Ancestor. The gush became a flood, a single jade-green column, as if the entire Irisian Ocean had been poured on them from above out of some upturned bucket. As the wall of green rushed toward them, Vansen had a strange moment's vision of a beautiful white youth trapped inside, burning and glowing like molten silver as he tumbled helplessly in the water's grip. Vansen plunged one hand as deeply as he could into the reeds of the boat, then wrapped his other arm around the limp form of Barrick's father, the king.

The speeding wave crashed over them and turned the world to silent jade. Bubbles floated before Ferras Vansen's blinking eyes, shining like stars lost from the firmament. The reed boat squirted up to the surface and for a brief moment he could suck in air, but the craft was being tossed like a wood chip by the crashing water. Vansen could not lift his head to look—it was all he could do to hang on to both Olin and the boat, bellowing with pain as the force threatened to yank his arms out of their sockets. They crashed against stone and the little craft turned over, then the boat was tossed out of the rushing green, spun, lifted, and tossed again. Once more they careened against a wall. Vansen thought he heard Barrick shouting and spluttering. Again the green covered them and spun them like a leaf in a powerful eddy. Deep beneath them, something still burned and smoldered in the depths, but even the god's flame was dying beneath the weight of so much water.

Up and out. Over, clinging without knowing which direction he was falling. Down again, then spat up and out once more. Water shook him like a dog shakes a rat. Vansen closed his eyes and hung on.

Briony was struggling to get back up when the first great shudder passed through the stone beneath her feet, knocking her to the ground again and almost rolling her over the edge and into the chasm. A roar as deep as some terrible beast of legend rose from the depths; even the Elementals slipped sideways in the air, surprised.

The roar from below had become a fierce and growing thunder. A howling gale burst up from the chasm deeps, and the rush of hot air threw Briony back from the edge and sent the Elementals flying like rags. The one with the glowing stone, the one named Shadow's Cauldron, hovered out of Briony's reach above the abyss, ready to throw down the Fever Egg and burst it on the stone to free the poisons inside.

"No!" shouted Briony as the sickly jewel rose higher and the ground shuddered beneath her hands and knees. "Don't . . . !"

A shape flew forward and threw itself off the edge toward the Elemental. At the last moment before falling into empty darkness it caught the floating thing and held on, grappling with Shadow's Cauldron's black insubstantiality as though the Elemental were a huge bat. The attacker was Kayyin, and for a moment it seemed his weight might pull the creature down with him, but the ragged black thing was too strong—it lifted itself and the half-fairy until Kayyin's legs dangled. Then, a moment later, another figure rushed past Briony—the girl Willow. She leaped after Kayyin, catching and clinging to his legs with a cry like a fearful child. She had surprised the Elemental. As Briony watched in horror, all three of them swayed for a moment and then tumbled away into the darkness, the Egg with them. The other two Elementals floated out over the abyss as if to see what had happened to their comrade, then abruptly vanished as if they had never appeared at all.

Breathless, horrified, Briony scrambled to the edge, staring down into the darkness, wondering if she would feel the poison when it came—would it be thick like smoke, like temple incense . . . ?

Something was climbing up the chasm from below, something big. The wind of its coming flattened her hair against her head, but Briony could see it only as a broad moving front pushing its way up through the darkness.

Water. The gigantic hole was filling with water, and it was rushing upward toward her. Kayyin and the girl and even the Fever Egg were gone beneath it, and in a few moments she and Chert would be swallowed up, too, left to drift in it until their bones settled to the bottom. Briony crawled back toward the place where the little man lay beside the wall, still fighting to get onto his feet. She sat down beside him and waited for the end, wanting to pray but not certain to whom she should address the prayer. After a few long moments the roaring began to quiet; the water still rose, but its speed seemed to have lessened. Briony clambered back to the edge and looked down, holding the torch out so she could watch the frothing shadow as it rose, as it swallowed level after level beneath her, until to her amazement it finally stopped rising only a few dozen yards below.

"Water," she said, still trying to understand it.

Chert had crawled to her side. "Fracture and fissure," he said. "We did it. Oh, my ancestors, we did it. . . ."

"And that Fever Egg fell into the water and didn't break," she said slowly. "Even now it's sinking to the bottom."

"Are you certain?" Chert asked, peering down into the darkness as if it might be floating there. "How can you know?"

"Because if the shell had broken, I imagine we'd be dead by now."

Chert was suddenly distracted. "Princess? Don't you see them?"

"See what? See whom?"

"Down there." But where he pointed, Briony could see nothing—it was too far and too dark. "None of them are moving," he said, "but there are four of them lying in the bottom of the boat."

"What do you mean?" She could not see in this dim light like a Funderling, and certainly could not see a boat, but as she stared, she saw a green gleam far down in the watery depths, growing as it rose toward the surface. For a moment, as if in a dream, she saw an impossible thing—a gigantic, glowing human shape struggling up through the fathoms of roiling water, thrashing toward the surface. Then it slowed to a drift. The light dimmed and nearly died, and the vast, manlike shape fell into dark, flickering pieces. A moment later the water was completely dark once more. It had been a dream, a vision, nothing more. Briony shook her head in confusion. "Do you still see the boat? Are there truly people in it?"

"Yes. Perhaps if I can get down to them with my rope, they can answer some of your questions. If they're still alive, of course."

"I think it unlikely." Briony stared down at the boat she could not see. What had happened here? More importantly, what had happened far below? To her family? To the autarch? The unsettled water still roiled and made waves along the edge of the chasm. How could any of them have survived? "Merciful Zoria, does anyone but us still live?"

But Chert had already gone looking for a place to anchor his climbing-rope.

Chert seemed unusually grim as he came back up the treacherous slope after tying a rope to one of the survivors, and he would not answer Briony's questions as they hauled up the first of the boat's passengers, a slender young girl with the dark skin and dark eyes of a southerner, her body cold and motionless. By the time they had untied her, the first of the Syannese troops began to appear on the path. Eneas had sent them, they told Briony, and the prince himself was close behind. With their help, the second victim came up much more quickly, and even before he had been unharnessed, she realized she was looking at her father's body.

As she lay weeping on Olin's cold chest, the guards drew up the last two from the boat. Her brother Barrick was laid out beside her father, then as she stared down at his pale, still features in growing horror, the last of the survivors was brought up. He struggled out of his own harness and walked unsteadily toward her, then fell to his knees, swaying like a tree that had been cut mostly through.

"At your command, Princess, I bring your brother back to you. I believe . . . I believe he yet lives . . ."

Then Ferras Vansen's eyes turned up and he fell senseless before her.

PART FOUR
THE PINE TREE

45
Only in Dreams

"For three days and three nights Adis went up and down across Kerniou singing the story of his sad life, and at last the goddess Mesiya, wife of Kernios, let drop a tear of pity. Kernios was so angry that he banished her forever . . ."

—from "A Child's Book of the Orphan, and His Life and Death and Reward in Heaven"

SHE WAS SO TIRED, so tired. All she wanted to do was sleep until the world was different—but that was very clearly not to be . . .

"And the Xixian enemy, Highness?"

Briony nodded. "The city is safe. Captain Vansen says they are scattered through the hills, Lord M'Ardall."

"But there are still many of them . . . thousands!"

She did her best to keep her voice measured. The young earl was one of the few who had resisted Hendon Tolly's rule. She would need men like him. "They have shown no sign of wanting to continue their autarch's lawless attack on Southmarch, and our soldiers are busy subduing the last of the traitor Tolly's men inside the walls." She did her best to smile. "I promise you, good M'Ardall, we are watching all our enemies. Let's not borrow trouble until we have a better chance of paying it back."

He bowed. "I hear your wisdom, Highness."

The Throne hall was in ruins, so the seat of power was now a quartet of dining hall benches set in a tent in the middle of the residence's front garden until the residence itself was sufficiently repaired. At the insistence of Prince Eneas of Syan, Briony alone had been given a chair, both to make sure she held pride of place in the makeshift throne room and to alleviate the misery of having to wear a dress and stays again. She hated it, but it was a sacrifice she would make to show her people that things had gone back to the way they were—even those things she had loathed.

If only my head didn't feel like an anvil, she thought. *If only their voices did not feel so much like hammers, beating on it . . .*

As she looked at the faces around her, many of them as familiar as members of her own family, she could not help a moment's pang at the strangeness of her situation: though a few still survived, not a single person around her now was an Eddon. Anissa had taken baby Alessandros and retreated to her old haunts in the damaged Tower of Spring. Her great-aunt Merolanna was in ill health and kept to her rooms. Briony's father lay in state in the one remaining public hall of the residence, his bier surrounded by candles. Briony had wept over him many times. And her brother . . .

Ah, Barrick, where are you . . . ?

"Princess? I am sorry, should I come back some other time?"

She opened her eyes to see Hierarch Sisel doing his best to look patient. If nothing else, having Hendon Tolly as a master had made the hierarch and other members of the aristocracy more cautious about angering their ruler.

So I suppose that's one I owe you, dead man. "No, Eminence, no," she said out loud. "It is my fault, not yours. Please, ask me again."

"It is just that we cannot put off your father's funeral much longer and there is much to decide. The Eddon family chapel is ruined, and the great temple in the outer keep has been badly damaged as well. . . ."

"Then we shall have his rites beneath the sky, Eminence. I think he would have preferred it that way."

"I will arrange it, Princess," Eneas said, heading off any objections from Sisel. "If you will permit me, of course."

She nodded. "That is kind of you, Prince Eneas." But his willingness to help troubled her, too. She could not lean on him too much: she still owed him an answer. "Now, what else? I find myself muddleheaded, and I fear I am not the best judge of things this moment. Nynor? It is good to see you back, my lord. What do you wish to say?"

The old man had been struggling to rise, but let her wave him back into his seat. "How could I stay away when my lady needed me? And your father was one of my dearest friends, a gem among princes, an example to ordinary men . . ."

Briony was trying to hide her impatience. Didn't people understand there was no time now for such formalities and pretty words? Things had to be done. The March Kingdoms, especially Southmarch itself, were in a shambles. Bodies still lay in the ruins as well as in the caves and tunnels beneath the castle, and they were starting to stink. The living needed to be fed, and Tolly had emptied the treasury. Briony doubted he could have spent everything—more likely he had shipped gold and jewelry back to his family home in Summerfield, so on top of everything else she had to contemplate waging war on her relatives to retrieve her own exchequer.

Nynor was still enumerating the ways in which the current state of finances—and in fact the entire day-to-day administration of Southmarch—was a disaster unseen since the days of the Great Death: " . . . And who will stand witness against the malefactors?" he complained, wagging a knobby finger. "It is virtually impossible to know for certain which of the people supported Tolly and which stayed loyal . . ."

Briony did her best to disguise a sigh as a change of position. Why was she tired all the time, every day? "That is not of chiefest importance, my lord," she told Nynor. "How could the men and women of Southmarch know what to do except support the throne and whoever sat on it?" She had thought about this a great deal on her way back from Syan, all those long days riding through what had been her father's orderly kingdom but had now, like a deserted farm, begun to go back to nature. "It is not up to us to punish them if they cast in their lots with Tolly, it is up to us to show them the way forward. Unless they used Tolly's rule as an excuse for crimes and cruelty! Then I will be as hard as steel."

Whispers passed between the courtiers and nobles and others gathered in the large tent, many of whom were wondering anxiously how their own actions over the last two years might weigh on such a scale. *Good,* she thought. *I will be fair, and even more merciful than some might, but I do not want the wicked to think their deeds will go unnoticed and unpunished.* But it pained her to think of all the work to come. And without her father, without many of the old advisers, and even more painfully, without her brother. . . .

"Where is Avin Brone?" she asked suddenly, interrupting Nynor in the middle of a disquisition about grain stores. "Why isn't he here?"

Nynor's wrinkled face flushed at the neck and cheeks. "Lord Brone said . . . he said he will come at your summons, Princess Briony. At any time of the day or night."

"But he does not feel obliged to be here at the time of our greatest need?"

Nynor cleared his throat. "He . . . he said you did not seem to need or want his help, so he would wait. He said he is at peace with the gods and his ruler, and will do as you wish."

She stared at the old courtier, wondering how he would feel if he knew the things she did. "I will see him, then. Tomorrow or the next day." She smiled in a way that made a few of the courtiers wince, even though they didn't know the reason for it any more than Nynor did. "Tell him it should be at his convenience, by all means." She turned to Prince Eneas. "And of course there are still a hundred or more of Tolly's men gone to ground in Funderling Town like rats under the rushes. Captain Vansen and your Lord Helkis will be occupied there some days, I think."

Eneas nodded. "As long as the traitors get no support from the Kallikans living there."

"Funderlings," she said a little more sharply than she had intended to. "They are called Funderlings and they are as loyal as any men."

"Yes, Princess, of course, Funderlings." Eneas did his best to smile.

"Forgive me," she said hurriedly. "I have a beastly ache in my head. I did not mean . . ."

"Forgiven and forgotten, Princess." He would have said more, but Briony's attention was drawn to a very arresting figure in the doorway being kept there by anxious soldiers. "I think we have an embassy to attend to," she said. "Guards, this visitor is welcome here."

The gray-skinned woman was now the center of all eyes. Some among the assembly only knew the Qar as the creatures that had tried to kill them; these stared at her with open dislike. Some even scurried back from the tall, slender figure. Others, like Sisel, who had escaped the castle before the siege began and had weathered the worst days on his family lands, watched her with less fear and more interest. But nobody, Briony felt certain, least of all herself, could look at the newcomer without mixed feelings.

"I am Aesi'uah, counselor to Barrick Eddon, the Lord of Winds and Thought." The fairy-woman had skin the color of a dove's breast and bowed like a willow in the wind. "I bring his greetings and his gratitude."

As the courtiers whispered at this, Briony stared at the woman, trying to see past her skin and robin's-egg eyes. "My brother seems to have found a home among your folk. I am pleased for him—it was not always easy for him here, surrounded by his family and people."

"You seem angry, Princess Briony," Aesi'uah said.

"Angry that I have scarcely seen my brother since we all nearly died?" For a moment it was all she could do to contain herself. She took a breath. "Yes, you are right. I cannot help wondering why he does not come to see me, or at least pay his last respects to his own father, who will be buried soon."

Aesi'uah nodded. "These are strange days, Princess. It is . . . difficult for him."

Briony could not help looking doubtful. "Do you think so?"

"Please, Highness, you sent a summons. Your brother did not answer it himself, but he sent me. Let me answer any other questions you have, and your brother will make the rest of his thoughts clear to you soon."

Briony looked at the confusion and fear on the faces of those around her. A little less than a month ago Southmarch had been at war with these same Qar. She did not want that fear to return—conditions were too volatile. She softened her voice. "Of course, Lady Aesi'uah. Your words make sense. I understand your folk are camped beneath us, on the outskirts of Funderling Town."

"Until the rest of your enemies are driven from Funderling Town, we thought it best that we remain there, yes. Along with our Funderling hosts, we have made certain your enemies cannot escape into the tunnels, especially those that lead up to the mainland."

"It is appreciated. And after these last enemies are captured? What will your people do then?"

"We will return to our country in the north. Many of our survivors left families behind all over the shadowlands, and Qul-na-Qar, the great house of our people, is almost deserted. We are too few now to remain scattered."

"Another question, one that must be asked—will there be peace between us?"

"I think in this one thing I can safely speak for your brother. Yes, there will be peace, if mankind will leave us in our freedom and our isolation."

The whispers began again; Briony ignored them. "If my brother is truly your leader I will need to hear that from his own lips before I . . ." she turned guiltily toward Prince Eneas, " . . . before we could promise to honor such a pact on behalf of our peoples."

The eremite bowed her head. "As you say."

Briony took another deep breath, reminding herself that the business of caring for her people would always be a matter of compromises. "Thank you, Lady Aesi'uah. That eases my mind somewhat. Now, let us speak of other things. What happened down below the castle—I scarcely know how to talk about it. I've heard many stories, but I still don't entirely understand them. That . . . thing . . . the giant . . ."

"It was Zosim the Trickster, the lord of words and wine and fire. Zosim the Deathlord's son. Zosim the god."

The whispers became more urgent, more fearful.

"Forgive us if we doubt," Eneas said abruptly. "But this flouts everything we Trigonates believe."

"You need not take my unsupported word as truth, Prince Eneas," said Aesi'uah. "There are more than a few of Briony's own subjects who still live, and who saw much of what happened."

"Little people," said Eneas unhappily. "Kallikani."

"They are still my subjects, Prince Eneas," Briony said as politely as she could. *And Ferras Vansen, too,* she thought, *but he will not talk to me.* Scarcely a day passed after Vansen collapsed at her feet before he had gone off to join the Funderlings in hunting for Durstin Crowel and the rest of Tolly's partisans under the castle. "Even so, Lady Aesi'uah, it is hard for those of us who weren't there to understand. What happened to . . . Zosim?"

"He is gone, Princess. Even the oldest and wisest of our race who survived cannot tell for certain what that means. He is an immortal and immortals are, by definition, hard to kill, but it might be possible when they take mortal form. We can feel no trace of him in the waters that roil now beneath us—the inrushing sea quenched his blaze. Where is fire when it ceases to burn? That is where Zosim is."

"So you are telling me he . . . it . . . cannot come back? That we are safe?"

Aesi'uah's expression was strange—almost a smile. "None who draw breath are safe, Highness."

Briony checked her temper. It took a moment to answer. "Thank you for this report, Lady Aesi'uah. Have you anything more to tell me?"

"Nothing except that we regret the damage done to your people as well as ours."

"But it was you fairies who did much of that damage . . . !" said one of the nobles and the undercurrent of discontent threatened to break the surface and become a true wave.

"Murderers," called another, loud enough for everyone to hear. "Demons!"

Briony was angry at this, but she knew that many of her own people supported her only because of her family name, and others solely because of the prince of Syan and his soldiers. She could not afford to give her impatience full rein.

"Please," she said, holding up her hand to still the growing clamor. "Lady Aesi'uah is our guest. Whatever happened before, in the end the Qar fought as our allies and many of them died defending this city and stronghold. Do not forget that." She turned to the eremite. "But as you can see, our folk are not quite ready to extend the open hand of forgiveness—and who can blame them?"

Aesi'uah inclined her head. "As you say, who can blame them?"

It seemed to Briony there was a mocking undercurrent to the reply, and that decided her. She did not like smugness coming from these creatures, however justified. "Since we still have much to discuss," she announced, "and my brother will not come to me, then I will go to him."

She was satisfied to see something like surprise on the eremite's slender face. "Highness . . . ?"

"My apologies—was I not clear? I will go to speak to your Barrick, lord of fog and wind or whatever his grand new title is."

"But, Your Highness, it is . . . he is surrounded by . . ." Aesi'uah was clearly at a loss.

"He is what? He is my brother, yes. He is on the sovereign territory of Southmarch, capital of these March Kingdoms. He is surrounded by fairy folk, whom you have just promised me regret any damage they have done to my people. So why should there be any difficulties?"

Eneas was startled, too. "Briony . . . Princess . . . I don't think this is wise."

"But I do, Prince Eneas. More, I think it a grave necessity. The people with whom we were recently at war are encamped beneath our feet, within a short distance of miles of tunnels we know almost nothing about. If we are finding it difficult to root out a simple annoyance like

Crowel, can you imagine what a hornet's nest it would be to try to do the same with the Qar should things go badly between us?" She turned and saw, as she had hoped, that all eyes in the capacious tent were on her. "Of course I shall go." She raised her hand to forestall the prince's next words. "Alone but for a few guards—this is a parley between allies, after all. Lady Aesi'uah? You may go and inform Barrick that I will come to him today, before sunset."

Briony sat back in her makeshift throne as the eremite rose and made her graceful, unhurried way out of the tent. Her head was still throbbing but she felt a little better. At least she would finally have a chance to see her brother, face-to-face.

Tinwright crouched in the indifferent shade of a dying yew tree in the commons before the royal residence and watched Princess Briony march past with her retinue of guards. A group of nearby laborers also saw her and raised a ragged cheer. Tinwright hoped she hadn't noticed him. Only Elan M'Cory swearing to the princess that Tinwright had resisted Tolly long after others would simply have murdered Briony's infant brother had kept Tinwright from going back to a stronghold cell—or more likely to the headsman's block.

But was it really true, he wondered—what would he have done if things had been different? Would he have thrown away his own life, or would he have done what Tolly ordered?

Matty Tinwright had just finished his jug of wine and all he could think of now was that he wished he had been able to afford more. Prices were very high, and all the best things went to the Syannese soldiers—as it was, Tinwright had needed to steal coppers out of his mother's jewelry box so that he could get drunk and quiet the pain in his chest, which hurt every time he took a deep breath. Still, he supposed he should be grateful he was alive. If he had not had the Zorian prayer book in his breast pocket he would be having this drink in Heaven—or at least not in Southmarch.

"Who would ever think a book could save a man's life?" the Syannese soldier-surgeon who bandaged his wound had said. Tinwright had been in chains at the time so he had not agreed with the man about his luck. He was free now but didn't feel much better about things.

And there went the princess, he thought, less than a hundred paces away from where he sat, but it might as well have been a hundred miles. He could only watch as she and the soldiers made their way along the commons path toward the Raven's Gate—watch and wonder how things had gone so very wrong for Matt Tinwright, Royal Poet.

Elan M'Cory did not love him. She had made that plain. She had thanked him for helping to keep her alive and hidden from Hendon Tolly, but that, she had told him, was gratitude, not love.

"Duke Gailon needs me," she had said, pointing again at the hideous thing she had spent the last three days nursing. "He nearly died—he thought he was dead! How could I desert him now?"

Even had Tinwright not resented the man for the fortunate accident of his birth, he would have found it painful to have her prefer such a blighted creature to his relatively unblemished self. Gailon Tolly's face was a mass of open wounds and pocked with dirt and worse things beneath the skin, so that he seemed ravaged by plague. Still, Elan had told him that she wanted only to devote the rest of her life to nursing Gailon back to health. What could be clearer than that? Tinwright himself was of no further interest.

Love, he thought. *Subject of so many sweet verses, and yet it stinks like ordure.*

He levered himself to his feet and staggered across the green, which now was little more than mud and broken bits of rubble pierced by a few strands of dried, dead grass.

A map of my heart, Tinwright thought.

Would I have done it? Would I have killed the child to save myself—no, to save Elan? It was hard to say now—hard to remember anything except the confusion and terror of that moment. He stared down from wall the and across the outer battlements to the unending roll and crash of the sea. The looming Tower of Summer covered him in cool shadow. Tinwright's own thoughts on that night were as lost to him as something from the depths of history. How could anyone ever say with certainty what such and such a hero said, or thought, or felt? Tinwright had been in the middle of great events . . . although he had to admit his part had been a minor one . . . and could scarcely remember a moment of it except for Hendon Tolly's mad face glaring like a festival mask. *Like something from a play . . .*

He looked up at the sound of footsteps. A slender figure was coming toward him along the top of the wall, an old woman by her face, although she walked with strength and ease. Tinwright realized he was staring and looked out over the water again. The waves, whipped by early summer winds, spat froth as they raced toward the castle wall.

"Ah." The woman had seen him. "Forgive me. I will leave you alone and find another spot."

Tinwright shook his head. She was older than his mother, but he was tired of being alone with his own thoughts. "No, stay, please. Are you a priestess?"

"A Zorian sister," she said.

"So." He nodded. "No shortage of things for you to do these days, I'm sure."

"There is never a shortage of things to do, now or any other time." But she smiled as she said it. Tinwright liked the woman, liked her grave, somber features. "At the moment, though, I want to do nothing except feel some wind on my face."

Tinwright took this as a request for silence, so he turned away again to contemplate the restless ocean. People said that the sea had now flooded all the depths underneath Funderling Town; ever since he had heard that Tinwright half expected the castle to float away at any moment, like a boat lifted off the beach by a rising tide.

"Tell me," he said after a while. "How does it feel to know that the gods are not with us?"

"I beg your pardon?"

"You must have heard what happened here. Even in your temple or shrine you must have been told something of what happened."

The woman smiled again. "Oh, I know a bit about it, yes."

"Then tell me how you can still call yourself a Zorian sister when we are told the gods are asleep—that they have been sleeping for thousands of years. That Zoria herself was killed by her husband back in the beginning of Time. That all the things the priests have told us about Heaven have been lies." He could not choke off his own bitterness now. "Nobody watches over us. Nobody waits for us when we die. Nobody cares what we do in this world, for good or ill."

She looked at him carefully, then took a step closer and stood behind him, so that they both looked out over the moving water, which glinted like silver in the afternoon glare. "And how is that different?" she asked after a while.

"What do you mean?"

"How is that different from what we have always had, always known? The gods come to us only in dreams. We must make our own choices every day of our own short lives. Whether they will reward those choices or even notice them, we do not know. I see nothing changed."

"But it *is* changed! It was all a lie. We saw what the priests showed us, believed what they told us, but the gods they described to us were only puppets playing out a story. Now we don't even have the puppets. We don't have anything."

"We have the same troubles we always had, young man," she said sharply. "We have the same needs as always. I see you are injured." She pointed to the bump of the poultice under his shirt. "But there are many who are more sorely wounded. They need help here on earth, whatever the gods may do. Even if our faith was never anything but a shadow play, we can still learn from it. And it could be that even the gods themselves were only puppets—that there is a larger cause behind it all, for you and for me and for every person here." She shook her head. "Listen to me go on. Some comfort, eh? I fear I am out of practice." She patted his arm. "Take care, young man. Despair is the only true enemy. Make yourself useful. Nurse someone who has greater need than you. Feed someone who is hungry. Make something that will help another."

After the woman had left, Tinwright found himself still thinking about what she had said.

"Where are Crowel and his renegades now?" Briony asked Lord Helkis, who had been alerted to her coming and had met her at the front gate of Funderling Town.

"All but run to ground, Princess. They have been pushed back to the quarry on the edge of the town, I'm told. It will be over soon." Helkis seemed to have decided that since it was now all but certain she would marry his prince, he had better start treating her with respect. Briony wasn't at all sure about his reasoning, but it made for a nice change. "Crowel does not know these tunnels but that man Vansen seems to, and Vansen also has the help of the Kallikans, of course."

"Vansen makes himself very busy," she said. So busy that she had not seen him since his recovery. Between the guard captain and her brother, she was beginning to feel quite thoroughly avoided. *Does Vansen hate me?* she wondered. *Fear me? Or do both he and Barrick simply not care, as my brother did his best to make clear the last time?*

The Funderlings who had returned to the heart of their city came out to watch Briony as she passed down Gem Street, some of them cheering but the rest watching with fascination and worry on their faces. Apparently the Funderlings were not all happy with her, either.

"I feel the need to talk to Chert Blue Quartz," she said to Lord Helkis. "Will you ask the Funderlings to send him to me?"

"As you wish, Highness." He dispatched a runner to the guildhall at the far end of the long, winding street, where reconstruction had already begun on the damage caused in the last few days of fighting before Crowel's retreat. "No man would ignore your summons, Princess, I promise you."

Except the ones I truly want to see, she thought.

Aesi'uah came out to meet her in front of the chamber, and though the woman's face was as calm as always, Briony could not help feeling that the eremite was anxious about something. "He is waiting for you, Princess Briony." Aesi'uah gestured with her long hands toward the archway and the flickering lights beyond, then stepped discreetly to one side.

"He is my brother," Briony said when Helkis and his guards would have accompanied her. "Whatever else has happened, I feel certain he is no danger to me."

Lord Helkis did not look pleased to have to stand so near to Aesi'uah, but he was not going to move any farther away, either; Briony left them to sort it out.

Her brother stood looking down at a table made from two stones set one on top of the other where he had spread many slates and rolls of parchment. Barrick had taken off his armor, and wore only a loose-fitting white shirt with breeches of the same color. His feet were bare, and for a moment she had the illusion that the past year had not happened, that she had left her bedchamber and found him up before her, standing in his nightshirt waiting for her to rise as he had when they were children. Then he looked up, and the strange coldness in his face proved that such an innocent, mostly happy past was truly gone forever. "Briony," he said calmly. "You wish to talk with me, I hear."

It was hard to make herself speak. She wanted to rush to him, to throw her arms around him, even to hit him—anything to drive that look from his face. Instead, all she managed was a nod. "Yes, I thought that would be a good idea . . . since you would not come to me."

"My apologies," he said in the way he might have said it to a stranger after treading on her foot, "but it is not so easy. My people . . . well, they hate yours. That makes it difficult. They are still fearful, and many of them do not trust me completely."

"*Your* people? Are you talking about elves and goblins?" Briony realized her voice had risen almost to a shout, but she could not help herself. "You are calling these your people now, but you will not come to see your own sister? You will not come to see your father's body before he is buried?"

He turned his back on her as if to resume studying his papers and slates. "Of course you cannot understand."

Could this tall, flame-haired stranger really be Barrick? Or had the Qar somehow set a changeling in his place? Was such a thing even possible, or was it just another old wives' tale? These days legends and fairy stories seemed to be the only things that were unquestionably true. "Do you think things have not changed for me, Barrick? Our father is dead. I have walked all the way to Tessis and back as a traveling player. People have tried to poison me and shoot me with arrows. I met a demigoddess . . . !"

"I knew a demigoddess, too," he said. "But she was not the type who made friends with our kind."

"With our kind. Listen to yourself! A moment ago, the fairies were your people, now you speak as though you remember your true blood! You'll have to make up your mind, Barrick Eddon."

"You do not understand. The Fireflower . . ."

"Oh!" She turned and walked away, fighting back her anger. "Yes, things have happened to you. To me as well. Zoria's mercy, Barrick, I killed Hendon Tolly with my own hands! If you have been burned by Heaven's fire like the Orphan—well, then, so have I! We are both changed! But you haven't changed all that much—your suffering still must be unequaled by any other's . . . !"

He turned, his face tight with rage. "Don't talk to me about suffering, Briony! You will marry that prince—I have seen him moon over you like a calf following its mother. You will be the queen of Syan and the world will bow to you. What do I have? Do you even care?"

"Barrick, that is foolishness . . ."

"Do you know what is ahead for the Qar . . . and for me? Saqri, the queen of the People, is dying. She sacrificed herself so that Zosim could be defeated—dozens of arrows and rifle balls pierced her. Only her will and her love for her people keep her alive. When she is gone, half of what has kept the Qar race alive will be gone, too. Think of that, sister—when you are planning your marriage, I will be burying my queen *and* my beloved . . . !"

"Your beloved . . . ?" Briony could only stand and gape as if struck. "Who are you talking about—not that Saqri?"

"You don't understand anything," he said bitterly. "Come. Come and I will show you." He beckoned Briony to follow, then led her to a side chamber where a pair of female creatures in garb like Aesi'uah's, but whose angular shapes were less human, knelt in silence beside a makeshift bed of straw. On it, scarcely visible in the dim light of a few candles, lay a small, slender girl who could not be even as old as she and Barrick were.

"This isn't Saqri," she said. "This is the girl that was in the boat with you."

He stood over the head of the bed, looking down. "Saqri is in the center of the camp, surrounded by her people. This . . . this is the only person who truly cared whether I lived or died during this entire terrible nightmare. Her name is Qinnitan. For a year she was in my dreams and in my thoughts. She was my companion, my friend, my . . ." He stopped and shook himself angrily. "Now she is dying . . . and we never even spoke face-to-face. Never touched . . ." He turned abruptly and walked out.

Briony stood for a moment, gazing down at the motionless girl. If she lived, it was impossible to tell. She showed no movement of breath, no sign of the animation that plays over a sleeper's face even in quiet slumber.

Who are you? Briony wondered. *And what were you to my brother, really? Would you have loved him? Would you have cared for him?*

"How long will she live?" she asked the two Qar women, but although they both looked up at her words, neither answered.

"I'm sorry, Barrick," she said when she had found him again. "I didn't know. But that is all the more reason . . ."

"Cease, Briony, I beg you." He moved away when she would have touched his arm. "You will say it is all the more reason to cleave to the family I have, but you do not understand. *I am no longer one of you.*"

"What? An Eddon . . . ?"

He laughed harshly. "Oh, I am an Eddon all right. Everywhere I go others suffer in my stead. You must know that by now. How many of the men who came with you died so that you could regain Father's throne? How many others because the Tollys wanted it in the first place? And how many of the Qar have died because our ancestor stole Sanasu from her own family?"

A memory struck her, from the last time she had talked to their father. "There is something you must know . . ."

But Barrick did not seem to hear her. "In fact, now that I think on it, the number of current victims doesn't matter, because eventually the Qar will *all* have died because of what our family did to them. So if I can repay even a little of the debt that the Eddons owe to Saqri and Ynnir and even Yasammez, then that is what I must do."

The memory was washed away by anger. "You speak of *Yasammez* that way? The bitch that murdered so many of our people?"

He waved his hand. "Go away, Briony—you cannot understand. We have no more to say to each other. Soon enough the Qar will be gone from here and I will go with them. You can rebuild your houses in peace—we are too few to trouble mankind again."

"When I saw you, I wondered at how much you had changed, Barrick," she told him. "But now I see that in the most important ways you are no different. It's still your own sorrows you care about and no one else's, and you still turn away from love and kindness as though it were an attack."

Her brother's pale face showed nothing—he seemed as unmoved as the sea itself. Briony turned and walked out of the cavern.

46
The Guttering Candle

" . . . He told Zoria that if she could lead him out of Kerniou, the Orphan could return to the world and the sun, but if she faltered or failed, he would have to remain among the dead forever."

—from "A Child's Book of the Orphan, and His Life and Death and Reward in Heaven"

HE COULD FEEL HER TRYING not to be amused, although he did not know why. The exact nature of what Saqri found funny often eluded him. *Your sister has departed. Did it not go well?*

You know it didn't. You know it as well as I do, I'm sure.

I was not with you. I felt you, but at a distance. Still, the emotions were very great!

Even as she teased him with that strange indulgence she had begun to show toward him since she had been struck down, he could feel her fighting against her own growing weakness. Unlike Saqri, he was only just learning how to politely not notice things. *Don't mock*, he told her. *I am in pain.*

Of course you are. But it is unnecessary. The People have ended. Never was it promised that we would all meet our ends in the same instant, but I doubt not this will be our last generation, at least for those of the long-lived. A few of us shall straggle on for years, but the Defeat has finally come. Your people do not carry quite the same burden as we do, so you likely do not understand that knowing the end has arrived is almost a relief to us. I am sorry I will not be here to see the last, bright flowering that will come of it—I am certain the art and music will be glorious and frightening in a thousand subtle ways!

But if there is no longer a People, Barrick Eddon, there is no need for you to sacrifice yourself. The Fireflower of all our mothers will be gone soon. Then someday soon, even if your time is elongated by what has happened to you, it will happen to you, too, dear manchild—the last Fireflower will flicker and die. Without the Fireflower's light, the Deep Library will become a stagnant pond. And without the memory of who we are, we will dwindle and die like any mute creatures. The song will go on without our voices. . . .

It was as if the closer she moved toward death, the older she became. She seemed nearly as ancient as Yasammez now. *Perhaps it's the nearness of eternity and whatever it brings,* he thought, but did not share it with her.

When you have finished your moment with the mortal girl, she told him, *come to me. I would like to see you with my eyes.*

He stood over Qinnitan for a long while, trying not to think. Before he left he lowered himself to his knees and took her hand, but it was so limp and cold, he could not bear to hold it. He kissed it and laid it back on her breast.

Saqri was on a bed that Barrick had asked be made, although if the queen of the fairies had been given her way, she would have been laid on the naked rocks and covered only with her cloak. *If we are given the choice of how to die,* she had said, *we of the old ways, then we prefer the elements just as they are. It is good to learn to deal with the chill of night, because as it comes, death also blows its cold breath upon us. We learn to move less and think more.*

But you aren't being given any choice, Barrick had told her, and so the Daughter of the First Flower was kept comfortable and warm because she was too weak to have it be otherwise. *I will not let you die here in this place,* Barrick had sworn to her. *I will return you to the People's House.*

Foolish boy. Like Yasammez, I will die when the Book says I must die.

Liar. You are alive now when anyone else would have long since crossed the river. It is the strength of your will that gives us this time and you know it.

You saw your sister, she said. *She burns more brightly than I had guessed. She would have made a good mate for you.*

Barrick could only stare at her. *That is disgusting.*

Not among our kind—not in our ruling family. I loved Ynnir before I hated him, and hated him before I loved him. I knew him each moment of my life. That is how entwined we were. But your ways are not ours, I realize.

Don't say such things. Besides, she and I are no longer close. I've changed too much.

Have you?

You know I have!

She smiled at him. It was such a small wrinkle of her lips that someone watching less carefully might have missed it. *"All can be foretold," as the Oracles say. In truth, I think you should stay with your people . . . I am sorry, Barrick Eddon—with your other people.*

Never! I can never live among them again. I am nothing like that anymore.

She went on as though he had not responded. *I meant no insult. You have earned your blood with us as well, there is no doubt. Even the smallest and most distant of the People's clans will know about you.*

Barrick didn't care about such things—what did any kind of fame matter when the rest of his life would be little better than a long funeral procession as the Qar and their knowledge slowly died away? And at last he would die, too, either alone among a people that his family had helped destroy or as an alien in the land of his birth. Either way he would be a stranger to those around him.

Be of good cheer, Saqri told him. *Life is short at best. Even the long span of Yasammez was a mere flicker beside the stars, and the stars too will go dark some day.*

There was nothing to be said to such a blindingly joyful sentiment. Barrick nodded and turned away.

No, she said. *Come back. Please sit beside me.*

When he had seated himself, he looked at her more carefully. Saqri seemed almost translucent, like a candle that had become little more than a shell, its wick burned far down inside it. Though he knew her blood was red like his, it was not apparent from the outside just now; she seemed to be something other than flesh, like the petal of a white lily.

Why did it all happen? he asked at last.

She did not need to ask him what he meant. *It had to, dear manchild. The balance was too precarious to last forever. When Crooked finally died, everything tumbled loose. Now our time is over.*

But why? Even without both halves of the Fireflower, there must be something left for the People! They don't have to simply lie down and die.

Almost a smile again. *No, they need not lie down and die, Barrick—but our great age of blooming is over. Perhaps something will come after . . . perhaps . . . but I cannot see it. . . .*

She was growing tired, he knew, and he dared not waste her strength. Still, when she was gone, there would not be another person on all the earth who would understand him. *Have I told you what I have found?*

Her eyes fluttered but stayed closed. *No, tell me, manchild.*

It was just like the time before he knew the full horror of his father's illness, those days when Olin would move and talk like a man who had spent the previous days unpleasantly drunk. *Poor, blighted man. He understood what plagued him less than I do, and I still cannot fathom it all . . .* To Saqri he said, *I learned from some of the Xixian prisoners that there may still be tribes of the People living in the southern deserts and the hills—the Xixians call them Khau-Yisti. And there are tales of beings who must have some kinship to our People in the islands to the south and west of Xand as well . . .*

He realized that Saqri was not listening anymore—she had fallen back into her deep, deep sleep, a retreat to a place just this side of death. Each time it was harder to draw her out, each time she returned there more quickly. Soon the other half of the Fireflower would be gone forever.

Ynnir? What shall I do?

But that voice had also fallen silent.

"Elan, just speak to me. Surely that is not too much to ask from a man who has loved you as truly as I have?"

She frowned at him, but not in anger. "You know I care for you, Matt. I will always be grateful that you tried so hard to rescue me from Hendon."

"Tried? Did!"

"Of course. For a time. But things have changed now—you must see that."

"See what? That you are throwing me over for a dying man . . . ?"

She drew back from him. "Gailon won't die! Back at Summerfield Court, he will have the best physicians. He can't die! The gods would not let such a miracle occur only to snatch it away!"

After the past weeks, Matt Tinwright had a different view of what sort of thing the gods would and wouldn't do, but he knew it was pointless to argue. Elan had loved Gailon Tolly since she was a girl, and now she would be able to nurse the dying man through his last months.

"There are miracles all around you, Elan," he said. "I should be dead!

I was shot in the heart with a bolt from a crossbow. But the very prayer book I tried to give you stopped the arrow." He took the small book from his doublet and held it out. Torn parchment flowered from a jagged hole in the cover as big as a silver coin. "Look! My blood is on its back pages! If I hadn't had it, the arrow would have reached my heart, but instead it merely gouged me. Does that mean nothing to you?"

"It means that I was right to return it, Master Tinwright. If I had accepted your gift, you would have died."

Tinwright slumped. He had barely slept during the nights since Midsummer. Sometimes he thought that if he couldn't have Elan, his heart would break and he would die, too—sooner than Gailon Tolly, perhaps—and wouldn't Elan feel sorry then . . . !

"Come here," she said, lifting her pale hands. "Let me give you a kiss." And to his immense sadness, she did—a chaste, sisterly peck on the cheek. "I will never forget you, Matt. I will never forget you, or your sister, or your mother . . ."

"Nobody forgets my mother," he said bitterly.

"You could be a better son to her, you know. She only wants what is best for you. . . ."

Tinwright's aching heart immediately shrank inward a little, nestling deeper in his ribs. He began to say something sour, then realized that he and Elan were not even speaking the same tongue any more. "Best for me? You must think I'm a child."

"I think you are a good, kind man."

"Which it does not take a poet to understand is the same as saying, *'I don't need you any more,'* am I right?"

"Don't be angry, please."

"Angry?" He stood up and bowed. "Not at all, my lady, not at all. No, I am happy, because I have learned an important thing about love today—and that's a poet's proper study, isn't it—love? Farewell, Elan. I wish you and Gailon very well."

But when he looked back from the doorway after this noble, poetic leavetaking, Elan M'Cory wasn't even watching him leave with eyes full of regret and longing, as he had hoped. She had returned to her stitchery.

"I saw no sign of him," Chert reported to Opal as he slumped onto the seat. "I asked all over town, and no one else has, either."

Opal could barely muster the strength to look up. "Why did he lie to me? Why did he tell me I would see him again?"

Chert sat beside her on the bench and wished for the hundredth time that they didn't have to shelter in his brother's house, but their own place on Wedge Road was too close to the area where Durstin Crowel and the renegade Tolly supporters held out against capture.

As if to remind him of all the miseries in his life, Nodule Blue Quartz picked this particular moment to come down the stairs and into the dust parlor that was currently serving as his brother's and sister-in-law's place of refuge. "Ah, Chert. Sitting about, I see. Surely you can find some way to pitch in and help—the Elders know, there is plenty to do these days." He nodded slowly, as if the weight of his responsibilities made even such simple movements difficult. "And someone was here from the guildhall claiming you are wanted upground at the castle." He laughed, but there was more than a little anger in it. "I imagine someone has simply mistaken you for me, but the fool of a messenger kept saying no, it was you who was wanted, so I suppose you must go and find out." Nodule nodded to Opal, shouldered on his cloak, and went out the front door.

Chert had barely heard what his brother said about the summons; he was still chewing over the insult. *Pitch in and help? It was he who almost destroyed everything,* Chert thought. *My own brother. He tried to stop me without even bothering to find out what I was doing.*

Another thought came to him, one that had been there all along but he had been too busy to entertain. *I had something to do with all that happened—with things turning out better than they might have otherwise. With the end of that autarch fellow. With us all being alive.* For a moment Chert wanted to run after his older brother and skull him with a rock. *Me. Not him.* But so far most of Funderling Town knew only enough of what had happened to understand that Chert had been instrumental in destroying their most sacred places.

He was startled out of his reverie by Opal's hand closing on his arm, a hard squeeze with fingernails in it. "Go to her," she said.

"What? Go to whom? Why?"

Opal's deep, crippling sadness had fallen away, replaced by a feverish intensity only marginally less worrisome. "To the princess, of course, since you must go up to the castle anyway. You saved her life! She will help us!"

"Saved her life? Perhaps. But she also saved mine. I told you, it was nothing so simple as . . ."

"Tell her we need her to find our boy! Tell her all Flint did! She cannot turn you down—she owes you!"

"But, my love, Princess Briony has more than enough to do . . ."

"What could be more important than finding our boy, you old fool? You heard what Antimony said—he saved Beetledown so he could deliver the Astion! And the Qar—Flint did things for the Qar, too, although I never quite understood. But . . . but our boy *matters*. Tell her that. Flint matters. She must help him!"

Chert shook his head, though he knew the battle was already lost. "I cannot simply go to Briony Eddon, the princess regent of all the March Kingdoms, and say, 'You must find our son.' She will think me mad."

"She will think you a father." Opal had that look, the one she wore when something was agreed upon, even if she was the only one agreeing. "She had a father herself—in fact she has just lost him. She will understand."

Chert sighed. The pain of Flint's absence was terrible, but he felt certain that begging the mistress of all Southmarch for her help wouldn't change things. If he still lived, Flint would not be found unless he wanted to be found. A new thought chilled him. If they never found Flint, would Opal ever be happy again?

"Of course I will go to her," was what he said out loud. "Of course I will, my only darling."

Sister Utta came back from her walk along the walls heartened. It was good to see so many people already at the work of rebuilding Southmarch, although she knew a long time would have to pass before the scars of the conflict were even partially hidden. How much longer until people's hearts had also been mended? That Utta couldn't say, but she could smell summer in the air and that was good enough for now. The day after the ocean had crashed in and drowned the deepest caverns beneath the castle, black clouds had filled the sky over Southmarch, hurling down rain as if to soak all that was aboveground as well. In the storm's wake, little sprigs of green had already begun sprouting between the broken stones and out of the gouged, naked mud of the commons.

As if to underscore this theme of renewal, Merolanna was sitting up in her bed taking soup from one of her maids. The duchess had seemed at death's door only a few days ago, but today was feeling so much better that Sister Utta had been able to leave the nursing to others and go out of the house for a little while.

"Utta!" Merolanna pushed away her bowl with a trembling hand and shook her head sternly when the maid offered her more. "I have been asking for you, my dear. I feel as though I have been on a long journey. Tell me all the news, quickly—is it true Hendon Tolly and his bullies are gone?"

"Tolly is dead by all reports," Utta said, sitting on the edge of the bed. "But you should lie back and rest. We will have plenty of time to talk later."

"Nonsense. At my age?" Merolanna laughed, although her voice was still weak and reedy. "In any case, I have news of my own! I have met my son."

"What?" Utta's heart, so buoyant only a moment before at seeing her friend so much better, suddenly felt cold. Was it still the lingering fever, or was this madness something separate and deeper, something that would not go away even if the dowager duchess regained her health? "You saw him?"

"Not just saw him, met him! He came to me!" The old woman laughed again, then frowned as the maid dabbed at a spot of soup on her chin. "Stop that, girl. And Utta, don't frown. I can tell by your face that you think this some feebleness of mine, or else a piece of fever-foolery, but it was neither. He came to my bedside last night after you slept. I saw him and spoke to him. He even remembered his true name, the name only I know . . . Adis." She looked a little abashed. "I named him for the holy Orphan, yes. But even so, it did not protect him—the fairies stole him anyway."

Now Utta wondered if Merolanna had been tricked by some enterprising beggar-child who thought he had found himself a patroness that could strew the way before him with gold. Utta wasn't certain what she would do if that were the case. "Is he coming here, then? Did you invite him to stay with you?"

"Of course I did. But he has too much to do. He was very involved in the war against the fairies, you know." The old woman frowned. "Or was it the war against the southerners? I cannot quite remember. But in either case he has too much to do to stop here with an old woman. But he has scarcely changed since I lost him! Can you imagine!"

Now Utta felt a real chill. "But, Merolanna, when he was lost . . . that was fifty years ago."

"I know. Is it not a strange, miraculous thing?" The dowager duchess sat back among the cushions. "Still, I am happy, and he promised I would see him again. Now tell me everything that has happened while I was ill. I am hungry for more than soup . . . !"

Barrick looked down at the girl's face, so familiar and yet so strange. Only a short while earlier, Briony had stood in this same rock chamber, and she too had seemed an inexplicable mixture of the unknowable and the known. Could she really be his twin sister, the one who had sometimes seemed so close that she might have been just another part of himself? And could Qinnitan, lying here before him lit only by the deathly gleam of a few candles, really be a stranger he had never seen in the flesh until that moment down in the Mysteries?

Qinnitan? Can you hear me? He emptied his thoughts of everything—Saqri, Briony, all that had happened since the last spring moon began to grow—and tried once more. *Qinnitan. It's Barrick. I need you. I need to speak with you.* But he could feel nothing in that distant corner of his thoughts and his heart where she had once lived. *Qinnitan!*

He sat beside her. The Fireflower voices, quiescent and drowsy as sun-warmed bees, murmured to him of the Deathwatch Chamber, of quiet, dignified passage to the beyond, but he did not want to hear it. For once, the knowledge of the kings of the Qar meant little: they knew of no precedent for what was happening. Without the two halves of the Fireflower, there would be no Deep Library, and the voices there would drift into isolated madness. Qinnitan would leave him. Saqri would vanish, too. Soon his head would be empty but for the Fireflower. *All of them gone, across the river or waiting on its banks to ford those dark waters.* Even Ynnir had all but left him and was running in the far fields, soon to pass onto whatever was next as the earthly bloodline ended.

The idea came to him like a piece of distant music—only another sound at first, but one whose melody at last won out over more random, ordinary noises. *Ynnir. The fields. The river . . .*

Barrick sank down into himself, thinking. The candles glowed. After a time some of them had burned so low that they began to flicker and go out, but still he sat beside the motionless form of the dark-haired girl, considering.

47
Death of the Eddons

" . . . So she took him by the hand but Kernios sent the spirits of the fearsome dead to follow them and harry them . . . Zoria went so swiftly that she dared not even look at the Orphan, and he did not cry out or make a sound . . ."

—from "A Child's Book of the Orphan, and His Life and Death and Reward in Heaven"

BRIONY KNEW SHE SHOULD dress properly for the meeting, but it was easier when the time came to go to the duchess' chambers in her morning robes, with a soft cap on her hair and only one of her ladies to accompany her.

It's like being a child again, she thought—but, of course, it was nothing like that at all.

Utta met her at the door. For a moment the Zorian sister didn't seem to know what to do, whether to bow to her or embrace her. Briony relieved her of the decision by opening her arms. "Oh, please, Utta, don't be a stranger! Not after all that's happened!"

The old woman smiled and embraced her. Utta was thinner than she had been, as were most of the castle's residents: the siege had bitten hard in the last months.

"I am so pleased to see you, Princess," Utta said. "But like all of us, I grieve for your father."

"Of course." Briony wiped at her eyes and laughed. "It seems every hour I am either doing my best not to cry or trying to look stern and awful, like a true monarch. Ah, but it's good to see you."

"And you, Highness." Utta looked at her with obvious fondness. Briony was comforted to know that at least a few things hadn't changed.

Utta led Briony to her great-aunt's bedside. Briony had been prepared for the change, but seeing Merolanna still shocked her: only months before, the dowager duchess had been the very picture of a vigorous elderly woman. Now she seemed quite diminished, both eyes and cheeks sunken, as if she had begun to shrink inward on herself like fruit spoiling in a bowl. Still, the old woman's eyes were bright, and when she saw Briony, she was able to lift herself up onto her elbows.

"The Three be praised!" she said. "Utta, push these cushions behind me so I can look at my dear Briony properly." Merolanna shook her head. She wore only a coif instead of her usual wig and elaborate headdress—even her head seemed to have become smaller. "Come and tell me everything. Your poor father! Oh, what dreadful days we have seen here, dreadful days. But things will be better now."

Briony was still confounded. It was as if some other player had been brought in to play the part—her great-aunt might have aged ten years since last Winter's Eve.

"Of course," she said out loud. "Of course, Auntie 'Lanna. Things will all be better now."

"You look beautiful and strong, my lady," Rose Trelling told her. Briony's other companion Moina had been gone from the castle for months, returned to her family's great house in the east, but Rose had stayed in Southmarch with her uncle Avin Brone and now had taken back her duties as lady-in-waiting with alacrity. She fastened the clasp on the heavy necklace, which lay too brightly against her mistress' pale skin, like a string of stars.

"I do not feel much of either," Briony said, turning to examine herself in the mirror. "Especially today, when I must bury my father." She thought the huge, stiff dress made her look like a ship under sail, and not a fast brig, either. "A merchant's carrack," she said. "Wallowing under a full cargo."

"My lady?"

"Never mind." Much as she would have liked things to return to what they had once been, Briony could not make it so by wishing: just looking at Rose's sweet, open face reminded her of Brone, the girl's uncle. The time was coming fast when she must confront him with what the playwright Teodoros had seen. It was clear from the way Brone looked at her that King Olin's closest supporter knew something was wrong, but she could not bear to face him until after her father's funeral. Still, it could not wait longer than that. If the man was an enemy, as she had become more and more certain, wasn't it dangerous letting him walk free when he must know that she suspected him? No, she must deal with him tonight, after the funeral.

"Send for Tallow, the master of the royal guard," she told a waiting page. "I have an hour until the service begins, so I would see him now."

"Stop squirming!" Rose scolded as the boy hurried out. "If you don't let me tame this last unruly curl, you will have hair like a beggar woman's!"

To Briony's surprise it was not Jem Tallow who responded to her summons.

"Princess," said Ferras Vansen, kneeling just inside the doorway, "I heard your summons and took it upon myself to answer in Tallow's place. If I have done wrong, I apologize."

She sighed, but not so loud that he could hear it. "Apologies certainly seem to be your stock in trade, Captain Vansen. Do you truly think you have so much to be sorry for?"

He colored a little. "More than I would like, Highness. I spoke out of turn when I claimed I brought your brother back to you. The truth is, I left him in the shadowlands, although it was not by choice. He brought himself back to Southmarch."

It was strange how much he reminded her of Barrick—not in how he looked, or spoke, or acted, all of which could not have been more different, but in how he made her feel, frustrated and yet affectionate at the same time. But there was something more in what she felt for him than she had ever felt for her brother—something she did not know what to do with. And of course, there was Eneas, still waiting for an answer. . . .

She did her best not to show the confusion of her thoughts. "I have need of the guard tonight, after the funeral. Will you make certain that a troop of them come to me in the new throne room?"

"The tent?" He colored again. "I do not mean to make light of it . . ."

She laughed. "It *is* a tent. You only tell the truth."

"Of course, Highness. A half-pentecount of your best men will be there—I will see to it." He rose and would have backed out the door, but she held up her hand.

"We have scarcely spoken in this last tennight, Captain Vansen. I will have one of the pages bring you a chair, and you can tell me more about what you have gone through." She waved to one of the boys. "There is so much about what happened here that I still can't understand."

"Nor can any of us, Highness," he said somberly. "I suspect we would know more if we could hear from everyone who fought here, from Funderlings and upgrounders, even the Qar and the Xixians . . ."

"Upgrounders? What does that mean?"

"Your pardon, Princess. That is what the Funderlings call us—that and 'Big Folk.' It is strange how living among them I began to forget that I was not one of them, although I had twice their size!"

"Then tell me about them, Captain. Tell me about my brother, too, and what happened to you both in the shadowlands. Tell me everything you can. I bury my father this afternoon, and I dread it."

"I will never forgive myself that we could not save him," Vansen said, eyes downcast.

"Enough. You brought his body back to me. And I was able to speak to him once myself, before the final days."

"Truly?" He had not heard about this, it was clear.

"Yes. So let us talk, Captain Vansen." She looked around at the maids and the ladies-in-waiting, the half dozen young pages, the life that had recaptured her. "I fear we may never have such a chance again."

Vansen was ordinarily not much of a speechmaker, but the spirit of the tale caught him up: by the time he had finished telling of the last hours in the Funderling Mysteries, everyone in Briony's chamber had gathered around, servants and nobility together, all with open mouths and fearful faces. As he warmed to his task, he showed flashes of the dry wit he often hid, and although he downplayed his own role, Briony could see the many places where he shifted the credit to others. It reminded her a little of the way her father had told stories of his year fighting in Hierosol, and this in turn reminded her of the far less pleasant task that awaited her.

"Thank you, Captain Vansen," she said when he stopped to drink from a cup of wine one of the ladies had brought him. "It is a gift of Heaven that our beloved Southmarch survived, but we lost so many." She shook her head. "My father, dear Chaven, all your brave Funderlings, and so many more." She did her best to smile, but it was difficult. "Now it is time to go to the funeral. You will not forget your promise to me, will you?"

He looked startled. "I beg your pardon, Highness? My promise . . . ?"

"To see that the royal guard attends me tonight after the funeral?"

"Ah." He seemed both relieved and disappointed. What else had he been expecting? Some embarrassing display of gratitude? Had she been wrong about his feelings for her after all? Not that it mattered. With Olin dead and her brother determined to leave Southmarch behind, Briony knew she no longer had the right to her own affections—to anything except what was good for the land and its people. "Of course, Highness," he told her. "I will see that your guard remains with you after the funeral."

"Thank you, Captain Vansen. I owe you an apology and it . . . it troubles my sleep. I am truly sorry for the things I said to you in my time of pain after Kendrick's death. You are a good man and you have proved it many times over."

Something strange moved just beneath his calm features. Anger? Sorrow? "I seek only to serve you, Highness," was all Vansen said. "And the March Kingdoms, of course."

He rose quickly, bowed again, and hurried out. Briony sat for a moment, mustering the strength to rise and attend to her duties as chief mourner. Surrounded by her ladies and other folk, she still felt quite alone.

Vansen did not like Briony's choice to hold the king's funeral in the dubious safety of the commons outside the royal residence, although he understood her desire to give the castle's population a chance to mourn together. Still, even though Durstin Crowel had finally surrendered and had been taken to the stronghold with his last supporters, some of Tolly's most dangerous allies like Berkan Hood were still unaccounted for, and although the guards were still vigorously searching for Hood, Ferras Vansen thought it was unforgivably dangerous for Briony to put herself and her father's infant son out in the open where an arrow from some distant rooftop could leave Southmarch without a ruler no matter what the undermanned royal guard tried to do.

It only made him more confused about the days ahead. The royal guard, like the castle that housed them and the Eddon clan that employed them, had to be rebuilt. Jem Tallow had already tried to relinquish control to his former captain several times, but Vansen was not entirely certain he wanted his old position back. For one thing, it would force him to see Briony Eddon every day, and while that was in some ways his fondest wish, he also knew that being so close to her and unable to have her would be torment. And how long would it be until she gave herself to Eneas of Syan? What of Ferras Vansen, then? He would be little more than a page with a sword.

Somehow it also seemed pointless to go back to doing what he had done before, however necessary it might be. Once you had fought both a god-king and an actual god, it would not be easy to return to daily duty rosters and the other more mundane parts of his profession. He was looking forward to peacetime—what soldier who had survived this madness wouldn't be?—but not to the problems of keeping five pentecounts of men occupied and battle-ready while protecting the rulers at every moment.

Everybody had been waiting in the garden since midday as the long shadow of Wolfstooth Spire passed from west to east, but though the mood was somber, the people themselves seemed gathered for a more festive occasion, their places on the sunny grass marked off with blankets and cloaks, the remains of meals still to be seen. The royal family had been through the funeral service already as King Olin lay in state in the hall of the residence. Now, with his body hidden inside a somber, sparsely decorated coffin draped in the Eddons' wolf and stars, the mourning chorus sang the threnody and Sisel spoke the good words that had to be spoken over the dead. Olin the just ruler, Olin the protector of his people, Olin the diplomat—Vansen thought the hierarch spoke of him as though he were one of the deathless Trigonate gods. He thought he would rather have known the man who had fathered Briony, Barrick, and Kendrick, the man who had inspired so much feeling in all of them, but it was not to be. That man had been mortal and now he was dead. Now he was only a story.

"Though the terror and gratitude of those who pray fill thine ears always with myriad voice, O brothers who abide on the holy mountain Xand, yet hearken to us also, and grant this day your favor, that good Olin's exile now may have an

end, and that he may return to you and to his native land, at rest from labor of long journeys . . ."

The salt had been sprinkled and Sisel had just begun to chant the final prayer meant to guide the spirit of the departed king when Ferras Vansen felt a stirring among the mourners, as if the crowd were a field of flowers rippled by the wind. Was something amiss? He looked quickly to Briony, who had felt it, too.

A procession was coming up the road between the armory and Wolfstooth Spire; the people at the far end of the commons had already turned to watch it. At first Vansen could see little of the newcomers as they passed through the tower's shadow, but as their leader stepped out into the sun Vansen saw hair that dazzled like flame. Barrick Eddon had arrived at his father's funeral. The prince wore clothes of loose-fitting white cloth and a hooded white cloak, much as Queen Saqri had done the few times Vansen had seen her; Vansen realized now that white must be the Qar's mourning color.

He glanced again to Briony Eddon, but her expression was unreadable. Barrick and the company of fairies who came with him made their silent way up the colonnade beside the commons and then emerged into the sunshine again just short of the residence's front steps and the king's body, where Barrick stopped and stood, straight as a sentry.

After a confused few moments Hierarch Sisel continued the prayer. When it was ended the mantises came with their rattles and flutes to lead the procession, and the pallbearers lifted the coffin onto the wagon that would carry it toward the graveyard. It seemed the Eddons meant to keep using their family vault, Vansen noted, no matter what had taken place there or what lay beneath it. But before the pallbearers could take a step, Barrick abruptly stepped forward and laid two sprigs atop the coffin, one of meadowsweet and one of mistletoe, the Orphan's flowers of immortality. As he did so, he paused for a moment. A look of pain and confusion twisted Barrick's features and he snatched back his hand—the one that had once been withered and useless—almost as though he had burned it.

The prince and his followers did not accompany the coffin all the way to the graveyard, but turned away near the crumbled walls of the Throne hall and walked back toward the Raven's Gate and their camp in Funderling Town. Some in the crowd turned to watch them depart, making the sign for the pass-evil, but most paid scant attention, as if the king's son and his odd companions were only another clutch of mourners.

* * *

The funeral feast had ended nearly an hour before, and many of the guests had already retired, though a group of older nobles remained in the residence's long, low dining room drinking wine and telling tales of the late king and of all that had happened since last Olin had sat on Anglin's throne. Doubtless, many of them also expressed quiet reservations over the fitness of his daughter to rule, and questioned why her brother had made himself so absent from the business of governing the country, but Vansen ignored their conversations as he pulled a few of his more trustworthy guards from their duties in the dining room and led them to the residence parlor that served as Briony's royal retiring room. The princess was waiting there already, her face carefully empty. To Ferras Vansen, her expression was like a sort of wound: it hurt him to see it.

When his guards had filed in, he turned to Briony. "Shall I go and get Lord Brone, Your Highness?"

She nodded, but scarcely seemed to see him.

To Vansen's surprise, Avin Brone was waiting just outside the door of the hall—he had arrived while Vansen had been arranging the guards. The big man nodded. "It is good to see you, Captain Vansen. I assume you will not remain much longer in that low rank . . . ?"

"No one has spoken to me of any promotion, Lord Brone."

"Ah, but I am sure you will be rewarded. I hear you did noble, brave-minded work since your return to Southmarch. Many say that if you hadn't stiffened the Funderling resistance we would all be slaves now. You must tell me everything that happened one day, Vansen. I wish to hear what you saw. I trust your eyes and thoughts more than any others save my own."

"Thank you, your lordship."

The count smiled but he looked tired. "Let us not keep our mistress waiting. After all, she will soon be our queen." He walked past Vansen to the door.

When Brone had bowed to Briony (not without a little difficulty; the old man had gotten even stouter and his limp was now pronounced) she asked for a bench to be brought so he could sit down.

"Before we get to the meat of things," she said, "I have a question for you, Brone. Berkan Hood will soon be captured or dead. The post of lord constable is empty. Do you have anyone to recommend?"

Brone cleared his throat. "I can think of no one better than this man here, Ferras Vansen."

"Not yourself, Lord Brone? You held the post a long time. Do you no longer have confidence in your own abilities?"

"With respect, Highness, do not play games with me. I am too old for that, and also too old to try to be what I was. If you did not want my advice, you should not have asked."

"Very well, then, let's not circle like two tavern bullies." Briony's smile was hard. "You were my father's trusted adviser, Brone. You were that to my brother and to me as well."

"I have been lucky enough to serve the throne and the people of the March Kingdoms. That is well known. Many would say I did it well."

"Many would, yes—but that is not my complaint." For the first time, Vansen saw that the emotion she had hidden was not weariness or fear, but rage. Her cheeks were red and her eyes narrowed in fury; for the first time he saw how much like her brother she really was. "You betrayed us, Brone, or you planned to. You schemed to see us all dead—my father, my brothers, and me. What do you say to that?"

Brone did not burst out into a torrent of denials, which made Vansen feel even more that the world had tilted on its foundations. Instead, the old man pressed his chin deep into his beard and frowned with his bushy brows until he seemed like a bear staring out of a cave. "And why do you say that, Your Highness? Who has told you such a thing of me?"

"That is not your affair. But a person I trust has told me that you had a list, and on this list was the name of every member of my family and also the method by which each would be apprehended, imprisoned, and then murdered at your order. Do you deny it?"

Ferras Vansen realized he was holding his breath, and even the guards, his best men, looked startled. Only Avin Brone himself, of all in the long room, did not seem unduly troubled. "No," he said. "I do not deny it."

Briony let out a ragged gasp like someone struck a painful blow. "So," she said at last, her voice barely under control. "You told me to trust no one, Avin Brone. I thank you for the honesty of that lesson."

"Do you not wish to know the reason why?"

"No. No, I don't. Guards, take him away. The stronghold held a less guilty man in Shaso—it will serve for this villain, too."

Brone sat, unmoving, as at Ferras Vansen's signal a quartet of guards in Eddon black and silver surrounded him. "Will you really do this again, Princess?" the old man asked in a mild tone.

"What do you mean?" Briony had pushed her feelings back behind the mask again: she stared like a statue of Divine Retribution.

"You imprisoned Shaso dan-Heza without learning the truth. You regretted it later, as you make clear. Would you repeat that error?"

"Error?" Briony almost jumped out of her chair. "You have admitted you planned to murder my family, Brone! What could you say that would make any difference?" But she did not repeat the order for his removal and Vansen, sensing something afoot, signaled his men to wait. "Speak," Briony said at last. "It is late and I am tired and sad. I have just buried my father, and I want to go to bed."

"I loved him, too, Briony."

"But you planned to kill him!"

"My duty is first and foremost to the throne, Princess. That has always been true. Your father himself was careful to make certain I understood that. Yes, I planned his death—but it was with Olin's own knowledge."

"What?" Briony seemed about to spring from her chair and attack him. "Do you claim he wanted see his own family slaughtered . . . ?"

"No!" Now for the first time Brone lost his temper. "No, of course not, Highness! But your father knew he had an illness that no one could cure—an illness of the blood that brought raging madness upon him. For ten years or more, he also knew that Barrick had that same distemper of the blood. You and Kendrick did not seem afflicted, but who could tell?"

"What does my father's . . . blood have to do with . . . ?"

"He did not trust himself—and to be honest, I could not afford to trust him entirely, either. He was the king, but at least one night every month he was also a beast—a madman. How could I defend the country without planning to deal with the king himself if he went utterly mad? How could I protect the March Kingdoms if his heirs were also infected? If your father lost his mind beyond saving, I was under orders to lock him away—to lock you all away as well until we knew if one of you was trustworthy. And if none of you were, then there would be no point in leaving you alive to foster unrest among the people, who would not understand. I was prepared to put another relative on the throne if necessary, perhaps one of the Brennish cousins—yes, even to kill you all if no other choice was left to me! But I did not wish to, and I only imagined it because your father, may the gods bless his bravery and foresight, ordered me to do so." So saying, the count of Landsend folded his hands across his belly and stared back at her. "So if you still wish to execute me, Princess, then do so. I will not resist."

At first, Vansen thought Briony was going to scream at the old man—her face had flushed so deeply he feared for her health. But when she spoke, her words were little more than a whisper.

"Do you have some letter from my father that will prove this?"

He shrugged. "I have letters from him that allude to the plan. I can assemble them for you. All my papers from the time I served your father are yours now, in any case, Princess, though you might prefer to have someone more trustworthy than myself go through them. But choose that person carefully, Briony." His smile was mirthless. "I suspect there are traitors around you still uncovered. . . ."

"Get out of my sight, Brone." She spoke as if she had a mouth full of poison. "I will send guards with you to collect the papers. Until I decide what to do, you will confine yourself to the inner keep. You will most especially *not* return to your house in Landsend."

Avin Brone dipped his head in a small bow, scarcely more than a nod. "You are my sovereign, Princess. Of course I will do what you say."

Vansen had finished dividing the guard, keeping double Princess Briony's standard pair on duty but sending the rest away, and was waiting now as she had asked, but Briony deliberately ignored him as she finished a cup of wine.

Briony knew she should have been happy Brone had a plausible excuse—she could not remember ever dreading a meeting more—but instead she was just as angry as before but with no certain target for it. A tiny part of her had hoped he would laugh at the accusation, that it would turn out to be so transparently absurd she could soon laugh, too, but the greater part of her certainty had been that Brone was guilty, that his warnings to her to trust no one had been a form of thinly veiled confession. And when he had admitted it, every hard, protective thing inside her had clanged down like the portcullis of Raven's Gate. Now she was still furious with the old man, but just as angry with herself. If Brone's story was true, what else should he have done but followed her father's orders? But if he couldn't prove what he claimed? What then?

The chance that he might simply be dissembling—that she might still have to imprison and likely execute him—made things even worse, like being whirled around in a too-fast dance, stumbling and breathless.

Ferras Vansen was still waiting in the doorway, a look on his face that Briony thought a very annoying picture of noble suffering. She felt almost as unhappy with him as she had with Avin Brone. She beckoned him forward but gave him no indication of what to do. Vansen stopped before the throne, made an awkward bow, and then stood waiting again. After she had regarded him silently for a long moment, he finally said, "Highness?"

"Yes, Captain. Thank you for staying. I'm a bit weary just now, as you might guess, but I wanted to speak with you. What do you think of Lord Brone's proposal?"

He looked quite startled. "Highness?"

Briony was beginning to fear he would never say anything else. "He suggested you as an able candidate for lord constable, Captain. Lord Constable of Southmarch? You may have heard of the position? Rather well-known in these parts, I'm told."

He colored and Briony disliked herself more than she had when the conversation began. So many times she had longed to see this man—why did she find herself treating him in this unpleasant way again?

"I understood the question, Highness, but I didn't understand why you were asking me."

"Because I want to know if you're interested, Captain. As I said—and as I sincerely meant—you have done wonderful things for Southmarch. Not simply for my family, but for everyone who shelters under the Five Towers."

"I did only what any loyal servant of the Eddons would have done, Princess."

"What any would have *liked* to have done but few would have had the wit or courage to manage. Do not belittle your own deeds." He was coloring again. How could she have ever thought this man cared for her? Or that if he did, it was a passion any deeper than a little child's mute love for his nursemaid? How could such a tall, strong man seem so deep one moment, then so foolish the next? Were all his most appealing traits products of her own imagination? "What of the post, man?"

"I . . . I am no lord, Princess."

"A small enough matter. You would not have escaped your heroics without a title and some land in any case, Captain. Shall I make you a marquis? Though I fear you will not relish being a lord. You don't seem like the type to enjoy the preening and scurrying of court life."

"It terrifies me."

She laughed a little despite herself. "Poor Captain Vansen. It does seem a terrible thing to do to you. . . ."

He had been looking at the floor. Now he raised his gaze to hers and Briony felt a little shock. Ferras Vansen's dark eyes were fiercer than she had ever seen—fiercer than she would have imagined possible, like something that can retreat no farther and must now turn and fight.

"Why do you do this to me, Lady? Why?"

"What do you mean, Captain Van . . . ?"

"This! I mean this! This way of talking to me. I liked it better when you hated me. At least then being lashed again and again was no surprise. But now . . . you say you are grateful, you praise my deeds, but all the time you act like . . . like . . ." And although he was as flushed as she had ever seen him, anger mottling his cheeks and his forehead, he stopped suddenly. A moment later he said, in a far quieter voice, "Your pardon, Highness. I had no right."

"My pardon will not be given—not until you tell me how it is that I act."

"Please . . ."

"No, Captain Vansen, I insist. In fact, I command you—tell me how I act."

His eyes roved in desperation as though there might be some way out of the trap into which he had delivered himself, but all of the guards were working hard to seem as though they weren't listening, that they weren't even aware other people were in the room.

Vansen squared himself, took a breath, and said: "You act like a spoiled child given a pet with which she has already grown bored. Instead of simply sending it away when it displeases her, she teases and torments it only for her own amusement." His voice was thick now. "That is what you do, Briony Eddon. That is the part you act with me."

Part of her was enraged that he should speak that way to her, but close behind it stood a larger part that was horrified to realize what she had done to this kind, good man. "But I did not . . ." She could not make the words come out properly. "I never . . ."

Vansen, who a moment before had looked so resigned that he might have been a prisoner atop the gallows, now took a step nearer to her. He had a look on his face she could not understand—it looked something like exhilaration but also something like terror. "And I will say more," he told her in a breathless rush. "No matter what Avin Brone thinks, and even if you yourself do feel something like the gratitude you profess, I can never be the lord constable, nor could I hold a noble's place in your court—or, if it comes to it, be the captain of your guard. So, with gratitude for what your family have given me and the kindness you yourself have shown me . . . at times . . . I must resign my commission." He pulled his gloves from his belt and laid them on the floor at her feet, then unstrapped his sword and set it beside them. "May the gods watch over Your Highness and the throne of the March Kingdoms."

He had gone only a few steps before she called to him. "But why? Why would you turn your back on the rewards you have justly earned?"

He turned slowly, knowing that what he said now could never be unsaid. "Because I couldn't bear working within sight of you the rest of my life, Briony Eddon. I've loved you from almost the first moment I saw you, knowing also that moment that the gods in Heaven must be laughing until they wept . . . because who was I? A mere soldier."

"No! A brave man," she said, because it was so much what she had been thinking. "A kind man. A good man."

"Why do you speak kindly now when you wouldn't before, Princess?" He no longer seemed to care. "Pity for a fool?"

"I'm the fool, I think." She laughed. "But you are a fool, too, Captain! Oh, merciful Zoria, I thought you would never speak your heart. How could I let myself love a man who was too frightened to tell me how he felt?"

"You care . . . for me . . . ?" She thought he might laugh, or burst out into some kind of great oration like a character in a play, but instead he suddenly called out, "Guards! Go outside and guard the door for a short while. I have a sudden concern about the security of the outer passage."

"You don't have to send everyone away . . ." Briony began as the soldiers made their way out into the hall. Briony's heart was beating fast. She felt a strong urge to giggle like a child. "But I do," Vansen said. "Even if they are discreet, it's asking too much that they must pretend to be blind and stupid as well. We common folk still have our pride." He stepped up onto the dais. "And you may send me to the headsman for it tomorrow, Princess, but I must kiss you—I must! I've waited so long . . ."

At first Briony didn't speak, because it was all so strange and unexpected that she feared it might vanish if the moment was interrupted. She could scarcely breathe as Vansen reached out and drew her up from her chair, but the feel of his warm breath on her face made her realize how far she had kept from him all these months. "Yes, kiss me, Vansen," she said at last. "Kiss me, please!"

48
By the Dark River

"The kindly Dawnflower thought she had rescued Adis when she stepped into the sun outside the gates of Kernious and the underworld, but when Zoria looked down she discovered she was holding nothing more than one of the Orphan boy's wooden arms . . ."

—from "A Child's Book of the Orphan, and His Life and Death and Reward in Heaven"

BARRICK EDDON SCARCELY HEARD Aesi'uah's questions as they walked back through the Raven's Gate and into the outer keep. The guards in the gatehouse carefully looked the other way as the small procession passed, though Barrick could see both curiosity and fear in their postures. It might have been worse, but Barrick had chosen only the most manlike of the Qar to accompany him.

"Are you angry with us or your other people, Barrick Eddon?" the eremite asked him.

They stole Sanasu—she who was to have the Fireflower, the Fireflower voices reminded him—as if he needed reminding. *They killed her brother who would have been her husband.*

"It doesn't matter." He had no answers, and he had more pressing things in his head just now. When he had reached out to lay the offering on his father's coffin, he had felt a sharp stab of pain in his hand—pain he had not felt for so long he had forgotten how bad it was. It had receded again, but he could not stop thinking about it. Why now, after all this time, should he feel it again?

Barrick and the Qar continued across the outer keep in silence and into the shade of the harbor wall between the West Lagoon and the new walls. The gates to Funderling Town were guarded by more of Vansen's men, but Barrick's onetime companion had prepared the soldiers carefully, and they only saluted respectfully as the Qar passed. For a half a moment, Barrick even wondered if it might be possible for his two peoples to live in harmony again, as they had once centuries ago, but the looks of suspicion and even outright fear that he saw when he looked back at the guards' faces showed what a foolish dream that was.

Barrick flexed his aching fingers and thought about Briony.

The pain had returned to his left hand, and even the muscles themselves seemed to have shrunk again to the way they used to be, tightening like a drying hide so that his hand pulled into a tight clench. It had begun when he touched his father's coffin . . . no, it had happened a moment after that, as a memory of his father lifting him high in the air to show him the ocean from the top of the Tower of Summer. With the memory had come a wash of sadness, of missing the man he had spent so much time cursing. And with the memory had come the pain.

He did his best to uncurl his hand. Why should it happen again? Was it just the discomfort of being back among the people of Southmarch? Or of having to argue with his sister, who wanted so much more from him than he had to give . . . But she had always done that, always demanded his love even when he was too weary of life to give it.

The pain struck him so quickly and so suddenly that he dropped to his knees with a gasp.

She is your past, the Fireflower voices told him, but they seemed almost fearful. *Forget her. Forget this place. Be strong for your new people . . .*

Barrick sat on the stony floor and rubbed his aching hand.

The Sleepers took something from me in order to heal me, didn't they?

Saqri's sleeping face showed nothing—she was beyond that now, nearly as lifeless as Qinnitan—but he felt her words in his thoughts, thin as a breeze. *Everything has its price—life, love, even death. You know that. You know that better than almost any of your kind.*

But the price was my family! My love for my sister! He understood that now, although his feelings for Briony remained curiously distant. *They took it from me without asking!*

They did not take it. Her thoughts already grew faint again. *They used it. As a river dammed by stones will rise and flood in other directions, they only changed its flow. Love is a thing that cannot be destroyed, you see, only altered . . .*

Barrick knew he could not wait much longer. The queen of the Fay's strength was failing very swiftly now. He pushed the Sleepers' gift from his thoughts and knelt by her bed and took her hand. Sunset Pearl and the other healers stood back, doing their best to seem as if they did not disapprove of the strange thing he planned to do.

Enough of these other matters," he said. *It is time for me to make that journey we spoke of,* he told her. *To try to save what we can . . . if you will let me.*

He felt a faint sensation of amusement. *Why should I not, dear manchild . . . ?*

Two pale warriors of the Unforgiven tribe carried Qinnitan's bed into the rock chamber and set it beside Saqri's. The dark-haired girl seemed even smaller than before, as if with every passing hour she shrank farther in on herself, like something being slowly burned away. Her skin was as cold as if her spirit had already fled.

Leave us alone, he told them.

No questions, no argument—the Qar immediately left the chamber, leaving only Barrick, the two motionless women, and the unsteady candlelight.

He thought carefully about what Saqri had taught him back in Qul-na-Qar, as well as what Ynnir had said: "*The Fireflower is more than the knowledge of those who went before. It is the map of their journeys, the book of their rituals. But you cannot simply consult it as if it were a dusty scroll in a forgotten niche. You must make it a part of you.*"

Barrick fell back into the darkness inside himself; for a long span he simply floated in that emptiness. When he felt he was ready, he thought about Crooked, who had found a way to travel through so many different kinds of darkness, and then thought of himself and the blood they shared, however distantly.

I am a great-grandchild of Sanasu, he announced. *I travel where I wish in the lands beyond, the dreamlands of the sleeping gods. My blood is my safe-conduct.* There would be many in the darkness, though, who had no respect for such rituals.

A faint light kindled and began to form the void into recognizable shapes—into *here* and *there*, *up* and *down*. The light was his own, the gleam of the Fireflower on his brow. His feet touched the grassy ground, although he could see little of what was beneath him—two feet, no, *four*, his weight carried on hard hooves and powerful legs. As Ynnir here in these dreaming lands wore the form of a stag, and Saqri a swan, Barrick found himself in the semblance of a horse—a pale stallion. Overwhelmed by the new sensations, he began to trot, then to gallop.

Where am I? he wondered. *Are these Crooked's roads through the void, or is it the land of dreams where the gods still live? The country of the dead? Or some other place entirely . . . ?*

Barrick Eddon did not understand enough of the Fireflower heritage to know the answers, but he knew he was doing what he needed to do. He pushed his fears aside and kept moving, racing from shadow to shadow, through tangles of darkness so thick he thought he would never unmire himself, out into moments of blinding light that dazzled and confused him. Other shadows haunted that place, too—other beings like him, perhaps, or older, stranger things—but he dared not speak to them. It was too easy for a traveler to become lost here, to stray from the path, and although those that flitted around him now might mean no harm, there were others here that fed on solitude and suffering—he could hear them whispering to him as they followed, like the scrabbling of rats behind wooden walls: *Barrick Eddon, you owe the People nothing. We will give you the strength to do anything. Raise the girl from the dead. Command the allegiance of every creature you meet. Make yourself the greatest king that ever walked the earth! All will be yours . . . Just wait on the path for us. Let us join you . . . !*

He hoped the Fireflower's light would be enough to keep them at bay.

Barrick grew weary, but still the shadows seemed never-ending. He had encountered many sights he did not understand—doorways into nothing, moaning shapes like ghosts caught in their own dreadful dreams, even things that looked to be the ruins of ancient temples, monstrous slabs of tumbled stone as old as the stars. Once a great shape passed over his head, obscured by ragged vertical shadows that might have been trees. He looked up and thought he saw a ship far above him, half-hidden by silvery clouds, with a skeletal crew and only one passenger, a woman as perfectly pale as a full moon, sitting in a high throne upon the deck, but he could study it for only a few instants before it faded away again into the murky skies.

He traveled on until his weariness threatened to overwhelm him. The voices waiting in the shadows became louder, promising more but also demanding more, as though they scented his growing weakness.

You are nothing to me, he declared, and showed them the sign of *White Walls,* the inner swallowing the outer. They fell back, abashed but furious.

We will find you again, they promised, and he knew they spoke the truth: the things that lived in these places were like forgotten prisoners, with nothing to do but brood on escape. *We will find you when you are too weary for such wards. What then, manchild . . . ?*

He had traveled much farther now than he had ever gone with Saqri, but although he was not exactly certain what he sought, he knew he had not found it yet.

You have gone too far beyond the light, the shadows mocked him. *We will not just feed on you when you fall at last—we will make a doorway of you, so that we can feed on everything that lives. We will spread ourselves across the night, live in the owl's cry, hide in a baby's sudden stillness. We shall leap from this place in our countless numbers like bats flooding from their nests as the dark swallows the dusk.*

He knew that at least one thing the shadows told him was all too true: he no longer had the strength to turn back. If he failed in this gamble, every fearsome thing that hid in the darkness beyond sleep and life would fall on him and that would be the end; there was no one left who could save him.

As he stumbled ever more slowly through the outer reaches of dream, followed by a growing crowd of hungry shadows, he finally saw something that brought him hope: a pale, heather-colored glow in the distance (if such a word as "distance" could be used in this place) gave weight and solidity to the dreamscape: where that light lay upon it, the land had substance. A grassy hill now loomed before him, crowded with angular shapes, each with a crown of antlers as wide as a man's arms.

Barrick made his way toward the twilit hill. The creatures of the shadow-herd turned to look at him as he neared, and though recognition gleamed in some of those dark eyes, many of the other deer scarcely noticed him. Only one—the largest of the stags, or perhaps merely the closest—regarded Barrick as if he knew him. A cloud of lavender light hung above the beast's brow like an immeasurably distant star.

Manchild. You are a long way from what you know. Has your breath stopped so soon?

He knelt before the great beast. *Ynnir—my lord. I am sorry I must trouble you . . .*

Trouble? The mighty head dipped. *I am beyond that, child. Soon I will be beyond this as well.*

For a moment the mystery of it all drove his other thoughts from his mind. *Where will you go, Lord? What is next?*

It is not known until it is known, Ynnir said. *And even those who know cannot say. Why are you here, manchild? You have gone far beyond what you may safely encompass.*

I know. But I have a terrible need. He told the lordly beast of his fear and his hope. When he had finished, the stag waited silently for a moment.

If I do this I will not be able to remain here, it told him at last. *I will give my last strength and be forced to move on to whatever waits beyond—perhaps oblivion. And still it may not be enough . . .*

I can only ask you, Lord—for the sake of your sister and for the sake of the Fireflower.

The stag turned and walked away from him.

For a moment, Barrick was stunned, terrified that he had been rejected and would be left helpless in these bleak spaces, waiting for the hungry shadows to move in. But he saw that the great stag was moving through the herd. Each one of his fellows that he approached bowed its head as he came, then they stood together, antlers intertwined. Each time Ynnir stepped away, his own flame had grown a little wider and burned a little more brightly.

One by one, the members of the herd added their glow to Ynnir's until at last a great ball of cold violet blazed above his brow as he returned to the place where Barrick waited. Ynnir seemed fainter now—Barrick thought he could see the dark hills through his body.

Here, the stag told him. *The last of the kings by the river give their blessings, though it costs us all dearly. Bow to me and we will give you this last gift.*

Barrick lowered his head. The violet light seemed to surround him, warming everything he looked at, although the darkness still stood close on all sides. He could feel the glow inside him as well, strengthening him where moments before he had been as weary as death, lending him hope when he had been empty of all but need. The blessed strength ran through his veins like molten metal, like honey, like the song of a thousand birds. He blinked, and for an instant the dark hills were as bright as if the full summer sun beat down on them. The things in the shadows, panicky in their surprise, fled back into their hiding-holes.

Then the light faded, and Barrick found himself alone on the dark hillside where grass waved in an unfelt wind. Because the kings had made a sacrifice he did not fully understand, he now had the strength to grab at his last chance.

May the gods or whoever else watches you speed your journey, great kings, he prayed. *May you find shelter from the storms. May you find green grass and clear water.*

The Fireflower only touches something in us that is already there, Barrick thought, and it seemed like a great understanding. *Hatred alone can't take someone as far as I have traveled this journey.* He thought of Zosim waiting for centuries in the darkness of the nightmare lands. *Lust and greed aren't enough, either. In the end only duty, or the love from which duty springs, can provide strength for such a journey.*

He had left the hill behind him and traveled through another sort of dark land now, one where trees crowded thickly and the shadows were once more beginning to fill with watching eyes. Somehow he had left his four-legged form behind; he seemed to wear a man's body and move at a man's pace.

Exhaustion slowed him until it was all he could do to pick his feet up off the ground, but he persevered, and at last heard the sound he had been listening for for so long—a whisper at first, then a murmur that grew louder and louder until it seemed he was hearing the breath of everything. It was a river . . . no, it was *the* river, he knew, although he did not entirely understand. More than a passageway to whatever lay beyond death, it was an idea of what the darkness itself could become.

But most importantly for Barrick at that moment, it was the river. The last boundary before the lands of death.

He found her as he had thought he might, standing thigh-deep in the shallows and groping like a blind woman, as though she could not understand where she was. He went a little way toward her but stopped before he entered the river. He knew that would be a mistake, even here where it seemed so shallow.

"Qinnitan." He spoke quietly, knowing she would be dizzied, fearful. "I am here. Go no farther." Even these quiet words startled her. She took a teetering step backward and the opaque waters slithered and lapped at her slender hips. She was so young! How could it be that she had suffered so much, seen so much? "How little you deserved any of this," he said, half to himself.

She stirred. "Who . . . who's there?"

"Qinnitan, it's me. It's Barrick." But as he said the name, he suddenly didn't know what it meant—was it a mortal's name, or that of a half-blood mongrel of the Qar royal house? A man driven by love, or a man in whom nothing so soft remained? "Come with me, Qinnitan."

She still didn't move, and when she spoke, it was as if repeating a word she didn't understand. "Barrick . . . ?"

He slowly extended his hand and saw a little of the violet glow kindle on his fingertips. She leaned away but went no deeper into the water. When he touched her, she gave a little shiver but let herself be led toward the grassy shore.

Once her feet touch the earth you cannot look at her. The chorus of the Fireflower had returned as though awakening from a short sleep.

It is the Orphan's curse. The gods love their tricks, and dreaming gods are the most whimsical of all . . .

Hold her hand, but do not open your eyes.

We will sing you the path.

A part of Barrick feared it was only errant nonsense—sometimes the Fireflower voices seemed more like ideas than actual intelligences, fleeting phantoms without the coherence of a living person. Still, he knew he could not save her by himself—she was too close to death. He shut his eyes tight, took her hand, and let the voices guide him.

There were times as they walked away from the river that she seemed so insubstantial Barrick could not even be certain he still held her, but he knew he dared not look—that if he did, even the small chance they had would be lost.

Ignore all other voices, the Fireflower told him.

Even those that seem sweet. Keep your back to the river. Trust what you feel.

He let himself open to the darkness and the moving air, the damp air above the slow but powerful black river. He did his best to keep it behind him.

"Qinnitan? I'm here. Can you hear me?"

She did not reply, so he spoke to her again. At last, and from much farther away than should have been possible with her hand still clutched in his, he heard her say, "Who is calling? I'm frightened."

Words were little use—only her hand in his was real; he knew that as long as he held it she was still there.

They walked back across the dark lands for what seemed like years. At times, he saw and heard things that made him think they had almost found their way out, but the Fireflower voices warned him not to trust these phantoms, that it was only the lonely, bitter things that lived in this place laying snares for him. At last, Qinnitan became restive and began to fight him. He struggled with her for what seemed hours, trying to calm her but unable to do so. At last, overwhelmed by her terror and pain, he admitted to himself that he could not impel her any farther.

The Fireflower voices urged him not to give up, insisted that he keep fighting.

"No." He said it for them much as for her. "I will no longer force you. Why are you frightened, Qinnitan? I am trying to help you back toward the light. Why do you fight against me?"

But she couldn't hear him, or if she could she didn't understand, and only went on struggling like a frightened child. Barrick feared that if he continued against her will, he might lose her—might even destroy what little remained of her. He could think of nothing else to do, though it terrified him, so he let go of her hand.

"I am going on," he told her. "Follow me if you can—if you wish—and I'll lead you out of here."

And then, with the startled Fireflower chorus crying its anguish until his head echoed, Barrick again began to walk.

The voices gradually fell silent, but more from surprise than despair. Barrick felt his fear ease a little. Qinnitan must be following.

Now was the hardest time. He pushed his way through tangled branches that clawed and tore, and forded streams as cold and black as the river in which he had found her. He made his way down a long, dangerous slope into a valley where he saw lights twinkling in the dark, but when he got there, the place was empty but for a field of leaning stones.

Dozens of times he stopped himself from looking back. The Fireflower voices were almost completely silent now, but he felt certain he would know if Qinnitan fell away from him, whether they told him or not. Hadn't they found each other time after time in their dreams? Hadn't he found her here as well, on the very border of death's inescapable kingdom?

Then at last she did stop—he felt her warmth diminish. He stopped, too, and it took all his strength to keep looking forward.

"We're almost there," he told her. "Only a little farther. Don't fear!" But it was not her courage that had deserted her, he suddenly realized, but her strength.

They had been walking through a valley of high cliffs and deep darkness; now he moved slowly ahead, groping along the side of the path until he found what seemed like a crevice in the rocky wall.

"Come," he called to her. "Follow me inside. You can rest here and be safe from any . . . hunting things."

He made his way into a narrow space scarcely his own height and only a little wider and longer than he was, but he heard her moving behind him, and his heart once again grew light. He lowered himself to the cold ground, and when she reached him he opened his arms so that she could curl herself into his embrace like an ailing child. He could smell her now, a scent he had never known before but which seemed utterly familiar. He could even hear her breathing in his ear, fretful at first but slowing as she let sleep (or whatever passed for sleep in this nameless place) claim her.

Soon Barrick felt himself sliding away as well, and wondered whether he would wake again in this world or any other.

He didn't understand at first what was happening. He had been deep in an unremembered dream, but now he was awake in darkness. Something was wrapped around him. He reached out and found her face, let his fingers trail across her cheek to her mouth.

"Barrick?" she asked, startling him.

"Qinnitan! Yes, it's me. Can you really hear me?"

She did not answer for a moment. "Yes. But you seem far away. Why do you seem so far away when I can feel you next to me? Where are we?"

He didn't really know—even the Fireflower voices could not tell him exactly where he was. He also did not want to frighten her, because if he lost her now, it would be forever. "On our way home."

She touched his face. "Can you see me? I can't see anything."

Barrick was taking no chances—he kept his eyes tight-closed, even in utter blackness. "No, I can't see you, but that's only because we're in a dark place. Do you remember anything?"

"I remember you." She pushed herself close against him. She was taller than he would have guessed, her head just beneath his chin while her legs curled around his legs and her body pressed against him chest to chest and belly to belly. He had forgotten what it felt like to hold somebody, to be held. "And I remember the fire," she said. "Something burning. Something big."

Barrick remembered those terrible last hours in the deeps below the castle very well, but he had no urge to talk about it. Who knew if the god of lies was even dead? What if Zosim now roamed these dark places, too? "Don't think about it," he told her. "Think about leaving this place. Think about coming with me."

"But I'm so tired." She said not as someone asking for help, but as a matter of fact. "I can scarcely hold you."

"Actually, you seem to be doing that quite well." Unexpected joy bubbled up inside him. "You're holding me very tightly."

"Because I don't want to lose you in the dark. Do you realize how long I've waited to hold you . . . to touch you . . . ?" She tensed a little. "I am sorry. You must think I'm terrible. What kind of girl would say such things?"

"The right kind." He was afraid to speak now, fearful of anything that might end this moment. "You didn't recognize me before," he said. "When I found you in the river. Do you remember?"

"I don't remember anything except waking up here," she said. "Will you kiss me?"

"Kiss you . . . ?"

"No man has ever done that. I don't think we need to be able to see, do you?"

His heart felt as though it would burst in his chest. "No. No, I don't think we need to be able to see to do that."

Barrick marveled at how he could feel everything so completely, the warmth of her skin, the sweetness of her breath, the downy hairs of her cheek and the tickling softness of her eyelashes . . . even the wetness of her tears.

"Why are you crying?"

"Because I never thought this would happen—I prayed for it but I didn't believe the gods would let it happen. And I don't want it to end," she said. "But it is going to end, isn't it? You and I will never be together."

"No!" But at that moment he could not make himself lie. "I don't know, Qinnitan, truly I don't. Don't ask me to say more than that."

"I won't." But her cheeks were still wet. She pushed herself so close against him that she seemed to be trying to push herself *into* him as well, as though their separated flesh could somehow be blended into one body, their hearts into one pulse. "Kiss me again, Barrick. If we cannot be together, let's make a memory that neither death nor fire can take away. Stay here with me. Make love with me."

He kissed her again, as she asked. The darkness might have hidden them from other eyes, but it revealed far more to them than light would have, and the hours fled like minutes.

When he awoke again, Barrick was alone. Terrified, he scrambled out of the bower they had made for themselves with nothing more than the bliss of being together at last. At the last moment he remembered to close his eyes and thus escaped a more certain doom. "Qinnitan!" he called. "Where are you? Come back!"

At last he heard her voice, as if from a distance: "I'm here, Barrick. But you must go."

"What do you mean? You have to come with me!"

"I cannot." She sounded sad but certain. "I don't have the strength to cross back over. I know where I am now, Barrick, and I know what is possible. You have brought me as near to the lands of the living as you can. Now you must continue on your own."

"No! I'll never leave you! I will stay here with you . . . !"

"You will not," she said calmly. "We would have a little time, but then we would both have to cross the river and who knows what would happen after that?"

"But I won't give you up to death. I won't."

"You are too fearful. I will be able to remain here, close to the lands of the living—our love has made that certain. What we made together is strong, my sweet Barrick, like a great stone set deep in the ground. I can cling to it for at least a little while." She reached out then—he felt her fingers on his face, warmer now, as though some life had flowed back into them. "Go back now. I sense you had something planned—perhaps it will still save us."

He tried not to sound bitter. "It will save others. You will suffer from it, as I have."

She laughed, an astounding noise to hear in this place. "Then I will suffer, Barrick, and be grateful for it. What sort of life do you think I had before this? I would rather a hundred times the suffering if I also have your love."

He didn't even need to think. "You have it. You have it always."

"Then go, and trust that."

Never before had he felt so uncertain of anything. But never before had he known anything for which he was so willing to fight. Trusting, though—that was harder than fighting. "Wait for me, Qinnitan, my sweet voice, my dear one. Promise me that no matter how long it seems, no matter how impossible that I am still coming . . . that you will wait for me."

And then he turned and hurried toward the land of the waking and the living. Unkind Fate denied him even a last look back.

Barrick knelt beside Saqri. He could not bear to look at Qinnitan's face only a short distance away, so still, so much like death. "I have brought her as close as I can. Can you find her?"

Saqri's eyes were half open, a trapped creature breathing its last desperate breaths. *I . . . cannot . . . see . . . anything . . . beyond this . . .*

"Then let me help." He ignored his own bone-deep weariness to bend over. He lifted Saqri's dry, cold hand and placed it on Qinnitan's brow. A slight constriction of the muscles around Saqri's eyes was the only sign that she still survived. At last, her voice came, a murmur, a defeated sigh . . .

I cannot find her . . .

Barrick set his own hand on top of the Queen of the Fay's, then closed his eyes and let himself tumble down into the darkness he had just escaped. The Fireflower voices cried out in sudden terror:

Too weak, manchild! You are too weak . . .

You will die, too. You, Saqri, and the girl. Everything gone . . . !

Do not risk it!

But Barrick could do nothing else. Without Qinnitan, he would become something ugly—a cold, raging shadow of himself, a living ghost haunting his own life. Better to go now if he could not save her, to leap into the fire and make a quick ending.

Down, down Barrick Eddon fell. He could sense Saqri beside him, a white, winged shape diving beside him as though falling out of the clouds at the end of a long journey. The dark lands rose up and then rushed past as they skimmed over them, acres of silent forest and silvery meadows threaded with shining black streams. He led her as best he could, but it was not easy—her freedom returned and her crippled mortal body left behind, Saqri wanted to soar.

It was only as he realized he had reached the valley again that Barrick remembered he dared not look at Qinnitan, that like the Orphan, his eyes upon her would break the spell, and the black lands would claim her forever. He shut his eyes tightly, or dreamed that he did, but now he had to go blindly through a land far bigger than any earthly country. How could he find her? He reached outward, thinking that surely in this cold world she must be the only warm thing, the only thing that lived and cared . . .

I am here. The voice was faint as a cricket in a thunderstorm. *I am waiting.*

He turned toward her, letting the darkness shape itself as it would. He could only follow. He could only trust.

When he found her, he kissed her, his tight-shut eyes hot with tears. "Saqri!" he called. "She is here! Qinnitan . . . the one who also carries some of Crooked's blood!"

The great shape dropped out of the sky like a white storm, wings cracking.

"Has he asked you, womanchild? Has he warned you what it will mean if you take the Fireflower?" Saqri asked in a voice like solemn music. "Will you take this terrible burden onto yourself?"

"Yes." In that moment Qinnitan seemed to know all that she needed to know. "I will."

"She still cannot return, Barrick Eddon, even with the Fireflower," Saqri warned him. "In your world she will still sleep, even as I once did. She may never wake."

"I will find a way to wake her." He reached out to find his Qinnitan. He could feel the ripple and blaze of the Fireflower all around them, as if Saqri breathed cold fire. "If it takes me a lifetime, still I will do it. Do you hear me? I will wake you."

Qinnitan lifted his hand to her lips. "I wait for no man to save me—even you, beloved. I will find a way to wake myself."

Saqri laughed. "Well said, child—you may be a worthy successor after all. Take the Fireflower, Qinnitan, daughter of Cheshret and Tusiya. You and Barrick will hold all that remains of my family's long, painful legacy. May the Book record a new future for both our kinds."

And then it was done and Saqri was gone.

Barrick awoke slowly, as weak and sore as if he had been beaten. All around him the Qar were in active mourning, singing as they prepared Saqri's body. He crawled to where Qinnitan lay ignored beside her and rested his head on the girl's delicate chest to hear the slow but reassuring sound of her heartbeat. As he sat up he saw a faint silvery glimmer above her brow and the Fireflower inside him vibrated in sympathy like a plucked string. When he dragged himself to his feet, he was so unsteady that even the calmest of the attendants looked at him worriedly. "Fit a wagon to carry Queen Saqri's body," he said. "We will take her back to Qul-na-Qar so that she can lie with her ancestors, and so that her remaining subjects can mourn her as she deserves."

"And the other?" asked one of the healers. "The girl?"

"Dress her in bridal raiment," he said. "She is alive, although she sleeps. She, too, will go to Qul-na-Qar. See how the Fireflower glows in her? She is what remains of Saqri and all her grandmothers. Take care of her. Make her . . . make her comfortable." For a moment he could barely speak. "She is my love."

49
Two Boats

"Filled with despair, the goddess went to her father Perin and her uncle Erivor and begged them to intervene . . . But the other two brothers agreed that the Earthlord was within his rights, and that the Orphan could not live again because Zoria had failed to bring him out."

—from "A Child's Book of the Orphan, and His Life and Death and Reward in Heaven"

THIS HAS BECOME A CITY *of broken stone and silk tents—beauty amid the ruins. And what beauty . . . !* Ferras Vansen did not particularly like the new and unfamiliar, but he had already fallen out of the world he knew. There was no turning back—the impossible had become his lifeblood, and it seemed to froth inside him like sea foam. *Did she mean what she said? Of course she did, you foolish man, and showed you with her lips and arms that she meant it!* But would it make any difference when set against the hard facts of the world?

"Perin's Hammer, Dab, why are there no archers on the walls?" His good mood blew away in a moment, chased by fear. The responsibility of protecting Briony seemed almost impossibly large. "What do you expect the men up there to do if the Xixians play some trick? Spit on them? This is the life of the king's only daughter in our hands!"

"The archers are on the way, Captain Vansen," Dawley assured him. "Ten Kertishmen, good shots every one. They will be there as you ordered."

"I would have been even happier if you'd said 'ten Dalesmen.'" Vansen mopped his brow. He was terrified that something might go wrong, just when a happiness he had never believed possible was in his hands. "Tell me when these bowmen are in place." Vansen looked around. The pavilion that had been built covered much of the spit of land in front of the Basilisk Gate; the road up the rocky slope was all that remained of the near end of the mainland causeway. Vansen didn't really believe the Xixians planned any treachery, not with their own new monarch accompanying them, but Ferras Vansen didn't trust the Xixians not to do something arrogantly stupid. As Donal Murroy had always told him, it was better to be ready than to be sorry.

The day had turned out fine and sunny, with a fresh warm wind off the bay, and the attendants began rolling back the curtains of the pavilion as Briony arrived with the rest of her guards and Prince Eneas, who had brought a small company of his own men—"the Temple Dogs," as he called them. Ferras Vansen thought it a showy name for what was only another group of soldiers, after all. He had never held with the Syannese custom of self-glorying nicknames.

He approached Princess Briony, bowed, and said, "The guards are all in place, Highness. You will be as safe here as men can make you."

To his alarm, she laughed. He looked up, terrified he would see mockery, but the look on her face seemed to be a fond one. "Captain Vansen, we will have to return to the subject of your promotion soon. If you remain with the royal guard, you will drain the resources of the kingdom protecting me. I think I see three pentecounts of soldiers here!"

He felt himself flushing and cursed silently. "Your Highness is the heart of Southmarch. You have come through too much for us to risk losing you now."

"He is right, Princess," said Eneas in his soft midlander accent.

Vansen was doing his best not to hate the man. From everything he had heard, the Syannese prince was not only an honorable man and an admirable soldier but had been a gentleman and true friend to Briony as well; if Vansen had not feared him so much, he would have wished the chance to know him better. But Eneas had every right to marry Briony, while Ferras Vansen, however she might feel about him, had none. Even now, with his heart more firmly hers than ever before, Vansen felt certain she would do the politic thing—in truth, the only sensible thing—and marry the prince of Syan.

And then I will have to leave this place I love, as well as the only woman I desire. He did his best to push away self-pity. *But what can be done, after all? I am a soldier, she is my queen—the heights are not meant for such as me. At least I have the sun and the wind back again. . . .*

How long had he spent entombed in deathly twilight or under a terrible reach of stone? He had gone so long without open sky and bright sun in the year past that he had forgotten the simple goodness of its warmth on his skin, as well as the bewitching tang of sea air which to a boy of the distant hills still seemed a kind of magic, the stuff of his father's stories.

He must have missed it, Vansen thought. *Must have missed the sea when he left it and his home behind.* A thought was in his head now, and he had to dig at it carefully to find its true shape. *Even more, he must have loved my mother very much to give it up.*

"'Ware the ship!" shouted someone from the wall. Vansen turned to see a small, covered boat bobbing toward them over the swells, the oars on each side moving like the legs of a water beetle. It was painted and gilded in the full glory of the Xixian colors, a huge carving of a spread-winged falcon perched on its prow as if trying to lift the entire craft from the water and fly away with it.

A fitting symbol, Vansen thought with a twinge of satisfaction. *They thought they had the strength to take what they wanted here, but they underestimated the will of the Marchmen . . . especially the courage of the Funderlings. And now they come to us as humble as you please.*

When the boat had been drawn up to the makeshift dock, built from the last stones that remained of the causeway, a group of Xixian soldiers in leopard-spotted cloaks filed off it and lined up on either side of the causeway, followed by a slow-moving figure in an elaborate ceremonial robe. As this lean old fellow made his way forward, propped on the arm of a youthful servant, the soldiers still on the boat began to lift out a large, covered litter.

The old man reached the front of the pavilion where Briony sat with Eneas standing protectively beside her. The prince of Syan looked so much the handsome royal husband already that Vansen could have happily seen him shot with an arrow. The Xixian made an elaborate bow that did not quite cross over into actual humility. Then the youthful servant made a shrill announcement that his stumbling words suggested he had been forced to memorize, "I parsent His Revered Seff . . . Revered *Self,* the Wise Elder, Paramount Mis . . . Minister Pinimmon Vash."

"You are safe in our company, Minister Vash," Briony told the old man. "And so are all who travel with you."

The paramount minister pressed his hands together and bowed to her again. "Your Highness is too kind. Before we begin our formal discussion, may I take this moment to extend my deepest sorrows on the death of your father? I came to know him well in the last months—almost we were friends, I would say . . ."

"Friends?" Briony's voice had lost its smooth strength. "Your master killed my father, Minister Vash. Is this not hypocritical, to feign sorrow?"

"It is not feigned, Highness," he said with the ease of a veteran courtier. "And it is about my late . . . master that we wish to speak."

"We?"

"My present monarch . . . and myself. But I must beg your indulgence. Autarch Prusus has certain frailties that make it difficult for him to speak clearly. We hope you will indulge us and let me assist him."

"How do we know you will not simply say what you wish—that you are not the true ruler of Xis now?" demanded Eneas.

"Oh, my master can speak your tongue," the old man assured him. "He is a scholar. But it is difficult for him." At this, Vash turned and clapped his hands. The litter was carried forward and set down in front of the pavilion. When the curtains were drawn back even Briony had a difficult time hiding her surprise.

The new autarch was a simpleton, or so it appeared, his head lolling, a sheen of drool on his chin. Even his legs and arms seemed unwilling to be led by such a creature and seemed to be struggling clumsily to remove themselves from his trunk.

"Forgive me, but what is this?" demanded Prince Eneas. "Is this a jest or a trick, Xixian?"

"Please, Highness," Briony said. "Do not be hasty. Autarch Prusus, do you understand me?"

The man in the litter nodded, a complicated affair of wags and hitches.

"And do you truly speak our tongue?"

The autarch made a long series of stammering noises. Vansen actually heard a word he understood. " . . . *Dignity.*"

"He says he does, and he apologizes," Vash said. "The Golden One says the gods gave him more wit than dignity."

Briony smiled a hard smile. "Then he would be an ill fit in most courts, where it is generally the other way around—but come into our tent and we will speak. There is no forgiveness in my heart for Xis, but I want no more fighting if it can be avoided."

"Please, Princess Briony," said ancient Vash, "it was your father's own scheme that brought Prusus and I together—he alone saw through the scotarch's outer seeming and made me aware as well. That is why at the last I found a few sympathetic men to help me carry the scotarch and we escaped. That is why we did not die in the caverns beneath your castle. It was your father's cleverness that saved us."

"Do not think to flatter me with what my father did while he struggled for his life—a life your master eventually took from him." Vansen could see that Briony was fighting to stay calm. He longed more than anything to be able to put his hand upon her, to let her know she was not alone—but of course he couldn't. "From what I have been told about your people, it is scarcely worth our while to negotiate. As soon as you return to Xis, this man . . ." she gestured to the new autarch, who was being helped to drink watered wine by a servant, "will be replaced by another member of your mad royal family. So why should I not simply leave you all to make your way across Eion by land and let things fall out as they will?" Her smile this time was even harder. "I do not think you would have a happy time leading your survivors through Syan and Hierosol."

Vash nodded, but it was plain he too was nettled. "Yes, and more innocents would be killed. I do not speak of our soldiers here, Highness. We invaded you . . . or rather, the previous autarch forced us to invade. And ordinarily you would be correct—Prusus would have only a short time to rule before a successor was chosen. But he and I think we have a better plan. There is an old law among our people that the scotarch will rule until a successor has been chosen. However, if the autarch is not dead but simply gone, the successor cannot be chosen until five years have passed." Vash smiled. For all his age he had the confident smile of a younger man. "We will be able to do much in five years, I think, to change that which we like least about our country. For one, if you let us take passage from here, we will withdraw our army from Hierosol as well."

"Truly?" said Eneas. His skepticism was plain. "Why should you do that?"

Prusus abruptly spoke up. Vansen could make out an occasional word now, but much of it still sounded like animal noises.

"He says, 'Because conquest is expensive, and maintaining it is more so,'" the old man explained. "Xis has overstretched its boundaries and resources. We have enough to do taking care of our empire in Xand. All of the adventuring here in the north was the obsession of Sulepis, all bent toward what he thought to do here, in Southmarch." Vash bowed. "But Prusus says that he, who is scarcely a man, has no illusions that he is fit to be a god. He thinks he can be a goodly autarch, however, for as long as the gods give him to rule."

"You promise this?" Briony said, looking not at Vash now but at Prusus. "If we let you and your men take ship—and you Xixians will pay for those ships and pay for everything that goes upon them—then you promise you will withdraw your armies from the rest of Eion?"

Prusus' head wagged several times before he could get out the words. They were hard to understand, but not impossible.

"Yiy . . . I . . . do. I . . . puh . . . rah . . . misss."

"You and Minister Vash may return to your camp in the hills. My counselors, Prince Eneas, and I must talk together."

"I am disposed to trust them, not because I believe everything they say—Vash, it is clear to me, is a man who has long acquaintance with the manipulation of truth—but because I see no choice." In the privacy of the tent she had taken off her headpiece. A sheen of sweat flecked her brow. Vansen realized he was staring.

"I do not like it, Briony," said Prince Eneas. "Don't do it. I think it is a mistake."

She gave him enough of a nettled look to make Ferras Vansen happier than he had been in hours. "I'm grateful for your advice, Eneas, but please remember, this is Southmarch soil, and although I will never be able to repay all you have done for me and my people, I am still the mistress here, even if I have not yet been crowned."

She truly has changed, Vansen realized. *Most of the petty angers have gone. What remains is just and necessary . . . even queenly.*

Briony frowned. "In any case, what can we do? Imprison them all? Execute them . . . ?"

As she spoke a guard came in, clearly in haste. He bent and whispered his message to Vansen, who immediately stepped forward.

"Princess," he said, "my men say that a boat is coming, not from the Southmarch mainland but across the bay from Oscastle . . ."

"Surely that is not so unusual, Captain Vansen? Or is it a warship?"

"No, but . . ." He did not know what to say. "Perhaps you should come and see."

It took only a short time to throw back the curtains again and open the pavilion to the blue sky and the green bay all around. The Marrinswalk ship was impossible to mistake, a single-masted cog of the type usually meant for fast travel and vital news, but what caught Vansen's attention were the three flags she flew. One was the owl of the Marrinswalk's ducal family, but she also showed the black and silver of the Eddons and another pennant with a strange sigil that Vansen did not recognize.

"By the gods," said Steffens Nynor, his wispy hair a little disarranged with drink and the heat of the day, "they're flying the battle standard of the Southmarch master of arms. But we *have* no master of arms. Not since . . ."

"Do not say it," Briony told him. "Do not tempt the gods to cruelty or tricks."

The ship anchored a short distance out in the bay and a boat rowed across to the causeway and tied up on the opposite side from the Xixian falcon boat, which was just raising anchor. As if in studied imitation of the southern delegation, this boat too disgorged a man in dark traveling clothes and a broad hat; the man at the front of the landing boat was even darker of skin than Pinimmon Vash.

"Oh, merciful Zoria, is that truly Dawet?" Briony said. She stood up and waved her hand. "Master Dan-Faar, is it you?"

The newcomer waved from the end of the causeway, but Vansen thought it a subdued gesture. The dark man climbed out as the boat was still being tied and walked up the road toward the pavilion.

Briony clapped her hands. "I am so pleased you have come to us!" she called. "I feared something had happened to you—that you would never see the happy result of all our labors together in Syan."

The man Vansen had last seen as the envoy of Ludis Drakava mounted the wooden steps to the pavilion. He bowed and kissed Briony's hand. "I rejoice to see you back on your throne again, Princess." He turned and made a bow to the prince as well. "Your Royal Highness."

Eneas and Ferras Vansen looked at each other, unhappy with the arrival of this handsome newcomer and with Briony's obvious affection for him.

"But why did you come in such a manner, Master Dan-Faar, flying the flag of the master of arms?" Briony asked him. "Do you seek to fill the position?" She laughed, but suddenly looked unsure. "And why are you dressed so, all in black? Has something happened?

Dawet was still on his knees, as if he were too weary to rise. He took a square of parchment from his cloak and offered it to her. "Here, Princess. This is for you."

Watching the way Briony flinched at the letter, Vansen wanted to leap forward and snatch it from her hand, but he knew he could not. She took it and broke the seal, then spread it on her lap. For a moment she read it in silence, then held it out to Dan-Faar, blinking away tears. "I cannot . . . I . . ." She shook her head. "Please read it to me."

"To Princess Briony from her friend and servant, Idite ela-dan-Mozan, greetings.

On the night of the fire, we were able to bring the great man Shaso dan-Heza out of the flames of my husband's house, may the Great Mother guide and protect them both on their journeys. Shaso had taken great injury fighting with the men who set the fire, giving the women, children, and others a chance to escape the destruction, but he lived long enough to ask after your safety. When we told him you could not be found but had not been captured, he seemed satisfied, and died without saying more. Shaso was a man of great honor and wisdom. Tuan and Southmarch are both sadder places for his loss. . . ."

Dawet lowered the letter and turned to Briony. "I have returned a great man to Southmarch, my lady, so my ship bears his insignia. I am dressed in mourning because I bring back only his ashes." He lowered his head. "Princess, I come to confirm what was heretofore only a sad belief. Shaso dan-Heza is dead."

"Are you certain we are allowed to be here?" Opal asked again. Even the stolid presence of Brother Antimony did not seem to reassure her. The Tower of Summer, at the very heart of the castle, was not the kind of place where most Funderlings would ever feel comfortable, even though their ancestors had helped build it.

"The Big Folk owe a debt to the Rooftoppers now," said Brother Antimony. "I do not think they would grudge their use of an abandoned tower."

"Be grateful," Chert told his wife as they trooped up past another closed room. "When I wanted to visit them, I had to climb onto the roof."

"You? At your age? What were you thinking?"

"Fracture and fissure, woman, I'm not *that* old."

But he knew she didn't really mean it—like him, she was struggling to make sense of a world that had gone completely downside-up. Funderling Town remained a madhouse, with some neighborhoods still sealed off by the Guild and patrolled by the Big Folk's royal guards until the last of Durstin Crowel's men were rounded up. Almost every home had at least one survivor of the war, many of them wounded, not to mention all the surviving monks who had lost not just the Mysteries themselves but their temple home as well—and that, of course, had been mostly Chert's doing. And even though many of Funderling Town's citizens regarded flooding the depths as a heroic, brilliant act that might well have saved all their lives, Chert and Antimony and the engineers that had accomplished it were now despised by the most traditional and conservative of their kind, including the Metamorphic Brothers, many of whom had made it clear that Chert Blue Quartz would never be forgiven for what he (as they saw it) had taken from them.

"Here," he said as they reached the final landing. He pushed open the door. "The top floor."

Opal went through first. "Oh," she said in a faint voice. "Oh, look how *many* . . . !"

We'll be attending quite a few more of these, Chert thought. A vast assembly of such unhappy gatherings, funerals and memorials for fallen friends, awaited them in the days ahead. But in truth, he decided, what they watched now was more than a bit like a Funderling memorial ceremony, but one seen from the very back row of the guildhall: the tiny figures came out and performed their parts, but he and Opal could scarcely hear them and had to guess at what was being said and done. There was no coffin, of course, and no image of Beetledown the Bowman that he could see either, but the Rooftoppers' tiny voices were convincingly somber and the attitude of the mourners indisputably sad. Chert's friend had been well-loved by his people, that was clear, and understanding this reminded him that he would never see Beetledown's tiny, friendly face again. It was strange, because he had never known whether the little scout was married or had children, so he could scarcely claim to have been close to him, but they had been through adventures together nobody else could even imagine, let alone claim to have shared.

Chert found himself suddenly dabbing at his eyes with his sleeve, trying to hide what he was doing from Antimony and Opal. Because of this, he did not see the queen of the Rooftoppers' first steps out into the center of the empty fireplace, but he heard the tiny shell trumpets that announced her and hastily finished wiping away his tears.

She stood, smaller than a child's doll, in a beautiful dress of stiff, shiny fabric studded with beads so small Chert could scarcely even make them out. Beside him, Opal took a deep breath.

"My," his wife whispered, "isn't she so pretty!"

"That's the queen," he whispered back.

"Don't you think I could tell, you old fool?"

"Her most Insidious and Unalloyed Majesty, Upsteeplebat the Queen!" announced a crier the size of a darning needle, then blew on his fluted shell trumpet again.

"Upsteeplebat?" Opal murmured. "What kind of name is that?"

"Hush."

The queen looked up into the heights of the room—or so it must have seemed to her—where the faces of her giant guests loomed like three moons hanging in the sky. She nodded in a way that suggested that she was glad to see them, but she directed her words to the crowd of mourners.

"I do not come here to lament over the death of Beetledown the Bowman, chief of my Gutter-Scouts," she began in a surprisingly loud, high voice, "because we know that he is with the Hand of the Sky in the heights above the heights, and in that attic of delight there is no sadness, no pain.

"But I do stand before you to say that we will miss him, because our love for him was fierce—as was his love for his race and his nation, from the tip of the Iron Needle to the depths of the terrifying earth, from the Great Wainscoting to the fields of the South Roofs where our sky-steeds graze. Beetledown gave the greatest gift he had so that these things could survive, and so you and I could see our people prosper in a world that so often taxes us with hardship, but which is nevertheless the only world we the living have. . . ."

"She speaks wondrous well," whispered Antimony.

"She is their queen," said Chert. "She is altogether admirable."

Opal gave him a look that he could feel without seeing. "Admirable, is she?"

"She is their queen and a goodly one, that is all I am saying!"

"Bad enough you are a troublesome old dog who likes to roam," she said with quiet intensity, "but when you cast your eye on a woman no bigger than a baby's rattle . . . !"

"Oh, stop." He was mortified, and fearful that their voices might carry farther than they guessed among such small, sharp-eared creatures. "That is nonsense, woman, and you know it."

Opal sniffed, but fell silent again.

" . . . And without a moment's hesitation, after all that he had already given to his people and his queen, he said he would do it." Upsteeplebat was still extolling Beetledown's virtues. "Let those who are children this day look to his example—no finer one could have been set for you."

The thought of children made Chert's heart grow even heavier. Opal was not really angry with him, he knew, nor did she believe for a moment he felt anything for the tiny queen of the Rooftoppers. She was angry at him for letting Flint go, and angry at herself more than at him. This day's ceremony was no doubt reminding her of the day the boy had disappeared, that he had last been seen helping Beetledown escape a deadly attack to reach Antimony with the Astion, and that shortly after that sighting everything beneath that place, including the spot where Flint had been, had vanished in a remorseless crush of water. Corpses were still drifting up to the surface of the Salt Pool from its new tributaries below, bodies of Funderlings and Xixians and Qar alike. Chert knew Opal was terrified that Flint's fate had been the same as theirs, that their house would be one of those to receive a visit from a gang of men carrying a dripping body on a covered bier.

He lost track then of exactly what the queen of the Rooftoppers was saying, his thoughts spinning in unhappy circles until the ceremony was over.

★ ★ ★

The tiny man with the trumpet stood at Chert's feet, shouting at the top of his lungs. "Her Majesty wishes to speak to you, Chert of Blue Quartz."

Antimony patted him on the back. "You go. I will wait for you on the stairs. I am too fretful I will step on someone here."

"Don't take long with your flirtations, old man," his wife told him. "We have a great deal to see to at home."

"What are you talking about?" said Chert. "You must meet the queen, Opal. It is an honor. How many queens have you met?"

"Really? But I'm not dressed for it . . ."

"Gods of raw earth, woman, you spent the entire morning making certain you had on the right garb. Come along. Beetledown was my friend—and he helped rescue Flint, too."

His wife's face suddenly betrayed such deep unhappiness that he wished he hadn't said anything, but it was too late to take it back. He took her arm and led her forward, walking with small, sliding steps to give their hosts ample time to get out of his way.

Queen Upsteeplebat had been lifted up onto her saddled dove and waited for them with the serenity of a small but artful carving. When Chert and Opal had shuffled close enough, they carefully lowered themselves to their knees so they could see her better.

"You are very kind to come, Chert of Blue Quartz," the queen said. "And this must be your wife, the Lady Opal." She nodded. "We have heard so much good of you from Flint and Chert, Mistress. I thank you also for coming. Beetledown the Bowman meant much to us." She shook her head. "We will never forget him, nor will we ever be able to replace him."

To Chert's surprise and pleasure, Opal was clearly charmed by the miniature queen. "You are too kind, Your Majesty. I liked Beetledown so much, too. A lovely lit . . . a lovely man. So many have been lost in the war—what terrible times!"

As he listened to his wife and the queen, Chert's attention was caught by Antimony, who was standing in the doorway of the Rooftoppers' sanctuary trying to catch his eye, beckoning. Chert carefully made his way back across the floor.

"You had better come." Antimony's face betrayed nothing.

"What is it?"

"Bring your wife, too, Master Chert."

He went back and made apologies to the Rooftoppers' monarch, who did not seem either insulted or unduly surprised, and led Opal out.

"What is this about?" his wife demanded. "You wanted me to meet her, then as soon as we're talking friendly-like, you yank me off as though I were a . . ." She stopped in the doorway, looking past Antimony at something Chert could not yet see. "Oh," she said. "Oh!" And then she was hurrying across the landing. "Praise the Elders!" she shouted. "Oh, come see!"

It was the boy, of course—Chert had known that by the sound of his wife's voice. As Opal squeezed him and rubbed tears all over his shoulder and neck—he had grown even taller in the past days, it seemed—Flint gave Chert a look that seemed to mix amusement and bafflement.

"But Mama Opal, I'm well," he said as she wept and touched his face. "I said I would see you again. Didn't they tell you?"

She laughed through her tears. "Hark to the boy. As if I shouldn't worry when he's vanished and half the world's tumbled down—and him right at the center of it all!"

Chert joined the embrace, if a little awkwardly. The boy was almost a head taller than he was now but still looked as though he might have seen nine summers at most. "Still, you shouldn't have made your mother worry so, lad. We didn't know where you were . . ."

"Come home," Opal said. "Come home and I will make your favorite—muldywarp stew. Oh, Chert, let's take him home."

Chert could not help noticing that Brother Antimony looked uncomfortable, even troubled. As the boy tried to get down the stairs under Opal's continued assault, hugging him and trying to hold his hands and several times almost toppling them both off the steep steps, Chert slowed until he was walking beside Antimony.

"Why the worried face?" he asked the monk as lightly as he could.

"Oh, it is nothing," Antimony said. "It only troubled me that bad luck should have forced me to leave Beetledown behind just so I could carry Nickel to safety—that . . . that . . ." He looked around as though Brother Nickel's supporters might even be there, in the upper floors of the Tower of Summer. "That miserly, self-important creature. What a waste to lose little Beetledown instead of him!"

"The Elders' plans are not always written clear," Chert said.

"But then I was thinking about how Flint knew just where to be—just where to be! Of all the tunnels of the Mysteries, he knew just where

Beetledown would be coming and where the owl would catch him . . ." Antimony shook his head. "And I was thinking of that, and how he disappeared, and wondering how a mere boy could know such things . . . and then there he was! Standing directly in front of me on the stairs as if I had . . . as if I had conjured him up."

Chert felt a bit of a chill, too—not the first that his adopted son's actions had given him. "We have all had to get used to that. The boy . . . the boy is not like others."

Antimony's laugh was almost angry. "You are a wise man, Chert Blue Quartz, but that is far from the cleverest thing you've ever said. The boy is not like *any* other!"

"Chert!" Opal called back. "Did you hear what Flint said? You're going to have an audience with the princess—and *I* will be going, too!"

"What? Flint, what are you talking about?"

"An audience with the princess and many others, in two days' time," the boy said. "It is very important, Papa Chert. You really must go."

"With Princess Briony? And how did you hear of this?" he asked. "Did someone in the princess' household tell you?"

"Oh, no," he said, opening the door as they reached the bottommost floor. The late afternoon sun flooded in, so that for a moment Chert could not entirely make out the boy's shape and he seemed something else, something unknown. "No," Flint told him. "No one told me. I just thought of it."

50
Cuckoo in the Nest

"Great Kernios declared that that since he had sent his wife away he was in need of another wife, and that if Zoria would take Mesiya's place, Kernios would let the gods take the Orphan up into heaven to live with them . . ."

—from "A Child's Book of the Orphan, and His Life and Death and Reward in Heaven"

TO HIS ROYAL HIGHNESS, Eneas Karallios, Prince of Syan and North Krace,

My dear friend and protector,

It is with a heart still mourning my beloved father as well as pained by the loss of my twin brother, although at this moment he lives and breathes only a short walk from the room where I write this letter, that I come to this, a task I have been avoiding all day. I would rather tend to any number of dreary chores, such as the examination of the accounts with Nynor, which demonstrate my kingdom to be in just as shocking a condition of poverty and mismanagement as anyone might guess, than to write this. But write it I will, because the alternative would be to speak these painful words to your person, and to see their effect in your kind face.

Eneas, I cannot marry you. I promised I would consider it when I knew what fate awaited me here in Southmarch, and so I have pondered your proposal with the deepest and most grateful attention. Who would not be honored to have received such an offer? More importantly, what woman, even if she did not admire you as I do, would be foolish enough to turn such an offer down? Having traveled with you these months and seen your quality, I can promise you I am more honored than

I can ever say, but I still cannot be your wife. The woman who will someday have that good fortune and reign at your side as queen, whoever she may be, will be perhaps the most fortunate of my sex in all of Eion.

Please understand, noble Eneas, there is no failing in yourself which leads me to this decision, no insufficiency in either your character or your treatment of me which urge me to decline you. You have been nothing but honorable to me, and your kindness has been far more than I could ever deserve, were I to dedicate my life from this moment on solely to earning it. Rather, it is my country that makes demands upon me, my people who need me, and my ruined home that begs for my complete attention. I know that if I married you, I would not be discouraged from rebuilding Southmarch, or even giving the greatest part of my thoughts to my own people, but you would be doing your own subjects a disservice if you absented yourself from them, so we would marry division as well as each other. It also seems true to me that eventually, by the nature of your sex and the importance of your own country, Southmarch would become merely an outpost of Syan. That alone is enough to ensure that I marry no other monarch. Seeing what the last years have done to my beloved home has torn at my heart, and I have come to realize that I am, above all else, my father's daughter. I truly value my people more than my own happiness.

You will say that none of these are true impediments to a marriage, that they are the fears of a young woman who has suffered many losses. That may be, but you deserve better than to marry a halfhearted bride. You are the very paragon of Trigonate knighthood, dear Eneas, and you deserve a consort who can be always by your side without lamenting her own neglected kingdom.

But please know this—my debt to you is deep. Whatever happens, I pray that our two countries always remain friends, but even more so that you and I remain fast friends as well. . . .

The guards observed his expression with alarm, but he ignored them—it was not the guards who had earned his anger.

One of the maids let him in; he paced the antechamber until she returned and led him through into Briony's retiring room. The princess had been writing a letter; as he came in she blotted it, rolled the parchment, and put it aside. The summer night was warm but Briony wore a heavy sleeping robe, perhaps for modesty's sake. The rest of the maids were still dressed, which was a good thing considering Ferras Vansen's plans.

"I must have some time to speak privily with Her Royal Highness," he said. "Princess, will you send your attendants away? I apologize for the intrusion, but it is a matter of utmost urgency."

She looked at him, trying to read his face. "Of course, Captain Vansen. Give them a moment to compose themselves. Ladies, I know that Duchess Merolanna sits up late these nights because she has trouble sleeping. You can find a fire and some company in her chambers."

When they had all trooped out, whispering at this strange and sudden intrusion, Briony seated herself in a large chair and drew her feet up beneath her. "You have my attention, Captain Vansen." She shook her head. "I will not be able to call you that much longer, will I? Soon the coronation will come, and the honors will be given . . ."

"Hang that," he said. "I care nothing for honors or titles. You know that."

"Why such anger at me?" she asked. "I looked to you many times yesterday but all I saw was your frowning displeasure. You would not meet my eye." For the first time her mask slipped a little and her voice shook. "I offered you my heart and my lips the night before. Why should that earn your scorn?"

He stood in front of her with fists clenching and unclenching. "Scorn? It was you who would not look at me! I tried to catch your eye when you first came and you stared at me as though you had never seen me before! As though you were so choked in shame you could not bear to show me even the kindness you show to the youngest stable boy, or even old Puzzle!"

Briony laughed, a sudden burst of merriment that caught him by surprise. "Puzzle! Gods, are you jealous of the jester because I kissed his head and gave him a couple of coppers? He is a century old if he is a day!"

Vansen hated being laughed at; he would rather have been back in the depths of the Mysteries being strangled by the autarch himself than to have this woman, whom he loved so much his heart ached when he was away from her, laugh at him that way. "You mock me, my lady. You mock your servant because he is nothing more than that—a servant. Your pardon. I was foolish to think I could be anything more." He turned and walked stiffly toward the door, his head like a windy night full of blowing leaves.

"Wait."

He stopped. She was his sovereign, after all.

"Turn and face me, Captain. It is not proper to stand with your backside to your queen."

Vansen turned. "With respect, Highness, you are not the queen yet."

Her eyes were red, but she was fighting not to laugh, which confused Ferras Vansen mightily. "Merciful Zoria, you were right, Captain Vansen. You *are* a fool!"

"Then if my ruler has no further need of me," he said loudly, "perhaps she will be so kind as to release me . . ."

"Gods in heaven, Vansen, what is wrong with you?" She put her pale feet on the floor and stood up, her arms wrapped tightly around herself. "Release you? Are you truly upset with me because I would not gaze at you lovingly in front of all my subjects, in front of Prince Eneas and the new autarch? What do you want, man?"

"A sign." He did his best to calm himself. He had a sudden vision of Briony's ladies standing in the hallway with the guards, all of them listening at the door. "Some small sign that the other night meant . . . something."

Now she came toward him, spreading her arms. "Meant something? Oh, sweet Heaven, how can you ask? Does *this* mean something?" And as she pressed herself against him her robe fell open and he felt the length of her whole and warm, with only a thin cotton nightdress separating him from her flesh.

He pulled her close and for a long time only held her, squeezing until she could barely find her breath. "Oh, gods, I hunger for you, Briony. I am no poet, no courtier. I have never loved like this before and I do not know the rules of the game! I was frightened because I saw nothing in your eyes. It was as though . . . I could not . . ." He shook his head and buried his face in her golden hair, which was still so short he could feel the skin of her neck hot against his cheek. "It was as though everything else we had together . . . had been a lie."

"Fool, dear fool. I am soon to be a queen. I cannot show people my thoughts in the construction of my face. I would be dead today if I could not hide my feeling from others."

"But there are no others here now," he said, and lifted her chin until he could look into her face, the face he had been able to see only in memory for so long; for a moment it all seemed a dream again, but the feel of her reassured him. "No others. No one but us."

"Then you will see what our love is truly made of," she said, and brought her lips to his.

"Are you well, my love?"

She stirred. "Well, indeed. A little pain, that's all. They say the first time is always that way." She smiled. "You are my man now, forever and ever—the only husband I will ever have, even if a temple never hears our vows. Do you know that?"

"I would be nothing else." He traced circles on the skin of her belly, but could not do so for more than a moment before the urge to kiss her there became overwhelming.

"Stop!" Briony said, laughing. "We cannot! Just think of my ladies-in-waiting, who will be spreading this story all over Southmarch tomorrow morning if I do not bring them back from Merolanna's rooms before midnight."

"I told them it was a matter of grave importance," he said. "Did I lie?"

She smacked at his head and then rolled over so she could kiss him. "Oh, I wish we could be like this forever, Vansen."

"My first name is Ferras," he told her, almost shyly.

"Do you think I don't know?" She laughed again. "I know everything about you that I could discover. At first because I thought you the worst man ever. Later . . . well, my feelings changed . . . or at least became clearer." She looked at him, her face suddenly earnest. "Would you prefer I call you by your first name?"

"I don't care which you choose as long as you speak it with that look in your eyes, always," he said.

She rolled onto her back. "But I can't, you know. Not in front of others. You know that, don't you? Please say that you do."

"I suppose," he said. "But how can you love someone so much lower than yourself, that you must hide that love from everyone?"

"Foolish Captain Vansen! I could make you a noble in an instant. I *will* make you a noble—otherwise, you cannot be my lord constable. But even so, the way we feel for each other must stay a close-held secret."

"There are no secrets in a place like this—the servants and guards know everything, always." He shook his head. "I can live without marrying you, Briony, although I will die if you marry another . . . but why must our love stay hidden? Don't you feel the same for me?" He suddenly felt stricken. "You do, don't you? Feel the same?"

"Of course, you wonderful, truehearted man—but I have more than my own happiness to think about. If Kendrick or my father had lived, things would be different. Even if Barrick had not changed so greatly . . ." She shook her head, her expression darkening like a sky clouding over. "But an ordinary life is not what Fate has given me. I must keep myself aloof, or seem to. I'll have to pretend no man has won my heart . . . but that any man might, if he brings a useful alliance to Southmarch. That's how I'll make policy. That's how I'll keep our country free from the influence of powerful neighbors."

"Even Syan?" he said suspiciously.

She smiled, but it was a sad one this time. "Even Syan. Especially Syan."

He crept closer to her. "Let us not talk of Syan any more. Kiss me."

When they had done that and more for a while, he sat up.

"Don't go," she said, her voice growing a little slow and sleepy. "I take back what I said. The ladies can find beds in Merolanna's chambers. Tell me more of what you saw down in the caverns. I can scarcely believe any of it. Did you truly fight a god?"

"Not me, no. Not even your brother did. The creature was too far beyond any of us." He shook his head. "I don't want to talk about it. It is still too close."

She shook her head. "It's hard for me even to understand. You say my brother this, my brother that—he fought a hundred men! He swung down on a rope! Some powerful magic must be at work—that is not the brother I knew, who couldn't even cut his own meat without falling to cursing and knocking his trencher on the floor!"

Vansen smiled, but there was a touch of puzzlement to it. "Magic indeed. It's as if he aged ten years in a few months. And his arm is healed! He's changed so much that I hardly recognized him. When the stone-swallowing demons came at us, every last one of us would have died if Barrick and the Qar had not shown up . . ."

"The stone what?" She had a strange, troubled look on her face now. "Stone-swallowing . . . ? I have not heard this tale before. Tell me."

He pulled her closer. "Your maids and ladies . . . ?"

"Leave them be a little longer."

He described the final battle in the Maze in detail now, of how he and the Funderlings gave ground until there was no more ground to give.

"So brave!" she said. "And not just you, dearest Captain Vansen. Chert's people have astonished me."

"All of us," he said. "We did them a disservice for many years, it seems. But even they could do nothing when the Stone Swallowers came. I don't know what they were truly called—there were three of them. But each one placed a stone in his mouth and . . . and then began to change . . ." He hesitated, feeling her body grow rigid beside him. "Briony?"

"Are you certain they were men?"

He considered. "To be honest, I never saw them before they had already become those . . . things. . . ."

"Tell me again. Tell me what the stones looked like."

"I don't know," he said, laughing a little. "Perin's Hammer, girl, we were in almost complete darkness . . . !"

"Tell me all you remember!" There was nothing of the sweet young woman in her voice now.

And Vansen did, marveling to find that all this time he had been kissing not just his beloved, but also a queen.

Steffens Nynor was wrapped in a heavy wool cloak, but his ankles were bare of hose and he was clearly feeling the cold. "Is it truly necessary to do this now, Highness?" he asked.

"I have learned a lesson." Briony motioned for one of the guards to knock on the tower's heavy front door. The booming sound echoed and died. She was just about to order him to do it again when a quavering, childish voice from behind the door said, "Who goes there?"

"It is the Princess Regent, to see Queen Anissa," the guard said.

The door opened enough for the boy to peer out at the visitors, then the door swung wide. "But the queen is sleeping!" he said, as if the people knocking might not have realized that the time was well after midnight. "She is in mourning," he offered next, but the guards had already pushed past him and he was left talking to Briony, Vansen, and Lord Nynor.

"Of course she is," Briony told him, not unkindly. "And so am I. Do you see my black dress?"

He scuttled off up the stairs to the queen's bedchamber as if Briony had frightened him. The guards on duty in the reception hall had dropped to their knees; she waved them to their feet. Several of them looked to their longtime captain as though he might explain why this ordinarily sleepy duty had been interrupted, but Ferras Vansen took his lead from Briony and kept his thoughts to himself.

Anissa and her retinue were long enough coming down that Briony had begun to consider sending the soldiers up to get them when she heard the queen's voice preceding her down the stairs. *"But why? Why should she want to come here in the night this way? It frightens me!"* Now she appeared, accompanied by half a dozen women, one of whom held her little son, Alessandros.

Olin Alessandros, Briony reminded herself. *My brother. My father's child, too.*

The sight of Anissa in her nightdress brought back dreadful memories—memories of fire and living shadows, memories of last Winter's Eve when her entire world had been turned upside down—but Briony did her best to keep her voice even. "I am sorry to bother you at such a time, Anissa, but my sleep was troubled by a thought that you alone can answer."

Anissa turned to Nynor with a show of confusion, but the aged counselor had no duty here but that of observer. He nodded respectfully to her but made no other sign. "What is it?" she said. "What do you want of me, Briony, that you frighten me so?"

"I want to know how it was that your maid Selia came to you. Do not turn so pale, stepmother. I have recently learned something about the Autarch of Xis and now I need to know this from you. How did your maid come to you?"

"I . . . I do not know. I do not remember!" Anissa looked around as if one of her maids might help her remember, but none of them would meet her eye. Many of them were themselves from the queen's home in Devonis and knew themselves to be foreigners in the court, protected only by Anissa's position, but they seemed curiously unwilling to speak in her defense. "She . . . was sent to me," Anissa said at last. "I asked my mother's chamberlain to send me a good girl, someone to be my bodyservant. That is all. I scarcely knew her! I had no idea she was a witch! But I have told you this already, Briony—why do you tax me with this now, when your father is dead and I am so upset?"

"Why indeed?" Briony shook her head. "You ask a fair question. Nynor, did you find the letter?"

The old man was looking at Anissa with an expression Briony hadn't seen before. It took him a moment to realize she was speaking to him. "Oh. Oh, yes. Yes, it's here." He drew it out of the pocket of his cloak with a shaking hand. "I never throw anything away, and I am lucky that the fool who took my place did not change that." He held it out to Briony, but she shook her head.

"Read it to us, please."

"Let me . . ." he squinted, scissoring his spectacles until he could fit them properly over both eyes. "Let me find . . . ah. Here. From a letter Queen Anissa wrote to me in Heptamene of last year, a few months after the king had been imprisoned by Hesper of Jellon and then ransomed to Drakava in Hierosol."

" . . . And at King Olin's express wish, I have been bringing Lady Selia ei'Dicte, my dear friend of childhood, to be my companion in his absence. She is very close to me and of high birth, so please see she does not wait at the dock and is not put through some rude treatment like a common servant."

Briony stared at her. "So which was she—a dear companion from childhood, or a servant you scarcely knew?"

Anissa took a few steps back toward the stairs. Some of the guards tensed—Briony could feel it; the air in the tower's reception hall, large and drafty as it was, seemed to have grown tight. "How can I remember? I knew her, perhaps! That does not mean I had anything to do with what she did. I would never . . ."

"I know now that the stone your maid used must have come from the autarch—it was one of the same magical Kulikos stones he gave to others during the last hours of the fighting under the castle, changing them into dreadful, demonic *things*. Captain Vansen saw one of them putting the Kulikos in his mouth." She frowned. "No, not 'his mouth,' but 'hers.' The demons must have been women to begin with. Chaven said the stones only worked on women."

Briony moved closer to Anissa. "So I can only suppose that the autarch, who had several of these Kulikos stones, and also had several spies in the Tollys' Summerfield Court, gave one of these deadly talismans to your maid instead. But why? On the very unlikely chance she would use it to murder my brother Kendrick?" Just saying the words made Briony violently angry, but she forced herself to speak even more calmly. "Why? How would he know that Selia could be trusted, or would even do such a thing at all? Unless she was brought here with no other purpose in mind. Unless she was, perhaps, someone that had *already* been picked out for the task . . ."

The maids and ladies drew back a little, some of them whispering anxiously. Anissa's eyes were round. "What are you saying? That I knew? That is foolish! Why would I hurt Prince Kendrick?"

"I'm not certain," Briony said through her teeth, "but let me guess. You can answer one question for me, though, Anissa—did the autarch's servant first come to you before you left Devonis, or was it here, in Southmarch? My wager is that although you may have spoken to him before, when he finally approached you it was here, after you found out you were carrying my father's child."

"What do you say? I don't understand."

"This, Stepmother—although it galls me even to call you that. I think you *do* understand, all too well. I think that one of the autarch's spies came to you and told you that the child in your womb was doomed if Kendrick or either of the two younger children—Barrick or myself—took the throne. He told you that if Olin died in captivity, Kendrick and the rest of us would not stand any rivals for the throne, that Kendrick would have the baby done away with, and probably you, too. Am I right? Is that what he told you?"

"No! No!" But she had the sound of a woman in despair, not one protesting her innocence.

Briony, with a cold, sinking feeling in her belly, knew she had guessed correctly. "Tell the truth, Anissa. I am not the Autarch of Xis, but I'll not spare harsher means if I don't hear the truth from you now."

"Stop frightening me!" Anissa began to cry. For a moment, Briony almost felt sorry for the small, pretty woman who had brought her father such happiness, but she also remembered what had happened to her in Anissa's chamber the night her exile began—the night when the maid Selia had put the stone in her mouth and turned into something otherwordly and deadly. Briony couldn't bear to imagine what Kendrick's last hour must have been like at the hands of that monstrosity.

"Guards. She will go to the stronghold now, I think."

"No!" Anissa suddenly fell to her knees and scrambled forward, trying to throw her arms around Briony's legs. Ferras Vansen stepped out and blocked her, then lifted her to her feet with surprising gentleness. "Do not do that to me, please, Briony!" her stepmother wailed. "I was terrified, so!

He said that my baby would be taken and murdered! He told me I would never see my home again—that I would be poisoned here in Southmarch . . . buried in cold ground . . . !" She was weeping so hard now it was difficult to understand her. Briony looked at Vansen, whose face showed a complicated mixture of pity and disgust as he held Anissa upright.

"Who said that? Who approached you?"

"It was a man from my own country. A merchant. He told me he had news from home, so I let him come to me." She could barely stand. "Please, please do not kill me! Do not hurt my baby! I did not want to do it, but they said that Kendrick would murder me and the child. I was so frightened!"

"So you helped the autarch kill my brother instead." Briony felt as if she were a vessel full to the brim with caustic liquid, that if she spilled even a drop it would burn wherever it touched. "Lock her away," she told Vansen.

"In the stronghold?"

"No. That is no place for the mother of my father's child. She can stay here—under guard." She turned to Anissa. "But you will not keep the boy." She reached out her hands to the maid and took little Olin Alessandros while Vansen held the struggling Anissa. "He is something of my father, not of you."

"Do not murder me!"

"She must have a trial, no matter what, Highness," said Nynor. "Her father has been a close ally for years."

"A close ally who harbored agents of the autarch. Who allowed those same agents to send a witch here to murder my brother!" She wanted nothing more at that moment than to have done with Anissa once and for all, but she could not bring herself to do it. "Yes, you will have a trial, lady. Then you will be locked away so long that your name will be forgotten. You will die unremembered."

The child was crying now, too, moved by his mother's loud distress. As Vansen detailed new men to relieve those who had been guarding the Tower of Summer until he better understood their loyalties, Briony held the small body close to her breast.

As she reached the door and stepped out into the cold night air, Briony stumbled. The weight of what she had undertaken suddenly seemed too much—she felt she would never have the strength even to reach her chambers. But Ferras Vansen reached out and caught her arm to steady her, then they walked back to the residence side by side.

51
A Shared Admiration

"Zoria the Dove, of all gods and goddesses the kindest, agreed to marry her uncle if he would let the Orphan go, though all the earth and Heaven mourned to lose her."

—from "A Child's Book of the Orphan, and His Life and Death and Reward in Heaven"

IN HONOR OF THE ROYAL VISIT, Gem Street was ablaze with lanterns, so Funderling Town's famous ceiling and the faces of its public buildings could be seen in all their intricate, ornamented glory.

"It is quite astonishing," Briony said, staring up as Vansen led her horse along the narrow main road. "All this beauty. I knew it was here, but I scarcely noticed—my father brought me here several times, you know."

"Try to look down as well, Highness," said Nynor. "Your subjects desire your attention, too."

"Don't scold me, Count Steffens. I know they're waiting. That's why I'm here." But she made certain to wave and smile as they passed the junction of Gem and Ore where the crowds were gathered close together and had been waiting for some time. "There, I see the guildhall," Briony said. "Most impressive, isn't it, Captain Vansen?"

He grunted, being too engaged at the moment in trying to clear a path for Briony to approach the building's wide front steps. The castle was at peace in the largest sense, but a few of Hendon Tolly's most desperate supporters still lurked in the unfrequented outer reaches of Funderling

Town, and there were rumors that some Xixian soldiers and even a giant *askorab* or two might be hiding in the outer tunnels as well. After a time so strange it was hard to guess when anything would be completely ordinary again.

Several Funderlings called out Vansen's name, which surprised him. When he turned, he recognized men who had fought with him in the Maze and saluted them in return, but he felt awkward doing it. He was moved that they should consider him one of their own, but he didn't like being at the center of things and he never would.

And what will I let myself in for as lord constable, then? I will never be able to look the true nobles in the face . . . But, he reminded himself, many of the "true" nobles had managed to avoid fighting for Southmarch entirely. Many of those same nobles had also made it clear they would never come down into Funderling Town, even to hear what the princess regent had to say today. *Which shows that birth alone does not make or mar any man completely,* he thought, catching an upward drift of his heart and clutching it firmly for once. *Look at me! The princess says she loves me—do I have cause to complain of anything?*

It did not harm his mood that almost as many Funderlings seemed to be cheering for him as for Briony, though he carefully gave no sign of it. He helped her down from her horse in front of the guildhall and formed up her royal guards to accompany her inside.

"You are a well-liked man in these neighborhoods, Captain," said Briony, smiling.

"Any man who did not cut and run from trouble would be treated the same way." But he couldn't help being pleased she had noticed.

"Your Royal Highness," called out Malachite Copper, dressed in high finery, arms and neck glinting with gems and polished metal, "please forgive me for bearing bad tidings, but I must report that your captain is a terrible liar. There is no man more honored in our city, ordinary or Big."

"I know that, Master Copper," said Briony. "And it is a pleasure to see you again in less trying circumstances than on the day the ocean rushed in."

"The sentiment is mutual, Highness." He bowed and extended his arm. "Come, let me take you into the guildhall. You may leave your gloomy escort to join you when he is ready."

"She may certainly walk with you, Master Copper, but I will be right behind you," Vansen said firmly. "Her Highness goes nowhere without the captain of her guards along to keep her safe. She owes it to her subjects. Am I not right, Princess Briony?"

She smiled as she took Copper's arm. "Of course, Captain Vansen. You know best."

It was a baffling gathering, he thought—like something from the depths of the months just passed, when so many different kinds of folk had been thrown together by the desperation of their situation. A good number of the Southmarch royal court was there, and, of course, the Funderlings were present in force—it was their guildhall, after all—with the four Highwardens in their usual positions of power. That was not the end of those who crowded the council chamber, either. The Skimmers were present in large numbers as well, most of the men wearing ceremonial hats and mantles of fish skin—thoroughly dried and almost odorless, Vansen was glad to note, since the chamber was not large. The Rooftoppers had also made an appearance, their entire delegation seated on top of a Funderling ore wagon specially prepared for them. Even the Qar were represented, although only by the eremite Aesi'uah and a few silent, robed figures; like the rest of her kin, Aesi'uah looked as though she could wait politely until the sun itself was consumed if necessary. Barrick had not come.

One of the Highwardens, a Funderling named Sard who looked to Vansen's eyes to be older than the ancient building itself, opened the proceedings with words of greeting and extravagant promises of Funderling fealty which somehow had a less than sincere ring to them. Vansen wondered if he was the only one who noticed.

"And now, in a gesture which we must take as a show of great respect," the wizened elder finished, "she has come to our humble habitation to speak to us. Give heed to your monarch, the daughter of Olin Eddon and Princess Regent—yes, yes, soon to be crowned as queen, I'm told—Princess Briony. All bow."

Briony stood up in the general murmur and rustle of the Funderlings showing their respect. Of all those present only the Qar did not bow or salute. Many of Briony's courtiers saw that and did not like it, Vansen could not help noticing. *It is those who did not fight who have the least patience with our strange allies,* he thought.

"I accept this honor in the name of the throne, and of my father,"

Briony said loudly. "But I do not deserve it for myself. I hope one day it will be otherwise."

Some of the Funderlings murmured, confused.

"We have survived a terrible danger," she went on. "I believe that we were delivered from our doom by Heaven itself—but for a reason. Everything that we treasure was within a breath of annihilation—our kingdom, our city, our lives, perhaps even our souls. I cannot believe that such things happen without reason. And whether it was the gods my people worship, or the Earth Elders of the Funderlings . . ." A stir passed through the crowd as she listed the sacred names, "Egye-Var, Protector of the Skimmer-folk, or the Lord of the Peak," she nodded toward the Rooftoppers' wagon, "the matter stands thus—we were saved when it seemed certain all would die.

"We are here in part to thank those who fought for Southmarch, from the smallest to the tallest—I will speak of some of those contributions later—but perhaps even more importantly, we are here because I am determined that we should learn from what has happened.

"We may never know exactly what mysterious hand shaped the destiny of the people of this castle, the Qar, and the Xixians, and brought us all together in this place. What we can know is that only with the help of every single one of us were we spared a terrible doom. I cannot rule this kingdom in good faith without understanding Heaven's clear message to us.

"Funderlings!" Her voice suddenly rose. "My family, which once called you brothers, has in more recent years treated you poorly. We enjoyed the fruits of your work but gave you little say in your own governance. So, too, with the Skimmers. And you Rooftoppers—well, we cannot entirely be blamed for that, because you hid so well under our very noses that all but a few of us had forgotten you even existed." A shrill chorus of laughter arose from the delegation in the wagon bed, a little like the chirping of crickets.

Briony next turned toward Aesi'uah and the other hooded eremites. "And even the Qar deserved better of us." This caused a resentful murmur among the ordinary citizens. "It seems likely that we deserved better of them as well," Briony added, but without hurry or concern. "No one can answer that riddle yet. The hurts we have done to each other will not be unraveled in an afternoon.

"But now the time has come for us to rebuild Southmarch, from these beautiful streets and houses of Funderling Town, cracked by cannon's fire, to the deserted wilderness that the mainland city has become. We will need everyone's help. And thus, as we make right what has been harmed by war and treachery, we will need to work as one people. No longer will there be a royal council that has no Funderling members, or decisions about Southmarch that do not take into account all its residents. Do not mistake me!" And here Briony's voice rose a little as the crowd began to murmur. "Decisions will have to be made and not all will be popular. That is why the one who sits on the throne, whether it is I or perhaps one of my brothers someday, must have the weight of law behind them, just as before. But never again will that law be exercised without all Marchfolk being heard."

The voices of the crowd, which had grown louder during this strange and unexpected speech, became so loud that for a moment Vansen thought he might have to pull Briony from the dais for her own safety—some of the Funderlings were actually shouting. After a moment though, he came to realize that most of the noise was being made by a group of younger Funderlings cheering for the princess regent. The older Funderlings, as well as many of the courtiers and Skimmers, mostly looked dumbfounded.

"I come here today," she went on, "to proclaim a new synedrion which will advise the ruler of the March Kingdoms. This Council of Southmarch will be made of all the peoples of Southmarch, big folk and small, drylanders and Skimmers. Together we will keep safe this ancient seat that is home to all of us—dear to all of us . . ."

The long afternoon was finally ending. As Vansen waited, his beloved listened to Steffens Nynor, who was trying to speak to her confidentially in a guildhall full of Funderlings and others.

"But, Highness," he said in an agitated whisper, "there is no precedent for this!"

"Royalty makes its own precedents," laughed Dawet dan-Faar. "Briony begins her rule like a true queen. It is to be commended."

Nynor scowled. "There is no precedent for you, either, Master Dan-Faar. It seems to me that the last time we saw you, you were ransoming our king."

"It's true," Dawet said. "I am a busy man."

Vansen stepped between the two of them, not that he thought Nynor would do anything dangerous, but he did not like to see the old man teased, either, and Dawet was a bit like a cat. "Please, Highness," he said to the princess, "you should be getting back to the residence."

She gave him a look. "Why is it everyone seems to think I must be looked after like a child?"

"Because like doting parents, we none of us have anything else so precious and dare not risk it." Dawet was pleased with himself. Vansen found himself wondering when this smooth, dangerous fellow would move on to cause trouble in some other kingdom. For him, it could not be soon enough.

Vansen was startled to find Aesi'uah standing beside him. She had appeared as if from nowhere, and her coven stood with her, faces hidden in their hoods; everyone else on the guildhall platform seemed happy to give them a wide berth. "Princess Briony," the eremite said, "I beg your pardon for interrupting. I bring a message from your brother."

"Really?" Briony's voice was cool. "Surely it is not so far to your camp that he couldn't come himself."

"Do you wish to hear the message?"

The princess flicked her hand. "I suppose."

"He wishes you to know that we are leaving tomorrow. The survivors of the People will go back to Qul-na-Qar. But he said he would like to speak to you one last time, if you will come to bid him farewell."

"Where?" Briony looked angry, but there was something else in her face that Vansen could not quite understand.

"Where the two of you said good-bye the last time he left." She brought her hands together on her breast. "The Coast Road at sunset. If you cannot come so far he will understand . . ."

"I will be there." Briony turned from her as though the Qar woman had ceased to exist. "Come, Captain Vansen, round up your men. Nynor, you may tell the castle folk that we are going back now." She smiled, but it was the merest tightening of her lips. "We have given them all something to talk about today, haven't we?"

Nynor shook his head and sighed. "Oh, Highness, you certainly have. You are your father's daughter, true enough."

Rain had swept through in the morning but by the time Sister Utta was on her way back from the shrine, the skies had cleared to a blue just barely streaked with clouds. With the help of a few royal guards loaned to her by their handsome but reticent captain, she had set most of the worst damage to right, although the mosaics had been rattled to pieces by cannon fire and spread across the floor of the shrine. Separating and reassembling them would require months of careful work. Still, it was a grand feeling to be doing something useful, and especially to be doing something useful with Zoria's place of worship. After the events of the last months, Utta felt closer to her patroness than ever.

In fact, she thought as she made her way to Merolanna's apartments, why settle for just rebuilding the old shrine, which had always been small? Why not build a new one better able to serve the castle's populace? A bigger shrine could bring in more tithes, which would allow her to help some of the folk made homeless or destitute by these long seasons of war.

Utta was so caught up with these new ideas that she did not immediately notice the boy sitting on the bench in Merolanna's antechamber like a young scholar banished from the classroom to consider his sins.

"Oh!" She took a step back when she finally saw him. He was a young boy, perhaps nine or ten years old, with hair of so pale a yellow that in the dark room it seemed white. His clothes made her think for a moment that she was looking at one of the Funderlings; his face though, despite its solemnity, was that of a child. "Hello," she said, recovering a little. "The blessings of the Three on you, and the good grace of Zoria."

He slid from the bench and stood up. "Blessings to you, Sister Utta. I need to leave now, but I wanted to say something to you before I went."

The child was odd, although she could not say exactly why, but there was something so compelling about him that she did not back away again even when he came to her and took her hand. "Please, look after Merolanna. She is important to me and she will be sad when she finds I've gone. She doesn't have much longer—I fear she will be called onward before spring comes again—so I think the task will not be too much for you." As she stared at him in amazement and more than a little disquiet, the boy squeezed her hand. His eyes were as blue as a clear spring sky. "I must go to the stable now." He continued without explaining. "You have many years still, Sister, so you need not worry that your kindness to Merolanna will cheat you of your ambitions. I can tell you that you will bring many, many hearts to my mother's service in the days ahead."

With these words still ringing in her head, the child let go of Utta's hand and walked out of the dowager duchess' apartments.

"Oh, what a morning!" Merolanna said when Utta came to her bedside. "My son came to me! Here in my room! I wish you could have seen him!"

Utta could think of nothing she trusted herself to say, except, "That must have been a blessing."

"A blessing, yes, that is just the word. He came to me and told me so many wonderful things that he will show me one day! I can scarcely wait."

Utta looked at the old woman's smile for a long moment, then turned away to dab discreetly at her eyes. "All things come in the gods' time."

"You sound as if you don't think he'll be back soon," the duchess said, "but he had better not dawdle. After all, it is my coach and driver he's taken!" Merolanna arranged her cushions and sat back, then reached out for Utta's hand. "But until then, dear friend, sit with me for an hour, if you would be so kind. What is the weather like today? Is it truly summer at last?"

Utta let herself be pulled down into the chair, her thoughts skittering like mice. "Summer? Oh, yes, I . . . I think so, Duchess. It is not overly warm today, but the sky is bright and big . . ."

"She is guilty of murder. More importantly, she is guilty of conniving at the death of a ruling prince. You cannot let her live, Princess."

Rose was fussing with a loose ribbon on her stomacher and it was beginning to annoy Briony severely. She waved the young woman away. "Master Dan-Faar, this is my stepmother we are talking about—my father's widow. It is nothing so simple as you make it sound."

"It is *just* as simple as that. If there is discontent with your rule, Anissa will become the center of all resistance—she's the baby's mother, after all. "Put King Olin's son on the throne!" they will say. "We need a king!"

"As opposed to a queen?" Briony asked. "You do not know the history of my folk as well as you think you do, Dawet. . . ."

"Yes, we all have heard of Queen Lily, pride of the Eddons, yes, yes." He laughed in that infuriating way he had, as if everyone else's thoughts had already occurred to him, been considered, then dismissed. "But that was long ago and nobody dared speak against Anglin's blood. Times have changed, Highness. The world has turned topsy-turvy, especially here in Southmarch, and nobody will ever again feel quite so certain about what is important and what is not."

Briony shook her head. "Not all you say is wrong, Master Dan-Faar, but I am not you, this is not Tuan or any other Xandian satrapy, and we do not kill our relatives."

"Any prince would execute a relative who has already tried to kill him. We are not so uncivilized in the south as you think us, Princess."

She felt herself caught out. "I meant no offense, Dawet."

He made a little bow. "I know, Highness. But the facts remain."

"Enough. Tell me of something else. What of the Xixians? Did the last of them take ship this afternoon?"

"They did—the new Autarch Prusus and the minister and the remainder of the Leopard guards. They sailed in a Helmingsea coastal trader, so they will have a slow journey home." He grinned. "It was quite satisfying to watch, actually—what remains of the great Xixian army forced to hire ships and slink away. Perhaps someday my own country will joy in such a sight."

"Perhaps. And Prince Eneas?"

"He and his men are set to begin their own journey home tomorrow. As you know, his father is ill and he is needed at home."

"Poisoned by the bitch Ananka, I have no doubt. I hope Eneas can put things right there. Meanwhile, we will miss him. *I* will miss him." She sighed. "I am glad you are here, Master Dan-Faar. In a time when so much else is in doubt, you have been a good adviser and a good friend. I am grateful."

"I am happy to take your gold, Princess," he said, still smiling. "I assure you, my helpfulness is mostly mercenary."

She laughed. "Oh, yes, you are a famous villain, are you not? I had forgotten." Her brightened mood was short-lived. "I will never forget that . . . that you brought Shaso home. I know you were enemies in life, Dawet."

He shrugged. "In the end, I could not forget that he and I shared something important—a love and admiration for the same young woman."

"Ah." Briony nodded wisely. "Shaso's daughter—the one who died. Of course."

Dawet seemed surprised but did his best not to show it. "Ah. Yes, her. Of course."

52
The Crooked Piece

". . . And so the Orphan boy was taken up to heaven to live with the gods, where he lives still . . ."

—from "A Child's Book of the Orphan, and His Life and Death and Reward in Heaven"

VANSEN RODE AS FAR FROM THEM as he decently could, but wished Briony had not insisted he come along. Just the kindness and intimacy with which she spoke to Eneas, the obvious fact of her admiration for the Syannese prince, pained him.

"Do not take them yet," he heard her beg Eneas. "Let me thank them again."

He frowned. "They are soldiers, Princess. They do not expect to be thanked for what it was their honor to perform."

"Most men like to be praised when it is well deserved. I think your soldiers will not think too ill of me if I speak again of their bravery and sacrifice." She rode to the spot where Lord Helkis, Eneas' lieutenant, had assembled the troops at the crossing of the broad Coast Road. "Men of Syan!" she called. "I have been fortunate enough to ride with you. I count my pride at being allowed to ride as a Temple Dog as second only to the blood of Anglin running in my veins . . . !"

"She will give everything she has to this country of yours," Eneas said, watching the rapt soldiers. It took Ferras Vansen a moment to realize the prince was speaking to him. "Someone must watch over her. Protect her."

Vansen felt a moment of resentment. "We have soldiers in this country, too, Prince Eneas."

The prince laughed and turned toward him. "Did I say that aloud? My apologies, Captain. I meant no slight on you or the men of South-march—I only spoke what was in my heart. I knew I would never hold her, never tame her. She is too noble and singular a creature."

"She is not a creature, Your Highness." Vansen knew it was foolish to argue with a prince, but something more primal was going on beneath the words and he could not easily let go of it, either. "But we will agree that she is singular."

"Fairly spoken!" Oddly, the prince did not seem to take offense. "I meant only that her . . . determination is such a pure thing. Like a bird's need to fly . . ."

A great cheer went up, although it faded quickly beside the open, windy road. Several of the Temple Dogs were waving their swords and standards in the air, crowding around Briony to call their farewells, all semblance of military order gone. *But men are so few and the world is so big,* thought Vansen, looking from the knot of soldiers and mounted men to the empty hills. *How will we live without the gods?*

Fool, he chided himself a moment later. *We have exactly as much of the gods as we have always had.*

When Prince Eneas and the others had at last turned south toward their homeland, Briony rode with her retinue back through the mainland city, as empty and haunted as the places Vansen had seen on Northmarch Road that day so long ago, when he rode with Collum Dyer and the poor merchant lad, Raemon Beck.

"I go to meet my brother now," Briony told him. "There is much for you to do back home and Sergeant Dawley can look after me."

Young Dab Dawley, Vansen knew, was nearly as enthralled with the princess as was Ferras Vansen himself, and had no love for the Qar. Vansen had no doubt he would look after her carefully, but that was not his only concern. "No," he said. "You may dismiss me, of course, Highness, but if you will permit me, I would like to see your brother once more. We traveled together for a long time."

"What happened to him behind the Shadowline, dear Captain?"

He shook his head in frustration. "I cannot tell you, not truly. When I saw him last in Greatdeeps he had not changed much from what you knew. A little harder, perhaps. A little quieter. Becoming a man, I would say, because he wouldn't have survived that terrible place any other way." The sun was dropping down toward the tops of the western hills as they rode up Market Road toward the Coast Road crossing just outside the city. "Then Gyir, the fairy I've told you about, gave him a commission to take a mirror from Yasammez to the king of the Qar. I am still not entirely certain why, but it was meant to wake Saqri the queen, so he must have succeeded." He shrugged. "The next time I saw him was a few hours before you did. It was like meeting another person."

"Not entirely." She shielded her eyes against the sun as she looked up the road. "He was always full of secrets. It is just like him to wish to meet me out here, away from everyone else. When we were young we used to hide from our family and servants—or at least Barrick would. But I always found him." She looked so sad that Ferras Vansen almost pulled her to him and kissed her, despite the presence of all her guards and grooms and pages. "We would hide from the world together. I suppose that is what most galls me. Again, he runs away to hide, but this time I cannot go. Someone has to stay. Someone has to play the ruler."

The sun was very low, but the crossroad was still empty. At Vansen's insistence a tent had been erected so that the princess could rest out of the sun and the wind while she waited for her brother, and she was there taking a cup of wine and thinking her own silent thoughts when the scouts brought the news that someone was approaching. It was not the army of fairies Vansen had expected, but a single two-horse carriage that was rattling toward them along the rutted road.

If Vansen was surprised by the vehicle, which bore the crest of the late Duke Daman, King Olin's brother, and a coachman in full livery, he was even more surprised by the passengers who clambered down its narrow folding steps when it stopped—the Funderlings, Chert and Opal, followed by their adoptive child Flint.

"Master Blue Quartz!" Vansen said in astonishment. "What are you doing here, so far from Funderling Town?"

Chert did not speak until he was certain Opal's feet were safely on the ground. "I am not certain myself, Captain Vansen. It is all our son's idea—our son and Duchess Merolanna, whose cart this is."

"Good excuse to take it out of the stable, sir," said the coachman cheerfully.

"Did you come to see the princess?" Vansen asked. "Or to say farewell to Prince Barrick?"

Chert shook his head and pointed to Flint, who was already leading Opal toward Briony's tent. "You'll have to speak to the boy. I know it sounds foolish, but I promised I would ask no more questions until he was ready to explain."

Vansen knew the boy's history, so he was not surprised that Chert had been forced to come along, if only because Opal would have insisted. But why the strange child wanted to bring them here of all places, and just at this time, he couldn't understand.

By the time Vansen led Chert into the tent, Opal and Flint were sitting on cushions at Briony's feet. Chert reluctantly allowed himself to be convinced to sit beside them, but Vansen chose to stand beside the door flap so he could hear what was going on outside. He had no fear of Chert and his Funderling family, but he did not much like the notion of more unexpected arrivals.

"Well, Mistress Opal," Briony said, "we have not met before, but you must know that your husband means much to me. He likely saved my life."

Opal colored a little. "Well, he's always up to something, my Chert. It's a bit much for me to keep up with it all, sometimes."

"It has been difficult for all of us lately," Briony said. "These have been confusing, sorrowful times. But if I am not mistaken, we may learn a little more today about some of the mysteries that have plagued us."

"Not from me!" Opal said breathlessly. "Goodness, no, I don't think so . . . !"

Briony turned toward the boy. "You have flitted in and out through many of the tales I have been told in the last few days, young Master Flint. Is it time now to talk about you? It is plain enough that whatever your relationship with Chert and Opal, you are not a Funderling by birth."

"That is true, Briony Eddon," the boy said gravely.

Vansen was a little shocked. "Lad, it is polite to address the princess as 'Highness' or 'Your Royal Highness . . .'"

Briony lifted her hand. "Generally that is true, Captain. But I suspect we are facing something a bit different than the ordinary here."

The boy nodded. "I'm not Chert and Opal's child, that is commonly known." Watching the boy speak, Vansen felt the hackles lift on his neck and arms. He did not act like any child Vansen had ever known. Flint was not even acting much like himself—surely the child never spoke this formally when Vansen had seen him before.

"Where were you born, then?" Briony asked.

"Here in Southmarch . . . but it was a long time ago, as you measure it. Fifty years and more." The boy nodded. "Merolanna is my mother. My father is Avin Brone, count of Landsend."

Through everything that had happened, Vansen had never seen Briony truly astonished . . . until now.

"Avin Brone?" she cried. "Avin Brone was your father? He was Merolanna's secret lover? But she said the child's father was dead!" Her eyes narrowed. "And whatever else you may be, you are no comfortable old man of fifty years . . . !"

"The Qar took me when I was small. A childless Qar woman stole me from the house of my nursemaid, but they were disturbed in the doing and did not leave a changeling child to hide their deed. They took me to Qul-na-Qar and raised me. Although I aged but little, many years passed here during the time I was behind the Shadowline. At last Ynnir the blind king sent me here as part of his pact with Lady Yasammez—if I could bring out the essence of the god Kupilas to wake Queen Saqri, then the castle and its inhabitants would be spared.

"The queen was dying in slow drifts, like snow carried away by wind even as it falls—but the god was dying, too, and had been for centuries. Kupilas, as he is called by northern men, had long been failing from the treacherous wound Zosim had given him. But now his true end was upon him, and all who could sense such things knew it. In their place beyond this world, the sleeping gods could sense it. Even those only partly of the blood of Mount Xandos could sense it, too—Jikuyin, the great one-eyed demigod that Ferras Vansen met, and even your own brother and father, Briony Eddon."

Vansen was startled to hear his own name, but no more startled than was Briony. "Do you mean to tell me Father and Barrick *knew* what was coming?" she demanded.

"No, but the nearness of the dying god and of the place beneath Southmarch where Heaven touched earth when the gods were banished troubled their blood and their thoughts."

"But how can a child like you, even if you *were* raised by the fairies, know all this—know the business of all the gods and of my family, too?" A cold, hard sound had crept into the princess' voice, and for the first time Ferras Vansen recognized it for what it was—not contempt but fear: Briony was frightened by what she might hear from this prodigy, and when she was frightened, she hid behind her royal mask.

"That is part of the tale," the golden-haired child said. "It is what comes next—*my* tale. Only now can I see it whole and clear. It has the shape of a riddle." He nodded, almost with satisfaction. "My first mother asked my second mother to hide me. My third mother stole me from my second mother. My fourth mother took me in when my third mother lost me. And then my *first* first mother saved me."

Vansen did not like the aura of mystery that hung over the child's speech. Briony's discomfort was clear and the two Funderlings were no happier than she was. "What does that mean, 'First first mother'?"

"My first mother was the duchess, who gave me to my second mother the nursemaid in one of the farm villages outside Southmarch. A woman of the fairy folk stole me from the nursemaid, even though she had no changeling to give in turn, so the theft was discovered. My third mother in turn lost me to the blind king of the Qar, who had a higher purpose for me than simply to keep the thief-mother's fires tended and her house swept. And when I was taken across the Shadowline, Mama Opal and Papa Chert took me in."

"Yes, we did," said Opal with some feeling. "We wanted you. Didn't we, old man?"

Her husband did not hesitate. "Yes, we did, lad."

"And I have learned things from you that I learned from none of the others," Flint said. "In truth, I needed the wisdom of all my families, because the days ahead proved to be very, very dark.

"When I brought Ynnir's glass to the place where Crooked had banished the last of the gods, to the thing called the Shining Man, the vitality of Kupilas flowing into the glass threw me into a kind of ecstasy. Even a dying god is made of forces that mankind cannot understand, let alone harness, and a bit of the god's dying thought touched my own. For just that moment I could see as the god saw, I could look through mountains as if they were glass, I could see *what might be* nearly as well as I could see what was and what had been—and I could see them all at the same instant.

"And in that instant, though I did not realize it then, Kupilas of the

Ivory Hand and the Bronze Hand *left a piece of his godly essence in me*—a seed, as it were. And it has grown in my head and my heart ever since. More and more, it came to shadow my own thoughts with perceptions that were foreign to me—and yet not entirely so—and with understandings that were beyond me also . . . but not completely so. Slowly the presence grew, and slowly I grew with it, until I can no longer tell what is me and what is the seed of Crooked that has sprouted in me. . . ."

"It could be just a sprite," Opal said abruptly. "Some sort of earth-boggin deviling your spirit. We can ask the Metamorphic Brothers . . ."

"The Brothers probably would not help me if they could, Mama Opal," the boy said with a kind smile. "Do not forget, it is in part thanks to me as well as Papa Chert that they no longer have a temple."

"Good . . . !" Vansen laughed, but it was not a comfortable sound. "I nearly said 'Good Gods.' Can any of this be real? My head is spinning."

"Can any of this be true is the question, I think," Briony said. "I mean no offense to you, Flint, but why should we believe you? I have had my eyes opened to many things, but I am still not sure they are wide enough to see the god of healing hidden in the body of a little boy."

Flint smiled again. "You are right to be cautious, Briony Eddon . . . but I don't ask anything of you. In fact, I'm leaving Southmarch."

Opal's muffled cry of despair was immediately followed by a flurry of half-articulated questions from everyone present. The boy waited calmly until the uproar had lessened.

"I can't stay, Mama," he said when they were ready to listen again. He smiled sadly as Chert did his best to comfort Opal. "I've never been this sort of thing before, don't you see? A part of me feels as if it has been released after centuries in a prison. Even the part of me that's just Flint is a confusion of different things—not Qar and not Funderling, neither human nor immortal. I must find what kind of thing I am. I need to go about in the world, to wander . . . to learn."

"So is it you, then, who truly stands behind the defeat of Zosim, the demon-god?" Briony said. "I have heard many stories of those last hours, but all of them seem to be missing a piece."

"Any one of them, taken by itself, *is* missing a piece," the child said. "Without Vansen's courage and wit and the bravery of the Funderlings, no one could have held the autarch back long enough. Without the Qar's sacrifice of so many lives, the Trickster god would have escaped to the surface and then no one could have halted him. Without the Rooftopper

Beetledown giving up his own life, none of it would have mattered. Even with a piece of a god growing inside me, I did not understand until very late who the true enemy was and what he planned. Did I help here and there? Yes. But it would have meant nothing without the actions of others." Flint smiled and looked up, as if he meant his words for all of them together. "When you wonder in the days ahead if the gods are with you, think how even the smallest, cruelest whims of a sleeping god nearly became the end of all things. But if you think that means you are helpless in the hands of Fate, think of this: that same immortal god, master of fire and deceit, Death's own son, was brought down in large part by a man so small that my Papa Chert used to hold him in the cup of his hand." Flint stood up. "Now it's time for me to leave. Soon your brother will be here, Briony Eddon, and I think you still have things to say to each other."

"But . . . but why are you telling all this to us now?" The princess looked quite shocked, as close to helplessness as he had ever seen her. She turned to Vansen as though he might have some idea that had escaped her. "And why all the way out here?"

"Because first my parents must release me from a promise I made not to leave. Just as importantly, though, I want you to take them with you to the castle when you go back from here." He said this as though it should have been obvious. "I have learned enough about people to know that they will be sad when I'm gone, especially Mama Opal. Take her back with you so that she can help you care for your brother, little Olin Alessandros. She is a very fine mother. You will see."

Opal, who had calmed herself a little, started wailing again.

"Of course . . . of course I will see that your mother and father are . . . are well taken care of . . ." Briony began.

"No," Flint said firmly. "It does not take the god in me to know that you will be busy in the days ahead. Too busy to be a proper parent to a growing child. Do you want your father's youngest son, who might become either your own heir or your greatest enemy someday, to be raised by servants you scarcely know?"

"But . . . how . . . why . . . ?" Briony held out her hands; Vansen marveled to see the young woman who would in a matter of a tennight or two become queen of all the March Kingdoms rendered helpless by the arguments of a tow-headed child.

"To give things shape," Flint told her. "That is one thing the gods do. They give shape to the stories of men." He rose. "Now I must go, if you will let me. Papa Chert? You once made me promise not to leave until five years had passed. I cannot wait that long."

Chert spread his hands helplessly. "I could not hold you to a promise I forced on you when I did not understand everything. Of course—you are released. . . ."

"No! Don't go! It will be dark soon!" Opal cried.

"Mama Opal, do you really think I am afraid of the dark?" The boy looked at her sternly. "Even if I was only as old as I look, I would still have at least ten summers!" He went to her then and embraced her, holding on for a long time. Chert joined them and as Vansen watched, the three whispered to each other, heads close together; Chert and his wife both had tears in their eyes.

"Your other guests have arrived, Briony Eddon," little Flint said at last, pulling away. "I hear them now."

Vansen had only a moment to reflect that he himself had heard nothing, but then one of his guards called for him. He leaned out.

"A large force coming this way up the road," the soldier told him. "I think it's them Qar."

"It is," said Flint. "I will leave you to meet them. Farewell!"

❧

The sun had dropped behind the hills, but although the fire built outside her tent was bright, and was undoubtedly cheering the hearts of Ferras Vansen and the guards waiting for her there, the Qar themselves had built no fires and raised no tents. They waited beside the road in their silent hundreds while their leader spoke with the mistress of the mortal castle they had so nearly overthrown.

The mistress of the castle was also their leader's sister, a fact that Barrick Eddon seemed to remember now for the first time in a very long while.

"I'm sorry," he told her as they made their way slowly along the road, their backs to their obligations. His crippled hand, which had seemed quite cured the last time she saw him, was all white knuckled and cramping fingers, and he carried it like it had begun to hurt him again. "I see now that, in a way, I was blinded by all that has happened. I was wrong, Briony, very wrong—there is much for us to talk about, but we have no time for it now."

"What do you mean? We have all the time in the world. The war is over, Barrick. There is nothing to do now but rebuild, and trust me, there is enough of that to go around. Stay and help us. Do you mean to make me beg?"

He looked at her for a moment, then slowly shook his head.

"Curse you, Barrick!" she said angrily. "Can you never unbend enough to let someone reach out to you?"

"That's not what I meant," he said. "We don't have enough time because we don't speak the same tongue anymore, Briony. I have found some of what I lost—some of what I loved about this place and you—but for us to speak with true understanding, I would have to teach you all that happened to me in the time we were apart, and you would have to do the same so that I could understand everything you think and say. We have become . . . different." He lowered his chin toward his chest as though it were cold, although the early evening was warm and she doubted Barrick even felt cold much anymore. "And I do have to go, Briony. If I stay here, Qinnitan will surely die." He led his sister from the road and through the fringes of the waiting Qar, who watched her pass with the suspicious eyes of animals. "At Qul-na-Qar I might be able to save her, or at least learn how to keep her close enough that one day I can cure her."

"Qinnitan." Briony tried to swallow her unhappiness. How could so much be changing at the same time, and seemingly forever? "So that's it. Because of this girl you scarcely know, you will go away and I will never see you again? The only real family I have left?"

He stopped. She thought she had angered him and braced herself for his furious words, but when he spoke, it was something quite different.

"I had not thought of that," he said. "I . . . there is a part of me now, a large part, that does not easily remember those things—it has too many memories of its own to protect. My apologies."

She gasped a little at that, frightened. "Merciful Zoria, you sound just like that Flint. He told us he has a piece of a god inside him."

"He does." Her brother reached out and took her hand; both the unexpected gesture and the coldness of his skin startled her. "With me, it is something only a little less unusual. I am not the same, Briony . . . but a little of what I was has begun to come back, too." He held up his knotted hand; the knuckles were white from being so tightly clenched. After a moment, and with only a small grimace, he managed to uncurl his fingers almost all the way. He showed his hand to her, smiling through his pain, and although she did not quite understand, she knew he was showing her something important. Tears came to her eyes. "Perhaps someday there will be so much of the old Barrick that I will come riding up to the gate, shouting for you to let me back in!" He laughed at the notion. "Maybe I will even bring a wife and children."

"This will always be your home." She didn't want it to be a jest. She could barely keep the tears from overwhelming her. "Always. And I will always, always miss you."

They began walking again. For a while neither spoke.

"It is the place, not you," he said at last.

"What?"

"That which makes it hard for me to stay here, even if I did not need to take Qinnitan to the House of the People. This place, its . . . history. The Qar hate it here. They won no victory. In fact, this may still be the site of their final destruction. And it has not been good to me, either. But I can change things, I think, both for the survivors and myself."

"You are wrong about some things," she said.

He looked at her with a little surprise. "Tell me."

"The last time I saw him, Father told me a story about Kellick and Sanasu. He loved her, did you know?"

"What?"

"He loved her. Father said that in Kellick's own words, he meant only to find out what the Qar did beneath our castle, and so he took men to question them. But the first time he saw Sanasu of the Qar, his heart filled with love for her so completely that he could not imagine going home without her again. In the middle of dispute, anger, and suspicion, he told her brother, not understanding that Janniya was not just her brother but also her betrothed. Enraged by this terrible insult, as he saw it, Janniya struck out at Kellick and in the fighting that followed, Janniya was killed and the few Qar who survived fled. Kellick took Sanasu and before too much longer they were wed. Whether she was unwilling, Father told me, no one can say, but they lived together in what seemed like harmony until Kellick died."

"So the crime was no crime because it happened for love?"

"No." Briony reached out and took his cold hand again. "But even you must admit the crime is different than the stories have made it. Love and a foolish, deadly accident is a far cry from murder and rape."

He thought for long moments. "There's something in that," he said.

"I'll think about it. And I will tell the Qar about it, too. It may change nothing." In the dying light of evening Briony could see little of him except the hard angles of his face, and although it was her twin's voice that spoke, she could hear that it was different, too: Barrick was no longer the beloved, infuriating, pitiable companion of her childhood, but something altogether stranger and stronger.

"And now that you're going away, that's the Barrick I won't get to know," she said, airing her thoughts aloud.

He shrugged. "The old Barrick would never have survived without you. Besides, we shared blood in the pantry, remember? Even the new Barrick can't forget that."

She looked up in surprise. "I had never thought to hear that again."

"It could be that we'll also find ways to share our thoughts that you don't anticipate," he said with a serious face. "We will be two monarchs. Brother and sister rulers should stay in touch." He tapped his head. "I will give that some consideration, too."

Tears threatened again. "Still, it'll be years at best before we see each other again! The one thought that got me through all of this was that at the end, if we survived, we would be a family again."

"We *are* family, Briony. The more I change, the more I see that which will never change in me. I was an Eddon before I was anything else." He bent and kissed her forehead, then pulled her close. Surprised, she resisted for a moment, then wrapped her arms around him and clung. For long moments they just stood that way, two people on a green hill at the side of the Coast Road as the moon rose.

"Oh, Redling, I will miss you so!"

"I know, Briony." A smile crept onto his face. "I mean, 'I know, Strawhead . . .' and I'll miss you. But that means we will never be completely apart."

Vansen found it hard to think clearly on the ride back. Just helping the Funderling Chert to get his grieving wife back into the carriage felt like helping to betray someone.

"But how can he go off on his own?" Opal kept asking. "Our boy—what will he do? Who will feed him?"

"He will manage," Chert told her over and over, but the little man looked quite stunned himself. Vansen felt for him. He knew what it was like not to be able to mourn because others needed you. "Flint has always managed, long before we heard of any so-called god."

"Don't you believe him, then?" Vansen asked.

Chert scowled. "No, the wretched thing is, I *do* believe him . . . that is what is so dreadful. Even if we see the boy again, he will never be our Flint, not truly." He nodded toward the carriage where Opal waited for him and lowered his voice. "That is what makes her so sad."

"But your boy was always something other than what everyone thought him," Vansen said slowly. "We none of us truly knew him."

"And Opal knows that—she knows it better than we do." Chert reached out a small, callused hand so that Vansen could help him up onto the carriage steps. "Don't worry for us too much, Captain Vansen. We Funderlings are a thick-skinned race. We'll live."

"When you've had a little while to yourselves, bring whatever you need to the castle and we'll find you a place of your own there, in the royal residence." Vansen had spent so long without a real home that he couldn't quite think of what ordinary folk carried around with them. "Weapons, if you have them. Keepsakes."

Chert smiled despite the quiet noises of sorrow coming from the carriage. "Yes, my grand weapon collection, of course. To be honest, I won't need much room for that. But Opal may have a few pans." He nodded as he considered. "And I won't be sad to leave my brother's house. He'll be around the place a great deal more now that Cinnabar has convinced the Highwardens to remove Nodule from the Magisters' Slate for his dangerous meddling, and I'm certain he blames it all on me." Chert's smile became a wide grin. "Which gives me a great deal of pleasure, Captain—a great deal of pleasure."

When Merolanna's bewildered driver had at last been allowed to leave the crossroads and the carriage had become just another shadow ahead of them, Vansen and Briony rode back to the castle in the silent company of the royal guards.

The princess and the guard captain didn't have much to say on the way back, either. Vansen did not entirely trust words at the best of times, and just now could not summon even one word that would make sense of what he was feeling. Briony was as remote as he had ever seen her.

This "festive" mood was only enhanced when they were greeted at the causeway by another contingent of guards, this one led by a royal messenger who bowed only long enough for his knee to brush the ground before leaping to his feet and handing Briony a sealed letter from Steffens Nynor.

"Sweet Zoria," she said as she read it. "Or whoever it is now to whom we must turn. Mercy upon us all."

"What?" Vansen hated the look of alarm on her face, but he hated the look of pain and exhaustion even more.

"It is Anissa, my stepmother," Briony said, looking up at the looming castle walls. "She has fallen from her tower window—or she has jumped. She is dead."

53
Shadowplayers

" . . . And the gods have given him a pair of beautiful golden arms to replace those which were burned away by the sun. Tessideme, the village where the Orphan was welcomed and celebrated, became the city of Tessis, the center and heart of our Trigonate faith on earth. The Trigonarch himself lives there today . . ."

—from "A Child's Book of the Orphan, and His Life and Death and Reward in Heaven"

"YOU ARE LUCKY I didn't have you brought to me in shackles," Briony told him, her fists clenched so hard her knuckles had gone white. "How dare you!"

Dawet dan-Faar raised an eyebrow. "How dare I what, Princess?"

"You know precisely what, you rogue! While I was out of the castle, you went to the Tower of Spring. Anissa fell to her death while you were with her. Do you think I'm a fool, Dawet? You as much as told me you thought she should be murdered!"

He smiled. "I believe I suggested that it would be dangerous for you to let such a woman live. I was not aware a person could be killed with words."

"You were there! You were with her when she died—you pushed her from that window!"

Dawet cocked his head, his brown eyes as wide and innocent as a fawn's. "What makes you say such a terrible thing, Highness?"

"You were seen going in. One of the guards had stepped away—

doubtless pursuing some blind of your own—but as he came back, he saw you go inside the tower."

He shook his head gravely. "He saw an intruder but did not say anything to him? Did not try to stop the man? Did it ever occur to you that this guard is trying to make up for his own failing, Princess?"

"He saw you! He did not interfere because he knows you are a friend of the royal family."

"He was obviously mistaken, Princess. I was nowhere near the place. Several people will swear I was playing picket with them in a little establishment newly reopened near the West Lagoon."

"A gambling den," she said.

"You may call it such." He made a little bow. "Certainly there is an element of chance involved in the pastimes pursued there . . ."

"Enough! I thought you an honest man even in your most dishonest moments, Dawet. Why do you lie to me now? And why did you do what I told you I could not bear to see done? Kill that poor, stupid woman?"

"That poor stupid woman helped murder your brother." Dawet's voice was suddenly hard and serious. "In days to come she would have become a danger to you, too. As to lying—my lady, why would I lie? The only reason I can imagine why anyone who loved you and wished to help might lie to you is so that you can rule as you must, with a clear conscience. Because you, Briony Eddon, are no murderer."

She stared at him for a long time, then sagged back in her chair, her face sad and weary. "And what am I to do with you, Dan-Faar?"

"If I were truly the villain you think me, Mistress, I would suggest you keep me close to you where I might be useful. A prince never knows when he may need the service of a rogue, after all, and I suspect that things are little different for queens."

She stared at him for long moments, but the anger had gone from her eyes. "And of course your gambling cronies will swear you were with them all the day."

"Of course."

She waved her hand. "Go away, Dan-Faar. Go back to your cards and your convenient friends. I have another funeral to arrange."

"As you wish, Highness. But I would suggest you bury the late Queen Anissa with the full pomp of her position. She was the mother of your father's last child, after all. Her tragic accident, so soon after your father's death, has surprised and saddened all of Southmarch."

She could not stifle a bitter laugh. "Gods save me! As always, you are most helpful, Master Dan-Faar. Now go away and at least spare me seeing your face for a tennight or two."

"As you wish, Highness." He bowed, more deeply this time, and went out.

❧

Vansen was worried, even frightened, by what she told him in the privacy of her chamber. "You cannot let such a man stay in Southmarch! Even if nothing can be proved, you and I both know he is guilty. He is dangerous!"

"Perhaps. But not to me."

"You can't be sure of that!"

She reached out and took his hand. "The Kupileia is almost upon us, along with my coronation. I will be the queen. I *will* be the queen, my dearest captain, and much as I am almost foolish with love for you, I must be the ruler of the March Kingdoms, not you. I know something of Dawet, and I know that he thinks to help me."

"Help you . . . !"

She put a finger on his lips. "He is my problem, not yours, my brave knight. And it occurs to me that whether he meant to or not, Dawet has also proved that I owe Avin Brone an apology . . . but not tonight." She stood. "Now let's not talk about any of this any longer."

"I am your lover, yes, but remember I am also your constable."

"And you are admirable in both occupations. Come with me down to the retiring room. Some friends of mine have returned to Southmarch and I would like you to meet them."

"Friends?" Vansen had a dreadful vision of more suitors, more handsome foreign princes, a line of rivals stretching out until doomsday. "What sort?"

"The educated sort. Come, now—let me show you off to the only people who will not judge me badly!"

"Makewell's sister forbade him to come, Highness," said Nevin Hewney. "But we have found someone to take his place. I introduce you to Matthias Tinwright, poet."

Briony raised her eyebrow. The shamefaced Tinwright would not meet her eyes. "We've met. In fact, we saw each other rather recently. Master Tinwright was trying to kill my infant brother."

Now it was Hewney's turn to look bemused. "Truly? I never thought you disliked children so violently, Tinwright. I underestimated you."

While Vansen tried to make sense of this, Briony turned and threw her arms wide. "Finn!" she cried, embracing the third man with a joy that Vansen did his best to ignore. "It is so good to see you again! And you, too, Hewney, disreputable soul that you are."

The man named Finn Teodoros drew back, a little red-faced at his greeting. "All thanks to Zosim, patron of players, Princess . . ."

"Not him," Vansen growled.

Teodoros looked at him curiously for a moment, then back to Briony. "In any case, all thanks to the gods, we are here—and you are the queen! We should be down on our knees to you, not strolling in at this late hour with a couple of jugs of cheap wine!"

"By the time we finish both jugs, someone will certainly be on his knees," Hewney said, "but I suspect it will be young Tinwright."

"And this," said Briony, "is Ferras Vansen, captain of the royal guard and soon to be lord constable. He, more than any other man, saved this castle and my throne." She ordered one of her pages to fetch cups, then waved to Nevin Hewney. "Now bring that jug over here and let me tell you the truth about *everything*."

Vansen regarded his beloved with growing horror. "Highness . . ."

"You will have some wine, too, Captain. Tallow is in charge of the guardroom tonight and you are at liberty. These are my friends, and here we all are." She took a cup from the page. "Here—pour! And some for my captain, too. Did you know that he is my lover?"

"Princess!"

"It was not hard to guess, the way you keep clutching at his hand," said Finn Teodoros, grinning. "I hope you are more discreet in front of the paying public."

"Yes. But you are my only friends, and I am tired of secrets." She drank her wine at a gulp, then held out her cup again. "A few more of these, and I will begin declaiming Zoria's words." She smiled at Tinwright, who still looked a bit anxious. "I mean no blasphemy," she said. "Teodoros wrote them for a play, and I played the part of the goddess."

"No one could have played it better," said Finn Teodoros fondly.

"Chaste as old Zoria herself, too," grumbled Hewney. "No matter how often I tried to . . ." He blinked. "Why is this guard captain standing so close to me? And looking as though he might like to give me a thrashing?"

"If you are jealous of these fine folk, you haven't had enough wine yet, Captain," Briony said, then turned to give Vansen a kiss on the cheek. "I love you," she whispered, then said much more loudly, "Fill that man's cup again!"

Vansen and Finn Teodoros were deep in a slightly frog-mouthed discussion about the Qar, comparing their experiences, Vansen's mostly personal, Teodoros' mostly learned from study. Nevin Hewney, perhaps depressed by the lack of available female company or just overcome by all the wine he had downed, had fallen asleep between the two of them, so that they both had to lean forward to talk around his bobbing, bearded head.

" . . . But Phayallos says that when the gods walked the earth they could take any form, so why should Zosim, if it truly was him, not simply take the form of a bird or a fiery arrow and fly out of the deeps that way?"

Vansen shook his head firmly, then shook it again. "Because . . . because . . . curse it, Teodoros, I don't know. Why should I? He was a god! If you'd have been there, you could have asked him."

"I am not so brave, Captain . . ."

Briony, who had been admiring Ferras Vansen's face, the almost childlike earnestness that appeared so quickly even when he looked his most mature and handsome, did not notice for some moments that Matt Tinwright was standing beside her, swaying slightly from side to side.

"Yes, Master Tinwright?"

"Are you . . . do you still . . . I did not want to hurt your brother, Princess. Truly I didn't. . . ."

"I know, Tinwright. That's why you are standing free here before me, drunk to the gills on my good Perikal red wine."

He frowned. "I thought . . . that Hewney brought the wine . . ."

"We've moved on to the royal stores long ago," she said. "You should sit down again, man, before you fall and hurt yourself."

"I . . . I wanted to talk to you, Princess Briony. To thank you for making me your poet."

She smiled. "You are welcome."

"I have a question." He licked his lips, clearly uneasy. "Do you remember that . . . that I was writing a poem about you? How you were like Zoria?"

She nodded, although the memory was very vague indeed. It hadn't been very good was all she could recall. "Of course, Master Tinwright."

He smiled in relief. "Well, I was thinking I might go back to it . . . but I was thinking. That's what I was doing—thinking about the poem. I was thinking that I couldn't make a poem about you that didn't have anything about . . . about, you know, the things that happened. Here and while you were in Syan. I've been asking people. Trying to find out the truth."

"I'll be happy to answer your questions, Matt," she said kindly. "But not tonight. Tonight is for merriment."

"I know!" He waved his hands as though accused of theft. "But I was thinking and thinking about how the whole thing has been like . . . well, like one of Finn's or Nevin's plays from the very first."

"I'm not certain I understand." She looked over to Vansen and Teodoros, still talking like fast friends—or maybe Finn just fancied her guard captain. She could hardly blame him. "Like a play?"

"All of it. Like a puppet play. Someone was always behind everything we saw. From what I'm told . . ." he screwed up his face, trying hard to get it right, "from what I'm told, Zosim was behind it all, pretending to be Kernios. But Hendon Tolly thought it was someone else, a goddess—he sometimes seemed to think it was Zoria herself! But it was all Zosim wearing disguises, do you see? Just like a player!"

"I suppose . . ."

"All of it like a play. You were a princess, but you disguised yourself, just as in so many stories. The villain of the piece hid in the shadows and had others do his bidding, like that southern king, that autarch. That's just like one of Hewney's plays, too. But what really made me stop and wonder was when I thought, 'but if Zosim was behind it all, but he was beaten in the end . . . who did that?' "

Briony, a little the worse for wear herself after several cups of Perikal, could only shake her head. "Who did *what*?"

"Beat Zosim. Tricked him and defeated him."

"Well, the boy Flint, that I told you about earlier . . . *he* claims that part of Crooked lives inside him. . . ."

"Exactly!" said Tinwright loudly, then blushed. "Yes, Highness. And when you told me that, I really got to thinking. You know the stories from the old days about how Kupilas beat Kernios and Zosim both, right here!" He frowned. "I mean, down underneath the earth. You know, don't you?"

"I have heard many stories in the last year. But yes, I know about what Kupilas was supposed to have done to Kernios and Zosim and the rest."

"But who else was there all the time? Who else was present when that all happened?"

Briony was beginning to wonder if it might be time to end the festivities. "I don't know, Master Tinwright. Whom?"

He smiled in pink-cheeked triumph. "Zoria was—Zoria, the Dawnflower. She was there. Kernios killed her for betraying him—or at least that's what the stories say. But what if she didn't die, like Zosim didn't die? What if she stayed alive in those . . . whatever places?"

She looked at him and realized that he was not quite as drunk as he looked. "It's . . . it's a fascinating idea, Master Tinwright . . ."

"It was your Zorian prayer book that saved me from your archer, you know." He said the words very carefully, then smiled when he had successfully navigated the sentence. "It was over my heart and stopped the bolt. Zoria's hand. Your prayer book. Do you see?"

Briony didn't know what to say. "I suppose . . ."

"Very well. One last question, Princess. I heard you're building a shrine to the forest goddess Lisiya. Can I ask you why?"

"Demigoddess. Because . . . because I promised if I survived that I would build one for her. I would rather not say anything more about it. Why do you ask?"

He nodded. "Can I show you something I found in a book?" He reached into his pocket and pulled out a thin volume, then fumbled it open. "It's written by Phayallos. He wrote a lot about the gods . . ." Tinwright squinted as he turned pages. "Ah, here it is." He cleared his throat. *" . . . And these goddesses and demigoddesses, especially Lisiya of the Silver Glade and her sisters, were commonly called the Handmaidens of Zoria, and strove to see that the Dawnflower's wishes were carried out in the world, that Zoria's worshipers were rewarded and her foes were thwarted."* He closed it, spoiling his moment of triumph a bit by dropping the book on the floor.

"Master Matty is drunk!" laughed Finn Teodoros. "Time to take him home."

As Finn and Matt Tinwright helped Hewney onto his feet, Briony could not help asking the young poet, "And will you continue with your poem?"

"Oh, yes," he said, his eyes shining. "I have so many ideas—it will be the best thing I ever did! I was miserable because . . . because of a woman . . . but now I know why. I was meant to do this!"

He was still burbling as Vansen helped the three of them out the door. "Help them down the stairs!" Vansen shouted to a page. "We do not want the princess' guests breaking their necks. And tell the coachman to take them back to their inn."

"Oh, gods," groaned Hewney, waking up. "Not the Quiller's Mint! I'd rather sleep in the gutter."

Ferras Vansen came back in a little unsteadily and threw his arms around Briony. She kissed him, but she was preoccupied and he could tell.

"What were you talking with that fool of a poet about?"

"The gods," she said. "And whether or not earthly life is only a sort of play."

"I'm glad I missed it, then," he said. "I never had the wit for such things. Now come to bed, my beautiful Briony, and let me love you a while before we both have to get into costume and go back to playing our own parts once more."

54
Evergreen

. . . And that is the end of my tale, which is meant both to instruct and to please His Highness, and all other young people who shall read the Orphan's story."

—from "A Child's Book of the Orphan, and His Life and Death and Reward in Heaven", written by Matthias Tinwright and presented to His Highness Prince Olin Alessandros on the occasion of his first birthday.

THE MORNING DAWNED BRIGHT and much hotter than the day before. Barrick could smell the sap beginning to move in the pines and firs, the slow sweetness that ran through their veins as the Fireflower did in his. The Qar had traveled through the night, but slowly; now that Saqri had died, there was no need to go faster than what the many wounded could comfortably manage.

Duke Kaske of the Unforgiven brought the reports from the scouts: the road ahead was all but empty for several leagues. "But after that there are several mortal villages, and then a walled city with towers," Kaske said. His almond-shaped eyes were drawn up ever so slightly at their outer edges, which Barrick knew meant that the corpse-pale fairy was fighting with strong emotions. "We did not pass this way when Yasammez led us. We have not come against it before."

Barrick nodded. He leaned down to pat the neck of his horse, then drew back on the reins so that the black charger pulled up with anxious, skittering feet; even the horses didn't like this place and longed for the dark meadows of home. "Stop here," he called out, then repeated it again without spoken words. The procession behind him slowed and began to split into smaller pieces, horses and other steeds taken down the small slope to water, some of the Changing tribe joining them in four-footed form, which made the other animals restive. "Don't worry, Kaske, we'll go around it. There is no dishonor in that."

But the Unforgiven, a terrifying and fearless warrior, was still troubled. "But you know these mortals. We can avoid them now, but someday they will come into our lands. With the death of Yasammez the Mantle will vanish. How can we keep them out?" The skin of his face pulled ever so slightly tighter. "The Mantle—gone!"

"What do you care?" Barrick asked him. "You and your folk live in the snowy hills. Surely you will be grateful to see the sun again."

Kaske shook his head. "It . . . it will be strange. Everything will be strange now."

Barrick spread his fingers—*Tale of Years*—and said, "Yes, it will."

My love.

You are there! Barrick's heart, which for two days had felt like Kaske's mountain home, an icy stone beneath freezing gray skies, now suddenly was drenched with sunshine. *You came back to me! Oh, praise the Book, you came back. I feared . . . I feared . . .*

I was frightened, too, she said. Her thoughts, the voice, it was hers, blessedly hers . . . but so weak! *The Fireflower women—the mothers and grandmothers, they are so stern, so . . . beautiful and terrible . . . ! I thought they would sweep me away like a flooding river . . .*

I did, too! I was terrified! But I had Ynnir to help me. Do you know him?

Know him? He is my son, grandfather, my husband, Qinnitan said, still a little dreamy and confused. *I know what Saqri knew, and what all who came before her knew . . . !*

Ynnir helped me. I do not think I could have survived otherwise. Who helped you?

You. He felt it come from her like a caress. *The thought that we would be separated again if I could not find a way to live with it. I have had too much of that, Barrick Eddon.* Her thoughts twisted a little, took a tone of amusement and wonder. *And you are King Olin's son—of course! To think that all that time I didn't know . . . !* As she said it, he could see his father plainly, but it was a different Olin who faced him, the man Qinnitan had known, a kind, brave man unshadowed by rage, who valued his own life far lower than that of any innocent.

Tell me about him, Barrick said. *Stay with me as long as you can and tell me what I missed all those years that the shadows fell between my father and me . . .*

When she grew weary and her words began to slow, he stopped her, kissed her with a word and a thought, and let her go. Only when she had slipped down into sleep and he could no longer feel her did he let the sadness he had been holding at bay so long wash over him. He looked at the couch on which Qinnitan's small, slender body lay, in a wagon pulled by two patient nightsteeds. What if they never had more than this? Ynnir and Saqri had lived that way for centuries. That was some solace, anyway. Barrick doubted he would live so long.

He stood for a long time gazing back across the hills. The gleam in the distance was the tilted windvane on top of Wolfstooth Spire's shattered roof; the rest of the castle was invisible below the intervening hills. It was strange to be looking back on his old home. The last time he had stood in such a place he had wondered whether he would ever see it again, and this time was no different.

As he stared, he felt something strange happening all around him, a sudden warmth and a feeling of the air being pulled in many directions at once. Then something snapped like a large branch breaking and the space immediately in front of Barrick's face was full of flapping blackness. Without thinking, he reached out and grabbed the dark shape. It was feathery and fat and smelled like carrion.

"Don't hurt us!" it croaked. "Us be a bird of artfullest power—a wishing raven! Spare us and us'll grant you all manner of wishery, that you'll see!"

Barrick stared in astonishment. "Skurn? Is that you?"

The bird slowed its thrashing, turning its desperately shiny black eye on him. "Mought be. Then again, it equal-like moughtn't."

"Don't you remember me?"

"Well, doubtless that you look like the Barrick lad I helped so many times. But us has seen many a few others nearly as much like him since us first went through that darksome gate out of Sleep . . ."

"Where have you been, Skurn? You never reached Qul-na-Qar—I didn't see you after we escaped from the city of Sleep! And I never saw Raemon Beck again."

"Us hasn't seen that one either, though in our travels, us has seen a few creatures that were Beck-ish. Thanks mightily for telling where you've been—but not much help when us needed it, was it?" The bird fluttered up out of Barrick's open hand and onto a branch just a little overhead. "Been flapping in and out of some dreadful places since then. Some nice ones, too, to say fair, but still strange as down on a toad." He preened himself a bit. "Rather grand, our adventures have doubtless been, you and us. No doubt some fairy bard will want to make a tune of it all, with clever words to show how dangerous our fates narrowly was."

Barrick almost smiled, but was not going to be so easily lulled. "You talk more than you ever did, bird."

"It goes to show the gods live and the world be still full of miracles, as our mam used to say when us were scarce out the egg."

"And I suppose you'll want to go with me."

"Nay, don't think thyself so grand!" The bird looked up as if in search of some even higher perch more suitable to his stature. "Any bargain us made is long past. No need for us to follow all draggity-tail and call any-one master."

"Who said anything about calling someone master?" Barrick turned and called to Kaske and Sunset Pearl that it was time to gather up their people and return to the road. "I just thought you might like to keep company with me for a while. I'm more or less the king of the fairies now. Did you know?"

"King of the fairies?" Skurn hopped down the branch and looked him up and down carefully. "Them Qar must have lost a lot of their important folk somewhere." The bird made a harsh spitting noise. "Must be scraping the barrel now, us means."

My love?

So soon? I hoped you would sleep until tomorrow.

It is a beautiful night. I can feel it even if I can't see it. Is that horrible bird asleep?

Barrick looked down at Skurn bouncing on the front of the saddle. The raven's head was settled deep in his fluffed up collar of black-and-white-spotted feathers. *Yes. He's actually not as bad as he seems.*

He couldn't be.

Don't be cruel. He helped me many times. Saved my life at least once.

I'm sorry. In Xis they were birds of ill-omen. I will try to be kinder. My Fire-

flower mothers are scolding me, too. They say his kind are Whitefire's messengers . . . Oh, Barrick, there is so much to know!

Look, he said. *The Twilight Lands. I can see them in the distance . . . and I can see the stars, too!*

What do you mean?

The Mantle. The cloud of separation and protection that hung over this place so long. It's gone. Nothing left now but wisps like fog. He sighed, dazzled by the painful brightness of the stars in the night sky. *Ah, if you could only see this land of ours!*

I hear its beauty in your thoughts.

She went quiet then, but it was a companionable silence, both of them close despite their terrible separation.

My love? he asked sometime later. *Qinnitan, my heart, are you still awake?*

She stirred. *I drifted.*

I drifted with you.

I miss the House of the People, she said, *though I have never seen it with my own eyes. Is it as beautiful as my memories?*

It's a very old place. It has every kind of beauty. But there is more to it than that.

Of course, she said, then a moment later: *Barrick, I can feel the moon. Is it bright?*

It is.

It makes me stronger just feeling it. By the Hive, I think I can hear it, too . . . I feel as if I can hear everything!

He took a deep breath, in part to ease the rush of feeling. Even his thoughts were muddled, stumbling. *You do too . . . ? I thought I would be . . . I thought I would never . . .*

I know, she told him, and for just a moment he could feel her as if she were beside him, as if they again held each other in the dark dreamland. *Talk to me, Barrick.* It was close, as intimate as a whisper. *Tell me everything. I know everything the Fireflower knows, but the Fireflower knows scarcely anything about you. At least scarcely anything of the sort of things a lover wants to know.*

I will, he said. *And the first thing you must know about me is that I am not an ordinary person . . .*

He could feel her amusement. *Of course you aren't! As you told that foul bird, you are a mortal who became monarch of the fairies . . . !*

No, that isn't it. I was about to say that I am a twin. . . .

Epilude

THE MORNING SUN had pulled itself up above the eastern horizon, and the sky was brightening. Despite the paucity of clouds, a low rumble filled the air, beginning so low that it disturbed only a few slumbering creatures deep in the earth, but then rising until it made the slender branches of the birch trees quiver. Birds burst squawking from their upper reaches and a deer sprinted across the Coast Road.

The rumble grew until it sounded much like thunder, then the air seized, roiled, and cracked like a drover's whip. Something fell out of the nothingness onto brown Southmarch earth still wet with dew.

For long moments Raemon Beck, merchant's son, husband, and father, only lay facedown in the middle of the road, frightened by yet another forced, lightning-flash journey from one nowhere to another. At last, when the rumble of his arrival had subsided, he worked up the courage to lift his head. A moment later, he clambered up onto his feet, staring in astonishment to the southeast. There, across a short distance of green bay, stood the familiar towers of Southmarch Castle—some a little the worse for wear, scarred by fire and cannonballs, but unquestionably and recognizably the four cardinal towers and the even taller black-and-white prominence of Wolfstooth Spire.

Beck stared. He touched his own face as if unable to believe both he and Southmarch could exist at the same moment in the same place, then let out a whoop of delight and began a clumsy dance in the middle of the Coast Road. Two more deer, a doe and a fawn, sprang from the underbrush and bounded away into the depths of the woods, terrified by the disheveled man's capering.

"Praise the gods!" Beck shouted, tears streaming down his cheeks. "Praise all the gods! I'm back! I'm *home!*"

And then he dropped down to his hands and knees and kissed the ground over and over before he rose, still loudly thanking Heaven, and trotted off in the direction that would at last lead him again to Helming-sea and his family.

Appendix 1

PEOPLE

Adis—true name of Merolanna's son
Aesi'uah—chief eremite to Lady Yasammez
A'lat—a priest, servant of the Autarch
Akutrir—a Qar warror of the Unforgiven tribe
Androphagas—legendary monster, half-bull, half-serpent
Aristas—mentor of Adis, the Orphan
Avros—aka Little Avros, a Temple Dog
Aylan—Sulepis' great-grandfather
Beetlewing—a Rooftopper, Beetledown's father
Benaridas—a mercenary killed at Kleaswell market
Benediktos—Anissa's father, monarch of Devonis
Black Noszh-lah—Funderling version of Immon
Blackspine—Trickster
Bluedeeps—in the icy northern part of Qar lands
Buckle—a Summerfield guard
Calomel—Cinnabar and Vermilion Quicksilver's son
Chaffy—one of Brone's hired men
Cheshret and Tusiya—Qinnitan's parents
Chrysolite—a Funderling warder
Corundrum—a Funderling engineer
Dard, aka Dard the Jar—Hierosoline merchant
Dawet dan-Faar—envoy from Hierosol, late of Tuan
Dawn Flower—a Qar name for Zoria, mother of Kupilas
Dolomite—a Funderling, Jasper's lieutenant
Dordom—Parnad's oldest son
Duke Kaske of the Unforgiven—a Qar war leader
Duke of Veryon—a Syannese historical figure
Ekkadar—leader of the Qar at Kleaswell Market
Flightless—a Trickster Qar, son of Greenjay

Flowstone—a Metamorphic Brother
Gerasimos—Trigonarch who rejected Hypnologues
Gennadas—a Syannese knight
Gorhan—Tulim's uncle
Gunis—a Nushash priest with the Autarch's army
Hereddin—Xixian tactician, writer
Hypnologues—AKA "Hypnologoi", a heretic sect
Ice Ettins—one of the types of Ettins
Idite dan-Mozan—widow of Effir dan-Mozan
Jackdaw—a Qar, a Trickster
Karisnovois—Rooftopper name for Kernios
Kayne, Prince—Queen Lily's son who died young
Kelonesos—famous sea monster
Kernios Olognothas—the Earth Lord as All-Seeing
Kersus—Xixian tactician, writer
Khau-Yisti—Yisti (Funderling-type Qar) bred by Autarchs
Khobana the Wolf—a murderess and prisoner
Kioy-a-pous—Skimmer name for Crooked
Kirgaz—one of young Tulim's royal brothers
Kymon—a viscount of a county on the Syannese border
Leekstone—Opal's maiden name
Longscratch—Trickster
Mackel—Skimmer, Rafe's father
Mawra the Breathless—a Qar
Mehnad—a prince of Xis
Mihannid Blue Kings—ancient Xandian dynasty
Miron—Lord Helkis' given name
Morna—goddess of winter, victim of Zosim
Moros—treacherous servant of Adis
Moseffir—a Dan-Mozan grandchild
Mountain Korbols—a tribe of Qar
Okhuz—Xixian name for Volios the god of war
Okros Dioketian—a physician,
Osias—Tyrant of Hierosol during the Orphan's time
Oyler—one of Brone's pages
Paka—a Xixian soldier
Parak—former autarch of Xis, Sulepis' grandfather, Parnad's father
Pardstone Jasper, the last Funderling who had regularly contributed to the wide conversation of scholars
Pebble Jasper—wife of Wardthane Sledge Jasper
Perch—one of Brone's hired men
Phayallos—famous scholar
Pirilab—Xixian historian
Pyarin—Skimmer name for Perin

Rhantys of Kalebria—a scholar, author of "*The Agony of Truth Foresworn*"
Riddletongue—a Trickster
Salt Nitre—nephew of Ash
Selia ei'Dicte—Anissa's maid's real name
Shadow's Cauldron—an Elemental
Silvergleam—a Qar name for Khors the moon god, father of Kupilas
Singscrape—a Deep Ettin, Hammerfoot's son
Skollas—a historical dictator of Hierosol
Sorykidons—residents of Sorykos who claimed the Orphan had been born there
Spelter—a drow, related to Funderlings
Stephanas, Sir—a knight, one of Eneas' Temple Dogs
Sunset Pearl, aka Urayanu—aka She of the Strengthening Touch—Qar healer
Tirnan Havemore—Castellan under Hendon Tolly
Tulim—twenty-third in the line of succession
Tyron—famous Kracian bard and poet
Ultin—a prince of Xis
Unforgiven—a tribe of manlike Qar
Upsteeplebat—Queen of the Rooftoppers of Southmarch
Uwin—priest who replaced Father Timoid
Vasil Zeru—White Hounds quartermaster
Volofon—a mercenary from Ikarta in Krace
Weasel—one of the Temple Dog scouts
Whitewound—Ettin clan from Bluedeeps
Willow—A pixilated girl
Xergal—Xixian name for Kernios
Ximander—famous scholar
Xosh—Xixian name for Khors
Xyllos—a sea monster
Yermun—Xixian name for Immon the Gatekeeper
Zoaz—Xixian god, groom of the solar chariot

PLACES

Ancestor's Blood—Qar name for the Sea in the Depths
Anglin Parlor—Hendon Tolly's temporary throne room
Argas River Valley—in southern Silverside
Blue Lamp Quarter—a district of Xis
Brewer's Store Cavern—a cavern between the temple and Funderling Town
Cavern of Winds—a series of connected chambers in the Funderling Mysteries
Counting Room—a large cavern underneath Southmarch
Crying Hill—site of a famous battle between Qar and Dreamless

Dunletter—a town in the hills of Brenland
Frannac—Connordic island
Gem Street—the main processional in Funderling Town
Glittering Delights—Qar name for Sandsilver's Dancing Room
Grasshill Bridge—in mainland Southmarch
Great Delve—a large Stormstone tunnel leading under Brenn's Bay to the mainland
Initiation Hall—the center of the Maze
Iron Reach—passage above the Metamorphic Brothers temple
Kalebria—a southern city, once part of Syannese empire
King's South Cabinet—a room connected to the Erivor Chapel
Lake Strivothos—a huge inland sea in southern Eion
Last Hour of the Ancestor—Qar name for Southmarch Castle, esp. the deepest parts
Last Reach—a tunnel complex in the Funderling Mysteries
Millwheel Road—a major road that runs into the Coast Road near Southmarch Castle
Moonless Reach, a long, lightless cavern complex below Funderling Town
Mudstone Reach—another cavern system beneath Funderling Town
Ocher Bar—a clay pit near Iron Reach
Ocsa—Connordic island
Old Baryte Span—a series of tunnels off the Great Delve
On. Krisanthe—a Trigonate temple in mainland Southmarch
Onir Beccan—a town in Blueshore on the edge of Brenn's Bay
Potmis Bridge—scene of a famous Syannese military defeat
Prince Kayne Library—in the royal residence at Southmarch
Revelation Hall—the last chamber of the Maze before the Balcony over the Sea in the Depths
Sandsilver's Dancing Room—a large cavern near the Metamorphic Brothers Temple
Sharm—Connordic island
Shoremarket—a square in mainland Southmarch
Silver River Road—a main road through Kertewall and Silverside
Skean Egye-Var—Skimmer's name for M'Helan's Rock
Sycamore Tower—the tallest tower in the Orchard Palace
Stefanian Hills—hills between Brenland and Summerfield
Tessideme—name for Tessis when it was a village
Vale of Aulas—a forested stretch between Oscastle and Southmarch
Weeping Staircase—part of Qul-na-Qar
White Bank Road—a road near the lagoon in the Outer Keep of Southmarch
Xan-Horem mountains—Xixian mountains
Yenidos Mountains—Xixian mountain range

THINGS (AND ANIMALS)

A Diversitie of Truthfull Thinges—a book by Ximandros Tetramakos.
a-recking—toward the right side
Always Fire—the force that created the Book of the Fire in the Void
Askorab—AKA "skorpa" AKA "seliqet": scorpion
Chastiser—Hammerfoot's war ax
Day of Fires—Midsummer's Eve in Xis
Day of Smoke—Midsummer's Day in Xis
Ghostmaker—a Xandian knife
guruodir—heavy Funderling stabbing-spears with broad iron spearheads and shafts of oak
Hormos—a country dance in March Kingdoms
Kinwar—the Qar re-invasion of Southmarch
meadowqueen—a wildflower
Muckle Brown—a flittermouse, bat
Mykomel—AKA "mushroom jack", a Funderling liquor
Royal Spindle Shell—one of the Rooftopper's sacred artifacts
Sea Postern—a gate that the Skimmers use to slip in and out between Southmarch harbor and Brenn's Bay
Sealskin—the name of Rafe's boat
seliqet—Qar word for scorpion
Seven Gray Birds—a constellation and a group of semi-mythical Qar prophetesses
Third Hierarchical Conclave—a famous Trigonate religious council
Torvionos —a southern dance popular at the Southmarch court
Ul-Ushya Festival—important Xixian yearly celebration
Yah'stah's Eye—a Qar name for a star

Appendix 2

THE PRINCIPAL GODS OF THE TRIGONATE FAITH AND THEIR DIVERSE NAMES AMONG THE HEATHEN PEOPLES

PERIN the god of the sky and Thane of Lightnings is called *Argal* by the Xixians, *Cloudwalker, Skylord,* and *Thunder* by the Qar, *Hand of the Sky* or *Lord of the Peaks* by the Rooftoppers, and *Pyarin* by the Skimmers.

ERIVOR the god of the waters is called *Eshervat* in the south of Xand, *Efiyal* by the Xixians, *Egye-Var* by the Skimmer-folk, and *Ocean* by the Qar.

KERNIOS the lord of the underworld is named *Xergal* by the Xixians, *Black Earth* by the Qar, and *Karisnovois* by the Rooftoppers.

Together, Perin, Erivor, and Kernios are known as the Trigon, the Three, the Brothers, or the Three Brothers.

DEVONA, goddess of the forest, called *Devona of the Harp*

ERILO, god of the harvest, which is why the Qar name him *Harvest.*

HILIOMETES the mighty demigod is sometimes called (or confused with) Melarkh, hero of the Xixians.

HONNOS the god of travelers is called *Yunas* by the Xixians and *Red Stag* by the Qar.

IMMON the Gatekeeper of Kernios is called *Yermun* among the Xixians and *Black Noszh La* by the Funderlings of Southmarch.

KHORS the first god of the moon, named *Xosh* by the Xixians and *Silvergleam* by the Qar.

KUPILAS the Artificer, god of healing and making and smithing, is called *Crooked* by the Qar, *Habbili* by the heathens of Xis, and *Kioy-a-pous* by the Skimmers.

MADI ONYENA, mother of Zmeos, Khors, and Zuriyal, called Ugeni by the Xixians; *Umdi Onajena* by others of the southern lands, and Bird *Mother* or *Breeze* by the Qar.

MADI SURAZEM, mother of the Three Brothers, called *Shusayem* in Xis and *Moisture* by the immortal Qar.

MESIYA the goddess of the moon and first wife of Kernios, called *Nenizu* by the Xixians.

SIVEDA is the goddess of the night.

STRIVOS the god of the wind is sometimes called *Invisible* by the Qar.

SVA, the grandmother of the gods, is named *Void* by the Qar and *Zha* among the Xixians.

SVEROS the father of the gods, called *Twilight* by the Qar and *Zhafaris* in Xis.

VOLIOS, god of war, known as *Volios of the Measureless Grip* or *Volos Longbeard* is named *Okhuz* by the Xixians and *Bull* by the Qar.

ZMEOS the Horned Serpent, the Great Enemy, called *Nushash* by the Xixians and *Whitefire* by the Qar. His sword was also named Whitefire. (In the pagan rites of the Xixians, Zmeos stole and married Zoria to begin the Godwar, not his brother Khors, as our faith teaches.)

ZO, grandfather of the gods, is called *Light* by the Qar and *Tso* by the Xixians

ZORIA the daughter of Perin, mother of Kupilas, and later the wife of Kernios is called *Suya* by the Xixians and *Pale Daughter*, *Dove*, *Dawnflower*, or *Almond Blossom* by the Twilight Folk, or Qar.

ZOSIM the god of crossroads, poets, thieves, and drunkards, called *Salamandros* in his aspect as a fire god, *Shoshem* by the Xixians and *Trickster* by the Twilight Folk.

ZURIYAL the Merciless, sister of Zmeos and Khors, called *Surigali* by the people of distant Xis, and *Judgement* by the Qar.

The war between the children of Surazem and Oneyna, called the Godwar, is also named the Theomachy or Onyenomachy.